The BROTHERHOOD of the ROSY CROSS

IMMA
NUEL
IN HOC
SIGNO
VINCES

The BROTHERHOOD of the ROSY CROSS

A History of the Rosicrucians

ARTHUR EDWARD WAITE

BARNES & NOBLE BOOKS
NEW YORK

Frontispiece:

THE GOLDEN AND ROSY CROSS, understood in the secret circles as the Cosmic Cross of the Order, symbolizing universal manifestation, with the manifested Christ in the centre as the power and the grace of all things. The motto is: *Ego sum flos campi et lilium convallium.* This emblem appears on the title-page of GEHEIME FIGUREN, issued at Altona in 1785, and is characteristic of the theosophical spirit which permeates the whole work. It was attached evidently to a ribbon or collar, and is probably the reverse side of a Cross shewn in another plate, described as of fine gold and said to have been worn by each Brother on his breast. The inscription on the reverse is the well-known salutation of the Order which was repeated on exposing the symbol: *Benedictus Dominus Deus noster qui dedit nobis signum.* Beneath this inscription the signs of Mercury, Venus, the Moon, Mars, Jupiter and Saturn are written about a six-pointed star, having the Sun in its centre. On the uppermost arm of the Cross are the words: MAGISTER JESUS CHRISTUS, DEUS ET HOMO; the horizontal arms bear the signs of the three Philosophical Principles; and on that which is lowermost is inscribed: *Frater Rosæ et Aureæ Crucis,* i.e. Brother of the Rose and of the Golden Cross. The symbol illustrates the dedications of the Order at this period: but they were no new development, peculiar to the eighteenth century: they were in evidence even at the beginning and are characteristics of the present day more assuredly than ever.

This edition published by Barnes & Noble, Inc.

1993 Barnes & Noble Books

ISBN 1-56619-212-9

Printed and bound in the United States of America

M 9 8 7 6 5 4 3

CONTENTS

CHAPTER I

MYTHICAL ROSICRUCIAN PRECURSORS

CHAPTER II

MILITIA CRUCIFERA EVANGELICA

CHAPTER III

ALCHEMISTS AND MYSTICS

Contents

CHAPTER VII

THE CHEMICAL NUPTIALS

CHAPTER VIII

AUTHORSHIP OF THE CHEMICAL NUPTIALS

CHAPTER IX

DEVELOPMENT OF ROSICRUCIAN LITERATURE

Contents

CHAPTER X

ENGLISH ROSICRUCIANISM

CHAPTER XI

A GREAT GERMAN ALCHEMIST

Contents

PAGE

Contents

CHAPTER XXI

A MODERN ROSICRUCIAN ORDER

CHAPTER XXII

A KABALISTIC ORDER OF THE ROSE-CROIX

CHAPTER XXIII

THE AMERICAN ROSY CROSS

THE BROTHERHOOD OF THE ROSY CROSS

CHAPTER I

MYTHICAL ROSICRUCIAN PRECURSORS

THE Order of the Rosy Cross offers, on its external side, not only those general difficulties which are inherent to the subject of secret association but some others of a peculiar kind, chief among which are perhaps the successive transformations which it has suffered from within the groups and the actual circumstances of its origin, supposing that this is referable to the first quarter of the seventeenth century. It is much more difficult of approach than is, for example, the outward history of Emblematic Freemasonry. When the art and craft of building temples and houses began to be spiritualised is admittedly in a cloud of darkness, setting aside of course the casual symbolism which runs through all literature. We shall probably never know when men first took tools in their hands and began to moralise upon them, or when for such reason they might have called themselves speculative Masons—had a denomination of this kind come into their heads. But late or early—and not so late, I think—a time arrived when they issued out of their obscurity and held that epoch-making meeting which is connected for ever with the name of the London Apple-Tree Tavern. Thereon followed the institution of a Grand Lodge which became that of England—regarded now as the Mother Temple of the whole Masonic world. About the history henceforward there is no element of doubt on the broad scale, and so also we know the long story of spiritual and emblematic evolution which is that of the High Grades.

There is nothing corresponding to the year 1717 in the history of the Rosy Cross. Between 1614 and 1616 certain pamphlets appeared in German and Latin which affirmed that a secret and mysterious Order had subsisted in Germany for about two centuries; that it was full of light and knowledge, derived from a hidden centre in the Near-Eastern world; that it could and was prepared to transform and reform all the arts and sciences; and, in fine, that with this object in view, and for the personal benefit of earnest, prepared seekers, it was willing to admit members. The effect of this proclamation in Germany, Holland and even England is now a matter of notoriety: everybody who knows anything about Secret Societies in Europe has heard of the great debate that followed. But the first question for our consideration and the first difficulty before us is whether there was a Society at all in any incorporated sense when the documents which claimed to reveal it were first published as an appeal to *alumni* and *literati* of magian and occult arts. So far therefore from a visible and recorded convention held at an Apple-Tree Tavern, we are in the presence of a claim put out suddenly from the void: all that which lay behind it is the initial matter for our research, whether or not it may be possible to reach thereon any degree of certitude.

So also in respect of developments, that which in Masonry is moderately clear at least lies far behind the veil in respect of the Rosy Cross. The manifestoes of the early seventeenth century were either sent out by an incorporated society or led to imitative incorporation at an early stage of the story; and in either case there is sound reason for thinking that alchemy was the original concern-in-chief, however the theory of transmutation may have been understood and pursued within the particular circle. We know further that it was left for a period, at least in one of the branches, and there followed, as the fashion of a time, those astral workings which are heard of in the eighteenth century. We know, in fine, that there was a return to alchemy, and there are vague hints upon processes followed at that period. But what was included under the denomination of astral it is our task to learn if we can, and so also whether the Philosopher's Stone in the light of the Rosy Cross was a Mystery of Spiritual Healing and Divine Tincture, an ethical art of contentment or a method of raising so-called base metals into the perfect form of gold.

It is certain, again, that the great medley of theosophical Israel under the name of Kabalism was one concern of the Order, but there is no evidence on the surface to tell us why it was pursued ; now in the way of those Zoharic doctors who became—according to their legend—a sect of Christian *illuminati ;* now in the expectation of performing prodigies by virtue of inherent power attributed to Divine Names ; and now in the contra-theosophical sense of the dregs and lees of grimoires. We know in fine that at the beginning there was an Occult Order, that in some of the developments it remains at this day within those measures, but that at the apex or crown of its evolution it has emerged from all the vain observances, from all the seerings and the skryings, and has gone up into the mountain of the Lord—the fabled secret mountain of adeptship—in search of Divine attainment. But of these transformations and developments there are no records, except in so far as they may exist in the Secret Houses of the Brotherhood ; and to approach therefore the story of the Rosy Cross on this side of its subject demands access to sources of knowledge which are open to few persons—if indeed to any outside the hidden circles. The archives of Mary's

Chapel, of Mother Kilwinning and other "time immemorial" Lodges of the Masonic Brotherhood are available to Masonic students, but—on the hypothesis that they were and are—the Temples of the Rosy Cross may have indeed their names and local habitations, but they are as inaccessible to ordinary research as if they were in the "nowhere and the naught."

As I have intimated therefore, its external history is one of peculiar difficulty, and it requires to be approached from within as well as without in order to reflect any real light thereon. Its elusive nature and the charm of its mystery, not to speak of the tales of faërie which have been gathered about it by makers of myths for the past three hundred years, have drawn imaginations in literature, imaginations also in quest, who have woven about it another and iridescent veil. We have to find how far the Rosicrucian of romance has been made in the image and likeness of those Brethren of the Rosy Cross who pass—somewhat on the edges—across the horizon of history, and how far their quality of adeptship corresponds in the memorials concerning it with the radiant stuff of some of the modern dreams.

So far as obvious memorials are concerned, Rosicrucian history begins in and about the year 1614 with the publication of those documents which I have mentioned briefly, and by a highly speculative inference from these it has been supposed that the traditional founder died in 1484;[1]

[1] It is a date otherwise which recurs in Rosicrucian reveries, but only to betray research. Thus it happens that Mr. G. F. Fort recorded in AMERICAN NOTES AND QUERIES, Philadelphia, October 24, 1891, as follows: "In tracing out recently some lines of historical research . . . , I came upon a statement of fact that may be of interest, namely, the establishment in Sleswic, Denmark, *anno* 1484, of a Fraternity of Rosicrucians: *Fraternitas Rosarii Slesvici condita, anno* 1484." A Danish Guild of the Rosary suggests that someone has blundered, but it is not Mr. Fort, as it happens: his reference is to SPECIMEN HISTORICO-POLITICUM INAUGURATA DE GILDARUM HISTORIA, Amsterdam, 1834, the author being Cornelius Joscinus Fortuyn, who says,

but the later legends of the Order have combined with independent makers of myths to stultify this speculation in favour of various conflicting dates and other founders, more or less remote in antiquity. As there will be sufficient opportunity to deal with them in later places, I will mention here one only of the more recent legends which may be said to have grown up within the Order, far down in the eighteenth century. It has obtained a casual vogue, owing to dissemination through Masonic channels in France. It postulates a founder of the Rosicrucians in a certain Ormesius or Ormuz and affirms that he was converted to Christianity at Alexandria by St. Mark, A.D. 46. He is said to have purified the Egyptian Mysteries and married them to the new faith. His disciples followed their master, and with these as a centre he established the Society of Ormuz, or of the Light. The sign of membership was a red cross worn on the person. Essenes and Therapeutæ entered the ranks of this sodality, in which Hermetic Secrets were preserved and transmitted. The Baron de Westerode has been credited with putting forward this fiction, he being an adventurer among secret societies derivative from Masonry about the period of the French Revolution. An obscure figure in the annals, I conceive him nevertheless to have been connected with one of those

pp. 53, 54: *Religiosæ Societates, quæ sæculo XII jam reperiuntur, in Daniâ frequenter insecutis sæculis occurrunt. Sic anno* 1485 *in urbe Heligenhaven prostat gildaSanctæ Crucis, Flensburgi invenitur gilda Sanctæ Mariæ anno* 1514, *Fraternitas Rosarii* (Rosenkranz. Brüder-schaft) *Slesvici condita anno* 1484, etc. It is obvious that the reference is to a Catholic Association for promoting the devotion of the Holy Rosary and that Fortuyn's parenthetical gloss represents his own confusion. He quotes otherwise an authority to support him, and this is RIPÆ CIMBRICÆ SEU URBIS RIPENSIS IN CIMBRIA SITÆ DESCRIPTIO, EX ANTIQUIS MONUMENTIS, *etc. . . . Illustrata per* Petrum Terpager. Flensburgurgi, 1736, p. 438. However, the place in question contains *De Gilda S. Joannis* and opens *De Gilda S. Nicolai*, which concludes on p. 440. They offer no light on the subject. On p. 434 there is a short notice *De Gilda S. Crucis*, but I have searched the text in vain for any Guild of the Rosary and any reference to the Rosy Cross."

cliques which found shelter under the banner of Masonry, offering little distinction between Rosicrucian Rites proper and the numerous obediences of the Rose-Croix Grade in the old Rite of Perfection. These things merged into one another continually—or at least in the records concerning them. The alleged Society of Ormuz has been reflected into modern systems, like the confused and unwieldy Masonic Rite of Memphis. It is a characteristic specimen of spurious traditional history, to be met with everywhere in Masonry.[1]

[1] It would be interesting to follow this curious fable further and identify the Rite with which it may have been incorporated at first. Among English references there is Kenneth Mackenzie's ROYAL CYCLOPÆDIA OF FREEMASONRY, *s.v.* Ormesius. But he names no source. As a fact, however, he derived information from Thory's ACTA LATOMORUM. Quite naturally, the story has lost nothing in its travels from mouth to mouth. See in particular THE THEOSOPHICAL REVIEW, Vol. XXVII, pp. 422 *et seq.*, 1900–01. It produces some "Reasons" for believing that Francis Bacon was a Rosicrucian and leads up to this main subject in the manner following: (1) The Order of the Rosy Cross claimed Ormuz as its founder: it did nothing of the sort; the Ormuz fable was fathered on the Order at a late period. (2) It was allied closely to the Knights Templar and [or] the Knights Companions of St. John of Jerusalem. (3) Battista Porta in 1605 was a Chief of the Rosy Cross, who "under cover of his comedies instructed initiates in things human and divine"—not apparently under cover of his famous work on MAGIA NATURALIS. (4) Wickliffe, Lollard, Chaucer, Dante, Petrarch, Boccaccio, Voltaire, Goethe, Lessing, Swedenborg, Mesmer and Böhme "are to-day openly acknowledged as Brethren of the Craft," by whom does not appear, but by those presumably who regard Bacon as a Rosicrucian and as the "concealed poet" of the Shakespeare plays. It is scarcely necessary to say that no particle of evidence is produced in support of these statements: they are the vapourings of foolish dreams. Porta, for example, died in 1615, one year after the Rosy Cross made its public appearance on the stage in Germany. We may compare an essay on the Rosicrucians which appeared in THEOSOPHICAL SIFTINGS, Vol. III. All accounts are said to agree "in pointing to an origin outside Europe, in oriental lands." They do nothing of the sort, and in fact the Ormuz fiction appears to stand alone. It stands or falls on the authority of Thory, who says: (1) That a letter by the Baron de Westerode is in the archives of the PHILOSOPHICAL RITE; (2) that it was written from Ratisbon in 1784; (3) that it was addressed to the Head Tribunal; (4) that it contains the Ormuz story; and (5) that the story in question is described as "received in Sweden," which may mean that it is a traditional history be-

I have taken this particular illustration, not indeed that it is the best, or otherwise the nearest at hand, but as serving the purpose of a moment, to introduce the alternative fables which are not traditional histories, manufactured for Grade purposes—or to promote a particular claim—but views and opinions formulated in all seriousness as contributions to the Rosicrucian subject. I will cite them in that order to which they would belong in chronology, were there any chronology in reveries of this kind. We can pass over as simply fantastic some unsupported expressions of personal conviction like that of the French writer Sédir, who tells us (1) that the Middle Ages and Renaissance were united by a general belief in the existence of a Rosicrucian Order; and (2) that the Fraternity was at least coeval with the Christian era.[1] So also Cohausen speculates concerning

longing to the Swedish Rite of Masonry, an incorporation of many elements; (6) that, according to de Westerode, the Rosicrucians came to Europe in 1188—an important date connected with Templar history; (7) that three of the *adepti* proceeded to Scotland and there established an Order of Masons of the East. This legend is naturally set aside by Thory. There is very little doubt that he had seen the letter of Baron de Westerode, the present whereabouts of which are beyond speculation, as the archives of the SCOTTISH PHILOSOPHICAL RITE were dispersed on February 23, 1860. A catalogue was printed, but I have failed to obtain a copy. Baron de Westerode was on the Council of the RITE OF THE PHILALETHES and was present at the Convention of Paris summoned by that illustrious Masonic body. See ACTA LATOMORUM, I, 336, 337; II, 97.

[1] HISTOIRE DES ROSE-CROIX, 1910. *Préface*, p. x; *cap.* II, p. 31. The author qualifies subsequently by affirming that a neo-Rosicrucianism arose at a later period, meaning that the manifestation of the early seventeenth century was a revival of something much older. But for this there is no evidence. We may compare Kenneth Mackenzie in THE ROSICRUCIAN, August, 1874, being Transactions of the SOCIETAS ROSICRUCIANA IN ANGLIA. He appears to suggest in a confused paragraph that the Rosicrucian "system" was originally identical with the Chaldees or Culdees. So also in the same occasional periodical for 1900 another dreamer affirms on his personal authority, quoting nothing in support, that the " School " descended from the philosophers of Egypt and the Jewish rabbis. Compare Yarker, who describes the Fraternity as " inheritor of the Gnosis and mysterious wisdom of Egypt." See NOTES ON THE SCIENTIFIC AND RELIGIOUS MYSTERIES OF ANTIQUITY, p. 71.

Artephius, a supposed Arabian alchemist, placed far in the past of Hermeticism, and calls him the patron of Rosicrucians. The supposition is without warrant in the single Latin tract which is extant under this name.[1]

A considerable interest has attached always to the position of Raymund Lully—meaning the alchemist who adopted that name—as an exponent of Rosicrucian doctrine on the side of Hermetic physics, and all the makers of incautious hypotheses have passed from one to another a confused reference to one of his famous tracts. Their thesis intends to cite the TESTAMENTUM MAGISTRI RAYMUNDI LULLII, addressed to a Philip, King of France. In *Pars* I, *cap.* 87, of this work the adept states that he obtained the congelation of common mercury by means of its menstrual, and that he performed the experiment near Naples in *præsentia physici regis . . . et certorum sociorum.* As used by Cicero, the substantive word *physicus* signifies a natural philosopher, scrutator and student of Nature: it carries no suggestion whatever of adeptship, as understood in alchemy. In the adjective form it means natural, more especially in connection with philosophy. The expression *certi socii*—particular or faithful associates, may or may not imply a confederacy by way of incorporation, a companionship in terms of alliance; but it would be used also for adherents in a common bond of sympathy. The context of Lully's statement specifies that his companions or witnesses of the experiment included a brother of St. John of Rhodes and one Bernard de la Bret: he was not therefore referring to the members of a secret order. He adds also that—

[1] HERMIPPUS REDIVIVUS, *Tom.* II. Whether the tract of Artephius was written originally in Arabic I am—on the whole—disposed to doubt. Berthelot leaves the question open. In any case it is extant now only in the Latin form. The alchemist, who is otherwise unknown, claims to have attained the age of a thousand years by means of the Great Elixir. There is no need to say that his memorial does not contain a single reference to any secret association.

regia majestate salva, with due respect to the King—those who saw what he had done understood it only in rather a homespun manner. So much for the *Societas Physicorum* under the leadership of a *Rex Physicorum*, as the passage is interpreted by those who take it for a covert allusion to the Rosicrucian Order or some kindred antecedent fraternity.[1]

It remains only to say that in his work entitled *Experimenta*, s.v. *Aliud Experimentum* . . . XXXIV, Lully recurs to the congelation of Mercury, and says that his operation was performed in the presence of King Partinopeus, who appears to be purely mythical.

Benedictus Figulus, who wrote and edited alchemical treatises in and about the year 1608, appears to have understood the *certi socii* of Lully as referring to a society of alchemists, which society was established in Italy at the beginning of the fifteenth century, and he would be therefore the father of the notion ; but its later purveyors have derived it indirectly through Solomon Semler.[2]

[1] The TESTAMENTUM of Raymund Lully is found in THEATRUM CHEMICUM, *Tom.* IV, and in the BIBLIOTHECA CHEMICA CURIOSA of Mangetus, *Tom.* I. The first part of the TESTAMENT is called THEORICA and the second PRACTICA. Sédir affirms that the THEATRUM CHEMICUM was edited by Rosicrucians at Strasbourg, an entirely gratuitous notion. See HISTOIRE DES ROSE-CROIX. Yarker, in his ARCANE SCHOOLS, p. 49, describes Lully as the great pioneer of Rosicrucians, but as much might be said of any other important alchemist prior to the seventeenth century. Heckethorn, in his SECRET SOCIETIES OF ALL AGES, betrays his incompetence by referring to Lully the entire THEATRUM CHEMICUM, as if this were one of his treatises instead of a great collection of alchemical writings extending to ten volumes. Sédir suggests that the debated passage in the TESTAMENT was interpolated, for the inscrutable reason that Villanova's ROSARIUM is cited in *cap.* 38. But Arnoldus was a contemporary of the original Lully, who is to be distinguished from the later alchemist who adopted his name. See my RAYMUND LULLY : *Illuminated Doctor*, *Alchemist and Christian Mystic*, 1922.

[2] UNPARTEIISCHE SAMLUNGEN ZUR HISTORIE DER ROSENKREUZER. *Von* D. Joh. Salomo Semler. 4 vols. Leipzig, *bei* Georg Emanuel Beer. 1786, 87, 88. We hear also on Thory's authority of an Order of Magicians at Florence which is said to have merged into the Rosicrucians during the eighteenth century. He appears to reflect intimations, most probably

The addresses which occur in writers like Lully to Sons of Truth, Sons of the Doctrine and Sons of the Order have been applied, in much the same spirit of fantasy, to the Rosicrucian Brotherhood or their precursors. Arnoldus de Villa Nova makes use of such expressions,[1] but precisely the same formulæ recur incessantly in the ZOHAR, where they do not signify an incorporated society. The alchemical Sons of the Doctrine were the earnest researchers to whom the *adepti* appealed and for whom their tracts were written. They were also, and especially, the personal pupils of the Masters.

Much stress has been laid also on the fact that a certain Count von Falkenstein, Prince Archbishop of Trèves in the fourteenth century, was saluted once in the dedication of an alchemical work as "Most Illustrious and Serene Prince and Father of Philosophers." On the authority of this description it has been concluded that the prelate in question was at the head of an Occult Fraternity, which was that in fact of the Rosy Cross, whereas it is obvious in

mythical, in THE ROSICRUCIAN UNVEILED of Magister Pianco. Expanding all his precursors, Reghellini is said to state that Kabalists and Rosicrucians had settled from remote times at Florence, Vicenza and elsewhere.—LA MAÇONNERIE CONSIDERÉE COMME LE RÉSULTAT DES RELIGIONS JUIVE ET CHRÉTIENNE, *Tom.* I, p. 344. But I do not find the reference either at the place cited or anywhere in Reghellini's three volumes. He speaks of a Platonic Academy established at the place in question A.D. 1540, and terms it a Masonic Institution. III, p. 71. He quotes also a statement of Nicolai on the Order at Venice and Padua in 1622 and mentions a Rite of Alchemical R.·.C.·. at Padua in the eighteenth century.

[1] In Hermetic literature the custom is as old as the Byzantine alchemists, and is no more significant of persons addressing one another within the circle of a secret society than is the great debate of the TURBA PHILOSOPHORUM, which on the surface claims to be a Holy Assembly of Adepts, but bears the fullest evidence of a compiled dialogue. As regards Arnoldus, who has been quoted in this misleading connection, we have only to consult his LIBER DICTUS THESAURUS THESAURORUM ET ROSARIUM PHILOSOPHORUM to see that the implicit of *Filii Doctrinæ* is precisely the same as *Oportet igitur inquisitorem hujus scientiæ—Lib.* I, *cap.* 6—as *Studeas ergo, charissime—Lib.* II, *cap.* 7—and *Filius existens Philosophorum—Lib.* II, *cap.* 32.

sense and reason that his title is simply one of a patron of alchemists. It is not unimportant to follow out this misconception and mark how it has grown up. Among the tracts of that fourth volume of THEATRUM CHEMICUM [1] to which I have referred there is a PRACTICA ALCHEMIÆ ascribed to Ortholanus,[2] and it claims to have been compiled from his writings by an unknown Englishman named Joannes Dumbeler *ex mandato Illustrissimi et Serenissimi Principis Patris Philosophorum Domini ac Domini Comitis de Falckenstein, Divina Providentia sanctæ Trevensis Archiepiscopi, anno Domini*, 1386. Dumbeler, as I have said, is an entirely supposititious Englishman, unknown to the history of alchemy in this country, and the Lord Archbishop of Trèves, who is not himself imaginary,[3] is only a Father of Philosophers in the sense of an interested patron—as already stated. So far from proving the fact of an incorporated society of alchemists at the alleged period it exhibits the denseness of those who have sought to found an argument of this kind upon such an inscription.[4]

[1] THEATRUM CHEMICUM PRECIPUOS SELECTORUM AUCTORUM TRACTATUS DE CHEMIA ET DE LAPIDIS PHYSICI COMPOSITIONE, etc., 1613, *Tom.* IV, *Tract.* 135 : M. Ortholani PRACTICA ALCHEMIÆ, PROBATA PARISIIS, *anno* 1358. There is, of course, no evidence that this is a genuine date, but nothing attaches to the question.

[2] Ortholanus wrote two commentaries on the EMERALD TABLE of pseudo-Hermes and he is sometimes described as LE PHILOSOPHE DES JARDINS MARITIMES. He has been identified otherwise as *alchimiste Parisien.* He is better known in England as Hortulanus. The PRACTICA ALCHEMIÆ was translated into English and published under date of 1627, based obviously on the edition of THEATRUM CHEMICUM. Professor Ferguson is disposed to question whether Ortholanus and Hortulanus are names which represent one and the same person, but it is suggested by the French *sobriquet.* Hortulanus has been identified also with Johannes Garlandius, described as *Anglus.* BIBLIOTHECA CHEMICA, *s.v.* Hortulanus and Ortholanus.

[3] See CUNO VON FALKENSTEIN ALS ERZBISCHOF VON TRIER, etc. By Dr. Franz Ferdinand, 1886, in T. Lindner's MÜNSTERISCHE BEITRÄGE ZUR GESCHICHTSFORSCHUNG, etc. Old Series, *Heft* 9.

[4] The tract itself has nothing especially distinctive, but is clearly—indeed, lucidly—worded after its own manner, within its own measures of symbolism. It is said that the Work of the Elixir appertains to Quicksilver, Flying Citrine

Towards the end of the nineteenth century there came forward, however, a German claimant to distinction, named Karl Kieswetter, author of a brief monograph on the HISTORY OF THE ORDER OF THE ROSY CROSS.[1] He affirmed (1) that he was a direct descendant of the last Chief or Imperator of the Brotherhood; (2) that he was in a sense its literary heir and was in possession as such of many priceless Rosicrucian manuscripts;[2] and (3) that among these was one in particular entitled COMPENDIUM TOTIUS PHILOSOPHIÆ ET ALCHYMIÆ FRATERNITATIS ROSÆ [*sic*] CRUCIS, *ex mandato Serenissimi Comitis de Falkenstein, Imperatoris Nostri, anno Domini* 1374. The MS. was said to contain alchemical theories and practical processes. If it can be taken tentatively as in existence at the time of its description, there is no question that it is fraudulent, as the use of the word Imperator at the alleged period sufficiently shews. According to Kieswetter this is the first time that such a title occurs, but as a fact it is peculiar to the eighteenth century and later. We have the evidence of Michael Maier that the Order was ruled by a President in the early seventeenth century. It is to be added that the

Sulphur *vive*, Green Sulphur—which is Vitriol—and Fixed White Sulphur. Red Earth or Cinobrium, Silver and Gold also enter into its composition. There is also HORTUS AMORIS Joh. Dumbeleii, Angli, in the collection of Rhenanus called: HARMONIÆ IMPERSCRUTABILIS CHIMICO-PHILOSOPHICÆ DECADES DUÆ, 1625.

[1] It appeared in the year 1886 at Leipzig, in a German psychical and spiritistic magazine called DER SPHINX. It was translated into French by F. C. Barlet in 1898 and appeared in L'INITIATION. It is quoted in an uncritical and foolish little book called THE ROSICRUCIANS, by H. C. and K. M. B., n.d., *circa* 1915.

[2] The Imperator in question is said to have been his great-grandfather, a most zealous member of the Order during a long space of time. From 1764 to 1802 he was engaged in transcribing the archives, presumably for his personal use, and these are the MSS. which passed into Kieswetter's possession. But he speaks otherwise as if they were originals, each being inscribed with the date on which it was written and with the name of the Imperator by whose directions it was prepared. Those of the earliest period belonged to the year 1400.

claims of the German Rosicrucian inheritor are not of a kind to establish confidence apart from documentary evidence, and the documents—which have been sought eagerly—are not forthcoming.

The next mythical chief of the Rosy Cross is Aureolus Theophrastus Paracelsus, the occult master of Hohenheim. He has secured unwittingly a not inconsiderable vogue, though the FAMA FRATERNITATIS R∴C∴ happens to say in its sincerity that "he was none of our Fraternity." In the older days, as now, it was the habit of many to institute ascriptions within the circle of occult history without reference to its written memorials. It is difficult to say how and when the legend under notice arose. Miss A. M. Stoddart suggests that one of its earliest traces is in the woodcuts which accompany certain PROGNOSTICATIONS of Paracelsus in the collected edition of his writings by Huser, published at Cologne in 1589 and 1590.[1] One of these woodcuts is said to shew a heap of books, including a volume inscribed with the word *Rosa*. It is an exceedingly shadowy vestige and may be ignored as such. According to another story, Paracelsus was not indeed the founder of the Rosy Cross—which had existed in earlier days than those of Luther's contemporary—but he reorganised and established it on a new basis. Kieswetter puts forward this thesis and draws it from some apocryphal manuscript. His

[1] THE LIFE OF PARACELSUS, 1911, pp. 249, 250, and *ante*, p. 236. The illustration as described does not correspond with that which appears in the English PROPHECIES OF PARACELSUS, translated by J. K., 1915, though it claims to follow Huser. There are books and MS. fragments in Fig. xvi, but the word *Rosa* is wanting. Fig. xxvi, however, exhibits a great letter F standing on a Rose, beneath which is a crown. Two editions of the PROGNOSTICATIO appeared *circa* 1536 and 1600 respectively, according to bibliographical opinion, but the first is highly speculative, being that of the dedication *ad illustrissimum ac potentissimum Principem* FERDINANDUM ROMANORUM REGEM, etc. Both contain the Rose-Crown illustration, with the emerging letter F. I should not be at the pains to cite them were it not for Miss Stoddart's rather idle speculation.

precious invention has gone somewhat far in its travels among occultists and Masons.[1] It may be compared with the statement of John Yarker that, according to LE COMTE DE GABALIS, Paracelsus was elected Monarch of the Rosicrucian Society. What the famous occult romance actually says, however, is that the Sage of Hohenheim attained the Monarchy of Wisdom.[2]

Contemporary with Paracelsus was Cornelius Agrippa, who is alleged to have founded an alchemical or theosophical society at the beginning of the sixteenth century in Paris and to have brought it about the same period to London. It has been identified with the Rosy Cross and alternatively with an early form of Emblematic Freemasonry. On this subject Kieswetter and his manuscripts seem to have exceeded the reasonable limits of caution by affirming that the alchemist Eirenæus Philalethes, "when writing in 1650, expressely calls Agrippa Imperator." As nothing under the name of Eirenæus had appeared at the date in

[1] See Transactions of the Newcastle COLLEGIUM SOCIETATIS ROSICRUCIANÆ IN ANGLIA, Vol. I, p. 48; also ARS QUATUOR CORONATORUM, Vol. XVII, p. 32. The speculation unfortunately misled Archdeacon Craven in his excellent work on DOCTOR ROBERT FLUDD, 1902. See p. 34. Comp. ARS QUATUOR CORONATORUM, V, 67.

[2] Yarker's misstatement occurs in THE ARCANE SCHOOLS, p. 208. The remark of LE COMTE DE GABALIS appears in the *Second Entretien*. See ENTRETIENS SUR LES SCIENCES SÉCRÈTES, by the Abbé de Villars, Paris, 1670. There are many editions. Yarker's ignorant blunder has been reflected into the Manchester TRANSACTIONS FOR MASONIC RESEARCH. The article is entitled "Rosicrucianism and its connection with Freemasonry," by F. W. Brockbank, who says that Gioseppe Francesco Borri was a most illustrious Rosicrucian and left a record to which we are indebted for all our knowledge of the subject. That which he left was LA CHIAVE DEL CABINETTO *del* Cavaliere Gioseppe Francesco Borri, Colonia, 1681. It is supposed to have inspired the author of LE COMTE DE GABALIS, but the French work happens to have preceded the Italian. According to Charles Mackay, EXTRAORDINARY POPULAR DELUSIONS, s.v., *The Alchymists*, the literary cabinet of Borri is "a complete exposition of the Rosicrucian philosophy," which means, however, that it gives account of elementary spirits, a notion which did not originate with the Order but with Paracelsus, who—as I have stated elsewhere—was indebted to German folklore.

question, the Rosicrucian legatee and his pretended authority are confusing Eirenæus with Eugenius Philalethes, otherwise Thomas Vaughan; but the statement is a simple mendacity in respect of both, as their works remain to testify.[1]

We are approaching the seventeenth century when we arrive at the name of Dr. John Dee, that mathematician and astrologer of Mortlake who was a prime favourite with Elizabeth, Queen of England. He was precisely the kind of person who might have entered or possibly even founded a Secret Society like that of the Rosy Cross, and seeing that, having been born in 1527, he died only at the end of 1608, or some six years before the FAMA FRATERNITATIS was issued to the *literati* of Europe, it might seem feasible that he was actually connected with our debated subject during its embryonic period. He has been annexed accordingly, but it proves as usual to be by those who exhibit their inability to read the warrants which they cite. In the year 1618 there was published at Hamburg an

[1] Kieswetter's invention is, of course, reproduced by Yarker in THE ARCANE SCHOOLS as a matter of such complete certitude that it has not seemed even worth while to name his authority. The sole foundation of the story is that when Agrippa was sent as a young man to Paris by the Emperor Maximilian he is affirmed by Morley to have made himself "the centre of a knot of students," described otherwise as "a secret association of theosophists," who were admirers of Reuchlin, his doctrine of the Mirific Word and so forth. For the journey to Paris see Agrippa's EPISTOLÆ, Book I, Letter 2, in the OPERUM PARS POSTERIOR, published at Leyden *per Beringos Fratres*, n.d. There is no authority for theosophical activities in London, where Agrippa was the guest of Dean Colet. There is, of course, nothing *per se* improbable respecting such an institution in either city. THE QUARTERLY REVIEW of 1798 has been quoted for Cornelius Agrippa, his secret associations and Freemasonry, but it did not come into existence till 1809. See also Henry Morley's excellent biography of the occult philosopher, 1856, I, 25, 58, 59, 62, 63. I may add that Trithemius was the instructor of Paracelsus as well as of Agrippa, and in the ROSICRUCIAN AND MASONIC RECORD for 1891 a certain Dr. Lemon had the assurance to speak of Trithemius as a Brother of the Rosy Cross. In the case of a Masonic Rosicrucian it is usually safe to dismiss the charge of mendacity on the ground of invincible folly. In ANIMA MAGICA ABSCONDITA, 1650, Vaughan calls Agrippa "the oracle of magic" and the "master" of Wierus.

EPISTLE of Roger Bacon on the SECRETS OF ART AND NATURE AND THE VANITY OF MAGIC, which is said to have been "corrected after numerous copies" and edited by John Dee. In this case it will be seen that it appeared posthumously and at the height of a controversy which followed in Germany upon the issue of the First Rosicrucian pamphlets. The only sense in which it connects with our inquiry is that Dee is supposed to have dedicated his edition to the Rosicrucian Brotherhood, for which statement it would seem that Kloss, the German Masonic bibliographer, is the first authority.[1] On examination, however, it turns out that the Dee manuscript fell into the hands of an unknown person who undertook its publication for the benefit of seekers after knowledge, and it is to him only that the dedication in question is referable, together with an *Epistle to the Reader* which follows thereon.[2] I have no special concern in challenging the editorial attribution of the manuscript; apart from the preliminary matter it signifies merely that the Mortlake philosopher prepared a careful copy of Bacon's tract and it remains an open question whether he designed to publish it. In his catalogue of fifty private and imprinted works,[3] enumerated in a letter addressed by him to the Archbishop of Canterbury, 1594-5, there is no mention of his having edited the VANITY OF MAGIC, though he had a high opinion of Bacon as one "whose earthly fame can never die,"[4] though he

[1] I mean that he mentions the fact of the dedication in such terms that it might be supposed to have been written by Dee.

[2] The full title of the edition is as follows: EPISTOLA FRATRIS ROGERII BACONIS, DE SECRETIS OPERIBUS ARTIS ET NATURÆ, ET DE NULLITATE MAGIÆ. *Opera Johannis Dee, Londiniensis, e pluribus exemplaribus castigata olim et ad sensum integrum restituta. Nunc vero a quodam veritatis Amatore, in gratiam veræ scientæ* (sic) *candidatarum foras emissa, cum Notis quibusdam partim ipsius* JOHANNIS DEE, *partim edentis.* Hamburg, *anno* cIc Iↄ, cxviii.

[3] He admits, however, expressly that his list is incomplete.

[4] See Dee's preface to Henry Billingsley's English translation of Euclid's ELEMENTS, 1570.

sought after his works and transcribed more than one of them with his own hand. As regards the printed dedication I need say only that its anonymous author specifies in his opening lines that he was at Silesia in the year 1597, at which period Dee was in Manchester, being Warden of Christ's College.[1]

So passes the Rosicrucian claim in respect of John Dee, for I need not say that neither in the FAITHFUL RELATION[2]—so largely autobiographical in character—nor in his PRIVATE DIARY[3]—printed and in manuscript—is there the least indication that he belonged to any secret societies. During a six years' sojourn abroad he met with personalities dedicated to occult interests, including Heinrich Khunrath, whose AMPHITHEATRE OF ETERNAL WISDOM has long been held to contain Rosicrucian emblems. Dee also projected a treatise to be entitled DE HORIZONTE ÆTERNITATIS in reply to Andreas Libavius, who—in a book not named specifically but published in 1593–4—" hath unduly considered a phrase in my MONAS HIEROGLYPHICA . . . by his own unskilfulness in such matters." The Libavius in question was prominent in the Rosicrucian controversy over twenty years after. Finally, one of Dee's unprinted works, referred to 1573, is entitled DE STELLA ADMIRANDA IN CASSIOPEÆ ASTERISMO, recalling the Rosicrucian concern in new stars, e.g. in *Serpentarius* and *Cygnus*—which are mentioned in CONFESSIO FRATERNITATIS R ∴ C ∴[4]

[1] Charlotte Fell Smith : LIFE OF DR. JOHN DEE, *c.* 21.

[2] A TRUE AND FAITHFUL RELATION OF WHAT PASSED FOR MANY YEARS BETWEEN DR. JOHN DEE AND SOME SPIRITS. With a Preface by Meric Casaubon. London : 1659.

[3] THE PRIVATE DIARY, edited by J. O. Halliwell, F.R.S., and published by the Camden Society, 1842. It begins on August 25th, 1554, and ends on January 19th, 1601.

[4] The fifty works enumerated by Dee himself may be contrasted with a catalogue extending to 79 items, given in Cooper's ATHENÆ CANTABRIGIENSES, 1861, II, 505–9. No. 66 is called TREATISE OF THE ROSICRUCIAN SECRETS, and the reference given is to Harl. 6485. This is one of the fraudu-

I come now to the latest, most insistent and extravagant dream of all, being that which connects Francis Bacon, Lord Verulam, with the Rosicrucian Society as its founder and original head. The name of the Viscount St. Albans has been in the ear of most literate persons for far over twenty-five years—both here and in America—as the concealed author of the Shakespeare plays and poems. Ciphers and bi-literal ciphers have been discovered in the plays and offer proof irrefragable—in the opinion of those who have found them—that the great sanctuary of English literature, the true Helicon or Parnassus, is at St. Albans and not at Stratford-on-Avon. The question is none of our concern, except in one consequence of its growth. The great debate on the ciphers was preceded by a debate which was supposed to be founded on literary criticism, and for all reasonable persons the value of this criticism has been exhibited by its outcome: in other words, the canon of textual consideration which proves Bacon to have written the works passing under the name of Shakespeare makes it not less certain that he was also responsible for the bulk of Elizabethan literature—I speak of that which matters—and of much also which followed, down to the period of ROBINSON CRUSOE. Such being the putative Baconian output, under the veils of many names, it will be obvious that it was capable of yet further extension; and when in the year 1888 there appeared my first study on the subject

lent treatises known as the RUDD COLLECTION and belongs to the eighteenth century. I shall recur to it in a later chapter. As regards Libavius, he produced NEOPARACELSICA, written against the followers of Galen, in 1594, and TRACTATUS DUO PHYSICI in the same year. On alchemy and Hermetic Medicine he was the most voluminous writer of his period—almost of any period—and his OPERA OMNIA MEDICO-CHEMICA appeared in folio at Frankfurt, making three volumes, 1613-15. He died in 1616. I do not find any reference to Dee's MONAS in the texts which I have been able to consult. The MONAS itself is exceedingly curious, but contains nothing to our purpose. Its thesis concerning the symbol of Philosophical Mercury is reflected in Gabella's SECRETIORIS PHILOSOPHIÆ CONSIDERATIO, to which the Rosicrucian CONFESSIO was attached in 1615.

of the Rosy Cross it was seized upon with all eagerness by Baconian dreamers, who shewed to their own satisfaction that the Hermetic Order, clothed in mysterious veils, of anonymous and unknown invention, responded under so many heads to the mighty schemes of Verulam that it could have been conceived by no lesser mind.[1] Thereafter started yet another debate, which has continued with unthinkable developments even to this day. It happened in the fullness of time that—one in connection with the other—Bacon and the Rosicrucians were taken over by the Theosophical Society, which has the freedom of Akasic Records—an illimitable field for skrying—and has published the last word on the whole mystery. By the opening of certain " rifts in the veil of time " to the eye of vision there has unfolded a long scheme of successive incarnations, marking so many great epochs in occult history. I will omit the steps in personality which led up to Christian Rosy Cross, who attained a certain grade of adeptship—as it is affirmed—in the fourteenth century. He became Hunyadi Janos in a later embodiment, Francis Bacon, Thomas Vaughan,[2] a certain Rakocsky—of princely Hungarian birth—and thereafter the Comte de St. Germain, who is alive in the flesh to this day. It is " a story told for the truest," if not for " the holiest that is in this world," and it follows that the *mens sana et alta* of Bacon did not less found the Rosicrucian Order, if he did so under a more

[1] Dr. W. Wynn Westcott, Supreme Magus of the Masonic Rosicrucian Society, is content with affirming, in his DATA OF THE HISTORY OF THE ROSICRUCIANS, that Francis Bacon " became a Rosicrucian Adept." He has neither evidence nor authority, good or bad, to offer for this statement. I note also—not that it matters—his seeming conversion to the chief Baconian contention, for he adds : " And so Rosicrucianism may have been the means of prompting the introduction of many mystic notions into the Plays and Sonnets of Shakespeare." Dr. Westcott's opinion on any literary question is fortunately not of my concern.

[2] It happens, unfortunately, that Vaughan came to birth in 1622, when Bacon was still alive.

ancient personality and wearing another name in the annals of the past.[1]

I am not concerned with pursuing these famous inventions, which must be taken or left according to the quality of our distinctions in respect of psychic evidence and some of its cheap substitutes in common reverie. For my present purpose the one question that emerges is the historical position of the affirmations which link Francis Bacon with the Rosicrucian Brotherhood, in whatever capacity and whether brought forward by those who represent a psychic or presumably critical interest. Let it be remembered that Bacon was born on January 22, 1561, and died in 1626, so that he may be said to have witnessed the Rosicrucian Golden Dawn in 1614 and the setting of its second lustrum. In the year 1902, Mr. A. P. Sinnett, Vice-President of the Theosophical Society for a long period, wrote an article on THE REAL FRANCIS BACON, at the close of which he suggests that, " the student of the great Bacon

[1] An early memorial of this revelation will be found in MAN: WHENCE AND WHITHER, by Annie Besant and C. W. Leadbeater, from which depend many articles scattered throughout the periodical literature of modern theosophy. It may be said to have culminated in FRANCIS BACON, *Baron Verulam, Viscount St. Alban*, by E. F. Udny, M.A., which ran for many months in the columns of THE MESSENGER, an American magazine belonging to the same school The position assumed by this *deliramentum magnum* is that "St. Alban was an initiate of the Great White Lodge," described as a "Brotherhood of Divine Men, the firstfruits of our race, who have already trodden the Path and have become the 'Right Hand' of God, the agents behind the Veil of the Supreme for guiding and governing the world." There is also another book of Mrs. Besant's, entitled THE MASTERS, which summarises the actual findings as follows: "The last survivor of the Royal House of Rákóczi, known as the Comte de St. Germain in the history of the 18th century, as Bacon in the 17th, as Robertus the Monk in the 16th, as Hunyadi Janos in the 15th, as Christian Rosenkreuz in the 14th . . . was disciple through these laborious lives and now has achieved Masterhood, the 'Hungarian Adept' of THE OCCULT WORLD"—a book by A. P. Sinnett—"and known to some of us in that Hungarian body." Compare LE LOTUS BLEU, October, 1912, which claims that theosophy is in direct relation with the Founder of the original Rosicrucian Order. He is described as "an adept known to the initiates of our society."

mystery must turn to Mrs. Henry Pott's painstaking work, FRANCIS BACON AND HIS SECRET SOCIETY, where we get striking arguments to shew that the Rosicrucian movement in the early part of the seventeenth century was Bacon's doing." There is no doubt that this literary lady had a most intimate knowledge of the works of Lord Verulam, as of everything remotely or approximately connected with these, but respecting the nature of evidence she had no knowledge at all; her view that Bacon was the centre of a secret league for the advancement of learning is an expression of belief, and so is also her notion that the league in question was that of the Rosy Cross. We know exactly their root-matter and that the association which Bacon actually planned was in no sense secret at all. It was developed ultimately along similar open lines as the Royal Society. Though somewhat loose in the wording, Bacon's scheme is described tolerably by Bühle in his notice of THE NEW ATLANTIS and its Emblematical House of Solomon—as the idea of a Society of Scholars (1) to promote discoveries in physics by observation and research; (2) to displace the scholastic Aristotelian philosophy; (3) to dispel the theosophic, Kabalistic and alchemical illusions of Bacon's contemporaries; (4) to impel them towards a surer, more faithful study of Nature.[1]

An examination of Mrs. Pott's somewhat elaborate work[2] presents her from the beginning as her own court of appeal, as well as her own counsel. She has credited Francis Bacon, directly or indirectly, with the bulk of important Elizabethan literature, and as it is impossible that he could have produced single-handed so vast an output—

[1] J. G. Bühle: UEBER DEN URSPRUNG . . . DER ROSENKREUZER UND FREYMAURER, 1804, to which Nicolai replied in 1806 in a volume of equal pretensions called EINIGE BEMERKUNGEN ÜBER DEN URSPRUNG DER ROSENKREUZER UND FREYMAURER.

[2] FRANCIS BACON AND HIS SECRET SOCIETY, 1891. The publication of this volume took place in America only.

not to speak of the post-Elizabethan works which are also fathered upon him—she postulates "united efforts." In other words, Bacon was the centre of a "secret league for the advancement of learning." It will be seen that the thesis depends in this manner on the accuracy of her credit side of the account, with which no one is in agreement except a few kindred enthusiasts to whom I shall advert shortly. She tells us in the next place that she has searched the history of Secret Societies throughout the Middle Ages and has decided that the Rosicrucian Fraternity is "the one of all others which would have been best fitted to promote Bacon's lofty aims." There is no need to point out here, as an obvious answer, that the existence of a Rosicrucian Society in the Middle Ages happens to be one of the chief questions at issue: no doubt her purpose would be served equally well by saying that he founded the Order—which is one of her alternatives. It is enough that her contention is based on a question of Baconian authorship, about which neither she nor anyone like her has been able to satisfy a single reasonable mind. When the evidence has been based on supposed critical considerations we are embarked on a sea of false analogies and gratuitous speculations: when it is founded upon buried ciphers they prove to be arbitrary inventions by means of which any authorship could be got out of any document.

Let us admit, however, for a moment the ruling of the court of appeal and even extend its findings. Let us say that Bacon wrote all which matters in English literature from the CANTERBURY TALES to SARTOR RESARTUS.[1] Be

[1] The last suggestion may well appear incredible, but it has been made in THE MESSENGER, that American official organ of the Theosophical Society already quoted, by a writer who is entitled to place M.A., as a title of learning, after his name. From my own point of view the suggestion is of enormous value as an illustration of the canon of criticism which governs the Baconian aspect of Shakespearean research, more especially under theosophical auspices. They prove nothing whose thesis proves too much.

it granted also that a single Secret Society to furnish amanuenses, or even aids in research, seems strictly moderate. But what considerations are offered by Mrs. Pott to persuade us that he selected the Rosicrucians—supposing that they preceded him in time—or established them as a league of scriveners? I have searched the whole volume recommended by Mr. A. P. Sinnett and have found three pieces of alleged evidence. (1) It is said in the FAMA FRATERNITATIS: "After this manner began the Brotherhood of the Rosy Cross, at first by four person only, and by them was made the Magical Language and Writing, with a great Dictionary, which we still use daily to the praise and glory of God, finding great wisdom therein." Herein, as we are told, are the head and heart of Bacon discovered certainly, because one of his most cherished schemes was the compilation of dictionaries. Unfortunately, however, for Mrs. Pott, the Rosicrucian lexicon was obviously a glossary of words to accompany an invented language and its cipher alphabet, whereas Bacon's hypothetical dictionaries stood for encyclopædic compilations, for repositories of knowledge. That is the distinction between them, and thereon collapses the evidence.[1] (2) The second evidential point, according to Mrs. Pott, is that Bacon's College of the Six Days, described in THE NEW ATLANTIS, is the College of the Rosicrucians.[2] This, as she says, "we know," the rejoinder to which is an equally distinct negative. (3) For the third she produces a selection

[1] Were it otherwise, as there should be no need to add, the compilation of an encyclopædia, *ex hypothesi* in the fifteenth or any other century, would not prove that Bacon was connected with the compilers because he also had a kindred scheme in his mind.

[2] THE NEW ATLANTIS is an unfinished allegorical romance of the Utopian kind which was published after the author's death by Dr. William Rawley, being appended to SYLVA SYLVARUM and followed by THE HISTORY OF LIFE AND DEATH. A sixth edition appeared in 1651. The College of the Six Days was called Solomon's House alternatively, and was a place set apart from the rest, even in the Utopian community.

from fifty-two alleged Rules or Laws adopted by the original Rosicrucians ; but with due respect to the good intentions of a deceased lady I have to submit that, as enumerated by her, these Laws are fraudulent. The "original" Rosicrucians—according to their legend—had an agreement in common together, embodied in six clauses only, as we shall see in the proper place, and out of these she extracts three. The fifty-two Laws are those published by Sigmund Richter in 1710,[1] but Mrs. Pott has subjected them to a process of editing in the interests of personal predilections, as, for example, to shew that Rosicrucians were forbidden to issue Rosicrucian writings under the names of their authors[2]—presumably because the vast supposititious works of Bacon appeared under other designations than his own. Such are the heads of evidence that Francis Bacon belonged to the Rosicrucian Society, whether as member and chief at his period or as its original founder : they are of the same kind and the same value as those by which it has been sought to shew he wrote the plays of Shakespeare, THE FAERIE QUEEN, THE ANATOMY OF MELANCHOLY and so onward through the centuries, almost to our own day.

Next to Mrs. Constance M. Pott the most zealous follower of this Quixotic quest was Mr. W. F. C. Wigston, who between 1888 and 1892 issued four large volumes, in which the connection between Bacon and the Rosicrucians was put forward as strenuously as his authorship of the Shakespeare plays, the speculations being carried also

[1] S. R., i.e. Sincerus Renatus, i.e. Sigmund Richter : DIE WAHRHAFFTE UND VOLLKOMMENE BEREITUNG DES PHILOSOPHISCENS STEINS, etc. etc., i.e., THE PERFECT AND TRUE PREPARATION OF THE PHILOSOPHICAL STONE, ACCORDING TO THE SECRET METHOD OF THE BROTHERHOOD OF THE GOLDEN AND ROSY CROSS. *With the Rules of the said Order for the Initiation of New Members.* Breslau, 1710.

[2] It was decreed by Rule 13 that the making or printing of extracts from the secret writings could not take place except by licence of the Congregation, and that such extracts were not to be signed with "the names or characters of any Brother"—a reference most probably to their Sacramental Names.

a considerable distance forward owing to a better acquaintance with Latin and German sources.[1] Were it possible to accept them we should reach at least a *terminus* beyond which it would be impossible to go, looking back into the past after Rosicrucian origins, and a starting-point forward as from a basis in real fact. The vital points of Mr. Wigston's scattered and not a little confused thesis may be collected thus together: (1) That Bacon belonged to a corporate Society of which he was founder or head, and that it is described under veils in THE NEW ATLANTIS. (2) That this Society was actually the Brotherhood of the Rosy Cross, the manifestoes of which carry the chief marks and seals of his own mind and philosophy. (3) That Rosicrucian literature—which began in 1614—declined soon after his death in 1626. (4) That a notable Rosicrucian Emblem appears on the title-page of THE NEW ATLANTIS and on that of DE AUGMENTIS, being a heart placed in the centre of an open rose. (5) That all the curious and recondite doctrines held by the Rosicrucians are reflected by Bacon—including a restoration of knowledge, the music of the spheres, the doctrines of the spheres, and so forth. (6) That Rosicrucianism originated in England and not in Germany. (7) That the initials of Francis Bacon appear in the FAMA FRATERNITATIS, accompanied by a personal description, through which he is identified.

[1] BACON, SHAKESPEARE AND THE ROSICRUCIANS, 1888; HERMES STELLA: Notes and Jottings upon the Bacon Cipher, 1890; FRANCIS BACON—POET, PROPHET, PHILOSOPHER—versus PHANTOM CAPTAIN SHAKESPEARE, THE ROSICRUCIAN MASK, 1891; THE COLUMBUS OF LITERATURE, OR BACON'S NEW WORLD OF SCIENCES, 1892. The first of these volumes appeared in London and the fourth at Chicago. Mr. Wigston was an amiable and interesting man, whose zeal and devotion should have produced good fruit in legitimate fields of research. After the publication of his fourth volume he disappeared altogether from the arena of debate, and I have failed to trace him subsequently. Baconians of the present generation, outside theosophical circles, seem to have dropped the Rosicrucian thesis.

I have put these points concisely, yet with a certain force of expression, that they may lose nothing in the enumeration: I will now take them successively and exhibit their evidential values. (1) There is nothing whatsoever in the life of Bacon to shew that he was connected with secret associations of any kind, but on the contrary there is everything to indicate that he desired to bring the *literati* and learned of Europe together in an open manner, for the better advancement of learning.[1]

THE NEW ATLANTIS represents a commonwealth of learning established on those lines and is an allegorical picture of the scheme. It is a fable embodying a design. To suggest that it represents anything existing in time and space is equivalent to proposing that Campanella's CITY OF THE SUN or the RESPUBLICA CHRISTIANA of Andreæ belongs to annals of literal history.[2] (2) As there is no warrant for supposing that Bacon founded or belonged to any Secret Societies there can be none for his connection with the Rosy Cross, yet there is a certain very modified sense in which it is true to say that the FAMA FRATERNITATIS and its connections are in analogy with the mind of Bacon over things which are common to both. The reformation of arts and sciences, the appeal from scholasticism to Nature,

[1] The fact is on the face of his writings and has been recognised fully and frequently. It is indeed the whole motive and subject of Bacon's ADVANCEMENT OF LEARNING, which he was ready to promote by all reasonable means. If he speaks in one place of passing certain things "from hand to hand with selection and judgment," by a private reservation for "fit and selected minds," there is nothing in his life or his writings to shew that he pursued this method, which he regarded, moreover, as "an old trick of impostors," who have "made it as a false light for their counterfeit merchandises."

[2] REIPUBLICÆ CHRISTIANOPOLITANÆ DESCRIPTIO, 1619. An English translation by Dr. F. E. Held has been issued by the American Branch of the Oxford University Press, 1917. It is called CHRISTIANOPOLIS, truly "a neglected Utopia," as someone has said concerning it. Campanella's CITY OF THE SUN—CIVITAS SOLIS, IDEA REIPUBLICÆ PHILOSOPHICÆ, 1623—seems far-famed in comparison.

the dethronement of Aristotle, the longing for a better body of medicine and a purer body of religion began neither with Bacon nor the Rosicrucians, for their roots lie back in the centuries. The Rosicrucians and Bacon are in undesigned correspondence therefore one with another, not because the secret Brotherhood came to birth in a study at St. Albans or because German *adepti* inspired the *Novum Organum*, but because both belonged to their epoch and were products of their immediate past. (3) To affirm that Rosicrucian literature declined soon after the death of Bacon in 1626 is an arbitrary and *ex parte* statement for the sustenance of a particular thesis, and the bibliographical records are against it. So far as Germany is concerned it had declined previously; and publications on either side of the debate raised by the official pamphlets were few and far between after the year 1620. I can trace nothing in France prior to 1623, when Gabriel Naudé issued his hostile criticism, while in England Robert Fludd was still unfolding Rosicrucian theosophy and occult sciences in 1629. (4) The notable Rosicrucian Emblem proves on comparison not to be Rosicrucian at all. The heart placed in the centre of an open rose should have a cross inscribed upon the heart, in which form it appears—but very late indeed in the records—among THE SECRET SYMBOLS OF THE ROSICRUCIANS OF THE SIXTEENTH AND SEVENTEENTH CENTURIES, Altona, 1785–8.[1] Stripped as it is of this key-sign, the device of Bacon or his printer has no connection with our research. (5) The alleged analogies between Rosicrucian and Baconian doctrine have been discussed sufficiently in my consideration of the second point; and it remains only to say that such topics as the music of the spheres, the harmonies of the world and so forth are only treated incidentally and casually by the philosopher of

[1] There is also one example of a heart centred in a cross. See p. 14 of the reprint issued at Berlin in 1919.

St. Albans, whereas Robert Fludd—his contemporary—had taken them into his heart and wrote at large concerning them.[1] (6) As regards this point, it must be understood that the origin of Rosicrucianism in England rather than in Germany—though Christian Rosy Cross was a German by the hypothesis of history [2]—does not depend from any particle of direct evidence, but is an implication of the dream that Bacon was father or at least a sponsor of the Order. On such an assumption it is obvious that Rosicrucianism was conceived in England, even if it was born abroad; but there is no external fact or circumstance to render such a notion tolerable. Mr. Wigston [3] says that when Michael Maier, the alchemist, visited England, and perhaps stayed with Robert Fludd in his beautiful manor at Bearsted, he did not bring the Order of the Rosy Cross —so to speak—in his pocket: he carried it back rather on his return to Germany. But a little later on our apologist has perforce to admit that on his return Maier found the *literati* of his native land—all its theosophists, alchemists and astrologers, all the easy believers in tales of wonder and all the hard heads—waging one with another a royal battle on the claims of the Rosicrucian manifestoes. There is not the least reason for placing the origin of the Order otherwise than in the Teutonic fatherland, where all its antecedents lay: it bears the signs and seals of its German sources and is redolent of that environment. (7) To say, finally, that the initials of Francis Bacon appear in the FAMA FRATERNITATIS, together with a personal

[1] See the speculations on music in UTRIUSQUE COSMI MAJORIS. . . . PHYSICA ATQUE TECHNICA HISTORIA TOMUS PRIMUS, 1617; *ibid.*, TRACTATUS SECUNDUS, 1618, *s.v.*, *De Templo Musicæ; Anatomiæ Amphitheatrum*, etc., 1623, *s.v.*, *Monochordum Mundi Symphoniacum*, and elsewhere in his writings.

[2] The FAMA describes him as "the most godly and highly illuminated Father, our Brother, C.:.R.:.C.:., a German, and adds elsewhere that in his youth he was "of a strong Dutch constitution."

[3] See FRANCIS BACON, etc., *s.v.*, "Notes on Rosicrucian Literature."

description, is—in all frankness—to bear false testimony. The manifesto in question alludes to a mysterious Book T, being a parchment, described as a great treasure. It ends with a Latin ELOGIUM, after which the Brethren of the first and second circles are said to have placed their initials, by way of signature. Among those of the earlier group—and belonging *ex hypothesi* therefore to the fifteenth century—is *Fra* ∴ F ∴ B ∴ M ∴ P ∴ A ∴, described as *Pictor et Architectus*.[1] There is neither sense nor sincerity in affirming that these initials signify Francis Bacon, nor could he be identified otherwise under such denominations as Painter and Architect, though Mr. Wigston has dedicated several pages to an argument that he was both, if the words are understood within their figurative or emblematical measures.

We see, therefore, that so far as evidential values are concerned the deponent here cited is out of court or non-suited on every count of his affidavit. Were it possible to think for a moment that the Fraternity of the Rosy Cross had its concealed founder and chief in this country, Robert Fludd would be assuredly a far more plausible claimant than Francis Bacon; he corresponds to all the essential qualifications, generally as occult philosopher, especially as Theosophist, Alchemist, Kabalist, Magian and Exponent of *medicina catholica*, who taught from a seat of learning placed within the veil of a mystical sanctuary of healing, according to his own description. Bacon was none of these things, and Mr. Wigston has fallen into many signal errors of enthusiasm in attempting to shew that he was.

There is also Mr. Harold Bayley, who appealed long ago, for "further investigation and research" in respect of

[1] The same original member seems to be mentioned earlier as Brother B ∴, and the alleged personal description says that he was "a skilful painter," which cannot be called a characteristic definition of Francis Bacon.

Francis Bacon.[1] He lays down (1) that "St. Alban, poet and dramatist," belonged to "the mystic Brotherhood of the Rosicrucians," apparently because it was one of "their principles and rules to produce works under other names than their own"—being Mrs. Pott's thesis, as we have seen; (2) that the history of Bacon offers a parallel with that of Christian Rosy Cross, because at the age of fifteen he requested his parents to remove him from Cambridge, "as he had acquired everything the university was able to teach," while—according to the FAMA FRATERNITATIS—the Rosicrucian protagonist went Eastward in search of wisdom at about the same age; (3) that Mr. Bayley has discovered "peculiar and distinctive Rosicrucian symbols, cunningly but unquestionably concealed in the ornamental head and tail pieces" of Baconian books; (4) that certain watermarks on the paper used in printing THE ADVANCEMENT OF LEARNING shew the initials R. C., C. R. and "perhaps" C. R. C., while others include roses. The frivolity of these intimations is manifest on their surface. (1) The original Rosicrucian manifestoes were by their hypothesis on the part of the Society at large and could appear under no individual names, but the expository literature of the subject is under well-known names, like those of Robert Fludd, Michael Maier, Thomas Vaughan, John Heydon, whence it is the very reverse of the truth to propose that the mystical Brethren were accustomed to produce works under names other than their own. (2) Between the biography of Bacon and the traditional personality of FAMA FRATERNITATIS there is no analogy

[1] See TRAGEDY OF SIR FRANCIS BACON, 1902, and also JOURNAL OF THE BACON SOCIETY for the same year. I do not know whether Mr. Bayley has abandoned the views summarised above, but in his NEW LIGHT ON THE RENAISSANCE and LOST LANGUAGE OF SYMBOLISM, published some years later, the references to Bacon are few and far between and are confined to brief quotations, quite apart from any thesis, though he is dealing with watermarks and printers' ornamental blocks.

whatever. The one left Cambridge, weening himself stuffed with its knowledge, but the other went to the East, presumably in search of knowledge. It seems almost beneath the native dignity of criticism that one is called upon to point out a fact so obvious as this. (3) The alleged Rosicrucian symbols in the head and tail-pieces of Bacon's works can be dismissed in a no less summary manner, for the Brotherhood of the Rosy Cross has only one characteristic and exclusive emblem,[1] being that whence their name derives, and it appears nowhere in connection with the writings of Verulam, whether as a printer's ornament or as a watermark on the paper. (4) As regards watermarks, I make no pretence of distinguishing the specific edition of THE ADVANCEMENT to which Mr. Bayley refers, but it is certainly not that of the first two books, which appeared in 1605, is long antecedent to the original proclamations of the Order in Germany and could therefore—under any circumstances—prove nothing. I am of course far from admitting that the initials C. R. and their variants used as watermarks would prove anything at any period, and I remember Mr. Bayley's methods in two later books, where any watermark chalice is affirmed to be the Holy Graal, and any pictured castle is that of Corbenic or Mont Salvatch. It is not in such manner that great debatable questions attain a settlement.[2]

[1] It has been naturally a matter of convenience to father on the Brotherhood any emblems which happened to help the speculations of enthusiasts who have seen the Rosy Cross wherever they turned their eyes and would have liked to discover it everywhere. The pelican is one useful instance, but we shall find much later on its real position in our subject. As the Rosicrucians were alchemists, all the great cloud of pictorial symbols found in alchemical textbooks may have been part of their concern ; but they were not characteristic of the Order. So also on rare occasions we meet with figures and diagrams in Rosicrucian books which are suggestive of Masonic signs and moralities ; but again they are accidental or subsidiary, not essential to the Order and not belonging to its doctrine.

[2] See A NEW LIGHT ON THE RENAISSANCE, 1909, pp. 68, 69, where it is said that some writers represent the Castle of the Graal as situated on a moun-

Here are the findings of an exceedingly restrained criticism on the Baconian origin of the Rosy Cross, outside akasic records. The last state of the subject is far more frantic than the first in respect of these, for there has come about a kind of marriage between the two methods of research. The results of astral skrying have been fortified by gleanings from the Bacon-Shakespeare literature, while the pages of Mrs. Pott and her lineal descendants in the apostleship of literary unreason have been illuminated from time to time by the faculty of intuition and its substitutes, directed thereupon. There was never such a mad world, my masters, as that which has been formulated around the central figure of Viscount St. Albans. It seems idle to plead that for want of evidence—except in the opposite direction—we are unable to regard him as a Master of the Rosy Cross, or originator of the Rosicrucian Fraternity. or directly in touch with the Brotherhood and author of the allegory concerning C∴R∴C∴,[1] when these comparatively minor marvels are swallowed up in the shadow of truly cyclopean revelations, according to which (1) Bacon "created single-handed the literature and to a large extent the language of the Elizabethan age"; (2) was the real author of Pope's ESSAY ON MAN, of Addison's contribu-

tain. "Figs. 155 to 158 are representations of this castle." Again: "In Figs. 165 to 213 we have a series of designs embodying the manifold phases of the Graal cult." There is no evidence whatever and no process of interpretation could beg any question at issue more completely. See also THE LOST LANGUAGE OF SYMBOLISM, 2 vols., 1912. "The object surmounting Fig. 127 is the Sangraal," p. 51. Many other places could be cited, and the method adopted throughout—whatever the subject in hand—seems to me quite as arbitrary. It is characteristic of the kind of research. M. Eugène Aroux pursued it for years in France, and his MYSTÈRES DE LA CHEVALERIE is its illustration at large.

[1] See THE ROSICRUCIANS, by Brothers H. C. and K. M. B., which says: (1) that there is a strong probability that its author was Francis Bacon, Lord Verulam; (2) that THE NEW ATLANTIS is a sequel to FAMA FRATERNITATIS; (3) that seal, sign, secrecy and oath were identical in both works, which is utterly contrary to fact; (4) that as in Bensalem of THE NEW ATLANTIS

tions to THE SPECTATOR, of SARTOR RESARTUS—perhaps by way of inspiration—of THE ANCIENT MARINER and Fitzgerald's OMAR KHAYYÁM ; and finally (3) endured not only the incarnations and reincarnations which have been mentioned briefly but was the legitimate son of Queen Elizabeth and heir to the throne of Britain in place of James I. It seems incredible that a sane editor—if such a person exists in American theosophical literature—should publish month after month these vagaries of a literary mania in a periodical which pretends to be serious. But these on the one part are findings of the particular canon of criticism adopted in Baconian circles, and on the other are relations of ciphers and bi-literal ciphers, fortified by expert readings in the astral records of the past.

That which emerges from the research embodied in the present chapter is the signal importance attached to the idea of the Rosy Cross, its fact and the claims advanced concerning it, for several occult interests at this day and during two or three generations immediately preceding. There is no greater name in alchemy than is that of Raymund Lully, whether identified with the *doctor illuminatus* of the Balearic Isles or regarded as an Unknown Master, described vaguely as a Jewish neophyte, which might

there were " books pertaining to the Christian Revelation before they were written," so in the tomb of Christian Rosy Cross were unwritten works of Paracelsus, truly a striking evidence of *lapsus memoriæ* in both cases. The rest of the evidence for the Baconian authorship of the FAMA is of similar value. No doubt the canon of criticism represents a high-water mark of Baconian erudition acquired in the light of theosophy and its peculiar glass of vision. As regards the work which I have cited and its authors, Brothers H. C. and K. M. B. are to be understood as ladies, in accordance with the unspeakable terminology of Female Freemasonry. The little volume forms one of the TRANSACTIONS of the Golden Rule Lodge, under the obedience of Universal Co-Freemasonry. This body is to be distinguished from an independent obedience which came forth therefrom, and because it is the newest thing on earth is not unfitly denominated Ancient Freemasonry. The book is innocent enough by intention, but fanciful in its dealings with the facts of Rosicrucian history and of wild extravagance in speculation.

suggest a " proselyte of the gate," but was used to identify a convert from the religion of Israel. There is no occult personality to compare with Paracelsus, while that other ill-starred pupil of Trithemius, Cornelius Agrippa, is of traditional repute in magic. Lastly, Francis Bacon is the monitor and prophet of the new age which followed the Renaissance and Reformation. It is these who are marshalled successively to explain the Rosicrucian Mystery. The pleas fail, as we have seen, but there is something momentous in the ascriptions. It means that in study-groups, as among romance writers, the Mystery loomed largely, portending much more than was exhibited on its surface, however curiously blazoned.

CHAPTER II

MILITIA CRUCIFERA EVANGELICA

So far as the inquiry has proceeded, we have failed to find traces of any Rosicrucian Fraternity prior to the seventeenth century. Certain conspicuous personalities—occult and otherwise—have been cited as its founders or members, but the ascriptions have proved on examination to be based (1) on false inferences from the text of an early document—as in the cases of Raymund Lully, the alchemist, and a Prince-Archbishop of Trèves; (2) on the authority of archives which are not produced in evidence—as in the case of Paracelsus; (3) on the identification of any report or rumour concerning any Secret Society of past centuries—more especially of an alchemical kind—with the *Fratres Roseæ Crucis*, as in the case of Agrippa; (4) on the careless misreading of a printed text—as in that of John Dee; or (5) on the literary arguments of persons whose canons of criticism are beneath contempt, and on the ravings of occult dreamers—as in the case of Bacon. The speculations on Rosicrucian origins apart from specific or known personalities are also numerous and have one common characteristic, being the absence of evidence to support them. I will pass over Michael Maier, who decides on 1413 as the date of the Order's foundation,[1] because he and his claims will call for consideration at length. Solomon Semler also refers the Rosicrucians to the fifteenth century

[1] See THEMIS AUREA: *hoc est, de Legibus Fraternitatis R∴C...* Francofurti, 1618.

and says that the name Rosenkreutz—being that of the traditional founder—was borrowed from a Knight of the Golden Fleece.[1] His speculative dates are as follows: 1410, a Rosicrucian Society arose about this time, or was then existing in Italy; 1430, there was another established in Flanders; 1459, another was extant in Germany.[2]

It must be admitted freely and fully that there was nothing more calculated to produce casual and informal association for aid and support in common than the arduous pursuit of alchemy and its gropings in the dark night of physics. There are traces of such association, and I have no doubt in my mind that Italy, Germany and France were full of Secret Societies prior to the Reformation[3]—some for the advancement of science, of which alchemy would be then a branch; some for the liberation of religion, of which the Brethren of the Common Life, the Friends of God and the sects in Southern France are typical examples; some for the administration of occult justice, like the Secret Tribunal. But the point is that in respect

[1] UNPARTEIISCHE SAMMLUNGEN ZUR HISTORIE DER ROSENKREUZER. 4 parts, 1786–8.

[2] The facts—real or alleged—produced by Semler do not bear out his opinions. The so-called Rosicrucian Society is obviously the more or less mythical *Academia di Segreti*, of which we hear in connection with John Baptista Porta, who is supposed to have founded it in the second half of the sixteenth century.

[3] They were probably everywhere and for purposes of all kinds, England being no exception. Among Ashmolean MSS. at Oxford, the vellum fly-leaves of No. 360 contain (1) "Letters of Frater Johannes Gardianus . . . receiving Richard Ghonge (or Young) into a Fraternity. Dated in the Epiphany, 1450. . . . (2) Letters of Frater Wi . . ., receiving John Claxtone and Matild his wife into a Fraternity." See CATALOGUE of the MSS. bequeathed to the University of Oxford by Elias Ashmole. Ed. by W. H. Black, 1845, p. 271. The nature of these associations does not emerge, but the use of the term *Frater* in both cases carries occult suggestions, religious or otherwise. As regards Gardianus, see my note *ante*, p. 11, respecting Hortulanus. If this pseudonym and also that of Ortholanus covers the personality of Gardianus, writing in the mid-fifteenth century, it follows that Dumbeler's dedication to Falkenstein is antedated by nearly a century.

of alchemy every rumour—at however far a distance—of sporadic gatherings together has been at once labelled Rosicrucian by uncritical people in the past; and the qualifications of Semler are indicated by his last date. The year 1459 is that which appears at the head of the third Rosicrucian manifesto—being THE CHEMICAL NUPTIALS—and it is at once interpreted as evidence that the Order was extant in Germany at that period. But we shall see that the romance in question belongs, by the confession of its writer, to *circa* 1603.

Coming down to much later fantasiasts, there is John Yarker—always confused and confusing—who affirms that the early Rosicrucians were initiated by "the Moslem sectaries" and adds that the fact is "in evidence," but no authority is given.[1] It can be supplied, however, for according to the FAMA FRATERNITATIS the traditional Christian Rosy Cross visited Damascus and Fez, as well as a certain Hidden City, and was there instructed in the secret knowledge which became afterwards that of the Order. So does Rosicrucian myth become witness of Rosicrucian claims, according to the best spirit of Yarker's methods—other evidence being none. There is also the voice of Masonry, as it has been raised on the subject in Switzerland, and according to this the Rosicrucians were Gnostic heretics.[2] It is an exceedingly mixed instruction,

[1] THE ARCANE SCHOOLS, by John Yarker, 1909, p. 430. The chief point that is "in evidence" throughout this chaotic volume is the author's capacity for accepting anything that he has met with in print under practically any circumstances, so long as it serves his purpose. In his occasional periodical THE KNEPH, Vol. IV, No. 3, August, 1844, he alludes in similar terms of certitude to a "Rosicrucian MS. at Cologne, written by *Non Omnis Moriar*." But he is only quoting from THE ROSICRUCIAN UNVEILED of Magister Pianco, who cites nothing in support of his statement.

[2] MAÇONNERIE PRATIQUE: *Cours d'Enseignement Supérieur de la Franc-Maçonnerie, Rite Écossais Ancien et Accepté.* 2 vols, 1885. It is called *édition sacrée, s'addressant exclusivement aux Francs-Maçons réguliers*, and yet it is *publiée par un Profane.* The editor is an enemy of Freemasonry

which postulates Zoroaster as the fountain-source of Gnostic doctrine, but he derived apparently from India. It was after this manner—if I understand the deposition rightly—that Christianity itself came into the world, "a gnosticisation of the ancient symbolism." The Templars arose in their day and acquired Gnosticism at the feet of Persian Sufis. Being destroyed in due course, the "pure Gnostic symbolism" was inherited and preserved by the Rosicrucian sect. This is obviously matter of revelation—however and whencesoever inspired—so that it transcends the evidence which it is not in a position to furnish. We meet otherwise with the Order of the Temple, which—according to an alternative reverie—did not beget the Brotherhood of the Rosy Cross, this having been transmitted by Ormuz, as we have seen already; but the two Orders subsisted in close alliance.

These inventions might be multiplied almost indefinitely, but enough has been cited for my purpose, and I do not claim to have taken the entire annals of folly as my province. Not one of those which have been selected carries the thinnest colourable tincture of the plausible on its surface, while the seals of intellectual dishonesty are the sign-manuals which are marked on most.

As a possible counterpoise to the myths of cloud and moonshine, I shall take in the present chapter one case which stands out by itself and appears to offer something in the guise of concrete fact, whether or not it may prove to have been overlaid subsequently. Our initial knowledge on the subject throughout English-speaking countries is

and states that the work which he introduces is one of the worst of its kind. It claims to have been written *par le très puissant Souverain Grand Commandeur des Suprèmes Conseils confédérés à Lausanne en* 1875. There is, however, no Sovereign Commander of all Supreme Councils in the Scottish Rite. At the particular assembly or convention there would have been an elected President.

an essay[1] by Thomas de Quincey, adapted rather than translated from a German original,[2] the work of Professor J. G. Bühle, a writer of consequence at the end of the eighteenth and early in the nineteenth century. He is one also who followed the golden counsel of citing the authorities from whom he derived on his own part, and in this manner I have got so far to the root of the subject as seems possible at this day. Bühle derived his information from WIRTEMBERGISCHES REPERTORIUM DER LITTERATUR,[3] containing an historical monograph entitled NEW ELUCIDATION OF THE HISTORY OF THE ROSICRUCIANS AND ALCHEMISTS, on which the following account is founded. It tells of a certain enthusiast named Simon Studion, who was born at Urach in the State of Würtemburg in 1543.[4] He graduated

[1] HISTORICO-CRITICAL INQUIRY INTO THE ORIGIN OF THE ROSICRUCIANS AND THE FREEMASONS. LONDON MAGAZINE, Vol. IX, January to June, 1824. The successive papers were initialled X. Y. Z. It has been reprinted frequently in the Collected Works of De Quincey and in selections therefrom.

[2] J. G. Bühle: UEBER DEN URSPRUNG UND DIE VORNEHMSTEN SCHICKSALE DES ORDENS DER ROSENKREUZER UND FREIMAURER, 1804. It was delivered originally in Latin as a discourse before a Philosophical Society of Göttingen and is supposed to have been printed in this form, but all references which I have met with have proved to be false lights. The following brief report appeared in GÖTTINGISCHE GELEHRTE ANZEIGEN UNTER DER ANSICHT DER KÖNIGB. GESELLSCHAFT DER WISSENSCHAFTEN. 5 *Stück den* 8 *January*, 1803: "Göttingen: *Am* 18 *December vor. F. hielt der Hr. Professor Bühle eine historische Vorlesung in der Königb. Societat der Wissenschaften über die Entstehung der Freymaurerey, als einen Gegenstand, der in die Geschichte der Philosophie gehört*, p. 41.

[3] The REPERTORIUM appeared in three small volumes, 1782–3, and is a collection of considerable interest. The monograph under notice begins at p. 512 of Vol. III and is pseudonymous, but—as suggested by Von Murr—they were all possibly the work of J. W. Petersen, who seems to have been editor of the whole and is described as *Herzogl. Wirtemb. Unter-Bibliotheker.* His name appears after Tract 8 in the third volume. The second volume is almost entirely occupied by a life of J. V. Andreæ. Behind the REPERTORIUM there stands a much earlier reference, being that of Melchior Fischlin: MEMORIA THEOLOG. WIRTEMBERG, 1708, Supplement, pp. 204–5, *s.v.* Simon Studion. To this I shall refer shortly.

[4] It is said that there is much confusion as to the date and personality of Studion. His name is of considerable importance "for the history of

at Tubingen in 1565, under a master named Martinus Crusius.[1] At a later period—probably about 1572—he is said to have become a "preceptor" at the town of Marbach, near Ludwigsburg, which itself is at no great distance from Stuttgart. Among other activities he was occupied with the collection of precious stones and monuments which are now in the Stuttgart Library.[2] Memorials of these investigations are still extant in manuscript, but they do not concern our subject.[3] Simon Studion is affirmed

antiquarian work in Würtemberg," and his epigraphical writings are said to have been examined with great care in modern times. Mr. F. N. Pryce, of the British Museum, informed me that there is an account of his antiquarian activities in Haug: RÖMISCHE INSCHRIFTEN, etc., Bildwerke Würtembergs, Stuttgart, 1912, but it contains nothing to my present purpose. There is also a critical review of his epigraphical writings in CORPUS INSCR. ROMAN., Vol. XIII, Pt. 2, pp. 208, 209.

[1] I have searched the memorials of Martinus Crusius, who did not die till 1607. He was born in 1526 and was Professor of Greek at Tubingen. He wrote on Byzantine history and translated Homer into Latin. See ORATIO DE VITA ET OBITU. . . . D. MARTINI CRUSII, *Tubingensis Academiæ per annos octo et quadraginta Professoris nobilissimi ac celebratissimi . . . a clarissimo viro* D. VITO MYLLERO, 1608. Were there time in the world for everything, some of the Latin treatises of Crusius would repay reading. One at least on the Heavenly Jerusalem deserves more than the passing glance by which I have satisfied myself that it contains nothing regarding his pupils. But Crusius compiled also a Suabian Chronicle—SCHWABISCHER CHRONICK—which seems to have been first published in 1733, and a reference to Studion will be found in Part III, Bk. XII, cap. xi, p. 311. He is mentioned again in Moser's Supplement to the second volume. See p. 78, in connection with an Historical Calendar of Würtemberg.

[2] See C. F. Sattler: (1) ALLGEMEINE GESCHICHTE WÜRTEMBERGS UND DESSEN ANGRÄNZENDEN GEBIETHE UND GEGENDEN, etc. 5 *Theile*, 1764–8; (2) HISTORISCHE BESCHREIBUNG DES HERZOGTHUMS WÜRTEMBERG UND ALLER DESSELBEN STÄDTE, CLÖSTER UND DAZU GEHÖRIGEN AEMTER, etc. 2 *Theile*, 1752.

[3] See DIE HISTORISCHEN HANDSCHRIFTEN DER KÖNIGLICHEN ÖFFENTLICHEN BIBLIOTHEK ZU STUTTGART. *Beschreiben von Oberstudienrat Dr. W. von Heyd, Oberbibliothekar. Erster Band: Die Handschriften in Folio.* Stuttgart, 1889–90. (1) No. 57 in this Catalogue reads as follows: *Vera origo illustrissimæ et antiquissimæ domus Wirtembergiæ*, etc., *una cum venerandæ antiquitatis Romanis in agro Wirtembergico conquisitis et explicatis monumentis industria et labore* M. SIMONIS STUDIONIS *præceptoris apud Martisbacenses.* (2) No. 137 reads: *Ratio nominis et originis antiquissimæ atque illustrissimæ*

to have expended great pains and to have received considerable assistance from State grants of funds. He was more, however, than an antiquarian and *virtuoso* of his period. In the year 1586 he was at Lüneburg[1] in Hanover, where he either convoked or attended a memorable assembly of a religious character, out of which there arose the MILITIA CRUCIFERA EVANGELICA—otherwise, the Evangelical Brotherhood, according to a description in the REPERTORIUM. The REPERTORIUM adds (1) that this soon became " a strong sect " and (2) that it was a branch of the Rosicrucians, as is " well known." C. G. von Murr, a writer who was contemporary with Bühle, bears the same testimony.[2] If this be so, it will have to be admitted—in however broad a sense—that a Brotherhood or Society in the likeness of that with which we are dealing—and are now on the quest of its origin—had been established in Germany some twenty-eight years prior to the issue of the first formal Rosicrucian documents, and that this fact puts an end for ever to the most generally favoured hypothesis respecting the Order, being that which looks to the Würtemberg theologian Andreæ as inventor or founder, after one or another manner. The year 1586 was that of the birth of Andreæ.

domus Wirtembergicæ fideliter inquisita anno nostri salutis 1597 *authore* SIMONE STUDIONE *Uracæo apud Marpachenses præceptore.* See also *Ibid., Zweiter Band*: DIE HANDSCHRIFTEN IN QUARTO UND OKTAVO. Stuttgart, 1891.—No. 96. *Fragment einer Geschichte Schwabens ohne Titel, Aufang und Ende, lateinisch geschrieben von* SIMON STUDION.

[1] Wigston affirms in HERMES STELLA (1) that Lüneberg was " one of the head centres of the Rosicrucians "—but he means the MILITIA CRUCIFERA EVANGELICA—and (2) that De Quincey mentions a meeting of them at this place (p. 51). As a matter of fact, so far as De Quincey and his original are concerned, his brief reference to the MILITIA CRUCIFERA EVANGELICA is by no means a reference to Rosicrucians.

[2] Christoph Gottlieb von Murr is noted as born at Nuremberg in 1733, and he died on April 8, 1811. His Essay on the TRUE ORIGIN OF THE ROSICRUCIAN AND MASONIC ORDERS—ÜBER DEN WAHREN URSPRUNG DER ROSENKREUZER UND DES FREYMAURER ORDENS—appeared in 1803 and had an appendix on the history of Knights Templar.

The allegations concerning Studion and his MILITIA may be summarised briefly thus: (1) They accepted the occult teaching and philosophy of Paracelsus on chemistry and astronomy,[1] which would mean that the Hermetic Art was something far more catholic and important for them than the mere transmutation of metals one into another. We find also the FAMA FRATERNITATIS discoursing upon "the ungodly and accursed gold-making," and claiming on the part of the Brotherhood "a thousand better things,"[2] while the CONFESSIO dilates upon "the worthless books of pseudo-chemists," though testifying that it does not "set at naught" the transmutation of metals and "the supreme medicine of the world." This is precisely the position of Paracelsus. Astronomy of course included for the Helvetian Master of Secrets the signs and portents of the heavens, in accordance with which the CONFESSIO talks of new stars in Serpentarius and Cygnus as "powerful signs of a great council" and as evidence that the Book of Nature stands open for all eyes, though it can be read only by a few. (2) They looked for the renovation of the earth and a general reform to come, in other words, a Rosicrucian universal reformation, the correction of many "errors of our arts," a new order in "divine and human things" and, in fine, an "amendment of philosophy," which expectations were also the cause and reason of addressing the FAMA and CONFESSIO to the learned of Europe. (3) They regarded the revelations of Holy Scripture as *intus et foris scriptæ*—written within and without—like the

[1] In her LIFE OF PARACELSUS Miss Stoddart says that the MILITIA elaborated the views of Paracelsus "upon evolution, into an advanced theory." There is not a particle of evidence for this and no references are given. The speculations of the sixteenth century were not those of the twentieth.

[2] The heads of the criticism are (1) that under colour of alchemy "many runagates and roguish people do use great villainies," and (2) that even men of discretion are regarding the transmutation of metals as the highest point of philosophy.

Book of Nature. (4) They were an ultra-Protestant body, "heated by apocalyptic dreams," regarding the Pope as Antichrist and the Man of Sin—after the best manner of the CONFESSIO FRATERNITATIS R .·.C .·. (5) Finally, they used the symbols of the the Rose and Cross.

Against these arresting points of correspondence we have to place the fact that the MILITIA were ardent Second Adventists, according to their story, and that this enthusiasm did not especially characterise the later Order, though its documents shew certain traces. It constitutes—to my mind —a point of distinction, as between a transformation of the schools, effected *ex hypothesi* by communicating to Western scholars the treasures of a secret tradition hidden previously in the East,[1] and the creation of a new heaven and a new earth as a result of the Lord of Christendom coming in His good time to Judgment. The MILITIA CRUCIFERA were concerned therefore with a matter of religion and the enthusiasm arising out of a particular expectation based on doctrine, whereas the Order of the Rosy Cross might be said to cherish as its object the promotion of a religion of science. The marriage of a reformation in knowledge to a reform already affected in religious belief was at least their chief aim. However, as the years went on and a particular construction of the Book written within and without was not justified by the Second Advent coming to pass, it would not be impossible for a certain change of view to take place in the gospel sect, so that it could reappear under new auspices and characterised by a new name. The intimation here put forward is of course tentative in character and stands as such at its value : it will recur for consideration, and a conclusion will be reached later. We shall find that

[1] It will be seen later on that Christian Rosy Cross, the reputed founder of the Order, went in his youth to the East—that is to say, Arabia—and there met with wise men, who revealed to him many mysteries, in possession of which he returned ultimately to Europe.

as time went on there was a very good reason for a certain change of ground.

The REPERTORIUM LITERARIUM evidently derived its knowledge of the MILITIA in the main and it would seem exclusively from an unprinted work of Simon Studion, entitled NAOMETRIA, signifying a mystic measurement—that is to say, of the Temple—as if a deep understanding concerning it. The symbolical expression is reminiscent of Kabalistic or pre-Kabalistic tracts [1] on the DELINEATION OF THE CELESTIAL TEMPLES, the MEASUREMENT OF THE DIVINE BODY, and R. Eliezer's MEASUREMENT OF THE EARTHLY TEMPLE; but the immediate allusion is to the APOCALYPSE, X, 1: "And there was given me a reed like a rod: and the angel stood, saying: Rise, and measure the Temple of God, and the altar, and them that worship therein." For this reason the sub-title of the manuscript is termed "a naked and prime opening of the book written—within and without [2]—by the key of David and the reed like unto a rod." The book in question is presumably that which was sealed with seven seals, but was opened in heaven by the Lamb, standing before the Throne of God;[3] and NAOMETRIA is said to be a brief introduction to a knowledge of all mysteries in Holy Scripture and the universal world. It follows that Simon Studion, by the claim expressed in his title, had received the power which was given to the Lion of the Tribe of Juda and the Root of David.[4] Moreover, by the guidance of that Morning Star which appeared A.D. 1572, NAOMETRIA embodied a prophecy concerning the Second Advent of Christ, wherein He would restore His Church and assume the government of the world, while the Man of Sin—otherwise, the Pope—being destroyed, to-

[1] See my DOCTRINE AND LITERATURE OF THE KABALAH, Bk. IV, § 4, p. 154.

[2] Cf. "a book written within and on the back side." APOC., V, 1. The VULGATE gives: *Et vidi . . . librum scriptum intus et foris.*

[3] *Ibid.*, V, 6.

[4] *Ibid.*, V, 5.

gether with his son of perdition—meaning Mahomet—there would be henceforth but one fold and one Shepherd.[1]

The REPERTORIUM tells us further (1) that on p. 1673 of his vast manuscript Studion "derives long and obscure predictions" from Rose Symbolism, the comment on which is "true and original Rosicrucian wisdom"; (2) that his descriptions of the Rose and his auguries drawn therefrom fill many pages; and (3) that concerning the Cross, the people who are termed *Crucesignati* and the mysteries relating to them, "he knew so much that he has occupied two and a half columns with his table of contents alone." We hear also—on p. 1177—that in 1502 a Cross fell among the people in the Würtemberg town of Herrenberg, some of whom are mentioned by name, together with the other instruments of the Passion of Christ. Finally, the REPERTORIUM records how a certain Tobias Hess belonged—as it was held—to the MILITIA and we shall see that he was a friend of J. V. Andreæ, who is the chief storm-centre of Rosicrucian criticism. With all this we may compare the testimony of C. G. von Murr as follows: (1) The NAOMETRIA[2] was divided into two parts and

[1] The commentary of the REPERTORIUM hereon and on the farrago at large is that the work is a confused medley of absurd mystic computations, adorned with a great number of symbols and figures.

[2] NAOMETRIA was evidently in Latin, whether or not—after the fashion of such texts at the period—it may have lapsed occasionally into the German vernacular. The REPERTORIUM quotes its answer to the question: *Quid est clavis David?* as follows: *Est mensuratio seu dimensio omnium, non tam eorum quæ in S. Scripturis quam eorum etiam quæ in rerum universitate, seu in naturæ mysteriis a condito mundo usque ad ejus finem includuntur. Fit autem ea dimensio per calamum similem virgæ quem sibi datum esse, ut metiretur templum Dei et altare ejus et adorantes in eo ipse Johannes Apostolus de sese contestatur. . . . Quidnam aperitur per eam clavem? . . . Liber intus et foris scriptus, de quo D. Johannes prædicans: Et vidi, ait, in dextra sedentis supra thronum Librum scriptum intus et foris signatum sigillis septem*, etc. It follows in the obscure and contradictory symbolism that the Key of David is the rod with which the seer of Patmos made his measurements, but that, in addition to measuring, it opened also the Book with Seven Seals.

four sections. (2) It contained 1790 pages, not including the preface or the dedication to Frederick, Duke of Würtemberg, which account together for another 205 pages; (3) it is an interlocutory discourse between Nathanael and Cleophas, presumably imaginary characters; (4) its reflections on the renewal of the earth and a general reformation to come breathe the Rosicrucian spirit; and (5) it embodies real Rosicrucian doctrine. As regards Tobias Hess it appears, however, that he did not authorise his friend Andreæ to allude openly to himself in the matter of the MILITIA. It is certain that Von Murr was acquainted with NAOMETRIA at first hand and not only by reflection from the REPERTORIUM.[1] He is, therefore, the second witness whom I have cited.

We are now in the presence of that concrete fact to which I referred at the beginning of the present chapter, and we have found two direct or eye-witnesses testifying that in the year 1604 there was completed a work which is Rosicrucian in respect of doctrine and symbolism. The available summary of contents bears out these statements, and I have been able to indicate several strongly marked points of correspondence with known Rosicrucian teaching. So also the title of NAOMETRIA, which idiotically designates the prophet of Islam as the spiritual son of the Pope, recalls the CONFESSIO FRATERNITATIS R∴C∴ and its pretentious condemnation of the East and West—" meaning the Pope and Mahomet." We find under both denominations that the Rosy Cross signifies a gospel zealotry which recalls those later prophets, Cumming and Baxter, concerning the

[1] The REPERTORIUM says in its crude way that of all " objects and forms " none seemed more significant and mysterious to visionaries like those of the MILITIA than Roses and Crosses; that what is written in NAOMETRIA is " quite in the spirit of the Rosicrucians "; and that the MILITIA was evidently a branch of that body, or something made in its likeness. But the MILITIA and its NAOMETRIA anteceded the manifest epoch of the Rosy Cross and were therefore its first stage or its prototypes.

number of the beast and all the spiritual harlotry of the Scarlet Woman. We know that out of such things there evolves nothing but the mania in which they are begotten. It is not of Paracelsus nor of alchemy—physical or mystical; it is not of the inward meaning behind the Holy Scriptures, nor of that traditional history embodied by the FAMA FRATERNITATIS, which—as we shall see in its proper place—has been construed under other auspices into a real legend of initiation. A very curious literary document is this legend, a jewel in the brummagem setting of Reformation rubbish, those lees and dregs of the Luther aftermath, expressed in terminology to which Luther would have scarcely stooped. At this stage I need only add that the setting fell off quickly. So also the Second-Advent motive which appears to have marked NAOMETRIA with distinctive but once familiar seals remains only as a faint vestige when Rosicrucian manifestoes begin to appear in print. This has been intimated already. I may add that at a very early stage there were manifestations of grave doubts as to the kind of official religion which was professed in reality by the Brethren, and—as if they protested too much—it was suggested that they were the opposite of that which they appeared.[1]

We have no means of knowing the date of Simon Studion's

[1] According to Charles Mackay—MEMOIRS OF EXTRAORDINARY POPULAR DELUSIONS—the Jesuit Abbé Gaultier was at the pains of writing a book to prove that the Fraternity was Lutheran : one would have thought it proved sufficiently by the published documents of the Order. On the other hand, according to Kazauer, the letters F∴R∴C∴ signified *Fratres Religionis Calvinisticæ*. But finally Raphael Eglinus—DISQUISITIO DE HELIA ARTISTA, 1615—is said to have affirmed that the R∴C∴ were a Catholic Fraternity. I mention this as an illustration of the kind of bibliographical quests which I have been called upon to follow in the course of this involved inquiry. The disquisition in question was written in answer to two Jesuit writers on the transmutation of metals, and an *editio postrema correctior et melior* was published at Marburg, so far back as 1608. As there is little need to say at that date, the Rosicrucians are not mentioned, while much less is there any discussion of their official religion.

departure from this life. He would have been some sixty-seven years old in 1610, when there is reason to know that the FAMA FRATERNITATIS was circulated in manuscript form. He may still have been hale and vigorous when it was printed in 1614, and in this case it is barely possible that we may not have to look so far for its authorship as some have been wont to do. The first person who—historically speaking—married the Rose and Cross in symbolism may stand behind the figure of Christian Rosy Cross in the traditional story of the Order. We have also no means of ascertaining how things fared with the MILITIA after 1586. The REPERTORIUM says—and we know on our part already [1]—that it became a strong sect, but its sole annals [2] are in NAOMETRIA,[3] or at least I have sought vainly for other reports concerning it. German literature seems equally reticent on the subject of Tobias Hess, who —as we have seen—is stated to have been one of its members. I have found only one other memorial concerning him.[4]

[1] So also Von Murr, who calls them "a peculiar sect."

[2] It seems, in fact, the only printed authority for "the great gathering at Luneburg."

[3] The Latin title follows: NAOMETRIA, *seu nuda et prima Libri, intus et foris scripti per clavem Davidis et calamum virgœ similem, Apertio: In quo non tantum ad cognoscenda tam S. Scripturæ totius quam Naturæ quoque universæ Mysteria brevis sit Introductio. Verum etiam Prognosticus* (*Stellæ illius Matutinæ Anno Domini* 1572 *conspectæ ductu*) *demonstratur Adventus ille Christi ante Diem Novissimum Secundus, per quem, Homine Peccati, Papa, cum filio suo perditionis Mahometo, divinitus devastato, ipse Ecclesiam suam et principatus mundi restaurabit, ut in iis post hac sit cum ovili Pastor Unus. In Cruciferæ Militiæ Evangelicæ gratiam, authore* SIMONE STUDIONE *inter Scorpiones. Pars Prima. Interlocutores* NATHANAEL, CLEOPHAS. *Anno* 1604. The second part followed, but is not specified in the title. There was also an Appendix, which is described thus: HIEROGLYPHICUS SIMONIS STUDIONIS *versus de Christiana et fatali subequestris Ordinis titulo duorum Serenissimorum Heroum, primum Henrici IV, Navarræ et Franciæ, deinde Jacobi Angliæ, Regum, cum D. D. Frederico Duce Wirtemb: inita confœderatione, a* JOHANNE BRAUHART, *Scholæ Marpachianæ Collega sex vocum cantu, gratulationis loco, concinnati.*

[4] Joannis Valentini Andreæ: MEMORALIA, BENEVOLENTIUM HONORI, AMORI ET CONDOLENTIÆ DATA. *Argentorati. Anno* 1619. The second com-

I come now to that which, for so long a time, has been the crux of the whole subject. The author of the Essay in the REPERTORIUM fails to mention the location of NAOMETRIA at the time that he was able to consult it, nearly two centuries after the date of its completion. Von Murr also fails. Bühle makes no pretence of original research on the subject and simply reflects his authority. It was seen and consulted by C. F. Nicolai in or before 1806[1] and was then at Stuttgart, where Studion's antiquarian papers are still preserved, according to the printed catalogues already cited. On this basis I applied to the Landesbibliothek of that city and have learned that it has two copies: (1) COD. THEOL. ET PHILOS., No. 34, in folio, and (2) COD. THEOL. ET PHILOS., No. 23, in quarto. A verification sought subsequently of chief statements made by the old witnesses has proved negative and is therefore left regretfully to the care of those who can investigate on the spot. There is presumably no doubt whatever that the REPERTORIUM account is genuine throughout—all errors and omissions excepted: there is no ground on which it can be relegated to the region of wilful invention. We have also the evidence of Melchior Fischlin, to which I have referred in a note. The very title of NAOMETRIA and the exceedingly characteristic *additamenta* connected therewith bear all the marks of sincerity on the part of those who have described. Under

memoration concerns TOBIAS HESSI, *viri incomparabilis, immortalitas.* Born January 31, 1568; *ob.* November 24, 1614. It is a long panegyric and I note this only: *At hîc calumnia tripudiare, hîc jactare se illa, et quæ in Chymico nequicquam dentes impresserat, nunc Naometram, nunc Chiliasten, nunc somniatorem deprehendisse, ovans. Vide* p. 63. It is a document of unspeakable dullness, an expatiation which tells us nothing.

[1] See EINIGE BEMERKUNGEN ÜBER URSPRUNG UND GESCHICHTE DER ROSENKREUZER UND FREIMAURER ORDENS, Berlin, 1806, p. 91. It was written in reply to Bühle.

all proper reserves arising from the fact that I have not seen the MSS., I am satisfied that the Brotherhood of the Rosy Cross was in embryo prior to the year 1604 and that NAOMETRIA was its first memorial. An occult evangelical fraternity—a kind of spiritual chivalry—in respect of official religious belief, interpretation of astronomical signs and use of symbols, it is substantially identical with the record of the later Order, though somewhat distinguished therefrom by its Second Advent concern.

For the possible inward reason of this distinction we derive an unexpected light from the little monograph of the third witness, namely, Melchior Fischlin, my examination of which has been postponed for this reason to the present place. He tells us that the work of Simon Studion on the subject-matter of NAOMETRIA was in hand prior to 1593, for in January of that year the author was cited by Ludovicus, Duke of Würtemberg, to bring forward what he had affirmed therein respecting the Papacy. In this manner it transpired that Studion had committed himself to three prophecies concerning the immediate future: (1) that the last Pope would be crucified in 1612; (2) that among those who should condemn him to this death would be a future Frederic, Duke of Würtemberg; and (3) that the Second Advent would take place in 1620. Unfortunately for this notable forecast, the German Duke in question predeceased the supposed event in 1608, and such as it was therefore under the auspices of NAOMETRIA, the Rosy Cross had to revise its scheme. It would be subsequently to this that the FAMA FRATERNITATIS was devised, and it came to pass soon after, in view of the testimony according to which, as we shall see, Adam Haselmeyer had seen and read it in MS. in 1610. Otherwise there would be no reason to suppose that it anteceded 1612, which year passed quietly away, so far as the Sovereign Pontiff was concerned.[1]

The Würtemberg Repository preceded the work of Bühle by a considerable number of years, and its memorial on the Rosy Cross was calculated to furnish material for extracts and summaries in several directions, or alternatively there were other records of which I can find no trace, outside Fischlin. It is probably in this way that Nicholas de Bonneville heard a rumour concerning Naometria and fell into confusion respecting it, so far back as 1784, for in a work on the Jesuits in Masonry he assigns the manuscript of Studion to Dr. John Dee.[2] From this time forward, with the help of Professor Bühle, but above all of De Quincey in England and America, the report of Naometria and its maker has been variously reflected, and we meet on rare occasions with a witness who speaks as if he had really seen the manuscript; but he is only enlarging on

[1] I append the text of Fischlin: *Anno* 1593, *d.* 24 *Martii, utpote prim, die azymorum, quem observavit, primum Naometrici laboris specimen protulit in Curiam d.* 15 *Januarii ejusdem anni a Ludovico Wirtemb. Duce citatus ut ea quæ in opere suo contra Papatum collegerat, secum apportaret et quid fier, oporteat audiret. Ab eo tempore miserrime se ab inimicis exagitatum conqueritur. De cetero, quia de futuris vaticinabatur, idque ex numeris, domum remissus inceptum opus absolvit anno* 1604. . . . *In eo omnia mysteria quæ in S. Scriptura præsertim Ezechiele, Daniele, Apocalypsi leguntur, per numeros mire explicare conatur et omnino prophetam agere præsumit; falsus autem fuit in tribus præcipuis; ultimum Papam anno* 1612 *crucifixum iri; inter crucifixores ejus Frederic., Ducem Wirtemb.* (*qui jam anno* 1608 *vivis excessit*) *futurum; denique adventum Christi ad regnum Chiliasticum circa anno* 1620.

[2] Les Jésuites Chassé's de la Francmaçonnerie et leur poignard brisé par les Maçons. *Orient de Londres*, 1784. See Pt. I, p. 123, in a note on John Dee. It explains that Naometria signifies Measure of the Vessel, otherwise Measure of the Temple. Dee is described also as the author of a tract entitled Fasciculus Chymicus, which, however, is the work of his son, Arthur Dee. The date of De Bonneville's volume is notable in connection with that of The Würtemberg Repository, and the question arises whether the Frenchman borrowed from the slightly antecedent German work and got into confusion about it or derived from some misleading report at second-hand. It seems certain, in any case, that his source was not Melchior Fischlin.

the notice which lies already before us. Thus Kieswetter explains that the title signifies a new worship of the inner and outer temple, that is, a mystical description of man visible and invisible, phenomenal and noumenal, the true Temple of God.[1]

In the year 1905, and in America, a writer who styled himself Count St. Vincent and " Supreme Master of the Order," produced a volume entitled tautologically THE ORDER MILITIA CRUCIFERA EVANGELICA, otherwise SOLDIERS OF THE CRUCIFIXION, according to his amazing rendering. It affirms that this spiritual chivalry was founded by Simon Studion in 1587, being thirty-eight years before he happens to have been born, and even then—adds Vincent—it was not the beginning of the Order, which had pre-existed apparently under another name. It is represented as issuing a Manifesto at Lüneburg in 1530, of which a " liberal " translation is given. It proves, however, so liberal that it can only be characterised as embodying claims, every line of which betrays itself. It comprises: (1) A disjointed preamble, in which the Brethren are supposed to testify that they can no longer believe [*sic*] " in the universal Catholic religion as taught by our priests "; that the Pope is the Man of Sin (travestied from the title of NAOMETRIA); that the Book of Revelation [*sic*] is written within and without (compare *ibid.*); that it contains the " true secret of alchemy "; that the Universal Medicine includes the Catholicon or Elixir of Life and the Panacea, the first insuring to its possessor the prolongation or perpetuity of existence, the second restoring strength and health to debilitated or diseased organisms; that the Philosopher's Stone is " the great and universal synthesis "

[1] History of the Rosicrucians in THE SPHYNX, already cited. Kieswetter alludes also to Studion's mystical allegories and apocalyptic calculations, which he terms " perfectly unintelligible "—an expression transferred from the REPERTORIUM.

(a form of expression unknown in the sixteenth century). (2) A list of Rules, which have been taken—sometimes literally and sometimes varied or transposed—from the Laws of the Rosicrucian Society as published by Sincerus Renatus in 1710, these having no connection with the Militia of Studion. (3) A Pledge imposed on a new Brother, as given by Renatus in Law No. 45, but much altered and extended. (4) A Creed of the Order, which is modern and expressed in the English characteristic of the self-styled Count St. Vincent.

The script of a second manifesto is furnished also and is claimed to belong to the year 1598. Supposing that one could distinguish degrees in the products of such a mint, it would be accurate to characterise this rescript as still more ridiculous than the former, for the first at least was taken in the main from the work of Sincerus Renatus, whereas the second appears to be invention pure and simple. The preamble discourses of (1) students of the occult; (2) liberty of conscience; (3) clerical "prosecution" [*sic*] and esoteric Christianity; (4) the unity of spirit in all mankind; (5) the power of strong imagination; and (6) change from one plane to another. In a word, it gives expression to purely modern ideas, expressed in the familiar terms of current occultism on its most confused side. The replicas of Count St. Vincent are everywhere in the scheme of notions which are to be met with in the frivolities and brummagem of so-called "progressive thought"; but the pseudonymous Count is usually more banal, and much more contradictory than are his peers and co-heirs in these "foremost files" of folly. The preamble is followed by sixteen tautological rules, some of which stultify themselves, as for example (1) that no man or woman shall be accepted as members, but "they may be elected should they insist"; and (2) that a brother should work with a stranger rather than with one of the Order, because "no two men can work together for any length of time without thinking less of each other"—a caution which can justify nothing but work performed alone. These Rules are followed by "an oath" which travesties Masonic Obligations at the expense of English.

We have seen, however, that the Count St. Vincent is Supreme Master of the Order; but his incapacity for rational expression leaves it doubtful whether this qualification applies to the Western world, as we hear also of a Grand Master in the East and of a Grand Lodge which has chartered one in America. The result has been two American manifestoes, published respectively in 1902 and 1903, but about both I shall need only to say that they incorporate considerable materials derived from Éliphas Lévi.

CHAPTER III

ALCHEMISTS AND MYSTICS

THE antiquity claimed by the Order of the Rosy Cross in its original documents is that of the allegorical legend, which represents C ∴ R ∴ C ∴ as having been born in 1378 [1] and having established his Fellowship as an incorporation of four persons, himself included, at an entirely uncertain date subsequent to his return from the East. There is no sense of concern in antiquity *per se*, except in so far as it might serve to shew that schemes of reform were antecedent to the age of Luther. Even so, within the measures of the FAMA FRATERNITATIS, the claim was made on behalf of science and the arts, rather than on that of religion. The maker of this document—let us say, in or about the year 1609—was content with the Christian faith as he found it, under the providence of the Confession of Augsburg—*anno* 1530—or some analogous Protestant standard. For the rest, Rosicrucian philosophy and occult Rosicrucian knowledge were derived by the hypothesis of their legend

[1] Yarker alludes to some copy of an old manuscript in the possession of a German, to whom he will refer later, but does not seem to do so. He fell rather easily into lapses of this kind, not as the result of intention, but owing to a confused mind. The manuscript claimed to be of the year 1374, or alternatively this antiquity was advanced on behalf thereof. Furthermore, it is affirmed to mention the *Fraternitas Rosæ* (*sic*) *Crucis* precisely four years prior to the alleged birth of C ∴ R ∴ C ∴ which notwithstanding, the statement seems to have been quite satisfactory for the author of THE ARCANE SCHOOLS. I have followed the quest of this obscure treatise and have found that Yarker's information is derived from DER ROSENKREUZER IN SEINER BLÖSSE, under the name of Magister Pianco. I shall recur in its place to the subject: here it is sufficient to say that the date is not historical.

from the near East of Arabia and are described literally in terms which were familiar to learned persons at the period through the claims of Kabalism. They were received —*ex hypothesi*—by Adam after his Fall, were transmitted in the hiddenness to Moses and Solomon through Enoch and Abraham, were perpetuated not less secretly through subsequent ages and were the heritage which C ∴ R ∴ C ∴ offered to his companions and—by their intermediation—to the elect thereafter at large. In this manner the philosophical and theosophical position of the Rosy Cross *ab origine symboli* emerges with unchallengeable clearness; it belonged to the school of Mirandula, Reuchlin, Riccius and Archangelus de Burgo Nuova, or in other words to the line of Christian Kabalists who believed that Zoharic literature, its connections and dependencies, bore testimony to the fact that the expected Messiah of Israel had come in Christ. Supplementary hereunto there was unquestionably all that which is included by the so-called practical part of Kabalism and is comprehended under the generic term of Magia—the power of Divine Names, the art of invocation based thereon, the doctrine of correspondence between things above and below, of occult virtues and sympathies, of communication with spirits, but especially with those which—according to the FAMA—are "commonly called the dwellers in the Elements," and finally the transmutation of metals, followed in other ways than were set forth by the current literature of alchemy. Within this compass lies that projected reformation in arts and sciences of which we hear in the early memorials. The immediate *fons et origo* of all is to be sought in Paracelsus, but he is not the only source.

Now, the concern which was destined to overshadow and almost absorb the rest proved to be that of alchemy, and it comes about in this manner that the term Rosicrucian has been used synonymously and interchangeably with that of Alchemist, from the eighteenth century and onward to our own day. Both in reverie and practice, Germany was the chief stronghold of the art of transmutation, with Paracelsus for its central figure, Imperator and prophet-in-chief. When the sixteenth century melted into the century which followed, he came to be regarded by some of his disciples as himself that Elias Artista whose advent had been foretold by him, as the great revealer of mysteries, who was at once past and to come, the German Hermes, "the noble, beloved Monarch."[1] As past he was "of blessed memory," while his return was to be in the light of prepared minds—for in a spacious time to come they should be filled and refreshed by his doctrines, which were destined—in the dream—to prevail over all others in the world of Hermetic thought. Of faith and devotion like this a marked instance is offered by Benedictus Figulus. Paracelsus was for him removed indeed in the flesh but was ultimately coming into his own through an increased understanding and acceptance.[2]

We must remember that at this date the theosophical light of Jacob Böhme had been uplifted over the German

[1] The prophecy mentioned in the text was like a talisman to the Hermetic school in Germany, among greater and lesser alike. In THE BOOK CONCERNING THE TINCTURE OF PHILOSOPHERS, having dealt with Arcana which exhibit transmutations, Paracelsus affirms that the rumours concerning the Tincture and the art thereof are enveloped by a certain concealment, which the Almighty has given for their protection, "even to the coming of Elias the Artist, at which time there shall be nothing so occult that it shall not be revealed." (*Cap.* IV.) The prophecy recurs in other writings of the "Monarch of Arcana," and the Messiah of Hermetic Mysteries was expected ardently by several successive generations. When the mysterious adept, who "looked like a native of Holland," knocked at the door of Helvetius, as narrated in VITULUS AUREUS, he concluded that Elias had come, in view of the practical warrants which his unknown visitor carried.

[2] See A GOLDEN AND BLESSED CASKET OF NATURE'S MARVELS, one of the collections of Figulus, in which Paracelsus is called "our dear Preceptor," "our highly favoured Monarch," and the "noble, beloved Philosopher, Trismegistus." I refer to the English translation, edited by myself in 1893, and especially pp. 21, 26–9, as regards the panegyric of Paracelsus.

world, and it calls to be mentioned here because of the particular witness which his revelations bore to a spiritual understanding of the alchemical work and its symbolism. It was not that he established any school of interpretation, for the school—if such it can be called—was old already in the world; but he gave it a new impulsion and exercised the more influence because he was not concerned in any formal or deliberate manner with the general thesis of alchemy. He held up a glass of vision, under which the age-long familiar images appeared in a new atmosphere and seemed to radiate deeper meanings. By the hypothesis, they had belonged always to a Divine Art, whatever their modes and aspects; but Böhme's method exhibited the immanent Divinity shining through all the veils.[1] For him also the theosophical secrets of the *Magnum Opus* irradiated on every side the text of the Old and New Testaments. Jacob Böhme was born at Görlitz in 1575

[1] The editor of an American periodical under the familiar title of NOTES AND QUERIES, June, 1907, reproduces a "Rosicrucian Chronology," derived chiefly from the fabulous materials collected by Dr. Westcott and other luminaries of the Masonic Rosicrucian Society. Under the date 1612, it is said that about this time "Jacob Böhme was baptised by a Rosicrucian," and refers to "the collaborator of Böhme's work," an expression to which no assignable meaning attaches. J. G. Gichtel—born in 1638 and died in 1710—may be counted as an early editor, and Dionysius Freher was a commentator: they did much respectively for the collection and annotation of the Teutonic theosophist's writings; but he had no collaborator on earth. There is not one particle of evidence to shew that he was ever received into anything, except the Church of Luther, that he was ever baptised by anyone, except a Lutheran minister. The persons who make statements of this kind are not worthy of credit except by a jury of Bedlamites, but theirs is the quality of evidence which is borne always and everywhere in the history of occultism, so far as it has been written by occultists. As I have mentioned Gichtel, it may be added that he has been connected with the foundation of an Order of Angelic Brethren, otherwise a Society of the Thirty, which according to Woodford—see Kenning's CYCLOPÆDIA OF FREEMASONRY—was still in existence at the beginning of the nineteenth century and had Rosicrucian teaching. It is almost needless to say that no authority is cited, but if the statement could be accepted in its absence we should not be warranted in supposing that the Gichtel foundation had such teaching at the beginning.

and died at the same town of Upper Silesia in 1624. He saw therefore the genesis and development of Rosicrucian claims, and their first epoch was closing at the time that he passed away. His book on the root of theology, philosophy and "astral science," under the title of AURORA, belongs to the years 1610-12, and it was known somewhat widely by the circulation of copies in manuscripts prior to the publication of the FAMA, which appears also to have been going from place to place in the same manner, at much about the same time. As there is a story that Böhme in his boyhood was visited by a strange old man who took him by the hand and told him that he should become "such an one as at whom the world shall wonder,"[1] he is alleged by pseudo-historians to have been in the keeping of the Rosy Cross, to have been brought within the secret circle and even to have been a prominent member.

The Böhme affirmation belongs to the region of casual rumour and unblushing speculation which environs my whole subject. Whatsoever came into the nets which were cast at random into the waters of research proved good fish for the makers of foolish memorials, and every catch was as much material on the market to be raked over by the next comer, whether or not he had been at the pains of fishing a little on his own account. In this manner the supposititious finds have done duty over and over again, and the more frequently they have passed from hand to hand, the less has anyone been disposed to call them in question.[2] Moreover, the subject itself was by its nature

[1] See THE LIFE OF JACOB BÖHME, pp. xii, xiii, prefixed to THE WORK OF JACOB BÖHME, so-called edition of William Law, 4 vols. 4to, 1764–81. This is evidently the root of the fable concerning a baptism. Jacob was serving in the shop of his master, and the mysterious stranger insisted on buying a pair of shoes, after which he called the youth into the street and gave him the message that I have quoted. The story is Jacob's, and I suspect that the latter part at least took place in one of his visions.

[2] Perhaps the most typical examples are: (1) Raymundus Lullius and his *Rex physicorum*; (2) the legend concerning Comte de Falkenstein; and

only too open to uncritical adaptations. The title of Rosy Cross represented a Secret Order; it dealt in metallic transmutation, and alchemy was a cryptic literature: to merge one into another was more easy than the descent of Avernus. It happened also that certain Hermetic Masters appealed on occasion to their pledges,[1] whence it was concluded (1) that they obtained their knowledge by the path of initiation; and (2) that the initiating centre was the Order of the Rosy Cross. Again there are *bona fide* traces of mystical and other associations in Germany and elsewhere during the fifteenth and sixteenth centuries. Some of them were presumably more or less secret in character, but we know next to nothing about them;[2] some were a loose incorporation within the bonds of a common enthusiasm, e.g. the Brethren of the Common Life. I do not suppose for a moment that there was one of them which was secret in the sense claimed by the Rosicrucian Order, or even by modern Masonry; they were of the nature of sects or schools, in comparison with which the Monastic Orders, with their conventual houses and the curriculum maintained within them, bear outward marks

(3) Dee's supposed dedication of Roger Bacon's EPISTOLA to the Brethren of the Rosy Cross, which have been disposed of once and for all in my first chapter.

[1] It would be possible to collect a considerable *catena* of references in illustration of this fact, yet it would leave the whole question open. The pledges were either given to an incorporated Secret Society or by the pupil to his individual master. Now, it so happens that there is no particle of evidence to guide our choice between these alternatives, except that the alchemists refer occasionally to their Masters and never to a Secret Order of which they were members. There is no question that the Hermetic Secrets—whatever their value—were communicated from keeper to heir—sometimes *in articulo mortis*, as in the case of Elias Ashmole.

[2] Compare C. A. Thory: ACTA LATOMORUM, 2 vols., 1815. He mentions old German Secret Societies and a Hermetic Degree called *Yeldes*, a term to which I can attach no meaning. We hear otherwise of a mystical sect, said to have been established by Steinbach in the sixteenth century and to have been suppressed *circa* 1566, after being attacked by a pastor named Lutz.

of a more considerable mystery. But the drag-net to which I have alluded has taken in all these sources and the hand of the Rosy Cross has been seen in all, for the purpose of furnishing it with the credentials of a spurious antiquity.[1]

We shall see in what manner the particular concerns of material and mystical alchemy entered into the general dedication of the Rosy Cross. Prior to Jacob Böhme there was a more direct and representative exponent of both aspects in the person of Heinrich Khunrath. The name may signify little but a vague portent to most readers in England, except in so far as I have attempted on my own part to make it less unfamiliar. Khunrath's record in Hermetic archives is either in the Latin or German languages, while he was disposed to the disastrous literary fashion set by Paracelsus a few years previously: that is to say, he interspersed his Latin with German, and *vice versa*, so that he is a crux to the reader of either language only, not to speak of his other difficulties, which are common, less or more, to the subject. Even for an alchemist he was of a strange and exotic kind, and because of certain symbolical plates which are attached to his chief work he has been connected with the Rosicrucian Brotherhood, either as a precursor or a member.[2] Éliphas Lévi says

[1] The purpose is served occasionally by the myth direct. For example, according to Karl Kieswetter, Johann Karl Friesen was Imperator of the Rosicrucian Order in 1468. The authority is another of his unique MSS., this time under the title of CLAVIS SAPIENTIÆ, OR DIALOGUE BETWEEN WISDOM AND AN IMPORTANT DISCIPLE. It contains a collection of alchemical processes, which Kieswetter terms precious, adding that some of them were divulged by John Kunckel von Löwenstern, 1633–1702, the discoverer of phosphorus. I have not been able to trace the Dialogue, though I have heard of it in a printed form. It would belong to the great output of the seventeenth century and would certainly not contain the alleged Rosicrucian reference, which is peculiar to the alleged MS.

[2] Prior to the period of Éliphas Lévi the ascription rested solely on the so-called Rose-Pantacle, which is one of the page plates illustrating the AMPHITHEATRUM. Subsequently to that time it is referable to the French occultist's imaginative use of words.

that he deserves on every consideration to be hailed as a Sovereign Prince Rose-Croix, but this calls to be understood in a symbolical and not the historical sense—as if it were a point of fact respecting the Order and its headship.[1] The brilliant French occultist specifies indeed that he applies the title scientifically or mystically, much as it might be conferred on himself, and as he has said that he would seek to merit it.[2] In any case he did not use it by allusion to the historical Order.

Khunrath was an illuminated Christian Kabalist, and in so far as the Secret Doctrine of the Brotherhood shewed forth the mystical theosophy of Israel under the light of the New and Eternal Covenant, so far the author of THE AMPHITHEATRE OF ETERNAL WISDOM is on common ground with Rosicrucians and was to this extent their precursor. Being also, as I have said, an alchemist, though bizarre in his manner of expression, so far as the Fraternity represented Hermetic Mysteries—which it did indeed and certainly—so far it was in sufficiently near relationship to the German Hermetic philosopher. But Khunrath was born in Saxony about the year 1560; he died in 1601 before Rosicrucianism had emerged—at least definitely—above the horizon of history; and there is no evidence

[1] "He is a Sovereign Prince of the Rosy Cross, worthy in all respects of this scientific and mystical title." And concerning AMPHITHEATRUM: "A more complete and perfect initiation cannot be found elsewhere, unless it is in the SEPHER YETZIRAH and ZOHAR. (See HISTORY OF MAGIC, Bk. V, c. 4.) I have quoted from my own translation, published in 1913 and reprinted in 1922.

[2] "Albeit we have received initiation only from God and our researches, we shall keep the secrets of transcendental Freemasonry as we keep our own secrets. Having attained by our endeavours to a grade of knowledge which imposes silence, we regard ourselves as pledged by our convictions even more than by an oath. Science is a *noblesse qui oblige*, and we shall in no wise fail to deserve the princely crown of the Rosy Cross."—*Op. cit.*, Bk. V, c. 7. It should be added that *Prince Rose-Croix* was and is the title of perfection conferred on members of the Eighteenth Degree under the old Rite of Perfection, merged subsequently in the Scottish Rite.

(*a*) that he was concerned in any secret movement which led up to its foundation or (*b*) that he caused its antecedent existence to transpire, supposing it to be much older than the available records shew. One student of the subject with whom I was once in correspondence—Dr. George Cantor, of Halle—even went so far in the opposite direction as to suggest that there is a veiled attack upon Khunrath in the CONFESSIO FRATERNITATIS R∴ C∴ under the disguise of a stage-player "with sufficient ingenuity for imposition." [1] But this tract belongs to the year 1615, when the death of the supposed subject of reference should have tended to shield his memory, while the long period that had elapsed would have removed all point from the allusion, which is obviously to some man of the moment. Moreover, the obscurity of Khunrath, when he was yet alive, renders the proposition ridiculous; and finally the posthumous publication of the AMPHITHEATRUM [2]—a work delineating nothing but the mystical aspects of alchemy—should have drawn rather than repelled a Society which had protested against "ungodly and accursed gold-making."

There is some evidence in his books that Khunrath was irascible and abusive—like Thomas Vaughan—in dealing with those from whom he differed; but there is nothing tangible to shew that he made any figure at his period.

[1] This subject is postponed for consideration in a later chapter. I need say here only that the denominations of "stage-player" and man of "ingenuity" are about the last which could be applied reasonably to Khunrath.

[2] AMPHITHEATRUM SAPIENTIÆ ÆTERNÆ *solius veræ, Christiano-Kabbalisticum, Divino-Magicum, nec non Physico-Chemicum, Tertriunum, Catholicon: instructore* HENRICO KHUNRATH, etc. Hanover, 1609. Lenglet du Fresnoy says that there were several editions, including one at Magdeburg in 1608, but I have not been able to trace them. They extend in their legend from that alleged to have been published at Prague in 1598 to that of Hamburg in 1710. The posthumous character of the work is made more probable by the fact that the only known edition was produced by an editor, namely, E. Wolfart.

How obscure indeed he was seems evident from the few facts which have transpired concerning him. He was a native of Saxony, who led the errant life of so many struggling physicians before his day and after. Having taken degrees at Basle, he made a certain stay at Hamburg and settled ultimately at Dresden, where he is said to have died in poverty at forty-two years of age. He published three small alchemical tracts in 1599: one was entitled SYMBOLUM PHYSICO-CHEMICUM; another was on the Catholic Magnesia of the Philosophers; and the third was on the alchemical AZOTH, by which he understood the First Matter of creation—otherwise, the Mercury of the Wise.[1] One of these works at least was reprinted in the eighteenth century, but there is nothing to suggest that they were important at their own epoch, in the opinion of that epoch. His really memorable treatise did not appear till 1609. He is to be distinguished from Conrad Khunrath, a contemporary writer on the distillatory art and the Magian fire, whose works began to be collected in 1605, but they are not of consequence to our subject.[2] It was the AMPHITHEATRE OF ETERNAL WISDOM which occasioned the glowing panegyrics by Éliphas Lévi, who chose also for a motto on the title-page of his HISTORY OF MAGIC a definition which Khunrath gives of his own book: *Opus hierarchicum et catholicum*—a catholic and hierarchic work. Lévi points out, however, that in the matter of official religion, the German theosopher was a resolute protestant, adding that herein he was "a German of his period rather than a mystic citizen of the eternal

[1] SYMBOLUM PHYSICO-CHEMICUM, Hanover, 1599; MAGNESIA CATHOLICA PHILOSOPHORUM, Magdeburg, 1599; CONFESSIO DE CHAO PHYSICO-CHEMICORUM CATHOLICO, Strasburg, 1599.

[2] MEDULLA DESTILLATORIA ET MEDICA appeared in 1594. The two writers have been confused together, but Conrad seems to have survived Khunrath for many years. Professor Ferguson suggests that they were brothers, offering no evidence.

kingdom."[1] This is the *dictum* of a *magnus Apollo* rather than an *apologia;* but Lévi recognised assuredly that on another side of his nature Khunrath abode in the freedom of a spiritual Zion and not under the ægis of reform—in Germany or otherwhere. I have long felt that his apocalyptic presentation of the Kabalistic and Hermetic Mystery should be known among Students of the Doctrine in England; but the brief notice which is possible in the present place can only summarise the design. It will illustrate one understanding of alchemy which occupied the precincts and threshold of the Rosy Cross at the end of the sixteenth century.

As an exponent of the Hermetic doctrine of analogy, Khunrath believed in the physical Stone of Philosophy, but in his chief work at least he was concerned with the mystical side. He delineates the process as follows: (1) Purification of the personal part, that we may attain the vision of God; but he means that this vision is within and is a Presence in the hidden sanctuary of our noumenal being. (2) The closing of the avenues of sense, stillness of soul, sanctification, illumination, tincture by Divine Fire. (3) Hereof is the path of attainment, and it will be seen that it is a work of God, by which the soul is intincted and becomes itself the Stone, transmuted and transmuting. (4) But because it is a Divine Work and because God is the motive power and all the inward activity, the Stone is called the Living Spirit of the Elohim, and (5) the inbreathing of Jehovah, the Divine Power, the Word of

[1] HISTORY OF MAGIC, Introduction, p. 29. In one of his earlier moods Éliphas Lévi represents Khunrath as merely affecting Christianity, his Christ being really the Abraxas, "the luminous pentagram radiating on the astronomical cross, the incarnation in humanity of the sovereign sun."—TRANSCENDENTAL MAGIC: ITS DOCTRINE AND RITUAL, p. 348 of my revised and annotated translation, 1923. I mention this to register a definite denial. The Christ of Khunrath is the Christ of Nazareth, exalted in the centre of the sun, to indicate that He is the Sun of Righteousness.

God in Nature. (6) That Word is made flesh—so to speak—in the virginal womb of the greater world and (7) is manifested as Jesus in the virginal womb of Mary, but also (8) in the soul of man as a light superadded to that of Nature. Hereby is communicated the knowledge of God and His Christ.[1]

In addition to these heads of a thesis I offer for the consideration of my readers three reduced plates out of a total series of nine very curious engravings on copper, forming an integral part of the work with which I am concerned. They represent (1) the Oratory of an Alchemist, the device belonging to which is *laborare est orare*, carrying however—as I think—the sense of its counter-distinction, namely, that prayer is work. (2) The Gate of Eternal Wisdom, being that of the knowledge of God ; but he who opens any gate outside himself is working away from the centre and does not reach his end. (3) The sum and substance of the whole concern, termed by Éliphas Lévi the Rose of Light ; but it is an explanation of one symbol in the terms of another. This symbol signifies the central point of all wisdom, human and Divine, which point is Christ.[2] The suggestion of the designs as a whole is that the work of the spiritual alchemist—as shewn by the first plate—belongs to the path of devotion, notwithstanding the material vessels with which the kneeling figure is surrounded, but on which

[1] It is therefore Christ Mystical—that is to say, realised in the heart. This is the incarnation which has to take place in each one of us, and here is the efficient answer to the astronomical Christ of Lévi—crucified presumably in the heavens at the vernal equinox, as hazarded by Godfrey Higgins. There are several analogies between the doctrine of Khunrath and that which passed into expression a few years later in the revelations of his contemporary, Böhme.

[2] The so-called Rose of Khunrath is discussed in the next chapter. There is no question that the Rose of five petals and the Pentagram are both Christ-symbols, and both belong to the doctrine of the Rosy Cross at different stages of development. The pantacle of Khunrath is to be understood in an interior sense, as concerned with that Christ-Spirit which illuminates the world which is within.

his back is turned, somewhat significantly. I conclude that inward work is adumbrated. The suggestion of the second plate is that the Gate of Wisdom is one which is opened by prayer, but the latter is not to be understood in any formal and conventional sense. The gate opens in the darkness and seems like a journey to the centre, meaning the inward way and the great path of contemplation—but *contemplare est amare.* The third design indicates that Christ is not only the Way but the Truth—understood centrally—and the very Life itself. This is Christ Mystical and the Christ of Glory, no longer the Man of Sorrows and acquainted with infirmity. Yet is He still in the human likeness and not the Mystic Rose in the centre of the Macrocosmic Cross.[1] One reason is that as what is called theologically and officially the scheme of redemption is an operation within our humanity for the manifestation of a glory to be revealed, so in the uttermost attainment humanity is completed, not set aside. The Christ manifest is not apart from the Lord of Glory, and the Christ within is ever the Son of Man in us. So also our great Exemplar in Palestine could not do otherwise than come to us in human form, or He would have been never our pattern and prototype. He could not do otherwise than speak in the clouded symbols of our earthly language, or He would have brought us no message, except in the pageant of His life, though this indeed—in its plenary understanding—is the greatest message of all.

There is no question that in the opinion of Khunrath the living knowledge of Christ gave that of the Philosophical Stone in the ordinary alchemical understanding

[1] The figure is suspended in the sun with arms extended in the cruciform sign, and about it are written the words: *Erat ipse vere Filius Dei.* In the deep allegories of the Rosy Cross this symbol is that of the Christ-nature manifested in man incarnate. It is the glorified state of humanity, which has become the Cross. There is no distinction between this Cross and the Rose in the state of attainment.

of this term—in other words, for a medicine of metals and of physical human nature.[1] But—as I have said—he is dealing only with the mystical side of attainment in his AMPHITHEATRE OF ETERNAL WISDOM, though in such language that the likeness of alchemy shall be preserved. Many of the old seekers may have sought to understand him literally, and they went astray accordingly.

The thesis is veiled under the guise of a new translation—with commentary—of certain passages extracted from the BOOK OF PROVERBS and the Apocryphal BOOK OF WISDOM. The versicles are arranged so that there shall be one for each day in the year, and each—with its annotation—might well afford food for thought, even at this time, amidst all the hurry of our ways. The new rendering is printed side by side with the VULGATE and is in itself, I think, negligible.[2] The commentary explains that in

[1] The Son of God is called the Magnesia of Philosophers, the predestined and perfect subject of the Philosophical Stone. This *lapis philosophorum* is declared to be identical with the *Ruach Elohim* which brooded over the face of the waters during the first period of creation. The *Ruach Elohim* is called *vapor virtutis Dei* and the internal form of all things. The Perfect Stone is attained through Christ, and—conversely—the possession of that treasure gives the knowledge of Christ.

[2] For example, the *verba prudentiæ* in the Vulgate version of PROVERBS i. 3 is translated *verba intelligentiæ*, the Hebrew word *Binah* signifying both prudence and understanding. The *semitæ æquitatis* of PROVERBS iv. 11 become *semitæ rectitudinis*. The possession of wisdom in xvi. 16 appears as "acquisition" in the revision. *Scientia* is substituted for *disciplina* in i. 29. So also in the Vulgate rendering of WISDOM vi. 9 there is the word *cruciatio*, which is replaced by *inquisitio* in Khunrath's translation from the Greek. The Vulgate *sacramenta Dei* of vi. 24 becomes *mysteria* simply, and "emanation" is read "defluxion," vii. 25. I do not pretend to have checked the variations throughout, since it is obvious from these instances that it would serve no purpose. As regards the commentary, this note might be extended through many pages and yet give a few only among the curious findings of Khunrath in the consideration of individual verses drawn from his two sources. The synopsis in my text above will serve the simple purpose in view. Let us take, however, a single further specimen and one almost at random. The counsel of PROVERBS xxiv. 13 is *Comede fili mi, mel,*

alchemy, as in religion, Man is the Matter of the work, that subject which is to be purified by Art, the side that is physical being brought into subjugation by that which is within and above. God is the Soul which vivifies ; the Holy Spirit is the Bond of Union which leads to the Everlasting Kingdom, and makes possible admission therein—through the gate of regeneration. The co-operating office of the alchemist must be performed in the deeps and solitude of his own spirit—separated from sensible things—as by a withdrawal into God. The Way of Contemplation and Divine Colloquy will open the Book sealed with Seven Seals, which is the Divine Book of the Scriptures, Nature and the Self. The end is a marriage of Divine Wisdom with the soul, and therein is that Blessed Vision wherein all things are beheld.

In addition to the symbolical plates, the scriptural text and the commentary, there are certain curious tables, and the significance of one among these is likely to escape the penetration of all but the most careful reader. It is a summary of the whole subject, and it testifies that those who are called to the work must realise, under Divine leading, that the knowledge (1) of God, (2) of Christ Whom He has sent, (3) of the greater world, (4) of the self within each of us and (5) of the Stone sought by the Wise—though passing under so many names—is one knowledge, which is attained by virtue of a single gift, faculty or grace resident within seekers themselves and comparable to a clear mirror or fountain. Such was one aspect of *Ars magna Alchemiæ* in the year 1598, in the aftermath of the

quia bonum est, et favum dulcissimum gutturi tuo, according to the VULGATE, or in the AUTHORISED VERSION : " My son, eat thou honey, because it is good ; and the honeycomb, which is sweet to thy taste." The commentary explains that honey signifies the Doctrine of Eternal Wisdom, or the Bread of Life, and that when eaten by the mouth of the purified heart it gives back life to those who have been dead in sin and will redeem from that death which is eternal.

MILITIA CRUCIFERA EVANGELICA, and on the threshold of the Rosicrucian Mystery.[1]

As neither Jacob Böhme nor Khunrath cast light on the historical origin of the Rosy Cross, or give evidence of connection therewith, we must proceed on our way with caution and examine some further suggestions. It has been customary to speak of Gottfrid Arnold's monograph on the Rosicrucians in his HISTORY OF THE CHURCH AND OF HERETICS[2] in terms of high praise, and it is certainly creditable for the period.[3] I refer to it, however, for two

[1] It may be added at this point that the Supreme Council of the Ancient and Accepted Rite of Freemasonry had somewhere once among its valuable MSS. at the headquarters in London a work entitled: THESAURUS THESAURORUM A FRATERNITATE ROSEÆ ET AUREÆ CRUCIS TESTAMENTO CONSIGNATUS ET IN ARCAM FŒDERIS REPOSITUS SUÆ SCHOLÆ ALUMNIS ET ELECTIS FRATRIBUS ANNO MDLXXX. See p. 69 of the Catalogue printed under the editorship of Mr. Edward Armitage, where it is described as a German MS. "with emblematic coloured drawings." It was not to be found when I made inquiries concerning it, and in its absence I can only infer that it bears a false date, which may be of course a transcriber's error. There is no question that the descriptive title of Golden and Rosy Cross is not heard of till the early eighteenth century, while the manifest activities of the society so denominated belong, as we shall see, to the year 1777 and subsequently. The probable true date is therefore 1780.

[2] UNPARTEIISCHE KIRCHEN UND KETZER-HISTORIE, 4 vols. folio. Frankfurt-am-Mayn, 1700–15. The monograph in question will be found in Vol. II, Book XVII, cap. 18, i.e. VON DENEN ROSENCREUTZEN, pp. 613–28. See also Vol. IV, sect. III, No. XI, pp. 889, 900; and *ibid.*, p. 1035.

[3] Perhaps, after all, it belongs to the same category as the oft quoted or rather mentioned reference of J. L. von Mosheim, which occurs in his INSTITUTES OF ECCLESIASTICAL HISTORY, Book IV, s.v. SEVENTEENTH CENTURY, *Sect.* I. This contrasts very appositely the Peripatetics or followers of Aristotle—more especially his modern expositors—with the Fire-Philosophers or Chemists, who "roamed over nearly every country of Europe," assuming the "obscure and deceptive title of Rosicrucian Brethren." Unfortunately, the last clause is of itself sufficient to indicate that the reference is singularly uncritical, considering the name of Mosheim. It is he, furthermore, who is responsible for stating that Böhme was one of the Rosicrucian leaders, adding that the personalities of the first group were succeeded by J. B. van Helmont, his son Franciscus Mercurius, by C. Knorr von Rosenroth, Quirin Kuhlmann, Henry Noll, Julius Sperber and numerous others. With the sole exception of Sperber, who belongs to the informal debating society which filled Germany with printed polemics on the claims of the Rosy Cross, there is

reasons only: (1) Because Arnold suggests that Valentin Weigel may have founded the Rosy Cross; and (2) because he mentions—on the authority of a certain Breklingius [1] —that Ægidius Gutmann was a member. There is not the least evidence in favour of either ascription. Weigel was a Lutheran mystic of his period, who—like Jacob Böhme—offered too strong meat for the consumption of his co-religionists, and his writings were laid under an interdict in Saxony, about 1624. He was born in 1533 and died in 1588, or many years before the Rosy Cross had been heard of—even as a symbol. He is said to have illustrated his extravagance by maintaining that Jesus Christ came down from heaven ready clothed in flesh and blood.

The day of Luther and Melancthon was not a day of light, much less of wisdom in the spirit, so it came about that Weigel had his followers, some of whom saw to the publication of his works, while others proclaimed his coming as an advent of Christ. It is said that they were persecuted by the alternative class of maniacs who held to the Bible only, on condition that it was their exclusive province to affirm its meanings. There seems little to distinguish Weigelian theosophy from that of NAOMETRIA—so far as we can judge concerning it or concerning the MILITIA CRUCIFERA EVANGELICA. It has been regarded as a kind of marriage between Dionysian mysticism and Paracelsian reveries belonging to occult science. As such there seems no inseparable reason why Weigel should not have been founder and Grand Master *ad*

again no particle of evidence. But for Mosheim, as for so many, every alchemist, Kabalist and exponent of *Magia* was identified with the Brotherhood.

[1] Friedrich Breckling wrote REGINA PECUNIA, 1663; BIBLIA PAUPERUM, 1664; and LIBERTAS ET POTESTAS ECCLESIÆ VINDICATA, published in the same year. It will be seen therefore that he is a deponent long after the alleged event.

vitam of the Rosicrucian Order, except that he was too early.[1]

We are in much the same position with regard to Ægidius Gutmann, who is a little earlier in the chronology of German mysticism, a Suabian who was born at Augsburg in 1490 and died four years earlier than Weigel in 1584. His sole but sufficient memorial is REVELATIONS OF DIVINE MAJESTY, being a theosophical eduction of the inward sense of Genesis. According to R. A Vaughan, he "mingled, in hopeless confusion, religious doctrine and alchemic process, physics and scripture, tradition, vision, fancy, fact." I do not offer this citation as one who is satisfied with the verdict, because Gutmann has also strange, real lights scattered through his vast text, and there is no need to say that Vaughan—who knew the mystics only on their outer side—was in no wise qualified to find a guide therein. It enables us to see, however, the metaphysical personality with which we are dealing in Gutmann. He connects with alchemy on the spiritual side of its symbols, and when Arnold calls him a Rosicrucian it is manifestly incorrect

[1] I do not wish it to be inferred that Weigel is in any sense beneath contempt. On the contrary, he is a figure of some importance in the theosophy of his period and comparable as such to Gutmann. It is idle to judge these people on the side of their extravagance only. We need to know more about them, and that at first hand, in order to understand German theosophy and Hermetism at the end of the sixteenth century, and in order to appreciate the not unfruitful fact that the Brotherhood of the Rosy Cross, which brought all these enthusiasms and also their spiritual lights into a kind of informal centre, was by no means merely a school of Paracelsus, merely an occult cabal or an association claiming to possess the secret of transmuting metals. The tracts of Valentine Weigel are: (1) CHURCH OR HOSPITAL; (2) MASTER-TRACT ON TRANQUILLITY; (3) A GOLDEN STYLUS, *leading to the Knowledge of all things without Error*; (4) DIALOGUES ON CHRISTIANITY; (5) THE UNIVERSAL CONCERN; (6) A SHORT WAY TO UNDERSTAND ALL THINGS; (7) A LITTLE BOOK OF THE LIFE OF CHRIST; (8) A SHORT TREATISE ON PRAYER. He is treated somewhat tenderly by Jacob Böhme, in his Second Epistle, more especially on the subject of St. Mary as an Eternal Virgin and on the New Birth. See EPISTLES OF JACOB BEHMEN, English Translation, 1649.

in the corporate sense, though otherwise Gutmann represents the set of notions, the mental feelings and attitude to which the Order at a later period gave a more definite expression. In other words, he was a precursor but not a member, and—as I have mentioned elsewhere—his REVELATIONS[1] became a sort of Rosicrucian textbook, an inspiring spirit, much as L. C. de Saint-Martin's DES ERREURS ET DE LA VÉRITÉ was like a gospel for the theosophical side of High-Grade Masonry towards the end of the eighteenth century. The IMITATIO of St. Thomas à Kempis and the anonymous THEOLOGIA GERMANICA were other textbooks. I do not doubt that THE CLOUD OF UNKNOWING would have been of no less repute in the Order, had it been possible for an unprinted English text to have been known among them. The Rosicrucian maxim—*Summa Scientia nihil scire*—indicates that it would have been accepted in its true and vital spirit. I conclude that Weigel, Gutmann and the Rosy Cross were fashioned in one likeness and carried the same seals.

There are other claimants by proxy—meaning by their sponsors in speculation—but they will not detain us long. To his own satisfaction—and it would appear that he stood by himself therein—the Abbé Lefranc presented Faustus Socinus to an unbelieving world as the veritable founder of Emblematic Freemasonry, and having gone so far he turned an inquisitive eye on the field of possibilities opened by the Rosy Cross. He was not long in discovering that the same mouthpiece of heresy had also spoken great things of the

[1] According to Lenglet du Fresnoy, the REVELATIONS appeared at Hanover in 1609, but the copy in the British Museum is dated from the same place in 1619. As there is no trace otherwise of a second edition till that of Amsterdam and Frankfurt in 1675, I conclude that the French bibliographer erred or that his printer blundered. The full title is OFFENBARUNG GÖTTLICHER MAJESTAT, DARINNEN ANGEZEIGT WIRD, WIE GOTT DER HERR ANFÄNGLICH SICH ALLEN SEINEN GESSCHÖPFEN, MIT WORTEN UND WERCKEN GROFFENBARET, etc. Edited by M. B. M. F. C. I. 2 vols. 4to. Buchladen, Hanover, 1619.

occult and mystical Order, which had no other author and head. This was in the middle years of the eighteenth century. It signified little to his purpose that Socinus had carried his findings in doctrine beyond the gates of death many years before Rosicrucianism began to be a name in Europe.[1] The virus of such inventions has often a counter-nostrum provided by inventions of an opposite kind ; and we have therefore in this case the allegation that John Tauler—who is connected otherwise with the Brethren of the Common Life—was no stranger to the mystical concerns of the Rosy Cross and had a first hand therein. Such a myth being transparently absurd, the responsibility was shifted to an obscure namesake—possibly to the concealed personality behind THE FOLLOWING OF THE POOR LIFE OF CHRIST, which has been passed as the work of Tauler. Finally, there is Joachim Junge, who was born at Lubeck in 1587 and died in 1657 at Hamburg. When the FAMA was printed he was therefore some twenty-seven years of age.[2] In 1619 he is said to have planned a society for the advancement of natural science, to have substituted experiment for antiquated theories and to have been ranked by Leibnitz as the equal of Copernicus and Galileo. This is the sole colour for his alleged connection as founder with the Brotherhood of the Rosy Cross. He was a natural philosopher, geometrician and scientific botanist. His one link with occultism is that he was at

[1] As a fact, he makes it part of his evidence, because Socinus died in 1604, and this—according to Lefranc—was the epoch of the Rosy Cross, meaning presumably that it is the hypothetical date when the 120 years had expired since the alleged death of F∴R∴C∴ in 1484. Lefranc did not know that it is also the date of NAOMETRIA.

[2] M. Sédir is mistaken when he says that Junge was thirteen only " at the epoch of the apparition of the FAMA." He is still more seriously in error when he follows Hœfer respecting the writings of Tauler. According to this extraordinary biographer, the fictitious treatises ascribed to the disciple of Rulman Merswin are his authentic works and the genuine writings are forgeries. I prefer Surius to Hœfer.

issue with the Peripatetics of his day, preferring experience to scholastic debate.

In the year 1614, when the spirit of the new age gave up the first Rosicrucian documents, it produced also Michael Maier, the greatest of the literary alchemists at this or perhaps any period. I shall deal with him at length later on. Between the date just mentioned and the publication of AMPHITHEATRUM in 1608 there intervened two other alchemical writers and editors, to whom a false importance has been attributed in connection with Rosicrucian problems. We have to thank that patient but undiscriminating collector Solomon Semler for providing materials to some zanies of historical research by his reference to alleged travels and adventures of Nicolas Barnaud in search of Hermetic philosophers and to the activities of that impassioned idolater of Paracelsus who called himself Benedictus Figulus—a name which I have mentioned previously. They are both of moment to our subject, as representing the kind of occult atmosphere in which the Rosicrucian movement grew up. Barnaud was of Crest in Dauphiny—or more especially in the department of Drôme, according to present allocations. The dates of his birth and death are alike unknown, but he is said by Semler to have been travelling on the quest of Philosophers or Hermetic Masters in and about the year 1591, and to have had the intention of incorporating them into some kind of society. He is said also—in this year, or alternatively in 1601—to have issued an open letter to all French alchemists, exhorting the alleged Masters to employ their art in the interests of the Church of Christ and Prince Henry of Nassau.[1] What actually happened

[1] Semler dwells upon the fact that "about this time and onwards"—namely, 1600—various German princes became "lovers of secret chemistry." In addition to the Emperor himself he cites Ernest, Electoral Prince of Cologne; Duke Frederic of Würtemberg; Julius of Brunswick; the Landgrave Maurice of Hesse. Conradus Schuler, a Hermetic writer and collector, bears similar testimony.

was that in 1601 he issued a LETTER ON OCCULT PHILOSOPHY, which was addressed by a certain father to his spiritual heir or son.[1] Whether he was the father in question or merely an editor of the document remains doubtful.[2] He is known more especially as an editor—so far as his alchemical connections are concerned—and he brought some rare texts to light, e.g. the QUADRIGA AURIFERA, 1613, including tracts of George Ripley; but he wrote also on his own part an ELUCIDATION OF THE SECRET OF PHILOSOPHERS, while if bibliographers apart from occultism are to be trusted in their allocations he was the author of two very different works under the name of Nicolas de Montaud.[3] Notwithstanding his alleged but entirely mythical Epistle to the Masters for their enlistment in the service of the Church he was—in this case—on the side of drastic reform, recommending among other things the secularisation and marriage of the clergy. It is possibly for such reason that he has been even accredited with the authorship of THE THREE IMPOSTORS, that other mythical work which no one has read and no one has seen, but which is said to have been of peculiar infamy.

The authority for the travels of Barnaud—outside Semler

[1] DE OCCULTA PHILOSOPHIA, EPISTOLA CUJUSDEM PATRIS AD FILIUM, *a* NICOLAO BARNAUDO *Medico a Crista Arnandi Delphinate Gallo, nunc primum in lucem edita in gratiam omnium philosophorum, maxima vero Batavorum*—that is to say, Leyden, being the place of its publication in 1601.

[2] There is perhaps no substantial ground for affirming that he was author rather than editor, except the cloud of false-seeming which surrounded the publication of documents supposed to be antique all about the period in question.

[3] The works in question are: (1) CABINET DU ROI DE FRANCE and (2) LE MIROIR DES FRANÇAIS. Both appeared in 1582, the prefaces being dated October and November of the previous year. The CABINET was dedicated to Henri III and the MIROIR to the "reigning Queen." The first deals more especially with the corruption of the ecclesiastical hierarchy and the second with the miseries and burdens of the French people. It is perhaps on his alleged authorship of these revolutionary works that Barnaud is described as belonging to the reformed religion.

—in search of philosophers and the secrets of the *Magnum Opus* is said to be ECHO FRATERNITATIS R∴ C∴ which appeared in 1615.[1] There is nothing improbable in the story; the amateurs of the Hermetic Art were indefatigable in activities of this kind, and the wanderings of Bernard Trevisan in the fifteenth century are a memorial at large of the great zeal in quest. But Barnaud went, as we have seen, on a general research of Masters and not of Rosicrucian adepts, as mendacious witnesses have testified, while the EPISTLE of 1601 is an altogether different document to that which has been described: it is not written to alchemists at large, nor does it enlist anyone in the service of Church or State.[2] It opens with a promise addressed to a Son of the Doctrine on the part of his mystical father —that he will reveal to him the secret of all secrets, the most holy and excellent treasure, on the sole condition that he will hand it on to no one. The revelation of the secret opens in characteristic terms as follows: "Take in the Name of Christ our Blessed Stone, our Honourable Stone, Glorious and Incombustible Stone, that Stone which is hidden by all Philosophers and described only in parables: This Stone is most excellent Roman Vitriol.[3] Here is the Stone, my dearest Son, which all philosophers have concealed."[4] There is absolutely no reference to the Rosi-

[1] ECHO DER VON GOTT-HOCHERLEUCHTETEN FRATERNITET DES . . . ROSEN CREUTZES. Dantzic, 1615. It included a German version of the CONFESSIO FRATERNITATIS R.C., according to Lenglet du Fresnoy, but his reference is to a second edition, published in the following year. The statement is untrue in respect of both editions, and there is also no allusion to Barnaud.

[2] In the editor's preface, which of course is addressed generally to presumed readers, i.e. students of alchemy, there is a recommendation of this kind respecting (1) the Prince of Nassau and (2) the Duke Maurice.

[3] Rulandus gives Green Atrament and *Vitriolum Album* as alternative names. Alchemically, Metallic Vitriols are said to be Salts of Metals.

[4] Compare TRACTATULUS CHEMICUS and the process beginning: *Filat mea res, vel substantia una ex duobus*. There is also the PHILOSOPHICUM POCULUM of Nicolas Barnaud, which is POCULUM AMARITUDINIS. The separate letters of these two words form the following sentence: *Amore Mulieris*

crucians, and the extant remains of Barnaud will be searched to no purpose concerning them.[1] We are therefore in a position to estimate Kieswetter's talent for scandalous invention when on the authority of his supposititious manuscripts he affirms (1) That in the year 1601 Barnaud printed a Latin letter addressed to all Rosicrucians in France; (2) that he had therefore entered into close relation with the Order and was probably its Imperator; and (3) that his perambulation of Germany some ten years previously was undertaken in search of "the Hermetic Masters of the Rosy Cross."[2]

I suppose that Benedictus Figulus, as we know him by his memorials, was almost as the poles asunder from Nicolas Barnaud, the only link of connection between them being that they were both alchemists and both editors of curious

Ardens Ruffus Juvenis Transfigitur Venas Disrumpit Irascitur Nigrescit Inalbatur Sanguinem Postremo Ostendit Clarum Unctuosum Lapidem Universalem Medicinorum. This is probably a device of Barnaud, introducing his editorial work.

[1] In addition to the EPISTOLA . . . PATRIS AD FILIUM, the extant alchemical writings and compilations of Barnaud are: (1) BREVIS ELUCIDATIO ARCANI PHILOSOPHORUM. Leyden, 1599. I have mentioned this in the text above. (2) TRIGA CHEMICA, *seu De Lapide Philosophorum Tractatus Tres* Leyden, 1600. (3) QUADRIGA AURIFERA. Leyden, 1599, being tracts by various authors. (4) AURIGA CHEMICUS, *id est, Tractatalus Chemicus, Theosophiæ Palmarium Dictus Anonymi cujusdam Philosophi antiqui . . . nunc primum editus*, 1601. It contains fifty-eight propositions, mostly drawn from the TURBA PHILOSOPHORUM, and descants thereon.

[2] After notifying his astonishment that Rudolph II was never a member of the Order, Kieswetter proceeds to class Gerhard Doon and Thaddeus von Hayeck—as well as Michael Maier—among undoubted Brethren of the Rosy Cross, his evidence being of course wanting. Compare Hermann Fictuld: AZOTH ET IGNIS, to which is appended AUREUM VELLUS. Leipzig, 1748, p. 147, where it it said that after the death of Duke Charles of Burgundy, the possessors of the Great Secret—presumably like Doon and von Hayeck—retired with their exalted science, and a new Order was founded under the name of the Rose-Cross of Gold. But the denomination Rosy and Golden Cross belongs more especially to the eighteenth, not the seventeenth, century and appears to have represented two branches of the Order, which were at work together, as we shall see. We shall find, however, that Madathanus mentions the Golden Cross in 1621.

literary remains belonging to the Hermetic tradition. That either of them had put their hands to the practice, so-called, in the physical sense, I take leave to doubt, and in any case there is no evidence before us to suggest that they had. Barnaud was on the blind work in metals and wrote the common stuff of his period in that interest. Figulus was characterised by a devotional mind which lifted his occult wares above the dull and unintelligible groove of merely material dealings. Paracelsus was his great master; but for him—in his untutored zeal—all the literary vestiges which came into his hands shewed great lights, and he cherished superfervid hopes that he would reach the end of philosophy.[1] He also made journeys, seeking the wisdom of adepts and his beloved Sons of the Doctrine. According to his own description, he was poet, theologian, theosopher, philosopher, and even eremite, but not a doctor in alchemy or a student of that art. He was—I think—on a heavenly quest, " by means of the grace of God." He has been placed in the witness-box on the side of Rosicrucian antiquities by people who never in their lives have taken the pains to consult his various texts, but have depended on vague and antiquated reports which they have shaped and coloured to their liking. He is said to have mentioned that there was an association of physicians and alchemists in the fourteenth century, whose object was to discover the Philosopher's Stone. There is nothing more likely and nothing follows therefrom, unless it is the indubitable fact of their failure, which might serve as an object lesson. But Figulus is said further to have affirmed that this obscure body of research was merged

[1] Thus—in a Prolocutory and Dedicatory Speech, prefixed to the Golden and Blessed Casket—we find him guaranteeing to reward those who would assist him in the recovery of Paracelsian MSS. with " a grateful compensation when we (D.V.) shortly reach our goal in philosophy and medicine."

in the Rosicrucian Order about 1607.[1] The statement is invention as usual; the Paracelsian alchemist never bore testimony to the Order in any shape whatsoever, nor did he ever write anything which certifies in a cogent and convincing manner to the existence of corporate, occult or mystical association during his own period or before it. I have taken all the mediæval centuries as my province and all the Renaissance period in the hope of getting back this subject behind the Lutheran Reformation or behind, as an irreducible minimum, the unspeakable Andrean epoch of Würtemberg theology, and the materials are before my readers. It does not leave one stone standing on another of the house fantastic built up in clouds of pretence by the makers of false myths, the custodians of forged documents and those who pretend that one of their "ancestors" was once an Imperator of the Order. I could have wished that they bore true testimony, for then I should have reached my term.

Benedictus Figulus belonged to the Catholic school of alchemy, and herein—as in other matters—he differed widely from the College of Initiation which was typified by the Rosy Cross. He has left us indeed in one of his

[1] Mr. C. F. Gould has been misled by this story and reproduces it in his CONCISE HISTORY OF FREEMASONRY, giving no authority. See p. 73 of the work mentioned. He says also that—according to Figulus—there was one secret society which had existed for over two thousand years. Gould had no axe to grind and was incapable of inventing evidence, but he had only a passing acquaintance with Rosicrucian history and took the word of others. Professor Ferguson has drawn attention to a passage in Semler which discovers Rosicrucian ideas in the preface to the collection of Figulus published at Frankfort-on-the-Main in 1608 under the title of THESAURINELLA OLYMPICA AUREA TRIPARTITA. According to Heckethorn, it has allusions to an alchemical society and this has been expanded, of course, into a Rosicrucian reference. The prefatory matter of THESAURINELLA is comprised in a Dedicatory Epistle and an Address *ad lectorem philochemicum*. There is no such allusion in either. We hear of Elias the Artist, of *veritas hujus artis*, of the German Monarch Aureolus Theophrastus Paracelsus, of *antecessores*, Sons of the Doctrine, etc., but of Rosicrucians nothing and nothing of Hermetic Societies.

collections a most curious example of an Hermetic Mass, containing variations in the Introits, Collects, Antiphons and other parts of the ORDINARY: they have become Invocations for the Gift of Divine Light on the Secret of Philosophy. Figulus passes therefore, like Nicolas Barnaud, into the background, though he is left in a better position, as one who deserves by his dedications to be called a precursor of the Rosy Cross when it is taken at its best and highest—in the aspect, for example, presented by Robert Fludd, as we shall see later on. Barnaud, on the other hand, does not connect with the subject except in an accidental manner, as an alchemist on the material side and then only as speculative rather than practical, and chiefly as an editor of texts.

The general conclusion of Semler is that prior to 1597 there was a society of learned persons drawn from all classes, the members of which were engaged in the production of works on alchemy, theosophy and other subjects included, under the broad denomination of *Magia*. As he gives no reason to suppose that they were incorporated, his research tends simply to shew that like-minded people drew naturally together, went in search of one another and may, to some extent, have worked in common. The conclusion of M Sédir[1] is that there was no Rosicrucian Fraternity before 1600 or 1603, though Hermetic Fraternities had existed previously in several countries. But on the last count of his conclusion he can indicate only the supposed *Parliamentum Hermeticum* of Raymund Lully and his *Rex Physicorum*, which has—I think—been disposed of finally in my first chapter.

There are two last points and then we shall have finished the research in all its directions until the printed documents of the Rosicrucian Order come for consideration before us. As against all the rumours, speculations and mendacious

[1] HIST. DES ROSE-CROIX, pp. 42, 43.

inventions, it looks for one moment as if we should meet with a genuine and unchallengeable reference to the Rosy Cross—in the irrecusable plainness of print—in the year 1610. It has been said that Francis Allary, described as a visionary, was the author of a book published in that year under the title of BROTHER AND COUNT BOMBASTES, KNIGHT OF THE ROSE-CROIX, NEPHEW OF PARACELSUS. It has the aspect of a chap-book or one of those contributions to the literature of colportage which are first cousins in alchemy to the Grimoires of Black Magic; but as such it would be only the more remarkable if it should embody an allusion to the Rosy Cross, some four years before the Order began to be heard of by its own printed documents. It has been used accordingly to indicate the existence of a peculiarly early memorial. It is interesting also and even important after another manner, because the FAMA FRATERNITATIS tells us of FRATRES R∴ C∴ but not of a chivalry under that title. In the year 1616 we hear of the Founder of the Fraternity being made under very peculiar circumstances an *Eques Aurei Lapidis*, but the denomination of Chevalier de la Rose-Croix is a Masonic dignity which did not come into use until after 1750. On examination, however, we are confronted by another blunder, if indeed it is not to be characterised by a rougher term. In the year 1610 there appeared, presumably at Paris, a slender volume, containing a PROPHECY by the said Count Bombast, but it is anonymous and has no Rosicrucian reference in the title, which reads as follows: LA PROPHÉTIE DE CE GRAND BOMBAST [*sic*] *fidellement annoncée par le Trompette François dès l'année* 1609. *Sur la mort de Henry Le Grand, et sur le Règne de Louis traisième, Roi de France et de Navarre à present regnant . . . s.l.*, 1610. The publication forms therefore no part of our concern, but in the year 1701 there was issued PROPHÉTIE DU COMTE BOMBAST, *Chevalier de la Rose-Croix, nevue de* THÉOPHRASTE PARACELSE, *publiée en l'année* 1609, *sur la naissance miraculeuse de* LOUIS LE GRAND, *les circonstances de sa minorité, l'extirpation de la Heresie, l'union de l'Espagne à la Maison de Bourbon. . . . Expliquée et presentée au Roy par* FRANÇOIS ALARY, *Docteur en Médicine.* À PARIS, 1701. It follows that part of the title descriptive of the later publication has been transferred to the former in order to advance the claim and that an item of nomenclature which would have been historically of considerable consequence in 1610 is of no moment whatever in 1701, so far as Rosicrucian history is concerned. The unknown Dr. Alary most likely drew on his imagination for the decorative title which is conferred on the mythical nephew of Paracelsus; but CHEVALIER DE LA ROSE-CROIX, which is so familiar in High Grade Masonry after 1754, is not a little curious in 1701, from a Masonic standpoint, when it is moderately certain that there were not even three Masonic Degrees. The new edition of the PROPHECY is not a reprint of the first but reproduces its gist in the form of extracts, with commentaries thereupon. It has a dedication to the King and a preface, which seems to regard LE TROMPETTE FRANÇAIS (*sic*) of the 1610 title as signifying the original author.

There is finally the so-called DIARY of Hosea Lux and its alleged Rosicrucian pictures, the quest of which I followed, owing to a talismanic description by C. W. King.[1] He reports (1) that the unique manuscript was written between the years 1568 and 1612; (2) that it exhibits "the whole list" of existing Masonic Signs, but employed for Rosicrucian purposes. The "signs" enumerated by King are: (1) A bearded head placed upon a box on which are inscribed the letters X.P.S. (2) The same on a box inscribed with the Seal of Solomon. (3) The same, over an Ark of the Covenant. (4) The Pillars J. and B. (5) A human figure with uplifted hands, but having, instead

[1] THE GNOSTICS AND THEIR REMAINS, second edition, pp. 396, 397.

of a face, the Seal of Solomon enclosing a retort. (6) A naked boy extended on a wheel. (7) An egg containing a circle, whence issue rays of light. Such are the designs which King characterises as originally Rosicrucian emblems, but " now embalmed in the repertory of the Freemasons." My own examination of the DIARY, which is a minute, or midget volume, for many years in the collection of Mr. J. E. Hodgkin and now in that of his son, bears out neither dream, as might be expected from the particulars here enumerated. It is simply an alchemical manuscript, full of very curious designs in addition to those tabulated, but none of them are Rosicrucian in character, nor are any Masonic, except in rare cases belonging to universal symbolism. We know that pillars are everywhere, and so is the six-pointed star.

The sole conclusion which evidence permits us to draw from the inquiries pursued in this chapter is that Simon Studion and the reveries of NAOMETRIA are the *fons et origo* of the Rosicrucian claim and that its theosophical doctrine was held in common by many theosophists at the end of the sixteenth century, including zealots and enthusiasts. It is possible, however, to approach the subject of the symbolism from another and independent point of departure.

CHAPTER IV

SYMBOLISM OF THE ROSE AND CROSS

It is necessary to make a sharp distinction in opening the consideration to which this chapter is dedicated because of the uncritical methods which have been followed by several writers. They have met with certain vestiges of symbolism and tradition concerning (1) the Rose and (2) Cross in their natural separation from each other and have then sought to infer that the Rosicrucian emblem of Rose and Cross united is extremely old. Nothing of the kind follows in any rational sense of quest. I propose on my own part to look at the whole subject, critically and historically, under four heads, being (1) the story of the Rose in symbolism, so far as this symbolism connects with Rosicrucian tradition; (2) the Cross, under similar reserves; (3) the Rosicrucian symbol, as described and explained in Rosicrucian official publications and in works depending therefrom; (4) the antiquity of this symbol, with special reference to the question whether it was borrowed or devised by those who first used it in connection with the Rosy Cross of history.

We are concerned therefore with the Rose in the first place, and as I am dealing with a Christian Order, there is no occasion to dwell—except in summary form—upon its story in non-Christian symbolism, and above all in Pagan myth. I note therefore only: (1) That the Rose belonged as much to Iacchus as to Aphrodite.[1] (2) That, however,

[1] Respecting the silence of which the Rose was a symbol, compare the reticence and modesty by which the Perfect Mysteries of Love are environed and the stillness of that ecstacy implied by the higher understanding of Iacchic Mysteries.

it was sacred especially to Venus, considered as the goddess of love. (3) That it was a palmary symbol in the Thracian cultus of Sabasius. (4) That one of the principal festivals of the Thracian Dionysiacs under the Roman dominion was called Rosalia. (5) That the famous Rose-Garden of Midas, the King of the Phrygians, contained roses of sixty petals. (6) That it was at once an erotic plant and a safeguard against intoxication. (7) That it was also a funerary symbol. (8) That the Brahminical Garden of Heaven contains a Silver Rose, but the authenticity of this story might prove doubtful.[1] (9) That the Rose in ancient Egypt is said to have been a symbol of regeneration, but I have not found adequate authority for this statement.[2] (10) That the Mexican Eve sinned by gathering Roses.[3] (11) That when the angel of the Lord announced to the Mexican Eve respecting a conception to come, he placed a Rose in her hand; but this bears all the marks of an imitative or spurious legend.[4] (12) That the world-wide repute of the Rose as a symbol of silence originated in a classical story that it was consecrated by Cupid to Harpocrates as a bribe not to betray the multitudinous adventures of his mother Venus; but this is a vulgarian explanation.[5] (13) That it does not account for the pre-Christian German custom of the Rose-emblem in the ceiling of banqueting halls—as a reminder that whatever was said beneath it must not

[1] It is quoted at length in my REAL HISTORY OF THE ROSICRUCIANS p. 11.

[2] The authority—for better, for worse—is Mr. W. S. Hunter, of the *Societas Rosicruciana in Scotia.* He wrote on the Rose and its symbolism in the TRANSACTIONS of the *Soc. Ros. in Anglia* for 1898–9.

[3] See MEXICAN ANTIQUITIES, Vol. VI, p. 120 *et ante.*

[4] *Ibid.*, p. 177.

[5] The Rose—both red and white—was sacred to Harpocrates. See Nimrod: ALCHYMUS, i.e. HISTORY AND FABLE, Vol. IV, p. 557. The Hon. Auberon Herbert, who wrote under this name, speaks of red and white roses blossoming in the garden of Knights Templar, but it appears to be reverie. Whatsoever was dedicated to Harpocrates was sacred also to silence, as there is no need to say.

be repeated elsewhere.[1] (14) That the white Rose was especially sacred to silence. (15) That the colour of the red Rose was derived from the blood of Adonis, when wounded by the wild boar, or alternatively from that of Venus, who in her haste to assist Adonis was pierced in the foot by the thorn of a white Rose, which sprinkled the flower with her blood, and it has been incarnadined ever since. (16) That otherwise the white Rose was made red by Cupid upsetting a cup of nectar in the course of his dancing before the gods.

It will be seen that in this enumeration we have been dealing, for the most part, with varieties of legend and frivolities of cheap symbolism. If we turn now to the canonical Scriptures of Israel we find only two references, of which one is apart from symbolism.[2] There is the familiar promise that "the desert shall blossom as the Rose"[3] and there is the eloquent testimony of the SONG OF SOLOMON, which is translated in the Authorised Version: "I am the Rose of Sharon."[4] We are carried thereby into the realm of Christian symbolism, and it may be noted in the first place that the Hebrew text אני חבצלת שרון is rendered by the VULGATE *Ego flos campi*, while it appears to be an open question in the mind of Catholic commentators[5] whether the words are spoken by the Lover or

[1] I mean that the German allocation does not connote a classical origin. As regards silence, compare the three rosettes on a Master Mason's apron and their alleged reference to Fidelity, Secrecy and Silence.

[2] That it to say, the reference is by way of comparison and belongs to poetic imagery.

[3] ISAIAH xxxv, 1. Observe, however, the Vulgate rendering: *Lætabitur deserta et invia, et exsultabit solitudo, et florebit quasi lilium*—shall blossom as the Lily, instead of as the Rose.

[4] *Loc. cit.*, Cap. II, 1.

[5] Petrus de Mora refers the emblem to both in his allusion to three mystical roses: *Prima rosa est chorus martyrum; secunda, Virgo Virginum; tertia, Mediator Dei et hominum.* The first is red, the second is white, the third is red and white. Compare St. Bernard in his SERMO DE BEATA MARIA. *Maria rosa fuit candida per virginitatem, rubicunda per charitatem; candida,*

Beloved of the poem : in the mystical sense, they have been applied therefore indifferently to Christ and the Blessed Virgin. The latter allocation is illogical under any circumstances, as however spiritually understood the *personæ* of the SONG OF SOLOMON are in the relation of Bridegroom and Bride. It makes void also the arbitrary but far-prevailing interpretation of the poem as unfolding in earthly imagery the union between Christ and His Church. The fact remains, notwithstanding, that we have on the one hand the symbolical position given in the Grade of Rose-Croix, that Christ is the Rose of Sharon and was foretold in the SONG OF SOLOMON under this mystical title, while on the other we have a broad general connection instituted between the Rose and Mary.[1] The Rose of Jericho has been called St. Mary's Rose and tradition affirms that when Joseph and Mary were taking their flight into Egypt one of these flowers sprang up to mark every spot where they rested.[2] In mediæval times it was called *Rosa Mariæ*, while *Marien*

carne ; rubicunda, mente ; candida, virtutem sectando ; rubicunda, vitia calcando ; candida, affectum purificando ; rubicunda, actum carnalem mortificando ; candida, Deum diligendo ; rubicunda, proximo compatiendo.

[1] There is a remarkable symbolism concerning Christ and His Divine Nature in the Golden Rose, which is said to be blessed and carried by the Pope on the Fourth Sunday in Lent, called Mid-Lent Sunday, otherwise *Lætare Hierusalem* and *Dominica de Rosa.* See Durandus : RATIONALE DIVINORUM OFFICIORUM, p. 207. Venice, 1609. This is quoted by Soane in NEW CURIOSITIES OF LITERATURE, I, pp. 120, 121. But there is evidently a mistake, for there is no *Lætare* in Lent, and the Ceremony of the Golden Rose takes place on Easter Monday. See the Sermon of Innocent III (*ob.* 1216) : IN DOMINICA LÆTARE, SEU DE ROSA. It says that the Rose contains : (1) the gold of which it is made, (2) the musk, and (3) the balm, both of which it exhales. They refer to the three substances of Christ : (1) His human nature, represented by the unalterable gold ; (2) His immaculate soul, represented by the musk ; and (3) His Deity, represented by the balm.

[2] According to another legend, the blossoming of the Rose occurred for the first time when Christ was born ; its petals folded up at the Crucifixion, but opened again at Easter. Mr. W. S. Hunter, already quoted, mentions : (1) that no true Roses are found in Palestine, except on the Lebanon ; (2) that the Rose of Sharon has been sometimes regarded as a species of tulip or narcissus. I have seen a dried specimen of the Rose of Jericho, which

Roselen is a German title of the Virgin. I need hardly mention the devotion of the Holy Rosary, instituted by St. Dominic—the prayers of which appear to have been symbolised as Roses—or its close analogue, the Rosaries of Chinese Buddhists.[1] In its attribution to Mary, the Rose became a symbol of virginity.

Through the Christian centuries—from the fourth to the thirteenth—there grew up more or less secretly, under the ægis of the New Law, that Secret Tradition in Israel which is represented by the SEPHER HA ZOHAR, its connections and dependencies. This great work is rich with allusions scattered up and down the text to the Rose and its symbolism. Indeed, the first intimations on the subject occur in the opening words of the preliminary portion, where one of the mystical doctors initiates a certain conference with a quotation from the SONG OF SOLOMON: " As the Rose among thorns, so is my beloved among the daughters."[2] We learn in this place (1) that the Rose signifies the Community of Israel; (2) that its colour,

unfolds in water and for this reason is called the Resurrection Flower According to his traditional History, Christian Rosy Cross went to Damascus, the place of the Damask Rose, and Hakluyt—writing apparently in 1582—says that Dr. Linaker brought in " the Damask Rose in time of memory "—presumably within recent years. Dr. Linaker was physician to Henry VII and Henry VIII. See VOYAGES, Vol. II. The place to which it was brought was presumably England. This item of plant-lore might not be without consequence in the history of the Rosy Cross, but unfortunately the ARCHÆOLOGICAL JOURNAL, Vol. XIV, p. 271, gives a Bill of Medicine furnished for the use of Edward I—*tempus* 1306-7—as follows: *Item pro Aqua rosata de Damaso*, lb. xl. iiiili.

[1] In THE ROSICRUCIAN AND MASONIC RECORD, No. 1, 1876, a certain Dr. Bell ventured to suggest that the Rosy Cross may have been derived from the Rosary, which "has in German the appellation of Rosencrantz." The notion is of course preposterous, more especially as Rosicrucianism was a mouthpiece of Reform in Germany.

[2] Compare ECCLESIASTICUS: " I was exalted as a rose-plant in Jericho," *Cap.* XXIV, v. 18. The VULGATE renders: *quasi plantatio rosæ in Jericho.* As regards the Zoharic quotation from the SONG OF SOLOMON, the authorised Version reads: " As a Lily among thorns," for once agreeing with the VULGATE: *Sicut lilium inter spinas.*

which is red or white, has reference to the severity and mercy which alternate in the life of Israel; (3) that its five petals allude to the five ways of salvation and five gates of grace; (4) that it symbolises also the cup of benedictions and even the chalice of salvation.[1] We are told elsewhere that Adam, while still unfallen, tended the Roses of Paradise.[2] The Rose, however, is more especially a symbol of Shekinah, whose rule extends on the right and left side of the Tree of Life in Kabalism, and obtains also in the middle, because of her office in MALKUTH, considered as the kingdom of this world. On the severity side of the Tree HOD is in correspondence with the Red Rose, while NETZACH on the mercy side has the White Rose for its emblem.[3] The union of red and white produces the Rose of MALKUTH,[4] and the plural-form Roses has reference to the Shekinah above—in the transcendence—and in manifestation, or in the world below.[5] The Rose has also an important place as a symbol of sex spiritualised, for the name is applied to Shekinah in her desire after union with the King.[6]

Shekinah comes before us in the ZOHAR somewhat strangely confused amidst male and female aspects.

[1] ZOHAR I, fol. 1a. The five petals allude to the Rose-calyx. We hear otherwise of thirteen petals, which are the thirteen Paths of Mercy. See also ZOHAR III, fol. 233b., in which there is a legend concerning Solomon, to whom a Rose is brought by an eagle, as a symbol of the Community of Israel.

[2] See my SECRET DOCTRINE IN ISRAEL, p. 72. Compare Dracontius: CARMEN DE DEO, *Lib.* I, v. 437. He says of Adam and Eve walking in the garden: *Ibant per flores et lata rosaria bini*, i.e. amidst flowers and great bosks of roses.

[3] *Datur Rosa rubea et alba*, HOD *et* NETZACH; *quandoque autem rubedo prædominatur in rosa, quandoque albedo; sic aliquando* HOD, *aliquando* NETZACH *prævalet*:—Knorr von Rosenroth: KABBALA DENUDATA. *Apparatus*, p. 708.

[4] The Rose in MALKUTH it said to contain red and white—meaning a blush Rose—and these colours denote stimulation towards the right and the left side—a reference to the Sephirotic Tree of Life.—*Ibid.*

[5] *Ibid.*, p. 709.

[6] *Ibid.*, p. 333.

I cannot remember that she is ever saluted by the title of Rose of Sharon, which indeed is applied once to Rabbi Simeon, the head and fount of theosophical tradition in Jewry. The case of Shekinah seems therefore analogous to that other confusion which I have mentioned, namely, that the Rose of Sharon or *flos campi* is referred in Christian symbolism indifferently to Mary the Mother and her Divine Son.[1] But St. Mary, as the great patron and type-in-chief of virginity, appears as the poles asunder from the Most Holy Shekinah, who has a high office in nuptials and does not extend her protection to man except through the bond of wedlock. Yet is there the shadow of a link between them,[2] for she who above all in Christendom is *Virgo singularis et inter omnes mitis* is mother as well as virgin, and Shekinah presides over motherhood.[3] The idea of these two symbolical personalities, both full of grace and beauty, both uplifted beyond all heights of sanctity, yet—amidst their assumption and transcendence—both so near to earth, grew up in complete independence, each unknown to each. A Litany of Shekinah might, I think, be constructed out of the ZOHAR and would not be less decorative or less pregnant with meaning than the Litany of Loretto, though—as I have had occasion to point out elsewhere—she who was MATRONA in the heights and MATRONA also in manifestation was no object of ceremonial devotion, like Mary the Mother, among any sect in Jewry. Beside both emblems there persisted also the remanents of pre-

[1] Compare F. W. Hackwood: CHRIST LORE, 1902. "The Madonna is the Rose of Sharon," p. 26. It is an uncritical statement in the light of the dual attribution mentioned above.

[2] Mr. Wigston reminds us that Dante connects the Rose with "the ineffable Light of Shekinah."—THE COLUMBUS OF LITERATURE, p. 193.

[3] Compare Dante in Longfellow's translation:

> There is the Rose in which the Word Divine
> Became incarnate.—PARADISO, *Canto* XXII.

Mary is therefore the Christian Shekinah.

Christian myth and legend. The Rose of Mary was more especially the White Rose, and it is said that the Red Rose continued for long to be related with Holda, the Northern goddess. There is also the beautiful fable of Lauvin and his Rose-Garden, which takes us into the Land of Faerie, where the Rose was under special protection. In another category of symbolism the Rose is womanhood, and as such it is an erotic emblem. The presence of this intimation is, I think, to be found everywhere and has not been put away altogether but rather transformed and sanctified when the gracious type has been lifted into the spiritual world. Thus the Rose is a symbol of Mary because of her motherhood, but in relation to her it belongs to divine things, even as she herself stands on the threshold of Deity, being Spouse of the Divine Spirit and bearer of the Divine Word made flesh.[1] So also is the Rose of Shekinah a Divine Rose, as she whom it typifies is Divine Mother of souls.

But the material and sensuous aspects flourished in their own sphere, and in France of the twelfth century the symbol was enthroned in imperishable literature by the allegorical poem called THE ROMANCE OF THE ROSE. Therein it is said that the leaves of the flower enclose the Art of Love. In the four-square garden of the poem the Dreamer sees " a rose-bush, charged with many a rose," and

> Amongst them all,
> My rapturous eyes on one did fall,
> Whose perfect loveliness outvied
> All those beside it.

This is the Rose which he desires to kiss and is so enabled to do after many trials, for which rashness long suffering

[1] In Christian Iconography the Rosebud has been said to designate the Incarnation. See DICTIONNAIRE ARCHÉOLOGIQUE ET EXPLICATIF DE LA SCIENCE DE BLASON. *Par le Comte* Alphonse O'Kelly de Galway, *Tom.* I, 1901.

befalls him. On a later occasion he attempts to gather the treasure, hoping to possess it henceforth[1]—

> I raised my hand in hope to hold
> At last that lovely Rose that I
> Had craved so long and ardently.

But Danger, Fear and Shame combine to drive him away. Venus and Cupid intervene at the end to help him, and

> *La conclusion du Rommant*
> *Est, que vous voyez cy l'Amant*
> *Qui prent la Rose à son plaisir*
> *En qui estoit tout son desir—*

which means that the pilgrim of earthly love at last attained his guerdon, and the poem affirms in its final couplet:

> *Nature rit, si com moi semble,*
> *Quant hic et hec joingnent ensemble.*

The ultimate line unfolds in full the allegorical meaning of the Rose, according to LE ROMAN DE LA ROSE, or at least according to Clopinel, that minstrel by whom it was completed.

It must be said that it is the Rose in the ashpits, as other parts of the poem make only too clear; but there is another mediæval memorial, in which we are taken farther to the heights than Jean de Meung places his symbol in the depths. I speak of the Rose of Dante, the Rose of his Seventh Heaven, where the Beatrice of his blessed vision is enthroned in Paradise.

> There is a light above, which visible
> Makes the Creator unto every creature,
> Who only in beholding Him has peace,
> And it expands itself in circular form
> To such extent, that its circumference
> Would be too large a girdle for the sun.
> The semblance of it is all made of rays

[1] I have used the translation of Mr. F. S. Ellis, published in the TEMPLE CLASSICS, 3 vols., 1900.

Reflected from the top of Primal Motion,
Which takes therefrom vitality and power.
And as a hill in water at its base
Mirrors itself, as if to see its beauty
When affluent most in verdure and in flowers,
So ranged aloft all round about the light,
Mirrored I saw in more ranks than a thousand
All who above there have from us returned,
And if the lowest row collect within it
So great a light, how vast the amplitude
Is of this Rose in its extremest leaves ! . . .
Into the yellow of the Rose Eternal
That spreads and multiplies, and breathes an odour
Of praise into the ever-vernal Sun,
As one who silent is and fain would speak,
Me Beatrice drew on ![1]

And again :

In fashion then as of a snow-white rose
Displayed itself to me the saintly host,
Whom Christ in His own blood had made His bride,
But the other host, that flying sees and sings

[1] *Lume è lassu, che visibile face*
Lo Creatore a quelle creatura
Che solo in Lui vedere ha la sua pace ;
E si distende in circular figura
In tanto, che la sua circonferenza
Sarebba al sol troppo larga cintura.
Fassie di raggio tutta sua parvenza
Riflesso al sommo del mobile primo,
Che prende quindi vivere e potenza.
E come clivo in acqua di suo imo
Si spechia, quasi per vedersi adorno,
Quando è nel verde e nei fioretti opimo ;
Si, soprastando al lume intorno intorno,
Vidi specchiarsi in più di mille soglie
Quanto di noi lassù fatto ha ritorno.
E se l'infimo grado in sè raccoglie
Si grande lume, quant' è la larghezza
Di questa rosa nell' estreme foglie ? . . .—PAR. XXX, 100–17.
Nel giallo della rosa sempiterna,
Che si dilata e digrada e redole
Odor di lode al Sol che sempre verna,
Qual è colui che tace e dicer vuole,
Mi trasse Beatrice.—PAR. XXX, 124–128.

The glory of Him Who doth enamour it,
And the goodness that created it so noble,
Even as a swarm of bees, that sinks in flowers
One moment, and the next returns again
To where its labour is to sweetness turned,
Sank into the great flower, that is adorned
With leaves so many, and thence reascended
To where its love abideth evermore.
Their faces had they all of living flame,
And wings of gold, and all the rest so white
Not snow unto that limit doth attain ! [1]

This high mystical import of the Rose-symbol and the spiritual enfoldment thereof are things to be distinguished from Rosicrucianism *per se* in its early presentation : we shall find in due course that they belong to another category. The Rose of Dante recalls, however, the imputed Rose of Khunrath,[2] which is Christian Kabalism presented in summary form. It suggests on the surface that the German mystic had borrowed from the Italian poet, but a little examination will save us from being misled by one of Éliphas Lévi's recurring false analogies. There is no justification—as I have intimated—for regarding the ninth Diagram of Khunrath—or his editor—as intended to represent a Rose. It is a great pictorial circle, within which is

[1] *In forma dunque di candida rosa*
Mi si mostrava la milizia santa
Che nel suo sangue Cristo fece sposa ;
Ma l'altra, che volant vede e canta
La gloria di Colui che la innamora,
E la bontà che la fece cotanta,
Si com schiera d'api, che s'infiora
Una fiata ed una si ritorna
La dove suo lavoro s'insapora ;
Nel gran fior discendeva che s'adorna
Di tante foglie, e quindi risaliva
La dove il suo amor sempre soggiorna.
Le facce tutte avean di fiamma viva,
E l'ali d'oro, e l'altrio tanto bianco,
Che nulla neve a quel termine arriva.—PAR. XXXI.

[2] AMPHITHEATRUM SAPIENTIÆ ÆTERNÆ, 1609.

a figure of ten sides, containing the names or titles of the nine choirs of angels and the souls of the blessed ones. Within this figure is a ring of clouds penetrated by rays of light, representing the ten SEPHIROTH drawn into a kind of circle, in the uppermost part of which there is indicated the Divine Darkness of *Ain Soph*, or God in the unknowable Above this is a radiant triad of light, inscribed with the Sacred Name of ten letters, formed from the four consonants of Jehovah. The Sephirotic rays are an extension of the glory proceeding from a Great Sun of Righteousness, inscribed with the Hebrew characters composing JEHESHUAH, while in the centre of this Sun is represented FILIUS VERI DEI, the Christ of Palestine, an unclothed figure, " with arms extended in the sacred cruciform sign," encompassed by the Divine Names ascribed to the SEPHIROTH, and with a great phœnix at His feet.[1] There is nothing attaching to the question if we elect to call this a Rose of Christ in Kabalism, but two other diagrams follow immediately—being seven and eight in the series of Khunrath—and the designation—though it does not happen to have been made—would apply to these also with equal force. I am willing to add that the theosophical doctrine of the ninth diagram is so much in consonance with the theosophy of the Rosy Cross that it might have appeared in Robert Fludd's vast treatise on the Macrocosm.

Having thus described at some length a pre-Rosicrucian symbol, I will cite in conclusion of my study on the Rose in Symbolism the following intimations of Michael Maier,

[1] See my translation of Éliphas Lévi's HISTORY OF MAGIC, second edition, 1922, p. 354, note 2. The French magus misconceived the significance of the Rose in symbolism, whether Christian or Kabalistic. He calls it (1) the flesh in rebellion against the spirit ; (2) Nature affirming that she is a daughter of God ; (3) love refusing to be stifled by celibacy ; (4) humanity aspiring towards natural religion. All this is the imagery of romance and very suggestive as such ; but it is not the secret tradition or the doctrine of the Rosy Cross.

when he is not testifying as if an expert Brother of the Rosy Cross but as an alchemist only.[1] He says: (1) That the Rose is the first, most beautiful and perfect of all flowers. (2) That it is guarded because it is a virgin, and the guard is thorns. (3) That the Gardens of Philosophy are planted with many roses, both red and white. (4) That these colours are in correspondence with gold and silver. (5) That the centre of the Rose is green and is emblematical of the Green Lion, a familiar emblem to the Wise. (6) That even as the natural Rose is a pleasure to the senses and life of man, on account of its sweetness and salubrity, so is the Philosophical Rose exhilarating to the heart and a giver of strength to the brain. (7) That as the natural Rose turns to the sun and is refreshed by rain, so is the Philosophical Matter prepared in blood, grown in light, and in and by these made perfect. Hereof is the Rose in alchemy.[2]

I have quoted this only as presenting a point of view, possibly within the circle of the Order, but we shall see that Michael Maier differs from the majority of exponents respecting the sacramental name of the Fellowship. We have now to glance at the isolated symbol of the Cross and can set aside at once the mass-in-chief of its traditional history as extending beyond our concern. The archæology of the subject was of little or no consequence to the Brethren of the Rosy Cross, and they shewed an equivalent concern therein. We do not hear that it was uplifted in Egypt, either as a prophetic sign or otherwise as an important

[1] See Septimana Philosophica, *cap.* 4.

[2] It is at least one of the aspects, and perhaps the most fully developed, for—outside the lexicons, which tell us that *Rosa*=Tartar—the symbol enters commonly into the romance of imaginative titles, such as the Rosarium Philosophorum of Arnoldus de Villanova, the Rosarium Novum of Figulus and several others. Robert Fludd, who seems to have cared little enough for the interminable elaborations of conventional alchemical symbolism, saw nothing in the Rosicrucian Rose but an emblem of the Precious Blood.

symbol. They know nothing of the mythical or traditional crucifixions of deities in heathen religions.[1] They might have characterised them roughly—had they known—as inventions of that *diabolus* who is said to be the ape of God and produces blasphemous imitations because he cannot create. I question whether they were aware that there is an unrecognised cross in Zoharic Kabalism, drawn from the four cardinal points to a centre and that above this centre is the Sacred Rose of Shekinah. It is a matter of inference from the great text and not a formulated image, while the figure in question would delineate a Cosmic Cross—that is to say, having equal arms. Had the fact of this inference been known in much earlier days, the doctors of the ZOHAR would have been presented to our notice as Brethren of the Rosy Cross and Rabbi Simeon as the first Imperator. There is a cross also of the four elements among the types and images of alchemy: of this the Rosicrucians knew; on this also they dwelt—in the mind at least—because of another Cross with which we know that they were concerned, the Cross of Divine Mystery, raised upon the Mount of Calvary. There are testimonies concerning it in the writings of Robert Fludd and elsewhere in the literature.[2]

The Cross in alchemy will not detain us long: it is that of the four elements of ancient physics, and behind

[1] Most of these fables bear, however, very obvious marks of manufacture, among which may be specified (1) the alleged crucifixion of Indra or Buddha for robbing a garden of a flower, and (2) that of the air-god in Mexico, who is said to have been nailed to a Cross.

[2] They must be distinguished from the Cross-lore of Christendom, some of which is very old, as Graal literature testifies. Neither Robert Fludd nor any other of the Rosicrucian "fire-philosophers" was concerned with the side of legend. He might otherwise have found something to his purpose in the tradition that the Cross of Calvary was made from the wood of that Tree of Knowledge which looms largely in Zoharic reveries, and is said to become the Tree of Life when the soul ascends to perfection. He would remember of course that the Tree of Calvary is called mystically the Tree of Life.

these is an unity, which is called quintessence in the great veil of words, though it is known by many names. A mystical axiom found in Rosicrucian literature affirms that

> In Cruce, sub sphæra,
> Venit sapientia vera,

thus interpreting the astronomical sign of Venus as an emblem of the Life of life and the planet itself—understood of course spiritually—as representing, in the astrology of the soul, that law which governs the Second Birth. The wisdom reached in the Venusian Cross is that which follows the inward process of purification, effected in the four parts of human personality—or body, mind, desire and will in purpose—the Cross of our own nature, corresponding on the hidden side of Rosicrucian teaching to the Cross of the four elements. On this account the star Venus is said to shine before the Portal of Regenerated Life. There is, however, on the external side another axiom, namely, *In Cruce salus*, and although it may be taken assuredly to intimate the same spiritual mystery, it is understood alchemically as referring to the Cross of the physical elements, in which the matter of the quintessence abides, or otherwise of the Philosophical Stone. The wisdom of this Cross is therefore that of the Great Work accomplished; and Venus, who carries a Cross beneath the circle of her symbol, came to signify the Matter of the Work in one or other of its stages. An ingarnering of this kind might be carried much further, and we should find Arnoldus de Villanova and Jean de Roquetaillade comparing the Cross of the elements with the *signum magnum* of Calvary and the volatilisation of the fixed and igneous part of their Philosophical Matter with the uplifting of the Son of Man upon the Cross, a glorified state being that which followed by the hypothesis in both cases. But it is enough for the purpose in view to shew that there is a Cross in alchemy, as there is indeed also a Rose, which is said to signify *Tartarum Philosophicum.*

That the symbolism of the Cross in alchemy was reflected into the Order of the Rosy Cross there can be no need to debate, and from this it would seem to follow that their characteristic *signum* was a Cross with equal arms, otherwise a Macrocosmic Cross. There is, however, no means of knowing. We shall see that on a memorable occasion, in one of his traditional histories, Christian Rosy Cross bound " a blood-red ribbon, cross-wise upon his shoulder," presumably after the manner of a Knight Templar. It may have been a Calvary Cross or it may not. None of the early documents explain their chief symbol. On the other hand, it is inferentially likely that Simon Studion's allusions to the Rose and Cross may have corresponded roughly to the Rose-Croix definition, when it says that the Cross is the Cross of Christ, " red with the Precious Blood." So also in the hands of Robert Fludd it became, if it was not originally, a Passion Cross. As such it was regarded by John Heydon at a later epoch in the seventeenth century; but when the time came for the Rosicrucian SECRET SYMBOLS to be published at Altona the Cross of Calvary and the Cross with equal arms are both recurring symbols. Between these forms the question of the symbol lies: it matters nothing at the moment that it became in the seventeenth century the peculiar Patriarchal Cross delineated by the Tree of Life in late Kabalism. The St. Andrew's Cross lies outside our concern also until we come to adjudicate on a particular claim as to the foundation of the Brotherhood, and I have set aside implicitly whatsoever belongs to the *Crux ansata*, the Tau Cross and the Swastika. They entered neither into the mind of occult sciences in Germany of 1614 nor into Lutheran reveries of 1586. To make an end of this matter, we are not called upon to find judgment in favour of any one of the admissible forms, as there is no evidence before us.

I pass now to the conjunction of Rose and Cross, constituting the distinctive Rosicrucian emblem. The following points may be noted in the first place. (1) The earliest example of the Rose in union with the Cross is perhaps the frontispiece of a work by Jacob Locher, issued at Nuremberg in 1517. It exhibits a great circle of Roses, having a Cross in the centre and the figure of the Christ thereon.[1] There is, however, no reason to suppose that the circle is other than an ornamental border. (2) In what are called the "ages of faith," we hear of the Cross garlanded at Easter with wreaths of Roses; but these flowers were combined with lavender and other sweet herbs.[2] The fact belongs obviously to popular devotion. (3) Luther adopted a Cross emerging from a Rose as his coat of arms, and if this choice were of common knowledge at the period, it might well account for any wealth of Rose and Cross symbolism in the reveries of Simon Studion and his anti-papal apocalypse.[3] (4) The armorial bearings of Johann Valentin Andreæ were a St. Andrew's Cross, having Roses in the four angles; but this fact belongs to a later part of our inquiry. It is stated here so that no point of moment may be missed in a representative sequence. Meanwhile it belongs to heraldry. (5) The Cross in heraldry is called

[1] The work is called ROSARIUM.

[2] The authority in this case is the Rev. Hilderic Friend: FLOWERS AND FLOWER-LORE, 2 vols., 1892. But it does not appear that the devotional custom is represented by late or early memorials of Christian Art, so far as Roses are concerned. Louisa Twining's SYMBOLS AND EMBLEMS OF EARLY AND MEDIÆVAL CHRISTIAN ART, 1852, contains many examples of ancient Crosses, some decorated or encompassed with flowers and some with flowers springing from them. The examples are taken from the Catacombs, Lombardy and other parts of Italy, etc., but the Rose is not included.

[3] According to Sédir, *op. cit.*, the device of Luther was a Cross and four Roses, but he is thinking of the arms of Andreæ. Another story says that Luther adopted the Rose simply, which is certainly wrong.

" the first honourable ordinary," and the heraldic Rose is always full-blown, with the *petala* or " flower-leaves " expanded, " seeded in the middle and backed by five green barbs, or *involucra*," [1] between the five petals, the true Rosicrucian symbol being also a five-petalled Rose, like that of the ZOHAR. (6) Among coats of arms belonging to families in Great Britain there are examples of (*a*) a Cross between four Roses *gules*; (*b*) *Arg.* a Cross engr. sa., between four Roses ppr.; (*c*) a Cross patty between four Roses *arg.*; (*d*) Az., a Cross *arg.* between four Roses *or*; (*e*) Az., a Cross engraved *or*, between four Roses *arg.*[2] It is certain that these and many other analogous devices of Blazonry go further back than the end of the sixteenth century, and therefore unless the symbol described perhaps in NAOMETRIA and implied by the title of *Fratres Roseæ Crucis* in the first manifestoes of the Order was " a single

[1] See William Berry: ENCYCLOPÆDIA HERALDICA, Vol. I, 1828.

[2] These examples will be found in Papworth's ALPHABETICAL DICTIONARY OF COATS OF ARMS. In the DICTIONNAIRE ARCHÉOLOGIQUE of O'Kelly, already cited, it is said of heraldic Crosses that the red is more especially Spanish, and the golden Cross English. The French is silver, the Italian blue, the German black or orange, and the Saxon green. The *Crux rosea*, or Rosy Cross, might be simply a Cross of that colour—e.g. " red with the Precious Blood "—but the tradition and its memorials are both against this view. In my opinion Mr. Wigston is substantially right when he says that the Rosicrucian emblem was " a crucified Rose," whether or not the Cross was mounted on a Calvary. See FRANCIS BACON, *Poet, Prophet and Philosopher*, p. 317. I mean that this was the general or characteristic sign, adopted when the title of Rosy Cross was formulated as a symbol. When the Brotherhood in one of its revivals or developments became *Ordo Roseæ et Aureæ Crucis*, the emblem was a golden Cross emblazoned with a red Rose. It appears in this form as a Cross with equal arms in the SECRET SYMBOLS, but there are also examples of a golden Calvary Cross, charged in the same manner. I am not very often in agreement with Mr. Wigston, and I record this instance gladly, because he was a good knight-errant, on a forlorn and hopeless quest. He dwells much in another place on the Rose and Heart symbol in Bacon's " advertisement " of the HOLY WAR, saying—correctly, as I have no doubt—that it is found in no other volume printed by Haviland, but that it occurs many years after on the title-page of one of Heydon's works. In any case, however, the emblem does not belong to our subject, as the Cross is absent.

Rose upon a Passion Cross," it was neither unknown nor of great rarity.

I have not taken the whole emblematical science of heraldry as my province, but I have made such inquiries as are relevant to the case and sufficient, I believe, to establish the individual point, on the basis of which it appears correct to affirm that a Rose centred in a Calvary Cross at the meeting-point of the arms is not known in heraldry, while the same statement applies to the so-called Macrocosmic Cross or Cross with equal arms, bearing a Rose in its centre. Outside heraldry the marriage of Rose and Cross is not to be found in printed books prior to the seventeenth century, and I know not of any manuscript illustrated by such a device or alluding to such symbolism till long after the FAMA FRATERNITATIS was addressed to the *literati* of Europe—the unprinted NAOMETRIA of Studion being always possibly excepted. I have followed deceptive byways in many barren directions, seeking traces of the union. There is John Yarker, for example, who loved nothing better than enticing an unwary traveller into his pirate-bus and driving into a cul-de-sac. He mentions Jacobus Typotus, who wrote SYMBOLA DIVINA in 1601, and " under the symbol of the Holy Cross is supposed to shew his knowledge of Knights Roseæ Crucis." By whom supposed does not happen to appear, and an examination of the elaborate devices given in the work of Typotus fails to produce even one solitary example of the Rose and Cross in union.[1]

[1] The full title is SYMBOLA DIVINA ET HUMANA PONTIFICUM, IMPERATORUM, REGUM : *accessit brevis Isagoge Iac. Typotii.* 3 vols., 1601, 1602, 1603. Among many Eucharistic emblems, there is an altar inscribed on the front with a sun and the words : *Soli Deo Honos et Gloria* within the solar disc. In the centre is ✠ IHS. On the altar is a chalice inscribed *Et sanguis meus vere est potus*, completing the sentence on the Sacred Host raised above the chalice—i.e. *Caro mea vere est cibus*, surrounding a crucifix. A solar glory encompasses Host and Chalice, while a Dove—sign of the Holy Spirit—is

It is necessary at this point to make an apparent digression and to establish in the first place—as we shall see at length in the next chapter—that when the FAMA FRATERNITATIS first appeared at Cassel in 1614 it was described on the title-page as *Fama . . . des löblichen Ordens des Rosenkreuzes*, otherwise the Honourable Order of the Rosy Cross.[1] It follows that there was no mistake possible from the beginning as to the name of the Brotherhood or the significance of the letters R ∴ C ∴, when such an abbreviated form was substituted in later reprints. This notwithstanding, in the year 1618, the German alchemist Michael Maier, who became a chief spokesman of the Order, affirms as follows: (1) that when the Society first became known in writing the letters R ∴ C ∴ were taken to signify Rosy Cross; (2) that this is erroneous and, as explained by the Brethren themselves, the said initials denote the name of their founder. Where such an explanation is given I do not claim to know, but it is said to be in "subsequent writings." The contention is entirely hollow, for it transpired so early as 1616 that—mythical, traditional or historical, as the case may be—the name of the "careful and wise father" and founder was Christian Rosencreutz. *Ab origine symboli* therefore the Order was either that of the Rosy Cross or of the traditional person who was said to bear the name. It needs only to be

above the glory, amidst a radiant cloud. I have mentioned this emblem at length because late Rosicrucian Doctrine connotes a very high aspect of the Eucharistic Mystery. Another device is called *Symbolum Sanctæ Crucis*, and shews a pelican in its piety on the summit of a Calvary Cross, thus corresponding by antithesis to the Masonic Rose-Croix jewel, which has a pelican at the foot of the Cross. It is a well-known symbol of our Saviour, and the doctrinal reason is given in literal form in the Ritual of the Eighteenth Degree. The pelican has been described as an early Rosicrucian symbol, but I have not found the evidence.

[1] The fact disposes of a favoured thesis advanced by Mrs. Henry Pott in Baconian interests, namely, that "the title Rosicrucian was . . . never given or adopted until after the publication of the CHYMICAL MARRIAGE OF CHRISTIAN ROSENCREUTZ, in 1616."

added that Maier proceeds forthwith to stultify his correction by giving a personal interpretation of the letters R∴C∴, but it is unintelligible in the absence of a key.[1]

After an interval of some ten years Michael Maier was succeeded by a French writer, Petrus Gassendus, who in certain strictures on the philosophy of Robert Fludd, the

[1] See Maier's SYMBOLA AUREÆ MENSÆ, 1617. It affirms: (1) that R = Pegasus and C = Lilium, which appears nonsense, and the LEXICON ALCHEMIÆ of Rulandus, 1612, knows nothing of such terms. It is not till late in the eighteenth century that Antoine Joseph Pernety hazards a Hermetic interpretation of the winged offspring of Medusa and the Fountain of Hippocrene on Helicon, produced by a stroke of his hoof. He also explains *Lilium* as Philosophical Tincture, otherwise the Perfect Elixir of Hermetic Art. See FABLES ÉGYPTIENNES, *Livre* III, c. 14, §3, and DICTIONNAIRE MYTHO-HERMÉTIQUE, p. 249. (2) That the arcanum of the name reposes in the formula: d. wmme. zii, w. sgqq hka. x. It is concerned with the hoof of the Red Lion—i.e., the matter of the Mastery in the fixed or prepared state, "or the drops of the Hippocrene Fountain." This is the language of cipher: it is neither of Alchemy nor of the Rosy Cross. There was presumably a key to its meaning, but the keeper of that key was Maier and with him it was buried at Magdebourg. The antiquarian scholarship of 1836, represented by our old friend Godfrey Higgins, was cryptic after another manner on the same subject, as a characteristic specimen will shew. "Nazareth, the town of Nazir or Ναζωραιος, *the flower*, was situated in Carmel, the vineyard or garden of God. Jesus was a flower; whence came the adoration, by the Rosicrucians, of the Rose and Cross, which Rose was Ras, and this Ras, or knowledge or wisdom, was stolen from the garden, being also crucified, as he literally is, on the red cornelian, the emblem of the Rosicrucians—a Rose on a Cross. This crucified flower-plant was also LIBER, a book, a letter or tree, or Bacchus or IHΣ. This IHΣ was Logos, Linga, letters, LTR = 650. The God was, moreover, called Rose or Ras, because he was R ‖ 200, O = 70, Z = 90 = 360, or Rose = 365; RS = RST = 600; the Rose *of the Water*, or *Water-rose*, as it is termed to this day. But this Rose of Sharon, this Logos, this word, was called in Arabic and Chaldæan *werta* and *werd*, the same as our *word*. Thus it was both the Linga, the generative principle, and Lingua, a word, or words, language."—ANACALYPSIS, Vol. II, p. 240. Here is cipher also, but it can be decoded by going through the two quarto volumes. It is sufficient for my purpose to say that all these instituted analogies and identities between things lying far apart in myth, symbol and old religion, rest on etymologies as they stood at the Higgins period, with himself as chief mouthpiece, and for us at the present day they read like records of nightmare.

English Rosicrucian,[1] affirmed (1) that the name of the Order is not compounded of *Rosa* and *Crux* ; (2) that this and other interpretations have been put forward " by the chemists themselves " for the sake of imposing on others ; (3) that it is composed in reality of Ros=Dew and Crux=Cross ; (4) that Dew is the most powerful of all natural dissolvents ; (5) that the figure of a Cross exhibits the letters of the word Lux=Light, at a single view ; (6) that *Lux* signifies in alchemy the seed or menstruum of the Red Dragon, otherwise that " crude and corporeal light which, if properly concocted and digested, produces gold " ; (7) that a Rosicrucian is therefore a philosopher who seeks for light by means of dew, or otherwise for the substance of the Philosopher's Stone. There is nothing in antecedent Rosicrucian literature to sustain this statement and it must be placed in the same category as that of the alchemist Maier. The original manifestoes are against it. I do not pretend to understand how Gassendus proposed to revise the Rosicrucian name, so that it should tolerate his rendering and yet be intelligible Latin. Possibly his emendation would have been *Fratres Roratæ Crucis.* His criticism is, however, so obscure upon this point that yet another writer came forward and making short work of the Cross in previous symbolism, as well as of the evidence offered by Rosicrucian documents, substituted *Fratres Roris Cocti*, though I am not aware that alchemy had a process for the philosophical coction of dew.[2] The Rosicrucian SECRET SYMBOLS of the eighteenth century are an eloquent commentary unawares upon all these reveries, with which it has been necessary to deal and which may be set aside

[1] The tract was published in 1630 under the title of EPISTOLICA EXERCITATIO *in qua præcipue principia philosophiæ* Robert Fludd *deteguntur.* It was reprinted in the collected works of Gassendus as EXAMEN PHILOSOPHIÆ FLUDDANÆ. See OPERA, III, especially p. 261.

[2] Eusebius Renaudot : CONFÉRENCES PUBLIQUES, IV, 87.

once and for all, though two of them have held the field since they were popularised by Arnold and Mosheim.[1]

When a day came for the sacramental and mystical title of Rosicrucian and Rosy Cross to be explained in intelligible terms, the task—as already intimated—was undertaken in a treatise which Robert Fludd most certainly inspired and which embodies all his views, though it was not the work of his hand. The various propositions may be brought thus together: (1) The Cross is the sign or symbol of Jesus Christ, of the Brotherhood in its inward dedication, of pure mystical wisdom. (2) Its red colour represents the mystical and divine blood of Christ, which—according to the Apostle—cleanses from all sin. (3) It was borne on the breasts of Christian Chivalries in the wars against Turks and Saracens. (4) This red Cross is adorned with roses and lilies, because He unto Whom it refers is " the Rose of

[1] See G. C. A. von Harless: JACOB BÖHME UND DIE ALCHYMISTEN, 1870, pp. 114–16. Mr. Harold Bayley, *op. cit.*, is another who elects to derive the name Rosicrucian from " the words dew and cross," which he interprets cryptically by alluding to " the honey-dew of knowledge rising and falling again on the souls of men in odourous showers from the well of Truth." Where the Cross enters into this scheme of explanation does not appear. However, the Rosicrucians—understood as " a very secret society of learned men "—are described as " physicians in the highest sense of the term, because they aim at restoring the bodily powers of man through the action of the soul, fed by Divine wisdom and knowledge." This is Rosicrucianism as it is remade in the mind of reverie. It is to be understood that writers who reproduce the views of Gassendus derive their knowledge from Mosheim, whose ECCLESIASTICAL HISTORY became known widely through an English translation. We may account in this manner for the cipher F∴R∴C∴ being rendered *Fratres Roris Cocti* in Howard's NEW ROYAL CYCLOPÆDIA, 3 vols., n.d., but *circa* 1830. See s.v. Rosycrucians. The misstatements are scandalous even for that period. The Order is said to have been first heard of in Germany at the beginning of the sixteenth century; Fludd, Maier and Jacob Böhme are placed at its head. There is finally Mr. A. G. Mackey, a famous American Mason, who rejects the *Ros* explanation and suggests tentatively that " the Rose being a symbol of secrecy and the Cross of light " their combination was " intended to symbolise the secret of the true light, or the true knowledge, which the Rosicrucian Brotherhood were to give to the world."

Sharon and the Lily of the Valley." (5) Moreover, there is placed in its centre a Rose "of the colour of blood" to indicate the work of Sacred and Divine Alchemy in the purification of that which is unclean, the completion and perfection of which is "the full Rose on the Cross," as this is "offered and transfixed in the centre." The Brotherhood of the Rosy Cross is therefore *Fraternitas Christiana*, constituted by seekers for the Tree of Life in the Paradise of God, an incorruptible seed of the Spirit. In fine, their head is Christ, as "the head of Christ is God." The essential Rosicrucian symbol is therefore a Red Rose centred in a Red Calvary Cross, at the meeting-point of the arms.[1]

It may be urged with considerable force that Fludd as reflected in Fritz—was spiritualising the Rosy Cross; but if it be said that he advances a purely personal understanding, one answer to this would be that he may have been working from within. We shall see later on that he speaks with an authority which either connotes membership or is inexplicable, having regard to his known character. Moreover, he did not stand utterly alone: there was more than one Rosicrucian document in circulation on the Continent about the same period which suggests a similar concern, though they are not so lucidly worded. Our recurring source of reference, the SECRET SYMBOLS, is so much a witness in the same direction that it might be a collection bequeathed by Fludd himself to Rosicrucian

[1] See SUMMUM BONUM, published at Frankfurt in 1629, under the name of Joachimus Frizius. Also the Ven. Archdeacon Craven's DR. ROBERT FLUDD, pp. 142, 143. Elsewhere I believe that Fludd speaks of the Order symbol as "the Cross of Christ dyed by his rose-red blood." As regards No. 3 in the text above, this statement may account for Dr. Alexander Wilder in his usual state of confusion affirming that the "Rose upon a Cross" was a badge of the Knights Templar. See THE METAPHYSICAL MAGAZINE, Vol. III, pp. 417 *et seq.*, 1896. The reference of Joachim Fritz is to a cross of crimson colour, which was the Templar Cross. The allusions of SUMMUM BONUM to the Rosicrucian symbol are drawn from several places of that work.

posterity, though it is actually a work of the late eighteenth century. In and about the year 1650, the alchemist Thomas Vaughan, debating Rosicrucian theosophy, may obviously have reflected his precursor, the man of Kent; but it is a point to observe that he interpreted the claims of the Order, in the sense of that Holy Quest which is the Quest of Christ in God. And though others may have prompted his views, he was much too individual to reflect merely like a glass.

Among recent writers, Mr. Wigston, whom I have quoted previously, says that the crucified Rose of the Rosicrucian "hints at the entire Logos legend in a mystical sense."[1] Mr. W. S. Hunter, whom I have also cited, is a stultifying person, even for a Masonic Rosicrucian of the "Metropolitan College." After the manner of one who makes a personal discovery, he mentions that the Rose was "applied" to Christ, but the Rose on a Cross signifies "the secret of Immortality."[2] Why and after what manner he omits to explain. So also John Yarker affirms "a Masonic tradition," not otherwise specified, "which says that the first drop of blood which fell from our Lord's wounds was miraculously converted into a Rose," adding with inscrutable logic: "Hence the union of the Rose and Cross."[3] We may question others who pass as Masonic *literati* to the same or as little purpose. Reghellini, in

[1] It may be mentioned in this connection, apart from Rose-symbolism, that the word *Ros*=Dew—but no doubt in its Greek form—was a Gnostic emblem of Christ. The Ophites, moreover, held that the Dew which "fell from the excess of light was"—? represented—"Wisdom," understood as a Hermaphroditic Deity. Mr. Wigston alluded presumably to another Logos philosophy. W. F. C. Wigston: The Columbus of Literature, p. 195. See also B. Theodoreti Quæstiones in Genes., *Cap.* XXVII, p. 91, edition of 1772, and the same in Hæreticorum Fabulorum Compendium, *Liber* I, *Cap.* XIV, p. 307.

[2] Rosicrucian and Masonic Record, 1898.

[3] Notes on the Scientific and Religious Mysteries of Antiquity, 1872, p. 31.

comparatively early days, fulfils his duty towards the symbol by presenting the Cross as a sign of union and the Rose of Secrecy.[1] On the other hand, Marc Saunier, writing in 1911, is not alone assured that the secret science of Christian Rosy Cross was a synthesis of all accepted knowledge, but presents its characteristic symbol in terms hitherto unknown. It was a star of twelve points, on which a triangle was inscribed within a circle. A Cross within the Delta was emblazoned with a Rose in full flower, and beneath the Rose was a Pelican in its piety. The whole symbol was further decorated by five stars, each of five points, while a star of seven points was placed at the apex of the Triangle. It is possible that such an emblem is a Continental and probably French variant of the jewel worn by Masons of the Scottish Rite in the Eighteenth Degree of Rose-Croix, but it has certainly no connection with German Rosicrucianism of 1614 or any later period.[2]

A word may be said in conclusion as to the present theosophy of the symbol within the circle of initiation, it being understood that I speak under certain reserves, as the case demands. In its primary sense the Rose-Cross is the typical Christ-emblem, exhibiting the Divine Part in manifestation, not in immanence. A Calvary Cross bearing a Rose of five petals is the Mystery of the Incarnation. The

[1] Reghellini da Schio: LA MAÇONNERIE *considérée comme le résultat des Réligions Égyptiennes, Juive et Chrétienne.* We may compare the anonymous MAÇONNERIE PRATIQUE, 2 vols., 1885, which says that the Cross on the Rose (*sic*) typifies human reproduction, understood as the only mode of creation admitted by something termed "pure reason"—not otherwise defined. The Rose signifies *genitalia mulieris*, while the point of intersection of the four arms of the cross represents *membrum virile*. The authority is J. M. Ragon: RITUEL DU GRADE DE ROSE-CROIX, 1860, pp. 29 *et seq.*

[2] LA LÉGENDE DES SYMBOLES PHILOSOPHIQUES, RELIGIEUX ET MAÇONNIQUES. Deuxième édition. Paris, 1911. The symbol is interpreted as follows: (1) Star of Twelve Points = Signs of the Zodiac and their correspondences in humanity. (2) Triangle = the immutable Trinity, which Saunier understands in his folly as force, matter and movement. (3) Cross = the crucifixion of movement in matter; involution of the soul in the four elements;

Macrocosmic Cross bearing the same symbol in its centre signifies the Grace and Power of the Word ruling the whole creation. The Calvary Rose-Cross also represents man in the manifested state, having the soul abiding in the four parts of personality. When a certain sacramental sign is placed in the centre of the Rose, it is an allusion to the Christ-Spirit dwelling in the soul and also declared therein. When this sign is replaced by Dew, the *Ros Rosaceæ Crucis*, it conveys the same notion, and that also of the Spirit fructifying the soul. The most secret key is: *Angelus Domini nuntiavit Mariæ, et concepit de Spiritu Sancto.* It is the key also of that which out of all hymns and canticles is termed CANTICA CANTICORUM, the great Song of Espousals and of Solomon. After this manner is the pregnant and truly sacramental symbol elevated, as with great reverence, out of the hands of the honourable and Christian gentleman Robert Fludd. It is elevated also, as if above official altars, and exposed like a monstrance wherein is the Mystery of Christhood, "the truest and holiest that is in this world." We shall find the Rosicrucian Order among the purlieus of Protestant sects, among the money-changers of spurious alchemy; but we know antecedently in this manner that it is called and chosen for great transmutations to come, and that

incarnation and death; resurrection and immortality. (4) Rose = that which is born from the corpse and exhales itself in sweet odours. This Rose blossoms by following the example of the Bird, i.e. nourishing its starving young with its own blood. (5) Pelican = Infinite Love = the Phœnix, setting and rising Sun, Osiris and Horus, Christ accepting death for the weal of man. The young which it feeds are body, soul and spirit. (6) Star of Five Points = symbol of will transmuting passions and emotions. (7) Star of Seven Points = the seven rungs of that ladder which the sage must ascend if he would know the Holy Spirit—understood here as the Light in all its splendour. It is seldom that any canon of interpretation betrays its own invalidity so completely. Movement is not crucified in matter, which itself is a mode of motion; there is no analogy in symbolism between the Rose and the Pelican; while to speak of a Rose nourishing its starving young is to confuse the images concerned.

those among whom it originated knew not what they did.

The conclusion meanwhile to be drawn from the findings of this summary research is that if our first knowledge of the Rose and Cross in union comes to us from Simon Studion it brings with it an irresistible inference—but apart from any direct evidence—that it was suggested to his mind by the arms of Luther. Beyond doubt he dreamed, speculated and theosophised thereon, but the fact remains that there was no other antecedent source from which he could have drawn his symbol. On the other hand, it is not less certain that at an early period of Rosicrucian literature and history the symbol was changed over and became a Calvary Cross, emblazoned with a Rose of five petals at the meeting-point of the arms. By a process of exhaustion it is to be inferred that Robert Fludd was the author of this conversion, because he is the sole extant witness who describes the Order-symbol, awaiting that time when the authors of the SECRET SYMBOLS at the close of the eighteenth century presented the emblem pictorially, and they followed Robert Fludd—as John Heydon had done previously in England. Rose-Croix Masonry had taken a lesson from him also some thirty years previously. It should be noted in this connection that the allegations of Michael Maier are not concerned with the Rosicrucian symbol but with the style and title of the Order. As there is no suggestion at his period that the members wore jewels or badges, it may not have entered into his thought that any symbol was implied. Outside perhaps NAOMETRIA it is mentioned nowhere in the early documents, and Maier had passed from earthly life when Joachim Fritz testified in SUMMUM BONUM on the part of Robert Fludd.

CHAPTER V

FAMA FRATERNITATIS R∴C∴

It has been shewn that for any vestige of Rosicrucian history and symbolism at the dawn of the seventeenth century we depend upon the fact of a document which has been described by at least four writers who unquestionably had it in their hands. The most extended account is anonymous, though the author may have been identical with Petersen, whose name transpires as editor of the Würtemberg Repertorium Literarium. About the location of this document—so long uncertain, so long, it would seem unsought by those who speculate about the Rosy Cross, and even now uncatalogued—we have at length obtained a settlement. Behind it lies the convocation of a Militia Crucifera Evangelica, which has been called an assembly of Rosicrucians by various fools of research, who find anything that they want among the dubious memorials of the past. The more dubious apparently, the better is their purpose served. There is not the least reason to suppose that the *Militia* was other than a sect of Second Adventists, whose connection with the occult reveries and Paracelsian atmosphere of Naometria is borne out by no evidence. The all-important fact is not, however, the *Militia*, but the Studion document. I have summarised fully the extant descriptions and there seems no question—broadly speaking—that we can accept their evidence implicitly in respect of spirit and content. It follows in this case that Simon Studion made use of symbolism in which there was effected possibly a conjunction of the Rose and Cross. The casual reference to Tobias Hess by C. G. von Murr seems also to indicate a fact, and this is borne out by J. V. Andreæ's allusion to NAOMETRIA in his Latin memorial. It is certain, moreover, that prior to 1614 the peculiar set of notions and the prevailing atmosphere which characterised Rosicrucian documents are to be found in the writings of Valentin Weigel and Ægidius Gutmann.

We are now on the threshold of the time when official publications of the Rosicrucian Society began to appear in Germany, whether it was actually incorporated or had been devised by a few persons as what is termed an experiment on the mind of the age. The FAMA FRATERNITATIS was first printed probably in 1614,[1] but the bibliographical

[1] Professor John Ferguson states—BIBLIOTHECA CHEMICA, 2 vols., 1906, Vol. I, p. 27—that the UNIVERSAL REFORMATION was printed at Cassel by Wilhelm Wessell in 1612, together with the FAMA FRATERNITATIS and Haselmeyer's RESPONSIO, in small 8vo, pp. 147. Compare Dr. Begemann: COMENIUSMONATSHEFTE, 1899, p. 165. Ferguson says also that another edition was printed in 1614, with an EPISTOLA added. This was in sm. 8vo, pp. 152. There seems to be a mistake here. Kloss, the German bibliographer of Freemasonry, knows nothing of a 1612 edition, though it would help to explain a letter cited by Lenglet du Fresnoy as appearing in 1613 and also the testimony of Haselmeyer, if his possession of a manuscript version were not otherwise certain. In THE ROSICRUCIANS, by H. C. and K. M. B., it is said that the FAMA FRATERNITATIS was originally a Latin pamphlet of 33 pages, implying that it appeared by itself. As usual the authority for the statement does not emerge, and it is contrary to all bibliographical records. Du Fresnoy mentions COMMUNIS ET GENERALIS REFORMATIO TOTIUS MUNDI, ET FAMA FRATERNITATIS ORDINIS DE ROSEA-CRUCE, in 8vo. Casseliis, 1614. There is obviously no reason why the manifesto should not have appeared originally in Latin like the CONFESSIO. Kloss catalogues (1) ALLGEMEINE UND GENERAL REFORMATION DER GANZEN WEITEN WELT. *Beneben der* FAMA FRATERNITATIS *des Löblichen Ordens des Rosenkreuzes an alle Gelehrte und Häupter Europä geschrieben. Auch einer Kurtzen* RESPONSION *von dem Herrn* HASELMEYER *gestellt*, etc. Cassel, 1614. (2) FAMA FRATERNITATIS R∴ C∴ . . . *Benebst derselben Lateinischen* CONFESSION, *welche vorhin in Druck noch nie ausgegangen, nuhnmehr aber auff vielfältiges anfragen, zusampt deren beygefügten Teutschen version.* Cassel, 1615. (3) FAMA FRATERNITATIS R∴ C∴ *Beneben*

side of early Rosicrucian literature is full of pitfalls, and we shall see later on that the question is complicated, not alone by the errors of bibliographers and the conflicting statements of writers who did not know their subject[1] but by the fact that one important subsidiary text is introduced by a preface which is dated some years prior to the actual time of publication. As regards the FAMA it is known to have been issued originally accompanied by a reply thereto on the part of Adam Haselmeyer, who has been described as notary public of the Archduke Maximilian and subsequently as Imperial Judge in ordinary. He bears witness that he saw and read the FAMA FRATERNITATIS in the year 1610, when residing at la Croix, a small village near Hal, in the

der CONFESSION *oder Bekanntnuss derselben Fraternitat, an alle Gelehrte und Häupter in Europä geschrieben*, etc. Frankfurt am Mayn, 1615. Among other editions the British Museum has FAMA FRATERNITATIS *oft Ontdeckinge van het Broederschap des loflijcken Ordens des Roosen-Cruyces.* Followed by the CONFESSIE *van der Broederschap des Roosen-Cruyces ; Antwoordt van* ADAM HASELMEYER ; *Send-brief Aen de Christelijcke Broderen van den Roosen-Cruyces ; Discours van de alghemeyne Reformatie des ganschen wereldts. Sine loco*, 1615. A Dutch edition. There has been cited also FAMA FRATERNITATIS ET CONFESSIO FRATRUM ROSEÆ CRUCIS. Ratisbon, 1614. It would not follow that the text itself was in Latin, though the title was in that language, but I think that this edition is mythical. In 1615 the FAMA FRATERNITATIS appeared at Marburg, *ohne die Reformation*, as the title says. It should be added that my information is at second hand and that no copy seems extant. The COMMUNIS ET GENERALIS REFORMATIO would seem also to have been issued by itself in 1614, but at what place I am unaware. A complete bibliography is beyond the pretensions of the present note. A Frankfort edition of the FAMA appeared in 1617, together with the CONFESSIO, the SENDBRIEFF of Julianus de Campis and a FAITHFUL HISTORY of an unknown Brother of the Order of the R.·.C.·. It has been suggested that the FAMA of this edition has been largely rewritten, but according to its title-page the text and that of the CONFESSIO are only purged from errors and restored to their genuine sense. There is no question that this connotes important alterations. Finally, the FAMA and CONFESSIO appeared at Dantzic in 1618.

[1] There is, for example, the statement of Claude Jannet that the first work relating to the Rosicrucians appeared at Venice in 1612 or 1613, no title being given. On the authority of an obscure writer named Whytehed, concerning whom no details are given, he affirms that the FAMA FRATERNITATIS belongs to the year 1615—which is manifestly contrary to fact—and that its author was a citizen of Hamburg, named Jung—presumably Joachim

Tyrol. He seems to have been drawn towards the Order because he regarded it as a school of Paracelsus. There is no question that he was a personality of the period, and according to Semler he was a Knight of the Holy Cross.[1] The only difficulty respecting his testimony at the date in question is that it is practically borne by one witness only, unless we are willing to accept that of Julius Sperber —writing in 1615—who says that what is stated in the FAMA was known otherwise for over nineteen years before it was first printed.[2] Among the letters cited

Junge, of whom we have heard previously. Solomon Semler himself, though a patient and laborious investigator, contrived to create unawares numerous pitfalls of erudition in addition to those which opened naturally in the middle night of his subject. He says that between the years 1612 and 1615 the first writings bearing the name of *Fraternitas Crucis Rosaceæ* were printed several times in different languages and sent to all Europe. But the last point is the testimony of FAMA FRATERNITATIS on its own part, and it is not borne out by fact. I suppose that I need not mention seriously THE THEOSOPHIST—Vol. I, No. 5, February, 1880—which has an article on the Brethren of the Rosy Cross, by Alexander Wilder, M.D., described as Vice-President of the Theosophical Society—presumably in America. After a characteristic rhodomontade on blasphemy, iniquity and persecution, he proposes that a DISCOVERY OF THE HONOURABLE ORDER OF THE ROSY CROSS appeared in 1604, the result being war and massacre for thirty years. He belongs to that obscure Borderland where mendacity and mania meet.

[1] He is said by Sédir—on I know not what authority—to have suspected the hand of Jesuitry in the Order. The Responsion of Haselmeyer was printed by itself in 1612 and is attached to most editions of FAMA FRATERNITATIS. As regards Sédir, see HISTOIRE DES ROSE-CROIX, p. 51.

[2] The statement occurs in that ante-dated preface to which I have referred already, and it introduces a famous tract called ECHO FRATERNITATIS, to which I shall recur later. Publication took place anonymously and the authorship is not certain. Under the name of Julius Sperberus, Lenglet du Fresnoy catalogues otherwise two works having an identical title-in-chief with variant sub-titles, but they are really successive editions of the same tract, dated respectively 1672 and 1674. In 1728–32 it was translated from Latin into German by Friedrich Roth-Saholtz in DEUTSCHES THEATRUM CHEMICUM, Vol. II, and appeared as ISAGOGE *das ist Einleitung zur wahren Erkänntniss des drey-einigen Gottes und der Natur; worinn auch viele vortreffliche Dinge von der Materia des philosophischen Steins und dessen gar wunderbaren Gebrauch enthalten sind. Aus dem lateinischen ins deutsche übersetzet*, p. 119 *et seq.* The Latin titles were ISAGOGE, *in veram Triunius Dei*

by Bühle there is one also by I ∴ B ∴ P ∴, which states that the writer had seen the manifesto in question on June 28, 1613, his own communication being dated January 2, 1614.[1]

I have said that the RESPONSIO of Haselmeyer appears as a supplement to the first traceable printed edition of FAMA FRATERNITATIS, and the latter is preceded by a tract longer than itself, entitled AN UNIVERSAL REFORMATION OF THE WHOLE WIDE WORLD, which was accepted at the beginning as an official document of the Brotherhood. As a fact, it offers us spontaneously an useful criterion of distinction between the essential and accidental connection of works that pass as Rosicrucian. The mode of publication adopted was calculated to deceive at the period, and people were deceived accordingly, especially aspirants to the Order, and that considerable class which was prepared to find alchemy anywhere. In the case under notice they saw it to some purpose by writing Hermetic commentaries thereon.

However, in the year 1618, when Michael Maier published a treatise concerning the Laws of the Brotherhood, he explains that the COMMUNIS ET GENERALIS REFORMATIO was not a Rosicrucian manifesto but a work translated from the Italian which the booksellers bound up with the FAMA, as would seem to have been their frequent practice where small pamphlets were concerned. We shall see that something of the same kind happened in respect of the CONFESSIO, though it may not have been a bookseller's device. In this

et naturæ cognitionem, 1672, and ISAGOGE, *de materia Lapidis Philosophici, ejusque usu*, 1674.

[1] The title given by Bühle is SENDSCHREIBEN AN DIE CHRISTLICHE BRÜDER VON ROSENCREUTZ. I do not know whether this writer is identical with J. B. P., described as a physician writing from the Kingdom of Bohemia on June 12, 1614, and expressing the desire to become a member of the Order. But see Chapter IX of the present work for a fuller account of the testimony borne by the ECHO.

manner it transpired presently that the author of the Reformation tract was Trajano Boccalini, an Italian satirist of inconvenient opinions who was broken on the wheel in 1613.[1] It is conspicuously misplaced as preceding and apparently introducing the concise history of a Secret Society which had proposed *ex hypothesi* to effect a reform in science and art, if not also in religion, for it is a general and entertaining travesty of reformation schemes. It claims to have been issued by the Seven Wise Men of Greece, acting under orders of the god Apollo, to whom the Emperor Justinian had presented a plea for the promulgation of a new law against suicide, which his deposition affirmed to be on the increase. Apollo took pains to inform himself respecting the position of affairs in the world, and made such lamentable discoveries that he charged the Seven Wise Men, assisted by other *literati*, to produce a scheme. They gathered together in conclave and the tract furnishes a report of their debate at large, which took place in the Delphic Palace and may be summarised under the following heads.

(1) Hidden vices and perfidy in the cloak of simplicity being palmary causes of corruption, it was proposed by Thales that a window should be placed in the breasts of all human beings, exposing the heart and its workings and making concealment impossible. This scheme was abandoned ultimately because it would deform the microcosm. (2) Solon considered that disparity of means and the custom of *meum* and *tuum* accounted for hatred, envy and

[1] Generale Riforma *dell' Universo dai sette Savii della Grecia e da altri Litterati, publicata di ordine di Apollo*, being Advertisement No. 77 of Boccalini's Ragguagli di Parnasso, Centuria Prima, 1612. There were two Centuries in all, and they were thrice translated into English—by the Earl of Monmouth in 1656 and anonymously in 1704 and 1706. The ignorance of Kieswetter is exhibited by his statement that J. V. Andreæ wrote the Universal Reformation, the mendacious bibliographer of fraudulent or imaginary documents being unaware that whoever put this satire into German only translated from the Italian.

all uncharitableness, while an equal division of goods would remove prevailing disorders; but this opinion was set aside because fools would receive too much and the wise too little. (3) Chilo suggested the perpetual banishment of gold and silver; but it was pointed out that they would be replaced by substitutes. (4) Cleobulus appealed for the extradition of iron because it was maliciously applied to the forging of swords, instead of ploughshares; but it was agreed that force would be necessary to effect such a reformation, involving weapons of destruction and defensive armour, so that iron would be used to procure its own banishment and maintain its exile, or in other words, it would not be banished at all. (5) Pittacus appealed for the reservation of supreme dignities to those who sought them by the path of desert and under the guidance of virtue; but (6) Periander pointed out that these dignities were not conferred by princes on able and deserving men. (7) Bias regarded the evils and disorders of the times as materially referable to the fact that people were not content to live in their own countries, but were ever—as individuals and nations—exceeding their allotted bounds. The remedy of present disorders was to return every man forthwith to his native land and destroy thereafter all modes of communication between country and country. This having been rejected because the enmity of nation towards nation was due to the ambition of princes and not to national causes, while travel was necessary for those who would attain wisdom, (8) Cleobulus intervened a second time, demanding that the proposed reformation should be limited to the compensation of the good and the punishment of evil persons, since it was obvious that previous schemes were sophistic and chimerical fancies. (9) This enraged Thales, who demanded a canon of distinction as to those who were perfectly good and utterly evil, with another for the separation of counterfeits. (10) Periander affirmed that ambition and usurpation on the part of princes have filled the world with hatred and transformed human beings into beasts of prey. Their ambitious lust must be bridled and the extent of their principalities limited, since no overgrown kingdom could be ruled with care and justice. (11) Solon opposed this because it was too late in the day to root up so old an evil, while they were called to consider the disorders of private men and not those of princes. The faults of rulers should be corrected by the godly lives of their subjects. (12) The commendation which this speech elicited meant anything but practical assent, and thereafter Cato rose up, with much praise in his mouth for all the previous speakers, but so far the field of debate was rather for those who are acute in the diagnosis of disease than for those who prepare a medicine. He affirmed that the maladies which molested the age were like the stars of heaven in number and adjudged the case desperate. There was no cure possible except by another deluge, in expectation of which there should be built a new ark for the salvation of boys not above twelve years old, women being utterly destroyed, leaving only their unhappy memory and kind heaven being adjured to grant men the power of procreation, like bees and beetles, without the female sex. (13) The discourse of Cato was hated by the whole assembly, which prayed earnestly to be saved, alike from cataracts of heaven and the loss of womankind. Seneca came forward to deprecate extremes and violence but regarded all the schemes of reformation as paths travelled in darkness, for it was obvious that the assembled *literati* might be qualified by acquaintance to deal with the evils and vices which were common in their own class, but they were neither safe guides nor doctors for those of other walks in life. Persons of probity and worth should be told off therefrom to correct and purify the other trades and professions, in which manner there might be produced a reform worthy of the present deputation and of existing needs. (14) This proposal fared worse than Cato's because of its reflection on themselves and the dishonour which it did to Apollo, who had deemed them sufficient for the business. Seeing that he was only a novice, there was little hope to be placed in Mazzoni, but he spoke out unabashed and brought the subject in hand to a focus-point. The business was to cure the present Age of its many and foul infirmities ; they must therefore examine the Age *in corpore vile*. (15) The proposition was acclaimed by all ; the Age was commanded into the presence of the Reformers and was brought in a chair to the Delphic Palace by the Four Seasons. He was stripped of the gay vestures which concealed his real condition and was found to be encrusted beneath with a thick scurf of appearances, which had moreover eaten into the bones, so that in all the huge colossus there was not an inch of healthy flesh. Struck with horror and despair, they huddled on his garments and dismissed him. (16) Convinced that the disease of the time was indeed past cure, they shut themselves up and resolved to provide for their own reputations, to which end they prepared a manifesto, testifying to the solicitude of Apollo in respect of his faithful *literati*, and their own pains in compiling this General Reformation. Descending thence to particulars, they fixed the prices of sprats, cabbages and pumpkins, adding—at the request of Thales—a caution respecting false measures in the sale of peas and cherries. (17) The gates of the Palace were thrown open, the General Reformation was read to the people assembled in the market-place and was so ardently applauded that all Parnassus rang with shouts of joy. From this the author concludes that the rabble are satisfied with trifles, while men of judgment know that *vitia erunt donec homines* and that the height of wisdom lies in the discretion of those who are content to leave the world as they find it.

A very curious commentary in advance, lampoon and judgment by satire, on the pretensions of the FAMA FRATERNITATIS is this derisive pronouncement on the general advisability of letting ill alone, since it may be made worse by the meddling. It has been worth while to summarise it, that we may appreciate its complete distinction from the text which follows and estimate the intelligence of a bookseller who married such irreconcilables together.[1] For in the FAMA FRATERNITATIS the "Most Laudable Order of the Rosy Cross" (1) makes boast of the happy time—namely, that present age—in which all things hidden heretofore are being manifested and made known; (2) certifies that men are raised up, endued with great wisdom for the renewal of all arts, their exaltation and perfection; (3) looks to the realisation by man of his own worth and nobility, and of the measure of his knowledge in Nature; (4) cites "the most godly and highly illuminated Father, our Brother C∴R∴C∴," the "chief and original of our Fraternity," as one who laboured long in view of a General Reformation; (5) affirms that a Reformation is to come, that Europe is with child, that it will bring forth a strong child, and that a door shall open—as "already is expected by many with great desire"; (6) distinguishes the matter of reform into things human and divine; and finally (7) regards it as fitting that before the Sun uprises an Aurora should break forth, or some clear light in the sky—meaning the manifestation of the Brotherhood, as of those who have

[1] A few hostile writers of the past have regarded the Rosicrucian manifestoes as *jeux d'esprit*, mere hoaxes and camouflage. Had the notion come into their minds, they might have argued that the COMMUNIS ET GENERALIS REFORMATIO was joined to FAMA FRATERNITATIS not by a publisher's blunder but as a derisive challenge to the stupidity of the German mind. It did not so occur, and it is time—for the rest—to abandon the hoax hypothesis, which—in so far as it has any basis—rests only on alleged hedgings and insincerity of J. V. Andreæ, as we shall ascertain in the proper place.

made themselves ready against the coming of the New Age and hold the keys thereof.

The story of the FAMA FRATERNITATIS is that of the mythical founder of the Rosy Cross and of the circumstances under which the Order came—by its hypothesis—into being.[1] A mythical personality implies a mythical foundation, in the sense that it is falsified historically. The Legend of the Rosy Cross is in rigorous analogy with the Masonic Legend of Hiram Abiff, and the respective institutions are accounted for in both cases by invention instead of by history. The position of the FAMA, as regards the world and its learning, at the period [2] to which it is referable, locates it at once as belonging—somewhat late in the day—to the old encampment of revolt against Aristotle and Galen. It is at issue not only with the schools which held from these masters but with men of learning in general, because of their pride and covetousness. They are as a house divided against itself, but in union they might develop a perfect method of all the Arts. In respect of religion it allows that " the Church has been cleansed " [3]

[1] THE ROSICRUCIANS, by H. C. and K. M. B., describes the founder as sent forth with the warrants of a messenger by what is called the Grand, otherwise the Great White Lodge, a statement fully in accordance with the common habit of theosophists in presenting what they would regard as evidence.

[2] It was the eve of the Thirty Years' War—i.e. 1618–48.

[3] In the year 1900 Dr. W. Wynn Westcott published a pamphlet entitled A SHORT HISTORY OF THE SOC. ROSIC. (*sic*, i.e. SOCIETAS ROSICRUCIANA) IN ANGLIA, which contains several notable errors. It is affirmed, for example, that " if there is one thing clear it is that in the FAMA there is no reference to the Reformed Church, while in the CONFESSIO the whole tone is Lutheran." Hence it is inferred that the author of the one tract was not responsible for the other, and that presumably between the two there was precisely that lapse of time which must separate a pre-Reformation document from one that contrasted Lutheran views " with those of Roman Catholicism." It is said that this point has been missed by all writers. The answer is that Dr. Westcott—although a Supreme Magus of the so-called Rosicrucian Society—had failed to read the FAMA. What are the affirmations on the subject made therein? In addition to the clear statement quoted in my

and affirms that the Order confesses Jesus Christ, according to the faith maintained at that time in Germany and certain other countries. It makes use of two Sacraments, as instituted "with all forms and ceremonies of the first and renewed Church." In political matters it acknowledges "the Roman Empire and *Quarta Monarchia* for our Christian head," though it knows that there are alterations to come.

On the subject of occult science and philosophy it is to be inferred from the text at large that the Fraternity was versed—by its claim—in Higher Magia, pure Kabalism and a hidden art of healing.[1] Moreover, it had the secret of transmuting metals, and this is asserted expressly, though the text states that true philosophers—among whom they are presumably to be included—esteem little the making of gold, "for besides that they have a thousand better things."

text above, they may be taken out as follows: (1) That "in these latter days"—or when the document was written—God was pouring out His mercy and goodness so richly that the faithful were attaining "more and more to the perfect knowledge of His Son Jesus Christ and of Nature," whence the putative Dark Ages were over. (2) That Christian Rosy Cross returned from the East with a process for amending the Church. (3) That the world in those days was already "big with commotions" and was bringing forth worthy men—e.g. Paracelsus—"who broke with all force through darkness and barbarism." (4) That "if our Brethren and Fathers had lived in this our present clear light, they would more roughly have handled the Pope, Mahomet, scribes, artists and sophisters, and would have shewn themselves more helpful, not simply with sighs and wishing of their end and consummation." (5) That in respect of the religion professed by the Brethren, it was that which I have cited in my text—namely, Lutheran or Protestant, as proved by the "use" of two sacraments only. These are gleanings made from a small pamphlet, not from a considerable treatise, in which it might seem excusable for an undiscerning criticism to miss important points. The *congregatio omnium stultorum*—otherwise the "*Soc. Ros.*"—whom Dr. Westcott addressed in his pamphlet, were unqualified to correct their Magus, and this monument remains therefore, an unchallenged memorial in their archives. It should be added that the FAMA stultifies its own chronology by making C∴R∴C∴ a contemporary of Paracelsus.

[1] Kieswetter speaks of "magico-magnetic healing" as one of the chief studies of original Rosicrucians, as if the FAMA FRATERNITATIS were a post-Mesmer document. The expression was unknown at the period.

They do not rejoice therein, but rather—in the words of Christ—that they behold the Heavens open, the angels of God ascending and descending, and their own names written in the Book of Life. It is testified also that " under the name of *Chemia* many books and pictures "—meaning the symbolical designs which figure in the textbooks of Hermetic literature—" are set forth *in contumeliam gloriæ Dei*." It is prayed that all learned men will take warning against them, " for the enemy never resteth, but soweth his weeds till a stronger one doth root them out." Elsewhere it is said plainly that " we promise more gold than both the Indies bring to the King of Spain." The Order had therefore the Medicine of metals—as it is called in alchemy—but as regards that of men, even the early Brethren, who lived in the light of their founder, could not " pass their time appointed of God," though they were free from all diseases. Finally, they could behold, " the image and pattern of all the world," as discovered to them by one of their secret books ; but they had no glass which shewed to them their future misfortunes or their hour of death, the latter in particular being known only to God, " Who would have us keep in continual readiness." Astrology was not included therefore among their keys of science.[1]

Though qualified in this manner, the claims advanced on behalf of the Order were considerable enough within the measures of occult adeptship, at the time when the FAMA was published. The root of all was in certain written memorials, which were a heritage from the past. We hear of (1) THE BOOK M ∴, which does not seem to have been

[1] The position of the FAMA on the subjects of alchemy and astrology is of a certain importance, in view of later Rosicrucian developments. It puts open a door for the spiritual understanding of the Hermetic work on metals which was adopted by Fludd prior to 1630, and it does not exclude what may be termed a national astrology—or the witness of the heavens to coming events and epochs in human history at large.

identical with (2) ROTA MUNDI; (3) THE BOOK T∴[1]; (4) PROTEUS; (5) Certain AXIOMATA; (6) THE BOOK H∴; and (7) A Philosophical BIBLIOTHECA, which seems to have included an account of the first Brethren. These things notwithstanding, it was not known certainly whether the second line of adeptship, according to the succession of time, were of the same wisdom as the first and whether "they were admitted to all things." The deponents of the FAMA were of the third line, as the text states explicitly, and as would follow otherwise in the logic of the case.

That "high-illuminated man of God," Christian Rosy Cross, "the chief and original of our Fraternity," (1) had learned the lore of the East and was (2) in possession of "true and infallible" *Axiomata*, "out of all faculties, sciences and arts," directing to the middle point and centre, for the restoration of all things; (3) he had also the art of transmutation; and (4) acquaintance with the Elementary Dwellers—i.e. Elementary Spirits—"who revealed unto him many of their secrets." The manner in which he attained this occult knowledge constitutes the Legend of the FAMA and the traditional history concerning the Rosy Cross. It is said of him that he was descended of noble parents, or, in the words of a Latin *Elogium* purporting to be inscribed at the end of the BOOK T, *ex nobili atque splendida Germaniæ R∴C∴ familia oriundus.* It would appear to have fallen upon evil times, and in the fifth year of his age he was placed in a cloister because of his poverty. There he learned Latin and Greek,[2] and "being yet in his growing years" accompanied one of the monks on a

[1] Kieswetter claims to be in possession of a BOOK T∴—namely, TESTAMENTUM FRATRUM ROSEÆ ET AUREÆ CRUCIS.

[2] By the hypothesis of CONFESSIO FRATERNITATIS, C∴R∴C∴ was born in the second half of the fourteenth century, or at a time when the monasteries where it was possible to learn Greek were few and far between.

journey to the Holy Land.[1] This monk died at Cyprus, and though not possessing as yet the purse of Fortunatus, C∴R∴C∴ decided to continue his pilgrimage alone. With such object in view, he shipped himself over to Damascus, from which he proposed to reach Jerusalem. He remained, however, at Damascus, owing to "the feebleness of his body." Whether he was able or not to heal himself, he obtained "much favour with the Turks" by his skill in physic. Meanwhile a report reached him concerning (1) the Wise Men of Damcar,[2] in Arabia; (2) the wonders which they wrought; and (3) "how Nature was discovered unto them." The hope of reaching the Holy City now faded from his mind, and—being unable to "bridle his desires"—he "made a bargain with the Arabians that they should carry him for a certain sum of money [3] to Damcar." Notwithstanding his "debility of body," he was "of a strong Dutch constitution" and though only sixteen years old he accomplished this adventure happily.[4] The Wise Men welcomed and received him, not indeed as a

[1] According to Westcott, C∴R∴C∴ left Europe "with a member of a Christian Fraternity," thus suggesting that he was taken East by an initiate. The original says that he "was associated to a Brother P∴A∴L∴" This was of course a monastic brother, and the pair were on a pious pilgrimage.

[2] A Rosicrucian secret Ritual of the nineteenth century affirms that Damcar is a Hebrew word, signifying Blood of the Lamb—i.e. דם = Blood and כר = Lamb. In Talmudic Hebrew כאר denotes an ass and therefore the alleged signification might be as reasonably Blood of the Ass. Damcar is an invented name for a fabulous city and there is not the least reason to suppose that it has any derivation at all, while that which is offered is in no relation to the city or to anything that is said concerning it. The name seems later to have been regarded as a misprint for Damas, meaning Damascus, which, obviously, stultifies the story.

[3] After the common manner of the old romances, a fairy-gifted hero is provided with funds invariably, no one knows whence or how. Possibly C∴R∴C∴ earned fees by his "skill in physic."

[4] According to Westcott, he visited "the Sanctuary of Mount Carmel where he studied with the wise men," a peculiarly gratuitous substitution for the mythical Damcar, presented, however, as if there were no question on the subject, or as if the authority of the FAMA were behind it.

stranger but as one whom they had long expected; and in this Hidden City of Adeptship (1) he improved his knowledge of Arabic, (2) translated the Book M∴ into "good Latin," and (3) learned "his physic and his mathematics."[1] At the end of three years he "shipped himself over *Sinus Arabicus* into Egypt, carrying the Book M∴; but it was only for a flying visit, during which he noted "the plants and creatures." Afterwards he sailed the Mediterranean Sea and arrived at Fez, as directed by the men of Damcar, and there apparently he was taught how to communicate with Elementary Spirits. Though he learned their secrets—as we have seen otherwise—it is not perhaps surprising that in the opinion of C∴R∴C∴ the Magia and Kabalah practised by the people of Fez "was defiled with their religion," which notwithstanding he was able to adapt them, so that they served his purpose. He stayed for two years in Fez and then "sailed with many costly things into Spain,"[2] hoping that the learned in Europe would meet him with open arms and "order all their studies according to those sure and sound foundations" which he had reached in his travels. But the *literati* of Spain and also of other nations would have none of his new philosophy, his "sure and infallible *Axiomata*," or his reform of the arts and sciences. They had too much business in hand.

C∴R∴C∴ is said to have loved Germany, for which reason he betook himself to his native land, where he erected a "neat and fitting habitation," and "ruminated on his voyage and philosophy," reducing them into a

[1] Not—as Dr. Westcott suggests—"the old philosophies of Alexandria, and the Hebrew Kabalah, and the remains of the ancient Egyptian Mysteries." That is the *suggestio falsi* which abounds in the records of the *Societas Rosicruciana in Anglia*, and in records of kindred dreamers.

[2] C∴R∴C∴ came back like Noah in an ark, with growths and fruits and beasts, as if his proposition was to found a herbarium and zoological gardens.

true memorial.[1] He is said also to have made many instruments—*ex omnibus hujus artis partibus*—but few of them had come into the hands of the third line of succession. In this manner some five years passed away, and as will happen to *adepti*—so placed in a solitude—he began to "remember of this unstable world" and his desired reformation. He had been read a severe lesson, and it appears to have been a little in dejection that he decided to resume his work. This time, however, he set out from a different basis and selected three monks or friars from his ancient cloister, whom he bound to himself in fidelity, diligence and secrecy. Their business was to write as he might dictate or direct for the benefit of those who were to come. "After this manner," says the FAMA, "began the Fraternity of the Rosy Cross, at first by four persons only, and by them was made the magical language and writing"—presumably meaning a cipher—"as well as a large dictionary which we yet use daily to God's praise and glory, and find great wisdom therein." With the inevitable stultification of itself which characterises this kind of document, they made also the first part of the BOOK M.—which had been compiled long ago in Arabia, had been translated by C ∴ R ∴ C ∴ and carried by him to Europe.[2] It proved notwithstanding a heavy labour, while, albeit there were four only, abiding in secret, an "unspeakable concourse of the sick hindered them." Finally, C ∴ R ∴ C ∴ had been occupied in erecting

[1] Compare De Quincey: HISTORICO-CRITICAL INQUIRY INTO THE ORIGIN OF THE ROSICRUCIANS AND THE FREEMASONS. LONDON MAGAZINE, Vol. IX, Jan. to June, 1824. After his travels C ∴ R ∴ C ∴ is said to have "established himself in a grotto of his native country." See also William Hurd, D.D.: UNIVERSAL HISTORY OF THE RELIGIOUS RITES, CEREMONIES AND CUSTOMS OF THE WHOLE WORLD, pp. 699–701, *circa* 1794. The grotto story occurs herein, probably for the first time.

[2] The BOOK M ∴ has been identified with *Minutus Mundus*, about which we shall hear shortly, but the latter is distinguished expressly from certain MSS. of the Order, as if it might be an arcane instrument rather than a written volume.

a *Domus Spiritus Sancti.*[1] It came about therefore that when the last undertaking had been brought to a successful completion " they concluded to draw yet others into the Fraternity," making eight together in all. They were " bachelors and of vowed virginity, by whom was collected a book containing whatsoever can be desired or hoped for by man." In other words, the textual part of the scheme was at length finished, after which—as agreed, it is said, at the beginning—they separated into several countries, that their *Axiomata* might be examined by the learned in secret. Five of the Brethren departed and two remained with the Founder ; but in accordance with another undertaking, they gathered each year together " and made a full resolution of that which they had done."

It came about in the course of the years that one of the travelling Brethren died in England, and this caused

[1] According to Kieswetter, the House of the Holy Spirit was probably situated somewhere in Southern Germany. The suggestion is of course rubbish, an invention without a reason. More serious writers have discovered to their own satisfaction its analogy with a mysterious building erected at Cairo, our knowledge of which is clouded by myth and fable. It is said that Hugo of Cæsarea and Geoffrey, a Knight Templar, visited Cairo and the Sultan on Templar business. They were led by that potentate himself to the Palace Kashef and taken through various courts of very rich architecture, full of strange birds and beasts, and to an innermost chamber, where the Sultan invoked the Unseen Master. The curtains of gold and pearl were then drawn back suddenly, and they beheld that being seated in unspeakable glory on a golden throne, encompassed by his chief officers. This story is fathered on William of Tyre. An actual source of information is Von Hammer, who says that a Secret Society was founded at Cairo in the tenth century by a person named Abdallah, who divided it into seven classes or degrees of knowledge. The last and highest of these taught the vanity of religion and the indifference of all actions, because they were not visited with punishment or crowned by reward, either here or hereafter. The Society continued to exist and to develop its doctrines. In process of time it divided into two branches, otherwise Karmathites and Ishmaelites, the first of which was destroyed by fire and sword, for making war on the caliphate. The second was content to pursue its designs in secret and one of the members was placed at length on the throne of Egypt. After this piece of signal statecraft, the Society erected at Cairo that great palace described in this note and called it the House of Wisdom. It was provided with

Christian Rosy Cross to call the rest of them together. Ultimately he himself passed away, though those of the third succession knew not when nor how, for a hundred years and more had already elapsed.[1] There came, however, a novice—the pupil of one who had died *in Gallia Narbonensi*. Having taken " the solemn oath of fidelity and secrecy," he said that his spiritual father " had comforted him in telling that this Fraternity should ere long not remain so hidden," but should be helpful to the whole German nation. He completed his novitiate, and being then inclined to travel had been " provided with the Purse of Fortunatus." But seeing that he was " a good architect " —he proposed, before setting out, to alter and improve " his building." The intimation is curious because the sequel shews that no tenement personal to himself is really intended but a Hidden House of the Order, whether we

teachers, servitors, instruments and books. Von Hammer tells us that men and women were admitted on equal terms, without fees of any kind, and that the caliphs took part in the debates. I resume these points at their value, but some of them look dubious, and dubious is also the statement that behind this public institution there lay the mysteries of that Secret Order which has been mentioned, developed by the process of time into nine grades and unfolding finally the great arcanum of atheism, though it was political above all in its objects. These included the permanent overthrow of the caliphate race of the Abassides in favour of the Fatemite dynasty. There came a time when the Society was itself broken up, but a resurrection took place under the denomination of a New House of Science. C. W. King—in THE GNOSTICS AND THEIR REMAINS—and George Soane—in NEW CURIOSITIES OF LITERATURE—were both disposed to think that the College of Adeptship at Damcar was borrowed or reflected from the House of Wisdom at Cairo. It is not a very important question and may be dismissed as unproven. In any case, it is not worth debating. I do not remember that the House of Wisdom is supposed to have been the depository of a secret tradition connected with the Higher Magia and Hermetic Mysteries. According to the thesis of Von Hammer, it developed into the sect of Assassins, and I question whether the writers of the FAMA would intentionally have referred their theosophy to such a source, whatever may have been known or misknown concerning this sect at that period.

[1] *Vide* Westcott : " In 1484 the Founder and Imperator C. R. died." There was no such title as Imperator at that time in the Order, according to the records.

choose to understand it as that " fitting and neat habitation " in which Christian Rosy Cross " ruminated his voyage and philosophy," or the alleged " new building " which was *Domus Spiritus Sancti*. In the course of his labours—which were not pursued alone—he came upon a Memorial Tablet, inscribed with the Roll of the Brotherhood, and it was decided that this should be transferred to a more appropriate place. But it was affixed to the wall by a great staple, which had to be withdrawn forcibly and brought with it " an indifferent big stone." A secret door was uncovered partially in this manner, to the joy of those who were present, and when it was cleared completely they found thereon, written in great letters :

POST CENTUM VIGINTI ANNOS PATEBO [1]

" with the year of the Lord under it," but this is not given in the text. The Operative Lodge of these Emblematic Masons was then called off for the night, in order to consult the *Rota*. Their work was resumed next morning, and it came about that they opened the door, discovering a Vault or Sanctuary of seven sides and seven angles, every side of the width of five feet and eight feet in height. The sun never shone therein, but it was enlightened by another luminary in the middle place of the roof. On the floor was a circular altar, covered with a plate of brass, variously engraven as follows within concentric circles : (1) A∴G∴ R∴C∴ (2) *Hoc universi compendium unius mihi sepulcrum feci.* (3) *Jesus mihi omnia.* In the middle part of the altar were four small circles enclosing figures and about them the respective inscriptions : (1) *Nequaquam Vacuum.* (2) *Legis Jugum.* (3) *Libertas Evangelii.* (4) *Dei Gloria Intacta.*

Architecturally speaking, the interior of this Vault is

[1] A Rosicrucian Ritual of *circa* 1890 connects the 120 years with the number of Princes whom Darius set over his people, which is symbolism in a bankruptcy state as regards meaning.

not described intelligently: it is, however, an emblematic story and in the secret circles has long since been rectified. In the present place it is sufficient to say that each of the seven walls was parted into squares, while each square contained figures and sentences. There was a luminous triangle in the ceiling and another—presumably dark—on the ground or floor. In this latter were described "the power and rule of the Inferior Governors." The seven walls had seven doors, behind which chests were stored containing (1) all our books; (2) the VOCABULARIUM of Paracelsus, an ITINERARIUM and VITA;[1] (3) looking-glasses of "divers virtues," bells, burning lamps; and (4) "chiefly wonderful artificial songs."[2] In a word, everything was so arranged that if in the years or the centuries "the Fraternity should come to nothing," it might be restored again by the contents of this Vault alone.

The text proceeds to state that they "had not yet seen the body of our careful and wise father," so they placed aside the altar and raised up a plate of brass. In this manner they came upon "a fair and worthy body, whole and unconsumed," clothed in ceremonial vestments and holding that BOOK T, "which next to the Bible is our greatest treasure." Of this disinterment, which in better hands might have passed into an important figurative mystery, we find no further particulars. The narrative affirms

[1] The FAMA adds, "whence this relation is taken for the most part." The VOCABULARIUM, ITINERARIUM and VITA are of course imaginary texts. According to Westcott, the two last were those of Christian Rosy Cross, which is borne out by the Frankfurt edition of 1617 but not by earlier texts.

[2] Wynn Westcott makes the brilliant suggestion that the artificial songs were *mantras*. Having regard to his views as an occultist on the occult knowledge and science of the early Rosicrucians, I fail to understand why he should shrink from proposing that they were really phonographic records, in which case the mysterious *Minutus Mundus* might well be a phonograph itself—a little world indeed, full of expatiation and tales of little meaning, though occasionally "the words seem strong," like the depositions of Metropolitan Chapters of a "Rosicrucian Society of Freemasons."

further that there was another and smaller altar—"finer than can be imagined by any understanding man," and it is said to have contained MINUTUS MUNDUS, not otherwise described at the moment.[1] Elsewhere in the Vault there were also some further books—which were made by one of the sodality "instead of household care."

As regards the BOOK T∴[2], it contained at the end thereof the following

ELOGIUM:

GRANUM PECTORI JESU INSITUM.

C∴R∴C∴ ex nobili atque splendida Germaniæ R∴C∴ familia oriundus, vir sui seculi divinis revelationibus, subtilissimis imaginationibus, indefessis laboribus ad cœlestia atque humana mysteria, arcanave admissus postquam suam (quam Arabico et Africano itineribus collegerat) plus quam regiam, atque imperatoriam Gazam suo seculo nondum convenientem, posteritati eruendam custodivisset et jam suarum Artium, ut et nominis, fides ac conjunctissimos heredes instituisset, mundum minutum omnibus motibus magno illi respondentem fabricasset hocque tandem preteritarum, præsentium et futurarum rerum compendio extracto, centenario major, non morbo (quem ipse nunquam corpore expertus erat, nunquam alios infestare sinebat) ullo pellente sed Spiritu Dei evocante, illuminatam animam (inter Fratrum amplexus et ultima

[1] There is no warrant for identifying it with the Book M∴, which C∴R∴C∴ translated into good Latin, unless we elect to do so on the ground that the latter was otherwise absent from the vault or sepulchre. According to the ELOGIUM which follows immediately, *Minutus Mundus* was either a prophetic book or a divinatory instrument.

[2] This has been explained as *Torah*, the Book of the Law, perhaps a hidden understanding of Holy Scripture. The Hebrew word is תורה. In such case it would connote an interpretation like that of Ægidius Gutmann on GENESIS. Another speculation has referred it to the ancient Tarot cards, considered as a Book of Divination, but this is idle speculation. In 1620, however, there appeared LIBER T∴, *id est, Portus Tranquillitatis ejus*, to which I shall refer later.

oscula) fidelissimo Creatori Deo reddidisset, Pater dilectissimus, Frater suavissimus, Præceptor fidelissimus, amicus integerrimus, a suis ad centum viginti annos hic absconditus est.[1]

Beneath this inscription appeared the following initials, by way of signatures.

1. Fra ∴ I ∴A ∴ Fra, Ch ∴, *electione Fraternitatis caput.*
2. Fra ∴ G ∴V ∴ M. P. G.
3. Fra ∴ F ∴R ∴C ∴, *Junior Hæres S. Spiritus.*
4. Fra ∴ F ∴ B ∴M ∴ P. A. *Pictor et Architectus.*
5. Fra ∴ G ∴G ∴ M. Pi. *Cabalista.*

Secundi Circuli

1. Fra ∴ P ∴A ∴ *Successor Fra ∴* I ∴O ∴, *Mathematicus.*
2. Fra ∴ A ∴ *Successor Fra ∴* P ∴D ∴
3. Fra ∴R ∴ *Successor Patris* C ∴R ∴C ∴, *cum Christo triumphantis.*

Beneath these names was written :

Ex Deo nascimur, in Jesu morimur, per Spiritum Sanctum reviviscimus.

[1] It will be seen that this notable inscription constitutes a single sentence, and those who have affirmed that the early Rosicrucian manifestoes are the work of J. V. Andreæ have produced as part of their evidence an argument that their style is his style and their Latin is his Latin. I leave it to them, confessing on my own part that it would cost me considerable pains to express the ELOGIUM in reasonable translated form. But for the benefit of the English reader the heads of its instruction may be scheduled briefly thus : (1) That C ∴R ∴C ∴ came from a noble and illustrious family of Germany bearing that name ; (2) that on account of his subtle conceptions and untiring labours he became acquainted with Divine and human mysteries by way of revelation ; (3) that he collected a royal and imperial treasure in his journeys to Arabia and Africa ; (4) that the same was serviceable not only to his age but to posterity ; (5) that he desired to have heirs of the name, faithful and closely joined ; (6) that he fabricated a little world corresponding to the great one in its movements ; (7) that it was a compendium of things past, present and to come ; (8) that after living for more than a century he passed away at the call of the Holy Spirit and not by reason of disease, yielding his illuminated soul to its faithful Creator ; (9) that he was a beloved Father, a most kind Brother, a faithful Preceptor and an upright Friend ; and (10) that he is hidden here from his own for one hundred and twenty years.

I have compared all available German and Dutch editions with the English translation edited by Eugenius Philalethes, but owing either to original typographical errors or other reasons it is difficult or impossible to harmonise this Roll with the initials of Brethren about whom we hear otherwise. The original Brethren, taken out of his cloister[1] by Christian Rosy Cross, were *Fratres* G∴V∴, I∴A∴ and I∴O∴. The last died in England,[2] and—according to the story—it was subsequently to this that the mausoleum was erected, perhaps by the Founder himself, as intimated by one of the Latin inscriptions. The next recruits of the Order were R∴C∴, a first cousin of the founder, and described on the Roll as F∴R∴C∴, the "younger heir of the House of the Holy Spirit"; *Frater* F∴B∴,[3] who signs, however, as F∴B∴M∴, a skilful painter, according to the text of the FAMA, and *Pictor et Architectus*, according to the Roll; *Frater* G∴G∴, signing as *Cabalista*; and *Frater* P∴D∴, who was *cancellarius*, according to the FAMA, but does not appear in the document attached to the BOOK T∴. These were the First Circle. In what sense *Frater* C∴H∴ was *caput electione Fraternitatis* in the lifetime of the founder and in a circle of eight persons remains an open question, but he is implicitly excluded from the First Circle by the text of the FAMA. He was not a chief appointed on the decease of Christian Rosy Cross, because it is stated expressly in the Roll of the

[1] It is obvious that this statement belongs to the region of romance, a layman having no title to remove monks from their monastery.

[2] His death is said to have been foretold to him by *Frater* C∴—presumably *Junior Hæres*—but unfortunately such prevision, as we have seen, has been expressly denied to the Brotherhood in a previous part of the text. I∴O∴ is said to have earned fame in England "because he cured a young Earl of Norfolk of the leprosy."

[3] We have seen that the Baconians have claimed this signature as representing Francis Bacon, ignoring (1) that according to the BOOK T∴ he signed as B. M. and (2) that the first circle were all Germans, except I∴ A∴ whose nationality is not disclosed.

Second Circle that *Frater* R∴ was successor to Father C∴R∴C∴.[1]

It will be seen that as an historical memorial, the FAMA FRATERNITATIS is a confused and contradictory account. It is indeed so gravely at fault in this respect that it looks almost too bad to be regarded as a matter of invention: one would have thought that the concealed artist must have taken a little more pains. On the other hand, it is precisely in this manner that fictitious documents making mythical claims on the past invariably betray themselves, in accordance with a very wise, if hidden law which appears to protect history: in this case the manifold undesigned exposures constitute only a signal instance of the providential rule in its operation.

There are two other points which call to be mentioned briefly. It is stated expressly that the FAMA has been "sent forth in five languages," presumably that the "learned of Europe," to whom it was addressed more especially,[2] might have no difficulty in forming a judgment

[1] In his DATA OF THE HISTORY OF THE ROSICRUCIANS, second edition, 1916, said to be "revised," Dr. Westcott has the temerity to suggest that *Frater* D∴ was "chosen to be Magus"—a title unknown in the Order Manifestoes—after the death of C∴R∴C∴, and after his own death was succeeded by *Frater* A∴, on whom followed *Frater* N∴N∴, who, however, was a novice, according to the text and originally a pupil of A∴. The same spirit of incautious speculation expressed in terms of historical certitude characterises the so-called data throughout. There is, however, a *Frater* D∴ mentioned in the memorials. P∴D∴, according to Westcott, died after I∴O∴, in the lifetime of C∴R∴C∴. But the authority for this seems in the reverie of the Supreme Magus of the *Soc. Ros.*

[2] I have said that the FAMA was addressed to the learned in particular, as appears indeed by its title, but the following sentence is added as a kind of colophon to the discovery of the tomb of Christian Rosy Cross: "And so do we expect the answer and judgment of the learned and unlearned." One of the amazing suggestions put forward by Kieswetter is that the fact of the FAMA being translated into so many languages "shews that many persons possessed a key to its symbolism." It shews obviously nothing of the kind, and that the tract in question was so translated we have seen to be very doubtful.

concerning it in their own vernaculars; but so far as can be determined by the negative results of research, and so far as all records are concerned, the affirmation can represent a matter of intention only. The editions were German, Dutch and perhaps Latin; there is no trace of a concurrent French version, and nothing appeared in England till 1652. As the statement is repeated in the CONFESSIO respecting that manifesto, one would have expected the design to have been fulfilled, at least in the second case, but I have found nothing. However, the only real research on the bibliographical side of the Rosy Cross has been done in Germany and France, and it is not beyond possibility that something may have been produced in Italy, perhaps even in Spain. This is the first point, and as regards the second it should be mentioned that, while inviting answers and judgments, the FAMA FRATERNITATIS provided no means of communication except through the public press—e.g. by the voice of memorials and letters in printed form—as it did not disclose any place of convocation and the manifesto was quite anonymous. While the only courses open were adopted freely enough, the appearance of the CONFESSIO—recognising that it was of subsequent publication—must have been expected with much anticipation by a great many eager hearts, in the hope that it would provide more definite means of access. The assurance given in the first manifesto was perhaps a preliminary test applied by the Order to those whom it would call in good time to its service; but it could scarcely go on for ever. The covenant was expressed thus: "And although at this time we make no mention of our names or our conventions, yet shall every one's opinion come into our hands assuredly, and those who give even but a name shall not fail to speak with us, either by word of mouth or—if there be some hindrance—in writing."

Such is the first and only historical account of the Order

which was issued—so to speak—officially. Many apologists came forward in the early seventeenth century to espouse its cause, and other documents appeared, speaking with authority concerning it; but the story of its foundation and the myth of its sacred sepulchre stood high and clear above all. It is more especially in the eighteenth century that we meet with other claims concerning its antiquity and consequently with other personalities—for example, the sage Ormuz—as connected with its origin.

The one point of importance which emerges in the FAMA is the tomb of Christian Rosy Cross and the fact of its discovery. This is either an imaginative device to indicate the supposed or pretended age of the Society, or it contains a deeper meaning. It is difficult, from my point of view, not to take the legend seriously, but of course as an emblematical story. As such, it is in analogy with the finding of that temporary grave in which the body of Hiram Abiff had been laid hurriedly by his murderers, according to the traditional history of the Masonic Craft Degrees. The exhumation of that body is the central point in the myth of the Master-Builder, and about it the whole symbolism revolves. There is, however, no Raising in the Rosicrucian legend, and nothing follows apparently on that which is seen and done in the Vault. In the end it is testified (1) that the narrators replaced the altar, together with the plate of brass beneath it; (2) that they came forth from the heptagonal chamber; (3) that they shut the door and placed seals thereon; (4) that they departed one from another; and (5) that they "left the natural heirs in possession of our jewels." The last statement is inscrutable, but I conceive it to be simply one of those banalities of expression which abound in Rosicrucian as in Masonic documents. The "natural heirs" were certainly not the worms of the graveyard, for the body had remained *ex hypothesi* "whole and unconsumed" during one hundred and twenty years. Nor can it be intended to suggest that the freeholders came into possession, following the ordinary course, or that the goods were estreated because *Frater* N∴N∴ had omitted to pay the rent of his "building."

In concluding this chapter it ought, I suppose, to be mentioned that a few egregious persons, remanents of occultism as it was preached in Victorian days, maintain that the emblematical and symbolical myth of Father Rosy Cross represents literal history. They believe in "everburning lamps" because so much has been written on the subject that there must be something in it;[1] they regard the contradictions and stultifications in the FAMA and other texts as "blinds," meaning devices to mislead critical persons[2]; they are satisfied that if unique works of Paracelsus were not discovered in the Vault it had treasures of equal or greater value, which notwithstanding they were probably there in fact; they are convinced that the tomb of Christian Rosy Cross exists somewhere in Germany, and there is one favoured individual who knows where it is and could lead an earnest student to the hallowed spot, though he is not prepared to specify the place otherwise.[3]

[1] "There is a very large mass of references to such an invention to be found in old Latin literature, and there must have been some foundation for them."—Westcott: HISTORY OF THE SOCIETAS ROSICRUCIANA IN ANGLIA, 1900, p. 2. It is regrettable that radium had not been discovered at the date of the memorial.

[2] Compare Westcott, however, in his Rosicrucian DATA, 1916, p. 5. "It should be noted that although the FAMA and the CONFESSIO gave to the world a knowledge of the existence of the Rosicrucian Fraternity, there is no evidence that these publications were authorised; . . . certain discrepancies . . . in these tractates bear internal evidence that they were not written by anyone who had accurate historical information." But in the previous HISTORICAL NOTICE he sees "nothing unreasonable" in supposing that some "mystic student" should have been admitted "into the Order, should have written the CONFESSIO, and "should have been told off" to publish the FAMA.

[3] The favoured individual is not Dr. Westcott, who, however, testifies as follows: "It has been stated that this Tomb still exists, but its situation is only revealed to high Continental adepts."—DATA, p. 5.

They are a mad world, my masters, but they are *Magi*, *Magistri* and *Adepti*, *sub umbra alarum tuarum*, *O Societas Rosicruciana in Anglia*, and more especially under the zany's cap of the Metropolitan College.

There is one thing more: it is to be observed that FAMA FRATERNITATIS offers a clear issue in respect of its story and the claims connoted thereby. If it is not without discrepancies they belong to the *minima*. It is evident that the opening of the Tomb led, by the implied hypothesis, to the greater discovery, being that of the Rosy Cross, making an appeal in public to the mind of gentle and simple in the German world.

It seems evident also, at least to my own mind, that the text is typical of inventions which came into existence by scores, as from *circa* 1723 to about the same date in the nineteenth century. I refer to the fabulous histories of certain Rites and Orders, Masonic and super-Masonic. They were devised to justify the existence and pretensions of their particular institutions, and however fraudulent in fact were serious by intention. I shall indeed indicate later that there was from time to time a background of mental sincerity in those who made them. In some cases, moreover, as in the Third Craft Degree, they were parables as well as myths and were then comparable, within their proper measures, to the Mystery Legends of Eleusis, the Dionysiacs and Samothrace. The FAMA story is a legend which accounts, after its particular fashion, for the hypothetical transmission of secret knowledge from East to West, and there are many others in its likeness. There is not the least reason on the surface to assume that it was not intended seriously. There were numbers at that period and before it who believed themselves to have acquired an occult *theosophia*, *philosophia* and even *scientia*, drawn by their studies from various quarters and valuable in their own eyes. It is an arguable proposition that in the case with which we are concerned a few dreamers of this kind accounted in the FAMA by a fiction for that which they believed themselves to possess and thus drew attention to the fact, that they might extend their circle. The charge against them is not so much the figurative fable concerning C∴R∴C∴, as the mendacity which led them to claim the secret of transmuting metals.

CHAPTER VI

CONFESSIO FRATERNITATIS R∴C∴

THE FAMA FRATERNITATIS makes several references to a forthcoming CONFESSION of the Order, in which things left over by the original manifesto or treated shortly therein were to be communicated with a certain fullness. It would furnish (1) further information concerning the BOOK M∴; (2) a Table of thirty-seven reasons for making known the fact of the Fraternity and for offering such high mysteries without constraint or reward; (3) an elucidation on the subject of the *Rota*, which is mentioned twice in the FAMA as something to be consulted, but it is left uncertain whether it was a method of divination or a set of rules for guidance; and finally (4) a catalogue of sophistic works on *Chemia* which came under the sentence of having been written *in contumeliam gloriæ Dei*. The last point is only a matter of inference: the list in question is promised, but whether to appear in the CONFESSIO or in a separate form is not determined. It is affirmed also that the CONFESSIO, like the FAMA, would be "sent forth in five languages."

The bibliography of the second document is similar to that of the first, a matter of considerable confusion. We have seen that according to Lenglet du Fresnoy there was a Latin edition of the FAMA in 1614, but it seems unknown to other bibliographers, and I have failed to trace it, though I am satisfied as to the antecedent probability of such a Latin text, whether it was printed or not. In a Latin edition of the FAMA ET CONFESSIO, published together at Ratisbon in 1614, I must confess that I do not believe.[1] The internal evidence of the FAMA is against the simultaneous issue of these documents.[2] There was something to follow the FAMA, and it was described as "our Confession," while—uncritical as it was—the interest taken in the COMMUNIS ET GENERALIS REFORMATIO from the beginning

[1] It does not appear in the great bibliography of Kloss, but he is said to have heard of it by report, though the actual content of the alleged Ratisbon edition is not clear by his allusion. I find nothing to confirm this anywhere in his notes. When the FAMA was circulated in MS., as affirmed frequently, it is likely to have been in Latin and may have been read in this form by Haselmeyer, who had, however, no knowledge of the CONFESSIO at that time. Nicolai speaks of the FAMA and NUPTIÆ CHYMICÆ being reprinted at Ratisbon in 1781.

[2] Hereinafter follows a summary account of the texts with which I am acquainted at first hand and by report: (1) Philippus a Gabella: SECRETIORIS PHILOSOPHIÆ CONSIDERATIO, CUM CONFESSIONE FRATERNITATIS ROSEÆ-CRUCIS EDITA. *Francofurti*, 1615. This is in quarto, and is unquestionably the first edition of the text with which we are concerned. (2) The same in octavo, 1616, also issued at Frankfurt. (3) APOCRISIS, *seu Responsio ad Famam Roseæ Crucis, cum Confessione et Litteris quorundam, Fraternitatem se dare volentium. Francofurti*, 1615, 4to. (4) FAMA FRATERNITATIS ROSEÆ CRUCIS, CUM EORUM CONFESSIONE, *Latine et Germanice a Friedens Begierigen Philomago.* At Cassel in 8vo, 1615, and in the same year at Frankfurt, in 12mo. (5) CONFESSIO ET LITERÆ QUORUNDAM FRATERNITATI R.·.C.·. SE DARE VOLENTIUM. Francofurti, 1615, 4to. Probably identical with No. 3. (6) FAMA FRATERNITATIS R.·.C.·. *Das ist Gerücht der Brüderschaft des Hochlöblichen Ordens des Rosen-Kreutzes an alle Gelehrte und Häupter Europä. Benebst derselben lateinischen* CONFESSION, *welche vorhin in Druck noch nie ausgegangen, nuhnmehr aber auff vielfältiges anfragen, zusampt deren beygefügten Teutschen Version. In Druck gegeben von einem . . . Philomago.* Cassel, 1615. This was in 12mo. The statement that the CONFESSIO had never been edited previously would be exceedingly valuable, on the assumption that it could be taken literally, meaning that there had been no earlier Latin text. It would put an end to the fable concerning a Ratisbon edition in 1614 and give this publication a priority over that which is connected with the name of Philippus a Gabella. But the text of the CONFESSIO certifies that it was written in Latin, as we have seen. The edition under notice may be identical with No. 4, which I owe to Lenglet du Fresnoy, who in this case has shortened the title and turned it into Latin, justifying my opinion that Latin titles in old Rosicrucian bibliographies do not mean of necessity that the works were also in Latin. (7) FAMA FRATERNITATIS, *oft ontdeckinge van der Broederschap des loflijcken Ordens des Rosen-Cruyces.* The Dutch edition

of the Rosicrucian debate offers a presumption that they appeared together, and this is confirmed by the preponderating evidence of all bibliographical research. However this may be, there is and can be no question that the CONFESSIO itself was produced originally in Latin, for the text says: "It is no wonder that we are not so eloquent in other tongues, and least of all in this Latin." The year 1615 saw it translated into German,

noted previously as published, *sine loco*, 1615, in 8vo. (8) FAMA FRATERNITATIS, *oder Entdeckung der Brüderschaft des löblichen Ordens des Rosenkreutzes.* Francofurti, 1615, 8vo. (9) FAMA FRATERNITATIS, *beneben der* CONFESSION *oder Bekanntniss derselben Fraternitat, an alle Gelehrte und Häupter in Europä geschrieben. Auch etlichen* RESPONSIONEN *und Antwortungen, von* HERRN HASELMEYERN . . . *Sampt einem* DISCURS VON ALLGEMEINEN REFORMATION DER GANZEN WELT. *Nebst* 4 SENDSCHREIBEN *darzugesetzt, von vielen Erraten entledigt, verbessert und gedruckt zu Cassel.* 8vo, 1616. See my bibliographical note on editions of the FAMA, c.v. of the present work. (10) A reprint of No. 9, without the UNIVERSAL REFORMATION and the 4 SENDSCHREIBEN. Frankfurt, 1617, 8vo. (11) FAMA FRATERNITATIS, *oder Entdeckung der Brüderschafft dess löblichen Ordens des Rosen Creutzes. Beneben der* CONFESSION, *oder Bekanntnuss derselben Fraternitat* . . . . *Jetzo . . . zum andern mal in druck verfetiget. Sampt dem* SENDTSCHREIBEN JULIANI DE CAMPIS *und* G. MOLTHERI . . . *Relation, von einer dess Ordens gewissen Person.* Frankfurt am Mayn, 1617, 8vo. It is possible to extend this continental list, but my purpose has been served sufficiently, and so also, as I think, the requirements of any literate reader. It remains, however, to add (12) the FAME AND CONFESSION OF THE FRATERNITY OF R.·.C.·., *commonly of the Rosy Cross. With a Preface annexed thereto, and a Short Declaration of their Physical Work.* By Eugenius Philalethes. London, 1652. The publisher's Advertisement to the Reader explains that the translation "belongs to an Unknown Hand." See my WORKS OF THOMAS VAUGHAN, 1919, p. 490. This edition is misdescribed by Lenglet du Fresnoy as LA CONFESSION DE LA CONFRAIRIE DE LA ROSE-CROIX, par Eugenius Philalethes, in 8vo. London, 1652. The size is small 12mo. (13) There is also Ashmolean MS. No. 1459: THE CONFESSION of the Laudable and Honest (*sic*) esteemed Order, or Fraternity of the Rose-Crosse, written to the learned in Europe, with a preface to the wisdome-desirous reader. It occupies fols. 300, 301–11 of the volume cited, and is believed to have been transcribed from No. 1478, a folio volume divided into six parts, described as closely written in the time of James I or Charles I. According to Nicolai—who said that it had passed through his hands—the edition of Eugenius Philalethes was reprinted in 1658, but I find no evidence otherwise. See Kloss, *s.v.* No. 2435, p. 176.

and how frequently afterwards my note on the subject shews.[1]

The CONFESSIO FRATERNITATIS was introduced by a short preface addressed to " the reader who is desirous of wisdom," and it calls his attention to the " thirty-seven reasons of our purpose and intention " which had been promised in the FAMA and are contained in the new manifesto.[2] It will be as well at the outset to clear the issues by mentioning that we learn nothing whatever concerning the BOOK M∴, nothing as regards the *Rota*, and that in place of a catalogue of sophistic books we have only a further diatribe on " the worthless works of pseudo-chemists," with particular reference to one writer only, and he is not mentioned by name. Moreover, the thirty-seven reasons are not set out in an ordered manner—or indeed after any manner at all—but are left for extraction by the reader from the text itself. There was never a document pretending to advance further considerations in the matter of an important claim which has exhibited a greater want of method, not to speak of those difficulties and objections which will be dealt with as we proceed. The alleged reasons may be collected tentatively as follows: (1) The FAMA FRATERNITATIS is not to be believed hastily nor suspected wilfully. (2) Notwithstanding this counsel of caution, it is referable to the will of Jehovah, Who observes that the decaying world is now near its

[1] I may observe here that Claudio Jannet, who wrote LES PRÉCURSEURS DE LA FRANCMAÇONNERIE in 1887 and is an authority among French anti-Masons, because he is one of them, is in singular confusion on the Rosicrucian class of supposed precursors. He does not seem to have heard of CONFESSIO FRATERNITATIS and suggests that the manifestoes began to appear at Venice. He refers the FAMA to 1615.

[2] In the first edition it is also introduced or preceded by a Prayer, placed immediately after the text of Gabella's CONSIDERATIO and signed PHILEMON PHILADELPHIÆ, followed by the initials R∴C∴. The Order is mentioned also in Gabella's dedication to Uffel. The CONSIDERATIO itself is not of our especial concern.

end,[1] and therefore lays open that which heretofore has been sought with great pains and labour. (3) It will smooth the ways of the good and augment the punishment of the ungodly. (4) As regards the nature of the Order, it cannot be suspected of heresy or of schemes against the commonwealth, since it condemns the East and the West—meaning the Pope and Mahomet—and "offers the head of the Roman Empire our prayers, secrets and great treasures of gold."[2] (5) As regards the amendment of philosophy, which is altogether weak and faulty,[3] the way of its renovation in a new and renovated world is offered in the place of its disease—meaning Germany. (6) The philosophy of the Rosy Cross is the head of all the faculties, searching both heaven and earth. (7) It manifests the *microcosmus* or man. (8) It unfolds also the wonders of the sixth age. (9) If all books shall perish, "the meditations of our Christian father . . . are so great" that "posterity will be able thereby to lay a new foundation of sciences and erect a new citadel of truth."[4] (10) It must not be expected that new-comers shall attain forthwith the possession of all "our secrets": it will be a graduated process, from small beginnings to greater ends. (11) It is God Who has decreed at this time an increase in the number of our

[1] This is the NAOMETRIA formula and the accredited expectation of the MILITIA CRUCIFERA EVANGELICA; but it is connected by the fifth clause with the notion of a renewal to come, as if the Order of the Rosy Cross had a mission to restore all things, coincidently with the Second Advent, or as if its own manifestation were a kind of spiritual return of Christ.

[2] It is possible that this mendacious generosity was a device adopted to secure for the Order a certain State toleration, so that it might proceed on its path in peace. We shall see that in Holland at a later period there was a proposal on the part of the Magistrates and of a Theological Faculty to suppress what was called "the new sect."

[3] Compare the UNIVERSAL REFORMATION: (1) "The maladies which molest our age equal the stars of heaven"; and (2) "our business, gentlemen, is to cure the present age of the foul infirmities under which it labours."

[4] Compare the analogous statement in FAMA FRATERNITATIS, as noted in my previous chapter.

Fraternity: the task has been undertaken with joy and will be put in practice faithfully; but the good things can neither be inherited nor conferred promiscuously. (12) "The worth of those who shall be accepted into our Fraternity will not be measured by their curiosity but by the rule and pattern of our revelations." (13) The unworthy may clamour, but such is the Ordinance of God that we shall "hear none of them," and—encompassed by His clouds—no violence can be done "to us, who are His servants." (14) As only men of understanding rule in Damcar, so shall a government be instituted also in Europe, "according to the description set down by our Christian father."[1] (15) Whosoever can see and read "those great characters which the Lord God hath inscribed upon the world's mechanism . . . is ours already"; and (16) assured that such an one will not neglect our invitation, "we promise that no man's uprightness and hopes shall betray him who shall make himself known to us, under the seal of secrecy." (17) But those who look for other things than wisdom shall be partakers of that terrible commination announced in the FAMA, and their designs shall fall back upon themselves.[2] (18) God has decreed an influx of truth, light and splendour before the end of the

[1] It was therefore a bid for empire, brought about *ex hypothesi* by a conquest of science and wisdom. Compare the fourth clause, which affirms that there are no schemes against the commonwealth. *Ex hypothesi* also it would redound to the good of the commonwealth, and the head of the Roman Empire was offered a share in the supposed secrets. In this respect at least the CONFESSIO strikes a new note on the subject-matter of reform.

[2] The "commination" of the FAMA is perhaps more banal than terrible: it threatens false-hearted and covetous aspirants with "utter destruction;" but one would have thought it sufficient punishment for them to be left in the outer darkness, which of course also befel them, by the claim of the text. The CONFESSIO adds in the same connection that the treasures of the Order shall remain unrifled by such till the Lion shall arise and demand them, to aid in the foundation of His Kingdom—another Second Advent reference.

world,[1] so that darkness and bondage shall cease in the arts and governments of men. (19) A single and self-same rule shall be instituted.[2] (20) The Order by no means arrogates to itself the glory of this work, as if it " were imposed only on us " ; but " we testify, with our Saviour Christ, that sooner shall the stones rise up and offer their service than there shall be any want of executors of God's counsel." (21) He has sent His messengers already, namely, new stars in Serpentarius and Cygnus, the same being potent signs of a great council, for the Book of Nature stands free to all eyes, though few there are to read it. (22) The eyes and the ears have been opened for some in the ages going back, but there is a time coming when the tongue shall be loosened ; the world will then have slept away the effects of her stupefying chalice and will go forth joyously to meet the sun in the morning. (23) There are secret characters and letters in the Sacred Scriptures, and they are inscribed also on all the works of creation, the heavens, the earth and beasts. (24) " From these letters we have derived our magical writing," making a new language, in which the nature of things is expressed : it is the tongue of Adam and Enoch, contaminated subsequently by the confusion which came upon man at Babel, and very different from languages which have prevailed

[1] The NAOMETRIA formula, which recurs in this text, is found nowhere in the FAMA. It constitutes another distinction between the two works.

[2] Compare the fourteenth clause.

[3] The " new star in Serpentarius " was that of 1604 and was observed and described by Kepler. Serpentarius is known by its Greek equivalent Ophiuchus in modern maps of the heavens. The star in Cygnus—A.D. 1602—was brighter than that in Serpentarius and is said to have been visible in daylight. A *Stella nova Cygni* was seen in the same celestial region on November 24th, 1876. There was also the famous star which was described by Tycho-Brahe and appeared in 1572–4, as it had done previously in A.D. 945 and 1264. It was called the Star of Bethlehem. See Humboldt's COSMOS for the account by Tycho-Brahe. This was in Cassiopeia. A full account of it by William Hutton will be found in Zadkiel's ALMANAC for 1879.

since, wherein we lay no claim to eloquence.[1] (25) An excellent way to the Order is by the study of the Holy Scriptures, because these are " the whole sum of our laws." [2] (26) The Bible indeed is the rule of life, the end of all studies and the compendium of the universal world : its true interpretation should be applied to all ages. (27) No more excellent and admirable book has been given to man from the beginning of things. (28) " Blessed is he who possesses it ; more blessed is he who reads it ; most blessed of all is he who understands it truly," while whosoever understands and obeys it is one who is most like unto God. (29) Whatever was said in the FAMA against " the transmutation of metals and the supreme medicine of the world " was actuated by hatred of impostors and does not signify disdain for these great gifts of God. (30) There are, however, many other *magnalia*, while the observation of Nature and the knowledge of philosophy are preferable to the tincture of metals. (31) The worthless books of pseudo-chemists must be rejected ; they profit by the curiosity of the credulous, deceive men by monstrous symbols and enigmas, and apply the Most Holy Trinity to vain things. (32) The Order offers participation in its own treasures, putting forward no lying tinctures and seeking no goods of others. (33) It extends to those whom it invites within its penetralia the means of co-operating in the work of

[1] Compare Menken : DE LA CHARLATANERIE DES SAVANTS, 1721. He says that among the " admirable gifts " ascribed to the Brethren of the Rosy Cross the most remarkable was that of speaking perfectly the languages of the different countries through which they were dispersed. They shewed that kind of facility which would suggest that they were native-born. A writer named J. Berger is quoted as remarking that this aptitude is characteristic of Jews, which does not appear especially or generally accurate' at least as regards the present day.

[2] According to Mrs. Constance M. Pott " one great work of the Society was the publication and dissemination of Bibles," and this is said to be shewn by the testimony of Rosicrucian books, though not by the first manifestoes. As usual, there is no reference.

God, of being serviceable therefore to the age, having regard to the imperfection and inconsistencies of all the arts. (34) In this manner those riches of Nature which lie scattered everywhere on the earth will be gathered together, *tanquam in centro solis et lunæ.* (35) The things which obscure human knowledge and hinder human action will then be driven out of the world. (36) But those whom God wishes either to test or chastise will never be helped by opportunities extended from within the circle of the Order, even though there may be a Medicine which cures all diseases; and finally, says the official document (37), "we shall never be manifested to any man" except with God's concurrence; on the contrary, "he shall sooner lose his life in seeking us than attain his bliss by finding."

Here, then—duly drawn forth—are thirty-seven considerations or reasons of purpose, intention and what not imbedded in the CONFESSIO FRATERNITATIS, and they fairly exhaust the sense of that second discourse which claims to be addressed by the Order to the learned of Europe. It must be admitted that they could have been otherwise divided—at least here and there—as some few of them might have been drawn together and a few others split up.[1] There are

[1] In an ANALYSIS CONFESSIONIS FRATERNITATIS DE ROSEA CRUCE, Andreas Libavius made an extraction after his own manner of the thirty-seven reasons, and I will present them in summary form for purposes of comparison. They are termed *Argumenta* by Libavius, and it is to be understood that his examination is hostile to the claims of the Order, both general and particular: (1) The promised restoration of this world to the state of Paradise before the Fall of man. (2) The defects in Art, Science and Religion. (3) The free offering by Divine decree of those things which have been attained previously by great toil alone. (4) The possession by the Order of a healing balm for human trouble. (5) The Order can open a true medial way, by which the ills of our country may be healed and things can be made anew. (6) It knows the wonders of the sixth age. (7) It proffers great secrets and sets open a house of treasures. (8) And yet its arena can be in no wise made common or familiar. (9) It shews forth new truth and the building of an ark of truth. (10) The truth is to be found only in the Rosy Cross. (11) It is an asylum for those who would escape hunger, disease and old age. (12) It is the place also of those who would so live as if they had been from the

certain extraneous matters which are not in the nature of " reasons " and have not appeared therefore in the enumeration given above. (1) The CONFESSIO is a scurrilous and blatant document on the subject of Latin Christianity. One would think that its author had reflected on a remark of the FAMA concerning the original " Brethren and Fathers," who if they had lived in the " clear light " of the post-Lutheran period would have handled the Pope more roughly. And thus reflecting it was concluded, one might think also, that the time was ripe for *illuminati* of the third circle to give samples of their mettle, seeing that —according to the Advertisement—it was now quite safe to call the Pope Antichrist, and to say what they would do with him, if only he came into their hands. The valour of Alsatia and Whitefriars broke out accordingly in the

beginning and should prevail even to the end. (13) While remaining in that place in which it has pleased God to set them, the Brethren know things which occur at a distance, even by the Ganges and in Peru. (14) The Order promises the coming destruction of the Pope. (15) It seeks no man's money. (16) It would make others partakers of its own great goods. (17) It does not create deceptions by false tinctures and does not speak in enigmas. (18) It leads to a full and simple explanation of secrets and invites to royal palaces. (19) It has come forward by the impulsion of the Holy Spirit. (20) It communicates the good things which Nature scatters over the world at large. (21) It removes that which darkens and hinders human minds. (22) It confesses Christ sincerely. (23) The Father of the Rosy Cross lived for 106 years and saw many changes in the world. (24) Darkness and falsehood involve all arts and works of man. (25) Those who are desirous of light and truth in experience should seek within the Order. (26) It is in possession of a right and certain rule. (27) The happiness of the present age inheres therein, and this should not be neglected. (28) Many excellent men have promoted rapid reformation by their writings, and it behoves others not to be behindhand in respect of the Order. (29) The counsel of God is to raise up the humble and abase the proud. (30) He sends His angels to those who are secret and silent. (31) He abandons babblers to their own devices. (32) Be ye carriers of that which is noble unto all mankind. (33) Chrysopœa is the gift of God and is not to be spurned or rejected. (34) But it does not always give the knowledge of Nature. (35) Nature also proffers not only medicine but innumerable other secrets and wonders. (36) The first need is to follow after the knowledge and understanding of philosophy. (37) Great treasures are ours, and these we offer : come therefore to us.

terminology of Colonel Blood. The Pope was found guilty of blasphemies against Jesus Christ; it was proclaimed, in hot-gospel derision of merely historical fact, that—"after many chafings in secret of pious persons"—he had been "cast down from his seat by a great onset" and nobly "trodden under foot." But as he was enthroned actually at St. Peter's, or holding royal court in the Vatican, hearing nothing of these gutter-born ravings, the aspirations of the *adepti* went further, and they expressed three hopes for the future: (*a*) that his utter destruction was in reserve; (*b*) that he would be "torn in pieces with nails"; and (*c*) that a "final groan" would end his "asinine braying."[1] It may have been the manner born of the Holy Mysteries, as understood by the German mind in the early seventeenth century, and it may have breathed all the loving spirit of our highly "illuminated," "loving" and "Christian Father"; but to us at the present day it seems redolent of stables which have not been built in Bethlehem and in which Christ was never born. (2) The CONFESSIO parades that "unhoped for graciousness" which has led the Fraternity to come forward; seeks to reassure those who have been overwrought by "the surprise of our challenge"; assures all and sundry—in extension of Consideration X—that such as are received will be taken "step by step"[2]

[1] It is said also that the "Roman impostor," notwithstanding the full light which has been cast by Germany upon his doings, "will not abstain from lying," but is fulfilling "the measure of his sin," that he may be "found worthy of the axe." On a day to come, "the mouth of this viper shall be stopped." It it registered finally that Rosicrucians "execrate the Pope"—a redundant statement after all that has been mentioned previously. The text reads like a postscript to NAOMETRIA, added after 1612, when the crucifixion of the Sovereign Pontiff had failed to take place.

[2] It is said further on that the Fraternity is "divided into degrees," which has led the authors of THE ROSICRUCIANS to suppose that the Order worked in Ritual from the beginning; but the reference is to modes of government, questions of power and influence. It is pointed out, for example, that "those which dwell in Damcar have a different political order from that of other Arabians and that they make "particular laws" by

through the great mysteries which await them and will not be made free at once of the whole Pandora's box; comforts those who may "complain of our discretion, that we offer our treasures so freely"; repeats over and over that "the unworthy may clamour a thousand times" in vain; reiterates the assurance that God has decreed a numerical expansion of the Brotherhood; and yet appears to intimate that there are certain hindrances, some things which call to be removed, "some eagle's feathers in our way," as though people must be content to wait if they continue to hear nothing in respect of their chief desire. (3) As regards sophistic books on the subject of alchemy, it is said with great truth that "our age produces many." The CONFESSIO has also a notable personal statement, that one of the "pseudo-chemists" is a "stage-player" and "a man with sufficient ingenuity for imposition." The original Latin version calls him an "Amphitheatral Comedian," which I have compared carefully with available German and Dutch texts, as also with the English translation edited by Thomas Vaughan. The last renders as follows. "There are nowadays too many such books set forth, which the enemy of man's welfare doth daily—and will to the end—mingle among the good seed, thereby to make the truth more difficult to be believed, which in herself is simple, easy and naked." [1] It is hopeless at this day to speculate on the

the King's permission. It was not so in Europe at the period of the CONFESSIO, but a change would come about herein at a due time. There is no trace of Ritual procedure till 1710, and then it is a mere vestige. The second half of the eighteenth century saw great developments. Meanwhile it is clear from the FAMA that individual Brethren appointed their individual successors, who repaired subsequently to the place of convocation and took "the solemn oath of fidelity and secrecy."

[1] I do not know how the translation "stage-player" arose, but it is exceedingly loose, seeing that the Latin description is almost certainly figurative. The original, in the German CONFESSIO of 1617 reads: *unter welchen der Amphitheatralische und zum verfuhren genugsam sinnreiche*

question of identity, about which great nonsense has been talked, both here and in Germany. (4) The CONFESSIO FRATERNITATIS furnishes the first date in the history of the Rosy Cross, when it says that " our Christian father " was born in 1378. According to the FAMA, he reached Damcar at the age of sixteen years. On the basis of the same document, Michael Maier computes that he was absent for a period of six years from Europe and then proceeds to speculate that he " ruminated " in his " neat and fitting habitation " for thirteen years, at the end of which time, or in 1413, he began to recruit his disciples. He certifies that this is conjectural, and it is obvious that it contradicts the FAMA, which says that after five years " there came again into his mind the desired reformation," as a result of which he decided to " have out of his first cloister . . . three of his brethren."[1] According to CHYMISCHE HOCHZEIT, he was present at the Hermetic Wedding of the King and Queen in 1459, being therefore aged eighty-one years. By the hypothesis of the FAMA,

Histrio und Comediant ein furnemer ist. In BACONIANA, Vol. I, No. 3, May, 1893, a German writer—Dr. Georg Cantor—affirmed that the whole passage was an allusion—as I have mentioned previously—to Heinrich Khunrath, which appears improbable and has no better basis than the connection between *Amphitheatralische* and the AMPHITHEATRUM of Khunrath's *Magnum Opus.* The Hermetic theosophist had been dead—as we have seen—for some twelve years before the CONFESSIO appeared, and I should say that his work had made no particular mark on its period. Dr. Cantor seems to have held that the CONFESSIO was written by Dr. Dee, who had certainly met Khunrath in his travels abroad. The Baconians of 1893 and onward fell upon the allusion and at once attributed it to Shakespeare, as in their view the Rosicrucian documents were all written by Bacon. It may be left as an insoluble problem why the author, in such case, should have reviled himself in the person of his literary mask.

[1] According to the FAMA, he remained for three years at Damcar, thence proceeding to Egypt—" where he remained not long "—and afterwards to Fez, " where the Arabians had directed him." There he stayed two years and thence sailed to Spain, where we have seen that he, his discoveries and spoil of quest were flouted. The same experience awaited him from " other nations." According to this itinerary, he must have been absent from Germany for much more than the six years specified by Maier.

his tomb remained undisturbed for one hundred and twenty years, he having died—according to another speculation—at the age of one hundred and six, in which case the sepulchre was unsealed in 1604,[1] being the date borne on the title-page of Simon Studion's NAOMETRIA. It may appear illogical to debate the chronology of a legend or—more correctly—of a devised mythos; but the dates are not without consequence for the subject under other aspects. There is no doubt, for example, that on more than a single consideration the year 1604—or round about that period—is important for origins in respect of the Rosy Cross, while the two years by which it was immediately preceded will come before us in another unexpected connection in the next chapter but one.

I have now exhausted the content of the CONFESSIO FRATERNITATIS R∴C∴, and it will have been seen that it is not a satisfactory document, as produced in support of a considerable and ambitious claim. It dwells like the FAMA on a reformation other than that of Luther and yet scarcely apart from religion in the sense of Bible Christianity. As such, it offers, as we shall find, a marked contrast to the opinions and large-hearted sentiments of Robert Fludd, who held through all his days with zealous affection to the Church as established in England, and yet the Pontiff on the Throne of Peter is mentioned with respect by him, even when disallowing his claims. But Fludd's was no voice of an anonymous, without local habitation or

[1] The speculation seems based on the hypothesis that the *centum viginti anni* did actually end in 1604. The schedule may be taken out as follows: Birth-date=1378; age on reaching Damcar=16=1394; time at Damcar=3 years=1397; time at Fez=2 years=1399; speculative period spent in visiting European nations=5 years=1404; speculative "rumination" of Maier=13 years=1417, being date of recruiting disciples. C∴R∴C∴ was then 39 years old. But this allows nothing for time spent in transit from place to place after leaving Damcar. An alternative schedule is as follows: Birth-date=1378; Chemical Marriage=1459=81 years old; date of death=1484=106 years old; Opening of Tomb=1604=lapse of 120 years.

name. He graduated at St. John's College, Oxford, under influences in opposition to those of the Puritans and Calvin,[1] and during his travels abroad he made acquaintance with the Guise and Papal families. In conclusion, the CONFESSIO FRATERNITATIS follows logically at its value from the preceding manifesto and corresponds more or less to the actual document which is promised therein, though it does not include all that was announced in the FAMA. It is antecedently reasonable to suppose that there was something behind the texts, namely, a group of persons actuated by a certain motive and serious to that extent, precisely as Masonic Rites innumerable had Masonic personalities at their back, concerned seriously enough with the varied interests and schemes which are embodied in the Rites themselves.

[1] See Craven: DR. ROBERT FLUDD, p. 20.

CHAPTER VII

THE CHEMICAL NUPTIALS

THE third and most singular in several respects of early Rosicrucian documents—issued, so to speak, *ex officio*—is called THE CHEMICAL MARRIAGE—OR NUPTIALS—OF CHRISTIAN ROSENCREUTZ.[1] In a kind of romance or vision, it gives account at full length of a reception into the Greater Mysteries of Alchemy, presented as a dramatic pageant, in which the founder of the Rosy Cross took part, as one who mingles with a crowd, uncertain for a long time whether he is there by election or by a sufferance which may turn against him. The date assigned to this event is 1459, when—according to the mythical chronology of the

[1] There are no bibliographical confusions and no other difficulties respecting this text, for the editions are not numerous, and there was no pretence of its being translated into five languages. It will be sufficient to mention (1) CHYMISCHE HOCHZEIT CHRISTIANI ROSENCREUTZ, *Anno* 1459. First printed at Strasbourg and sold by the successors of Lazarus Zetner, *anno* 1616. (2) The same, but printed by Conrad Scher, 1616. (3) The same, under the same auspices, being a third edition at Strasbourg, 1616. (4) The same, according to Kloss, 1617. So far as I have been able to trace, there were no other German editions. There are reports of a French translation published in 1600, or alternatively at Ratisbon in 1603, both of which dates are impossible and blunders of a catalogue-maker. I question whether such a version was ever made, as there is no trace of it in any authoritative bibliography; but nothing attaches to the question in either case. (5) THE HERMETIC ROMANCE, OR THE CHYMICAL WEDDING. *Written in High Dutch by* CHRISTIAN ROSENCREUTZ. Translated by E. Foxcroft, late Fellow of King's College in Cambridge. Licensed and entered according to order. Printed by A. Sowle at the Crooked Billet in Holloway Lane, Shoreditch, and sold at the Three Keys in Nag's Head Court, Gracechurch Street, 1690. The British Museum has a curious transcript in manuscript of this English version, and I shall recur to it at a much later stage.

literature—the first Master of the Order was more than eighty years old. So far as it is possible to judge, the same hand never reappears in the documents.

We have seen that THE UNIVERSAL REFORMATION is more or less literally translated from an Italian author, Boccalini, and that it has no title to count as a Rosicrucian publication. It differs in every respect from the FAMA and CONFESSIO, the latter of these being written in a stilted style, devoid of any literary method: it is noticeable also as the work of a militant partisan of the Reformation inaugurated by Luther. THE CHEMICAL NUPTIALS, regarded from a literary standpoint—and also in other respects—differs from all three, irradiating a rare splendour of seeming Hermetic parable. With its innumerable quaint devices, its trumpets of beaten gold, its spangled and sky-robed dames, its doves and ravens, its badges of symbolic roses, its banners, wreaths and scarves, its pages and maidens, its mighty palaces, having rare halls and bedchambers, its wonderful adventures and dramatic mysteries, it is rare reading even at this day, independently of any possible hidden meaning.

The motto on the title of THE CHEMICAL NUPTIALS is—

> *Arcana publicata vilescunt et gratiam profanata amittunt:*
> *Ideo ne margaritas objice porcis, seu asino substerne rosas.*

But the author of these lines—whom I do not claim to identify—had forgotten Apuleius and his GOLDEN ASS. The great parable of the Hermetic Marriage is divided into seven books, representing seven days in the dramatic development of its mysteries. It should be noted that—according to the title—the wedding which is celebrated in the story was that of Christian Rosy Cross: CHYMISCHE HOCHZEIT CHRISTIANI ROSENCREUTZ; but seeing that the Master of the Rosy Cross is telling that which he witnessed in a Secret Palace, it is understood to be his marriage in the sense only that he has written the minutes of the spectacle. If I happened to be an occultist, seeing greater things behind the written word than any of those who wrote, I should call this title the veil of a singular mystery and should remind readers that French bibliographers always speak of LES NOCES CHIMIQUES DU PÈRE CHRÉTIEN ROSEN-CRUZ and not THE CHEMICAL WEDDING, written by him in High Dutch—as Mr. Foxcroft put it. It would follow that the Teutonic Master was recounting in a figurative form the adornment of his own spiritual espousals, his own golden marriage. But—not being an occultist—I know that Mr. Foxcroft was really right in his rendering, and that, by the hypothesis of his story, Christian Rosy Cross beheld in pictured symbols the accomplishment of the *Magnum Opus*, as the marriage of a King and Queen. My readers may judge for themselves.

The Master at that time was tarrying in a little house upon a hill, and on the eve before a certain Easter he was—according to his own symbolism—preparing unleavened bread in his heart and in the presence of the Paschal Lamb. In the midst of meditations he found, unawares, behind him " a fair and glorious lady," wearing a sky-coloured vestment bespangled with golden stars. She was a winged woman of the height, and her wings were full of eyes, like the cherubim. In her right hand she carried the fame of a golden trumpet and in her left a great garner of letters in all languages, as one who is commissioned to make known in the four quarters the glory of the Rosy Cross. She kept the silence of the threshold, and in such reverence laid a letter on the table, departing thereafter and mounting upward, while the hill re-echoed with a mighty blast of proclamation from the golden clarion. The Master fell upon his knees and so examined the letter, on the seal of which was a cross—not, apparently, a Rosy Cross—and the inscription : *In hoc signo vinces*. Within he discovered an invitation to the Royal Wedding, about which he had been told in a vision some seven years ago and had awaited it with great earnestness. The missive was written in golden letters on an azure field, and beneath it stood *Sponsus* and *Sponsa*,[1] by way of signatures. Over this he prayed fervently and had mystic visions in the night. In the morning he prepared himself for the way by putting on a wedding-garment, binding a blood-red ribbon, cross-wise—upon his shoulder and setting four red roses in his hat. Here ended what is called the First Day of the CHEMICAL NUPTIALS.

Provided with bread, salt and water, Christian Rosy Cross left his humble habitation and entered a forest, observing that heaven above, the earth beneath, and all that lived thereon were adorned against the coming marriage. He went singing through the woodland till he reached three cedars, on one of which was a tablet of welcome in the name of the King and Bridegroom.[2] It contained an inscription which told him of four ways to reach the Royal Court. The first was short, dangerous and led through a region of rocks; the second was long and circuitous, while he that travelled it must turn neither to right nor left, for there were many bypaths; the third was a royal road and a journey amidst joyful pageants, but it was scarcely for one in a thousand; the fourth and last could no man take because it was a consuming way, encompassed

[1] In this manner the form of invitation determines the personalities of the marriage and reduces Christian Rosy Cross to his proper status as a guest and witness thereof, or coadjutor therein. The celebration, by the wording of the message, was to take place on a mountain, where stood "three stately Temples." The fact is forgotten, however, in the general development of the romance, part of which takes place in a palace on the sea-shore, or actually within sight of a harbour, and partly in a tower on an island. The letter is in rhymed verse, and the sign of Philosophical Mercury appears in the margin of the text.

[2] The tablet is described in the margin as *tabella mercurialis* and the cedar to which it is affixed is termed *arbor mercurialis*.

by fire and cloud: it was reserved for incorruptible bodies. Christian Rosy Cross was now in no little perplexity, and being seized with hunger and thirst he had recourse to his bread, which a white dove came down to share. The dove was attacked by a raven, also in search of food, and took refuge in flight, whereupon the traveller pursued the one in order to deliver the other. In this manner he found himself entered unawares into one of the paths, leaving the rest of his food behind him. A great wind made any return impossible, but the road was clear in front, and was that of the second or circuitous path. With the help of a compass he kept to the meridian line, and at the hour of the setting sun he beheld a stately portal far off on a high hill. It was reached by expedition before night set in, and he found it enriched with noble figures and devices, while a tablet thereon was inscribed with the warning words: *Procul hinc, procul ite, profani.* He was greeted by a porter habited in sky-blue, who demanded his letter of invitation, and on receiving it bade him welcome as an acceptable guest. He asked also for the wayfarer's name, when C∴R∴C∴ described himself as a Brother of the Red Rosy Cross. He was invited finally to purchase a golden token, in exchange for which he delivered his flask of water. In fine, he received a letter for delivery to another porter, who was keeper of a second gate, and under the light of a flaming beacon—put up unawares as a guide to those on the way—he drew to the end of his journey.

The tablet on this second gate was inscribed with the words: *Date et dabitur vobis.* A chained lion was on guard, but he was put back by the second porter, who received the traveller's letter and afterwards saluted him with marked respect, even in the Name of God, as one whom—"of long time"—he would have seen gladly. It was evident—except to himself—that Christian Rosy Cross was coming unto his own in the Hermetic Palace of the

King, as he did—in the other legend—among the wise men of Damcar. The porter required, however, that he should purchase a further token, and when it proved that the postulant had nothing but salt to offer, it was received with thankful heart. The first token was inscribed with the letters S.C. and the second with S.M. among the respective meanings of which were *Sponsus carus* and *sal mineralis*.[1] But that which remained to be done he was warned that he should do quickly. He made speed therefore and having entered, the door shut so suddenly behind him that part of his wedding garment stuck fast therein and he was forced to tear it away. On the further side of this portal he was given a true guest-token, inscribed with the letters S.P.N., signifying *sponsi præsentandus nuptiis* [2] and also a pair of new shoes. He was presently within the castle, where two pages led him to a small room, and his grey head was tonsured. A bell rang without and he was again led forward, but this time through man, corridors and up winding stairs into a spacious hall, wherein was a great multitude, not alone of emperors and kings, princes and lords, but all sorts of people, poor and rich, including persons of his own acquaintance, otherwise those sophisters in alchemy who are denounced in FAMA and CONFESSIO. His presence on such an occasion was a matter of great mirth among them, and when trumpets sounded to the table they scrambled for the highest seats, so that Christian Rosy Cross " and some other sorry fellows " found room hardly at the lowermost end. A goodly feast followed, and when they were warmed with wine the babblers grew louder in their boasts and contention, till the stately musick of stringed instruments charmed all into silence. Thereafter opened a great door in the hall,

[1] Alternatively: *Sanctitati Constantia* or *Spes charitas* and *Sponso mittendus* or *Sal menstrualis*.

[2] Otherwise: *Salus per naturam*.

amidst a blare of trumpets within ; a procession of tapers entered the banqueting-room, some thousands in number, but those who bore them went invisible. At last came the two honourable pages who had escorted C∴R∴C∴ within the castle precincts. Their torches lighted in a radiant Maiden, drawn on a self-moving golden throne. She was clothed in a snow-white robe, sparkling with pure gold, and is described as *Virgo Lucifera*. The company at the board stood up, and she made her proclamation in the name of the Bridegroom and the Bride, who had witnessed the arrivals with joy. She reminded them, however, that none had been called to the nuptials but those who were prepared thereto, and that all the artists must be therefore weighed on the morrow. Those who misdoubted the ordeal might remain where they were and then be dismissed from the castle. The trumpets sounded again and the Virgin departed on her throne. The majority of the guests resolved to await the weighing ; but Christian Rosy Cross—convinced of his own unworthiness—held back with some others in the *Refectorium*, making nine in all. While the confident were lighted to their separate chambers, those who had abased themselves were bound with cords and left in darkness to contemplate their presumption in coming to this amazing marriage.

The night-visions and vigils of Christian Rosy Cross attained their end in the dawn of the Third Day. The brave champions who had settled to withstand the ordeal now trooped into the hall, and beholding the nine in their bonds reproved their cowardice ; but there was no loud cry of the business, for the morning brought sober reflection. The trumpets sounded once more and *Virgo Lucifera* entered, crowned with laurels, arrayed in red velvet and girded with a white scarf. To those who had been bound she promised on behalf of her Lord that it should fare better than with many of the presumptuous who yet remained at liberty. Certain golden scales were now placed in position and the work of weighing began. Of emperors, kings and lords, few withstood the test, but there is particular mention of one who proved Imperator in the truth of the Rosy Cross, as in royalty of the world without: he was therefore given a gown of red velvet, a laurel wreath and a seat on the steps of the Virgin's throne. Of the gentry—both learned and unlearned—some two only were found in perfection; and then it was the turn of "those vagabond cheaters" and makers of false stones, to be jerked out of the scale with whips and scourges. It appears, however, that among this motley crew there were a few of another category, who earned their wreaths and robes. This business being also over, one of the captains of the castle demanded that the poor bound brothers who had "acknowledged their misunderstanding" should be set also on the scale, but without danger or penalty. The greater part miscarried and were placed peaceably on one side. One of the first seven held out bravely and received his reward. The ninth failed, but the eighth—who was C∴R∴C∴—"outstayed all the weights," and when three men hung on the other side of the beam, nothing could prevail against him. Thereupon one of the pages stood up and proclaimed with a loud voice: "That is HE." After such manner was the pious pilgrim honoured, and it was given him to release at will one of the captives. He chose the first emperor, who was liberated and seated among the victors. Meanwhile C∴R∴C∴ had removed the roses from his hat, and while they were held in his hand the Virgin saw them and "graciously requested them of me."

This ended the trial, about ten o'clock in the forenoon. But judgment had yet to be given and so a council was convened, with the Virgin as president, and it found as follows: (1) That the lords should be dismissed the castle, yet with befitting respect; (2) That some of the rest should be caused to run out naked; (3) That yet others, being stripped, should be scourged away from the precincts; (4) That those who had surrendered willingly should depart without blame; (5) That those who had misbehaved at the dinner should be punished in body and life. The candidates who escaped lightly were told that they had given credit to false books and had come uninvited to the castle. To others it was said that they had forged the false books, had befooled and cheated many, diminishing regal dignity, and seeking to ensnare the guests. In particular they had made use of "ungodly, deceitful figures . . ., not even sparing the Divine Trinity."[1] An unescapable execution followed all the sentences, and this took place in the garden about the castle, the King and Queen being present, in a curtained gallery, so that they sat and watched invisible.

When all was over, those who remained as guests ad-

[1] Compare the FAMA FRATERNITATIS R∴C∴, which says: "We must earnestly admonish you that you cast away . . . the worthless books of pseudo-chemists, to whom it is a jest to apply the Most Holy Trinity to vain things, or to deceive men with monstrous symbols and enigmas." This part of THE CHEMICAL NUPTIALS is important for the authorship of the early Rosicrucian documents. It provides, moreover, a graphic picture of the parlous condition into which German alchemy had fallen, or of the repute in which it was held at the beginning of the seventeenth century. For example, the makers of false books are compelled to affirm that their lucubrations "sold so mightily that whoever had no other means to maintain himself was fain to engage in this cozenage." As part of the sentence there is published also a proclamation of the King's Majesty, in the course of which it is stated that he has "resolved to communicate shortly" a "CATALOGUE OF HERETICS OR INDEX EXPURGATORIUS," recalling the promise of the FAMA, that the Brotherhood will "name in due season" those books and pictures which are "set forth *in contumeliam gloriæ Dei*" and "will give to the pure-hearted a record or register of the same." There is little need to say that no such Catalogue or Index is included among Rosicrucian publications at any period. It should be added that pictorial symbols abound in alchemical literature, including works of reputed Masters, like Basil Valentine.

mitted to the marriage washed their hands and heads at a certain fountain and were led back into the castle. They had been invested already with the Golden Fleece and a Lion volant, being counselled to maintain the repute and dignity of that Order which royal favour had deigned to confer upon them. A page was set apart for each guest, and they were taken to visit various portions of the building. In this manner, by an apparent mistake of his guide, C∴R∴C∴ was permitted to examine a certain royal sepulchre, and there it is claimed that he learned more than is extant in all books.[1] He was ushered, moreover, into a very noble library,[2] "as it was altogether before the reformation." In fine he had experience in a kind of *camera obscura*, wherein he was able to contemplate the stars "glittering in an agreeable order" and "moving so gallantly" that—as it seemed to him—he could have looked for ever. It fell out for these reasons that he was almost the last at table when the party was called to supper, yet the waiters treated him with so much "reverence and honour" that he dared not look up for shame.

The Virgin presided,[3] and the discourse was cheered by enigmas and counter-enigmas.[4] The meat being finished and grace said in due order, the President asked whether they "desired to begin the wedding," and there is no

[1] It is said that in contiguity to this sepulchre there stood a glorious Phœnix, about which Christian Rosy Cross had published a small discourse two years previously. There will be occasion to consider this testimony in my next chapter.

[2] The romance explains why there is no account of its contents—namely, because the "catalogue is shortly to be published."

[3] *Virgo Lucifera* is also described as the Lady Chamberlain. On this occasion she wore the insignia of the Golden Fleece and Lion.

[4] One of the riddles concerned the name of the Virgin and ran as follows: "My name contains six and fifty, yet has only eight letters. The third is a third part of the fifth, which added to the sixth will produce a number, the root whereof shall exceed the third by the first precisely, and it is the half of the fourth. The fifth and seventh are equal; so are the last and first. These

need to testify concerning their zeal. A page was therefore despatched and a procession of virgins entered with lights carried before them, chief among whom was one wearing a coronet and " looking towards heaven rather than earth." She was mistaken by all for the bride, whom it is said that she much surpassed in honour, riches and state. In a word, it was she who would rule the whole Marriage.[1] The company of guests fell on their knees before her, but she offered her hand to each, admonishing them to remember their Creator and so proceed in their enterprise. But to Christian Rosy Cross she uttered these memorable words : " Thou hast received more than others ; make therefore a larger return." After this the procession turned about and the guests were so led into another chamber, but each in fine to his own apartment, that which was assigned to C∴R∴C∴ being furnished royally with rare tapestries and paintings.

The proceedings of the Fourth Day began at a Fountain in the Garden. The Lion of the Garden was beside it and a tablet inscribed strangely recited the virtues of the water, which had become a healing medicine by the aid of Art. The counsel was therefore : " Let him drink of me who is able : let him who will, wash ; let him trouble me who dares." And again : " Drink, Brethren, and live."

make with the second as much as the sixth has, and this contains four more than the third tripled." The hidden Name was

A= 1	
L=12	
C= 3	Three—as will be seen—is the value of the third letter,
H= 8	being one-third of nine, the value of the fifth letter. Add
I= 9	9 to 13=value of fifth and sixth letter, and the result is
M=13	22=4, which exceeds the third=3 by the first=1. The
I= 9	fifth and seventh are both 9, while the first and last are one.
A= 1	
56	

[1] She is called *Virgo præstans* in the marginalia of the romance and also the Duchess or Queen.

The guests washed at this Fountain and drank also thereof out of a golden cup; but it does not appear that any great renovation followed. Thereafter a certain door was opened, and the Virgin Guide of the Paths led them up three hundred and sixty-five stairs, following a band of musicians, till they paused under a painted arch and were joined by a notable train of maidens, apparelled richly. The musicians were dismissed; a bell rang; and another most beautiful virgin brought wreaths and branches of laurel, which were presented to the guests and the ladies by whom they had been joined—as it might be, unto each visitor his proper dedicated maid. A curtain was then drawn up, and they beheld the King and Queen, as they sat in their majesty in a room gleaming with gold and precious stones.[1] C∴R∴C∴ bears witness that the Queen's robes were so radiant that he was not able to behold them. The *Virgo Lucifera*, who presided over the proceedings, presented the guests to that royal pair as those who had adventured thither "with peril of body and life." They were received joyfully and grace was assured to all. As regards the royal persons, the description baffles the reader. We have seen concerning their state, majesty and in particular the vestment of the Queen. But we are told subsequently that at the western end of the room there were three thrones and two seated in each of them: in the first a very ancient king, whose consort was fair and young; in the third a black king, of middle age, and by him "a dainty old matron, covered with a veil"; but in the middle sat "the two young persons, wearing wreaths of laurel," while "over them hung a great and costly crown." These were the two lovers, and about them was a Cupid,

[1] The Latin marginalia of the text describes the vestibule of this chamber and the throne-room itself as *laboratorium*, to intimate that the whole pageant of the nuptials concealed—*ex hypothesi*—an experiment in secret chemistry.

who also flitted from point to point, tormenting all and sundry.

The guests were led forth, after the formal presentation, and C∴R∴C∴ records that the youthful royal pair were not at that time so beautiful as he had imagined previously to himself. In a later period of that day the guests were present at a comedy—which was attended also by the royalties—in what is called the House of the Sun. There also was that " unknown Queen " who has been named previously and is to be distinguished from *Virgo Lucifera.* The latter was President and Guide of the guests at large; the former ruled, as we know, over all that concerned the Hermetic Marriage.[1] The play-scene over, its spectators returned to the throne-room, where the evening feast was prepared, and the royal persons sat down to it in glittering, snow-white garments. Notwithstanding the sallies of Cupid, it was, however, a feast of sorrow, fulfilled for the most part in silence. When it was finished, a book —covered with black velvet and gold—was brought to the young king, and this he laid open. By the royal command, an elder of the castle demanded whether the guests were resolved to abide by the King, for better, for worse, and all consenting wrote themselves down in the book, after which the whole company—from the first even to the last—drank the Draught of Silence, like a pledge taken in any House of the Mysteries.

The cloud on the sanctuary of the festival was to be explained speedily, for a bell began to toll; the royal personalities put off their white garments and assumed those of mourning; the guests also were clothed in black; and the room was draped in like manner. The tables were

[1] The House of the Sun was entered in processional form, thus: (1) The Unknown Queen; (2) Six Virgins carrying " the King's jewels "; (3) the Three Kings, having the Bridegroom in the midst of them; (4) the Three Queens; (5) the Guests and their Virgins; (6) One who is called " Old Atlas " and otherwise the Astronomer.

removed and the place of banqueting was changed into a place of holocaust. The Virgin President of the Mystery bound the eyes of the six royalties with black taffeta scarves, after which six coffins were brought in and set down, with a low black seat in their midst. A giant negro entered with naked axe and proceeded in a solemn and reverent ceremony to decapitate the kings and queens—male and female indifferently. This terrific pageant began with the ancient monarch, who—so far as alchemy is concerned—may possibly have represented Saturn. The king, who was of a middle age, may correspond to Jupiter, and he suffered in the next place, each presumably with his royal consort. The king who was to come, for as yet he does not seem to have been crowned, must have represented Sol, and I take it that he was last in the sacrifice. The business had been done expeditiously but there was to be yet another episode, for when the headsman prepared to retire he was added also to the shambles. The blood of the kings was received in golden goblets, which were placed with them in their coffins, and these were duly covered. As regards the executioner, his head was deposited with the axe in a certain chest. Christian Rosy Cross adds—not without warrant—that it seemed to him a bloody wedding. But the Lady President bade her auditors rest content, for the life of the victims stood now in the hands of the guests and, if they followed her, " this death should make many alive."

The guests meanwhile were counselled to seek their repose, for the business of the fourth day was over, and her own part was a vigil beside the bodies. Their respective pages conducted the visitors presently to their proper lodgings. The room of C∴R∴C∴ had windows looking on to the lake, and about midnight—he being far from sleep—there was a great glow over the water, and he beheld from afar " seven ships making forward, all full of lights." Over each of them hovered a flame, which he judged to be "the spirits of the beheaded." When the vessels had come to land he saw the Queen-President[1] going towards them, bearing a torch and followed by the six coffins, as also the chest. Each of these was laid secretly in a ship; the lights were extinguished, save one for a watch on each vessel; and the spiritual flames "passed back together over the lake." It is said that there were hundreds of watchers encamped on the shore; but as for the Virgin she returned to the castle and carefully bolted up.

Very early in the morning, being that of the Fifth Day, C∴R∴C∴ rose up, and—seeing that no one was stirring—he entreated his page to take him about the castle. In this manner he visited the Royal Treasury, in which—out of common expectation—he found a noble "sepulchre," or rather a triangular monument. "Here," said his page, "lies buried the Lady Venus, whose beauty has undone so many in fortune, honour and blessing." He led him therefrom, through a copper door, far down into the earth to another chamber, wherein was a rich bed, hung about with curious curtains. The page drew one of them, and—looking even beneath the coverlets—they saw the Lady Venus in the incredible beauty of her nakedness. This was a most secret visitation and there was trouble afterwards to keep it in the place of hiddenness, above all from Cupid, as jealous of his mother's honour. Indeed he heated his dart when he found Christian Rosy Cross in proximity to the so-called sepulchre and pricked him with it on the hand.[2]

[1] Alternatively, *Virgo Lucifera*. The text says merely "our Virgin."

[2] We hear also of an "unknown tree," the fruit of which fell into a copper kettle and was turned into water; but the heat of burning pyrites caused it to produce new fruit continually. It is said that when the tree is melted down, "then shall Lady Venus awake and become the mother of a King."

But there was now other business to transact and the President appeared in black velvet with her virgins, whom the guests followed into the court before the Castle. They came upon six coffins, by each of which stood eight muffled men. The guests generally supposed that they contained the bodies of the kings and their consorts, but C∴R∴C∴ remembered what he had seen upon the lake. The coffins were borne into the Garden, where a "wooden edifice" had been erected, standing upon seven columns and having "a glorious crown" in the roof. Within this structure were six sepulchres built over six graves, wherein the coffins were laid, the chest containing the head of the executioner being put in the middle of all.[1] After the interment was over the Virgin exhorted the guests (1) to keep their engagements faithfully; (2) not to repine at their pains; (3) to be helpful in restoring the Royal Persons to life; with which object (4) they must accompany her to the Tower of Olympus and bring thence the medicines required for this purpose. They repaired therefore to the shore and found the seven ships, in three of which the Virgin arranged her party; whereupon the voyage began, with the ships in due order, as shewn in the following diagram.

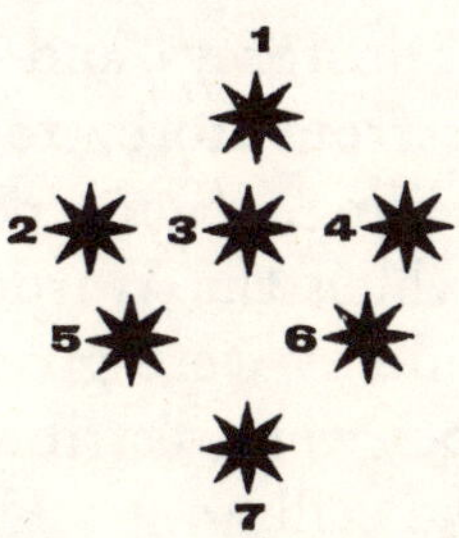

The distribution was as here follows, according to the numbers of the ships:

(1) The Moor or Negro, and twelve musicians; (2), (3),

[1] "Herewith were my companions deceived," says the supposititious C∴R∴C∴, "for they imagined that the dead bodies were there."

(4) the guests at the Wedding, Christian Rosy Cross being an occupant of No. 3, together with the Lady President; (5), (6) having no passengers, but " stuck about with many branches of laurel"; (7) Forty Virgins in all.

The ships sailed over the lake and then through a narrow arm into the open sea, amidst sirens and sea-goddesses, chanting the victories of Love. After some hours the voyagers reached a four-square island, on which was the Tower of Olympus, by wall within wall environed. They were greeted by the Warden, described as " a very ancient man," and led into [1] a subterranean laboratory, where they extracted the essences from plants and precious stones, receiving at the end of these labours some scant refreshment, and a mattress laid on the floor for each to rest as he could. But Christian Rosy Cross went out to contemplate the stars, and from one of the walls he beheld not only a memorable conjunction of planets, but the Seven Spiritual Flames passing from over the sea to rest on the summit of the Tower. After this manner the fifth day came to an end in wonders.

Of that which followed on the Sixth it is scarcely possible to speak in a summary manner, as it is exceedingly involved. Above the subterranean laboratory the Tower of Olympus was raised in eight stages or storeys, and—so far as the Guests were concerned—access from storey to storey was through a trap opened in the ceiling. Some performed the ascent by the help of wings which the Warden fastened to their shoulders; to others ladders were given, e.g., to Christian Rosy Cross; while ropes were distributed to the rest and fastened on hooks in the ceiling.

To the seven floors there were allotted seven stages of work, the particulars of which follow: (1) The laborious experiment of ascent from the laboratory or first conclave

[1] In such a manner, says the text, that the coffins were brought in without observation on the part of the visitors.

to the second or floor above. (2) A period of prayer therein for the life of the King and Queen, performed in separate oratories, after which a great oval chest was brought in, containing the six royal bodies, and was placed beneath a fountain, the waters of which were shut off at the beginning. The Virgin [1] entered, bearing a casket, in which was the Moor's head. Her attendants carried lamps, and torches were given to the Guests, all present being gathered about the chest. The Moor's head, covered with green taffeta, was placed in a kettle and the liquid essences prepared on the previous day from plants and precious stones were poured therein. The fountain played, and its water was delivered through small pipes into a smaller kettle, heated by the lamps of the attendants. So far as it is possible to understand a confused text, the contents of both kettles "fell in upon the bodies" and dissolved them. The liquid formed thus by the bodies was received in a golden globe, which became exceedingly heavy and was taken out of the chamber with great labour. Thereafter the Guests ascended as they could to the third conclave. (3) They found the golden globe suspended from a strong chain midwise in this apartment, which contained many windows, with polished mirrors between them, "so optically opposed" to one another that the image of the sun, shining through one window, was multiplied everywhere and refracted upon the golden globe, which was thus raised gradually to a desired state of heat. The mirrors were then shut off and the globe was left to cool, after which it was cut open with a diamond and a great snow-white egg was discovered therein. This was carried away by the Virgin, and after a certain space of time the Guests ascended in the same miscellaneous manner to the fourth floor. (4) They discovered herein a great copper kettle, exactly

[1] She is called "our Virgin," but was presumably the President of the Work and not *Virgo Lucifera.*

square in shape, filled with silver sand, having the egg deposited therein, that it might be brought to perfect maturity by a gentle fire, kindled beneath the vessel. The said condition being reached and the egg removed, a Bird with black plumes broke through the shell and was fed with the blood of the beheaded kings and queens—but diluted with prepared water. It grew in the sight of all, the black feathers being replaced by others of snow-white, and afterwards by yet others, so curiously coloured that there was nothing like them for beauty. In this state the Bird was carried away by the Virgin, and the Guests ascended presently to the fifth floor. (5) The work was now concerned with the bath of the Bird. He was placed in a vessel of water " so coloured with a fine white powder that it had the appearance of milk." The vessel was heated by lamps placed beneath till the Bird's feathers came off and the water was turned blue, looking afterwards even as a blue stone. This stone was pounded and the Bird painted therewith, the head only excepted, " which remained white." The Virgin departed with her Bird, and the Guests were thereafter called up to the sixth storey. (6) In this place the Bird was fed with the blood of a white serpent and then decapitated, the body being burnt to ashes, which were deposited in a box of cypress-wood. Christian Rosy Cross and three of the other workers were driven out at this stage by the door on the pretence that they had proved idlers ; but in reality they were led up a staircase to the eighth floor, while those who were left behind ascended to the seventh. (7) The chosen three were welcomed by an ancient Warden of the Tower, to whom entered the Virgin and deposited the ashes of the Bird in another vessel, after which she departed to " cast a mist before the eyes of the remaining artists." [1]

[1] They were apparently set to work in maintaining a furnace and believed that they were much preferred before the other ill-starred guests. A little

The work of the triad was to moisten the ashes with prepared water till they became a thin dough, which was then heated over the fire and cast " into two little forms or moulds," where it was left to cool. Subsequently the moulds were opened, discovering " two bright and almost transparent little images, a male and a female, the like to which man's eye never saw." They were " limber and fleshy as other human bodies," but had as yet no life within them. Now, the blood of the Bird had been received into a golden cup, and the next duty was to instil it drop by drop into the mouths of the little images which, under this ministration, continued to increase in size; and when all the blood was exhausted, " they were in their perfect full growth, having gold-yellow curled hair." Their flesh was now of a lively, natural colour, though they were still " dead figures." They were veiled by command of the Warden, and in that which followed the Guests had no share. Moreover, the intention on the part of the official *dramatis personæ* was that they should see and understand little. The actors included the Virgin and her attendants. That which took place was the entrance of the souls into their bodies through tubes placed in the mouths, an event which was seen and understood clearly by Christian Rosy Cross alone. He testifies that the souls descended through an open space in the vaulted roof, after the manner of streams of fire poured through the tubes, and thence into the two bodies. This operation or ceremonial was performed three times, after which the now living bodies were placed in a " travelling bed" and curtains drawn about them. They were left to sleep in this manner for a considerable time, but were ulti-

later on, their satisfaction was increased because they had " to work in gold," of which it is said that it belongs indeed to the art but is not chief and most necessary therein. They had also part of the Bird's ashes and imagined therefore that the dead bodies would be raised up to new life by means of gold. Owing probably to a *lapsus memoriæ*, the story does not relate what happened when the two classes of artists were ultimately reunited.

mately awakened by Cupid, were vested by the Virgin in white garments and seated in certain very curious chairs, where they received the congratulations of all present.[1] It is said that the young King and Queen "imagined that they had slept from the hour in which they were beheaded." In fine the royal personages were escorted to the waterside, where a ship was waiting and presently put forth to sea, the guests proceeding to supper and thence to rest for the night, after their long toils.

On the morning of the Seventh and last day the guests were clothed in yellow garments and golden fleeces, the Virgin declaring that they were Knights of the Golden Stone.[2] Each of them received also a golden medal, bearing the following inscriptions: on the obverse—*Ars Naturæ Ministra*; on the reverse—*Temporis Natura Filia*. The company returned across the sea in twelve ships, under the care of the old lord. There were guards of honour on board, together with many musicians, and the ships' flags carried the twelve zodiacal signs, the guests sitting under *Libra*. As they drew to the mainland a great fleet came out to meet them, including one vessel which sparkled with gold and precious stones: it carried the King and Queen, with many lords and ladies of high degree. All were brought to, and then Atlas—on the deck of the royal vessel—welcomed the arrivals in the King's name. The harbour reached and all in fine landed, the King and Queen presented their hands; the guests were mounted on horses; the old lord and Christian Rosy Cross were caused to ride with the King, who saluted the latter as his father.[3]

[1] There is no suggestion that their extraordinary ordeal had transformed them in any visible manner, nor does any purpose appear to have been served thereby.

[2] Of which we were ignorant heretofore, says the text in its most banal manner.

[3] The reason not emerging in the course of the story, which indeed represents Christian Rosy Cross as chief and most observant, as obviously most favoured among the seven guests, but allocates the vital part of the work to the Lady-President and her coadjutors.

They reached the first palace-gate, the keeper of which —with whom C∴R∴C∴ had exchanged his flask of water against a golden token—now presented a petition, begging him to intercede with the King on his behalf. In this manner it transpired that he was a famous astrologer who had been guilty of a misdemeanour against Venus by beholding her in her bed of rest, as a punishment for which he had been put to serve at the door until such time as one who had transgressed in like manner should take his place. It follows that the petitioner was actually in the presence of his successor and appealing as if unawares to him. Moreover, when the document came to be read later on in the proceedings, it certified that "Venus was already uncovered" by one of the King's guests. There was much perturbation in consequence, which notwithstanding a great feast followed in the palace, and then the new Knights of the Golden Stone were pledged to observe the following Laws of the Chivalry[1]: (1) That they should ascribe the Order only to God and His hand-maid Nature. (2) That they should abominate all uncleanness. (3) That they should be ready to assist all worthy persons who had need of them. (4) That the honour conferred upon them should not be applied to works of worldly pride and ambition. (5) That they should not desire to live longer than God willed. They were installed Knights thereafter, and "set over ignorance, poverty and sickness, to handle them" at their pleasure.

It is said that Christian Rosy Cross hung up his golden fleece and hat in the chapel of the Order, as an eternal memorial. Moreover, as each was required to write his name—in a register, presumably—he set down on his own

[1] It is obvious therefore that the romance is concerned with the Order of the Golden Stone and not of the Rosy Cross. It is merely incidental that the narrator happens—as his name suggests—to be already a Brother of the Red Rosy Cross. The distinction is important and will call for further consideration in the next chapter.

part as follows: *Summa Scientia nihil scire:* FR.·. CHRISTIANUS ROSENCREUTZ, *Eques Aurei Lapidis. Anno* 1459. In fine, a royal reward had been adjudged to each, and each was called upon to prefer his request in private. But Christian Rosy Cross decided on his own part to ask for the release of the doorkeeper, which involved a confession of his own vision of Venus on the fifth day of the Marriage. The King told him that he could not "transgress his ancient usage," which appeared to signify that C.·.R.·.C.·. must take his predecessor's place at the gate, notwithstanding the intimations of the story, that it was chiefly through his offices that the royal personages had been brought again to life.

He was told, indeed, that this was the last time when he should see the King as he now looked upon him, meaning as a guest at the palace. The King took him in his arms and kissed him, and he was committed to the Divine Protection, all of which he regarded as a form of dismissal. However, the Lord of the Tower and he who bore the mythological title of Atlas, conducted him to "a glorious lodging, in which stood three beds." The last lines specify that "each of us lay down in one of them," at which point the narrative closes abruptly in the midst of a sentence, the following statement being added by way of colophon: "Here are wanting about two leaves in quarto, and he (the author hereof), whereas he imagined he must in the morning be doorkeeper, returned home."

The German occult mind of 1616 concluded that Christian Rosy Cross had attained the secret of the Hermetic *Magnum Opus*, had performed the transmutation of metals with his own hands and had elected to put on record the particulars, including the process, in the guise of an exceedingly picturesque allegorical romance. The promises of FAMA FRATERNITATIS had not been fulfilled in the CONFESSIO; but there is, I suppose, no question that the publication of NUPTIÆ CHYMICÆ must have raised expectation and desire to a fever-heat—at least on the part of the alchemists.[1] It did not go through so many editions as the two previous tracts, and there was no pretence—as we have seen—of its translation into other languages than the German in which it was written. I do not think—or at least have been unable to trace—that it had even the honour of a Dutch rendering; but more than one laborious commentary unfolded its hidden meaning. For reasons which will appear in the next chapter it is unnecessary to do more than specify therein by title one of these hermeneutical experiments. The question before us is not that of significance but of the tract in respect of its origin: it so happens that the settlement of this point will dispose effectually of the other.

For the rest, the position of NUPTIÆ CHYMICÆ on its open surface is—as I have indicated—that of an allegorical romance or parable woven about the legendary Founder of the Order, and it does not contain as such any further contribution to Rosicrucian history. At most it illustrates the alleged fact that C∴R∴C∴ attained the ends o. alchemy. In reality it embodies an exposition at length of the claim made in the two previous manifestoes that the Adept Brethren were in possession, through the work of their Master, of that Great Secret which is summarised in the CONFESSIO as "transmutation of metals and the supreme medicine of the world."

[1] Compare Findel: HISTORY OF FREEMASONRY: "The beautiful embellishment of the subject in THE CHEMICAL NUPTIALS caused the desire for initiation to be increased everywhere, especially in the Rhine country, which was the chief seat of the Society." Reghellini says also in his loose and inaccurate manner that "the taste for occult sciences and theosophy on the part of the R∴R∴✠∴✠∴ is to be found permeating various German works, which made a considerable stir, especially in England." The history of occult thought in England is against this view. Reghellini adds that the works in question were the CHEMICAL NUPTIALS OF ROSEN-CRUX (*sic*) and the UNIVERSAL REFORMATION OF THE WHOLE WORLD, by Valentine Andreæ.

CHAPTER VIII

AUTHORSHIP OF THE CHEMICAL NUPTIALS

In the year 1614, when the Fama Fraternitatis created its first public sensation, a young man named Johann Valentin Andreæ, who has been already the subject of more than a single allusion, had attained the age of twenty-eight years, having been born at Herrenberg in Würtemberg on August 17, 1586. The family appears to have been rich in theologians and Lutheran pastors. His immediate progenitor belonged to the second category and his grandfather, Jacob Andreas, has been called famous in divinity, while an uncle James is said to have been known through all Germany as a second Luther. Johann Valentin received the elements of his education under a certain Michael Beumler [1] and afterwards at Tübingen, in connection with which we hear of Martinus Crusius,[2] the preceptor of Simon Studion, but without mention of the latter.[3]

According to Hofelius, Andreæ fell into bad company at Tübingen, squandering some years of his youth and leaving the university in 1610, full of repentance and hoping to recuperate by travel. This stands at its value and is not exactly borne out in the confessions of his autobiography. In any case he travelled, in and around the year 1610,

[1] Joannis Valentini Andreæ Vita, ab ipso conscripta, 1849. Printed *ex autographo in Bibl. Guelferbytano recondito, adsumtis Codd. Stuttgartianis, Schorndorfiensi, Tubingensi.*

[2] *Ibid.*, pp. 8, 9.

[3] It seems possible that Studion was an assumed name, though I find no such suggestion in any of the past records.

visiting Switzerland, France, Austria [1] and Italy. In 1614 he married Agnes Elizabeth, who was a daughter of Joshua Grüninger. The successive appointments which he held as a minister of the Lutheran Church need not detain us. In 1620 he became superintendent of Calva and filled this office for nearly twenty years. In 1654 he died at Stuttgart on the eve of accepting the post of prelate at Adelberg.

There is one other point only in respect of his external life. Having been accused of heresy and of defending the Rosicrucian Fraternity, he issued his profession of faith, certifying his detestation of papal tyranny, the pride of Calvinism, the hypocrisy of Anabaptists and registering his adhesion to the Confession of Augsbourg. The Rosicrucian impeachment appears to have been passed over, but the connection with the Order which is implied in the charge against him happens to be our sole concern. It takes us at once to his literary output, which was large enough in its way, consisting of numberless little books written in Germanised Latin, with little grace of diction through all their pomp of pages.[2] I conclude that they have been praised in proportion as they have been read the less by those who have pronounced their panegyric. It has been said that he devoted his learning, talents and imagination to direct his contemporaries into the true path, being that of Bible Christianity. There is no room for doubt ; but men of God or men of the Devil, they were one and all an impossible crowd—these *literati* and *theologi* and *philosophi*, in their sacrosaintly fatherland of the early seventeenth century, agaze

[1] This is the fact which lies behind the muddled thesis of Heckethorn, according to which Andreæ established " Rosicrucian Lodges " in Austria in 1612.

[2] Compare De Quincey, following and reproducing Bühle : " Besides Greek and Latin, in which languages he was distinguished for the elegance of his style," etc. etc.

and clamorous in the aftermath of the garish light of Luther. Whether it is possible or not to say anything in *la grande manière* of literature which shall take people who are disposed into a path of Bible Christianity I do not pretend to know: what is certain, however, is that it was never said by Andreæ. His books—with a single exception which is a thorn in the flesh of my subject—are dull with a dullness which surpasses all vexation.[1] One of them has been translated recently, and those who challenge my ruling are in a position to estimate for themselves the price they might be prepared to pay for deliverance from the yoke of his CHRISTIAN REPUBLIC, supposing that the world were debating its own reconstruction along such lines as his.

I do not question of course that in his day and generation he was a shining light in Lutheran letters and theology: it is the theology and the letters which no light can enlighten and no Confession can redeem—of Augsburg or otherwhere—either in this world or that which is to come. The sin of Luther and the rest of the German Reformers was not their revolt against the Papacy, but their substitution of a religion of lead. It was ingots of lead on the eyelids and lead in the heart and head for the generation which came after and held up cudgels of debate "as a challenge to all the field." It follows that Andreæ *et hoc genus omne* were products of their period—*infelices theologi*—exponents of a chaotic reform. They are forgotten now, when there is no dew of Protestant praises to keep green their dejected memory. I am not suggesting that Andreæ fell below the better measures of his period: he may rank high in its classes; but there remains the irrepealable platitude of the

[1] Compare therefore *Bruckeri Historia Critica Philosophiæ*, *Tomus II*, p. 740. It registers that Andreæ was very learned and a very elegant genius. Other deponents speak of his satirical powers and even of his wit. I would persuade the modern reader to draw, if he dare, a few drafts from that Castalian fount in dereliction which is called VITA AB IPSO CONSCRIPTA.

whole subject—that dullness is still dullness and that its deeps are still the deeps.

There must now be placed before my readers—I mean, those who are otherwise unversed in the subject—an almost incredible proposition, and it is one which cannot be dismissed, unhappily for the romance and mystery-side of the Rosy Cross. With all its banners and pennons, its virgins and light-bearers, its palaces and towers, its astrological ship sailing over Hermetic seas, its transformations and resurrections in parable, its *Equites Aurei Lapidis* and intimations above all concerning the Red Rosy Cross, the author of the CHEMICAL NUPTIALS was no other and more concealed genius than Johannes Valentinus Andreæ. It is true that the testimony is his own and is not only devoid of all contemporary support but—so far as I am aware—of all suspicion of the fact. But in VITA AB IPSO CONSCRIPTA, already cited, he registers the point, as one speaking in humility concerning a youthful indiscretion, of which he was almost ashamed.[1] He is reciting his early literary efforts belonging to the period *circa* 1602 and 1603, in which he had attained the respective ages of sixteen and seventeen years.[2] Though enumerated in Latin, it seems fairly certain that most of them were written in German, as their author's native tongue. They included (1) the Comedies of ESTHER and HYACINTH;[3] (2) THE CURSING OF VENUS; (3) certain Dialogues, to the number of three, under the title of TEARS;[4] and (4) THE CHEMICAL NUP-

[1] Solomon Semler did not know the VITA, which was still unprinted in his day. He affirms that the CHEMICAL NUPTIALS was written by Caspar Rosencreutz, a man of learning, otherwise unknown, but there was also a Christian Rosencreutz. ELUCIDARIUS MAJOR and ELUCIDARIUS CHEMICUS, 1617, were written to combine their legends.

[2] *Jam a secn do etuteteio post millesimum sexcentissimum cæperam aliquid exercendi inergo rpgeniiangre.*

[3] As to what remained of these at the time of writing, he says: *pro ætate non displicet.* They were imitations of English comedies.

[4] The description is: LACHRYMÆ *tribus dialogis satis prolixis.* It is possible that these Dialogues were in Latin.

TIALS. As to the DIALOGUES he says that *invito me perierunt*; but as to NUPTIÆ CHYMICÆ, the annotation is *superfuerunt e contra.* They perished but this survived, "with its fœtus fruitful of monsters." It is described as a jest—that is to say, *ludibrium*—and Andreæ supposes that his readers will be astonished to hear of its being esteemed by some and explained with subtle ingenuity.[1]

The autobiography from which these excerpts are taken was written late in life, and we cannot do otherwise than accept the statement made, for it might be unreasonable to suppose that Andreæ advanced a false claim, after the lapse of long years, were he even capable of such a dishonesty, which I am quite sure that he was not.[2] There would be nothing to gain by assuming such a mask, and, moreover, the publication of his memoirs during his life-time was probably not intended. As a fact they remained in manuscript for one hundred and forty-two years and were issued even then only in a German version.[3] The original Latin

[1] His note-books had records of yet other productions, e.g. JULIUS, otherwise POLITIA, in three books, and ASTROLOGICAL JUDGMENT AGAINST ASTROLOGY, the latter indicating his bent against the occult sciences at that early age. They contain, however, no reference to a tract on the Phœnix. Had such a performance been included among his JUVENILIA, it would have helped us to understand the statement made in NUPTIÆ CHYMICÆ about a work on this subject having been published by Christian Rosy Cross two years prior to the marriage. Otherwise it remains inscrutable. The Phœnix is a familiar alchemical symbolism and has been said to recur frequently in Rosicrucian literature, which, however, is not the case.

[2] In my REAL HISTORY OF THE ROSICRUCIANS, 1888, p. 231, I indicated that NUPTIÆ CHYMICÆ was incredible as a boyish effort. The difficulties which I felt then remain now; but I am conscious at this day that it is at least equally difficult to suggest that Andreæ lied in his testamentary memoirs. I have taken therefore in the text above what seems to me the better part and have preferred the honour of a long departed theologian before the validity of a literary judgment, however strong in itself. I think also that the place of the romance in Rosicrucian debate can be assigned more easily by accepting its author's statement.

[3] They appeared in 1796 in Seybold's collection of AUTOBIOGRAPHIES OF CELEBRATED MEN.

text did not appear till 1843.[1] Evidently he regretted the romance, as shewn by the allusion to a brood of monstrosities which were begotten thereby.[2] We have therefore to recognise that Andreæ wrote in his 'teens a work called CHEMICAL NUPTIALS and in after years at least regarded it as a jest, unless I may venture to render *ludibrium* as a sufferable equivalent of "fantasy."[3]

We have seen that THE CHEMICAL MARRIAGE was published in 1616, and it goes without saying that it had all the appearance of a third Rosicrucian manifesto. There is no question that it was taken as such by the rank and file

[1] VITA AB IPSO CONSCRIPTA, already cited.

[2] In his PRONAOS OF THE TEMPLE OF THE ROSICRUCIANS, Dr. Franz Hartmann says that Andreæ wrote THE CHEMICAL NUPTIALS at Tübingen in 1602 and (*read* or) 1603—or prior to the completion of NAOMETRIA—and states in his autobiography that "he intended to give a true picture of the follies of that time." No such testimony is borne. The full passage is as follows: *Superfuerunt e contra Nuptiæ Chymicæ, cum monstrorum fœcundo fœtu, ludibrium, quod mireris a nonullis æstimatum et subtili indagine explicatum, plane futile et quod inanitatem curiosorum prodat.* This has been loosely translated: "After them"—i.e. the Dialogues of LACHRYMÆ—"came CHEMICAL NUPTIALS, teeming with fanciful monstrosities: a playful delusion, which you may wonder by some was esteemed truthful, and interpreted with much erudition, foolishly enough, and to shew the emptiness of the learned." It is obvious that an alchemical romance, whether written in jest or earnest, is not calculated to exhibit a picture of the time, though a romance written on the subject would indicate that alchemy was in vogue. I have rendered *cum monstrorum fœcundo fœtu* "with its fœtus fruitful of monsters," as one who offers a literal meaning crudely. "Teeming with fanciful monsters" is paraphrase rather than translation and inexact even as such. The meaning of the Latin clause is that Andreæ's juvenile book of wonders proved a prolific source of other ridiculous inventions—e.g., alchemical commentaries thereon. The passage in any case does not signify an allusion to two works: (1) THE CHEMICAL MARRIAGE and (2) some other production, not named by its title but described as begetting a brood of nightmares—e.g., the FAMA. As one instance of the alchemical commentaries see the anonymous PRACTICA LEONIS VIRIDIS, published in 1619 under the initials C. V. M. V. S. For the rest, it is obvious that the MARRIAGE, published in 1616, did not produce the FAMA of 1614 or CONFESSIO of the following year.

[3] Compare p. 46 of the VITA and its reference *ad Fraternitatem Christi* as formulated in his INVITATIO and described as *Ludibrio illi Rosicruciano oppositam.*

of enthusiasts who had received FAMA and CONFESSIO into their heart of hearts. Whether it was regarded seriously by the better class of expositors on the defensive side may be open to question. It is significant, at least, that it was never mentioned by Maier, among the fervent German apologists, and never by Robert Fludd. One must be cautious about definite statements, but I do not remember that it was a subject of either criticism or allusion on the part of hostile writers—for example, Libavius. Commentaries notwithstanding, it is probable that neither class knew how to regard it, and it was avoided prudently by both—notwithstaning the impression produced on the German world of alchemy.

It is, however, of palmary importance on the historical side. If it was produced by Andreæ in 1602 or 1603 as an excursion in the world of fantasy, or otherwise as a kind of hoax, to palm off on alchemists a mere boyish invention as a thing of serious importance, it is to be observed that his production remained in manuscript till he was nearly twice the age at which it was written and that he published it in 1616, unquestionably as a contribution to the Rosicrucian subject of debate. He did this either as one who was working from within the circle out of which the manifestoes came or as one who was without, acting on his own initiative. In either case—according to his personal testimony—it was jest, hoax or fantasy. I can understand the *ludibrium* designation more easily by supposing that he was without and that he issued NUPTIÆ CHYMICÆ to confuse the issues of debate. The internal evidence of the text lends colour to this speculation in a rather curious way. The honour conferred therein on those who attended the marriage was the Order of the Golden Stone, not of the Rosy Cross. To this they were bound, this and no other they were pledged to maintain inviolable, subscribing to its various laws. Nothing in the story itself arises out of the fact that it is told by Christian Rosy Cross; nothing again follows from the fact that he called himself a Brother of an Order which bore his own name. So far as the story—under the circumstances of its production—can be said to have any sub-surface meaning, which is of course in pretence only, it belongs to the literature of the Philosophical Stone and takes its place as such among alchemical texts. Supposing that Andreæ was not himself initiated—if I may use such a term—however well he may have been acquainted with those who were, and supposing that he regarded then, as he certainly regarded afterwards, the whole movement as a thing of folly, the fact that he had in some pigeon-hole his boyish fantasia may have prompted him to foist it on apologists and accusers as a priceless contribution to the story of the mythical R∴C∴ founder. To the words CHYMISCHE HOCHZEIT—*id est*, NUPTIÆ CHYMICÆ—of the original title he added Christiani Rosencreutz, with a few lines in the text,[1] and the trans-

[1] I imagine that no one has realised previously the very slender connection between the CHEMICAL MARRIAGE and the Rosy Cross, outside the ascription of its title and its reference to ungodly alchemical books, making use of Divine Emblems. Let us see, however, what was actually done by Andreæ if, according to the hypothesis above, he converted it into a document of the Order. (1) He represented C∴R∴C∴ as placing four roses in his hat when he set out to attend the wedding. (2) At the Portal of the Hermetic Castle he caused C∴R∴C∴ to describe himself as a Brother of the Red Rosy Cross and to be greeted by his own name of Rosencreutz when his fellow-alchemists accosted him. (3) Virgo Lucifera is made to ask C∴R∴C∴ for the roses in his hat. (4) At the triumphal return to the Hermetic Castle on the seventh day, he and the Warden of the Tower ride with the young King, each bearing a white ensign embroidered with a Red Cross. (5) However, at the end of all C∴R∴C∴ writes his name in the Chapel of the Knightly Order to which he has been admitted, the inscription being Fr∴ Christianus Rosencreutz, not adding, however, *In Ordine Roseæ Crucis*, but—on the contrary: *Eques Aurei Lapidis*. It follows that THE CHEMICAL MARRIAGE is inwardly, outwardly and only as if a memorial extracted from the chivalrous archives of an Order of the Golden Stone, which was also arbitrarily connected by the fact of its badge with the Order of the Golden Fleece. The latter was instituted at Bruges in 1429 by Philip III, Duke of Burgundy, to commemorate his marriage with Isabella, daughter of John, King of Portugal.

formation was complete for his purpose. My suggestion is that the original manuscript was interpolated to this extent, that the additions thus made were quite unnecessary to the text, the issues of which are indeed confused by the introduction of matter belonging to the Rosy Cross. If this hypothesis is justified, the later literary history of Andreæ in connection with the Order falls into its logical place. It has been pointed out that he never denied his connection with the Rosy Cross, but his unwise act made him the author of its third presumed official document, being that also which was next to the first in apparent consequence. He could not therefore deny, and the whole truth he was apparently unwilling to tell; there were alchemists of the period who might have turned to rend him. Long after only—in the unpublished VITA—he registered the bare fact of authorship at a period when the subject seemed to all intents and purposes dead and done with for the time being in Germany. The subsequent publication of this memorial he bequeathed apparently to future generations and the care of time and circumstances. Meanwhile the issue of THE CHEMICAL MARRIAGE anonymously in 1616 was followed presently by tracts of identical authorship, whether issued or not under the name of Andreæ, in which his hostile and derisive opinion of the Rosicrucian subject appears in unmistakable terms. The Rosicrucian who was not a Rosicrucian, the alchemist who was not an alchemist, the Lutheran theosophist who had no part in the sciences called occult, no doubt repented at his leisure of that which he had done in his haste.

It will be observed that my colourable hypothesis, thus tentatively expressed, accounts in a natural manner for the fact that NUPTIÆ CHYMICÆ was printed some thirteen or fourteen years after it was written. But I will now take the other side of the question and assume for a moment that Andreæ was connected directly with the Rosicrucian movement, conspiracy or experiment, *ab initio.* He may have founded the Order or been connected intimately therewith as one of those who did; it may have existed on paper, or he and his coadjutors may have incorporated themselves. He may have written FAMA and CONFESSIO, or he may not; but if not he was one—let us say—of a close corporation from which those tracts emanated. For the moment at least, mere questions of detail do not signify. In any case he wrote NUPTIÆ CHYMICÆ when he was sixteen or seventeen, and as I am abandoning for the time being my previous speculation, I will set aside also for a moment that which belongs thereto, the alleged interpolation of this text for specific reasons on its publication in 1616. Now it is obvious that allusions to an "Order of the Red Rosy Cross" in a work of Andreæ belonging to the year 1602 or 1603 and written then as a *ludibrium* imply one of two things—either that having for the purposes of his romance invented an alchemical Order of the Golden Stone he added casually thereto, for no reason connected with the story, another fictitious fraternity and that, some ten or fourteen years later, it began to be heard of in the world, issuing manifestoes concerning itself and making great claims; or alternatively that such an institution was subsisting already in the hiddenness. On the side of the first proposition there is whatever we may choose to infer from the decorations which I have cited already as worn by Christian Rosy Cross when he started to attend the Marriage: (1) a blood-red ribbon, cross-wise upon his shoulder, and (2) four red roses in his hat.

Now it so happens that the arms of Andreæ, were a St. Andrew's Cross, having a rose in each of the angles.[1] There is nothing in the text to shew that C∴R∴C∴ fixed any-

[1] Wigston points out, in BACON, SHAKESPEARE AND THE ROSICRUCIANS, that the name Andreas signifies Andrew, the patron saint of Scotland, to which also belongs the St. Andrew's Cross, embodied in the family arms.

thing but an ordinary Calvary Cross to his shoulder, and if Andreæ was borrowing from his own heraldic bearings it is difficult to see why he dismembered these by placing the roses in the hat of his hero, so the point stands at its value, with perhaps little therein. But if, on the other hand, in the year 1616 he added the Rosicrucian allusions to his original draft, it was natural that he should interpret the name of the Order in the light of his own armorial device. On the side of the second proposition there is whatever attaches to the symbolism of the Rose and Cross in the NAOMETRIA of Simon Studion, and we have seen that this work has certain points of correspondence with the FAMA and CONFESSIO. If, however, Studion can be said to have founded anything it was the *Militia Crucifera Evangelica* rather than the Rosy Cross, though the first may have developed into the second or given birth thereto. Now, there is evidence, as we shall see shortly, in Andreæ's TURRIS BABEL that he did connect Studion with the Fraternity of R∴C∴, though the allusion is rather indefinite; and this being the case, it has to be remembered that we are not dealing with a casual deponent, putting speculations on record, but with one who had means of first-hand knowledge and unquestionably knew at first hand. He was either acquainted personally with Martinus Crusius, the preceptor of Studion at the University of Tübingen, or with survivors of that generation; he was acquainted with NAOMETRIA—completed subsequently to his own NUPTIÆ CHYMICÆ—though it existed only in manuscript; and he exhausted language in the laudation of Tobias Hess who was connected with *Militia Crucifera Evangelica* and was apparently joined with its activities. It was the comet of a season, for although the memorable REPERTORIUM says that it became a strong sect, we have no other record concerning it; but it is probable that Andreæ saw it shine for its brief period in his precocious childhood and would remember 1604 when he was at Tübingen or in the society of Hess. In the last place, it is possible and not unlikely that he knew Studion himself, though perhaps under another and Germanic name. If the Rosicrucian claims and legend were hatched under the wings of the *Militia* he would be acquainted with the fact at least: he was sufficiently in the hiddenness of the fact for anything that was going on not to be veiled from him. But as there is nothing to shew that he belonged to the *Militia*, so there is no evidence that he was joined to any Rosicrucian activities which may have emanated therefrom. Were it otherwise, it would seem impossible to account on any colourable hypothesis for the alleged fact that he wrote NUPTIÆ CHYMICÆ, containing Rosicrucian references, as what he called a *ludibrium*, subsequently, or again for its publication in the high tide of Rosicrucian controversy, unless all the publications were part of a planned hoax.

Now this last thesis has been put forward, with much care and elaboration, by Professor Bühle, whose considerations on Simon Studion have been cited in my second chapter. Both in Germany and among English writers, here and in America, all hostile scholarship has followed the lead of Bühle; but my position is that everything which has been advanced under this aspect of the subject calls to be unsaid. The thesis—made familiar enough by De Quincey—can be summarised briefly thus. (1) That Germany was a prey to enormous evils in the first quarter of the seventeenth century—notwithstanding apparently the great light of Lutheran Reformation and the lifting of the Papal yoke. (2) That a cry for reform rose up therefore on all sides, as for a second and greater dose of the vaunted nostrum. (3) That in spite of his twenty-six years in 1610 and the unexampled precocity which produced NUPTIÆ CHYMICÆ in 1602-3, Andreæ was an inexperienced young man, on whom the fever of reform had fallen, and he imagined that it might be encompassed easily. (4) That he proposed to work towards it by means of a secret society. (5) That he travelled in search of like-minded enthusiasts, though it is not added that he found them. (6) That he decided on appealing to the follies and manias of the period, or the passion for occult sciences, especially the transmutation of metals and the elixir of life. (7) That he would collect zealots and enthusiasts in this manner and would select afterwards from among them those who might be fitted for his purpose, this being the quest after true philosophy and religion. (8) That to secure efficiency in his appeal he invented an Order drawing secret knowledge from the East and having already a respectable antiquity of more than one hundred and twenty years. (9) That he wrote FAMA and CONFESSIO, which were sent abroad into the world, but—for some obscure reason lying behind the hypothesis—without the author's knowledge. (10) That they produced an uproar of hostility, which convinced Andreæ that he must renounce, disavow and discredit them, or imperil his ultimate schemes. (11) That being gratified, however, by the universal delusion which he had created, he cast more fuel on the flames by further publications—e.g., presumably THE CHEMICAL MARRIAGE. (12) That when he found the delusion growing and taking a firmer root it is said that he was shocked, but apparently all that he did was to satirize the Society in some of his later writings, which are like the tea-pot of De Quincey, unending, *a parte ante et a parte post*, or like a circle, without beginning or end, for their origin is in the cloud and darkness of VITA AB IPSO CONSCRIPTA, hinting at things *quae invito me perierunt*, and their term is in things unknown, which a branch of the Andreæ descendants is said to preserve in its archives to this day. I was planning a quest of these once upon a time, but life is short and the art of this kind of research is long and wasteful. I made an end therefore by ascertaining that none of the unknown treasures were to the purpose of the Rosy Cross.

Such is the thesis of Bühle [1] in rough summary and I will take it clause by clause. (1) Let it be granted in the first place that evils of many kinds were rampant in Germany. The Church Catholic and Latin had been succeeded by a raging crowd of sects, mostly with knives in their boots and clawing at each other's throats ; moreover, the Roman Empire was shaking on the threshold of the Thirty Years' War, so that there was worse to follow, all schemes of further reformation notwithstanding. (2) The schemes were many and were in harmony at one point only, that all of them came to nothing. (3) Perhaps also, whether the persons concerned were young or old, there may have been a general tendency to think that a reformation *coup* could be brought to pass easily : Martin Luther stood alone by his chained

[1] Dr. F. C. Held, the American translator and editor of Andreæ's CHRISTIANOPOLIS, is not only entirely convinced that the FAMA was written by Andreæ, but is either unaware that the allocation has ever been challenged or ignores it in his total assurance. He shews no knowledge of the literature or of the debates arising therefrom. The publication of the FAMA concurrently in five languages is mentioned as if these versions were ready to the hand of the student, whereas those alleged to exist in Latin, French and Italian are utterly speculative, or have been cited in any case by persons who have never seen them. That he should justify CHRISTIANOPOLIS itself is obvious and reasonable enough, but the alleged attempt to class it with the FAMA as to intent and scheme is a travesty on the serious criticism of a very difficult subject. CIVITAS SOLIS, the NEW ATLANTIS and CHRISTIANOPOLIS—with all their differences—abide on a common ground, being all philosophical, ideal commonwealths. Moreover, they share in common an atmosphere of utter artificiality, apart from a single gleam of likelihood. The least preposterous of all is possibly the imaginative excursion of Francis Bacon, which had the good fortune to escape completion. The prototype of all is the UTOPIA of Sir Thomas More. On the other hand, the FAMA relates the obscure beginnings of a supposititious secret society : it is neither of commonwealths nor empires, has no direct eye on the seat of government and no avowed concern with the body politic, except in so far as it might be ameliorated by the substitution of alleged Arabian occultism for the methods of art and science in the Holy Roman Empire. I should add that the ill-starred analogy is not instituted to sustain a claim of authorship, but as a literary point of view which has occurred to the translator.

Bible and alone he shook the Papacy. (4) There is the fullest evidence in his writings that Andreæ saw the evils, with a great longing to reconstruct Society, German philosophy and even German religion, or at least its screaming sects: there is no evidence at all that he ever dreamed of doing so by means of secret societies. His projected *Fraternitas Christi* was neither to be a secret order like later Masonry nor an occult order like the Rosy Cross. (5) He did not travel in search of collaborators, for he was at the University of Tübingen till 1610, in which year—as we know quite certainly—Adam Haselmeyer already had a written copy of the FAMA, he being then in the Tyrol. On the contrary, Andreæ—as we have seen—travelled in search of health. (6) For his alleged decision to utilise the follies of the period there is of course no other foundation than the dream of Bühle. (7) It did not occur to this German Professor that the occult zanies and impostors whom Andreæ despised and denounced were neither likely to be sought by him nor to provide material for his purpose, at least by his own hypothesis. (8) Those who affirm, like Bühle, that Andreæ invented the legend of Christian Rosy Cross affirm obviously that he was a liar and a literary cheat. (9) They have never produced a single point of fact to support their hypothesis, the alleged similarity of literary style between the FAMA and acknowledged writings of Andreæ being precisely the kind of rock upon which many better theses have split before and since. It is the kind of likeness which is recognised by those who want to find it. For a person such as myself who does not, in the last resource, care two straws about the authorship of the early Rosicrucian manifestoes, the only similarity that I can see between FAMA and CHYMISCHE HOCHZEIT is that both are occult fables. Their distinction is that the latter is rich in episode, diversified in pageant and brilliant in colouring, while the former is tame and thin, the great allegorical opportunity offered by the opening of the tomb being missed completely. As to the CONFESSIO, which Bühle fathers also on Andreæ, the anonymous hand which emerges in that wretched performance is far worse than the German hand of the FAMA, and in its Latin I can see no likeness to the Latin of Andreæ—for what such a point is worth. (10) When Bühle dwells on the uproar of hostility caused by these pamphlets, he stultifies himself and the facts. There was hostility of course, but it was out of all proportion to their welcome, in view of the royal news which they brought to all concerned in their subject-matter. (11) They were received with open arms and, as Bühle shews himself, that which on his own hypothesis faced Andreæ was not the hostility but the universal delusion which he had created. (12) The suggestion that he was shocked thereby is assumed simply to account colourably for the fact of Andreæ's severity towards the Order when he wrote about it less or more openly in later tracts. I conclude, therefore, that so far as the Göttingen professor is concerned and so far as those are concerned who have followed him to the present day there remains nothing in our hands to justify or even excuse the alleged authorship of FAMA and CONFESSIO.

In presenting such a conclusion it is a satisfaction to know that it exonerates the memory of Andreæ from a charge which is not less disgraceful because it was preferred by a friend rather than an enemy, and was, on the whole, intended to glorify its subject, not to place a stigma upon him. Whatever our opinions concerning the occult sciences, whether we regard them as connoting a body of secret knowledge or as fantastic and illusory arts, there is no question that at the beginning of the seventeenth century they were pursued with the uttermost zeal by untold numbers who were in search of light and certitude on the mysterious relations between God, man and the universe.

There is little question that at such a period the occult sciences were no manifestly impossible direction in which to turn for aid. Their position was not unlike that of modern spiritualism or psychical research of all grades at this day: (1) in respect of their attractions, (2) of their claims, and (3) of their distinguished exponents. Then as now there was a mass of deception and self-deception; then as now there were innumerable impostors pretending to dispense a knowledge which they did not possess—by means of books and otherwise. Little tracts on alchemy and magic were things of common colportage; needy authors and commercial booksellers lived by and because of them. But those on whom they lived were mainly genuine inquirers, however easy of belief, seeking a guide in the unknown darkness of chemistry and the yet more cimmerian gloom of the unseen side of things. There could be few conspiracies more villainous at that period than an attempt to mislead defenceless students further. If, therefore, Andreæ put forward the FAMA and CONFESSIO, knowing them to be false in claim and fictitious in story, the act was scandalous, and furthermore, in so doing, he entered into distinct covenants for the communication of treasures of secret wisdom which he did not himself possess, and he was therefore like "the rogues and runagates" who are attacked in Rosicrucian manifestoes and in his NUPTIÆ CHYMICÆ. He would have known unfailingly that he was at work for the misery of many. I have indicated in no uncertain manner the very little use that I have for Johann Valentin Andreæ in any of his moods or ways, but in his sincerity I believe at least.

Before, however, dismissing Bühle and his thesis it is desirable to add certain considerations which may tend to exonerate him, at least in part. He was by no means the first person who referred the early Rosicrucian documents to Andreæ as their author. The argument from literary style seems to have been put forward originally by Arnold in the first years of the eighteenth century.[1] He affirms (1) that when Andreæ was of "the ripe but ardent age of twenty-eight years" a book called FAMA FRATERNITATIS was published in 1614; (2) that this was followed two years later by CHYMISCHE HOCHZEIT; (3) that these are the first works [2] in which any notice is given concerning the Order of the Rosicrucians; (4) that they differ totally in character from anything produced by later writers, such as Maier and Fludd; (5) that they correspond so entirely with the acknowledged works of Andreæ that, from internal evidence, they have been ascribed unhesitatingly to his pen.[3] To these opinions and impressions Arnold added an involved story which passed in his mind for evidence and which I will endeavour to elucidate as follows: (1) Among the contemporaries of Andreæ was M. Christoph Hirsch, otherwise Hirschen. He has been identified with Joseph Stellatus, who published PEGASUS FIRMAMENTI during the stormy debate of pamphlets which followed the Rosicrucian manifestoes. (4) He was a pastor at Roba and Eisleben, and he left certain writings which were published posthumously. (3) In these, testifying at third hand, he mentions having learned in confidence from Johann Arndt how the latter had been told by Andreæ—also *sub rosâ*—that he and thirty others, described as theosophists, had sent forth FAMA FRATERNITATIS, so "that under this screen they might learn the judgment of Europe thereupon, as also what lovers of true wisdom lay concealed there and here, and would come forward in consequence." This testimony must be left to stand at its value, seeing that I

[1] See the HISTORY OF THE CHURCH AND OF HERETICS, already quoted.

[2] It follows that Arnold did not know of the CONFESSIO and hence did not know his subject.

[3] He offers no means of dentifying his precursors in this criticism.

have failed to trace in this country a copy of the posthumous writings.[1] It is obviously not evidence that would be accepted in any court of law, and equally certain that a tract with pretensions like the FAMA could bring forward only lovers of occult wisdom or its substitutes, while the judgment of *literati* in Europe would be upon the validity of the claims advanced and—whether confirmatory or otherwise—little to the presumed purpose of Andreæ and his "choir invisible."

I do not pretend to do more than report briefly respecting Johann Arndt and his vast array of volumes, with their loaded pages. He was assuredly a theosophist of his period and might well have been one of the thirty whose combined wits were necessary to produce a pamphlet of approximately as many pages. I imagine, however, that he was nothing of the sort in fact; but he wrote on Jacob Böhme, Valentine Weigel and earlier mystics than either. It appears, moreover, that M. Christoph Hirsch may himself have been a friend of Andreæ and might therefore have learned at first hand what he owed to a third party. There was, finally, another friend, to whom Andreæ dedicated Book III of MYTHOLOGIA CHRISTIANA in extremely laudatory terms, as to *clarissimo et consultissimo viro*. This was Christoph Besoldt, otherwise Besoldus, who wrote at large and too often for our patience in these days. He died in 1646, and is said to have left some record about the plain character of FAMA and CONFESSIO, a sufficiently oracular statement, though believers in the Andreæ authorship have found it plastic and have bent it accordingly to their purpose. But so far as I am aware no reference to the alleged source has been given by anyone. In the memorable year 1614 Besoldt was discoursing on SIGNS OF THE TIMES, but

[1] Or indeed anything in our public libraries under the name of M. C. Hirschen.

the portents of the Rosy Cross do not appear among them.[1]

In the year 1619, and at Argentorati—that is to say, Strasbourg—there appeared TURRIS BABEL, being a judgment concerning the Brotherhood of the Rosy Cross, or otherwise the voice of Fame pronouncing against the FAMA.[2] The publication was anonymous, but it is certain, and there is no question, that it was the work of J. V. Andreæ, after whose familiar manner it comprises a series of dialogues, twenty-five in all, each having three interlocutors, who differ in every section. The seventh dialogue has reference to Alchemy, while the tenth denounces Necromancers, Kabalists, Chemists and other occult schools as plagues of the Republic. Fame, in the last of all, addressing *Obstinatus* and *Resipiscens*, exclaims: "Men have been deceived enough and indeed more than enough: it is time now to set free those who are bound, to confirm the wavering and make the sick whole. Woe is me, O Mortals, from this Fraternity there is nothing left to look for. The comedy is played. Fame erected, Fame demolishes; Fame asserted, Fame denies." This has been quoted in part by nearly every critic, from Bühle downward: I give it for the first time in full. It is beyond question that the voice and witness of Fame—a play upon the title of FAMA—is the witness and voice of Andreæ. Otherwise, the allegorical persons of the sections—*Curiosus*, *Supinus*, *Solicitus*, *Scrupulosus*, *Securus*, *Prudens*, *Astrologus*, *Calculator*, *Conjectans*, several bakers' dozens—represent various opinions, as on the main subject so also on subsidiary matters. A chief point of

[1] SIGNA TEMPORUM, *seu succincta et aperta, rerum post religionis reformationem, ad hoc ævi in Europâ gestarum, Dijudicatio. Auctore* CHRISTOPHORO BESOLDO, Ic. Tubingæ, 1614. It contains two tracts: (1) *De Reformatione Religionis, paceque religiosâ in Germania constituta;* (2) *De Rebus post pacem Religionis a Germaniæ ordinibus constitutam, in orbe Christiano gestis.*

[2] It may be said that in the first section there is an address to the Brotherhood on the part of Fama personified, but it is meant of course in mockery.

interest centres in *Calculator*, who is actually Simon Studion, as appears by the text itself. One of the interlocutors has expressed admiration at the spectacle of heaven on December 20, 1603, to which Studion replies by citing NAOMETRIA *mea* and its deductions from mystical numbers concerning the restoration of Jerusalem and the fall of Babylon. For his companion the position of the stars certifies the solemn pledges and immunities of the Royal Fraternity, while according to Studion the Holy and Roseate Brethren are those whose advent was promised by Abbot Joachim, St. Bridget, Lichtenberg, Paracelsus, Postel and other *Illuminati.* As I do not suppose that Andreæ would have foisted on the author of NAOMETRIA opinions which he was unlikely to have held, I regard as significant the statement thus put into the mouth of Studion. He appears only once in the recitals, and there is no means of identifying the other characters with living personalities of the period. The dialogues are dull and tiresome : they offer, moreover, very little to our purpose on either side of the debate. In the nineteenth section we hear about Fortunate Isles and places more safeguarded, like Fessa and Damcar ; but the reference serves nothing. *Resipiscens* in the final colloquy, speaking after *Fama*, says that he dismisses the Fraternity, meaning as denounced by her, but that it is impossible for him to let down those who grow Roses under the Cross and keep themselves unspotted from the impurities, confusions, delirium and vanities of the world—namely : *vera Christiana Fraternitas.* He aspires to be joined therewith. The allusion is to a Brotherhood of Christ which Andreæ proposed to form and which is here invested with the insignia of the Rosy Cross. It may have been a subtle device in his own view, but it may be questioned whether it recommended the new scheme to any side of the debate. For the rest, I conceive that the various colloquies might confirm in their scepticism those who were disposed to unbelief; but that one among hundreds who were drawn by the talismanic magic of Rosicrucian claims should have been directed into other courses by the declamations of TURRIS BABEL is a proposition which I reject utterly.

In conclusion, as to this text there are certain misstatements concerning it which have passed from hand to hand. (1) Reghellini mentions one, according to which it intimates that Andreæ had demitted from the Rosy Cross, that he might join the Brotherhood of Christ. The French historian of Masonry thinks that the reference is vague, but no such intimation is found in TURRIS BABEL. (2) The English translators of Mosheim state, on the other hand, that it implies or admits that Andreæ "was himself concerned" in spreading the reports concerning the Rosy Cross. It does nothing of the sort. (3) It has been said also to mention M. C. Hirsch, to whose story of the thirty theosophists I have referred already. It would be unnecessary, however, to point out that the name does not occur in TURRIS BABEL, had it not also been added that the mythical story itself is found therein.

A considerable tract, entitled THREE BOOKS OF CHRISTIAN MYTHOLOGY, is also referable to the year 1619, and though anonymous so far as the title-page is concerned, the dedication is signed by Andreæ on October 18 of the previous year. It must be admitted that he who reads it from cover to cover is like a barefooted pilgrim treading a stony road; but in any other subject I should count it a strange thing that most of those who have cited it have gone so far astray. There is Nicholas Bonneville in 1784, who descries the Rosy Cross in all our Masonic symbols and claims to have discovered the characteristics of a Masonic Tracing-Board in CHRISTIAN MYTHOLOGY. Where he does not say, and I confess that his meaning eludes me, having searched in vain for these needle-points of supposed symbolism in the mythological bundle of hay. There is also the Honourable Auberon A. Herbert, who is responsible for stating that the German *Illuminati* of St. Christopher Rosy Cross were a society founded by one faithful brother out of the ruins of the Knights Templar. The authority is MYTHOLOGIA CHRISTIANA, pp. 305, 306, and Herbert adds an explanatory suggestion that the *Frater fidelissimus* was one Sir Richard de Heredom, otherwise Brotocanus or Carbonatus, the last being an anagram of the second name. In his casual and trusting way Mr. Wigston quotes this statement without reference of any kind, it being only too evident that he has not gone back to the source. Andreæ says nothing of the kind at the place cited, or anywhere else in the volume. The section in question is entitled *Ordo Crucis*, and it speaks of the Church having created Christian chivalries—as, for example, the Templars, though none of them are mentioned by name. At the end, instead of an allusion to St. Christopher Rosy Cross, Andreæ speculates why "our elders"—*majores nostri*—attributed the stature of a giant to a certain martyr in the days of Decius who assumed that name which signifies *Christum ferens*, Christ-bearing, exoterically as if he were like unto the Cross of Calvary, but inwardly because he bore the Christ Mystical in his heart. It calls to be said that Herbert had no purpose to serve by wresting the remarks of Andreæ, so it follows either that he mistranslated incredibly or that he reproduced an anterior blunder which I have not been able to trace. These are the kinds of quest that one follows in Rosicrucian research, and this is the profit attached to them. I question whether the many makers of reverie who have quoted Andreæ in the particular connection can have read a single sentence from beginning to end—not to speak of the context.

The THREE BOOKS OF CHRISTIAN MYTHOLOGY contain the now famous paragraph beginning *Planissime nihil*, which has been quoted everywhere as the final judgment of German good sense on the claims of the Rosy Cross, when the debate concerning it was beginning to manifest a certain sense of weariness. It has been favoured especially by those who regard Andreæ as author in chief of the manifestoes, whether as a *jeux d'esprit*, experiment on the mind of the age or planned imposture of a satirist ; but it has proved no less serviceable to those who regard the subject from one of these points of view apart from any definite thesis as to authorship. The observations are placed in the mouth of *Alethea*, the personified Spirit of Truth as conceived at the period by a spokesman of Würtemberg theology under the ægis of the Confession of Augsbourg. " Most indubitably I—*Alethea*—hold nothing in common with this Brotherhood. When it came about, no long time since, that some on the literary stage were arranging a play-scene of certain ingenious parties, I stood aside as one who looks on, having regard to the fashion of the age, which seizes with avidity on new-fangled notions. As spectator, it was not without a certain quality of zest that I beheld the Battle of the Books and marked also subsequently an entire change of actors.[1] But seeing that at this present the theatre is filled with altercations, with a great clash of opinion, that the fight is carried on by vague hints and malicious conjectures, I have withdrawn myself utterly, that I may not be involved unwisely in so dubious and slippery a concern."

The oration stands at its value, which is *nil* on the question of authorship, though presumably the Andreæ hypothesis would postulate that he, speaking in the person of Truth, certifies that he has washed his hands of the whole

[1] The meaning of this statement can be only that those who moved first in the foundation of the Rosy Cross—as e.g. Studion—found others intervening—namely, makers of later pamphlets, who will come before us in the next chapter.

business. It is of course an impossible construction, the testimony being that *Alethea* has never had a hand in the business and now leaves the auditorium. In the address to the reader at the beginning of the third book there is a much more significant passage, which—so far as I am aware—has not been cited at all. The author appeals to God on the audacity of slander against him. He has been represented as a chemist, though he had no furnace ; as a caster without brass ; a brother, when he has no society ; and as a prophet, though he is destitute of oracles. It will be seen that popular report has connected him with the Rosy Cross and has doubtless imperilled his position as an orthodox theologian and minister of reformed religion, and he intervenes to rebut the charge or appeal against it. If there is a halting accent in the process, as it will be seen, I think, that there is, we must remember that there was a skeleton in his cupboard, and the inscription thereupon was NUPTIÆ CHYMICÆ, written at sixteen and published at thirty years old.[1]

There is nothing further in MYTHOLOGIA CHRISTIANA which need, I think, detain us. The tract was followed by a century of " satirical dialogues " under the general title of MENIPPUS. It is supposed to be anti-Rosicrucian, but I do not find that the Order is mentioned by name, though it seems evidently the subject of reference in *Titulus XII*, which is called BROTHERHOOD. A later section is headed AUTHORUM CATALOGI, and alchemists are mentioned therein, but the allusions come to nothing. The last Title is INSTITUTIO MAGICA, and this is the longest of all ; but again it is little to our purpose, except as indicating the unqualified disdain of Andreæ for everything—root and branch—which belongs to occult sciences. This is the prevailing

[1] This notwithstanding, the vital issue is simple : Andreæ denies categorically that he belongs to any Society, and he is lying if his testimony is false. He is guilty of *suggestio falsi* if he belonged to it once and left.

characteristic of all his undoubted writings at this period, and it does not in my opinion connote a revulsion of feeling or a change of view. It is certain that he did not issue FAMA FRATERNITATIS, as one who wove a gracious and talismanic fiction about a circle of secret practices in which he believed and which it was his hope to elevate above the realm of mania and imposture. That is an impossible hypothesis. The alternative advanced by Bühle is merely ridiculous because it postulates Andreæ as imbued with an earnest zeal for reform and seeking to promote it by circulating fraudulent fictions for the advancement of beliefs which he hated, as if these would draw about him the right thinking, right acting and mentally qualified circle essential to his scheme in hand. According to one of his early biographers, he desired earnestly to infuse " a new life into the religious feelings of his age." What manner of new life would he draw from those whom he deemed to be either quacks or zealots, the knaves and fools of false science and false philosophy? But we have seen that, according to others, he, being a young man, a wit and satirist of his day, foisted a cruel hoax upon the German occult mind for the poor purpose of fooling it. This is a possible proposition, but I have shewn why it must be rejected. We may or may not admire Andreæ as a theologian and religious author of his period, but at the very least he was a man of blameless life, while as he understood and realised them he strove for the betterment of his land and period: it is intolerable to fasten a gross slander upon him in the absence of adequate as indeed of any evidence.

I conclude therefore that whether or not the House of the Holy Spirit—as the FAMA testifies concerning it—was built on sands, or was comparable to a house of cards, it was not built by Andreæ.[1] I have given, as it seems to me, the

[1] MYTHOLOGIA CHRISTIANA, Book III, even if it stood alone, is an adequate justification of this view.

only possible explanation of his possible connection with it.[1] In his early life he was acquainted with Tobias Hess, whom he admired, respected and commemorated in glowing terms; he was almost certainly acquainted with Crusius, who did not die till Andreæ was twenty-one, and may even have had a hand in his education; and it is by no means unlikely that he was acquainted with Studion himself. If the Rosicrucian claim and legend were hatched under the wings of the *Militia*, he would be familiar with the fact at least, and perhaps intimately. But as there is nothing to shew that he belonged to the *Militia*—though Tobias Hess presumably did—so there is no evidence that he was connected by membership with any Rosicrucian Brotherhood, either before or after the publication of the FAMA. If there is any one point which emerges with irrecusable clearness from the vast literary output of J. V. Andreæ, it is that he had no concern with the occult sciences, except as a hostile satirist It is true that he wrote NUPTIÆ CHYMICÆ, but that was a boyish romance, and he was not for such reason an "occultist," any more than was William Godwin because he was the author of ST. LEON. When VITA AB IPSO CONSCRIPTA was penned in the old age of the Würtemberg theologian, the *ludibrium* description expressed his way of regarding it after the lapse of a lifetime: in reality it

[1] In this connection I should perhaps mention and dismiss the gratuitous hypothesis (1) that Andreæ was not the founder but the spokesman of the Rosy Cross; (2) that he was appointed to issue the manifestoes; (3) that he restored the Order, this having existed previously. The first view is advanced by Sédir, the second by the authors of THE ROSICRUCIANS, while as regards the third it is to be met with in several quarters. No one has ventured to offer any evidence for these speculations. Compare Dr. Westcott, in the Transactions of the *Soc. Ros.*, on the subject of NUPTIÆ CHYMICÆ. He testifies to "grave reasons for believing that the kernel of the work, the original scheme and the mystical basis was derived from C∴R∴ and his personal pupils in their Temple House of the Sanctus Spiritus one hundred and sixty years before the time of Andreæ," who may have published or edited it. The commentary on this farrago is VITA AB IPSO CONSCRIPTA.

was *fantasia magna*, and it does great credit to his years, as yet untouched by the depressing spirit of homily, not overweighted as yet by the mill-stone clauses of the Confession of Augsbourg. Moreover, he wrote in his own tongue and was not engaged, as subsequently, in the smartness of everlasting somersaults turned in the turgid Latin of the cumbrous German schools. As I intimated over thirty years since and have reaffirmed now, I believe that he dressed up his juvenile extravaganza with a few Rosicrucian tags and tie-ups, to express his detestation of the FAMA, its claims and all its ways, by making confusion worse confounded in respect of the debate, then raging at its highest. It is probable that he knew enough and too much of the zealotry and false enthusiasm which lay behind it. The fact of such detestation appears everywhere, in the important VITA, in the texts already cited, in CHRISTIANOPOLIS and in a comparatively obscure effort like DE CURIOSITATIS PERNICIE SYNTAGMA. The FAMA is always delusion and the Brotherhood always folly.

On the other hand, FAMA FRATERNITATIS is a purely occult document, based on an alleged secret knowledge brought from the Near East. The sole point at which the manifesto can suffer comparison with the aim of Andreæ is over the question of reform. But that which FAMA desired was a better understanding of certain *Magnalia Naturæ*, especially the transmutation of metals and *elixir vitæ*. There is little to shew that it had any job in purely official religion, any more than in politics, being content with the German Reformation as regards the one, and on the other with the Roman Empire. Andreæ, on the other hand, is reported by all his apologists and shewn in all his writings to have been out for religious reform, grounded on the Confession of Augsbourg and directed against Calvinists and Anabaptists. There is no analogy between these things, except in the shibboleth of reform, while the answer to both on the plane of events was one—namely, the Thirty Years' War.

That which the FAMA offered was an open entrance to a House of Great Mysteries, an *aureum sæculum* in prospect, a medicine of men and metals, and yet these things were only *res minores* in the treasury, while it was indicated that they would be made available to those only whose hearts were fixed on some other and *majores res* which were kept in the hiddenness of the House. In this manner the document has the air of dealing in a veiled theosophy: I mean to say that a theosophy of the period seems to be at the back of its claims. We shall see how Fludd transmuted it in the limpid light of his own qualified mysticism, reposing under the wings of the Christian Church in England, as then by law established.

This is how the case stands in respect of all that arises out of the authorship of NUPTIÆ CHYMICÆ.[1] It takes us back to the fact of NAOMETRIA as the first intimation in symbolism concerning the Rose and Cross. Here is the direction to which we are justified in looking for the origin of FAMA FRATERNITATIS, either as we now have it or in its root-form. The text and its legend are to be judged by German occult thought of the period, by the influence of Paracelsus, by the apocalyptic astrology which followed in the wake of Reformation, by the expectation of the Second Advent.

[1] I set aside utterly an allegation reported by Miss Stoddart in her LIFE OF PARACELSUS, namely, that on his death-bed J. V. Andreæ made confession about certain "fictitious pamphlets" which were intended as satirical fables, but they had gone forth into the German world and Rosicrucian Societies had been founded at Nüremberg, Hamburg, Dantzic and Erfurt. The "infection" spread also to Holland and Italy—more especially Mantua and Venice. Miss Stoddart gives no authority, formulates her statement in a curiously confused manner and proceeds to describe the official clothing of Rosicrucians; but it happens to be that of the eighteenth century. In a word, she does not know the first elements of her subject. Pahl, who was one of Andreæ's early biographers, would have been acquainted with death-bed confessions—if any—but he sought to free his subject from the taint of

Simon Studion and his *Militia* stood for these enthusiasms, which are reflected in the Rosicrucian manifestoes, and I should expect to find that these were descendants, lawfully begotten, of NAOMETRIA, were it possible to examine more fully that all-important text. Emanating from such a source in zealotry we need no longer regard them as products of conscious fraud, while we are also saved from accepting the alternative of modern occultism, that they were the work of veiled Masters. Their extravagant fixed beliefs were centred about a mythical or allegorical figure. The FAMA is, in fact, an early vestige of a design which developed subsequently under the ægis of the Rosy Cross—namely, the spiritualisation of alchemy, of which Jacob Böhme offers an independent and contemporary example. The treasures of gold which were offered to the Roman Emperor in the generosity of the CONFESSIO were in reality a wealth of doctrine, while its reformation of all the arts was an apocalyptic light on Scripture. I trace also a certain clouded reflection of old Lullian *philosophia*. It is precisely one of those cases in which a common accident of fortuitous analogy may be taken for something which had a purpose behind it, and I am by no means intending to suggest that the inventor of a so-called Universal Science or the traditional maker of the *materia aurea* of Rose Nobles by way of transmutation is the historical personality

Rosicrucian connections, either as founder or member of that mysterious body. He explains also how the supposed relation arose, namely, that Andreæ conceived various projects for infusing new life into the religious feelings of his age by means of societies and when the Rosicrucians sprang up, claiming a similar programme, the projects were identified, the known personalities in the one case being held to stand behind the *anonymi* in the other. I set aside also an allusion in a letter written by Andreæ to Comenius, date 1629, concerning his *Fraternitas Christi;* saying that it was planned "about eight years ago," *post famæ vanæ ludibrium.* It is quoted by Begemann and I know of it only through the good offices of Mr. F. N. Pryce. No special pleading can suggest that it throws light on the authorship of the Rosicrucian texts.

which is clothed in the vesture of legend by FAMA FRATERNITATIS; but Raymund Lully looks like a kind of prototype in the actual and outer world, as the following tabulation shews:—

(1) C∴R∴C∴ acquired an *Ars magna*, as against the invention of one by the theosophist of Majorca. (2) It included the Secret Medicine of Metals and the Great Elixir. (3) But these, according to his legend, were possessed by Lully. (4) The Universal Science was a great scheme of reform to displace the systems and conventions of established authorities in seats of learning—Aristotle, Averroes and scholastic philosophy at large. (5) But C∴R∴C∴ returned from *Arabia Felix* and the City of Dreams at Damcar on a quixotic mission expressible in the same terms, though the seats of intellectual thought in the German Fatherland had not exactly the same occupants when the FAMA passed into writing. (6) The reform of C∴R∴C∴ was a laughing-stock to the learned of Europe, and Lully—notwithstanding life-long efforts—could gain scant hearing from Church Councils or the Papal seat of authority at Rome and Avignon. (7) The refuge of both was to reduce their systems to writing. (8) In this manner there emerged the Lullists in the one case and the Rosy Cross in the other. (9) Lully was tinctured with Kabalism and so also was the German Order, while the dream of both was to realise the unity of science. (10) In fine, at the period of Studion, the *doctor illuminatus*, Raymund Lully, was still remembered in Europe, his Universal Science was still extant and still had its apostolate. He has been classed among heretics, but he died a martyr at Bugia, preaching to the followers of Mahound, and the process of his beatification was begun. His proposed reformation was anti-scholastic but not anti-papal, and C∴R∴C∴ was a reformer, by the hypothesis of his legend, mainly in the matter of arts and sciences. Lully became a centre of romantic

myth—*il magico prodigioso*—a son of Hermes, with his life prolonged through centuries, at once a saint and an adept. Whosoever wrote the FAMA may have had his story in mind.

We have seen that according to REPERTORIUM the *Militia* became " a strong sect "—that is to say, of Second Adventists, hot gospellers, readers of celestial signs and calculators of mystic numbers. They would have represented as such a consensus of mania which must have been abominable in the sight of Andreæ, for it has to be remembered that he was a man of clear and sane mind, holding to a reasonable mean in the matter of reformed religion, to that, in a word, which—as we have seen—is called Bible Christianity. *Cœteris paribus*, he is most comparable among modern types to Dr. Clifford, whose salient contrast was the Rev. M. Baxter, of THE CHRISTIAN HERALD and the number of the beast. Studion was the contrast of Andreæ—on the one hand, theosophy in the tatters of Barnaby Rudge, and that, on the other, which is represented by THEOLOGIA GERMANICA. There was no sect at the period so likely to have produced the Rosicrucian claim as *Militia Crucifera Evangelica*, and no person so likely to have written the Rosicrucian manifestoes as Simon Studion or his immediate successor, if any, in the " strong sect." I make this statement, remembering that Studion, according to one of my correspondents who speaks with official knowledge, is of serious importance for the history of antiquarian work in Würtemberg, and that his " epigraphical writings " have been carefully " worked through." It is obvious that his qualifications as an antiquary are without prejudice to his extravagance as an enthusiast in sectarian religion. For the rest, and because it is important not to cloud the issues, we shall do well to remember that the manifestoes of the Rosy Cross are not to be judged out of hand and sentenced on the evidence of one of their aspects. When Éliphas Lévi had occasion to put on record that Khunrath was a zealous adherent of the reformed religion, he added—as we have seen—that in this he was "a German of his period, rather than a mystic citizen of the Eternal Kingdom." The Rosicrucians were Germans of their period. But Khunrath was also a catholic and hierarchic mystic, dealing with spiritual mysteries under the veil of alchemy. The Rosicrucians, in like manner, had other doctrines than those of Protestantism and other aims than "the ungodly and accursed gold-making." However vaguely, the fact emerges in the FAMA, amidst the pretence of its occult claim; it comes into full view not long subsequently to the publication of that document; and in fine, but after generations and centuries, it shines radiantly in *lumen vultus Christi*. I conclude that Andreæ, as one standing without, knew all the occult claim *ab origine symboli*, and that he loathed it—also *ab origine*.[1] I conclude also that after its own manner the Order was in earnest as was he himself: that it desired earnestly "the supreme medicine of the world," those other *magnalia* of which the CONFESSIO speaks, the "amendment of philosophy" along the lines of its own zealotry, and a better government to come. There came a time, after many changes, when it began to understand these things in another and higher way.

[1] Compare the article on Andreæ in ALLGEMEINE DEUTSCHE BIOGRAPHIE, I, 441–6. It happens that I have consulted it only after this chapter was completed and am therefore the more gratified to find that it is in general agreement with my own conclusions, namely, that Andreæ was most probably acquainted with the entire "mystification" but was not the author in chief. The article suggests further that he may have tried to turn it towards his own serious purposes, but this seems dubious, especially as it is admitted that he could not fail to recognise the inevitable fact that Rosicrucian fables would unmask themselves.

CHAPTER IX

DEVELOPMENT OF ROSICRUCIAN LITERATURE

It is a matter of common knowledge in almost any handbook of historical reference, that the publication of Fama Fraternitatis created a very considerable stir in Germany. It was hailed with enthusiasm in what must be called the occult circles—not that there is real evidence of ordered fellowship or manifest combination of experimental research anywhere—and the emotions of the moment found vent in pamphlets, corresponding to its own form of appearance—rough and ugly enough—while a cloud of eager aspirants took, as they could take only, the course suggested by the manifesto and formulated their desire for admission into the ranks of the Brotherhood by means of printed letters. The Confessio, of course, stimulated production of all kinds—I mean, judgment and appeal—though the second document proved no more helpful than the first in disclosing the whereabouts of the Order or identifying the persons of its members. As we have seen, there was a suggestion also of let and hindrance, to increase the difficulties and underscore the disappointments of many. For this and for other reasons, amidst the chorus of approval, there arose presently a hostile element in the debate. Not all the alchemists of that period, not all the Lutheran theosophists were prepared to accept blindly an unsupported account of itself which the Brotherhood had been pleased to put forward as the warrant for a proposed amendment of that crooked and misguided time, nor was the necessity of reform to be admitted without demur by all and sundry, or the kind of remedies proposed to be passed without challenge, especially in view of their vagueness. But it was the frustrated aspirants for admission who had printed their forms of profession, their letters of humble supplication, who had magnified the unknown Society and found all its claims true: it was these who began ultimately to find themselves on a solid ground of complaint, when they came to compare notes in the booths and the market-places, the academies and colleges, for it appeared that all applications had been made in vain. There was not one of them who was nearer the desired goal than if the Brotherhood of the Rosy Cross had never issued invitations, and they had never responded, accepting all the claims—with a tongue in the cheek or otherwise. As it was an open question whether anyone had been admitted at all, so it began to look doubtful whether such a Society existed. There was too much of uncritical reliance on the fact of the written word and far too much dullness in the mind of German occultism to encourage that side of the question; but it was to be met with here and there. Nor did it occur to any that their canon of judgment was worthless, because it was possible—on the hypothesis at least—that there were receptions of certain candidates; but those who were drawn within the circle and its sanctuary passed into a place of silence, while the clamours increased without on the part of those who were rejected.

I do not doubt that Bühle is right in affirming that some of those in the school courtyards and taverns began to compare notes in a very adverse sense, to say that they had been fleeced and flouted, which notwithstanding, to all intents and purposes, it is clear that they were Rosicrucians themselves, makers of gold in prospect, holding the keys of knowledge or at least beginning to know. In this manner a few may have sought to incorporate themselves fluidically, much as Alsatia and Whitefriars worked more or less in gangs, for the good of the secret commonwealth of rogues and runagates. Beside that which was sincere—if anything—within its own measures, there arose up therefore sporadic impostures, mostly mushroom growths, and they are heard of from time to time. A little later on we shall meet with a supposed case in point at the Hague, but at present we are concerned only with early memorials. Their development and the debate connoted thereby—a thing *sui generis* in literature—may be considered under four aspects, it being understood that I am dealing in the present chapter with publications up to and including the year 1620. (1) By far the most considerable numerically are pamphlets, for the most part in the form of letters, being those to which I have referred, and embodying applications for admission within the ranks of the Order, not only—as I have stated—accepting all its claims, but often couched in extravagant terms of laudation. (2) The issue of independent tracts on Alchemy, Magic and other branches of occult science or philosophy, but prefaced by a fervent dedication addressed to the Brotherhood. They may be regarded generically as theses written with a view to admission by persons who wished to exhibit their qualifications and ardour more elaborately than was possible within the few pages of an epistle. (3) Tracts of a critical character, in examination of Rosicrucian principles, whether the conclusions reached were favourable or hostile. In a few cases it is difficult to determine whether they were written by friends or enemies. (4) Further missives which have the appearance of being issued officially, but dubious for the better part and in some cases almost obviously fraudulent.[1]

[1] They would be the work of those "new actors" mentioned in the *Address* which introduces Book III of MYTHOLOGIA CHRISTIANA.

We may take these classes successively in the order thus tabulated, and as regards applications for admission they connoted in all cases professions of faith not only in the Order itself, its affirmations and titles of sanctity, but in its peculiar religious, philosophical and pseudo-scientific principles. In a word, the postulants were anxious to establish that they were protestants of their period, who loathed the Man of Sin; that they denounced Aristotle; and that they were true disciples of Hermes. They signed their productions occasionally with names which may be taken as real, more often with symbolical titles and even with initials only. Some of them supplied addresses, obviously to encourage communication, but many letters were anonymous and left the identity of their writers to the wisdom of the Brotherhood. On the external side, the most noticeable fact concerning them is the early date at which they began to appear, lending colour to the story that the FAMA was circulating in manuscript prior to its appearance in print—as we know by the notary Haselmeyer—or alternatively that the Cassel edition of 1614 was not the first published. An EPISTOLA AD REVERENDAM FRATERNITATEM R∴C∴ came to light at Frankfurt in 1613, and is identified with a German SENDSCHREIBEN of January 12, 1614. The author in the latter case is veiled by the initials I. B. P. and offers his assurance that he had read the FAMA on June 28 of the previous year. He had seen also an answer sent by the Order to an application of a personal friend. Other printed applications appeared (1) at Lintz in Austria, under the initials M. V. S. and A. Q. L. I. H., also on January 12, 1614; (2) under the initials M. H. and I. I. on August 14, 1614, from which it follows that the FAMA had come also into their hands; (3) under those of G. A. D. in November of that year. By the hypothesis of Bühle these three publications were prior to the Cassel FAMA, being the first edition of that text which had come within his knowledge.[1] The month of December, 1614, is for some reason the approximate time of publication most favoured by bibliographers, in which case it must have appeared concurrently with Σοφία Παναρετος by Paulus de Didis, but my knowledge of this tract is confined to bibliographical lists.[2] According to the title, it was concerned with that wisdom which leads to the attainment and fruition of a good and happy life, in conformity with the mode and spirit of the favoured Order of Brothers R∴C∴.[3]

As communications addressed to the Order did actually precede the appearance of its first printed manifesto, it will be easy to understand how they multiplied after the FAMA was published and became available throughout the German world. The *literæ quorundam Fraternitati R∴C∴ se dare volentium* would form an exceedingly large collection, could all of them be drawn together. We hear of the Latin CONFESSIO appearing at Frankfurt in 1615, bound up with a sheaf of applications, so described in the title. They came out separately also in all forms and sizes, duodecimo, octavo, quarto, folio, while the fashions in which they addressed the Brotherhood are similarly varied. Among writings belonging to the year 1615, a correspondent, anonymous like themselves, issued a DIAGRAPH at Augsbourg

[1] There would be priority also in the case of Andreas Hoberwechsel, who speaks of the *Fraternitas Crucis Rosaceæ* in a letter dated from Prague on September 1, 1614. See M. Sédir: HISTOIRE DES ROSE-CROIX, p. 82.

[2] It appeared in 1614 without particulars of place or publisher.

[3] As there are very few examples in England of the petitions put forward by candidates, I may mention for those who are curious on this unprofitable subject a folio volume labelled Liber H, being No. 1459 of the Ashmolean MSS. It contains in the writing of Ashmole: QUINQUEGENARII CUJUSDAM VIRI, *qui per* 20 *annos arcana investigarat*, EPISTOLA *ad Fratres Roseæ Crucis, in eorum Fraternitatem se recipi petens.* It occupies folios 280–2 of the volume and a note says that the petitioner *anagrammatice se nominat in calce —Tellus Astri Solis.*

and dedicates it simply *Fratribus Roseæ Crucis.*[1] Another who offers no indication of place, explains that he is a friend who is devoted especially to the glorious Fraternity and most Illustrious Order.[2] In the opinion of L. G. R., it is not only illustrious but reverend, and his considerations are submitted to their Worships in metrical form, as one who would give a test of merit.[3] Under date of January 12, an apostle of the absolute wisdom proffers a simple response to the highly illuminated Order.[4] It is called honourable by another, as if one who reserves his speech, but for him the mysterious sodality dwells in some thrice-guarded island of the blessed.[5] On September 4, M. B. chooses a laconic style and sends forth a RESPONSION at Amsterdam which does not waste words in the matter of laudation.[6] For C. V. H., it is a Christian and High Fraternity.[7] But the superlatives tend to predominate, so that the simple prayer of a Frankfurt layman, who is however a friend of wisdom, has rather a cold air and contrasts with him—H. R. —who on September 17 wishes eternal salvation in God to the Sons of True Wisdom, or with the splendid intent of an unknown who has neither local habitation nor name, but in answering the Illustrious Brotherhood proposes to

[1] DIAGRAPHE *Fratribus Roseæ Crucis*, Augsburg, Schultess, 1615. It appeared in quarto.

[2] SENDSCHREIBEN *an die Glorwürdige Brüderschaft des Hocherleuchte Ordens vom R.·.C.·.*, etc. Dated from Camposala on Jan. 29, 1615.

[3] EPISTOLA *ad Illustrem ac Reverendissimam Fraternitatem* R.·.C.·. *metro legata, ad eosdem missa a* L. G. R. Frankfurt, 1615.

[4] SENDSCHREIBEN *oder Einfeltige Antwort an die Hocherleuchte Brüderschaft dess Hochl. Ordens dess R.·.C.·.*, etc. Frankfurt, 1615. Compare in respect of terminology a letter signed J. D. Z. L. and addressed to the high, laudable Brotherhood of the enlightened, inspired, noble and dear Men of the Rosy Cross. A confidential and benevolent Epistle. The date is Aug. 10, 1615, and the motto is taken from PSALM xxxvii. 10.

[5] MISSIVE *an die Hochw. Fraternitet des R.·.C.·.*. 1615, *sine loco.*

[6] ANTWORT *oder* SENDBRIEF *an die Brüderschaft vom R.·.C.·.*, etc., 1615.

[7] EINFALTIGE *und* KURZE ANTWORT *über die ausgegangen Fama und Confession der Christl. Hocherl. Brüderschaft des löbl. Ordens vom R.·.C.·.* (C. V. H.). 1615, *s.l.*

rebuild the Palladium, or ruined Athenian edifice.[1] The palm, however, is perhaps due to one who supplements his missive by a concise philosophical discourse and addresses it to the Godwise Order, which is said to be regarded unanimously as dedicated to Natural and Divine Wisdom, whereunto the anonymous writer is also zealously attached.[2] "The secret of the Lord is with them that fear Him," according to PSALM XXV. 14, and this is the text of the thesis, as it is also the message of its argument. The mottoes behind the title are *In silentio et spe erit fortitudo vestra* and *Nil prophanum in philosophia*. It is a broadsheet of eight pages, dated July 10, the first part being in German and the second in Latin. The few Rosicrucian references make the usual exclamatory display and, of course, convey nothing. What remains is designed to indicate the Hermetic qualifications of the Candidate. The occult name *Lili*[3] is ascribed to the First Matter and is well known to students of the literature as one of the veils of the work. Regeneration and renovation are said to be the beginning, middle and end of fixion, which is certainly true of the alchemical experiment on its mystical side. Another significant allusion is: *Omnia ab uno et omnia ad unum*, and this is a doctrine of experience on the deep spiritual side. It seems otherwise familiar, but I do not remember the source. The philosophical process is: R. *Quinti esse Macro et Microcosmi sine* (*sic*, read *sive*) *Mercurii Philosophici, Ignis Invisibilis cœlestis vivi Salis metallorum ana q.s. Fiat arte magi-philosophica rotando, solvendo, coagulando et fixando.* This is seemingly *Medicina Summa*, and a true process, at least on the spiritual side of Hermetic

[1] REPARATION *des Athenischen verfallenen Gebeuws Paladis samt vorhergehenden proœmium und folgenden angehängten Appendice, etc.* 1615, *s.l.*

[2] SENDSCHREIBEN *mit Kürtzerm philos. Discurs an die Gottweise Fraternitet des löblichen Ordens des R∴C∴.* 1615, *s.l.*

[3] See Pernety's DICTIONNAIRE MYTHO-HERMÉTIQUE, 1787.

Philosophy. Understood thus mystically, it is a key to the following lines :

The Matter, Vase, Furnace, Fire and coction—these are one thing only :
The one thing and the sole one, the beginning, middle and end.
It suffers no foreign substance and is performed without any alien thing.
Behold, in Mercury there is that which the Wise seek.

As it is clear that applications for admission can be matters of curiosity at most, and whatever they may tell us of their writers can throw no light upon the Order to whose consideration they appeal, we can dismiss in a few words the epistles which were printed during the five years subsequent to 1615. The majority continued to be the production of concealed writers and many of them are known only by their descriptions in catalogues. It is interesting to note an example in Italian, addressed to the Most Laudable and Most Virtuous Order, on March 7, 1616, by an unnamed person writing from an unnamed place.[1] On the other hand, Valentin Tschirness has left us the benefit of his identity in full, as a philosopher and licentiate of medicine at Görlitz, when he published, as if at full-finger speed, his RAPID MESSAGE to the Philosophical Fraternity at the place in question, adding his publisher's name, that there might be no doubt on the matter.[2] So also we have cause for contentment with J. Irenæus for his frankness respecting himself on December 3 of the previous year, when he issued an epistle as a disciple of Divine Wisdom at Frankfurt and described the Lords

[1] BREVE ET SIMPLICE RISPOSTA *alla dignissima Fraternita del virtuosissimo Ordine di R.˙.C.˙. Stampata addi 7 di Marzo*, 1616.

[2] SCHNELLE BOTSCHAFFT *an die Philosophische Frat. vom R.˙.C.˙. durch* Valent. Tschirnessum, etc. Görlitz, 1616. Published by J. Rhambaw. The writer says that the denomination Rosicrucian is a popular error, taken from the name ascribed to the founder. Why it was conferred upon him is kept secret. Compare Maier.

and Brothers as venerable, most instructed and highly enlightened men.[1] Intermediate between both are certain students of three liberal and most respectable Arts—not more specifically described—who addressed the August Fraternity from Rostoch on June 11.[2] There were many other missives to the glorious sodality in the same year, and among those of 1617 I note an anonymous answer—to the FAMA specifically—in Dutch,[3] a reply dated from Leipzig on November 16,[4] and a benevolent message from two courageous *anonymi* issued at Oppenheim on March 20.[5] There was also a *Sendschreiben* addressed to the Fraternity at the centre of Germany, but I have no particulars concerning it.[6] In 1618 it is only necessary to mention an Address to the Decemvirate of the Brotherhood on the part of a secret key to the Castle which can scarcely be opened—but this I suppose to be fooling;[7] two missives to the Glorious Fraternity which appeared at Frankfurt;[8] and a

[1] *Ad Venerandos, Doctissimos et Illuminatissimos Viros, Dom. Fratres S Roseæ Crucis* EPISTOLA J. *Ειρηναιου, Divinæ Sophiæ alumni.* Francofurti, 1616

[2] EPISTOLA trium liberalium et honestissimarum artium studiosorum ad Augustam Fraternitatem R∴C∴. Rostochii, 1616.

[3] *Ontdeckinghe van een onghenoemde* ANTWORDE *of der Famam Frato, sine loco,* 1617. The author, according to Kloss, was Andreas Hoberveschels von Hobernwald.

[4] EINFALTIGS ANTWORTSCHREIBEN *an die Hocherl. Frat. des löbl. R∴C∴.* Datum Leipzig, den 16 Nov., 1617.

[5] WOHLGEMEYNTES AUSSCHREIBEN, *an die Hochw. Frat. des R∴C∴. zweyer ungenannten biederleuth.* Published at Oppenheim by H. Palthenius, 1617.

[6] SENDSCHREIBEN *an die R∴C∴. in Centro Germaniæ,* 1617. The things which I have been unable to consult are no doubt in analogy with those made available in my research. The particular " Missive " under notice would be as much and as little to our purpose as BREVE RESPONSUM *ad amicam invitationem celeberrimæ Fraternitatis Roseæ Crucis utcunque concinnatum,* published in 1617, the text being dated October 23 of the previous year. It is a pamphlet of eight unnumbered pages and is a medley of prose and verse in praise of Paracelsus : after such strange manner does an anonymous aspirant reply briefly to a friendly invitation.

[7] SENDBRIEF *an die Herren des Decemvirats der Frat. der R∴C∴. vom geheimen Schlüssel des fast uneröffentlichen Schlosses.* 1618, *sine loco.*

[8] ZWEI SENDSCHREIBEN, *etc.* They appeared in a single pamphlet.

RESPONSUM[1] with an unintelligible epigraph concerning a lion which trusts in the cross and a light sufficing for those who advance in faith. I note under date of June 14, 1619, a letter to the Holy Fraternity,[2] introducing an appended parable and the explanation thereof. It is the last which needs to be cited, for by this time the controversial aspects of the subject had put an end to the letters of simple believers. Those who desired the Society went to work in another way, it being tolerably evident that a Rosicrucian Order was about somewhere in Germany, whether or not it was identical with that which first published the FAMA.[3]

There is no cause to particularise at length on works dedicated to the Brethren of the Rosy Cross, having explained already the motive which actuated the procedure in most cases. I have shewn in my first chapter that the occasional practice was likely to dig pitfalls for unwary modern writers, the case in point being Dr. Dee's edition of the VANITY OF MAGIC. Probably the first dedication in point of time was inscribed by Johann Faulhaber, " with humility and sincerity," to the " most enlightened and famous Brothers R. C." It was prefixed on September 1615, to his ARITHMETICAL MYSTERY.[4] Faulhaber was a professor of mathematics at Ulm and a writer on this subject ; but he had also alchemical interests and was

[1] RESPONSUM *ad Fratres Rosaceæ Crucis Illustres.* 1618, *sine loco.* The writers were Hercules Ovallodius, Hermannus Condesyanus and Martinus a Casa Cegdessa Marsiliensis, who pleaded for admission because of the evil times. They regarded the Brethren as instruments of Divine vengeance in the consummation of the age.

[2] DEMÜTIGES SENDSCHREIBEN *an die Hoch. Gottselige und Heilige Frat. der R.∴C.∴, etc.—sine loco,* as usual.

[3] I have been unable to trace particulars of Kloss, No. 2509, in which the Fraternity was supposed to answer certain communications received. It appeared in 1617.

[4] MYSTERIUM ARITHMETICUM, *sive Cabalistica et Philosophica Inventio, nova admiranda et ardua, qua numeri ratione et methodo computantur . . . illuminatissimis laudatissimisque Fratribus R.∴C.∴ Famæ viris humiliter et sincere dicata.* Vlmens. *Calendis Sept.,* 1615.

doubtless drawn by these to the claims and pretensions of the Rosy Cross. Much about the same time Jacob Schelling published his work on the nature of the eyes, entitled OPTHALMIA, which he submitted for judgment and criticism to the Honourable Order. This dedication is dated April 9, 1615, and the folio appeared some time in the same year.[1] A late dedication to the Brethren of the Rosy Cross was that of Thomas Vaughan's ANTHROPOSOPHIA THEOMAGICA in 1650, and—as we shall see in its place—the motive was identical with that which I have ascribed to those who first made the experiment.[2]

My third section will call for consideration in detail as it stands for the great debate which proceeded without intermission during the five years ending with 1620, though we shall find later that it had not finished altogether at that date. It is exceedingly various in character and is difficult to present synthetically, as it lends itself to numerous distinctions. I shall set aside from the present consideration all tracts which, in virtue of any pretence, may be regarded as official publications, including those —if any—which claim, falsely or truly, to be written by individual members of the Order. They belong to my

[1] Jacob Schelling: OPTHALMIA, *sive Disquisitio Hermetico-Galenica de Natura Oculorum.* In Latin and German. Erfurt, 1615. There was also M. Potiers' NOVUS TRACTATUS CHYMICUS, *de vera materia, veroque processu Lapidis Philosophici.* It was dedicated devoutly to the Brotherhood and included a true and sincere judgment on the claims of the Order. The place of publication was Frankfurt, *anno* 1617. There was finally RAPTUS PHILOSOPHICUS, 1619, a book of revelations addressed to the Brethren in humility.

[2] It was in reality the last, because CABALA, SPECULUM ARTIS ET NATURÆ IN ALCHEMIA, 1654, is a Latin translation of CABALA, *oder Spiegel der Kunst und Natur in Alchemie*, which appeared at Augsbourg in 1615. The preface is signed Stephanus Michelspacherus Tirolensis, who terms himself an ardent worshipper of wisdom. The tract is designed to shew that the Stone of the Wise is three and yet one. The dedication on the title-page reads in the Latin version: *A strenuo Sapientiæ cultore, et una cum præstantissimi cujusdam Philosophi Diagraphe hujus ipsius argumenti, Roseæ Crucis Fraternitati dicata edita, quo hac in materia amplius nil desideretur.*

fourth section. It will be understood that in 1614, during the first flush of enthusiasm, there was only the voice of praise. It was raised by the anonymous APOCRISIS, called otherwise a lawful response to the greatly renowned FAMA, and is of course an affirmation of its claims, apart from criticism or question.[1] For the rest, it is not to be confused with applications for admission to the Order or pamphlets in the class of petition, as, e.g. those, otherwise negligible, which entreated the wise Brotherhood to issue its promised catalogue of false and sophistic works on alchemy. Speaking generally of tracts written in defence of the Order, there are those which stand at their value as individual testimonies but are without consequence, since they evoked no response or counter-criticism from anyone. There are a few very curious pamphlets which have the air of apologies but are in reality hostile works. There are, finally, those which are answers to direct attacks, and there are the attacks out of which they arose, altogether a notable group.

As regards the first on my list, there was nothing likely to be said about certain JUDGMENTS concerning the Status and Religion of the Brotherhood which were formulated at Frankfurt in 1616 by several anonymous but "well known and most learned men," who are described as separated from each other by their distant places of abode.[2]

[1] APOCRISIS, *seu* RESPONSIO LEGITIMA *ad Famam Laudatissimam Fratrum ac Societatis R.·.C.·.* Frankfurt, 1614. It was reprinted or reissued at the same place in 1615, *cum* CONFESSIONE ET LITTERIS *quorundum, Fraternitati se dare volentium.*

[2] JUDICIA *Clarissimorum aliquot ac Doctissimorum virorum, locorum intervallis dissitorum, gravissima de Statu et Religione Fraternitatis Celebratissimæ de Rosea Cruce, partim soluta, partim ligata oratione conscripta.* Francofurti, 1616. We may compare another but quite worthless performance of the same year which is also of multiple authorship, the persons concerned with the production of its eight unnumbered pages terming themselves Sadrach, Misach, Abednego, Pegasus, Aristæus and Serpentarius. They are Lutherans who regard the Pope as Antichrist, and their

The judgments are affirmed to be important, even to a high degree, but the tract is filled with perfervid adulation of the "holy and enlightened" Brotherhood. It is in reality a bid for initiation and might well have been placed previously with others of its own kind, except that it claims to pronounce as well as to apply. There is also another reason: its medley of verse and prose is like a herald going before and preparing the way for Robert Fludd at his best on the Rosy Cross, when he spiritualised the whole Order and its claims—as we shall see in the next chapter. The aspirants before us are in search of no material gold, whether that of Nature in the mines or of Art in the alembics of adepts; and this is their title to consideration, assuming implicitly that the all-wise Order stands guard over the true philosophical and spiritual treasure, a single particle of which is efficacious to transmute the soul. In a word, it is gold of knowledge, by which the pure mind—set free from earthly concerns—ascends to the Courts of Heaven.

Passing over some items which I can speak of by report only,[1] there are two tracts which have been the subject of a previous note, in connection with NUPTIÆ CHYMICÆ, otherwise ELUCIDARIUS CHYMICUS and ELUCIDARIUS MAJOR. The first is concerned more especially with unfolding Rosicrucian intentions on the subject of world-wide

discourse is concerning the star followed by the Magi at the nativity of Christ and the new star "seen by many for years in the German firmament," presumably that in Serpentarius. The pamphlet is entitled: *Ad Fratres illustres nec non doctrina sapientes ροδοσταύρου* EPISTOLA.

[1] As examples of these I will mention: (1) JUDICIUM THEOLOGICUM pronounced on the FAMA and CONFESSIO of the Laudable Brotherhood of R∴C∴ and determining—apparently in the affirmative—whether a Christian can be affiliated to the Order with a good conscience, or without offending against the Majesty of God. It was completed on Jan. 27, 1616, by David Mader, a theologian of Osterfeld and pastor at Nolra. (2) FIDELE ANIMI FIDELIS SPECULUM, by Rudolph de Bry, 1620, *sine loco*. This "faithful mirror of a faithful soul" is an example of official publications—real or

reform and recalls therefore the Universal Reformation translated from Boccalini; but, as indicated by the sub-title, there are many references in the second to the significance and importance of The Chemical Marriage. The author was Radticho Brotoffer, i.e. Christoffer Rotbart. It is the larger and more important of his two tracts, but is in reality a sequel to Elucidarius Chymicus, comparatively a small pamphlet of the same year and both embodying an explanation of the projected reform as an allegorical veil of the secrets symbolised alternatively under the name of the Philosophical Stone. I characterised these tracts long ago as curious and perverse, which remains their proper description. It should be added that although their interpretations are couched in terms of certitude, they do not suggest that Brotoffer wrote as an initiate, testifying from within the Order.[1]

The next work which calls for consideration, entitled Confessio Recepta, was composed in the month of March, 1617, and appeared in the course of that year,

supposed—which have not passed through my hands. It is described in the sub-title as a collection of letters sent abroad by the hands of a certain Fraternity, belonging to no bastard and adulterous generation but to the true and legitimate R.·.C.·., residing secretly over the whole earth. The description is useful for comparison with the testimony of Julianus de Campis, affirming on the basis of his own initiation that the world itself contained only four members of the Order, and also as another indication on the activities of impostors masquerading in its name.

[1] The titles in full are: (1) Elucidarius Chymicus, *oder, Erleuchterung und deutliche Erklerung, was die* Fama Fraternitatis *vom* R.·.C.·. *für Chymische Secreta de Lapide Philosophorum, in ihrer Reformation der Welt, mit verblümten Worten versteckt haben.* Von Ratichs Brotoffer, 8vo, pp. 85. Published at Gosslar in 1616. A second edition appeared in the following year. (2) Elucidarius Major, *oder Erleuchtungen über die Reformation der gantzen Welt.* F.·.R.·.C.·., *aus ihrer Chymischen Hochzeit und sonst mit vielen andern Testimoniis Philosophorum.* 8vo, pp. 234. Published at Lüneburg in 1617. After what manner the two tracts were supposed by Semler to combine the legend of Christian Rosencreutz with that of Caspar Rosencreutz, of whom no one has heard otherwise, it is impossible to conjecture.

without imprint, under the initials A. O. M. T. W. It was written—as the title indicates—to approve the CONFESSIO FRATERNITATIS, which it describes as the Order's act of faith, and the consideration is certified as useful for those who have regard to their temporal and eternal salvation. The Society is not only good and profitable but righteous in the eyes of the Almighty and charged with many great secrets. The Lord Almighty reveals Himself in many ways, and those who follow the Divine counsels can enter into paths leading to true knowledge, with the consequent possession of transcendental secrets. The quest involves, however, considerable study and even indefatigable research, as well as personal sacrifice of other kinds. The Brethren of the Rosy Cross are exhorted to press on with their sublime work. The pamphlet is one of many which in addition to destitution on matters of fact respecting the Order were characterised by extreme poverty of thought and complete lack of suggestion. In what manner the reader's salvation was at stake does not emerge in the pamphlet.

In 1618 it cannot be said that simple applicants, accusers or defenders had learned anything by the experience of debate, but the arena was clearing slowly. Some interest attaches to PEGASUS FIRMAMENTI,[1] because it is held to

[1] PEGASUS FIRMAMENTI, *sive* INTRODUCTIO BREVIS *in veram Sapientiam quæ olim ab Ægyptiis et Persis Magia, hodie vero a Venerabili Frat. R.·.C.·. Pansophia recte vocatur, in piæ ac studiosæ inventutis gratiam conscripta a* JOSEPHO STELLATO *Secretioris Philosophiæ Alumno* 1618. We may compare with Stellatus a GEISTLICHER DISCURS UND BETRACHTUNG, by a doctor who styled himself Gratianus Amandus de Stellis, which is in the best manner of Rosicrucian sacramental names. The tract appeared at Oppenheim, also in 1618, with a Rosicrucian reference on the title-page and the following symbol: a Rose encircled by a Crown of Thorns, a St. Andrew's Cross superposed on the flower and a large C at the extremity of each arm, being the initials of a sentence which serves as an inscription, namely, *Crux Christi Corona Christianorum.* The Spiritual Discourse and Consideration is on the proper manner of creating that piety and love which are presupposed on the part of

have been written by Christopher Hirsch, the pastor of Eissleben, at the request of John Arndt, whose acquaintance we have made previously in connection with Andreæ. The name which appears on the title of this pamphlet is however, Josephus Stellatus, described otherwise as "a pupil of the Secret Philosophy." It was published by the favour of Apollo and with the special privilege of the Muses, though the content cannot be said to justify such exalted patronage. It refers to the "Glorious Society" as people dedicated to God wholly and only, while as regards their status they "flourish triumphantly in the fell labyrinth of this world," even as the rose amidst thorns. The Sibylline Oracles are taxed for their homage, and the writer seems to regard them as in some sense the successors of Christ. The tract, speaking generally, possesses all characteristics of its class, or all marks by which we are able to distinguish the typical German advocates of the Rosicrucian Order: (1) Strenuous impeachment of what is called the ethnic, i.e., the Aristotelian philosophy; (2) enthusiastic devotion to the principles of the Reformation and laudation of Martin Luther, who is termed unconditionally "a man of God"; (3) similar praise of Paracelsus, whose allusions to Elias the Artist had caused him to be regarded as the special prophet and preceptor of the Rosy Cross, for the promised *adventus Artistæ* was identified with the coming of the Order. According to Stellatus, there are two chief interpreters of Nature, Hermes Trismegistus and Theophrastus of Hohenheim, after whom—but obviously at a distance—comes the Benedictine monk, Basil Valentine. Beyond this common ground of all the apologists, Stellatus exhibits a great

those who would share in the communion, science, wisdom and fraternal fellowship of the Brethren R.·.C.·., who are said to despise the whole universe and yet to be held in esteem and friendship by God. The counsel is not to love only in words but in deed and truth. There are references to John Arndt, Valentine Weigel and to a so-called EVANGELIUM of Tauler.

respect for his contemporary, the alchemist Michael Maier, and he refers also frequently to THE CHEMICAL NUPTIALS, about the great impression created by which there can be no question, for it had the outward aspects of a romance embodying an ordered meaning. The main inspiration, however, is that of Maier, described as "the most famous poet and doctor of medicine," who furnishes proof infallible from monuments of antiquity that Colleges of a Rosicrucian kind have been always in the world, although not visible to all. Whether Maier succeeded in establishing a valid analogy will be seen in the chapter devoted to this famous Son of Hermes. Stellatus seems further to infer from the testimony of Bernard Trevisan that the celebrated TURBA PHILOSOPHORUM originated from some such source as a secret society and was therefore edited rather than written by its reputed author Aristæus.[1] There is a reference also to a congress of "certain brethren," held from time to time at such towns as Frankfurt. That there were conventions of this kind is perhaps inevitable rather than a matter of possibility, just as there was a *Militia Crucifera Evangelica* and a conference which formulated the Confession of Augsbourg; but as a contribution to Rosicrucian antiquities they are cited to little purpose.[2]

[1] The TURBA was a great authority for Trevisan, but he says nothing of the sort. The reference of Stellatus is probably to a passage in THE NATURAL PHILOSOPHY OF METALS, which represents Aristæus or Arisleus (1) as Governor of the universal world for sixteen years, owing to his great knowledge and understanding; (2) as convening the disciples of Pythagoras who—"as we read in the Chronicles of Solomon" (*sic*)—was the most wise of men after Hermes. The TURBA is "the code of all truth" and truth above all falsehood. Hereof is the witness of Trevisan. The Rosicrucian apologist accepts the *Dramatis Personæ* of the old debate, explicitly and implicitly, as those whose names they bear and as assembled in actual session, however divided in time, in which case, since they were adepts of a secret science, they would constitute a secret society. But I have stated elsewhere that the TURBA bears all the marks of a manufactured thesis, not of a report.

[2] There is nothing in the tract of Stellatus which lends any colour to a supposition that he was himself an initiate of the Order or one of its

"To you it is given to know the Mysteries of the Kingdom of Heaven" are words of Christ which the Echo applies to the Order. There were darker things in the mind of yet another anonymous who penned a Judicium on the Seal and Trumpet, and on the Mystery of the Reformation to come, according to the Fellowship of the Rosy Cross.[1] The Trumpet is that of the last Jubilee, and the Seal appears to connect with those ominous words of the Apocalypse: "One woe is past; and, behold, there come two woes more hereafter." There is much on the Key of David, the Corner Stone and the coming of the Holy Kingdom. We hear also in strange symbolism concerning the Fount of Life, and although there are no Rosicrucian references anywhere in the text itself, we are assured at the end of all that whosoever has doubted

early substitutes, nor indeed that he was acquainted with anyone who occupied such a position. What is more, the same statement, without need of modification, applies to the anonymous and pseudonymous partisans practically all round, the few excepted—well under six—who, at least by their own hypothesis, wrote officially as members. The others discuss divisions of philosophy, the several pillars of science—*de omni re scibili*—but leave their readers no wiser than before on the true issues of the whole investigation.

[1] F.∴R.∴C.∴ Fama e Scanzia Redux. *Buccina Jubilei ultimi. Eoæ Hyperboleæ prænuncia montium Europæ cacumina suo clangore feriens, inter colla et convalles Araba resonans.* 1618, *sine loco.* The last sentence reads in English: "Hyperbolic prediction of Eos, smiting with resplendent noise the summits of the mountains of Europe, sounding amidst the hills and valleys of Arabia." The English, however, is one thing and the meaning—if any—another. As regards the settlement of all doubts concerning the Order, the affirmation is expressed in the two following lines:

Quisquis de Roseæ debitas Crucis Ordine Fratrum,
Hoc lege, perlecto carmine certus eris.

To quote them reminds me of another pamphlet, containing some twenty pages of German verse, said to have been written originally in Latin by a Brother of the Society and printed by I. S. N., described as *Publicus et Poeta Coronatus*—perhaps a laureate of the Order. The preface is dated September 16, 1617, and the pamphlet was published at Neustadt in the following year. The title is Ara Fœderis Teraphici, followed by the letters F.∴X.∴R.∴, meaning *Frater Crucis Roseæ.*

concerning the Order will be assured after reading, which notwithstanding I am unable to determine whether it is a defence of the Order or a judgment which relegates it among the seven last plagues. It is not unlikely that the Unknown Superiors of the Mystery were in a similar position at the time. If anything on the Rosicrucian subject fell still-born from the press, amidst all the curiosity and fever, it was surely FAMA E SCANZIA REDUX.

The REDINTEGRATIO of 1619 places on its title-page an epigraph from Holy Scripture which is in strong contrast to that of the preceding tract: *Omnes de Saba veniunt, aurum et thus deferentes, et laudem Domini annunciantes.* There are obviously all things good to follow from the coming of the Order. There is not only such an institution but it is in possession of great secrets—*Magnalia Dei et Naturæ.* The activities of the Brotherhood may be shared by all and any with a good conscience and with due regard to the sanctions of their Christian faith. The reproaches which are cast at the Order are therefore of no effect, as for example (1) that its members are enemies of lawful governments; (2) that they are Calvinists or Jesuits; (3) that the whole business is farcical, having some undisclosed purpose in view. There is a bid for initiation in certain prefatory verses dedicated to the *pia turba sophorum*, in which the author describes himself as a friend, hoping to be regarded propitiously and admitted within the ranks.[1]

[1] Φλενσθιουρε ανδας, *id est* REDINTEGRATIO *an die Frat. vom R.·.C.·. dass man sich mit gutem Gewissen derselben mag theilhaftig machen.* 1619, *sine loco.* It does not appear in what sense the Order was renewed by affirming that it could be joined with a clear conscience. This tract may be compared with THEOSOPHI EXIMII EPISTOLA . . . *de Sapientissima Fraternitate R.·.C.·.*. Frankfurt, 1619, the text itself being dated September 3, 1617, and signed with the initials C. R. E. The person addressed is Anastasius Philaretus Cosmopolita and the letter replies to a question raised by him in regard to the Brotherhood. It is a defence of the Order on the ground that its religion is that of the Word of God and the Catechism of Luther. There is

The last tract offers a path of transition to the next stage of our research, for it indicates that the religion of the Order had become a rock of offence. I have mentioned already an implied suspicion that the original manifestoes protested too loudly and that Adam Haselmeyer—perhaps with a bee in his bonnet—scented the Jesuits at work behind the pamphlets. This—as we know—was in 1610 or thereabouts, and there could be nothing more fanciful on the surface. In 1616 Daniel Cramer, a Protestant theologian who taught at Wittenberg and Stettin, produced a tract entitled SOCIETAS JESU ET ROSEÆCRUCIS VERA,[1] which connected the two institutions, and the fact was not likely to be lost at that period, though it was not a polemical treatise but a collection of forty emblems and letterpress on the name of Christ Jesus. About the same time and at Frankfurt, Christianus Philadelphus, described as a lover of *pansophia*, the catholic wisdom, produced a meditation on the symbol, cipher or sign of the father original of the Rosy Cross, leading up to an inquiry concerning the religion of the Brotherhood.[2] It is obvious, the seal of Martin Luther notwithstanding, that the Rose centred on a Cross is not suggestive of the Protestant Reformation in any of its forms or ways. Moreover, the

a vague suggestion that the writer was speaking with first-hand knowledge of the subject. There is also WOHLGEMEYNTES ANTWORT-SCHREIBEN *an die Frat. von R∴C∴*, the text of which is dated July 8, 1618, but it did not appear till 1619, when it was published at Frankfurt. It is a pamphlet of eight pages, signed S. V. S. P., and deals generally with FAMA and CONFESSIO, giving reasons why all pious persons should be ranked on the side of the Order. The title claimed by the writer is that of *Philotheosophus*.

[1] The sub-title reads : *Hoc est, quatuor decades Emblematum Sacrorum de Nomine et Cruce Jesu Christi*. D'Alembert's ENCYCLOPÉDIE, *ou Dictionnaire Raisonnée des Sciences, des Arts et des Métiers*, T. XIV, 1765, mentions a counter-charge on the part of Christophorus Nigrinus, namely, that the Rosicrucian Brethren were disciples of Calvin.

[2] EULOGISTIA *e Symbolo Patris Primarii Roseæ Crucis, qui dicitur, cujusnam sint Religionis, Scripta a Chri : Philadelpho, Pansophiæ Amatore.* Francofurti, 1616.

vaunted new philosophy was admitted to contain "much of theology"[1] and implied a general reformation respecting Divine Things as well as those that are human.[2] It was to be expected therefore that many would ask, with Libavius in 1615: "What manner of new theology is this . . . ? Again, where is its novelty, if it be that of the primitive Church? Is it of Gentile, Jew, Mahommedan, Papist, Aryan, Anabaptist, Lutheran, or follower of Paracelsus?" The most definite charge—though still in a manner of questioning—was formulated in 1619 by a tract entitled ROSA JESUITICA,[3] otherwise Companions of the Jesuit Band. The proposal put for consideration was whether the two Orders, being the chivalry of the army of Jesus and that of the Rosicrucians, were not in reality one and the same body, as if the one had been driven into concealment, to emerge later on as the other. The authorship has been referred to J. Themistius de Melampage. I conceive that the pretensions of the publication may be judged out of hand by the writer's alleged protecting office and that the place of original publication was perhaps part of the camouflage.

There should be no need to say that about the last charge which can be brought in the likelihood of things against Rosicrucians of the early seventeenth century is one of being papal in disguise. To prefer it seems comparable to the counter-folly of a certain Jesuit, Abbé Gaultier, who is cited by Charles Mackay as devoting a book to prove that the Fraternity was Lutheran.[4] On

[1] CONFESSIO FRATERNITATIS R.·.C.·., cap. II.

[2] FAMA FRATERNITATIS R.·.C.·., following the description of the Tomb.

[3] ROSA JESUITICA, *oder Jesuitische Rottgesellen . . . von* J. P. D. a S., *Jesuitarum Protectorem* (*sic*). It claims to have been done at Brussels on the day of St. John, 1619, which of the two saints bearing this name not appearing. There was a reprint at Prague in 1620.

[4] *Memoirs of Extraordinary Popular Delusions*, s.v. Rosicrucians, edition of 1852, Vol. I, p. 171.

the surface, it is sufficiently proved by the FAMA and CONFESSIO, and these therefore, still at their surface-value, dispose of the papal charge. The matter of fact behind the whole business is that in a great and ever-expanding cloud of speculation no one knew anything certainly and that almost any view was tenable. Amidst a multitude of applicants some—as we have seen—may have been received within the secret circle, but they did not emerge to testify. It was therefore an open question whether any appeals had been answered; but if they were, there was no knowing whether the replies came from a genuine source. It is very clear that impostors were thought and known to be about.[1] It is to be observed further that there was a strong element of hostility manifested at a fairly early period, the chief case in point being that of Libavius, whom I have quoted already. He was no anonymous, unknown or obscure person, but perhaps the most prolific writer of his period on Hermetic Medicine and Alchemy. He was, moreover, of notable attainments in experimental research, the first person to speak of the transfusion of blood from one animal to another, while a preparation called "the liquor of Libavius" was long used in laboratories. Andreas Libau was born at Halle *circa* 1560 and died in 1618. He has been represented by Lenglet du Fresnoy as a follower of Paracelsus, but was really opposed to the school and recommended it on one occasion to slumber in its own absurdity. The point does not signify, for his firm belief in alchemy might have drawn him well enough in that direction. Among his Hermetic writings may be mentioned DEFENSIO ALCHEMIÆ TRANSMUTATORIÆ,

[1] See Dr. Georg Molther's RELATIO DE QUODAM PEREGRINO, *qui anno superiori Wetzlariam transiens, se Fratrem R.·.C.·. : confessus est et mira fecit.* Francofurti, 1616. It had been preceded in 1615 by "a true history of what passed at Wetzlar with a Brother of the Order of the R. C.," i.e. WAHRHAFTIGE HISTORIE, *so sich zu Wetzlar mit einem Bruder des Ordens der R. C. zugetragen.* Frankfurt, 1615. This was the original German version.

OPUS ALCHIMIÆ PRACTICUM, APOCALYPSIS HERMETICA and ALCHEMIA TRIUMPHANS. They may be termed the records of a worker who had long laboratory experience, which is more than can be said of Michael Maier, though he is a much greater contemporary name in German alchemy. As the warfare of Libavius was less against the doctrine and practice, the claims and *philosophia sagax* of the sage of Hohenheim himself than it was against the *neo-Paracelsica* of his own day, so was his hostility to the Rosy Cross more especially an opposition to its methods rather than its pretensions otherwise. He had written so much and so long upon Alchemy and Hermetic Medicine that he could feel little tolerance for these anonymous upstarts who affirmed in their superciliousness that the art of transmuting metals stood last in the inventory of their secret treasures. He knew in his heart and no doubt reflected bitterly that after long years of labour he had failed to produce transmutation, though he could prove its possibility as he understood the nature of things. Who were they that had done far differently and better, according to their boasting hypothesis, and by what warrant did they denounce "the ungodly and accursed gold-making" or affirm that many books "under the name of *Chymia* were set forth *in contumeliam gloriæ Dei*"? It must be said that Libavius is captious enough in some of his criticisms, gratuitous in his own assumptions, and that—worst of all—he misses the obvious points and the strongest points badly. It is idle to belittle the alleged journey of Christian Rosy Cross in search of Eastern magicians because there were magicians and to spare at home. It is impertinent to affirm that a society ordained by God should be able to prove its mission, for in 1615 there was no such point at issue. It is feeble and sorry commonplace to condemn the secrecy of the Order on the ground that those are lovers of darkness whose deeds are evil. But these are the kind of considerations which fill two folio tracts devoted to the Order alone. The supposed makers of a new theology are recommended to make also a new god, but above all to beware of going headlong into the old perdition; and those who would unveil the *Mysteriarcha Dei* are warned that the "searchers of majesty shall be overwhelmed with glory."[1] It is obvious that the Rosicrucian House of the Holy Spirit—even if more properly it was a House of Dreams—was not likely to collapse when trumpets like these sounded before its gates and walls. The truth is that Libavius was strong in hostile purpose but he had no offensive materials, or only instruments of debate. I have given already his analysis of the CONFESSIO FRATERNITATIS in quite another connection; but having produced the "thirty-seven reasons" of Rosicrucian "purpose and intention," his objections to all and several do not bear citation.

Now, it happens that the star which ruled the fortunes of Rosicrucian hostile criticism must have been provided with a sense of humour which the criticism itself lacked, and it was able to promote in its subjects a marked disposition towards change of mind. It began early with Libavius and continued till late in the story. I do not suggest that he had read over his folios and in cooler moments had found them weak or inconclusive; I do not suggest that they were written prior to NUPTIÆ CHYMICÆ and that because he was an alchemist the glittering pageant of the MARRIAGE brought him to another frame of mind; I am scarcely prepared to affirm that he would have recognised a new spirit intervening in his Rosicrucian reverie, yet it came about that in a final treatise Libavius changed

[1] The Rosicrucian vision of a possible Paradise on earth connoted the Anabaptist heresy, according to Libavius, and he seems generally to have regarded the Order as an Antichristian movement.

his ground.[1] He wrote forty-three chapters, *de omnibus rebus Rosicrucianis*, the Stone of Philosophers, the Magical Language, the Spheric Art, the Universal Reformation as a prelude to the Day of Judgment, the restitution of all arts, the wisdom of Adam, Enoch and Solomon, the Earthly Paradise to come. He was prompted, as he tells us, by the desire and command of certain worthy persons and confessed to a spirit of friendly criticism, by the inspiration of which he proceeded to affirm (1) that the Rosicrucian Order was no mere figment of debate, but a Society which existed in fact; (2) that all persons would be well advised to join it; (3) that there was much to be learned thereby and considerable wisdom to be attained; (4) that it was graced by sound doctrine in things belonging to religion; (5) that it was to be praised for denouncing the Pope; (6) that it had laudable views on Mahomet; and (7) that the value which it set upon the Bible redounded to its great credit. The one thing needful, however, was that seeing the corruption of the world and its incapacity for improvement prior to the Judgment Day, the Order should relinquish forthwith any programme of universal reformation, the same being left to God, and should set its heart upon one of a private kind, restricted presumably within its own ranks and working in the hearts of its accepted postulants.[2]

[1] The Rosicrucian writings of Libavius are (1) De Philosophia Harmonico-Magica Fratrum Roseæ Crucis, incorporated with Examen Philosophiæ Novæ, *quæ Veteri abrogandæ opponitur*, 1615; (2) Analysis Confessionis Fraternitatis de Rosea Cruce, 1615; (3) D. O. M. A. *Wolmeinendes Bendenken von der* Fama *und* Confession *der Bruderschafft dess Rosencreutzes*, 1616. These have been noticed in the text. He wrote also Admonitio de Regulis Novæ Rotæ, *seu Harmonica Sphæræ Fratrum de Societate Roseæ Crucis*, incorporated with Appendix Necessaria *Syntagmatis Arcanorum Chymicorum* Andreæ Libavii. Francofurti, 1616.

[2] It must not be supposed that the Well-meaning Objections did in no sense correspond to their title. Libavius had little use, as we have seen, for the school of Paracelsus, but it was indubitable to him that the Order had sprung therefrom. I suppose that he held himself a Lutheran in the

The hostility of Libavius offered a plain issue on the part of a plain man, though somewhat dull of wit and missing great opportunities, even when he discovered errors and contradictions in Rosicrucian texts. It provoked a reply on the part of Robert Fludd, who is the subject of my next chapter. I refer to the TRACTATUS APOLOGETICUS, published at Leyden in 1617 to clear the Society from "the calumnies of Dom. Libavius and others of his kidney," but especially from charges of diabolical magic and superstition. The mistake of the German accuser was to regard all magic and Kabalism as abominable arts and all astrology as foolish; but the Brethren of the Rosy Cross were concerned only with their higher aspects and practice. The views of Libavius were, however, only a peg on which Fludd suspended an elaborate discourse; but the German critic has the merit, such as it is, of having opened the debate on its hostile side, and this in his own name. The pamphlets which followed seem endless, but we know them in most cases only by their titles in bibliographical lists. Among those which I have been able to see or of which it has been possible to find sufficient descriptions a selection must be made, as it would serve little purpose to analyse obscure pieces which do not count in the debate on either side.

An anonymous FAMA REMISSA appeared in 1616, and the title makes evident its hostility, the manifesto called FAMA being returned to those who had sent it forth.[1] There were in particular two reasons: (1) that the proposed reformation of the whole world was ridiculous as well as

"best sense" of the Church of Luther, but the Rosicrucian expectation of Paradise regained on earth connected it with the Anabaptist sect. A second edition of WOLMEINENDES BEDENKEN was printed at Erfurt in 1617. It must be distinguished from D. O. M. A. CRUX ABSQUE CRUCE . . . *Auctore Vito del Capo de la Bona Speranza*, 1617—a pamphlet of eight pages.

[1] FAMA REMISSA AD FRATRES ROSEÆ CRUCIS, 1616—*sine loco.* There was no second edition.

impracticable, and (2) that the religion of the Brotherhood was abominable in the eyes of the writer. It must subscribe to the Confession of Augsbourg in public and unmistakable terms before it could be regarded as organised for the good of any reform in the German world. An appendix discusses the doctrine of transubstantiation in terms of Bedlam, but it is notable as indicating that at this early stage there was a disposition to connect the Rosy Cross with a peculiar teaching on the Mystery of the Eucharist.[1] The tract produced no answer from any quarter, so far as I can trace: it may have commanded a certain agreement in many directions at a period and in a place which had partisans innumerable of the secret sciences, and an audience for all claimants on this subject, but no toleration whatever for the apostles of a secret religion, which seemed to be represented by the Order.

Among the prophecies of Paracelsus there is one to which I have adverted on several occasions, and previously in the present work, as something that was taken into the heart of all subsequent Hermetists: it is that which foretold the coming of Elias the Artist, in whose glorious day whatsoever had been hidden in the deeps would be proclaimed on the heights, and by inference the secret science would be known throughout the world.[2] So the alchemists looked for his advent. There was, however, a tendency to believe that Paracelsus himself, hailed by his admirers as the great monarch of arcana, was in reality the expected Messiah of Hermetic lore, otherwise Elias the Second. When the Rosy Cross emerged in part from its penetralia by means of

[1] I have failed to meet with a later tract which appeared at Hanover in 1618 and may have carried the Eucharistic question further. This was SYLLOGE, *an Hostia sit Verus Cibarius, a Fratribus Roseæ Crucis donata Rhumelio et Puello.* The author was Theophilus de Pega, an assumed name. The title is varied by Kloss.

[2] Paracelsus; OPERA OMNIA. Geneva, Vol. II, 1658, in the treatise DE MINERALIBUS, and elsewhere in his writings.

published documents, I infer that enthusiasts regarded it as a corporate Elias, who would be therefore Elias the Third. I account at least in this manner for the title selected by a Silesian named Adam Bruxius when he wrote ELIAS TERTIUS[1] in August, 1615, and published it in the following year, as a "judgment and opinion on the Most Illustrious Order of the R ∴ C ∴," in reply to the FAMA and CONFESSIO. Whatever the analogy between the Rosicrucian promised restoration of all things and the saving mission of the promised grand adept, the Order for Adam Bruxius was a false Elias and his judgment concerning it was uncompromising in hostility. The name of the Hermetic Messiah was presumably talismanic and there were new editions of the tract in 1618 and 1619.[2] There is nothing otherwise in the author's record to indicate that he was concerned with the *theosophia* of his period, its theology or even occultism, so why he intervened and pronounced judgment on the Rosy Cross and what his warrants may have been are questions to which no answer is forthcoming.

In 1617 a certain Johannes Sivertus came forward with a proposal to strip off a fantastic mantle, mask or veil, otherwise to produce a "Christian refutation"[3] of CONFESSIO FRATERNITATIS, and to prove that the new self-

1 HELIAS TERTIUS, *das ist Urtheil oder Meinung von dem Hochl. Orden der Brüderschaft des R∴C∴*, etc. 1616, *sine loco*.

2 The second and third editions suppress the name of the writer. That of 1619 specifies the place of publication for the first time—that is to say, Frankfurt. Another ELIAS ARTISTA was issued anonymously in the same year at the same place and included "a benevolent judgment on the new Brotherhood R∴C∴," together with a reply to their two manifestoes, namely, the FAMA and CONFESSIO. It is a German pamphlet of twelve pages, signed L. C. There are references to Galatinus, who wrote DE ARCANIS CATHOLICÆ VERITATIS, Reuchlin, Mirandula and to Paracelsus, especially his TINCTURA PHYSICORUM, *cap.* 4, at the well-known point where Elias the Artist is foretold.

3 ENTDDECKTE MUMMENSCHANTZE ODER NEBELKAPPEN, *das ist, Christliche Wiederlegung der negst von Cassel ausgeflogenevi Stimpelconfession, etc.* 1617, *sine loco*.

styled Brethren of the Rosy Cross neither came with a mission from God nor belonged to Him, but were emissaries of the Father of lies and working to the confusion of discipline. I have no particulars concerning the writer, and as more important criticisms were ignored it is difficult to understand why H. S. F., described as *philophilos*, should have been at the pains of examining, discussing and "demolishing" the arguments of Johann Sivert.[1] He did more even than this, for he followed up EXAMINATIO BREVISSIMA with a second German pamphlet, containing an equitable answer to the same attack.[2] There is said also to have been an EXPLANATORY LETTER on the subject which may have been Sivert's rejoinder, but it seems to have been heard of and not seen,[3] or if seen has been for some reason described only by the bare title.

I proceed now to a summary enumeration of certain hostile critics who occupy a different position from those already mentioned, because their attacks were answered by writers claiming to testify concerning the Rosy Cross from within the circle of its members. The earliest in point of date is Henricus Neuhusius of Dantzic, some of whose findings were dealt with by a writer using the pseudonym of Eucharius Cygnæus. Neuhusius is described on his title-page as physician and philosopher. His PIOUS AND MOST USEFUL ADMONITION[4] on the subject of the Rosy Cross is more properly challengeable in respect of its

[1] EXAMINATIO BREVISSIMA, *das ist, Kürtzliche Erörterung, worinnen sich* JOH. SIVERTI *in seiner* . . . NEBELKAPPE *wider die vom R∴C∴ zeimlich verhauen, von* H. S. F. 1617, *sine loco.*

[2] ANTIPANTZERFEGERIANUS, *das ist, rechtmässige Antwort auf die Scharteke* JOH. SIVERTI, *durch den Autorem der* EXAMINATIO. 1617, *s.l.*

[3] EPISTOLA COMMENTATORIA, *über der Mummeuschantze.* 1617, *s.l.*

[4] PIA ET UTILISSIMA ADMONITIO DE FRATRIBUS R∴C∴ . . . *Conscripta a* HENRICO NEUHUSIO, DANTISCANO, *Med. et Phil. Mag. Prostat apud Chro.* Vetter, 1618. A French translation appeared at Paris in 1623 under the title of AVERTISSEMENT PIEUX ET TRÈS-UTILE *des Frères de la Rose-Croix, escrit et mis en lumière pour le bien public par* HENRI NEUHEUS DE DANTZIC.

statements rather than a hostile tract. It deals especially with the purpose of the FAMA FRATERNITATIS, real or alleged. A preliminary question is one which we know to have been exercising the German world, though I have indicated that prior to 1619, when Neuhusius wrote, there was a sense in which it was settled. The question was whether the Order had any existence in fact. He propounds the question and answers in the affirmative, producing also his proofs, namely, that he had met with members. The next question is as to what manner of men they were, but he was not in their particular confidence, he was not within their circle, and though his note is one of warning there is no grave or specific charge. He dwells most on Rosicrucian religion and thinks the Brethren open to the accusation that they were Anabaptists or even Jews. There is a word also on their horror of Latin Christianity and their disinclination to mix with persons of that faith. There are, further, indications that he regarded the Rosicrucian projected reformation as almost connoting revolution. In fine, however, he reports the removal of the Order to India, presumably a derisive commentary on its manifold activities at the period in the German press. Eucharius Cygnæus replied in CONSPICILIUM NOTITIÆ,[1] the "Observatory of Knowledge" in question being presumably the Order House of the Holy Spirit. The admonition of Neuhusius was in his opinion futile. I do not think that the admonition matters greatly, or the answer.

A more notable opponent of the Order wrote under the name of F. G. Menapius, who has been identified as Johannes Valentinus Alberti—according to Bühle and others—a personal friend of Andreæ. There are alternative

[1] CONSPICILIUM NOTITIÆ, *inserviens oculis ægris, qui lumen veritatis ratione subjecti, objecti, medii et finis ferre recusant. Oppositum Admonitioni futili* HENRICI NEUHUSII *de Fratribus R.·.C.·. ab* EUCHARIO CYGNÆO PHILADELPHO ET PHILALETHEO. 1619, *s.l.*

attributions, but one and all seem hypothetical in the highest degree. His first attack on the Society was written under date of June 3, 1617, and was in Latin, a German version following on July 15. This is certain from particulars furnished by Florentinus de Valentia, who in the autumn of the same year replied to the "inconsiderate calumnies" by issuing ROSA FLORESCENS;[1] but I have been unable to trace under what title Menapius opened the debate.[2] Valentia wrote as "an unworthy servant of the Blessed Order of the Rosy Cross." In the case under notice the kind of service connoted membership, and it must be said that Valentia, whose Rosicrucian accent is eloquent, appears as an adept rather than a mere initiate.[3] In his manner and in the impression that he creates, he is much more important than Eucharius. But it is to be observed that Menapius himself, his hostility notwithstanding, also made a claim upon membership, as we shall see. On November 29 he replied to the response of Valentia, and his pamphlet appeared at Cologne in 1618.[4] The controversy

[1] ROSA FLORESCENS, *contra* F. G. MENAPII calumnias, *das ist*, KURTZER BERICHT UND WIDERANTWORT, *auff die sub dato* 3 *Junii*, 1617, *ex agro Norico in Latein, und dann folgends den* 15 *Julii obgedachten Jahres Teutsch publicirte unbedachte calumnias* F. G. MENAPII, *wider die R∴C∴ Societet, durch Florentinum de Valentia, Ord. Bened. minimum clientem.* Francofurti, *ipsis nundinis autumnalibus*, 1617. Further editions appeared in 1618 and 1619. The calumnies of Menapius—among other impeachments—described the Brethren not only as sorcerers and black magicians, but as incarnate demons.

[2] It has been described as a printed letter which terms the Order a faction of men *qui sceleribus suis, non benedictam et roseam sed malam crucem promereantur.*

[3] I must not be understood to mean that the rejoinder contains anything of real importance as an exposition of the Order or from any other point of view. To serve God, to discover the *arcana* of Nature, to promote true faith in Christ and Divine Glory are the aims of Brethren. Those who love God and therefore live to please Him are few in the world, and they should be like Adam in Paradise. The secrecy of the Order is defended, as a part of which its manifestoes appeared anonymously.

[4] ANTICRISIS *ad Responsum* FLORENTINI DE VALENTIA, *das ist, Kurtze Duplic und Defension auff die Widerantwort, Replic, oder Confutation der Missiven, von* F. G. MENAPIUS, *unlengst an die R. C. abgangen, etc.* 1618.

closed at this point, so far as Valentia was concerned,[1] but it was not otherwise the end of the matter, for in April, 1619, Theophilus Schweighardt, acting as Secretary of the Order—and of whom we shall hear further—issued a pamphlet entitled MENAPIUS ROSEÆ CRUCIS,[2] which (1) posed for consideration the question whether that pseudonymous writer should be regarded as a Brother, presumably in accordance with his claim; (2) cited him to appear at a full meeting of "our Supreme Council" on account of having slandered Valentia—not, it will be observed, the Order; and (3) summoned all members of the Rosy Cross to attend at its Invisible Stronghold. *Ex hypothesi*, initiates would know the locality of the Stronghold and so also would Menapius, if his claim was genuine, but it does not appear that they and he were commanded on a specific date. There is no account of what followed, if indeed anything, but the name of Menapius is not heard of subsequently in the arena of public debate.[3]

Florentinus de Valentia also "fell into himself and was missing ever after," but his intervention places us in a better position regarding the claims of the Order if we can accept him at his own valuation as a witness from within the secret circle. His affirmations fall unawares into two categories, of which the first is purely mythical, otherwise

[1] I should add that Menapius made two further attacks in CENTO VIRGILIANUS DE FRATRIBUS R.·.C.·., *authore* F. G. MENAPIO, published with CENTO OVIDIANUS DE FRATRIBUS R.·.C.·., *auctore* F. GENTDORP, *cognomento* GOMETZ MENAPIUS. 1618, *s.l.* They are known to me by their titles only.

[2] MENAPIUS ROSEÆ CRUCIS, *das ist, Bedenken der Gesambten Societet von dem verdeckten und ungenandten scribtore* F. G. MENAPIO. . . . *Auff gnädigen Befehl der Hochl. Societet publicirt von* THEOPHILO SCHWEIGHARDT, *Ord. Bened. Grafiren, im* April, 1619.

[3] The pamphlet of Schweighardt is almost obviously a piece of farcical writing, but a question arises as to what may be behind it, considered as the final result in print of two Rosicrucian initiates falling foul of one another, an example to be followed by others—as we shall see—almost concurrently.

occult fooling, unless a symbolical significance can be assumed. The mirrors of Archimedes, the automata of Roger Bacon and Albertus Magnus, the use and composition of the wheel of Pythagoras, the everburning fire, perpetual motion, the quadrature of the circle, the key of the music of Nature and the harmony of all things are among the treasures possessed by the Order. The explanation is that those who understand the characters and signatures which God has inscribed in the great book of the cosmos, and who contemplate the origin and interconnection of creatures, will discover things that seem impossible to the hostile critic. But the enumerations of the second category belong to a different class. It is said that the Brethren seek the Kingdom of God and regeneration in Jesus Christ; that they study the Book of life; that they hearken to the Spiritual Word in a still Sabbath. The explanation is that the book which contains all things is within us; that it is this which leads the wise into all knowledge; that the Word is the Wisdom of God, His image, His spirit, His law; that this is the Christ in man; and that the part of those who would attain is the resignation of their will to God, seeking before all things for His Kingdom to reign within them. It is like the voice of THEOLOGIA GERMANICA, behind which is the voice of Tauler, and we shall see in the next chapter that the Rosy

As regards Menapius, he was so well acquainted with the Order, according to his claim, that when he wrote in the first instance, it was possible for him to describe the habitation of the Rosy Cross in a decorative fable. It was a castle encompassed by clouds and apparently built upon a rock supported by four pillars and approached by seven marble steps. The rock being surrounded by deep water formed a sort of island and was reached by a boat covered with a blue canopy, the master and his servants being clothed in red mantles. Those who would reach the castle had to pass the Tower of Uncertainty and the Perilous Tower, to vanquish a wolf and a goat, after which they had free entrance and received the reward of their labours. They were crowned by a virgin, clothed in a robe of yellow silk and enthroned in heavenly and earthly magnificence.

Cross was understood after this manner by its great English exponent, Robert Fludd.

In 1618 an entirely unknown person—Mundus Christophori Filius—produced a polemic in quarto, called obscurely enough GREASE FOR THE FALL,[1] otherwise observations on "the craft and knavery of the newly constituted Brotherhood of the R∴C∴," which brought forth a reply, also anonymous but ascribed to Irenæus Agnostus, who, as we shall see, was another official apologist and the most prolific of all. This was SPECULUM CONSTANTIÆ,[2] the said mirror being otherwise an exhortation to steadfastness and firmness addressed to all and sundry "whose names have been submitted to the Holy and Blessed Fraternity," lest they should be led away by "certain wicked and perverse writings." Mundus rejoined in 1619 with ROSEÆ CRUCIS FRATER THRASONICO-MENDAX,[3] being a response to the alleged libel of the MIRROR OF CONSTANCY, described as "put in circulation recently by a so-called Rosicrucian" and directed against his own "catholic treatise." The result in due course was VINDICIÆ RHODOSTAUROTICÆ,[4] issued by Irenæus Agnostus under date of September 5 in that year and described as a radical denial of the insults, defamations, lies and calumnies spread abroad by Mundus, son of Christophoros, against the Illustrious Society.

The debate closed at this point, but it leaves us confronted by a very curious problem, because GREASE FOR THE FALL claims in the first place to have been compiled at the

[1] SPECK AUFF DER FALL, *das ist, List und Betrug der newenstandenen Brüderschaft oder Frat. derer vom R∴C∴, durch* MUNDUM CHRISTOPHORI FIL.

[2] SPECULUM CONSTANTIÆ, *das ist, eine nohtwendige Vermahnung an die jenige, so ihre Namen bereits bey der heiligen, gebenedeiten Frat. dess R. C. angegeben*, etc. 1618, *s.l.*

[3] ROSEÆ CRUCIS FRATER THRASONICO-MENDAX, *das ist, Verlogner Rhumbsichtiger R∴C∴ Bruder, oden Verantwortung auff die Skartecken* SPECULI CONSTANTIÆ, etc. 1619, *s.l.*

[4] VINDICIÆ RHODOSTAUROTICÆ, *das ist, Warhaffter Gegenbericht der Gottseligen Frat. dess R∴C∴*, etc. 1619, *s.l.*

solicitation of a highly distinguished person, not otherwise specified, and to have been written in the second place *Permissu Superiorum*, which can signify only the licence of the Order itself. This notwithstanding, the preface proceeds forthwith to affirm that the Brethren are judged out of their own mouths and by their own writings, though Mundus adds that he does not attack their morals or even their curious arts. In the eight chapters comprised by the tract he marshals his alleged evidence, based (1) on the origin and founders of the Order; (2) their religious belief; (3) their opinion of "papal holiness"; (4) their worldly policy; and (5) their occult claims. As regards the matter of faith, they are a sect equivalent to Anabaptists, not Christian in the true sense, which is that of the Catholic Church. It is evident throughout that Mundus, though self-described as a lover of *pansophia*, belonged to the old religion. In respect of "the purse of Fortunatus" and the "Parergon of gold-making," the Brethren "promised more in front than was to be seen behind." The conclusion is that there is nothing to warrant anyone in abandoning the Catholic Faith to join the Rosicrucian Society. Mundus cites the testimony of an alleged Brother, according to which he was on probation for over seven years before he was received into the Order. The tract on the THRASONIAN LIAR terms Irenæus Agnostus, firstly, a vainglorious Brother and, secondly, a self-styled Rosicrucian. It warns everyone against falling into the heretical trap, its position otherwise being summed up in the following lines:

> Quod ergo scit Roseæ Crucis Frater? Nihil
> Quam quod crepat creata cuncta esse ex tribus,
> Sale, alazothe, fœtidoque sulphura.

On the surface, therefore, we are in the presence of two Brethren denouncing one another, owing to their divergent views about an Order to which both belong. But if we elect to decide that Mundus gave false testimony when he implied the fact of his membership, we shall find ourselves shortly facing another problem respecting Irenæus himself.

When Mundus ceased from testifying, he was replaced in the lists by ISAIAH SUB CRUCE, who attacked Irenæus Agnostus in MIRACULA NATURÆ,[1] otherwise seven admirable mysteries regarded hereunto as fabulous, owing to "the philosophical and astronomical operations" of the R∴C∴, who are yet designated as a "highly illuminated Fraternity." Isaiah undertakes to shed new light on the "seven wonders" in question. The pseudonymous writer has been identified —speculatively or otherwise—as a professor of Latin at Ulm, namely, Zimpert Wehe. On June 13, 1619, Irenæus Agnostus came forward with TINTINNABULUM SOPHORUM,[2] being "a further and fundamental discovery of the godly and blessed Fraternity" and of the illustrious Order, chiefly directed against the self-styled Athenian ISAIAH SUB CRUCE, but also condemning the SPECULUM as written in extravagant and ironical terms. It would seem therefore that the latter tract has been ascribed in error to Irenæus. On August 18 Isaiah completed his VIII MIRACULUM ARTIS,[3] the alleged eighth wonder comprising a "fundamental, perfect and decisive revelation" of many *arcana* concerning "natural, supernatural and infra-natural sciences," but embodying for the most part a "condign declaration" on the last tract of Irenæus. It includes also and curiously

[1] MIRACULA NATURÆ, *das ist sieben überaus treffliche, sonderbare und bisher unerhörte Arcanen und Wunderwerke der Natur, durch* HISAIAM SUB CRUCE Ath., etc. Strassburg, 1619.

[2] TINTINNABULUM SOPHORUM, *das ist, Fernere gründliche entdeckung der gottseligen, gesegneten Brüderschaft dess löblichen Orden dess R. C.*, etc. Nürnberg, 1619.

[3] VIII MIRACULUM ARTIS, *das ist, gründliche, vollkommene und endliche Offenbarung vieler Geheimnussen, so wol in Natürlichen, als über und under Natürlichen Wissenschafften*, etc. Strassburg, 1619.

the horoscope of Irenæus Agnostus, who illustrated his indefatigable zeal for the Order on three further occasions. Under date of October 21, 1619, he issued a "brief but well-founded refutation of every charge brought falsely and wickedly against the Brotherhood by ISAIAH SUB CRUCE. The general title was APOLOGIA FRATRUM R∴C∴[1] It was followed on April 13, 1620, by PRODROMUS FRATERNITATIS R∴C∴,[2] the Herald or Messenger announcing the speedy advent of a great APOLOGIA in detail for the further exposure of Isaiah's fabulous stories. The promise was fulfilled under date of July 30 by the publication of LIBER T, or alternatively PORTUS TRANQUILLITATIS,[3] recalling, and intended to recall obviously, that "parchment inscribed T" found in the tomb of "our careful and wise Father," when the early Brethren beheld his body in the tomb. It may be remembered that this was their "greatest treasure" after the Bible, and was to be protected from "the censure of the world." The tract of Irenæus may have signified a precious possession to those whom it concerned, but was more by its own claim, that is to say, a "magnificent and most consoling relation concerning that Supreme Good which, having been so highly desired, has been at length and recently obtained by those who have renounced the

[1] APOLOGIA FRAT. R∴C∴, *das ist, Kurtze, jedoch wahrhafte und wohlbegründte Ablehnung aller der Beschuldigung, die in verwichener Frankfurter Herbstmäss, von* HISAIA SUB CRUCE ATHEN, *fälschlich und bosshafftigklich beschwert worden, etc.* 1619. There was a second edition at Nuremberg in 1620.

[2] PRODROMUS F∴R∴C∴, *das ist, ein vorgeschmack und beyläuffige Anzeig der grossen aussführlichen Apologi, etc.* 1620, *sine loco.*

[3] LIBER T.. *oder* PORTUS TRANQUILLITATIS. *Durch* IRENÆUS AGNOSTUS. 1620, *sine loco.* If this tract fulfilled one promise of PRODROMUS it left another in suspension, namely, a new commentary on Genesis, which was to unfold the true matter of the heavens and the universe, explain how water is coagulated, etc. It has been said that the reference is almost unquestionably to Gutmann's REVELATIONS OF DIVINE MAJESTY, which deals with these subjects, but this work had appeared already at Frankfurt in 1619.

Papacy and have been admitted into the Order and College of the R∴C∴." [1]

The debate ended at this point on the part of all disputants. We hear nothing further of Isaiah, Irenæus passes from the field, though we shall recur to him immediately in connection with other writings, and—real or alleged—the official publications of the Order were soon to be suspended for nigh on one hundred years. The controversial side of these documents has been now dealt with as fully as my materials permit, and it is necessary to retrace our steps for the purpose of my fourth section and its further illustrations of the Order as affirmed and explained by itself, premising that in all cases the official character is that which can be ascribed to individual expositors testifying from within the secret circle: they are distinguished in this manner from FAMA and CONFESSIO.

(1) The earliest in point of time was a Swiss Protestant theologian named Goetz, who was ruined by alchemical experiments and leaving his debts behind him in his native land because a resident of Marburg. In 1614, under the name of Raphael Eglinus, he published at Frankfurt an ASSERTIO FRATERNITATIS R∴C∴, [2] in which he termed himself *socius ejus*, a Companion of the Brotherhood. Prior to this he is said to have written a DISQUISITIO DE

[1] According to the APOLOGIA of Irenæus, the Order existed long before Christian Rosy Cross, whose office was one of reconstruction. The legend of the FAMA is thus demolished in a sentence. It is added, moreover, that C∴R∴C∴ knew everything in temporal philosophy but was deficient in matters of faith, for which reason he was no more the founder of the Brotherhood than Solomon—the explanation of this statement being that "doctrines exist before their human representatives." He that has ears to hear this kind of reasoning must be left to hear.

[2] ASSERTIO FRATERNITATIS R∴C∴, *quam Roseæ Crucis vocant, a quodam Fraternitatis ejus socio carmine expressa.* Francofurti, 1614. The imprint of Bringer the publisher appears on the title-page. He appears to have been the chief Rosicrucian bookseller in that city. There was a second edition of the ASSERTIO in the following year, and it was translated into German and

HELIA ARTISTA which appeared at Leipsic in 1606 and has been falsely affirmed to contain Rosicrucian references.[1] The ASSERTIO is a Latin metrical discourse which at this early date alludes to adventurers claiming a connection with the Order and affirms, for the rest, that its name is not to be identified with that of the founder.[2] The publication of THE CHEMICAL NUPTIALS of Frater Christianus Rosencreutz, in 1616 is a notable commentary on this statement.

(2) The second and by far the most interesting exposition on the affirmative side of debate, is an ECHO OF THE GOD-ILLUMINATED BROTHERHOOD OF THE VENERABLE ORDER R∴C∴,[3] dated November 1, 1615, and published at Dantzic in that year, the reputed author being Julius Sperber, whose collection of KABALISTIC PRAYERS had appeared at Magdebourg so far back as 1600.[4] The ECHO

published at Dantzic in 1616 and 1617. So far back as 1591 there had appeared at Tiguri a tract entitled ORATIO DE CONCORDI FRATRUM SOCIETATE. *Ps.* cxxxiii *celebrata: in solenni ecclesiæ Antistitum, Professorum et Studiosorum conventu Tiguri à* RAPHAELE EGLINO, *alumnorum collegii Tigurini Pædagogo, habita.* It was a commentary of seven pages in small quarto on the three verses beginning: *Ecce quam bonum et jucundum.*

[1] The full title is HELIOPHILUS PHILOCHEMICUS: *Disquisitio de* HELIA ARTISTA, *in qua de Metallarum Transmutatione, addressus* HEGELII *et* PERERII *Jesuitarum Opiniones, evidenter et solide disseritur.* It appeared at Frankfurt in 1606 and at Marburg in 1608, being described in both cases as *editio postrema correctior et melior*, but I am unacquainted with its earlier bibliographical history. The preface raises the following pertinent question regarding the Heavenly Jerusalem: *Si urbs est aurum, et eadem est pellucida ut vitrum, ergo quiddam quod est substantiæ et naturæ aureæ, quod est pellucidum instar vitri.* The tract has also certain Hermetic Canons on the spirit, soul and body of the greater and lesser world. It is unnecessary to say that the Rosicrucians are mentioned nowhere, nor do I know why the anonymous work is ascribed to Eglinus.

[2] There appears to have been another ASSERTIO attached to a Cassel edition of FAMA ET CONFESSIO in 1616 and claiming to be official in character, but I have met with no copy.

[3] ECHO *der von Gott Hocherleuchteten Fraternitet des Löblichen Ordens* R∴C∴, etc. . . . Danzig, Andreas Hünefeldt, 1615.

[4] He is described as of Anhalt, Dessau. It is to be noted that Lenglet du Fresnoy catalogues two alchemical works under the name of Julius Sperberus, both appearing at Hamburg, respectively in 1672 and 1674, and both

claimed to embody (1) absolute proof that the statements of FAMA and CONFESSIO are possible and true ; (2) that the facts have been commonly familiar to certain God-fearing people for more than nineteen years ; (3) that they are on record in secret writings ; and (4) that the evidence is a "magical letter" issued by the Venerable Brotherhood and printed in the German language—referring presumably to the FAMA. Were these promises fulfilled the beginnings of the Rosicrucian Order would antecede the completion of NAOMETRIA and belong possibly to the activities of the *Militia Crucifera Evangelica*, but unhappily the proof is wanting.[1] That which is furnished, however, is a second preface under the date 1597, which may not be so manifestly fraudulent as appears on the surface and is meant to indicate an embryonic state of the Order at that time. It recommends the establishment of a Fraternity or the erection of some great College, but there is no reference to Christian Rosy Cross or his own traditional foundation. Apart from my hypothesis concerning it, there is no purpose in the document,[2] but from this point

entitled ISAGOGE, the first concerning the true knowledge of the Triune God and of Nature, the second on the matter of the Philosophical Stone and its use. They are presumably posthumous writings. Sperber is said to have died in 1616.

[1] The German historian of Freemasonry, Findel, considered that the ECHO is not unimportant for the origin of the Swedish Rite, apparently because he traced in it some vestiges or reminiscences of the Order of Knights Templar. The opinion in either case is not likely to be shared by those who know the tract, the most important point in which is the sincerity with which it seems to be imbued.

[2] It cites Ægidius Gutmann of Suabia and his REVELATIONS OF DIVINE MAJESTY, published in 1619 and thus antedated by twenty-two years. He is described as a wise man who was a lover of God and his work is compared in respect of value to the traditional seventy volumes which God dictated to the prophet by His angel. There is no question that the REVELATIONS were of great moment in the mind of the Rosy Cross and this panegyric appearing four years before the volumes were printed shews that it was known in manuscript previously, like the FAMA itself. There is evidence otherwise of the fact, as we have seen.

of view it is easy to understand why in addition to the proposition itself there comes—at the end of the tract—a schedule of the Laws which should govern it. The first or later preface is addressed to the Brothers R∴C∴, and implores them in the Name of the Holy Trinity to meet together and teach the True Light to the world, being that of Holy Scripture and of Nature, according to their secret meaning. The CONFESSIO had just furnished the German world with the birth-date of him whom the FAMA calls the "chief and original of our Fraternity," but the text of the ECHO makes short work of a claim so modest by affirming that the first Rosicrucian of the Old Testament was Adam, while Simeon was the last. One is disposed to speculate whether the early Masonic *literati* who said practically the same thing of their own Brotherhood had taken a lead from the ECHO.

The antiquity of the Order being such, it might be supposed to have spread widely in the long course of the ages, but the recipients of its wisdom are described as few, owing to insufficiency of zeal in the quest of Divine Things. The analogy cited is the great audiences that heard the Christ of Nazareth and the three among all who were chosen to learn the deep mysteries of His teaching, namely, Peter, James and John. It was these also and only to whom it is said that "He shewed the same vision which God had granted to Elias and Moses," meaning the Transfiguration. The Divine Wisdom being the antithesis of the wisdom of this world, it follows that the hidden *theosophia* can be revealed only to those who renounce the *sapientia mundana*, the world which cleaves thereto and the fleshly lusts thereof. It appears, for the rest, that Christ, who came not to destroy but to fulfil, maintained the old tradition of the Rosy Cross—otherwise, of the Ancient Mysteries—and in establishing a new College of Magic did not depart therefrom. The Laws of the Order, according to the ECHO,[1] reflect apparently from this source, but they are more properly golden counsels and, of course, familiar in our mouths as the proverbial household words or the teachings of the Sermon on the Mount. To be faithful, modest and obedient; to love the neighbour and share our fortune with him; to respect the secret studies and keep silence regarding them: hereof is the yoke imposed on those who would follow in the footsteps of Christian Rosy Cross. We are far indeed from the FAMA and that anti-papal spirit which succeeded the Reformation in CONFESSIO FRATERNITATIS R∴C∴. Other rules of conduct impose the fear of God as the root and crown of wisdom; the will to discipline; piety, purity and holy horror of sin; prudence and equipoise; contempt of riches; realisation of this world's friendship as connoting enmity with God; disesteem of human wisdom and foresight; ardent desire for Divine Wisdom; and gratitude towards one's own master. In the following of this path it may be that a disciple will find in the inward and secret sense of the Word of God that there are Great Mysteries which are undreamed by those who cleave to the external meaning of Scripture, and that—God willing—those who seek for His light in all sincerity will indeed find the light, an illumination at once temporal and eternal for the desiring soul.

The ECHO, for the rest, affirms three classes of Magic, of which only the first is lawful: it is called *Magia Cœlestis*, and this is *Divina Sapientia*. The second is *Magia Humana*, defined as Platonic doctrine, presumably the wisdom of man at its highest. The third is superstitious and diabolical, using conjurations and charms: it includes necromancy.

[1] The ECHO was reprinted, or at least reissued, at Dantzic in 1616, again in 1620, and finally in 1656. The work is divided into twenty-one chapters, which treat of Divine Wisdom, its origin and source, the means by which it is attained and the fruit which comes therefrom.

The Magic which is of heaven is Magic which comes from God and tends to union with Him. It gives true understanding concerning the sacred writings, with gifts of vision, revelation and working of miracles. The tract adds that those who are proficient in Magic of this denomination are few and far between, because infidelity advances with rapid strides, the teaching of Christ is neglected, religious devotion turns more and more to the outward side—as if to that letter which killeth—and in its activities to the acquisition of ecclesiastical possessions, understood as the goods of this world.

The ECHO is altogether an important official document, and I am disposed to believe that something lay behind the seeming fraud of its predated supplementary preface. I mean that there was something fermenting in the hiddenness at the end of the sixteenth century, of which Simon Studion was a mouthpiece and that it was growing up into manifestation between 1604 and 1614.

(3) The year which produced the ECHO saw also the publication of a certain OPEN LETTER under the name of Julianus de Campis. It defended the Order against accusations abroad in the world, but they were those of ecclesiastical censure rather than of Libavius. The representatives of German theology were informed that the Order was beyond their province because it was a group of theosophists and not of *theologi*. It was the repository, moreover, of a secret art, in comparison with which the praise or blame of the world could count for nothing. The tract was addressed to all who had heard, by report or otherwise, of the new Brotherhood and admonished them not to be influenced when judgments were delivered by the ignorant. The writer testified (1) that he was himself a member of the Order; (2) that he had met only with three other members in all his travels; and (3) that presumably they were the sum total of those then on earth who were

worthy to possess its mysteries. It followed that many compete for the pearl of great price, but those are few who gain it. It followed also that there could not be said to be any definitely incorporated society. The position of Julianus de Campis might have been enviable for those who could tolerate his claim, but on our part we need observe only that his open letter stultifies FAMA and CONFESSIO still more than the ECHO. Where now is the House of the Holy Spirit, and where even are those who put forward the first manifestoes, that the *literati* and others of Europe might judge thereon? It is answered only that the incorporation of the Order and its COLLEGIUM will come to pass in the future. Notwithstanding these difficulties Julianus found favour with two other claimants to initiation whom we shall meet shortly. He is cited by Theophilus Schweighardt and quoted by the author of FRATER CRUCIS ROSATÆ.[1]

(4) As a rejoinder to various slanders, not otherwise specified, Theophilus Schweighardt of Constance, who has been identified as Daniel Mögling, produced under date of June 1, 1617, a tract entitled PANDORA SEXTÆ ÆTATIS,[2] otherwise SPECULUM GRATIÆ, which claimed to communicate the whole art and science of the Brotherhood established by Christian Rosencreutz, to trace its development and to shew that it could be utilised without endangering health of body or soul. There is further ascribed to Schweighardt

[1] Mr. F. N. Pryce has drawn my attention to a CHRISIS AD LECTOREM, signed by Julianus de Campis and placed between the dedication and preface in TETRAS CHYMIATRICA, by Arnold Kerner, published at Erfurt in 1618. It is a violent attack on Andreæ, under the name of Menippus, because he had published a tract so entitled, as we have seen, in that year. *Ad Orcum, ad Orcum, Menippe, cum tuis comitibus* is an exclamation which strikes the keynote. There are also references to the FAMA. The plausible explanation is that Julianus attacked Andreæ because he was an enemy of the Order, and I must suppose that this is how it stands.

[2] PANDORA SEXTÆ ÆTATIS, *sive* SPECULUM GRATIÆ, *das ist, die Ganze Kunst und Wissenschaft der von Gott hoch erleuchteten Fraternitet* CHRISTIANI ROSENCREUTZ . . . *Durch* THEOPHILUM SCHWEIGHARDT. 1617, *sine loco.*

a DESCRIPTIO FRATERNITATIS R∴C∴, *anno* 1618, according to Kloss. His name is connected also on the same authority with another work of 1618 entitled SPECULUM SOPHICUM RHODO-STAUROTICUM,[1] dedicated to all those who, being eager for true wisdom, await further information on the Brotherhood of Christian Rosencreutz. The author describes himself as *Dei gratia tertriunius catholicæ Promotor indignus*—i.e. *Promotor Ordinis*. His discourse concerns the College of the Order and its axioms, understood as an extension of knowledge.[2] It is addressed to the "imbecile" followers of Zoilus, as accusing critics, but for their everlasting shame and scorn. We hear also that aspirants sought instruction concerning the Order among booksellers and engravers. I have dealt already with the last publication of Schweighardt when, in his alleged official capacity, he cited F. G. Menapius before the Council of the Order.[3]

[1] The title continues: *Das ist, Weitläuffige Entdeckung dess Collegii und Axiomatum von der sondern erleuchten Fraternitatis* CHRISTIANI ROSENKREUTZ . . . 1618.

[2] I should add here that "an unnamed but notable Companion of the Fraternity" published at Frankfurt in 1617 a "fundamental relation" of the designs and objects of the Order: GRÜNDLICHER BERICHT *von dem Vorhaben, Gelegenheit und Inhalt der Löblichen Bruderschaft des R∴C∴*. His initials were E. D. F., O∴C∴R∴Sen. It contains a parable concerning the Mountain of the Wise, to which I shall recur subsequently.

[3] The author of the SPECULUM would seem to have regarded the IMITATIO CHRISTI, and especially its first chapter, as the chief key to the Rosy Cross. Those who conformed their life exactly thereto would be visited by a Brother, bearing the *Parergon* of the Order. It it explained that the *Ergon* is purification of spirit, glorification of God on earth. It is the work of all true Christians as well as of the Brotherhood. The *Ergon* is otherwise the right eye of the soul, by which it looks to the eternal; the left eye looks towards time, and this is the *Parergon*—the criterion of things good and evil for the life of the body. The College of the Holy Spirit, according to Schweighardt, is not less marvellous than the Castle described by Menapius. It is suspended in the air wheresoever God wills, for it is He Who directs it. It is mobile and immobile, stable and unstable, goes on wheels but also on wings. The Brethren have the gift of ubiquity and are nearer to the seeker than he thinks. The PANDORA speaks of Virgin Wisdom and her garden, which must be traversed to attain the end of the great research.

(5) The most important and problematical of all the apologists is he whose acquaintance we have made under the pseudonym of Irenæus Agnostus, and we have seen that he wrote many pamphlets in reply to MUNDUS and ISAIAH SUB CRUCE. They do not, however, exhaust his contributions to the Order subject. It is possible that we meet with him for the first time as J. Irenæus, that "disciple of Divine Wisdom," who addressed—as we have seen—a letter to the Order on December 3, 1615, and it appeared at Frankfurt some time in the following year.[1] He has been accredited, but by mere affirmation only, with the authorship of some "philosophical revelations"[2] communicated to the Brotherhood in 1619. The discourse in question actually appeared under the name of Rhodophilus Staurophorus, August, 1618, but this designation is pseudonymous like that of Irenæus and therefore affords no light. Under date of March 16, 1619, he would seem to have issued FRATER NON FRATER,[3] exhorting the Rosicrucian *adepti* to be on their strict guard against pretended Brethren and false prophets, who are going up and down in the world wearing the mask of the Society. There had been warnings of this kind previously, as for example the ANWEISUNG[4] of 1616, published at Frankfurt, which "indication" pointed a straight way to the Brotherhood of the R∴C∴ and included an instruction to those postulants of the Order who had antecedently entreated it to beware of false

[1] *Ad Venerandos, Doctissimos et Illuminatissimos Viros Dom Fratres Sanctæ Roseæ Crucis* EPISTOLA J. Ειρηναιου, *Divini Sophiæ Alumni.* 1616.

[2] RAPTUS PHILOSOPHICUS, *das ist, Philosophische Offenbarungen, etc.* 1619, *sine loco.* The author narrates a vision in which a virgin presented him a book called AZOTH, signed with the letters F. R. and treating of Magic, Hermetic Medicine, Philosophy and Mathematics.

[3] FRATER NON FRATER, *das ist, eine Hochnothdürflige Vermanung an die Gottselige, fromme Discipul der gebenedeyten Societet des R∴C∴, dass sie sich für den falchen Brüdern und Propheten fleissig vorsehen, etc.* 1619, *s.l.*

[4] ANWEISUNG DES RECHTEN WEGS ZU DER FRATERNITET DES R∴C∴, etc. 1616.

brethren. But it must be added that Irenæus pretended to furnish the particular marks and signs by which true members might be distinguished indubitably from such persons.[1]

A tract entitled CLYPEUM VERITATIS, otherwise THE SHIELD OF TRUTH, which appeared early in 1618, is a typical deliberation on the *pro et contra* side, and I am taking it out of due order as it connects with the next tract. It claims (1) to deal with everything which "hereunto has been set forth openly, either for or against the Most Honourable and Blessed Brotherhood of the Rosy Cross," and (2) to exhibit once and for all that which zealous disciples may expect confidently therefrom. The author in this case also was Irenæus Agnostus, who subscribes himself (1) as writing from Tunis on February 21 of the year mentioned, (2) by special command of the glorious Brotherhood, he being (3) its "unworthy notary" throughout Germany. It affirms (1) that our highest good and way to the blessed life lies in the knowledge of God; (2) that the man who is devoted to the word of God is ever proceeding further in the quest of wisdom; and (3) that learning must be maintained for the propagation of celestial doctrine. In some manner which must have been conclusive to the writer himself these considerations lead up to the Christian and theological reflections of "our Society," which testifies its approval of what Michael Maier delivered from a solid foundation and "published in our defence," referring apparently to his enumeration

[1] The signs were: (1) unity of doctrine; (2) modesty of garb; (3) taciturnity, beneficence, humility, chastity; (4) power to cure leprosy, gout, epilepsy and cancer. But Irenæus adds fabulous things, viz. the possession of two instruments called respectively *Cosmolothrentes* and *Astronikita*. By the first any building could be destroyed, and the second enabled the user to see the stars through clouds. Other warrants were the gifts of interpreting dreams and discerning things to come. Finally, the Brethren know everything contained in books, yet they appear of small consequence outwardly.

of other Colleges of Wisdom in past ages. As regards the teaching of the Order it has been inherited through a valid and unbroken succession; it is the custodian of things hitherto regarded as lost; its vocation is to bring errant wanderers to the light of virtuous and true knowledge; it has never designed that all men should accept its teaching "before the end of the world," but those alone who from the beginning have been called thereto by God. As the foolish old Masonic *literati* declared that their Speculative Art began in the Garden of Eden, so is it said—like the ECHO—that the succession of the Rosy Cross goes back to "our first father Adam," descending from him to "our still surviving president, Hugo Alverda."

The intermediate custodians of the Mysteries were Seth, Enoch, and Noah, with other familiar names according to the normal transmission of the Secret Tradition in Israel, so forward to Christian times, the succession in which I will give at length as follows: Philo, Rabbi ben Thema, Schmuel Jarchinas, R. Asse Rabbena, Marcus Eremitas, Dado Episcopus Rotamagensis, Beda, Walafrid, Archbishop Turpin, Moses bar Kephas, Almansor, Peter Damian, Hugo de Saint Victor, Rabbi M. Maimon, Abraham aben Ezra, R. Moses Kimchi, Jacobus de Voragine, Alanus, R. Moses, Aben Tafon, R. Mordechai, and Hieronymus à Sancta Fide. Finally, the Lord illuminated Hugo Alverda, "our excellent Chief, to commission his brethren into the whole world," for the annunciation of this "godly and wholesome philosophy."

The genealogy being such—indiscriminately among Jews and Christians—it will be understood that the Hidden Temple had not only its treasures of oral tradition but lost and unknown books, probably beyond computation. A few are promised categorically "at the expiration of a brief time," among which I need mention only those of King Solomon and the magical works of Apollonius of Tyana. In the presence of such an equipment the Order can afford to be merry, and is so after a German manner, when "inconsiderate and unskilled people" deny that it can add to the general sum of knowledge, more especially seeing that its members "can speak and write not only all languages but also all dialects." As regards complaints respecting the silence of the Order, the pamphlet appeals to its notorious cures of diseases "without reward," and to the counsels on matters of government which it has addressed to those who rule. We hear no longer about false books on alchemy and lists which are going to be published for the protection of sincere students, but much on the age and importance of the metallic art, with hints as to all that could be unfolded by those who write, were they called so to do. There is also a synopsis of the virtues possessed by "our artificial gold." In fine it is testified that the legality or otherwise of "our College" does not tolerate debate, the reason given being curious: "For we have had and may have still in our Fraternity, Popes, Cardinals, Emperors, Kings, Bishops, Abbots, Prelates, Earls and Lords"—a notable list truly, having regard to the Reformation rant of CONFESSIO FRATERNITATIS.

In the year following, 1619, the same "unworthy German notary" issued FONS GRATIÆ, the FOUNTAIN OF GRACE, being a brief declaration concerning the precise time when those who were "accepted as Brethren of the Holy and Blessed Brotherhood of the Rosy Cross" should make a beginning in respect of their "redemption and perfection," or in simpler words, when Postulants might look for reception. It sounds like a clear issue and was written by "special command of the aforesaid high Society." The colophon, however, quotes—perhaps advisedly—the familiar text: "Blessed are those who have not seen and have believed." It calls upon those "humble Brethren who are enrolled in our Society" to praise the Lord. Yet a year hence and they shall reach their plenary salvation. The document is "given at Aleppo" on November 29, 1618, and the great day of election is that date precisely in the following year. Then, as it is certified, there will be sent to those who tarry "one of our Society, *videlicet*, Elman Zarta, who will assemble you and bring you to our dwelling, with very great triumph and rejoicing, from this vale of woe." Whatsoever is said by this ambassador on "our behalf" shall be fulfilled truly, and that with faithful diligence. Readers are referred for the rest to Maier's THEMIS AUREA, "wherein he made manifest that we belong in unbroken succession to the medical faculty." [1] In fine the Selected Brethren and Sons of Wise Humility must understand that they are coming into a still Sabbath and the narrow way to eternity.

So far as any records are concerned, it does not appear that the "humble Brethren," or Postulants at the gate of the Temple, received the promised visit or entered within the precincts; but as regards the alleged envoy it may be mentioned that a tract or manifesto entitled FORTALITIUM SCIENTIÆ,[2] published in 1617, was signed by (1) Hugo de Alverda the Phrisian, in the 576th year of his age; (2) François de Bry, the Frenchman, in his 495th year; and Elman Zarta, or Zatta, the Arab, at the age of 463.[3] The FORTALITIUM was written under the pseudonym of Rhodophilus Staurophorus, an alleged alternate, as we have seen, to that of Irenæus.

[1] Irenæus affirms elsewhere that while the Rosicrucian habitation is normally invisible, the compassion of the Order has caused it to be seen frequently by the poor and sick.

[2] The FORTALITIUM affirmed that the glorious and enlightened Fraternity have proffered the unerring art of all arts to worthy and virtuous persons who study the sum of wisdom.

[3] The signatures attached to FORTALITIUM excited the ridicule of Mundus in GREASE FOR THE FALL, and it may be noted as a curious point that he refers the tract itself to the authorship of "Rosencreutz."

On April 3, 1619, Irenæus Agnostus put forward an "indispensable advertisement to Novices,"[1] exhorting them to persevere even to the end (1) in faith towards God, (2) the love of others, (3) patience, and (4) in their trust of the Order and its goodness. On August 16 he produced a RULE OF LIFE[2] for those who had not yet been incorporated by the Order, notwithstanding their earnest desire for this privilege. The next and last item which stands to the credit of Irenæus in this connection —rightly or wrongly—is dated August 25 and is called EPITIMIA FRATERNITATIS R∴C∴,[3] being a final revelation, discovery and *apologia* in respect of the Most Enlightened Order of the R∴C∴, and of its sincere and truthful Confession. It claimed to be written, printed and published by the ordinance of the Society itself. So far as we have proceeded, and whether writing, so to speak, at his own instance or officially in reply to hostile critics, we are acquainted with Irenæus only as a fervent champion of the Order, in and out of season. He has seemed sometimes an admirer from a certain distance and sometimes speaking from within. On the present occasion he is vested with official authority, but the unaccountable fact emerges that EPITIMIA is against the Rosicrucian claims and unfriendly to the persons of the Brethren. He informs his peers and co-heirs, otherwise, "my Brethren of the R∴C∴," that he knows not how to regard them or what manner of men they are. They have produced so far in their writings only familiar things and things full of contradictions. On the supposition, however, that they are the keepers of a real knowledge which might redound to

[1] THESAURUS FIDEI, *das ist, ein nothwendiger Bericht und Verwarnung an die Novitios*, etc. 1619, *s.l.*

[2] REGULA VITÆ, *das ist, eine Heylsame, Nützliche und Notwendige Erinnerung*, etc. 1619, *s.l.*

[3] EPITIMIA FRATERNITATIS R∴C∴, *das ist, Endliche Offenbarung, oder Entdeckung und Verthaydigung dess hochl. Ordens dess R∴C∴.*, etc. 1619, *s.l.*

the benefit of mankind, they should come forth into the open day and communicate it in public teaching, not in anonymous pamphlets. Then, warming as he proceeds, there are the following more serious affirmations: (1) That the Brethren are mere magicians, making false claims on power; (2) That their wisdom is hollow pretence; (3) That he has visited many lands and has heard nothing concerning them; (4) That in reality the Order was founded by the Jesuits as part of their secret warfare against the religion of reform. It follows (1) that its members, as he says indeed categorically, are ignorant persons and that when he terms them most enlightened in his title he himself has lied; (2) that he has not published his pamphlet by their command; and (3) that if he has failed to meet with them in his travels or even gain tidings concerning them, he cannot belong to them as he claims.

One would think that in the sense and reason of things, even at that bewrayed period, it was impossible, without preface or explanation, to take up suddenly a new position like this. It must be remembered that the period elapsing between the unconditional defence of REGULA VITÆ and the radical hostility of EPITIMIA is the space between August 16 and August 25 of the same year. There is neither situation to save nor axe to grind so far as I am concerned, but as a matter of logic and likelihood my inference is that Irenæus Agnostus did not write EPITIMIA, the fact notwithstanding that this pseudonym appears on its title-page.[1] It is more likely to have been the work of Menapius, to whom also it has been attributed, and in this connection

[1] There is, of course, a strong possibility that some Rosicrucian texts were like some texts of alchemy, namely, speculations of unprincipled booksellers, produced to their order for the exploitation of a public demand. And yet if EPITIMIA was ascribed falsely, why did not Irenæus repudiate it in yet one other pamphlet? The problem baffles ingenuity.

it may be noted that at the end of LIBER T, or bound up therewith in that copy which came into the hands of Kloss, there is a missive or SENDSCHREIBEN of Menapius in which he pretends that the author of FAMA ET CONFESSIO and also Irenæus Agnostus had foisted a hoax on the public.[1] It is added that a certain J. Procopius bore similar testimony in the same place, but I have not met with him among the numerous *interlocutores* of the long debate.

It remains to say that according to Sédir the identity of Irenæus has never transpired, though he is able to tell us (1) that he was Chancellor of Westphalia ; (2) that he was the best Catholic theologian of his time ; (3) that he debated *incognito* at Frankfurt with Jean de Martoff and others, presumably Lutherans ; (4) that he conferred with Henry IV of France in 1606 " on the best manner of terminating the war " ; and (5) that he discharged public functions at Lubeck, Hamburg, Luneville and elsewhere. On the other hand, Kloss says, but I know not on what authority, that Irenæus was Gotthardus Arthusius of Dantzic, joint rector of the Gymnasium at Frankfurt-on-the-Main, in which case we have met with him already as a Candidate for admission into the Rosicrucian Order so early as 1614. There is nothing attaching to the question of

[1] He claimed also that he was perfectly well acquainted with the author of the FAMA and knew better than anyone what to think on the reality of the R.·.C.·.. The letter cited by Kloss is by Gometz Menapius, supposed to be a variant pseudonym of F. G. M. We may compare SPHYNX ROSACEA, Frankfurt, 1618, which—according to Kloss—was written by C. Nigrinus, a theologian and friend of the Muses. It claims to be an " inoffensive hypothesis " concerning the origin of the " illustrious Order " as well as of the FAMA and CONFESSIO. As regards the legend of Christian Rosy Cross and the Brethren whom he incorporated, the author had " certain originals " in his mind. It states further that C.·.R.·.C.·. was an adventurer known as Andreas von Carolstadt. Various names are assigned to the other seven originals, one of whom was Zwinglius. This tract has been attributed also to Florentinus de Valentia, with whom I have dealt as an early official apologist. Nigrinus has been mentioned in a previous note concerning the alleged Calvinism of the Order.

identity for any purpose of my own, but it may serve to introduce a further point, on which also opinion is divided. According to Bühle and others, Irenæus was a hostile satirist who posed as champion of the Order with his "tongue in his cheek," in which case it might be presumed that he varied the farce by subsequently turning against it. Nicolai takes the opposite view, regarding him as a serious defender and expositor; but the German bookseller of the *Illuminati* period was probably unacquainted with EPITIMIA, while he mistook FONS GRATIÆ for a work of Robert Fludd. This notwithstanding, I conclude that Nicolai was probably in the right: it is quite impossible to read CLYPEUM VERITATIS or FONS GRATIÆ, not to speak of other texts, and suppose that they were the work of a concealed enemy or of a *farceur* producing dull hoaxes by the score for the confusion of German occult minds. The notion is really a derivative of the Bühle and Johann Georg Walch hypothesis, which postulates Andreæ and thirty so-called theosophists conspiring together—as we have seen—to fill the press with lies. My opinion of German theosophy in the first decades of the seventeenth century is my opinion of the Lutheran strife of sects, but it will be remembered that I have rejected this unworthy view. Its second derivative proposes, for the ease of the creaking hypothesis, to identify apparently independent Rosicrucian apologists, as Irenæus and Schweighardt, but no evidence is produced. In its absence I conclude on grounds of simplicity that the Order had apologists and critics, who stand as such at their value in the usual way, and that it must be left an open question whether those on the affirmative side and Menapius on the side of denial, who claimed to be members, told the truth or not. There is no means of knowing. On the assumption of their good faith it must be said that the Rosy Cross of 1614–20 could have been hardly in a position to communicate anything that justified its claims, if the records of apologists and defendants offer—as I think they do—some criterion for judgment.

The year 1620 saw two further publications, a note on which may close the present chapter. The first is SPECULUM AMBITIONIS[1] by Johann Hintnem, described as HISTORICUS TREFERENSIS. It indicates that onward from the world's beginning the Devil has made use of ambition to engender idolatry, heresy, factions, sects, but especially to spread new Orders, an example of which is the new Fraternity R∴C∴. The charge against this is a further ringing of changes on the vexed question of religion: its principles are contrary to those of Luther, though it has adopted his seal, and for this reason no one should join it. The circulation of apocryphal manuscripts is also laid at its door, while generally as regards its claims, and notwithstanding its proud titles, the Order is reminded that the seven wonders of the world, the glories of Greece and Rome, and all that is serviceable to life, owed nothing to the Rosy Cross. The second tract is perhaps most curious of all, for it is entitled the WORKSHOP OF THE SISTERS OF THE ROSY CROSS,[2] containing a discovery of its nature and what can be found for religion and science therein. It claims to be printed at Parthenopolis and to be written by a Franco-German Famagusta. It may have been about as serious at its period as Leo Taxil's Y-A-T-IL DES FEMMES DANS LA FRANCMAÇONNERIE, and yet the suggestion is notable, for we shall come later on to consider the important question of Woman and the Rosy Cross.

If there is one thing which can be said to emerge clearly from all the chaos of debate, it is that J. V. Andreæ knew

[1] SPECULUM AMBITIONIS, *das ist, Spiegel des Ehrgeitzes . . . Durch* JOH. HINTNEM TREFURENSEM HISTORICUM. 1620, *sine loco.*

[2] FRAWEN-ZIMMER DER SCHWESTERN DES ROSINFARBEN (*sic*) CREUTZES . . . *Durch* FAMAUGUSTAM FRANCO-ALEMANNICAM. 1620.

what he was saying when he spoke in MYTHOLOGIA CHRISTIANA of "a complete change of actors." Whatsoever personalities were veiled by FAMA and CONFESSIO they are represented no longer in the subsequent memorials which claim to speak officially. I do not believe that the two original manifestoes were the work of one person, but I think that they belong to each other. The third, or NUPTIÆ CHYMICÆ, represents the intervention of Andreæ, but it stands outside the general controversial region. The ECHO FRATERNITATIS manifests a new spirit and a new claim on the past, but it is not otherwise militantly at issue with the set of notions represented by the original sources. These are stultified, as I have said, by Julianus de Campis, and they might have been withdrawn from circulation when the procession of apologists began to fill the stage. As to what was transpiring in secret it is impossible to have any but the most tentative hypothesis and every speculation is likely to be out of court. The "change of actors" may signify groups which had agreed independently to adopt the style and title of Rosicrucians for their several purposes, whatever they happened to be, and then a time came when their representatives fell foul of each other. Meanwhile it is colourably possible that the old group went on but was found on the stage no longer, or in other words that they gave no sign in pamphlets.

CHAPTER X

ENGLISH ROSICRUCIANISM

THE Kentish village of Bearsted[1] lies at a distance of almost three miles eastward from the county town of Maidstone, just off the main road in a peaceful, pleasant vale, ringed by hills in the distance. It is a sweet and scented place, green with a hundred gardens of hops, an illustration of perfect retirement, but marked otherwise by no special individuality. The church above the village, on the descent from the main road, belongs to several periods, having even Norman vestiges, and is fair to look at, above all on the ivied side. It is dedicated to the Holy Cross, the later architectural style being mainly perpendicular—for example, the picturesque tower and the eastern window. There is an aisle on the north and a chantry of the fourteenth century. On the southern side of the chancel a minute organ has been placed within comparatively recent times. The stained glass window of the chancel depicts somewhat vividly the Descent from the Cross, and there are panelled figures, on the walls, of apostles and holy women. On the floors and walls of the aisle are many memorials of the Cage family, numbers of whom are interred beneath their tablets. With these I have no concern; but on the eastern wall of the aisle there is an elaborate commemoration which he of whom I must speak—a most illustrious "philosopher by fire"—erected

[1] Otherwise Bearstead and Bersted.

to the memory of his mother.[1] Besides the armorial bearings at the top of this tablet there is a curious winged skull, the wings being painted blue, while the skull is an earth-brown. Some interest attaches to the memorial, more especially because the inscription happens to have been the work of the son. Far more important, however, is a cross on the floor of the chancel hard by the altar-steps and bearing the following legend:

**In Jesu qui mihi omnia
in vita morte resurgam.**

Under this stone resteth the body of Robert Fludd, Doctor of Phisicke, who changed this transitory life for an immortall the viii day of September A° Dni MDCXXXVII, being LXIII years of age: whose Monument is erected in this chancel according to the forme by him prescribed.

[1] The inscription is as follows:—

Mors ei quae bene vixit Lucrum.

Elizabeth Andros being of the Ancient Familie of the Andros of Tavnton in Somerset Shire was ye first wif unto Sir Thos Fludd of Millgate Knight: By whom he had divers sonns and davghters whose names are expressed on his Monument. What her matchless Industrie in Housewifry was, and how amply she expressed herself in the entertainment of her friends and in what lavdable manner her hospitality was extended towards ye poore we need not to expresse in writing, seeing that ye essentiall characters thereof are engraven even to this very day in the hearts of such as are yet living who were conversant with her in her lif time: she changed this mortal life for an immortal the 25th day of January, 1591.

"Accept, O blessed soul, as sacrifice,
A filial signal of obedience,
And let this marble memorie suffice,
Altho' but in a part of recompense,
To manifest the loyal duty of your sonne,
Before his toilsome pilgrimage of life be done."

The son erected also a monument to the memory of his father, Sir Thomas Fludd, but the exceedingly long inscription is very much defaced.

Somewhere about the year 1855 this monument was unfortunately removed from the chancel to the vestry under the tower. It is in marble and includes a bust of Robert Fludd, with the right arm and hand resting upon an open book. The inscription in this case is as follows :

Sacred to the Memory

of the Illustrious Physician and Man Robert Fludd, alias De Fluctibus, Doctor of both Faculties, who after some years of travelling beyond seas, undertaken successfully for the improvement of his mind, was at length restored to his Fatherland and was not undeservedly received into the Society of the London College of Physicians. He exchanged life for death peacefully on the 8th day of the month of September A° Dni MDCXXXVII, in the 63rd year of his age.

No costly perfumes from this urn ascend ;
In gorgeous tomb thine ashes do not lie ;
Thy mortal part alone to earth we give ;
The records of thy mind can never die :
For he who writes like thee—though dead—
Erects a tomb that lasts for aye.

Thomas Fludd of Gore Court, Otham, in Kent, Esquire, erected this Monument to the happy Memory of his most dear Uncle on the 10th day of the month of August, MDCCXXXVIII.[1]

It has been reconstructed by Dr. Craven and will be found in the fourth chapter of his work, already cited. We learn from this source that Robert was the fifth of six sons and that two daughters were also born to his parents. Thomas Fludd came of a Shropshire family and was knighted by Queen Elizabeth for his military services.

[1] *Sacrum Memoriæ Claris : Doctissq : viri* Roberti Fludd, *alias de Fluctibus, utriusq : Medicinæ Doctoris, qui post aliquot annorum perigrinationem quam ad recipiendum ingenii cultum in transmarinos regiones fæliciter susceperat, patriae tandem restitutus et in celeberrimi Collegii Medicorum*

The entire monument is enclosed by an arch; there are armorial bearings behind the head of the bust; and on each side there were originally four books arranged one above the other. Two only remain and are inscribed respectively *Mysterium Cabalisticum* and *Philosophia Sacra*.

A rugged and precipitous footpath brings the traveller —proceeding south-east from the church—once more to a main road and opposite the lodge-gate of Milgate House, in which Robert Fludd was born.[1] The manorial residence itself is in one of the best manners of the country-seat of its period. At the time of my visit—now twenty-five years ago—the lodge was empty and open-windowed; the bosky, winding drive which led from gate to manor was somewhat wild and weedy; amidst ferns on the left, with an occasional glimpse of deer, was a cluster of tiny cottages, all untenanted; and the house itself was empty. For the

Londinensis Societatem non immerito electus vitam morte placide commutavit viii die mensis viibris, Ao Dni MDCXXXVII œtatis suœ LXIII.

Magnificis hæc non sub odoribus urna vaporat
Crypta tegit cineres nec speciosa tuos
Quod mortale minus tibi te committimus unum
Ingenii vivent hic monumenta tui,
Nam tibi qui similis scribit, moriturque, sepulchrum
Pro tota æternum posteritate facit.

Hac monumentum THOMAS FLUDD, *Gore Courte, in Otham, Apud Cantianos Armiger in fœlicissimam charissimi Patrui sui memoriam erexit, die X mensis Augusti MDCXXXVIII.*

The rendering of the Latin verses given in the text above is that which appears in Archdeacon Craven's DOCTOR ROBERT FLUDD, THE ENGLISH ROSICRUCIAN.

[1] Speaking of its proximity to the church, Archdeacon Craven says: "Not far off stands the more modern house of Milgate"; i.e., modern in respect of the church. Presumably on this basis Dr. Westcott says that "the site of the house where Robert Fludd was born is now occupied by a more recent building." See TRANSACTIONS of the Metropolitan College, 1907, p. 47. According to Hasted—HISTORY OF KENT, II, 486, 487—Sir Thomas Fludd improved and augmented it. Whether it was ever entirely rebuilt I have not been able to ascertain. It is not as it stands exactly an edifice of the sixteenth century, but when I went over it many years ago, I have a pious hope that it was at least in parts the house in which Fludd was born and not something altogether different erected on the same site.

first time on record, whether for Kentish histories—like that of monumental Hasted—or for still more archaic "Visitations," the house was explored, as I need not tell, even from roof to basement. As one who goes back through the centuries to a desired place and time, I saw the strange mythological paintings which adorn the fine staircase, trod the echoing floor of the library and admired its beautiful oak panelling, paused a little before the spacious chimney-corner of the great kitchen, passed upstairs to the quaint and not too roomy drawing-room, perchance a retreat for ladies of quality in the reign of James I, and traversed the innumerable bedrooms, in one of which it might be dreamed that Fludd was born. From almost every window there are charming views of a well-kept English lawn and English woodland vistas. The whole impression was delightful, though again there was nothing that could be called especially distinctive, and Milgate House, like Bearsted Church, may be seen in one of its varieties in many a shire and county, provided that manor or church be "four miles from any town."[1]

[1] On September 14, 1907, the Masonic Rosicrucians of the London Metropolitan College determined to visit Bearsted and the tomb of Robert Fludd. The date contained a sacrament, for it was the Festival of the Holy Cross or, more correctly, that of its Exaltation, a double of the first class in the Calendar of the Latin Rite. Presumably it connoted the Rosy Cross in the mind of Masonic Rosicrucians, who do not seem to have been aware that the church—as I have said in the text—was dedicated to the Holy Cross. But it was also a few days after the 270th anniversary of Fludd's death, and their object was to place "a memorial wreath on his monument." They termed the excursion a pilgrimage, but it was performed by train. They were aware in their zeal that the excellent Hargrave Jennings had made such a journey previously, or at least dreamed that he did. His lucubration on the subject in THE ROSICRUCIANS is quoted in a memorial of the later adventure in the TRANSACTIONS of the Metropolitan College for the year in question. The Supreme Magus was moved so much beyond his wont by the occasion and its circumstances that he delivered no less than two Orations, one before the monument beneath the tower and one subsequently at the Ancient Bell Hotel, Maidstone, where the Rosicrucians took their tea. In the earlier discourse Dr. Westcott states that Fludd "may be well called

There is full opportunity for the ordinary literate reader to make acquaintance at this day—at least in a preliminary sense—with Robert Fludd of Bearsted, reputed Rosicrucian and memorable occult philosopher. If a student of animal magnetism, one may meet with his name and a summary account concerning him in Joseph Ennemoser's attempt

the first and chief of English Rosicrucians," ignoring the preliminary and vital question whether in the absence of all direct evidence it is legitimate to term him a Rosicrucian at all—except by mental dedication. We can say only that he was the first English expositor and defender of Rosicrucian claims and principles, as they were put forth in Germany. Westcott speaks further of Fludd's "intimate connection with the great German Rosicrucian Magus Michael Maier, whom he greatly admired and respected" and by whom he was led "to enter with the greatest ardour into Rosicrucian studies." To these positives and superlatives I will add merely that the statement is *ludibrium magnum*. There is no evidence of intimate acquaintance between Fludd and Maier; there is so little evidence of admiration and respect that Maier seems mentioned nowhere in Fludd's writings. The story that they met in England is a precarious inference from the fact that Maier came over, by his own testimony, to England and afterwards is said to have published a work of Fludd's in Germany. That Maier was a Rosicrucian Magus there is no scrap of direct evidence to shew: such a denomination appears—as I believe—for the first time in a work of Magister Pianco belonging to the year 1782. Having testified thus in the Church the Supreme Magus proceeded to testify in the hostelry, where he affirmed that Fludd during his foreign travels "became acquainted with the Rosicrucian Fraternity and"—it being desirable apparently to accentuate the previous point—"made a notable friend of the famous Magus and adept Michael Maier." It will be seen that the latter has taken another grade in the occult hierarchy. But Fludd, by his own shewing, returned to England in or about 1604, at which date neither Westcott nor another can bring forward any proof that the Fraternity was in existence, except possibly in the mind of Simon Studion, while as regards Maier he had published nothing and was utterly unknown. Elsewhere and long previously the "Supreme Magus" affirmed that Fludd was initiated abroad. See ARS QUATUOR CORONATORUM, Vol. VII, p. 41. The story of his initiation is old—much older than the Metropolitan Chapter and all its lights of learning. Reghellini, in the year 1833, offers the following statements: (1) That the R∴R∴✠∴✠∴ appeared in England; (2) that Robert Fludd wrote a book in defence of the Rosicrucian Brethren; (3) that he was initiated and had a large number of disciples; (4) that he applied the principles of the Gnostics to physics; and (5) that, as a sequel of his system there followed that great revolution which came about in English science.—LA MAÇONNERIE, etc., already cited. But in the last clause Reghellini appears to confuse Fludd with Bacon.

to explain the whole history of magic by means of the force which Mesmer found or recovered at the close of the eighteenth century.[1] If drawn alternatively to investigate the origins of the Masonic Fraternity, he will have seen certain dubious and somewhat sensational references to Fludd in that fantastic exposition which Thomas de Quincey adapted from the German Bühle, under the title of ROSICRUCIANS AND FREEMASONS. But if his interest be rather towards the mysterious and elusive Brotherhood which united the Rose and Cross in a single symbol, he may have met with Fludd's literary and philosophical portrait at much greater length in one of my early studies of this subject,[2] or with the connection between Fludd and alchemy in my *Lives of Alchemystical Philosophers*[3] and elsewhere. Finally, he may have had recourse to the excellent monograph on DOCTOR ROBERT FLUDD by Archdeacon Craven, of whose great care and sympathy it is good to offer this brief word in recognition.

I have mentioned here the most available sources of information in what is practically a chronological order, but those who would still pursue the subject must have recourse to the philosopher's chief writings, which are buried —with one exception—in Latin of the seventeenth century and are mostly books in folio. They perplexed the scholars of their own period and they perplexed rare readers in later generations, till it seemed to be understood that the author might be named indeed but not consulted. Yet a good deal of curious lore has accreted about his memory, and he stands now somewhat as a figure in philosophical romance. Mr. Craven has dealt as he could with Fludd's involved system and has furnished most material help, taking the texts successively. The works treat of life,

[1] See HISTORY OF MAGIC, 2 vols., in Bohn's translation.
[2] REAL HISTORY OF THE ROSICRUCIANS, 1887, *cap.* XI.
[3] Published in 1888. See p. 16, *s.v.* Michael Maier.

death and resurrection; the macrocosmos, or greater world; the world in little, or the microcosm; Mosaical cosmogony; the universal medicine; above all the claims put forward by the Rosicrucian Brotherhood and the recognition due to these. According to his own description—as we shall see shortly—he was a seeker through all and in all for "the unknown basis of true philosophy and the supreme secret" of healing. At the beginning of the seventeenth century, as it did for some time afterwards, this quest signified a Kabalistical interpretation of the universe and the pursuit of alchemy. The theosophical tradition of Israel—represented by the word Kabalism—was a great intellectual puzzle and wonder of that time, and Fludd was one of its students, so far at least as its literature had passed into the Latin tongue. William Postel had translated THE BOOK OF FORMATION.[1] Riccius, Reuchlin and Archangelus de Burgo Nuovo had brought back glad tidings from Hebrew and Aramaic texts.[2] Portent and comet of a season, Picus de Mirandula had flashed much earlier across the horizon of Europe and passed too soon; but he had left his THESES CABBALISTICÆ and the amazing report of Esdras manuscripts, which embodied all mysteries of Israel from the days of the patriarch Abraham.[3] Like all those who preceded him, Fludd construed the tradition in the light of Christian revelation. As to the alchemists whom he followed, "their voices were in all men's ears." Both subjects belonged to the romantic mind of the period,

[1] Gulielmus Postellus: Abrahami Patriarchæ LIBER JESIRAH. *Parisiis*, 1552.

[2] There was also Petrus Galatinus: DE ARCANIS CATHOLICÆ VERITATIS, 1602, being twelve books in folio of Dialogues between himself and Reuchlin. It is followed by Joannes Reuchlinus: DE ARTE CABALISTICA, *Libri Tres*.

[3] The texts which came actually into his hands were those comprised in the SEPHER HA ZOHAR. They are described briefly by Jacques Gaffarel in *Codicum Cabbalisticorum Manuscriptorum quibus est usus Joannes Picus Comes Mirandulanus* INDEX. Parisiis, 1651.

and—so far as England was concerned in the days of James I—it is this romance which has taken name and shape about Fludd. It was not a time of tolerance, as people may know if they read or remember history ; but the Reformation meant qualified liberation here and in Germany. The horizon was extending everywhere ; the study of different philosophies, of theosophical systems more than these, and above all of Nature, working in her secret laboratories, offered an escape from the narrow measures of reform in official doctrine and practice, without rejecting the reform and without ceasing to be " a true Protestant in the best sense of the Church of England "[1] or of Luther.

It was further a period of great claims in the so-called occult world, and not long after Robert Fludd " was at length returned to his Fatherland," after those " years of travelling beyond seas " mentioned on his monument at Bearsted, the star of Rosicrucianism rose over the German world. His six years' tour had included Germany as well as France, Spain and Italy, and one of his biographers suggests that during its course he imbibed that taste for Rosicrucian philosophy by which his after life and all his writings are coloured.[2] I am perhaps a little surprised that the makers of imaginative history have not found material more to their purpose in this travelling. We have seen that speculation adorned in pontificals of certitude supposes a first meeting with Maier the alchemist abroad, thus beginning an acquaintance which was to be renewed and improved in England at a later date. But what was to prevent Fludd from seeing and even instructing the famous Johannes Valentinus Andreæ, then a precocious boy in his 'teens ? And if indeed the Order of the Rosy Cross lies hidden as to its origin behind the year 1614, should it not be possible

[1] It is the quaint testimony of Thomas Vaughan concerning himself.

[2] See Munk's ROLL OF THE ROYAL COLLEGE OF PHYSICIANS, Vol. I, p. 150.

for one who carried all its seals of dedication to have come across Simon Studion and even to have inspected NAOMETRIA on the eve of his return to England? The opportunity would appear to have been missed because, according to all use and wont, the occult fiction must be not alone contrary to fact but against all colour of reason and all traceable likelihood.[1]

Fludd returned from abroad in or about 1604 to graduate in medicine at Oxford on May 16, 1605[2] and after several difficulties—owing to his opinions and apparently his personal manners—he was admitted a Fellow of the College of Physicians on September 20, 1609.[3] It was not till 1616, being forty-two years old, that he first appeared in print, when he wrote in defence of the early Rosicrucian pamphlets and the claims embodied thereby. He was drawn to them in three ways: (1) By an innate love of the marvellous, accompanied by credulity which was extraordinary even for his period and for the particular bent of his interests; (2) by the fact that the Rosicrucians purported to be an association of masters keeping guard over those very possessions to which Fludd himself aspired—the basis of philosophy and the supreme secret of medicine; and (3) by the fact that he may have been acquainted—we have seen that this is a thorny question—with one of identical dedications, who became himself a German exponent of the Order and whom there is considerable reason for connecting later on with the society at its headquarters, assuming its corporate existence at that period—I mean, the alchemist Michael Maier. The publication to which I have alluded is called A COMPENDIOUS APOLOGY *for the Fraternity of the Rosy Cross*, *pelted with the Mire of Suspicion and Infamy*, *but*

[1] Witness occult reveries on the Bacon-Shakespeare question and generally on Rosicrucian history and doctrine.

[2] Munk, *op. cit.*, p. 150. [3] *Ibid.*, pp. 150–3.

now cleansed and purged as by the Waters of Truth.[1] Though his name appears on the title, it has been stated that this minute tract was not the work of Fludd, on the authority of what evidence I have never been able to ascertain. The point is not unimportant, for it is not only the first work ever penned in England on the Order of the Rosy Cross, but if correctly attributed, it follows that Robert Fludd preceded Michael Maier in that defence and exposition of the Fraternity which engrossed the zeal of both. It is possible fortunately to determine the question by recourse to a manuscript in the Library of the British Museum. It is a thin quarto volume in the handwriting of the period, exceedingly clear and beautiful, but unfortunately regarded as the copy of a destroyed original, in which case there is no known autograph of Fludd now in existence. It is entitled: A SHORT DECLARATION, *addressed to the Most Serene and Potent Prince and Lord, the Lord* JAMES, *King of Great Britain, France and Ireland, and Defender of the Faith: Wherein is made clear the true purpose of a certain published Work on the part of the Author himself, to wit,* ROBERT FLUDD, *Esquire and Doctor of Medicine, unto the King's Majesty.*[2] The published work referred to is called TRACTATUS MEUS APOLOGETICUS.[3] The curiosity and probably the suspicion of the royal mind had been excited by the defence of an occult Order on the part of his

[1] APOLOGIA COMPENDIARIA FRATERNITATEM DE ROSEA CRUCE *suspicioni. et infamiæ maculis aspersam, veritatis quasi Fluctibus abluens et abstergens*: *Auctore* R. de Fluctibus, M.D., Lond. *Leydæ apud* Godefridum Bassons 1616. But see later on respecting TRACTATUS APOLOGETICUS, which appeared in 1617.

[2] DECLARATIO BREVIS, *Serenissimo et Potentissimo Principi ac Domino, Domino* JACOBO, *Magnæ Britanniæ, Franciæ et Hyberniæ Regi, Fideique Defensori dedicata, in qua sincera operis cujusdam publicati intentio Majestati ipsius Regiæ luculenter per ipsum auctorem* ROBERTUM FLUD, *Armigerum et in Medicina Doctorem Regiæ Majestati subditissimum explicatur.*

[3] A second and more extended tract of Fludd's, described subsequently. It embodied the first pamphlet, as we shall see.

Kentish subject. He may have doubted the Rosicrucians because rumours of witchcraft would be abroad already concerning them, while we know that he believed in witchcraft and feared it. By consequence, he would also be doubting Fludd, who followed strange ways in medicine and whose ways may not have been unknown. It would appear that the SHORT DECLARATION was penned in obedience to the royal demand, not perhaps without some trepidation on the part of the "philosopher by fire." Be this as it may, the opportunity was favourable for compliment, and though Fludd's explanation is manly and honest enough, it is sweetened at the beginning by just that measure of adulation which was to be expected under the circumstances. This finished, he proceeds to clear his treatise from any suspicion of heresy or desire to make innovations in religion, explaining that the reformed faith —"as in use amongst us in England"—was infused into him almost with his mother's milk and had been adhered to faithfully ever since. Then next on the question of immorality, he affirms "in the sight of God and of your Majesty" that he had lived always as *virgo immaculata*.[1] With regard to the Rosicrucians, that school of philosophers is acknowledged by the Germans—whether Papists or Lutherans—to have embraced most firmly the religion of Calvin, in support of which statement Fludd cites a letter received by him from a friend at Frankfurt, named Justus Helt, and refers afterwards to the CONFESSION issued by the Fraternity, "wherein it is most openly declared that they belong to the reformed religion." That which attracted Fludd towards the Rosicrucians he admits to be their revela-

[1] We know him otherwise as a high-minded Christian gentleman who—for reasons which do not transpire—never entered into the bonds of wedlock. Was it because in undertaking to defend the Rosicrucians he modelled himself on the rule of the first members, who are described in the FAMA as "all bachelors and of vowed virginity"? Was it because he was incorporated and living under their rule?

tion[1] of a hitherto unknown basis of true philosophy and of that supreme secret of medicine to which I have referred already. On these points he submits certain propositions for the royal assent, and proceeds to develop various considerations concerning them, after which there are matters connected with the dedication to the King of his forthcoming work on the MACROCOSM ; but this is outside our inquiry.[2] The manuscript ends with citations of commendatory letters received by the author from various foreigners of philosophical or other eminence, including the beforementioned Justus Helt, Jean Balthasar and others. There is a final commendation of his cause to the justice and wisdom of his king.

While this very curious document, so long unaccountably passed over, establishes the authorship of the TRACTATUS APOLOGETICUS and exhibits the alleged religious tenets of original Rosicrucianism to some extent in a new light, there is nothing which predisposes a critical reader to include Robert Fludd in a list of the Society's initiates, for —taken by itself—the reference to a new basis of philosophy on which I have annotated is wholly inadequate as evidence. It may be warrantable to urge that he would have concealed the fact of his membership from the curiosity of a suspicious king, but this argument scarcely concerns our inquiry, which is a quest after information. For its absence there may be good reason, but the information is not there.

[1] The fact of such a basis is affirmed but cannot be said to be revealed by Rosicrucian early literature. If Fludd spoke from within the circle we should understand his statement better.

[2] The reference is to UTRIUSQUE COSMI MAJORIS SCILICET ET MINORIS *Metaphysica, Physica atque Technica. In duo volumina secundum Cosmi differentiam divisa.* The first tract of the first volume appeared at Oppenheim in 1617, the dedication in question being preceded by a dedication to God. The second tract was published in 1618. Vol. II began publication in 1619, was continued in 1621, but never completed.

It will be noted that the APOLOGIA COMPENDIARIA appeared at Leyden in 1616, but the SHORT DECLARATION refers to a TRACTATUS APOLOGETICUS, which belongs to the following year and had the same place of publication.[1] I have dealt with them so far as if they constituted a single tract and this is essentially correct, the first having been reprinted in the second as a *Proœmium* thereunto. It was therefore no more than an *avant-courier* or advertisement of the more extended work which followed it. In both there is a memorable epilogue addressed to the Brethren,[2] wishing them salvation in Jesus Christ, whom they worship sincerely and purely. For the errors which may be found in his treatise the author craves forgiveness, saying that he is but a rude philosopher and an unworthy publisher of their praise. As regards his own personality, he is one of a certain nobility—in respect of his nation, birth, status and earthly name. His bride is the desire of wisdom; his children are those fruits which are thence begotten; his body is accounted as a prison; for him the pleasures of the world are vain and deadly to the mind. He desires to be a glass unto himself, wherein he may contemplate what he is. He describes how in mind and in body he has traversed the chief countries of Europe, dared the depths and tempests of the sea, withstood the toils of mountains, the slippery descents of valleys, rude and savage shores, hostile cities, the pride, ambition, avarice, deceit, faithlessness, ignorance and indolence of men; but he has

[1] TRACTATUS APOLOGETICUS, *integritatem* SOCIETATIS DE ROSEA CRUCE *defendens. In qua probatur contra* D. LIBAVII *et aliorum ejusdem farinæ calumnias, quod admirabilia nobis a* FRATERNITATE R.∴C.∴ *oblata, sine improba Magiæ impostura aut Diaboli præstigiis et illusionibus præstari possint. Authore* R. DE FLUCTIBUS ANGLO, *M.D.L. Lugduni Batavorum apud* GODEFRIDUM BASSON. *Anno Domini* 1617. Dr. Westcott calls the minute APOLOGIA COMPENDIARIA a "volume" and says that it was republished in 1617 under the new title—a very misleading reference from a bibliographical point of view. TRANSACTIONS, 1907, p, 45.

[2] The Epilogue of the first work is amplified slightly in the second.

discovered nowhere anyone who has attained to the height of felicity or has come truly to know himself. Vanity of vanities is to be found everywhere, and all things are as vanity and wretchedness. Finally, he prays and beseeches the Brothers of the Rosy Cross—by their faith and by the ignorance of the age in true and pure philosophy—to be with him and to protect him, to be mindful of him and of their promises.

What those promises were may be determined by a simple reference to the text of the FAMA FRATERNITATIS: (1) That those who communicate their minds by print or otherwise shall hear from the Order, by word of mouth or in writing, and (2) that whosoever has affection thereunto shall benefit "in goods, body and soul." These assurances are checked in the CONFESSIO by two qualifying affirmations: (1) That "we shall never be manifested unto any man unless God should favour it" and (2) that he "who thinks to be partaker of our riches against the will of God . . . shall sooner lose his life in seeking than attain happiness by finding us." Alternatively, the promises of which Fludd asks the Order to be mindful may be of a more intimate kind and connote things personal to himself. While this is pure speculation, it may not be without a reason that the Epilogue of APOLOGIA COMPENDIARIA says simply: *Valete nostrique memores estote*, which carries no implication and is little more than a courtesy of diction in drawing an address to its conclusion; but the enlarged Epilogue to the TRACTATUS APOLOGETICUS says: *Valete, Fratres suavissimi, in illo ipso quem syncere colimus. Valete, inquam, iterumque valete, et mihi (per vestrem fidem, perque hujus sæculi in Philosophia vera et pura ignorantiam vos oro atque obtestor) favete, adeste: meique et promissorum vestrorum memores estote.* The extension is significant, and though it is not strengthened by the context as quoted, it seems to me—under all necessary reserves—that it could have been addressed by the novice of a Secret Order to Superiors by whom he had been admitted.[1]

The TRACTATUS APOLOGETICUS is not otherwise a work which brings any especial conviction, save only on its writer's sincerity.[2] The story of Christian Rosy Cross is affirmed to be important for its traditional value and very high from the ethical standpoint, but the tract is in particular a defence of the Order as an advocate of general reform—reform in Natural Philosophy, nothing short of revolution in Medicine, and a radical change in all that concerns Alchemy. Now, the quality of championship must be judged in respect of Natural Philosophy by Fludd's militant hostility to experimental methods, his appeal from particulars to universals and his insistence on the secret wisdom which unveils Nature and draws from the Fountain of Life. So also in respect of Medicine, for him it is in a state of widowhood, apart from the Universal Medicine which is like a crown of all art in healing. As regards Alchemy, a different note is sounded when it is affirmed to be enveloped in a maze of processes, buried under a cloud of symbols and lost utterly amidst a great multitude of arbitrary and fictitious terms. Hereof are the impediments of science, which must be taken out of its way. The remedy in respect of Natural Philosophy is by recourse to the ancient philosophers and by decoding their occult meanings, holding fast—for example—to the doctrine of actives and passives and contemplating the wisdom of

[1] So expressed and so guarded, my suggestion is to be distinguished from the speculations expressed in terms of certitude which characterise manufacturers of dream like Dr. Wynn Westcott, who, without a particle of evidence to justify, affirms (1) that Maier visited Fludd in London and (2) that "the result of his visit was, we know, the publication of his"—meaning Fludd's—"APOLOGIA, written in Latin and published in Leyden in 1616." See ARS QUATUOR CORONATORUM, Vol. VIII.

[2] Mr. Wigston thinks that it gives evidence of a reconstruction or remodelling of the Rosy Cross in England. As a fact, it is evidence only of Fludd's point of view.

universals with eyes of understanding. The reform in the department of Medicine is in the recognition and attainment of the one and only medicament, being that of Hippocrates, and an accurate understanding of its composition, virtues and operations. In Alchemy the way of advancement is to realise that its true work is a work of Nature only, and that he who would co-operate therewith must use natural matrices in place of artificial furnaces, applying natural things to things which are also natural and " species to their congruents." But the canonical writers on alchemy had borne their testimony to these irrepealable canons of the art through several generations prior to Robert Fludd.

Like Simon Studion and like Paracelsus yet earlier, the TRACTATUS maintains that there are Books of God, both visible and invisible, that Nature herself is written within and without, that the universe around us is full of mystical characters, and that because of these things " day unto day uttereth speech and night unto night sheweth knowledge." The stars also are a voice in the silence, and astrology carries a great book of portents for those who can read therein. The distinctions of Fludd on the kinds and classes of Magia are unfolded with considerable elaboration, to exonerate the Rosicrucian Order from charges advanced by Libavius and others on the subject of the Black Art. Venific, necromantic, goetic, malefic and so-called theurgic Magic are set apart as so many forms of diabolical commerce ; but that which concerns the Order is of another category, inspired by other motives and derived from a celestial source, being that perfect knowledge of natural things, above and below, in heaven and on earth, by which the three Kings of the East were led in the light of a new star, even to the cradle of Him Who—because He is the Sun of Righteousness—is the true Light of the World. After this manner is Robert Fludd led on in fine to treat of the Mysteries of Light and the blessed state of those who have come to understand its virtues as the cause of all energies.

It is in moments like these that the Kentish theosophist becomes worthy of a higher title than the technical designation of a Philosopher by Fire—which was held in the past to characterise the alchemical fraternity at large.[1] He was a philosopher by the Light in Christ: whether at his best or worst, he wrote always therein; and as I believe that he lived under it, so I have no doubt that the light abode within him. With the sole exception of PHILOSOPHIA MOSAICA his chief works have never been put into English, and only in the case of TRACTATUS APOLOGETICUS was a second edition attained. It was translated into German in 1782 by Adam Booz at Leipsic,[2] who appended certain annotations which are curious contributions to the text and reproduce its spirit after the lapse of over one hundred and sixty years. We hear of the art of Palingenesis, said to have been discovered and made known by the naturalist

[1] It is used by Anthony à Wood in his description of Fludd and of other Hermetic *literati* whose biographies are found in ATHENÆ OXONIENSES. When it first began to be current remains an open question but certainly it did not originate with the pupil of Peter Sthael.

[2] "DEFENCE OF THE GENUINE CHARACTER OF THE SOCIETY OF THE ROSICRUCIANS, *by the Englishman* ROBERTUS DE FLUCTIBUS, *Doctor of the Medical Fraternity of London. Translated from the Latin into German by request, and on account of its great rarity and importance, together with certain annotations, by* ADAM BOOZ. Leipsic: *published by* ADAM FREDERIC BÖHME. 1782." It is probably to Booz in the first instance that Kloss was indebted for the story that John Dee dedicated his edition of Roger Bacon's tract to the Rosicrucian Fraternity. The note of Booz is as follows: "The annotations of John Dee upon the treatise of Roger Bacon entitled THE WONDERS OF ART AND NATURE AND THE NULLITY OF MAGIC are included with the said tract in THEATRUM CHEMICUM, vol. 5, and are prefaced by a dedication to the Rosicrucians which is couched thus: *Clarissimis Restitutionis Universi Phosphoris Illuminatis* ROSEÆ CRUCIS FRATRIBUS *unanimis.* Herein is the Society overwhelmed with powerful and deserved praises. Robert Fludd is mentioned—in a most complimentary manner—in the preface, while the objector Libavius is completely and properly despatched." Like those who repeated this unhappy reference subsequently, the excellent Booz had failed to read his text intelligently.

Buoss in Aura, though I think that the mythos goes back into a much further past[1]; of everlasting books and ever-burning lamps,[2] like those which were found in the sepulchre of Christian Rosy Cross, according to his legend in the FAMA.

The TRACTATUS APOLOGETICUS was followed by a TRAC-

[1] It is explained that by means of a magnetic electrum the rays of the Sun and Moon are drawn out of a viscous water and thus it becomes crystalline. There is nothing added, but in the space of four weeks wonderful starry flowers grow up herein. These flowers can be resolved again into water by a little *aqua de nubibus* and can be passed through blotting-paper. But in the space of another four weeks the flowers will be produced once more, reassuming their former shapes. "When the sun shines they diffuse such a radiance that the eye cannot support it." Adam Booz adds that an experiment of this kind took place on May 28, 1776, before "many noble persons," and it seems to have been recorded in THE HAMBURG CORRESPONDENT, IV, 127, of that year. "Should lovers of these wonderful flowers . . . desire ocular demonstration," he affirms finally, "it will be supplied with full instructions, so that no one can fail therein." It is said that the flowers could be transported from place to place, either in dry or fluid condition.

[2] It is related that the Count of Carburi at Venice rediscovered incombustible paper, and that the Senate caused a medal to be struck in his honour *ad perpetuam rei memoriam*. The paper was made in the first instance by Marco Antonio Castagne, overseer of some mines in Italy, where he found a great quantity of amianthus stones, out of which he prepared incombustible skins, paper and lamp-wicks. I may explain here that Amianthus, according to Rulandus in his LEXICON ALCHIMIÆ, is practically identical with asbestos and mica. It is described by Dioscorides and Pliny. Booz goes on to point out that "if the famed incombustible oil were discovered once again, everlasting lamps and eternal fire would become ours," adding that they were frequent among the ancients. The artist Castagne, on the basis of his own achievement, is said to have promised a book made of amianthus, "as to binding, paper and thread." He would write in it with letters of gold, "so that the volume would not only be incombustible but would be safe from the effects of water and air, and might truly deserve the title of Book of Eternity or The Everlasting Book." Booz refers to the PHILOSOPHICAL TRANSACTIONS of June 19, 1671, and THEATRUM CHEMICUM, Vol. V, p. 435, but I have not carried the inquiry further. Readers—if any—of Fludd's TRACTATUS APOLOGETICUS may remember that he constructed a wooden bull "which lowed and bellowed after the fashion of the living animal." Booz caps this story by his account of an automaton chess-player, which was not only ready to compete with anyone but "there was no recorded example of the figure having lost a game."

TATUS THEOLOGO-PHILOSOPHICUS, concerning Life, Death and Resurrection, which was dedicated in the sub-title to those who are called Brethren of the Rosy Cross.[1] There is a story—originating with Bühle—that when Michael Maier left England he carried the manuscript of this work to Germany and saw it through the press in that country; but I have failed to find anything in support of the statement. It is a strange, enchanting book, perhaps with regard especially to its speculations concerning Paradise and how—as we learn otherwise from the ZOHAR —there is a Paradise here below but a Paradise also above: *unus erat ille terrestris, seu supra terram descriptus; alter supercœlestis et quasi intra novam Jerusalem situs, quæ totaliter spiritualis est.*[2] But I am concerned with the TRACTATUS only in so far as it can be gleaned for occasional references to the Order. It is divided into three books, corresponding to its three subjects. Towards the end of the first there is a consideration of the admirable knowledge enjoyed by Moses and Elias, and it is said to be a true key of wisdom. Out of this arises the question whether it has been taken utterly away from mankind, having regard to the fact that—according to the BOOK OF WISDOM— the spirit of God fills the whole earth and God has sent down His wisdom from the holy heavens, that it may dwell with man and with him also may work. The answer is that the delight of the Spirit of God is with the sons of men, that even unto this day it has remained with elect persons who are pure of heart, that the Sons of God have

[1] TRACTATUS THEOLOGO-PHILOSOPHICUS, *in Libros tres distributus, quorum de Vita, Morte, Resurrectione. Cui inseruntur nonulla Sapientiæ veteris, Adami infortunio superstitis, fragmenta: ex profundiori Sacrarum Literarum sensu et lumine, atque ex limpidori et liquidiori saniorum Philosophorum fonte hausta atque collecta,* FRATRIBUS A CRUCE ROSEA *dictis, dedicata, a* RUDOLFO OCREB BRITANNO. Oppenheim, 1617. There has been no question as to the authorship of this tract, and the adopted name decodes by transposition into Roberto Fludo.

[2] *Op. cit., Lib.* I, *cap.* 9.

been always in the world, that to such has been given the Tree of Life and to such the Hidden Manna. But the powers of men like these are unknown at this day and unknown are their Holy Houses. They abound in heavenly riches but are poor in the sight of the world. They are not doctors in theology, nor is the Pope himself one of them, though he appears to possess the seat of Jesus Christ. The real and efficacious gifts of the Spirit are prophecy, miracles, tongues, healing: those who come forward to proclaim hidden truths must manifest these powers, must be able to drive out demons and in their own lives must observe the Divine precepts, doing nothing contrary to the word of God.

Who were the representatives of this elect school in the days of Robert Fludd? They were the Brethren of the Rosy Cross, whom he proceeds to address at length: (1) As a result of close investigation, he has been led to the conclusion that they are illuminated truly by the Spirit and that to them are unfolded those things which the sacred texts have foreshewn mystically as preceding the end of the world. (2) They have been endowed with spiritual virtue and the higher Divine Grace. (3) If their deeds correspond to their words—and he can doubt no longer that they do—that which they prophesy on their own part must be accepted in faith, more especially as it is in perfect harmony with the sacred source of truth. (4) By an attentive study of their writings he has found that they act under the impulsion of the Holy Spirit. (5) They have knowledge of the true mystery and of that key which leads to the joy of Paradise. (6) They have therefore the freedom of Paradise, even as Elias of old. (7) To them it is no cause of pride that they are able to make gold, but they rejoice when the heavens open and at the sight of their names written in the Book of Life.[1]

[1] Compare FAMA FRATERNITATIS.

(8) Transferring the appeal to those whose minds are obscured by a cloud of ignorance, Robert Fludd invites mankind at large to agree with him that the Brethren of the Rosy Cross are guided by the Spirit of God, that their asylum—the House of the Holy Spirit—is situated at the world's end, and is there encompassed by clouds, or that it is on the apex of a high mountain and that those who dwell therein breathe in the sweet and rarefied air of the Psyche, or the life of true wisdom.

In the book concerning resurrection the Brethren are said to abide in a light which is greater than that of the rising sun. Their celestial treasure is contrasted with the metallic gold which is sought after by errant and false alchemists. The sun in the roof of the tomb of Christian Rosy Cross is said to have been an emblem of Christ, the Sun of Justice, and there is another reference to His advent. It will be seen that thus early in Fludd's defence of the Order, and thus early in its manifest history, the process of its spiritualisation had begun in the hands of the Kentish mystic; but it was to be carried yet further. Already in his prevision concerning the New Jerusalem, descending four-square out of heaven, it would seem that the Rosicrucians were warders of the gates and keepers of the sacred precincts, if they were not also the priests and rulers therein, under Him Who is the light thereof and the Tree of Life in its midst.

Supposing the Rosicrucian manifestoes to have emanated from a corporate society or that they led—as perhaps intended—to such a foundation soon after they were issued, the TRACTATUS APOLOGETICUS lends some colour to a supposition that Fludd was acquainted with the Order "as to their persons," to cite the quaint expression made use of by Thomas Vaughan in a similar but reverse connection.[1]

[1] THE FAME AND CONFESSION OF THE FRATERNITY OF R.∴C.∴ . . . *With a Preface annexed thereto. . . .* By EUGENIUS PHILALETHES. 1652. Preface, c. 3 (obverse). See also A. E. WAITE: *The Works of Thomas Vaughan*, 1919, p. 365.

But again it is entirely a matter of inference, and amidst its quaint and melancholy panegyric upon the majesty of the science of the past there is no light of detail shed upon the original documents or upon the association which it defends. The fact may seem explicable on its surface by regarding Robert Fludd as a novice *in absentia*, far away from the seat of authority, and we shall see that at a later period he adopts another tone. But one of the amazing things connected with the whole debate is the existence of so considerable a literature dealing, or professing to deal, with a single subject, which neither friends nor enemies have succeeded in elucidating. From one point of view the subsequent writings of Fludd—which are of some importance as a presentation of the Secret Tradition in Christian Times, coloured in its passage through the alembic of a singular mind—might be called a development at large of Rosicrucian philosophy. Putting aside some few things which are purely polemical, like a negligible answer to Foster on the question of the Weapon Salve, they might have been issued from first to last with the *imprimatur* of the Rosy Cross, as they contain no line or word which is not in complete consonance with the claims made by the Order and with the teaching thereto ascribed by all its German literature. I am concerned, however, only with the works of Fludd in so far as they cast direct additional light on the doctrine of the Rosy Cross. For a most careful and satisfactory account of those vast treatises which are concerned with the Macrocosm and Microcosm, with MEDICINA CATHOLICA, Mosaical Philosophy and Anatomy the reader may be referred with full confidence to Archdeacon Craven's study of Fludd and his philosophy.[1]

It was not until 1629 that Robert Fludd was called again to the defence of the Rosicrucian Brotherhood, and then

[1] *Op. cit., passim.*

it was owing to charges brought against himself and his system by Marin Mersenne in a certain commentary on Genesis.[1] Fludd answered under his own name in SOPHIÆ CUM MORIA CERTAMEN,[2] but this was a defence of himself and his principles. Book I deals with the Kentish philosopher's views on the science and philosophy of the Macrocosm, the harmony of the world, etc. So far from being new, it is affirmed that the wisdom of past ages is embodied therein, and the charge of atheism preferred ridiculously against him is exposed in its true light. The second book maintains in opposition to Mersenne that there is a soul of the world. In the third Fludd puts up a powerful defence against the charge of evil magic, which would not have been advanced had Mersenne known the subjects with which he was seeking to deal. In the fourth and last book Fludd vindicates his particular construction of Kabalistic tradition, not—however—that Mersenne can be looked upon as a serious assailant who regarded the tradition as wrested. These four books may be called, I think, an *apologia* at large for the philosophical life of its author. The *Fratres R∴C∴* are mentioned on the crowded title-page but not in the text. It was, however, a year of peculiar activity in the literary concerns of Fludd, and the publication with which I am dealing included also a tract called SUMMUM BONUM, issued under the name of Joachim Fritz.[3] There would not be the least doubt in

[1] QUESTIONES CELEBERRIMÆ IN GENESIM, *cum accurata textus explicatione, in quo volumine Athei et Deisti impugnantur.* Paris, 1622. Archdeacon Craven says that Mersenne was a literary friend of Descartes and "a man of universal learning."

[2] SOPHIÆ CUM MORIA CERTAMEN, *in quo Lapis Lydius a Falso Structore*, FR. MARINO MERSENNO, *Monacho Reprobatus, celeberrima Voluminis sui Babylonici (in Genesin) figmenta accurate examinat. Authore* ROBERTO FLUDD, *alias* DE FLUCTIBUS, etc. Frankfurt, 1629.

[3] SUMMUM BONUM, *Quod est Verum Subjectum Veræ Magiæ, Cabalæ, Alchymiæ*, FRATRUM ROSEÆ CRUCIS *verorum, in dictarum Scientiarum laudem, et insignis calumniatoris* FRATRIS MARINI MERSENNI *dedecus publicatum, Per* JOACHIMUM FRIZIUM. *Anno* 1629.

my mind that this also was the work of Robert Fludd, were it not for his own testimony. Everything about it recalls the man and his methods, including the elaborate tables, the setting forth of Mersenne's criticisms and of the replies thereto. Moreover, the style, spirit and views are those of the English Rosicrucian. But on p. 20 of CLAVIS PHILOSOPHIÆ ET ALCHYMIÆ FLUDDANÆ, referring to SUMMUM BONUM, Fludd remarks as follows: *Licet hoc non meum, sed amici mei intimi opus esse alibi asseverarim*, adding, however, the following qualification: *tamen ad omnes Lanovii Theologo-militis, gladio malevolentiæ me petentis, objectiones (quippe mere frivolas) respondebo*, the explanation being that Lanovius had attacked Fludd in attacking SUMMUM BONUM. I have only to add that there is and can be no appeal from the testimony of the Kentish philosopher.[1]

It will be seen that SUMMUM BONUM was a further reply to Mersenne and as regards three-fourths of the contents it covers much the same ground as the CERTAMEN. Book I treats of Magic; Book II is a study of Kabalism, regarded as a Mystery of God and Nature transmitted in secret; Book III deals with the *essentia* of true Alchemy, understood as a spiritual science and distinguished therefore

[1] Archdeacon Craven, who is unacquainted with this testimony, registers a taking but not convincing point when he cites from SUMMUM BONUM an affirmation on the part of the author that he "had already defended" the Rosicrucian Brethren in a tract. It seems obviously a reference to the TRACTATUS APOLOGETICUS, but it does not warrant us in saying with Craven that "whoever was author of the TRACTATUS APOLOGETICUS was also author of the SUMMUM BONUM." Joachim Fritz was not Robert Fludd, but he may have written one of the other apologies which came out by the score or the hundred before 1629. It is to be noted, in conclusion as to this question, that on p. 26 of the CLAVIS Fludd makes his printer responsible for placing SUMMUM BONUM at the end of the CERTAMEN against his own mandate to the contrary. He desired it to appear separately and in octavo, not in folio. The printer excused himself, maintaining that if both tracts, seeing that they belonged to one and the same subject, were included in one volume, it would be more useful and convenient.

from "vain tinctures" and sophistic operations. There is finally Book IV, "wherein the cause of the Brotherhood of the Rosy Cross . . . is strenuously and powerfully defended." [1] The memorable points in connection with this exoneration are: (1) The entire Rosicrucian claim is transferred to the spiritual plane, shining in the light of an exalted Christian Theosophy: it has become a Hidden Church of the Elect, in striking analogy with the Sanctuary of Karl Eckartshausen, the Interior Church of Lupukhin and the Mystic Temple of the Philadelphian Society. (2) The author of SUMMUM BONUM bears his testimony with the plenary certitude of one speaking from within: it is expressed with fervent devotion; and that it should be the work of an enthusiast about a House of the Holy Spirit of which he knows only by report appears incredible. But finally (3) as to their persons, names, places or anything concrete concerning them and their doings—in a word the external evidences—the apologia tells us nothing respecting the Brotherhood of the Rosy Cross. Once more, there may be good reasons, because it was a secret society and must be concealed even in manifestation, but the information is not there and SUMMUM BONUM leaves the historical position of the Order precisely where it was previously. Mersenne and many hundreds before him had asked "Where is the dwelling of the Brethren?" understood as an incorporated Society which had offered initiation at large to suitable persons in an official publication called FAMA FRATERNITATIS.[2] To answer that it is

[1] *In quo causa* FRATRUM ROSEÆ CRUCIS (*quos etiam petit malevolus iste per calumniam et malitiam*) *strenue et viriliter defenditur.*

[2] The position is that after the manner of their mystical founder they had taken credit for a bountiful readiness to impart all their secrets to the learned, that "the number and respect of our Fraternity" may be increased thereby, an offer which is bequeathed in the FAMA for those who are concerned to ponder. In this connection I may mention that Fludd is quoted as follows by Alexander Wilder: "There is scarcely one who thinks about us who does not believe that our Society has no existence, because, as he truly

in a house not made with hands, eternal in the heavens, transfers the question to a very high region indeed but can satisfy no one under all the circumstances. With the Holy Assemblies, Interior Churches and Hidden Temples which have not issued *pourparlers* the case is different: they have been heard of under other warrants—to be taken or left—and they have promised nothing.

On this understanding and under such reserve, the intimations of SUMMUM BONUM are exceedingly curious as the defence of an Order which less than twenty years previously had claimed incorporation in space and time, a local habitation and the palladium of a hallowed tomb, somewhere in the German Fatherland. The heads of the Fritz consideration are as follows: (1) The counsel at large of the Order and its object—expressed briefly—are embodied in the pregnant sentence: *Ascendamus ad montem rationabilem et ædificamus Domum Sapientiæ*, thus defining the Brotherhood as a Company of Spiritual Builders. (2) The corner-stone of this Building is Christ, while those who are integrated in the House are the Living Stones thereof. (3) The qualification required of aspirants is promulgated in a Rosicrucian Epistle attached to SUMMUM BONUM: *Transmutemini, transmutemini de lapidibus mortuis in lapides vivos philosophicos.* (4) I shall shew in a later chapter that the *mons rationabilis*, the Secret Mountain has entered into Rosicrucian allegorical literature independently of Robert Fludd and has been called a philosophical Horeb. (5) That which is built thereon, according to SUMMUM BONUM, is a Spiritual Palace, a House founded on the rock, the Holy Place of a Holy Priesthood. (6) The

declares, he never met any of us. And he concludes that there is no such Brotherhood because, in his vanity, we seek not him to be our fellow." I do not happen to have met with this passage in Fludd's writings, nor has Archdeacon Craven apparently, so I quote it under all reserves. From what I know of Dr. Wilder's methods, it is probably drawn at second hand, and in any case no reference is given. See THE THEOSOPHIST, I, p. 110.

place and its priesthood are filled with all heavenly riches, though the Brotherhood are poor and unknown in the eyes of the world.[1] (7) The dwellers in the House are those who are instructed, like Solomon, in true and Divine Magia, the true Kabalah and Chemia. (8) There have been a few always in the world who have gone in through the gate of this Temple, to be numbered among the Sons of God, who have shed their light upon humanity and illuminated the cloud of darkness which covers earthly things. (9) Temple, Palace or Cœnobium, the House of the Holy Spirit and House of the Rosy Cross—as may be collected from the words of the Brotherhood—is that of which the sacred pages speak. (10) It is the House of God, while the Stone of Foundation is that which was cut out without hands, which broke the feet of "the statue of false worship" and became a great mountain, filling the whole earth. (11) The House itself is no work of human construction, as foolish alchemists and sophistic Magi dream: it was built of old in wisdom. (12) It is the mystical Citadel of Bethlehem[2]—a House of Bread and Warfare, of Living Bread, even as that Manna which came down from Heaven. (13) *Escam dedit timentibus se*, and by such Food of Angels it is possible for every man to live without mortal bread.

Two things remain to be noted: (1) at the end of SUMMUM BONUM its concealed author anticipates the question whether he is himself a Brother of the Rosy Cross. The answer is skilful, implying a decisive affirmative while on the surface pretending to leave the question open. Such a grace from God has he least of all deserved: "it is not of

[1] Compare FAMA FRATERNITATIS: (1) "That there might be also a Society in Europe which should have gold, silver and precious stones, sufficient to bestow upon kings for their lawful use and purpose"; (2) "We do promise more gold than both the Indies bring to the King of Spain."

[2] The name Bethlehem is supposed to have signified House of Bread or alternatively House of War. Fludd connects it with Bethel, the attributed meaning of which is House of God.

him that willeth, nor of him that runneth, but of God that sheweth mercy."[1] Yet, if it have pleased God to have so ordained, this shall be enough.[2] (2) The Rosicrucian letter appended to SUMMUM BONUM was addressed, it is said, by the Brotherhood to a certain German, Dr. Fludd obtaining a copy from a Polish friend of Dantzic.[3] In Archdeacon Craven's opinion it conveys " a poor idea of the teaching or erudition of the Brotherhood." If, however, it can be regarded as a genuine official document, it is exceedingly important as indicating the spiritual dedications of the Order at the period to which it belongs. It is, of course, unsupported by anything which can be regarded as legal evidence and must therefore stand at its value according to the impression which it may convey to the literary sense of the reader. It is undated and there is hence no means of knowing how far it anteceded the year of publication, namely, 1629. The content may be scheduled in summary form as follows:

(1) The unknown person to whom it is addressed has completed the first year of his nativity, meaning his birth into the Order, and he is wished a felicitous " entrance into and exit " from life—an allusion to the life of initiation and the kind of departure which will be reached when he is raised to Heaven. (2) He is counselled to make progress in true knowledge, on the understanding that God is both the circumference and the centre. (3) It is small cause for wonder that an ungrateful world persecutes the professors

[1] Romans ix, 16.

[2] *Anne tu ex* ROSEÆ CRUCIS FRATERCULIS *unus? Ad ultimam interrogationem dico, me minime tantam unquam a Deo meruisse gratam, agnoscentem cum Apostolo, non est istud donum volentis aut currentis sed Dei miserescentis: si Deo placuisset voluisse sat erit.* The VULGATE reading of the text is: *Igitur non volentis, neque currentis, sed miserentis est Dei.*

[3] One is disposed to speculate whether the Polish friend may be the concealed author of SUMMUM BONUM, whether he was the recipient of the letter—perhaps several years previously—and was therefore a neophyte of the Order in one of its developments or variants.

of true arts, or indeed the truth itself. (4) For the sake, however, of their neophyte, the Order proposes to deal with three recurring questions among those who are without, being firstly its existence as a Brotherhood, secondly the activities with which it is concerned and thirdly the limits of its powers. I am afraid that no subtlety of interlinear reading can extract any answer to these questions from the text of the perfervid oration,[1] but the Fellowship of the Order is with the Father and Jesus, for which reason the Brethren address their recipient, so that he may rejoice "because God is light and in Him there is no darkness whatever." (5) Those who would come to them must have a gift of discernment in this light, for in any other it is impossible to behold the Brethren, unless they will it.[2] (6) An answer is not vouchsafed to all because there are many of deceitful mind.[3] (7) Those who are alienated from God are contrary to the Brethren and it would be folly to permit their entrance. (8) Be they changed therefore from dead stones into living philosophical stones.[4] (9) Let them follow the counsel of the apostle and have the same mind within them as there is in Christ Jesus. (10) The office of the Order is to lead back lost sheep to the true sheepfold. (11) Its Immovable Palace is the centre

[1] An old English version of the EPISTLE printed *in extenso* was in my REAL HISTORY OF THE ROSICRUCIANS: it must be admitted that the confused expression and continual deviation from the proposed subjects justify the opinion of Archdeacon Craven.

[2] This is quoted—without reference to the source—in the ANIMA MAGICA ABSCONDITA of Eugenius Philalethes. See my WORKS OF THOMAS VAUGHAN, 1919, p. 107. See also p. 364, where it is quoted again in the Introduction to the FAMA and CONFESSIO.

[3] It seems to me that this remark indicates that the EPISTLE was written somewhat early in the Rosicrucian debate. Disappointed applicants for admission had wearied of the subject long before 1629, and new applications had ceased.

[4] This aphorism is found also in the Rosicrucian document published by Eugenius Philalethes in LUMEN DE LUMINE. WORKS OF THOMAS VAUGHAN, pp. 259 *et seq.*

of all things, but it is concealed by many names. (12) It is the gate and school of Philosophical Love, wherein everlasting charity is taught. (13) It is that resplendent but invisible Castle which is built upon the Mountain of the Lord, " out of the root whereof there flows forth a fountain of living water and a river of love." (14) It is lawful to know Heaven by Heaven, not by earth, but the virtues of earth are known by those of Heaven. (15) Virtue is the supreme truth, and it will confirm those daily more and more who follow it with all their might in words and works. (16) The writer affirms in conclusion that the said Lady Virtue has commanded him to make these communications at this time to the recipient, but he shall be taught more largely hereafter, if he will keep surely that which has been committed to his trust.

There is no doubt in my mind that this document was going about at the period as a missive which had emanated from the inner circle of the Rosy Cross. When we come to examine the testimony which was borne to the subject by Thomas Vaughan at a later period in England we shall meet with several analogies, and it would appear therefore that the construction placed by Joachim Fritz on the ends and objects of the Fraternity was not exclusive to himself, though it was illuminated by Fludd's genius. The ordered contentions of SUMMUM BONUM—which he must have inspired, though he did not write—compare very favourably with the hectic and confused Epistle, but the issue and intention are one in both cases.

It has been said with considerable force by Bühle—and Archdeacon Craven who has followed the debate at first hand adopts the same view—that Mersenne was no match for Fludd and one who was much more able came to the rescue in the person of Petrus Gassendus.[1] Fludd was

[1] He was a French astronomer and philosophical writer, born on Jan. 22, 1592, and he died at Paris, Oct. 24, 1655. His first published volume

embroiled also with Franciscus Lanovius,[1] as he had been previously with Kepler. In 1633 Fludd published his last words on the general subjects at issue in CLAVIS PHILOSOPHIÆ ET ALCHYMIÆ FLUDDANÆ,[2] already quoted; but we are concerned with his answer only in so far as it connects with the problem of the Rosy Cross. Except when he speaks for himself—as it were, from his own platform—and then only on his personal understanding of Mystical and Divine alchemy—it is the dull record of an arid scholastic quarrel, about which we need note only that Fludd, with his vast learning, rather disdained Mersenne, while Fludd and Gassendus really respected each other.[3] Lanovius seems to have been of no particular consequence on either side of the debate. It appears that the Brethren of the Rosy Cross had been called libertines by this writer, and having

was certain EXERCITATIONES PARADOXICÆ ADVERSUS ARISTOTELÆOS. It appeared at Grenoble in 1624. The work in reply to Fludd was published at Paris in 1630 under the title: EPISTOLICA EXERCITATIO, *in qua præcipua principia philosophiæ* ROBERTI FLUDDI *deteguntur, et ad recentes illius libros adversus* PATREM MARINUM MERSENNUM *scriptos respondetur.*

[1] I have failed to trace Lanovius. He is not to be identified with François de la Noue, called Bras-le-Fer and also *un moraliste militaire du seizième siècle.* He is included among the great captains of France. Among his books is a DEFENSIO VERITATIS *adversus assertiones Catholicæ Fidei repugnantes.* 1594.

[2] CLAVIS PHILOSOPHIÆ ET ALCHYMIÆ FLUDDANÆ, *sive* ROBERTI FLUDDI *Armigeri et Medicinæ Doctoris ad Epistolicam* PETRI GASSENDI *Theologi Exercitationem Responsum. . . . Francoforti, Anno* 1633. A thin folio set closely in small type and an unfavourable specimen of the Fludd mode of book-production.

[3] Archdeacon Craven tells us, however, that Mersenne was also a man of learning, as we have seen in a previous note. His methods in criticism are characteristic of debate at the period. Isaac Disraeli reminds us in AMENITIES OF LITERATURE of Mersenne expressing astonishment that King James I should allow such a man as Fludd to live. The latter thereupon obtained an interview with his sovereign, to clear himself of "the Friar's scandalous report"—i.e. that Fludd, among other things, was an atheist. He found the King, as he says in his own words, "royally learned and gracious." Finally, "I found him my Kingly patron all the days of his life." Where this account is located in Fludd's writings does not appear. I have failed to find it in SOPHIÆ CUM MORIA CERTAMEN.

affirmed that on the contrary they were true seekers of Divine Mysteries, Fludd volunteers the following explanation, which is at once remarkable for its period and significant, in view of the anti-papal mouthings in CONFESSIO FRATERNITATIS R∴C∴.[1] He establishes *ex cathedra* that seekers of this kind are to be found in all religions—Papal, Lutheran, Calvinistic and so forward. As such, they adhere to the external Rites and Ceremonies which characterise their particular form of faith, not that they regard truth as concealed within outward observances, for truth is divine. They are so many forms and offices which express the principles of the sects, each after its own manner, and they are diligently observed and respected by every Brother of the Rosy Cross in accordance with the religious school to which he belongs. They are of the laws and politics of this or the other Church, and he regulates his life in their path, lest he be a source of scandal to his neighbours. So passes out of sight for ever the FAMA's boasted dedication to the "forms and ceremonies of the first and renewed church," its limitation of the sacraments to two, and its knowledge of Jesus Christ according to the self-styled orthodoxy of Lutheran reform. So passes CONFESSIO FRATERNITATIS, its execrations of the Roman impostor, its expected fall of the triple crown. The outward forms have become types of convention, while as to their variations, each follows the rule of his own conscience, and the elect are everywhere.

This is like a new star in Serpentarius or Cygnus; but Fludd goes further still and puts on record his personal conviction that all persons whatsoever may and shall be accounted as true Brethren of the Rosy Cross if they are

[1] I observe that according to Kieswetter CLAVIS PHILOSOPHIÆ FLUDDANÆ states (p. 50) that the prosperity of the Rosicrucian Order was short lived and hints also that it was transformed into Freemasonry. There is no such statement, neither is there such indication.

(1) rooted firmly in the Christian faith, (2) confirmed in the knowledge of themselves and (3) consciously built up on that corner-stone which is Christ Spiritual. The head of all is Christ, of whose mystical body there are many members. The point has become of such importance that he returns thereon and repeats it with a slight variation of form: "I affirm that every *Theologus* of the Church Mystical is a real Brother of the Rosy Cross, wheresoever he may be and under what obedience soever of the Churches politic." Finally, he informs us that those who used to be called Brethren of the Rosy Cross are now termed the Wise—men of wisdom here on earth, conditioned either in the search or attainment of Divine Wisdom.

We may compare these affirmations and findings with that commentary on the Laws of the Fraternity which was published by Michael Maier in 1618.[1] As we shall see, he testifies to the fact of an incorporated Order in unmistakable terms: for him it was a College of German Philosophers of R∴C∴. It was not apart from things spiritual, but it was of the occult rather than of any mystical movement. In the hands of Fludd it has been spiritualised out of all likeness to its own earlier records, while in CLAVIS PHILOSOPHIÆ it has evaporated to all intents and purposes, unless indeed we elect to conclude that under his headship, or that of others who were men of his mind and spirit, the corporate body had transformed into a secret House of spiritual election, the tradition, knowledge and practice of which were concerned only with the life that is hidden with Christ in God. We shall see

[1] Maier had been dead for many years when Fludd published the CLAVIS. We should understand many things better if we could suppose that the Order had fallen into the hands of the English theosophist in succession to the German alchemist. But neither positive nor negative evidence is available in this direction.

whether there are later memorials which offer any indications along these lines. Meanwhile, in the symbolism of the Latin Church we have heard of the Church Militant, the Church Suffering and the Church Triumphant; but of a Church Mystical—within that obedience or without—I think that we hear for the first time from Robert Fludd. I speak tentatively, as the reason of things requires, for in the presence of the vast literature of theology, it is impossible to speak certainly: if I am right, the use of such a term in the particular set of connections is exceedingly significant. It would not be without importance, had it been used previously.

As he spiritualised the Rosy Cross—or bore witness alternatively to the transfiguration which it may have undergone otherwise—so Fludd spiritualised alchemy. Even in the early days of TRACTATUS THEOLOGO-PHILOSOPHICUS the "divine balsam" of Paracelsus and his followers had become celestial grace, but in CLAVIS PHILOSOPHIÆ the work in creation of Christ the Word—*per quem omnia facta sunt*—is called "Divine Alchemy," and it is more than a figure of speech. The work of the human alchemist—all that which is characterised broadly as belonging to the *Magnum Opus*—is in analogy with the operation of the Holy Spirit, of the Word and the Wisdom of God. The Philosopher's Stone is most truly theosophical in its virtues, or at least "theo-philosophic." It is the power of God breathed forth and the influx of His Glory. The fixed gold of the alchemists abides in the soul of man, which is not only purified and exalted by the Christ-Stone but is raised into eternal life. The Rosicrucians are therefore concerned with no gold of the *profanum vulgus*, no common silver or fire. The alchemical sublimation signifies progression in virtue and ascent in the contemplation of God which follows therefrom: it brings the soul of man into the likeness of angels. Finally, in his catholic manner Fludd says that the Rosicrucian's subject of chemistry, their Stone, their Regimen, being concerned with the Corner Stone, or—as I read him—the attained state of the Christhood, in no wise differs from that of all holy and truly wise men.

Now if this were the testimony of one speaking alone and awaking no echo anywhere in the second quarter of the seventeenth century, it would still be difficult to suppose that Robert Fludd, revolving in his scriptorium at Bearsted, or by Mason's Hall in Coleman Street, London City, the claims of a Brotherhood of which he knew at first hand nothing, should have reached such a grade of certitude, not alone concerning their pursuits and dedications but also concerning a new spirit which had passed over them, transforming both name and nature. But he does not stand utterly alone, as we shall see when we pass to the consideration of the Rosy Cross in its connection with Maier, from 1621 onward to 1624. He is certainly more highly inspired than are any other voices, and he is at once the most responsible and ascertainable of all the witnesses. We shall see further that in and around the epoch of the French Revolution there was an activity of the Rosy Cross in Germany and Russia which at least appears to connect it with the spiritual side of things. Of that for which, in some at least of the circles, it stands at the present day we shall learn also, of *pars hæreditatis suæ et calicis sui*, and that if it were mindful of personalities in things past or present, the Imperator *in temporibus omnibus* might well be Robert Fludd. But the Head is Christ. My inference is therefore that the Kentish occult philosopher is more likely, in the general reason of things, to have borne his witness on the basis of what he knew at first hand than to have talked through long years in a dream-state about the glories of the Rosy Cross and the high attainments of those who carried its symbol in their hearts and perhaps wore it on their breasts. Beyond this tentative view the question cannot be carried. It is an interesting fact that Fludd was abroad during what may be called the Rosicrucian formative period, or from 1598 to 1604, when Simon Studion was preparing an *avant-courier* of all the symbolism in his vast treatise NAOMETRIA. Were I a spokesman of Masonic Rosicrucian Societies, I should proclaim in all their Colleges—as I have intimated—that Fludd was acquainted with Studion and was by him brought within the circle of adeptship. As it is, I remember only that his natural and acquired dedications were after the manner born of those to which the Order itself confessed; but he had no part in Second Advent zealotries, and he had no cause against the Pope. If there be any call to say so, I am quite certain that he did not found the Order of the Rosy Cross, but he may have belonged to something at work under that name, perhaps in 1617, and perhaps later. The last point is speculative, but its consideration in the light of other possibilities will be resumed at a later stage.

I have not dwelt upon the external life of Fludd, which is of no importance to my subject; but as it may be desirable to fix periods, let it be added that he was born in 1574, while we have seen already that he died in 1637. He graduated in arts at St. John's College, Oxford, and in medicine at Christ Church, on his return from abroad. His history thereafter is practically that of his books, but he has been called "eminent in his medical capacity." In so far as he was an occult philosopher and an occult practitioner in medicine he seems second to none in his follies; but on the religious side of his nature, his personal sanctity is reflected into his works and it is correct to call him a notable Christian theosophist. It is this side of him which comes into prominence in his later controversies on the subject of Rosicrucian claims. If he was ever connected with the Brotherhood as a member, either he found it holy or sought to hallow it.

I should add that in THE FREEMASON for January 22, 1910, an anonymous contributor furnished a mendacious account of Fludd in connection with a quarterly meeting of the SOCIETAS ROSICRUCIANA IN ANGLIA. At this assembly there was exhibited the photograph of an alleged Rosicrucian Cross and Chain said to have been worn by him as head of the Order in England. The statements concerning it were (1) that the originals were in the possession of a gentleman in Hampshire who was a descendant of Sir Kenelm Digby of the seventeenth century; (2) that this Digby was Rosicrucian Chief in succession to Fludd; (3) that the articles had been handed down from generation to generation; and (4) that they had been identified by experts as being the work of Southern Germany at the Fludd period. The part of fact in this story is separable easily from the invented part; we can accept the gentleman of Hampshire who possesses a Digby heirloom which is indubitably a Rose Cross, and the photograph of which was lent or given to the Soc ∴Ros ∴. Had it been accompanied by those particulars of its history which appear in the anonymous account it is obvious that the writer would have mentioned a matter of such importance. In its absence he had recourse to old fictions which speak of Fludd and Digby as heads of the Rosicrucian Order in England, as they speak of Thomas Vaughan in the same connection. The historical and evidential value is much less than that which attaches to Isaac Disraeli's "mysterious announcement" made in 1626, being an offer from an ambassador or envoy of a "President[1] of the Society of the Rosy Cross,"

[1] It is to be noted that according to Burton, whose ANATOMY OF MELANCHOLY first appeared in 1621, the founder of the Rosy Cross was alive when that work was being prepared for press. But it is obvious that Burton knew of the Order and its claims only by hearsay.

offering three millions sterling to enrich the royal coffers, if only King Charles I would follow his advice.[1]

[1] The story is extant in certain letters of the period, and according to these it appears (1) that a mysterious stranger had been resident for two years in London; (2) that he was, or claimed to be, the President of the Rosy Cross; (3) that he proposed, with the King's "allowance," to send his anointed messenger, being a "young child," otherwise "a youth," on the Sunday following November 20, 1626, presumably to ascertain whether His Majesty would accept and follow his advice; that in this case the promised millions would be paid in the coming month of May; that the proffered counsel would enable the King "to suppress the Pope," to "advance his own religion," to bring "the Catholic King on his knees" and to convert the Turks and Jews. The ambassador failed, however, to appear at Whitehall on the day appointed. See CURIOSITIES OF LITERATURE, *s.v* *Secret History of Charles I.*

CHAPTER XI

A GREAT GERMAN ALCHEMIST

In or about the year 1568 and at Rendsberg in Holstein, there was born Michael Maier, who became body-physician to the Emperor Rudolph II and was ennobled by him.[1] He became in this manner Count Michael Maier. A doctor of philosophy as well as of medicine, he was also an alchemist, and by his contributions to the literature of Hermetic Art he stands not only head and shoulders above his occult contemporaries in Germany, but in comparison with him there is no writer of any consequence on the subject—assuredly not Libavius. I am speaking, however, within narrow limits, for Maier's literary activities, which began in 1614, were closed by his death at Magdebourg in 1622. Another great name contemporary with his own was that of the Hermetic mystic who wrote AMPHITHEATRUM SAPIENTIÆ ÆTERNÆ, but Heinrich Khunrath—as we have seen—died in 1601, long before any tract appeared from the pen of Maier, his Hermetic co-heir. There was also Jacob Böhme, but he is not to be included among alchemists, though he adapted some of their terminology to his purely theosophical purpose.

Maier was a Lutheran of his period and by his hostility to the Church and Court of Rome he would have been

[1] I am concerned only with three points in the life of Maier, (1) his visit to England, (2) his literary output and (3) his connection with the Rosicrucian Brotherhood. I refer on other matters to the extended and excellent monograph of Doctor J. B. Craven: COUNT MICHAEL MAIER: *Doctor of Philosophy and of Medicine, Alchemist, Rosicrucian, Mystic.* 1910.

recommended to the high consideration of those who produced the CONFESSIO FRATERNITATIS R∴C∴. He appears like Fludd to have been a man of personal devotion, and in the preface to a work published after his death he is described by a friend (1) as a regular attendant at the House of God; (2) as a Christian in life and conversation; and (3) as one who practised on his own part the charity recommended by Christ in the parable of the Good Samaritan. I mention these facts at the beginning of my analytical account of his writings, from the standpoint of their Rosicrucian connections, to establish the position of their author. As a follower of Martin Luther, he accepted that reformer's doctrine of consubstantiation, which places the Christian Mystery of the Eucharist in a very different light from the commemorative observance of common English protestantism. One of his publications, with which we shall be concerned shortly on account of its Rosicrucian references, is entitled SYMBOLA AUREÆ MENSÆ and has been termed a symposium, presumably because of the word Table in the title; but it is a treatise in twelve books, each of which is devoted to one of the most famous alchemists, e.g., Raymund Lully, Arnold of Villanova and so forth. Their particular presentation of the Art is set forth in the first place, followed by a counter-thesis and finally by a rejoinder and summary, as a judgment on the side of the alchemist. I am concerned, however, with a single case only: the eleventh book is devoted to Melchior Cibinensis, described as a Hungarian Adept, but he is unknown otherwise in the golden chain of Hermes, and it occurs to me that, by possibility, he has been invented by Maier for the purpose which I am about to unfold. He is described as one who has graduated in "the Hidden Mysteries of the Hidden Science" and also in some form of Christian priesthood, but whether official or secret does not emerge from the story. A copperplate in the text depicts him celebrating Mass in elaborate sacerdotal vestments. In the person of this exponent of the debate, Maier represents the Mass as a work of the hidden science and the sanctuary of its Mysteries, which are those of the Philosopher's Stone. It is said also (1) that in the Sacrament of the Altar are concealed the most profound secrets of spiritual Alchemy; (2) that the perfection of the Great Work is the birth of the Philosopher's Stone in the Sacred Nativity; (3) that its sublimation is the Divine Life and Passion; (4) that the black state represents the death on Calvary; and (5) that the perfection of the red state corresponds to the resurrection of Easter and the Divine Life thereafter. It is added that "these earthly things are a picture of those which are heavenly" and finally that *Lapis itaque ut homo.*

There is no question that these citations from a work at an early stage of his literary life are very important for the mystical dedications of Michael Maier, though the scope of their meaning may be exaggerated. It must not be taken to signify that German alchemy at its highest—either generally or in many particular cases—was a Mystery of Divine attainment reached through the Eucharistic sacrament, but rather that through this channel of grace a transmuting tincture was communicated to the soul which was in rigorous analogy, *mutatis mutandis*, with the physical tincture which transmuted base metals; and otherwise that the states and stages of the material alchemical work were in correspondence with the redemptive work of Christ. But having established this on the evidential basis of the wording in SYMBOLA AUREÆ MENSÆ it follows notwithstanding that Maier regarded the Eucharist from the standpoint of a true sacramentalist and was eminently one who might have passed over from a quixotic concern in physics to the transcendental science of Spiritual Alchemy, for which "the sacred forms of the Mass" are either its representative, veridic symbols or Spiritual Alchemy is the science of a super-valid Eucharist. There is no doubt in my own mind that these purposely contrasted alternatives are differentiated aspects of one Great Mystery, which has also other aspects in the natural and sacramental worlds.

The first publication of Maier is referable or at least referred by bibliographers to the year 1614, there being no date on the title-page, and is called ARCANA ARCANISSIMA, a discourse in six books, which are occupied in placing on Egyptian and Greek mythology the same kind of alchemical construction as was performed long afterwards and on a much larger scale by the French Hermetist, Abbé Pernety. It would be interesting, though here impossible, to compare the two schemes of interpretation, the second of which owed almost certainly nothing whatever to the former. It remains to point out that ARCANA ARCANISSIMA was published in the same year as FAMA FRATERNITATIS, probably prior thereto, and that no rumours of the Rosy Cross appear in its discussions. It seems quite certain that Michael Maier was not *ab origine symboli* connected with the Order and was in any case not one of the hypothetical theosophists who put forth its first manifesto to learn the judgment of Europe thereupon. We shall see in due course that his entrance into the debate is posterior to the chief official publications—if I may venture so to term them—and is sufficiently late to present a silent but eloquent commentary on certain reveries which suppose that he visited England as if carrying a commission to spread knowledge concerning the Rosy Cross and its claims.[1]

For the fact of this visit there is very full evidence, both positive and presumptive, in the writings of Maier.

[1] Mr. Wigston is one who offends in this manner, but it is owing to mental confusion among a mass of undigested material and not to the familiar disposition to sacrifice fact on the altar of hypothesis.

The period at which it occurred and the length of his sojourn must remain open questions. As a matter of mere speculation, I incline to think that it was in 1614, but subsequent to the appearance of ARCANA ARCANISSIMA[1] and he had returned to the Continent when DE CIRCULO PHYSICO QUADRATO was published in 1616, being the second work proceeding from his pen. The latter was followed by LUSUS SERIUS, which belongs to the year 1617. So far as evidence is concerned, Maier was not preoccupied with the honour, dignity or interests of the Order when he came over to England, though there is no question that he travelled as an alchemist. It is generally reported that he undertook many journeys—doubtless, for the most part, over the wide field of his fatherland[2]—for the purpose of conferring with persons of the same dedication, to extend his own and general knowledge of Hermetic Art, and perhaps to acquire tracts, like those of Norton and Cremer. The English visit had unquestionably the same object in view. Now, it is out of this pilgrim-motive that there has arisen the hypothesis of his acquaintance with Robert Fludd. I have no wish to cast ridicule on the notion and no intention to reject it. There is a colourable presumption in its favour ; but from the days of Bühle, with whom it seems to have originated, to

[1] This is on the assumption that bibliographers are right in referring the tract to 1614, and it is subject to whatever may follow from the fact that it is dedicated to Sir William Paddy—1554–1634—who was four times President of the College of Physicians, London. This dedication suggests, though it does not presuppose, personal acquaintance. Paddy was of eminence in his own country and was probably of repute in Germany, though he seems to have written nothing, except some verses on the death of Queen Elizabeth and the accession of James I.

[2] This is the statement of Craven, but no authority is given. Mr. F. Armitage in his SHORT HISTORY OF FREEMASONRY expands the story, saying that "having become initiated by some adepts," Maier travelled over all Germany, looking for other members and collecting the laws and customs of the Order "from their confidential instruction." This is rubbish.

the last maker of worthless Rosicrucian myth, and the last compiler who follows antecedent statements blindly, it has been expressed in terms of certitude, as if there were records on the subject or even an extant correspondence between the two notabilities. Maier did meet with like-minded people in London, as at the period there is the best reason to expect that he would, and he makes mention of a few. But there is no mention of Robert Fludd. It is true that the latter was then unknown to fame and had published nothing. That this might account for the omission is of course colourable, but the suggestion is also a presumption against the alleged meeting, for Maier was naturally in search of fellow-alchemists who were in evidence as such, and there is not the least reason to suppose that he had ever heard of the Kentish mystic. The meeting therefore, if indeed it ever took place, could have come about only by accident. On the other hand, so far as Fludd is concerned, we have found that not once in the course of his writings did he quote or mention his supposed German familiar.

We have seen that Michael Maier returned to his native land in 1616, and that one year later there appeared his LUSUS SERIUS,[1] which was not dedicated—as might have been expected—to the Rosicrucian apologist Robert Fludd, but to the Englishman Dr. Francis Anthony among other people, being one who is in comparison unknown.[2] It was not—as might have been expected

[1] LUSUS SERIUS, *quo Hermes, sive Mercurius, Rex mundanorum omnium, sub homine existentium, post longam disceptationem in Concilio octovirali habitam, homine rationali arbitro, judicatus et constitutus est.* Francofurtum, *apud* LUC. JENNIS, 1617. The dedication is dated at Frankfurt, *ipso ex Anglia reditu, Pragam abituriens, anno* 1616, *Mense Septembri.*

[2] Francis Anthony was a Spagyric doctor of the period, with immeasurable faith in the medicinal virtues of *Aurum Potabile*, on which he has left a tract delineating his " way and method." He had no other medical qualifications and was continually embroiled in consequence with the College of Physicians, who procured his imprisonment on one occasion at least.

also—a Rosicrucian treatise, but a typical German work of its period belonging to the lighter kind of Hermetic motive. He must have found the Rosicrucian controversy literally raging round him, but no allusion to the Brotherhood occurs in its pages. LUSUS SERIUS contributes therefore nothing to our subject and yet a word about it is desirable in this place, to indicate the particular aspect of alchemy which had been occupying the mind of Maier—presumably in England—at such a moment in the Hermetic history of Western Europe, and in view of the important place which he was destined to fill for all too brief a period in the story of the Rosy Cross. Those who are acquainted with alchemical literature will know that there was a child's work, boy's work or woman's work from the standpoint of the adepts, signifying something that was *ex hypothesi* far more easy than those more ordinary practices which connect with the idea of transmutation. The *ludus puerorum* and its analogues may not have proved simpler to follow by the unaided student than were other courses in the thorny path of Hermes, but they stand at their value in alchemical bibliography and can be checked by those who choose.[1] I mention them because it may seem on the surface of its title that LUSUS SERIUS belongs to this class; but as a matter of fact it has nothing to do with transmutation on any side of the practice. It is a

[1] An old song provides the quotation which might appear as an appropriate text for every authoritative discourse on alchemy:

> Let us be open as the day,
> Each mask does to the other say,
> That he may deeper hide himself.

The Hermetic Masks reproached one another and taunted even one an other with their envy towards zealous seekers, but they practised it without exception, in the so-called *Opus Mulierum*, which may be compared with *Ludus Puerorum*, as in tracts on the Sealed Palace. A tract entitled LUDUS PUERORUM will be found in ARTIS AURIFERÆ QUAM CHEMIAM VOCANT VOLUMEN DUO, I, 5.

chronicle concerning a fantastic Parliament of Beasts and other creatures who lay before man—in the position of an appointed arbiter—their respective claims to pre-eminence over all sublunary things. Ruminating animals are represented by Calf and Sheep ; the Goose answers for birds ; the Oyster typifies the denizens of the sea ; the Bee does duty for winged insects ; and the Silk-worm for creeping things : it will be observed that one and all are of conspicuous utility to man. Flax for the same reason represents vegetable things and in fine there is Mercury—as a veil presumably of the First Matter of metals. The Judge is to choose a King from among them, and he sums up after hearing their pleadings. The claims of each are recognised, but Mercury is found to be the miraculous splendour and light of all the world. It receives therefore the Royal Crown as monarch of visible things under the command of man. It is difficult to see that a *jeu d'esprit* of this kind has any title to existence,[1] but it found appeal in two quarters, being reprinted at Oppenheim in 1619 and translated into English.[2]

[1] The representations submitted by the various creatures are almost exclusively concerned with their various ministries to mankind. There is a long discourse on the part of Mercury, and though the crown is adjudged to him he points out very honestly that it is gold which has the prerogative over all other precious things, that nothing is so durable, nothing so strong in fire, or of greater value and beauty. As regards Mercury itself, (1) it is an antidote against the plague ; (2) in combination with gold or " any other body " which is neither corrosive nor noxious, it is the best natural purgative ; (3) it is valuable as a semi-metal, and (4) when mixed with certain salts it becomes a poison. There is not a word upon the Mercury of the Philosophers, and although Francis Anthony is described as a " jocund " friend I question whether the medicinal recipes included in the discourse could have proved useful in his practice.

[2] Lusus Serius : *or Serious Passe-Time. A Philosophical Discourse concerning the Superiority of Creatures under Man.* Written by Michael Maierus, M.D., London (*sic*). Printed for Humphrey Moseley at the Prince's Arms in St. Paul's Churchyard and Thomas Heath in Covent Garden, near the Piazza, 1654. The translator signed himself J. de la Salle, i.e. John Hall.

The year 1617 was exceedingly prolific in respect of published works under the name of Michael Maier or at least written by him. Their chronology is of course untraceable, but in addition to LUSUS SERIUS there were SYMBOLA AUREÆ MENSÆ,[1]—already cited—JOCUS SEVERUS[2] and EXAMEN FUCORUM PSEUDO-CHEMICORUM DETECTORUM,[3] besides one contribution devoted exclusively to the elucidation of the Rosy Cross. It is called SILENTIUM POST CLAMORES[4] and is further described in its title as (1) an answer to the calumnies and affronts poured out by turbulent persons who desire to be received into the Fraternity of the R∴C∴ but have failed in obtaining an answer; (2) a substantial demonstration why the said Fraternity have hesitated to reveal themselves and receive such people into their Society. The preface refers to an opinion entertained by many that the Order

[1] Maier is distinguished from his peers in German alchemy by an extraordinary obscurity of style and by a passion for extensive titles, of which this work offers an exaggerated instance.

[2] JOCUS SEVERUS, *hoc est Tribunale æquum, quo noctua Regina Avium, Phœnice arbitro . . . pronunciatur.* Francofurtum, 1617. It will be seen from the title that this tract is concerned with a Parliament of Birds, with the Phœnix as President and Judge. There is a debate after the manner of LUSUS SERIUS, in which the Owl, Goose, Raven, Crane, Crow, Nightingale, Swallow, Jackdaw, Sparrow-Hawk, Heron and Cuckoo take part. On account of its traditional wisdom the Owl is made queen and is duly crowned. In what way this jest deserves the title of *severus* I do not pretend to say, or in what way it would appeal to all lovers of chemistry in Germany; but it is inscribed to these and more especially to that Order hereunto lying concealed which the admirable FAMA ET CONFESSIO have declared. This dedication was written on the return journey from England to Bohemia. Archdeacon Craven—following Bühle—suggests in an excellent bibliographical note that the work itself was written in England.

[3] EXAMEN FUCORUM PSEUDO-CHYMICORUM DETECTORUM *et in gratiam veritatis amantium succincte refutatorum; authore* MICHÆLE MAIERO, etc. Francofurtum, 1617.

[4] SILENTIUM POST CLAMORES, *seu Tractatus Apologeticus quo causæ Revelationum* FRATRUM ROSEÆ CRUCIS *et silentii eorum demonstrantur.* Francofurtum, 1617. Lenglet du Fresnoy, in his valuable Bibliography of Alchemy, calls it *très curieux etrecherchés des Amateurs.*

has disseminated innumerable delusive writings almost simultaneously in different parts of Europe [1]—much after the manner that swift-footed Thales of old was supposed in the space of three days to have erected Tablets of the Laws in one hundred cities of Crete. They have been stigmatised also as pilferers, after the mode of Autolycus, and as begetters of a monstrous brood.[2] Maier regards such judgment as not only rash but wicked and affirms—as if with the authority of personal knowledge—that the Fraternity does in no wise act in opposition to truth or morality. The testimony of ancient philosophy and of natural law is in agreement with their programme, after which declaration there follows the curious suggestion that in such a case ocular demonstration is to be preferred before mere rumour. It has no relation with the antecedent context, nor with that which comes after. According to this, anyone who denies the testimony which Rosicrucians offer concerning themselves must—to be consistent—deny everything, like the Pyrrhonists and New Academics.[3] "In my opinion," says Maier, "those who published the FAMA and CONFESSIO have done their duty and are therefore not to be blamed by rash critics—about whom, however, they concern themselves very little, but refer them to their Master.[4] They prefer to

[1] An allusion to the statement in the FAMA that this manifesto and its sequel were "sent forth in five languages"—on which see text and annotation, p. 137.

[2] It will be remembered that these are the very words used by Andreæ in his autobiography when alluding to NUPTIÆ CHYMICÆ.

[3] The alchemist's notion of evidence is precisely like that of Emily's maid in THE MYSTERIES OF UDOLPHO, when having shewn the cannon on the battlements by which the ghost appeared as so much ocular demonstration concerning the apparition she failed to understand why her mistress remained sceptical.

[4] Recommending the sceptics to the devil, not to the Hidden Master of the Rosy Cross.

exhaust calumny by silence rather than to increase it by writing further."[1] Then as if drawing himself up suddenly, lest he should be accused of being acquainted with the Brethren "as to their persons," the apologist concludes his preface with these qualifying words: "Meanwhile, I do not consider this Society stands in need of my insignificant patronage and apology, while I myself expect nothing from its members but goodwill, which they as honest and upright persons extend willingly to all who are upright and pious. Yet I could not omit to defend the truth therein, so at least that they should not be more oppressed by the ill-favour and envy of the ignorant than exonerated by the uprightness of intelligent and good-hearted persons."

We can take our choice between two ways of regarding this preliminary discourse, either as an *ex parte* argument on the part of one whose congenital credulity has been stimulated by desire to recommend himself in the eyes of an Order which he believes in on its own warrants and desires to be received therein or as a defence issued from within the occult circle,[2] which—while advancing what it can on its own behalf—is determined to remain anonymous and requires its champion to dissemble. The difficulty about the second view is in the text itself and in the fact that so many declared aspirants followed strictly analogous ways to earn a title of admission. Let us see, however, what light—if indeed any—can be derived from a brief analysis of the work itself.

The alchemist sets out with an intention of proving

[1] We have seen, however, that there were other official documents—whether real or simulated.

[2] It seems certain, however, that in 1617 Maier wrote as one defending the Society from outside its ranks, but we shall see that in 1618 the testimony of THEMIS AUREA appears to come from within. I am reminded that among rumours current at and about the period there was that reported by Garasse, according to which Maier was Secretary of the Rosicrucian Brotherhood.

various points but offers in reality only long and mostly arbitrary argumentations to the following effect: (1) That the majority of Nature's secrets are still hidden. (2) That these secrets are exactly such as they are declared to be in the CONFESSIO FRATERNITATIS R∴C∴. (3) That the Universal Medicine is comprised among them, and this is the highest good—after the knowledge of God. (4) That the said Glorious Medicine is found in Nature. (5) That there have been Philosophical Orders and Fraternities among other nations and peoples in ancient times; that these also studied the secrets of Nature and in particular of this Medicine with the highest diligence; that they transmitted it to successors through the centuries, choosing them from among other philosophers. (6) That the existence of such a Society at the present time is not therefore incredible, especially when it is manifested by written and published works.[1] (7) That, according to its own Confession, the Society has existed already for a considerable number of years, watching over the glory of God and the welfare of men, in order to manifest ultimately, which it has now done. (8) That this manifestation could and ought to take place only through the FAMA and CONFESSIO—a fact which has come to pass.[2] (9) That these publications contain nothing which is contrary to

[1] Maier not realising that printed and published works might proclaim a Society which had no existence outside them.

[2] I do not cite the arguments on which this contention is based: they are available to those who are concerned—if any—at the present day. The supposition is that the FAMA is true historically and that the CONFESSIO represents the faith of the Brotherhood. Both are relevant therefore to the act of manifestation, as *pièces justificatives*. The will to believe was obviously much too predominant in Michael Maier for him to see that there was another point from which it might be possible to approach the subject, namely, that statements in anonymous documents which offer no evidence and cannot be checked otherwise can at most be left only as open questions and are certainly not justified by the appeal to an alleged possibility of things.

the nature, rationality, experience or possibility of anything. (10) That for cogent reasons many are called by this Society but few are chosen. (11) That the god Harpocrates and the Sphinx were placed upon Egyptian altars to signify silence, that the Pythagoreans had to keep silence for five years and that the Fraternity must do likewise, lest the secrets of Nature should be revealed to the unworthy. (12) That the Order was actuated by good reasons when it resolved on manifestation up to a certain point and on ascertaining the judgment of the world, while it is on grounds not less solid that it has again decided on concealment for a given space.[1] (13) That the manifestation by means of the FAMA and CONFESSIO was received variously, some denying the existence of such an institution as the Order. (14) That certain people are opposed to the Order owing to their ignorance of chemistry. (15) That others disapprove owing to self-esteem and vanity. (16) That there are those who accuse it of Necromancy, Sorcery and such evil practices. (17) That there are yet others who, perceiving that they are not accounted worthy by an Order so highly exalted, have given up their hope concerning it and impeach it in all ways. (18) That there are many who approach the Society by means of letters, asking to be received therein, to be healed of their sicknesses, or to be visited in a certain place and answered according to their desires, but when they fail to succeed herein they find a refuge in slander. (19) That impostors have shielded themselves under the cover of this Order and have cheated the foolish of their money, which persons shall be brought to condign punishment.[2] (20) That

[1] It is to be noted that this statement was made in 1617, after the publication of the three chief manifestoes of the Rosy Cross and that all subsequent official documents—real or supposed—are different in tone and nature.

[2] The statement, which may be accepted as one of fact, is not without

yet others have resorted to other evil practices for their own profit. (21) That these facts have been turned to the prejudice of the Society, whereas it is much to be desired that such judges should seek to understand it better, because it is entitled to all honour, desiring as it does only the general good.

The kind of validity which may be credited to these representations does not need to be recited: they are a testimony to the writer's sincerity and his personal *a priori* belief in the actuality and honesty of the Order, because its claims are, from his standpoint, without offence to possibility. It is probably on these considerations rather than on any first-hand knowledge that Maier represents the Order exhibiting the Rose as something far off in respect of attainment, while the Cross is offered to Candidates. He held also that the Masters desired rather than expected a reformation of the world and of science. Meanwhile, the therapeutics which was their chief study had three objects in view, being body, soul and spirit. In other words, they healed on all the planes, as those who had the freedom of all, holding the keys of life by derivation from that Source which Itself is Life of life. Thus equipped and warranted, they went about doing good to others in humility and the abnegation of self, pursuing an honest and moderate mean, inconspicuous by their clothing and frugal in their food. It is true that they were distinguished from the crowd, but this was by veneration of God and by hatred of evil things.

Another text to which I have referred previously was

consequence in the early history of the subject. The "rogues and runagates" pilloried in the FAMA would of course bring grist to their mills and at the the same time avenge themselves by claiming that they belonged to the Order. But while individuals went to work in this manner it is probable also that there were cases of grouped imposture.

a much more considerable and ambitious work entitled SYMBOLA AUREÆ MENSÆ,[1] in which—as I believe, for the first time—the Brotherhood is referred to as a College of German Philosophers R∴C∴. The denomination was perpetuated by occasional use among later German writers and in the nineteenth century was remitted from one to another by various imitative Societies, some of which still maintain it. According to Maier, the Rosicrucian establishment was preceded by a College of Gymnosophists among the Ethiopians, a College of Magi among Persians, a College of Brahmins in India. Of such is the genealogy of the Order, though according to a certain spiritual descent, for there is no suggestion of lineal succession, as if one derived from another. I question whether German occultists of the seventeenth century followed any quest of origins in this direction. A long preface to the work explains that the Golden Table is that at which Triumphs were celebrated among the Romans, but Maier is concerned with the victory of *Chymia*, " than which there is nothing more sublime." The Rosicrucian references, which are comparatively few, considering the bulk of the text, may be thus collected together.

(1) As against modern gratuitous inventions which represent Michael Maier carrying the Rosy Cross in his pocket to England and initiating Robert Fludd in Coleman Street or Bearsted, he states in his sub-section entitled *Collegium Philosophorum Germanorum de R∴C∴* that the report of it reached him when he was at work in

[1] The work extends to seven hundred quarto pages, with copper-plates by Rudolph de Bry. It appeared at Frankfurt *apud Lucam Jennis.* It is impossible to quote the entire title, but a shortened form begins: SYMBOLA AUREÆ MENSÆ XII *Nationum, hoc est Heroum XII Selectorum Artis Chimicæ, usu, sapientia et autoritate, parium augmenta, quibus adversarius jam tot annos ipsi, tam vitiosis argumentis, quam argutis convitiis, injuriam atrocissimam inferens, confunditur et exarmatur, etc. etc.* 1617.

England on the business of Alchemy—meaning probably that he was in search of fellow-students—and that he regarded it doubtfully.[1] (2) He mentions a certain prophet, said to be of the number of the wise, who had sprung up in the vicinity of Morocco and Fez and whose wonderful innovations were credited to the College. This was in 1613. (3) His return to Germany and consequent first-hand acquaintance with the subject of debate must have brought him in a short time to a different point of view, for his conclusion regarding the FAMA is: *Magna sane res est.* (4) It seems evident, however, that he is still speaking as one who is outside. (5) In the next sub-section, which is called *Dubia habita a quibusdam de Collegio Hermetico nostri temporis celeberrimo*, he recites and explains away as he can certain contradictions in the text of FAMA and CONFESSIO. There are eight of these difficulties in all, but it will be sufficient to mention three: (*a*) C∴R∴C∴ is represented as falling sick at Damascus and afterwards being carried thereto; but Maier fails to recognise the distinction between that city and the hidden place called Damcar in the FAMA: it may be added that German printers fell into similar confusion. The point is notable because it indicates that the apologist in chief of the Order in its own country was not a member three full years after the publication of its memorials began. (*b*) Paracelsus is represented as reading the Rosicrucian BOOK M∴ before he was born, but this misreads the FAMA, on the hypothesis of which all the documents treasured by the early Brethren were in existence early in the fifteenth

[1] I give the Latin passage in full: *Fama illa dictæ Fraternitatis, quæ hic in plurimorum auribus oreque jampridem perstrepuit, adque exteras oras circum circa vagata latissimas regiones pervolavit, mihi quoque tum in Anglia agenti, reique Chemicæ unice invigilanti, obscuris quibusdam rumusculis, incredibilibus ipsaque veritate longe majoribus insonuit, cui fidem, pro referentis fide, dubiam prima vice adhibui.*

century and could have been read by Paracelsus, supposing that he had access thereto.[1] (*c*) A VOCABULARIUM of Paracelsus is said to have been found in the tomb of C∴R∴C∴, but this is impossible, as the Sage of Hohenheim was not in existence when the Mystic Vault was sealed up for a period of one hundred and twenty years.

In the next sub-section Maier presents various metrical enigmas on the part of Apollo and the Nine Muses concerning the College of Philosophers and their Hidden House—*eorumque locus*—but it need only be said concerning them that their business is to darken counsel. It is obvious that the physician of Emperor Rudolph II was not in a position to disclose that with which only the initiates were acquainted. After these barren ingenuities there follows a summary history of Frater C∴R∴C∴, reproduced from the FAMA to determine some points of chronology, as for example that the Master died in 1484 at the age of one hundred and six years, whence it would follow that the one hundred and twenty years during which his tomb must be concealed ended in 1604. The successive circles into which the Order was divided by the effluxion of time are set out in the last place and it will be seen in the following tabulation that they are at variance with the original lists.

FRATRES PRIMI ORDINIS ET SÆCULI: (1) *Fr*∴C∴R∴, *Author et Inceptor*. (2) *Fr*∴G∴V∴ (3) *Fr*∴I∴A∴ (4) *Fr*∴I∴O∴, who was the first to die in England. (5) *Fr*∴R∴C∴, *patris ejus filius*. (6) *Fr*∴B∴ (7) *Fr*∴G∴G∴ (8) *Fr*∴P∴D∴ FRATRES SECUNDI

[1] There was a tradition that Paracelsus had visited the East and had drunk at its founts of wisdom. The suggestion of the FAMA might be therefore that he also visited Damcar and knew something of its archives; but the real meaning is that *Liber M*∴ contained the Principles of Nature, which Paracelsus also had mastered.

ORDINIS ET SÆCULI : (1) *Fr* ∴C∴H∴, *electione caput Societatis.* (2) *Fr* ∴R∴C∴ Junior, hæres S. Spiritus, Successor *Fr* ∴C∴R∴, *cum Christo triumphantis.* (3) *Fr* ∴M∴P. (4) *Fr* ∴P∴A∴, *pictor, architectus, mathematicus.* (5) *Fra* ∴B∴M∴ (6) *Fra* ∴P∴I∴, *Cabalista* (7) *Fr* ∴C∴ (8) *Fr* ∴A∴ *successit ipsi* P∴D∴, *et cum multis vixit tertii Ordinis.* FRATRES TERTII ORDINIS ET SÆCULI : (1), (2), (3) *Tertius in Ordine, qui Wetzlariæ,* A. C. 1615, *se fratrem ore est confessus et multis modis demonstravit.* (4), (5), (6), (7) B∴M∴I∴, *qui Hagenosæ scripsit quædam impressa, A.* 1614, *Sept.* 22. (8) N∴N∴, *bonus architectus ; casu aperuit fornicem sepulchri Fr* ∴R∴C∴, *anno Christo* 1604, *aut circiter.*

The Rosicrucian subject was taken more seriously in hand when Maier published his THEMIS AUREA[1] in the following year, the Golden Rule in question being the Laws of the Fraternity, which are said to have been discovered in the tomb of Christian Rosy Cross, inscribed in a golden book, though the traditional history of FAMA FRATERNITATIS does not favour the invention. They are those with which we are acquainted and not, as might have been expected, a new catalogue or enumeration. It follows that THEMIS AUREA, though in its dimensions a considerable tract, is merely an exposition and defence of six very simple rules which stand at their individual value and by no means call for comment, much less at inordinate length. It is explained that the senary is a perfect number, free from the confusion which

[1] THEMIS AUREA, *hoc est, de Legibus* FRATERNITATIS R∴C∴. *Tractatus* . . . *Authore* MICH. MAIERO. Francofurti, *typis* NIC. HOFFMANN, *sumpt.* LUCÆ JENNIS. 1618. The addendum to the title affirms that the said Laws are shewn in the text to be "in conformity with the truth of their object and contribute to public and private utility." A second edition was called for in the same year and also a German version. Finally, an English translation appeared in 1656 and was dedicated to Elias Ashmole as "the only philosopher in the present age."

might follow from greater magnitudes and simple to this extent, like the great laws of Nature, for which reason the adepts or epopts of the Order adopted six rules. It cannot be said otherwise that the *Apologia* of Maier itself makes for simplicity. We know that according to the Third Law of the FAMA all Brethren were required to be present at the House of the Holy Spirit on a certain *Dies C*,[1] " or write the cause of absence." The commentary offered hereon certifies in the first place that " we are unable to specify the Houses in which they meet " and thereafter proceeds thus : " I beheld on a day the Olympian Towers shining by a certain stream and famous city, which we have consecrated by the Name of the Holy Spirit. I speak of Helicon—or double-peaked Parnassus—whereon the steed Pegasus opened a fountain of perennial water, flowing unto this day. Therein Diana bathes ; therewith are associated Venus as a waiting-maid and Saturn as a patient client." We know that the House of the Spirit is a House of Holy Inspiration and Divine Rapture ; we know also —or some of us—that there is a Helicon which is not of this world and a Parnassus which is not in any earthly Greece ; and it may be that the Brethren of the Rosy Cross, as conceived if not known by Maier, observed the High Festival of *Dies C* ∴ in the Hidden Church of Eckartshausen ; yet I cannot think that the direction thus given is of the kind which those who run may read, nor do the alchemical references make for understanding, even if the Copper and Lead of the Wise assist at those ceremonies in the course of which Adept-Hermetists testify that they have seen Diana unveiled. Maier is,

[1] In the opinion of M. Sédir the formula *Dies C* signified the " Day of the Cross," presumably the Invention of the Holy Cross, but he does not say why, and it is unlikely that such a purely Roman Festival would have been countenanced by the Lutheran FAMA. *Op. cit.*, p. 69.

however, of another opinion and adds: "These are words which will say too much to those who understand, but to the inexpert little or nothing."

The heads of the consideration [1] otherwise may be summarised briefly thus [2]: (1) The Rosicrucians are servants of the King of kings. (2) Religion is held by them at a higher value than is anything in the whole world. (3) In the Book M ∴, as in a glass and clearly, they behold the anatomy and idea of the whole universe. (4) Their Medicine is comparable to the marrow of the great world, but also to that fire of Prometheus which he is fabled to have stolen from the sun. (5) It is brought to perfection by the help of a fourfold heat. (6) It is to be understood, however, that the Brethren make use only of lawful and natural remedies. (7) It is perhaps in this sense that they are certified as dedicated only to the study of Natural Magic. (8) With further reference to the Book M ∴ it is affirmed to comprehend "the perfection of all arts," beginning with the Heavens—probably in an astrological sense—and coming down to the inferior sciences. (9) As against current exaggerations and enthusiasms on the part of postulants and defenders, the disposition of Maier throughout is to paint his portrait of the Brotherhood in sober terms. (10) It is said that they are mortals only and will therefore cease to be, meaning of course that they will die in the physical sense when their time comes. (11) As custodians of their Mysteries they are secret, true in their dealings, and—for the rest—frugal, temperate and laborious. (12) They are anxious for the reservation of their hidden

[1] I should mention that Themis Aurea has a preface addressed to the Brotherhood and to a certain S. P. D., described as *Theod. Verax.*, *Theophil. Cælnatus.*

[2] It will be observed that the thesis throughout is written as if by one who is initiated and is speaking in the name of his Brethren.

knowledge to those whom God may call. (13) Its unbroken transmission is therefore an important point. (14) They have always "had one among them as a Head and Ruler, unto whom all are obedient."[1] (15) In this manner there is no confusion among them, and from one to another their secrets are handed on, after the manner of ancient knowledge. (16) So also they follow the custom of Colleges in past ages, which were composed of "the pick of the most able, and these were few." (17) It is claimed finally that the Order has one secret of "incredible virtue," and by means thereof they can cause piety, justice and truth to predominate in any person who is brought under their influence, suppressing the contrary vices. It will be observed that several of these testimonies appear to come from within the secret circle.

THEMIS AUREA is the last publication in which Michael Maier espoused the cause of the Rosy Cross to the exclusion of all else, and he died—as we have seen—in 1622.[2] His VERUM INVENTUM of 1619—otherwise MUNERA GERMANIÆ—could scarcely do otherwise than include the Order among the Fatherland's gifts to the world, but it deals with such inventions as printing and other discoveries innumerable, not to speak of the religion of reform. SEPTIMANA PHILOSOPHICA, 1620, is described as Golden

[1] It would follow that the Order was governed by an Imperator from the beginning, though he may not have been distinguished by this title, which is characteristic of a later period.

[2] A manuscript of Michael Maier is preserved in the University of Leipsic and is mentioned by Fessler in his HISTORY OF FREEMASONRY. There is also an account of Yarker, published in THE KNEPH, Vol. IV, August 3, 1884. As usual, this is a tissue of inextricable reveries, reproducing matter from THE ROSICRUCIAN UNVEILED of Magister Pianco, concerning the year 1570, when the Old Magical Brethren are said to have been re-established as Brethren of the Rose-Cross of Gold. Pianco's story is confused, moreover, with the history of the German Steinmetzen and their Head-Lodge at Strasbourg. The testimony of Magister Pianco will be reviewed in my sixteenth chapter.

Enigmas on the whole system of Nature. It is in the form of Dialogues between Solomon King of Israel, Hiram King of Tyre and the Queen of Sheba, who is characterised, however, as Saba, Queen of Arabia. They embrace the whole scheme of the cosmos, from the firmament and the four elements to fossils beneath the earth. The animate creation is represented by vegetables, animals and man. It happens that the Rose is described, but Maier's testimony concerning it has been quoted in my fourth chapter, and it remains only to note that the obvious opportunity to mention the Brotherhood of the Rosy Cross seems missed on purpose, possibly because Maier had a counter-explanation of the letters R∴C∴. In a posthumous tract, published long after his death, SCRUTINIUM CHYMICUM, 1687, it is said (*Emblema* XVII) that the ROSARIUM of Arnoldus de Villanova was the progenitor of Maier's Rosicrucian writings. It is difficult to understand how, because the latter are apologetic and polemical, while the former contains a presentation of the author's theory and practice of Alchemy. But the meaning may be that as Maier valued the ROSARIUM, Rosary, or Rose-Garden of Arnold, so he was drawn to the Rose-Cross of the Order before he questioned the correctness of this denomination.[1]

We are concerned more directly with another posthumous work which appeared at Frankfurt in 1624 and is entitled ULYSSES,[2] alternatively, Wisdom or Understanding, regarded as a certain ray of celestial beatitude,

[1] Norton's ORDINAL OF ALCHEMY and Cremer's TESTAMENT, two precious English MSS. obtained by him in his travels were translated by Maier into Latin and published, together with the TWELVE KEYS of Basil Valentine, under the title of TRIPUS AUREUS at Frankfurt in 1618.

[2] The text occupies 31 pp. only in a duodecimo book. Ulysses is regarded as a symbol of absolute human wisdom. Maier affirms: (1) that only the wise are blessed, (2) that the unhappy are those who are foolish—*intellectus dextere non utens.* According to one of the aphorisms, *Diadema coronat Regis exterius, et Sapientia interius.*

by the help of which those who are shipwrecked as regards benefits of body and fortune can retire on their oars into the harbour of meditation and patience. It will be seen that it is an exhortation of a moral and spiritual kind, shewing that other side of the author's dedications to which I have referred previously. It is not of great importance otherwise and there is no space for its analysis. On the other hand, a singular interest attaches to certain additamenta, being two tracts which follow in the same volume, and the prefatory remarks of its editor, who appears to have been an intimate personal friend.[1] I have quoted the latter at the beginning of this chapter, as regards the Christian piety of Maier. He makes two further statements concerning him: (1) that he did not know whether the famous alchemist who had defended the Brothers R∴C∴ ever became a member of that Fraternity; but however this might be (2) that he was assuredly integrated in the Brotherhood of the Kingdom of Christ and in the Order of the Christian Religion. A so-called appendix, occupying the bulk of the volume, is specified as containing tracts on the Fraternity of the Rosy Cross. These are four in number. The first is entitled COLLOQUIUM RHODOSTAUROTICUM, and was published originally in German, 1621.[2] It is described as a colloquy between three persons on the subject of the Rosicrucian Brotherhood, as made known by the FAMA ET CONFESSIO.[3] Tyrosophus, the

[1] He describes Maier as *Amicus et Favitor meus honorandus*, and says that he paid the debt of Nature at Magdeburg in 1622, *in tempore æstiva*. The tract ULYSSES was received by its editor from Maier himself.

[2] COLLOQUIM RHODOSTAUROTICUM *Trium Personarum, per Famam et Confessionem quodammodo revelatum, de* FRATERNITATE R. C. 1621, *sine loco.*

[3] The writings of Maier are quoted, and so also are Schweighardt, Irenæus Agnostus, Menapius, the PRODROMUS and TINTINNABULUS. There are allusions, moreover, to Gutmann and Weigel. One subject of debate is the relation of MOLTHERUS WETZLARIÆ, *qui a viro quodam qui anno* 1615 *illic transierat, testatus est quod non solummodo sese* ROSEÆ CRUCIS FRATREM

third of these, makes reference to Michael Maier and speculates whether his labour of love was barren to himself of fruit. There is nothing else to our purpose. This tract bears the date of February 13 in the year mentioned. In the second and more important Benedict Hilarion came forward with an ECHO COLLOQUII RHODOSTAUROTICI[1] in German, claiming that his answer was given by command of the Superiors, otherwise the Masters of the Rosy Cross. It is a pamphlet of considerable interest, more especially in respect of two statements addressed to Tyrosophus of the Colloquy: (1) He is assured that Maier should not work to no purpose in his notable defence of the Order, which can carry one meaning only, and indeed it is intimated to all intents and purposes that he would be brought ultimately within the circle.[2] (2) It is testified further

professus fuisset, sed etiam multifaria eruditione, omnisque generis rerum scientia, verbis et operibus ita sese tum temporis exhibuisset, ut ejus singuli mirati fuerint.

[1] The tract is dated *Mense Martis, anno* 1622, so that Maier was still alive. That which it registers concerning him is actually a record of intention. I quote from the Latin edition. *Quemadmodum etiam Dominus* MICHAEL MAIERUS, *tamquam vir clarissimus, illud ipsum scribendo egregie præstitit, veluti ejus rei luculentum præbent testimonium, ipsius* SILENTIUM POST CLAMORES, THEMIS AUREA, VERUM INVENTUM, SYMBOLUM AUREÆ MENSÆ, etc.; *quæ scripta etiam a Domino Authore ipso, non frustra scripta esse debent, sed illum, haud immerito, ante mortem ipsius, tam ingentibus honorariis, quam non minus singularium mysteriorum communicatione, beabimus.*

[2] There is indeed a very general promise of reception, and it seems to stand upon the threshold. *Cum enim nobis omnium actiones hinc inde satis superque notæ sint, iccirco nuperrimo tempore iterum non contemnendam partem bonorum, bene affectionatorum moderatorumque hominum in Fraternitatem nostram recipiendi, eosdemque nostræ tam spiritualis, quam secularis a divina bonitate acceptæ sapientiæ participes reddendi elegimus.* Benedict Hilarion proceeds next to enumerate pious and steadfast theologians, proved Christians, lawyers, doctors, philosophers, poets and other lovers of liberal arts. He gives even the initials of alleged personalities. There is an allusion also to the number of appeals put forward in the course of the years: *A publicatione* FAMÆ *nostræ insuper huc usque non pauci, tam docti, quam indocti homines nos tentarunt, an videlicet nos commovere possint, ut in Fraternitatem nostram reciperentur.*

that the possibility of their reception is still held out to others in a due time to come.[1]

Benedict Hilarion is a new name and does not recur in the debate, which was now practically at an end. It ought to be unnecessary to indicate, even in those places of folly which are called occult circles, that his statement, had it been put in much more positive terms, would not constitute evidence and leaves everything doubtful as it stands. But if it proves nothing I think that the fact of its existence is more difficult to explain on the ground of lying fable than on the supposition that there was something behind it. We must remember that seven long years had worn themselves slowly out since the strife of words began: in the nature of things it would have been exhausted much earlier had there been nothing to support it but its own verbose extravagance, stimulated only by occasional contributions on behalf of the alleged Order itself. I feel certain that the report of an Order was being heard of from time to time outside documents, that a general feeling was abroad concerning something which was alive in the world, that the debate was sustained thus and could not have been otherwise. The people who issued the first manifestoes may have gone about their ways in other directions: on this question it is impossible to hold a decisive opinion for or against; but, if they had so scattered, something sprang up in their place, and the rumour of it was current in Germany. It may have been framed seriously on the plan outlined in the early memorials—we cannot tell: it may have

[1] The text of the Latin edition covers 20 pp. It is addressed more especially to Tyrosophus as *Christiano innominato et omnium artium amatori verissimo*, and affirms that the COLLOQUIUM *nobis Collegio Ordinis* ROSEÆ CRUCIS *satis maturo tempore acceperimus*. One of its mottoes is a promise of a good time in prospect—presumably for worthy aspirants:

Post pluvia formosa dies, post nubila Phœbus,
Post lacrymas tandem cælica hora venit.

been rank imposture—again, we do not know; but that there was something which people could join who had a lucky star in their heaven I shall always think. Into this something Maier may have been brought ere he died—in which case the intention expressed by ECHO COLLOQUII connoted a hidden fact accomplished—and if it lied to him in respect of claims and antecedents there is no question that he would have believed. That he founded anything on his own part which by intent and otherwise was fraudulent I want no evidence to disbelieve otherwise than is furnished by the man himself and his writings. While on the tentative hypothesis here outlined it may seem as easy to suppose that the little loosely interlinked circle which issued the FAMA continued in secret activity, I feel this explanation precarious. If Benedict Hilarion writing *mandato Superiorum* represented a Society in fact under the Rosicrucian name, it had undergone a new birth in time, of which there are indications otherwise. The virulent sectarian spirit in respect of religious reform is absent from ECHO COLLOQUII; the traditional history of the Order and its founder has faded into the background; there is no offering of gold to princes; there is a spirit of theosophical religion on a reasonably broad basis. It is by no means the later mind of Robert Fludd testifying to the spirit and the truth of a regenerated Rosy Cross; but on a lower level it is like a herald of that mind to come.

At the end of ECHO COLLOQUII there are certain Declaratory Canons, specified as *Ergon et Parergon F∴R∴C∴*, otherwise a Kabalistic Chart from the Terrestrial Olympus, setting forth after what manner Nature, whose mastery is concealed chiefly in the earth, follows in the steps of her Creator, tingeing and transmuting metals. The Canons establish (1) that from the

Eternal there was the Father God, without beginning or end, an incorruptible fire, an everlasting light, filled with spirit and eternal splendour ; (2) that this Spirit in God is stronger than His body because it is vivified by fire ; (3) that the soul of the Creator dwells in this life of fire ; (4) that the said Spirit in Divinity, united in itself and fortified, brings forth a third, to wit, a soul which hath dwelt in the Spirit from eternity, being the very Word ; (5) that in and by the Word the Spirit is fire ; (6) that this Spirit of fire abides without end by the fire of love in God ; (7) that it is the Divine all-powerful Spirit which spake and all things were made, even by the power of the Word ; (8) that the Spirit which moved upon the waters was in the Word ; (9) that the eternal Wisdom and Word of the Father God, Spirit and Soul of God, invisibly and incomprehensibly perfected all things in itself ; (10) that for the manifestation of the most high mysteries of the Fire and Spirit of God in God, the Fire and Spirit of God descended and came forth in bodily form, and commanded that the Fire and Spirit within it should be poured forth therefrom into a virginal human body ; (11) that the hidden should be manifested thereby ; (12) that the Fire and Spirit of God from God should be glorified throughout all Nature ; (13) that by means of the Spirit moving upon the waters the Creator divided His eternal creative fire from the outward bodies of created things ; and (14) that such division being made in the mind of the Creator, God ordained the four elements.

The first cosmic epoch being thus completed, the recital goes on to affirm (1) that the Fire and Spirit of the Creator poured out on the stars and firmament ; (2) that the Most Holy and Blessed Essence of the Creator was hidden in each and all of these, as Soul is hidden in Spirit ; (3) that it went forth afterwards through all its marvels of created things, as through bodies; (4) that hence also the divine cognition of things was sealed upon the inward side of that which was created; (5) that inferiors were thus drawn to superiors; (6) that from this divine soul bodies imbued by its law proceeded and were multiplied; (7) that the Fire, Spirit or Divine Essence being provided by the Creator's blessing and the thing thus confected, it was developed as a beautiful, pure and pellucid body, and the Creator fumigated that which was pure, pellucid and beautiful out of earth, and drew the same from the hiddenness and made it manifest by forming an image in His own likeness, namely, man, whom he built up out of the quintessence of Olympian earth, which consists in spirit and soul through the Spirit and Soul of the Creator, which in earth is most brilliant Salt, Sulphur and Mercury.

The alchemical thesis follows and is to this effect: (1) that metals and the other minerals are found only in mountains and under earth of Salt, Sulphur and Mercury; (2) that this earth is impregnated by Nature with mineral water; (3) that whilst the metals grow undisturbed the root of all metals comes forth; (4) that this is the First Matter of all the wise, whom God hath made glad by knowledge of the most High Mastery of Nature; (5) that the virtue of this Nature is in the body, that is, in Salt, which Salt or the body maintains the Sulphur and Mercury, otherwise spirit and soul with itself; (6) that the matter of Highest Mastery is found in fire and water or in impregnated water, which water is not moist and does not wet the fingers; (7) that all things are one thing only; (8) that this water cannot abide without earth, which earth nourishes fire and air by the active Spirit of the Creator; (9) that there is a perpetual intercourse of the Divine Essence with created bodies; (10) that the Divine Essence is manifested through fire and water, as through Spirit and Soul; (11) that created things are brought forth and manifested by earth and water, as through bodies; (12) that herein lies the sacrament and mystery of the correspondence between the philosophical work of highest science and the harmony of the Sacrosaintly Divine Trinity, even as *Ergon* with *Parergon*. Glory unto God alone.

I have quoted these Canons in full as a specimen of affirmed Rosicrucian doctrine and theory during the first decade which followed the FAMA FRATERNITATIS. Their arrangement has been simplified as far as possible for the sake of the general reader, while recognising that a process of tabulation will not make them intelligible. I can say only concerning them that they seek to illustrate and justify the dream of metallic transmutation by establishing its theosophical correspondences. It may be observed in this connection that the seventh paragraph in the alchemical thesis is an arbitrary introduction without reference to what precedes or comes after, and yet it provides a keynote of the whole intention. The words in the Latin are: *Omnia sunt res una*, and their analogies are recurrent in Hermetic literature, the most notable being: *Est una sola res*. The last as it stands, apart from any context, is an unconditional affirmation of the doctrine of unity—namely, that God is All, rather even than All in all. I have cited it, however, because as such it is to be distinguished from the Declaratory Canons. To say that *Omnia sunt res una* is very like saying *Est una sola res*, but the sentences are not synonymous; the one is the doctrine of multiplicity becoming unity, while the other denies multiplicity. Moreover, as it seems to me, the *res una* of the Canon signifies an unity of concordance rather than oneness of essence, and this is illustrated throughout the text. I do not remember that a correspondence has been established in other alchemical writings between the Trinity in Unity of the Divine Persons and the kind of hypothetical unity which can be predicated as subsisting between Salt, Sulphur and Mercury according to the mind of Hermetic literature, but the work in the alembic has been compared to the work of God in creation and to the redemptive work of Christ in the soul of man.

CHAPTER XII

LATER CONTINENTAL HISTORY

THE testimony of Robert Fludd brings the literary history of the Rosy Cross in England to the year 1629 and closes its first period. So far as records are concerned, it is the story of a single individual and of that which he was able to find in his glass of vision. With the exception of MOSAICAL PHILOSOPHY, which does not belong to our subject unless in that almost spectral sense which might be suggested by far-off analogies with the theosophy of Ægidius Gutmann—a writer favoured by early memorials or traditional concerns of the Brotherhood—and with the exception of PARSON FOSTER'S SPONGE, which is of no consequence or interest from any standpoint whatever, all writings of Fludd—his Rosicrucian apologies included—were published abroad, and there is no direct evidence forthcoming that they created any concern or had a circulation to speak of in England. Dr. Craven has given us a careful summary account of Hutchinson and his system and has shewn us that he was to all appearance unacquainted with his predecessor of a few years back, yet he was perhaps the most likely of all to have known him. It is to be questioned whether there was any Rosicrucianism at all in these islands during the first quarter of the seventeenth century beyond that which was centred in the person of Robert Fludd—a restricted circle of course—and the whole subject may have fallen into complete desuetude at his death in 1632.

We have now to return on the years, so far as the Continent is concerned, to see what took place in Germany and elsewhere during the period immediately subsequent to 1620, until we reach a date, about 1630, when the records and doings of the Rosy Cross passed into apparent suspension for a space of seventy years. The halter of the Thirty Years' War had tightened about the neck of the German people; the miserable strife of sects was another yoke upon the land; the blessing brought by Luther was as much qualified in respect of reform as it was dubious in the matter of freedom and desolating in the religious sense.

After 1620, but few and far between, there still emerged for a moment some apologies for the Order, recalling those which served no purpose in the past but to exhibit the zeal of their writers and—in most cases—to notify that which they sought. Among all it will be sufficient to cite the following casual examples: (1) SCRIPTUM AMICABILE, in which the piety of the Brotherhood is defended against impostors.[1] (2) A CHRISTIAN EPISTLE addressed to the Brethren R∴C∴ respecting its doctrine.[2] (3) THE GARDEN OF ROSES,[3] comprising a fundamental and apologetical account of the new heavenly prophets, Rosicrucians, Chiliasts and Enthusiasts, by George Rostius, who seems also to have investigated alleged Rosicrucian calculations on the subject of the Last Day. But this was in another tract entitled PROGNOSTICON THEOLOGICUM, about which I know nothing except that the date of publication was

[1] SCRIPTUM AMICABILE *ad venerandam Fraternitatem R. C., in quo pietas eorum contra Impostores defenditur.* Francofurti, 1621.

[2] CHRISTLICHES SCHREIBEN *an die Bruderschaft R. C. wegen ihrer lehre, ihren meinungen, etc.* Frankfurt, 1621.

[3] Literally the HEROIC BOOK concerning the Garden, etc., which seems nonsensical. The full title is: HELDENBUCH VOM ROSENGARTEN, *oder gründlicher und apologetischer Bericht von dem newen himmlischen Propheten, Rosenkreutzern, Chiliasten und Enthusiasten, durch* Georg Rostium. Rostoch, 1622.

1621. Some attacks of the same period were more to the purpose—in violence of language at least. A notable specimen is called WARNING TO ROSICRUCIAN VERMIN,[1] by Philipp Geiger. It appears to have evoked a reply on the part of J. H. Cochheim, described as of Holbrieden, but the witness which he bore in defence of the Order, thus scurrilously attacked, has eluded my research, even in the matter of its title.[2] Equally explicit in a different sense seems another tract which I know only by name, that is, THE FAITHFUL ECKHART[3]—reflecting in its title an old German legend. It speaks of Rosicrucian heresies relative to baptism and conversion, evidently a recurrence to the Anabaptist charge of earlier years. It describes the Brotherhood as a disordered troop going to and fro in the country and as a brigandage which slaughters souls. I am unacquainted also with J. Brenna and his WOOLCOMBER'S FAIR of the Brothers of the Rosy Cross, which appeared in 1625, but it may be judged from the title. In conclusion as to miscellaneous hostile criticism, I may mention Johannes Robertus, a Jesuit of Luxembourg who died at Namur in 1651. He was an opponent of Fludd, Goclenius and others on the subject of cure by sympathy and the so-called magnetic cure of wounds. One of his treatises was published posthumously in *Theatrum Sympatheticum*, Norimbergæ, 1662, and was entitled *Goclenius Heautontimorumenos.* It contains two sections, (1) on the *Acheruntici Fraterculi* who call themselves Brethren of the Rosy Cross

[1] WARNUNG *für die Rosenkreutzer Vngeziefer.* Heidelberg, 1621.

[2] See Franz Fendenberg: *Aus der Älteren* GESCHICHTE DER ROSENCREUTZER, a small treatise, issued undated and with no place of publication.

[3] Valentin Griesmann: GETREWER ECKHART, *welcher in den ersten neun Gemeinen Fragen der Wiedertaüferischen, Schwenkfeldischen, etc., Rosenkreutzerische Ketzereyen im Lande herumstreichende wüste Heer zu flichen . . . verwarnet, etc.* 1623. It might be useful to know more of this lucubration, because of the suggestion in the title that there were many going about in Germany using the name of the Order to substantiate their claims.

and (2) on the said Brotherhood as exhibited by their own writings.

Of tracts which claim to speak with individual or official authority from within the circle of initiation there is no question that the most important and interesting is the Echo Colloquii of Benedict Hilarion noticed in my last chapter; but there were other sporadic testimonies. I have mentioned J. H. Cochheim—otherwise Kocheim von Hellrieden—on the authority of Freudenburg, but he can be traced in a more direct manner, for he entered the field of debate for a second time in 1626, and now as a professed alchemist who was able to lead those who wandered through devious paths into the only straight way respecting the true matter of the Philosophical Stone. His "firm, irrefutable and fundamental" relation on these subjects appeared at Strasbourg and was dedicated to the Landgrave Maurice of Hesse,[1] who is described as his friend. It is of our concern only because it describes the Brotherhood as the Order of the Fleece, otherwise the Golden Cross, recalling the insignia worn by *Equites Aurei Lapidis* in the Chemical Marriage. It is said also that the association ought not to be too easy of access and that persons of vulgar status should not be admitted at all. It may seem arbitrary to suggest that these statements are intended to imply membership on the part of the writer and if I incline in this direction it should be understood that the view is tentative, while on either side it is not of particular consequence. The new designation is in any case of some importance, as it is the second of two early allusions to the Society as an Order of the Golden Cross and the first and only time that it is connected by a distinct designation with the Golden Fleece—outside the Chemical Marriage.

[1] Tractatus Errantium *in Rectam et Planam Viam Reductio*, with a long sub-title in German. It is an octavo pamphlet of 117 pages and was issued on December 1 of the year 1626.

According to Lenglet du Fresnoy, Peter Mormius attempted to revive the Rosy Cross in Holland about 1630[1], and we shall see shortly that there is some evidence for its existence at the Hague in 1622. Moreover, he sought audience of the States General as ambassador of the Order, to lay before those august legislators the nature and importance of its secrets. The States General saw fit to refuse him audience, having possibly enough business in hand, and at that time and in that place the story is that the projected second birth also proved a failure. Mormius is represented as indignant, more especially at his own treatment, and to mortify " those wise republicans " he issued a treatise at Leyden on the most hidden secrets of Nature, brought to light by the *Collegium Rosanium.*[2] As understood and represented by him the Order was alchemical and concerned with nothing but alchemy, the Universal Medicine and the secret of perpetual motion. We have had ample evidence already that it stood always and only for that which appealed to its exponents, for spiritual mysteries according to Robert Fludd, because in the last resource he understood everything spiritually, but for the letter of occult claims according to Peter Mormius, because the letter to him was life. It is very probable that Temples and Colleges—or whatever the title assumed by such fluidic foundations—rose up there and here in Germany to represent the dedications of those who after this manner sought to incorporate their concerns.

It will be observed, however, that in this case the new designation of *Collegium Rosanium* is not synonymous with a College of the Rosy Cross. Mormius ceased from testifying, but if in the absence of any quoted authority we

[1] Histoire de la Philosophie Hermétique I, 379.

[2] Arcana totius Naturæ Secretissima, *nec hactenus unquam detecta, a Collegio Rosanio in lucem produntur, opera* Petri Mormii. Lugduni Batavorum, 1630.

can trust Lenglet on the question of fact and admit that the alchemist applied to the States General, his rebuff is explicable on other grounds than those of preoccupation or simple scepticism. There was Rosicrucian activity in Holland prior to 1625 and in that year. It is said to have been "old" in Amsterdam[1] and generally in the Netherlands.[2] We hear also of nocturnal meetings at Haarlem. In the year mentioned the Court of Justice in the Dutch Province of Holland sent to the Theological Professors at Leyden for an opinion on certain printed books which accompanied the letter of inquiry, and were concerned with the "creed and doctrine" of the Rosy Cross. The Leyden Faculty replied, reciting the claims and tenets found in the FAMA, from which manifesto it was concluded that the sect in question was founded by Christian Rosencreutz, that it was spread by initiated Brothers and that it pretended to be a leading power in "the domain of religion." Examination shewed, however, that it was nothing but false doctrine, fanaticism, magical art and so forth. It should be therefore opposed in good time, as prejudicial to Church and Republic. The best way of stopping the proceedings of the sect must be left to the judgment of the Court, but the members might be dealt with as people on the verge of insanity, unless they attacked the inviolability of the Church and the peace of the State, in which case they should be punished more severely. The document setting forth these views is dated at Leyden on May 10, 1625, and is signed by four members of the Faculty. It resulted in a letter addressed to the Officers, Mayor and Rulers of Haarlem, reciting what had been done and further stating (1) that Rosicrucians from Paris had appeared in the Provinces, (2) that the sect was increasing daily, (3)

[1] P. P. Reubens: LETTRES INÉDITES, 1840.

[2] See L. Ph. C. van der Bergh: GRAVENHAAGSCHE BYZONDERHEEDON, 1857, I, 66, 67.

that its doctrines were heterodox and hurtful to the Commonwealth and (4) that its meetings were held at unreasonable hours and in different places. The instructions were that the sect was to be watched and in particular one of the principal members, named Thorentius. There is no account of what followed, but the three documents—thus fully described—are extant among the State Records,[1] and if only five years subsequently Peter Mormius came forward with pleas for a hearing on the subject of the Rosy Cross, it is rather curious on the whole that he escaped so easily.

There is another story of Holland and the Rosy Cross, the scene of which is at the Hague, and it offers considerable difficulties to research, owing to the mixed and elusive nature of the evidence. It begins on the authority of Nicolai, who says (1) that in the year 1622 there existed at the place just mentioned a society which had adopted the title of Rosy Cross and was concerned with alchemy; (2) that the founder was Christian Rose; and (3) that the said Order had other assemblies at Amsterdam, Erfurt, Nuremburg, Hamburg, Dantzic, Mantua and Venice. This distribution suggests, however, the original establishment—whatever it can be held to have been—with Rose as an envoy, rather than an invention of his own devised in the likeness of the FAMA. It must be said, further, that Christian Rose seems to be a name rather than a person who can be brought to book with a reasonable account of himself. In so far as it responds to any test of identity we find a Christian Rose in the last years of the eighteenth century as a Knight of the Holy Sepulchre discoursing

[1] My authority for this account is a manuscript in the Library of the Quatuor Coronati Lodge, No. 2864, entitled: REPORT READ BY THE HISTORICAL COMMISSION *at the Meeting of the Supreme Head Chapter of Higher Degrees, held at the Hague on the 21st of May*, 1864. I have given a simple summary.

on the subject of Freemasonry.[1] As such he is nothing to our purpose, nor do we fare better when his name is transformed into Frederick by the *fabulator magnus*, Kieswetter. On the authority of Peter Mormius, we hear of a certain Rose, not otherwise designated, who was very old in 1620 and dwelt on the frontier of Dauphiny.[2] He affirmed that he was a member of the Golden Rosy Cross, which was composed of three persons only and refused to accept Mormius, who had come over from Spain in the hope of securing this advantage; but in the end Rose permitted the future author of ARCANA TOTIUS NATURÆ to remain as his servant or *famulus*, and the latter obtained sufficient knowledge to warrant in his own opinion the attempted inauguration of *Collegium Rosanium*, as already seen. The octogenarian or what not of 1620 could not well have been the Christian Rose of 1622, and the Order with three members which refused a fourth could not have been the Hague foundation, dwelling—as it has been said—in a palace. To make an end of enumerations *sub nomine*, an apothecary named Jacob Rose is reported as founding a Rosicrucian Society at Paris in 1660 which lasted till 1674, when it was dissolved, owing—unaccountably enough—to the Brinvilliers case. This is how the records stand with the Hermetic Sodality at the Hague, as regards the allegation of its origin. The Rose mythos would seem to have originated with Mormius about 1630, and as regards Christian Rose a moment's reflection will tell us that he stands for Christian Rosencreutz, "the chief and original of our Fraternity." How and with whom the misnomer first arose it would seem impossible to trace.[3]

[1] FREYE BERMUKUNGEN *über die politische Verfassung des Ordens der Freyen Maurer, von dem Bruder* CHRISTIAN ROSE. 1787.

[2] It is perhaps on this authority that Morhof speaks of a *Collegium Rosanium* founded by Rosay, 1620, in Dauphiny. See POLYHISTORY, Book I, c. 15.

[3] It is possible that Mormius spoke at full length of Christian Rose,

The authority for Nicolai's Hague story is Ludovicus Conradus Orvius, whose testimony by its claim is contemporary, though it first saw the light in 1737. The most extraordinary confusion has been handed from one to another in his respect, and when this is cleared up it must be said that little remains, and that he is himself, after the manner of a myth, represented by a single memorial which claims to be the work of his hand. It is a tract of some eighty pages in German, entitled OCCULTA PHILOSOPHIA, *oder Cœlum Sapientum et Vexatio Stultorum*, the preface to which contains autobiographical matter of singular interest and told in the opinion of Nicolai with convincing simplicity. It affirms (1) that Orvius became a Rosicrucian under the obedience of the sodality established at the Hague; (2) that he undertook many journeys at their instance; (3) that his considerable patrimony was dissipated, as well as that of his wife, which amounted to eleven thousand crowns; (4) that he lived miserably, while his chiefs led a sumptuous life in magnificent palaces; (5) that he discovered a book containing their pretended secrets and much more; (6) that he was reprimanded sharply and the work was burnt; (7) that he gave a remedy for dropsy to a sick friend—presumably a Rosicrucian nostrum; (8) that he was hailed before a convention of adepts, whom Orvius describes as "these great Pharisees" and was expelled; (9) that he was threatened with death if he betrayed their secrets; (10) that he went forth ruined; and (11) that he had done as demanded, "but after the fashion of women, who guard a secret religiously, above all when they do not know it."[1]

giving the full name. I have been compelled to derive information from there and here, as I have met with no copy of the text. It is presumably by reflection from him that Gmelin regards the Hague Fraternity as originating from Christian Rose on the borders of Dauphiny, but he has confused two distinct and mutually exclusive accounts. See GESCHICHTE DER CHEMIE, 1797, 98, I, 566, and II, 331

[1] Compare De Quincey's improved version: "Which secrets I have

In 1751 Johann Ludolph ab Indagine produced a new edition of the Orvius tract, altering title and text, and excising the most incriminating references to the Hague Society.[1] He styled his author L. C. von Bergen, otherwise Montanus, an ascription rejected by Semler and one which has helped to increase the general confusion, as among later writers some speak of Montanus instead of Orvius while others represent Orvius as editing a work of Montanus with a preface concerning himself.[2] Three points remain to be stated, namely, that Orvius is responsible for the story of the wide distribution of the Order, which in the opinion of Christopher von Murr is utter fabrication; that he pretends to have been misled by its chiefs for a period of thirty years;[3] and lastly that he represents members as wearing in their secret assemblies a broad blue ribbon, from which was suspended a gold cross

faithfully kept, and for the same reason that women keep secrets, viz. because I have none; for their knavery is no secret." It is pointed and brilliant, but unhappily rather far from the original.

[1] It was now called GRÜNDLICHE ANWEISUNG *zu der wahren Hermetischen Wissenschaft*. There are no particulars forthcoming of J. L. ab Indagine. He is to be distinguished from Johann ab Indagine, a writer on chemistry, astrology, physiognomy and chiromancy in the seventeenth century commonly identified as Jæger of Nuremberg, and from Innocentius Liberius ab Indagine.

[2] Compare Thory's ACTA LATAMORUM, II, 255: "These details and many others are said to be in the preface of L. C. Orvius to the works of Montanus entitled PRINCIPLES OF HERMETIC SCIENCE." For the rest, Thory's account of the Hague Rosicrucians is taken almost bodily from ESSAI SUR LES ACCUSATIONS INTENTÉES AUX TEMPLIERS, . . . *avec une dissertation sur l'origine de la Francmaçonnerie*, Amsterdam, 1783, translated from the German of Nicolai. I suggest that the translation has been followed as something readily available. The original appeared in 1783, i.e. VERSUCH *über die Beschuldigunger welche dem Tempelherrenorden gemacht worden und über dessen Geheimniss*, etc.

[3] M. Sédir points out that if Orvius was expelled in 1622 he must have started working with the Rosicrucians in 1592, and this would be very important from my point of view, were it possible to establish. But even if we accept Orvius as giving a more or less true account of his experiences, it is difficult to accept the date on which he was driven out of the Society.

surmounted by a rose. They were distinguished in public by a small black ribbon, having apparently no jewel attached to it.[1]

There is no need to join issue with Nicolai on the convincing note of the recital here summarised. I am in complete agreement with von Murr about Rosicrucian places of assembly in palaces scattered far and wide between the Hague and Mantua: there is not only no truth in such testimony but no ring as of truth. It is possible that Orvius was a personality of the early seventeenth century and not an invention of more than one hundred years later;[2] but—to define the position clearly—we do not know, and to say that there is anything evidential in his story would be to talk against sense and reason. At the value of such an opinion under such circumstances, but remembering the many rumours of errant impostors under the mask of the

[1] On the evidence of one of his alleged MSS., Kieswetter provides the following variations: (1) that Rosicrucian neophytes at the Hague received a black silk cord to be worn on the "top buttonhole," commemorating the penal clause of their pledge, by which they agreed to be strangled with such a cord rather than break the silence imposed upon them; (2) that the blue ribbon and golden cross "with a rose on it" were also conferred at reception; (3) that on the top of the head they wore "a shaven spot about the size of a louis d'or; (4) that most of them had recourse to a wig for the concealment of this tonsure; (5) that at sunrise on high festivals they left their residence by a door facing East and waved a small green flag, awaiting a similar signal from any Brother in the neighbourhood. These are the kinds of meetings that take place in penny dreadfuls and not in real life, even with occult dedications. We shall find, however, that they are a variant of procedure belonging to the Laws of the Order in the early eighteenth, not in the seventeenth century.

[2] Findel calls him "the faithful Urf," to confuse the issues further and says that he "frankly exposed the cunning doings of these Rosicrucians," without mentioning where or when. Moreover he knows so little of the subject and its criticism that he suggests L. C. von Bergen as perhaps the founder of the Hague Society in place of Christian Rose. Kenneth Mackenzie, substituting the *suppressio veri* for his more usual *suggestio falsi* in Rosicrucian matters, summarises and accepts the Orvius story, but takes care that the Order does not appear in the matter. He says merely that Orvius "fell into bad hands."

Rosy Cross, it is more than credible that a gang of them may have gathered at a specified point of the Netherlands and pursued the avocation for which they were banded together: it may be that one of their victims may have left a record of his experiences under the name of Orvius, and that it is less or more accurate. I claim only to put an end here—as I hope, once and for all—to the gospel aspects presented previously and repeated from mouth to mouth by those who have made no attempt to investigate the story. It is certain that when the Court of Justice applied for information to the Theological Faculty there must have been more than a rumour abroad of the Rosy Cross in Holland, and the Hague was a likely place for activities of a central kind. This is how the research stands in respect of net result, and this is how it must be left.

The consideration of a tract on The Golden Age Restored[1] belongs to a later chapter for reasons which will appear therein, but as it was published originally in 1621 or 1622 the fact of its existence should be noted at this point, since it claims to be written by a Brother of the Golden Cross and speaks with high authority on the Hermetic Mystery. The preface is dated March 23, 1622, but according to Kloss it was published in the previous year under the name of Hieronymus or Henricus Madathanus, a pseudonym adopted by Adrian Mynsicht according to Lenglet du Fresnoy, who fails to cite his authority. Four other alchemical treatises[2] are ascribed to this author, but

[1] AUREUM SECULUM REDIVIVUM, issued *sine loco* in 1621. It is described in the sub-title as a rare and precious treatise, otherwise a seed, imparted to Sons of True Wisdom and Sons of the Doctrine. In 1625 it was reprinted as the first tract in MUSEUM HERMETICUM, published at Frankfurt, and as the second in Museum HERMETICUM REFORMATUM ET AMPLIFICATUM, of which I edited a translation in 2 vols., 1893. Finally, it reappeared—as we shall see—in THE SECRET SYMBOLS OF THE ROSICRUCIANS at Altona in 1783, the pseudonym being given as Henricus Madathanus Theosophus.

[2] THESAURUS MEDICO-CHIMICUM, *cum Tractatu* DE LAPIDE AUREO PHILOSOPHORUM, Lubeck, 1638, reissued at Leyden in 1645 and again at Lubeck in

they do not mention the Rosy Cross and are therefore not of our concern. It has been pointed out that the name Hadrianus a Mynsicht can be written in an anagram as Hinricus Madanathys (Madathanys). The fact did not transpire in England till 1895,[1] but was no doubt derived from some old published source to which Lenglet had access previously. The title of Count is conferred sometimes on Mynsicht, but there are no particulars of his life. He calls for remembrance because he is prized by Hermetists who are not of the occult order and because there are certain intimations in THE GOLDEN AGE which are above the level of common alchemical literature and the common quests that some pursued with egg-shells and some in a chariot of antimony. When Madathanus certifies that he belongs to that or this—be it Rosy or Golden Cross—it is obviously not evidence, but we have had good reason to see that he does not stand alone, that there is in reality a succession of witnesses, each at his value, and I feel for one that it is following a line of less resistance to tolerate the supposition that they belonged to something, whatever it was, rather than to conclude that they were all lying. Some of the deponents lied almost certainly, some of them who may be taken to have borne tolerably faithful witness seem, on the assumption that they were members, in a state of such serious confusion that they had no means of knowing

1646. ARMAMENTARIUM MEDICO-CHIMICUM, Rothomagi, 1651 and TESTAMENTUM DE LAPIDE PHILOSOPHICO, 1664. According to Sédir, Madathanus worked with his *alter ego* Herman Datich, who is mentioned in THE GOLDEN AGE, at a marriage between the theosophy of Böhme and that of the Hermetists, but Sédir is confusing Madathanus and THE SECRET SYMBOLS.

[1] See a letter contributed to a magazine then edited by myself under the title of THE UNKNOWN WORLD, Vol. I, p. 281. The communication in question was signed Resurgam, Fra.·.R.·.R.·. et A.·.C.·.. In connection with THE GOLDEN AGE, it may be noted that I have also left over for later consideration the anonymous AUREUS TRACTATUS, which appeared originally in German, *anno* 1625, *sine loco*, namely, EIN GÜLDENER TRACTAT VOM PHILOSOPHISCHEN STEINE, *etc.*, addressed to the Brotherhood of the Golden Cross, another early illustration of the use of this variant.

whether a contemporary pamphleteer was himself initiated or not. It is possible—as we have seen—that there was already more than one group of putative adeptship, and a hostile criticism put forward by a *soi-disant* Brother may not mean that its author was fooling or had intervened in the debate to make money with a saleable article but that he had outlived any belief in his particular obedience. In the last resource, however, we have to recognise that there were the "rogues and runagates" who plied their trade in a topic of the time which was also a burning question, while through all and in all there were the booksellers with their vested interest, ready to sell anything on any side of everything to all comers, asking no questions either of those who bought or of those who brought them copy.

We have seen how the case is left when the year 1620 was drawn behind the gates of an irrepealable past, and this is how it stands now when the sinews of assault had wearied and the weapons of defence were blunt. Does it signify if PALMA TRIUMPHALIS derides the Fraternity because it arrogates to itself such glorious titles, because it poses as a Congregation of the Elect and the flower of the human race, because it claims to be inspired divinely for the reformation of the world, because it can restore all sciences, prolong human life and transmute lead into gold?[1] And what if Père Garasse the Jesuit pillories those whom he calls *Fratres Rosarum Crucis* as sorry rascals and a gang of

[1] See Fredericus Fornerus, Episcopus Hebronensis: PALMA TRIUMPHALIS *Miraculorum Ecclesiæ Catholicæ*, Ingolstadii, 1621, pp. 437–39. It is an exceedingly rare work and—as might be expected—there is no copy in the British Museum. There is no year on the title-page, but the *Epistola Dedicatoria* to Emperor Ferdinand II is dated Sept., 1620, while the *Approbatio Facultatis Theologicæ* is dated April 23, 1621, and the *Concessio Authori* was granted in December of that year. The views which I have cited occur in *Lib.* I, cap. 45, which is entitled *Quid de Roseæ Crucis Fraternitate, cornicula, tot prodigiorum plumis picturata, sentiendum?* The forty-eighth chapter contains a diatribe against the transmutation of metals, which has never been practised apart from fraud and the deception of man.

drunken impostors,[1] or that Kircher, who knew all things and much that had no existence, regards them as an impious race?[2] Is it worth while to travel far through the works of Campanella, or even through his SPANISH MONARCHY, to choose between rival rumours, according to one of which he lampooned the "Illuminated Brothers of Rosy Cross," but according to another was a noted member of the Order, as was also his amanuensis, Tobias Adami.[3] I have wasted some days to no purpose over Jan Amos Komensky —better known as Comenius—to find that Mrs. Cooper-Oakley and some of her precursors were dreaming—as expected—when they called him "a great and moulding force on Freemasonry" and one who was "actively interested in the Rosicrucian movement."[4] It is not

[1] The reference is to R. P. Garasse: LA DOCTRINE CURIEUSE DES BEAUX ESPRITS DE CE TEMPS, Paris, 1623. He calls them a faction of idlers, whose proper title is Brothers of the Cross of Roses—*Fratres Rosarum Crucis*—the reason being that they were good drinkers who carried their wine well and published their secrets only in taverns, the parlours of which had always a crown of roses hung from the ceiling above the table, imposing silence on all things spoken in the heat of wine.

[2] Athanasius Kircher: MUNDUS SUBTERRANEUS, p. 298.

[3] It is Gabriel Naudé who says that Adamus belonged to the Brotherhood, as shewn by his preface to Campanella's REALIS PHILOSOPHIÆ EPILOGUSTICÆ PARTES QUATUOR, Frankfurt, 1623, but it shews nothing of the kind, for it contains no Rosicrucian allusions. Wigston affirms that Campanella was "a noted member." See BACONIANA, Vol. I, new series, August, 1893, probably following the author of NIMROD, who terms him "one of the reputed founders of the association or gang called the Illuminated Brothers of Rosy Cross." On the other hand, Sédir, *loc. sit.*, p. 90, says that Campanella pilloried the Rosicrucians in PRODROMUS PHILOSOPHIÆ, 1617, as well as in THE SPANISH MONARCHY. In the last there is an Appendix to the second edition of 1623 which contains Christopher Besold's statements (1) as to the transparent character of the FAMA, (2) as to the fact that the R.·.C.·. Brotherhood was the fiction of a playful mind, and (3) that men of learning were fooled thereby. These are expressions of individual contemporary opinion, of the same and no further value than might be that of a non-Mason delivering his judgment on those activities of 1717 which created the Grand Lodge of England. There is nothing in PRODROMUS PHILOSOPHIÆ.

[4] See her TRACES OF A HIDDEN TRADITION IN MASONRY AND MEDIÆVAL MYSTICISM, 1900. One of her authorities is Ludwig Abafi: GESCHICHTE DER FREIMAUREREI IN OESTERREICH UND UNGARN, 1890–91.

true, for example, that he joined J. V. Andreæ, for the latter was in Würtemburg and he in Austria, while about 1618, at the beginning of the Thirty Years' War, he was exiled, ruined and took refuge in Poland. You can follow quests like these through the long succession of years and come to nothing; I have followed them from time immemorial in respect of the Rosy Cross and have gained only a touchstone of experience by which I seem to know occult impositions and exaggerations at sight: of a truth their name is legion.[1]

The tracts which I have mentioned briefly on both sides of the debate do not pretend to exhaust the list, but between 1630 and 1690 there was practically nothing save the occasional reprint of a pamphlet already known to us.[2] In the year last mentioned Adam A. Lebensevaldt, as one looking back upon the past and taking stock thereof, delivered his opinion on the craft and imposture of the devil in false alchemy, with special reference to the "surprising Fraternity" of the R∴C∴, whose medley

[1] For example, Mackenzie, ROYAL CYCLOPÆDIA OF FREEMASONRY, includes among members of the Rosy Cross a certain Benjamin Joehla, said to have been of Jewish birth but Christian faith. In proof of this there is reproduced from AURIFONTINA CHYMICA, London, 1680, a letter addressed to Frederick, Duke of Holstein and Schleswig, which document proves only that the personage in question was an alchemist of his period. There is not one word of reference to any Secret Order.

[2] There are sporadic reports which I have either found it impossible to follow up or they prove to lead nowhere, as usual. In 1882 Dr. von Harless published at Leipsic a second edition of his work on JACOB BÖHME AND THE ALCHEMISTS, in which he mentions a Rosicrucian Society at work in 1641. The authority is a manuscript seen by the writer and entitled TESTAMENTUM: it contained statutes, alchemical operations and so forth. But Dr. Harless does not state where it is deposited, and he is dead long since. Here is one indication which must be left to stand at its value. Another is in the theosophical magazine LUCIFER, Vol. II, 188, containing an article by Karl X X X, entitled *Finger-Posts in the Middle Ages*. It pretends to explain how the Brothers of the Rosy Cross taught "the finding of the Way," citing certain instructions alleged to date from 1675 and beginning with "a letter of warning against the effort to obtain wealth and power by easy ways." This letter states that the Brothers R∴C∴, "impelled by the Spirit of

of claim and doctrines is described as a devil's brew for poisoning souls.

The subject was now dead and done with, to all intents and purposes, so far as Germany is concerned. Those who defended and those who attacked the Order, without claiming to be acquainted with it at first hand, had exhausted the general considerations which arose from official texts and the occasional aids of rumour. They could contribute nothing to knowledge, and their numberless productions belong solely to the arena of debate. On the other hand, those who claimed to speak from within the initiated circle, if they are to be accepted on their own terms, present us with new claims respecting the Order, the traditional history of which, according to FAMA FRATERNITATIS, has passed out of sight. They have gone back upon the centuries to seek and find their origin. It is as if a new generation had arisen with new views, or as if the influence of Michael Maier had satisfied them that they were much older than they had dreamed. We have seen also that some of the official documents are exceedingly suspicious in character. In so far as there are traces of a claim in respect of dedication and purpose akin to those of Robert Fludd, I am disposed to think that it was put forward seriously and represented a secret theosophical group interlinked for the study of the relations between God, man and the universe, and that in such pursuits they had made a certain progress, as—on the assumption of their zeal and sincerity—they could not fail to do. Benedict

God " have already in various languages " pointed out the Way " but have been misunderstood by " the Masses " (*sic*), who imagined that they " desired to teach the art of making gold by alchemical means." The secret must be attained, however, in quite another manner. There is no need to say that the locality of the alleged instructions does not transpire, but some of the excerpts are referable to the old communication concerning the Mountian great and small *in medio terræ*, with which I have dealt elsewhere in the present work.

Hilarion's ECHO COLLOQUII may have issued from a group of this kind. On the other hand, it is a colourable proposition that certain later documents analysed in my ninth chapter and swarming with exaggerated claims were the work of pretenders who were also grouped together. The kind of theosophy which I attribute to the first class would most probably have evolved from a blending of the IMITATION OF CHRIST, the POOR LIFE of pseudo-Tauler and THEOLOGIA GERMANICA with the REVELATIONS OF DIVINE MAJESTY and the deep searchings of Jacob Böhme. It would have been subject to many errors of enthusiasm, but it might have learned certain lessons of caution from those of Simon Studion and his fatal prophecies. It had lost interest in the Man of Sin and may have been disposed to substitute a spiritual return of Christ in the hearts of dedicated Brethren for the apocalyptic Second Coming in the clouds of a visible heaven.

The later Continental history of the Rosy Cross is not confined entirely to the German Fatherland, and though French translations of FAMA FRATERNITATIS and NUPTIÆ CHYMICÆ belong to bibliographical dreams, its rumour passed over the Rhine in the year 1623, for there seems to be no question that on one occasion at least the walls of Paris were placarded with a manifesto which has been quoted in different terms by different contemporary writers. According to Gabriel Naudé, it was worded as follows :[1] " We, the deputies of our Head College of the Rosy Cross, now sojourning, visible and invisible, in this town, by grace of the Most High, towards Whom the hearts of sages turn, do teach, without the help of books or signs, how to speak the language of every country wherein we elect to stay, in order that we

[1] INSTRUCTION À LA FRANCE SUR LA VÉRITÉ DE L'HISTOIRE DES FRÈRES DE LA ROZE-CROIX.

may rescue our fellow-men from the error of death." It will be seen that the purport of this proclamation remains obscure, it being difficult to understand how the acquisition of this or that language is going to save a learner from the common fate of mortality. An alternative version was as follows: "We, who are deputies of the College of the Rosy Cross, do counsel all who seek entrance into our congregation that they should become initiated into the service of the Most High, in Whose cause we are at this day assembled. Our part shall be then to transform them from visible into invisible beings and again from invisible into visible. They shall be transported, moreover, into all countries whither their desire may lead them. But let him who reads be warned that we are able to divine his thoughts and that if in seeking to arrive at a knowledge of such wonders, and in his desire to see us, he is prompted by curiosity alone, let him rest assured that he shall never establish communication. If actuated on the other hand by a true desire to be inscribed on the register of our Confraternity, we will make evident to such an one the validity of our promises, but will not unveil the place of our abode, seeing that simple thought, joined to a resolute will, shall be sufficient to make us known by him and him reveal to us." [1]

[1] EFFROYABLE PACTIONS FAITES ENTRE LE DIABLE ET LES PRÉTENDUS INVISIBLES, *avec leurs Damnables Instructions, perte déplorable de leurs Escoliers et leur Misérable Fin.* Paris, 1623—a pamphlet of the period, belonging to the *colportage* class. Éliphas Lévi quotes this version of the proclamation, adding the following remarks: "Public opinion took hold of this mysterious manifesto, and if any one asked openly who were these Brothers of the Rosy Cross, an unknown personage would perchance take the inquirer apart, and say to him gravely: 'Predestined to the reformation which must take place speedily in the whole universe, the Rosicrucians are depositories of supreme wisdom, and as undisturbed possessors of all gifts of Nature, they can dispense them at pleasure. In whatsoever place they may be, they know all things which are going on in the rest of the world better than if they were present in the midst of them. They are superior to hunger and thirst and

Whatever its original form, the proclamation was in manuscript and was evidently put up as a jest to set Paris by the ears. Naudé calls it a comedy and accounts for it by supposing that French booksellers had returned from the fair at Frankfurt with some of the German pamphlets concerning the Order. He adds that the King was at Fontainebleau, the realm at peace and that there was a scarcity of topics on 'Change, whence some one undertook to supply a subject of gossip, reckoning that there were fools enough in Paris to prevent the folly from stagnating. We might leave it at this, with an encomium on the good sense of the INSTRUCTION and its author; but unfortunately Naudé goes further to fare worse and forfeit our conditional esteem, for he affirms elsewhere not only that there were Colleges of the Rosy Cross in Canada and India, but also an establishment of the kind in "underground Paris," and that its members were precursors of Antichrist. It seems peculiarly hard after bearing such unqualified testimony that Gabriel Naudé should be classed by the egregious Kenneth Mackenzie as a Brother of the Rosy Cross.[1]

have neither age nor disease to fear. They can command the most powerful spirits and genii. God has covered them with a cloud to protect them from their enemies, and they cannot be seen except by their own consent—had any one eyes more piercing than those of the eagle. Their general assemblies are held in the pyramids of Egypt; but even as that rock whence issued the spring of Moses, these pyramids proceed with them into the desert and will follow them until they enter the Promised Land.'" See my translation of Lévi's HISTORY OF MAGIC, second edition, pp. 358–9. I have very little doubt that the French occultist manufactured this encounter with a putative adept, turning up at convenient moments to answer a supposed question of the hour. The pamphleteers of the period and that general reservoir of current gossip, the MERCURE DE FRANCE, know nothing about it.

[1] In reality he is reflecting, without reference, from Clavel. See ROYAL CYCLOPÆDIA OF FREEMASONRY, 1877, p. 631, s.v. EMINENT ROSICRUCIANS. Notwithstanding his classification, Mackenzie admits that Naudé was opposed to Rosicrucian theories, as appears in his "several works" on the subject. Naudé, however, wrote only one tract on the claims of the Brotherhood.

The anonymous author of another pamphlet [1] is much more fully informed and does not falter for a moment over the grave subject. A fell intention lay behind the placard, for Satan himself was chief of the execrable College, the Rules of which were (1) denial of God, (2) blasphemy against the Holy Trinity, (3) trampling on the Mysteries of Salvation, (4) spitting in the face of the Holy Mother of God and at all the Saints, (5) renunciation of Baptism and the intercession of the Church, (6) sacrifice to Satan, (7) Black Magic and frequenting the Witches' Sabbath. The placard, for the rest, was a summary of "flagrant blasphemies." On the other hand the FRIGHTFUL COMPACTS, already cited, was the work of a venal pamphleteer who saw money in the madness and fed it with incredible stories of drowning and suicide which followed the experiences of initiation. For example, an Anglo-Frenchman who had taken the fatal step, being anxious to revisit England, was at once translated to Boulogne, but the demon who bore him flung him headlong into the sea between Calais and Dover, "with a frightful noise." No less than two hundred Dutch ships, on their course from Amsterdam to India, were present at this catastrophe. As regards the College of Rosicrucians and its history, there were certain Articles of Agreement with a Necromancer named Respuch, and these had been signed by members with their own

[1] EXAMEN SUR LA NOUVELLE ET INCONNUE CABALE DES FRÈRES DE LA CROIX-ROZÉE, *habituez depuis peu de Temps en la ville de Paris. Ensemble l'Histoire des mœurs, coutumes, prodiges et particularitez d'iceux*, Paris, 1623. There was a second edition in 1624, and this was reprinted by Édouard Fournier in the first volume of his VARIÉTÉS HISTORIQUES ET LITTÉRAIRES, 1855. Fournier states that the Rosicrucians began to make themselves known in 1604, "after the opening of the tomb of their Master had delivered to them great secrets written in letters of gold." He was further of opinion that NUPTIÆ CHYMICÆ includes a criticism of Rosicrucian doctrine. The points are worth noting as illustrating the extent and limits of French knowledge on the subject in the middle of the nineteenth century.

blood. They correspond substantially to the Rules already mentioned and were executed in the presence of Astaroth, manifesting as a beautiful youth and ratifying them on behalf of his Master Satan. In consideration of this concordat the Rosicrucians had power to go invisible, to pass through locked doors, to read the most secret thoughts, to be carried from place to place at will, to speak with talismanic eloquence in every language and to wear each of them a gold ring enriched by a sapphire, to which was bound a demon as guide and mentor. It is understood otherwise that all of them renounced Christ and the grace of Christian sacraments. They were thirty-six adepti in all, of whom some were commissioned to France, others to Germany, Italy, Spain, Switzerland, Sweden, Flanders, Lorraine and Burgundy, or—as it is alleged—into Catholic countries only, the lands of heretics and infidels, without the pale of the Church, being "already in the claws of hell." Those envoys who carried the French powers reached Paris on horseback, July 14, 1623, and ultimately took up their quarters in the Marais du Temple,[1] soon after issuing the placards which introduced France to a knowledge of the debatable Order.[2] It is said to have raised curiosity, alike among learned and simple, on account of the great gifts claimed by the Brethren, but especially those of going invisible, speaking all tongues and discovering inward thoughts. As it was agreed generally that such powers could not come from God, the intervention of the Devil was assumed.

So far the FRIGHTFUL COMPACTS, and its revelations of a lying spirit for the delectation of fools. But there is also the MERCURE DE FRANCE, which has claims on sober

[1] They met, however, where the resolution of the moment took them, to-day in the quarries of Montmartre, to-morrow on the height of Parnassus.

[2] A much fuller account of all the inventions will be found in my REAL HISTORY OF THE ROSICRUCIANS, c. XIV.

history, however often its plain tales suggest the hand of fiction. It says (1) that a popular panic was created by fear of the mysterious sect; (2) that ridiculous stories were circulated day by day and found a ready ear—presumably like those of the COMPACTS; (3) that hostelries reported strange guests who vanished in a cloud when the time of reckoning came, or paid in gold coin which proved slate on the next morning; (4) that peaceable citizens awoke in the middle night to find mysterious visitants at their bedside and that when an alarm was raised they became invisible suddenly; (5) that people began to sleep with loaded muskets at hand; and (6) that strangers in the public streets were liable to be stoned if they could not account for themselves in a way which gave satisfaction. It is pretended that suspicion and excitement lasted for two years, but this is on other testimony than that of the periodical print. Hereof is the Rosy Cross in France of the seventeenth century; and when at last the agitation died Paris forgot the Order till High Grade Masonry gave to it the Rose-Croix degree, or till Lenglet du Fresnoy wrote his HISTOIRE DE LA PHILOSOPHIE HERMÉTIQUE a few years earlier. The FAMA FRATERNITATIS and NUPTIÆ CHYMICÆ remain untranslated to this day. We know only that the French philosopher Descartes sought tidings of the Rosy Cross—as it is said, throughout Germany—and heard from impostors but nothing on the genuine side of the subject.[1] Presumably, like Leibnitz after him, he concluded that the Order and its story belonged to the realm of romance.

[1] It calls to be said that this inquiry was made *circa* 1619—when Descartes was in Suabia—and therefore prior to the time when Rosicrucian placards appeared on the walls of Paris. The story respecting Leibnitz is that he heard of a secret society of chemists at Nuremberg, under the name of the Rosy Cross; that he applied for admission; that he was received with honour and was offered the position of secretary at a salary. I think that the story in this form is told by Fontenelle in ÉLOGES DES ACADÉMICIENS.

CHAPTER XIII

THE AWAKENING IN ENGLAND

It is very difficult—in the absence of all records—to hold any opinion, however speculative, on the influence of Robert Fludd in England during his life-time and on what he may have left behind him. There is evidence, though it is confined to his own writings, that he was a *persona grata* to the restless and suspicious mind of King James I, but he who cultivated "the divine art of poesie," feared witchcraft and misliked tobacco, was succeeded by Charles I in 1625, and there is nothing to shew that the White King and martyr, who perished for the royal prerogative, ever saw the Kentish philosopher, though we have found that the latter survived his royal patron for twelve years. Whether Fludd's translation from earthly to heavenly life on September 8, 1637, left vacant the place of a Master in some Hermetic Circle offers a tempting field of debate, but if it should be travelled on our own part it would be found that there is unfortunately no expectation that it will become a field of knowledge. We are never likely to know what kind of procession—if any—what mourners but near kinsmen, accompanied the remains of Fludd from his London house in Coleman Street to the parish church of Bearsted. Except in the minds of villagers along that countryside, the act of death may have put his very name to sleep. So far furthermore as all evidence is concerned, it would be difficult to say that anything but the vaguest rumour of the Rosy Cross had reached England, except in the studies of a few Latin-reading scholars—with Fludd as their possible centre. There was nothing available in the vernacular, not even the memorial addressed by Fludd to King James being hidden in the court archives. If I express my personal opinion, it is probable enough, it seems indeed especially likely, that—however restricted—there was a living circle of which the centre was Robert Fludd. I have said that he was a man of considerable personality, of fervid zeal in conviction, and by no means of that kind whose light would be under a bushel ; but there is not one scrap of paper to testify in this direction. We know that at Mason's Hall, a few yards from his house, a Lodge of non-operative Masons was meeting in the year 1620 and thence onward. We know that among its records was a BOOK OF CONSTITUTIONS, "which Mr. Fflood gave." It is idle to assume that this donor was Robertus de Fluctibus or to affirm that he was therefore a member ; but again the facts offer an attractive field of speculation. The list of Accepted Masons belonging to this Lodge was destroyed in the Fire of London. What if the Rosicrucian apologist, as a later Hermetist turned to Operative Masonry—the great antiquary Elias Ashmole—had looked for something to his purpose in this mysterious Acception, about which we can ascertain so little and would give so much to learn ? What if his circle were there ? It can be said only that in such case an old feeling of Masonic *literati* that early Speculative Masonry grew up under a Rosicrucian ægis would become a much more colourable hypothesis than it has proved so far. Had most of the writers who have preceded me been acquainted with these facts they would have seen no field of speculation but a wide world of certitude, and as if in possession of inexpugnable documentary evidence would have affirmed that Robert Fludd was the father of Speculative Masonry, that it was he and no other who founded the Lodge of Acception. Had they carried investigation a few paces further, they would have found that the meagre traces of this fellowship begin in the year which I have mentioned—namely, 1620—and it would have been like a light descending from heaven to support the view. I hope at least that I have forestalled any "rake's progress" of the future and closed this house of call against them.

So far as our knowledge goes—whatsoever of occult or spiritual mystery was connoted at that period by the Rosy Cross fell asleep in England and was buried for the time being with its great protagonist in the Church of the Holy Cross at Bearsted. It may have been asleep previously, for CLAVIS PHILOSOPHIÆ ET ALCHYMIÆ, though not the last work from the pen of Robert Fludd, is the last in which he refers to the German Brotherhood, and it was issued in 1633. The question of the Order rose up once more in the year 1650 with the first publication of the famous alchemist and mystic Thomas Vaughan. It is necessary, however, in the first place to consider what I must term the legend of Elias Ashmole, prominent as he otherwise is in the literature and history of his period.[1]

[1] It is an inchoate and contradictory story in all its variations, as there is no need to say, and began presumably with Nicolai, according to whom—writing in 1783—the persons present when Ashmole was made a Mason at Warrington in 1646 were members of the Rosicrucian Fraternity. In 1784 Nicolas de Bonneville recounts that London Rosicrucians and Masons were united by General Monk to promote the return of Charles II—after what manner does not emerge in the fable, except that according to Yarker they added five symbols to their collection drawn from the work of Typotius, to which I have referred elsewhere. There is no truth in this story, and it would signify nothing if there were. Anthony à Wood describes Ashmole as "a certain Rosy-crusian" in his account of Edward Kelley, otherwise Talbot (ATH. OX., I, 639 *et seq.*, ed. of Bliss). Heckethorn improves previous accounts by alleging that Ashmole, Lilly, Wharton, J. Hewitt and J. Pearso formed a Rosicrucian Society in London, *anno* 1646, on the plan of Bacon's NEW ATLANTIS. The Meetings were at Mason's Hall. He is evidently following Reghellini, according to whom (1) Ashmole and others modelled their foundation on the Hague Rosy-Cross and undertook to write somewhat more clearly than the German Brethren, yet were unwilling to communicate their discoveries outside the pale of their Society—"through fear of

In my NEW ENCYCLOPÆDIA OF FREEMASONRY it has been analysed at a certain length, but more especially in its Masonic bearings, which are not of our concern here. I have shewn, however, (1) the fact of a recurring legend that Ashmole belonged to a Rosicrucian Brotherhood established in England, whether by himself or others, about or before the year 1646; (2) that there is no evidence to support it, except indeed (3) that his introduction to a notable collection of ancient Britannic tracts on the subject of alchemy impresses me as "a faithful reflection of Rosicrucian doctrine"; and on this account (4) that it is perhaps possible to presume his membership tentatively, as also, in such case (5) that he did not stand alone. How guarded these statements soever, it seems to me that they err on the side of toleration, for the legend itself is founded on no considerations of internal evidence offered by an extant text but on matters of pure invention. Having dealt with them adequately for my purpose in the work already cited, it must be sufficient to state here as typical examples (1) that according to Eckert, Elias Ashmole founded an English Order of the Rosy Cross in 1646 on the plan of the Brotherhood in Germany; (2) that, assisted by his fellow-Rosicrucians—according to Ragon—he transformed Operative into Speculative Masonry for ulterior reasons cherished by the Hermetic Order; (3) that in other words, and now according to the reveries of Dr. Papus, Freemasonry was established in England by the Fraternity of the Rosy Cross and still carries, for those who can read, the outward and inward marks,

persecution." (2) He says also that Ashmole rectified the formulæ of reception, basing them almost entirely on those of the old Egyptian and Greek Mysteries. The Hague formulæ, however—if any—are unknown, and the last statement is literally taken from Thory—ACTA LATOMORUM—who follows De Bonneville, and he appeals in turn to BIOGRAPHIA BRITANNICA, 1778, s.v. Ashmole, but it contains nothing to the present purpose.

characteristic signs and seals of its occult origin.[1] These are peremptory statements, at once unqualified and apart from all foundation, nor—except by a bare possibility in the case of the German Eckert—can they be explained by the invincible ignorance which has used Rosicrucian and Alchemist as synonymous or interchangeable terms for considerably over a century.

Were it possible in the light of his dedications and the peculiar Hermetic complexion of his religious and philosophical sentiments to regard Ashmole as integrated in the Rosy Cross, I have said that he would not stand alone, meaning that I should regard the fact as connoting something perpetuated through the few years which intervened between the death of Fludd and the publication of THEATRUM CHEMICUM BRITANNICUM, the connecting links being furnished by people like William Backhouse, who was Ashmole's teacher in alchemy and confided to him its root-secret concerning *materia prima*. There is nothing that is difficult or arbitrary in such an assumption, but on the other hand there is nothing to support it. Elias Ashmole was born on May 23rd, 1617, and died at the age of nearly 75 on May 18th, 1692. His living memorial is the

[1] As I have mentioned Wood's reference to Ashmole, I may add as a curious point under all the circumstances that he himself has escaped unaccountably the honour of being classed among Brethren of the Order in England, having regard to the fact that in his own autobiography he records, under date of April 23, 1663, 14 Car. II, how he "began a course of chimistry under the noted chimist and Rosicrucian, Peter Sthael of Strasburgh in Royal Prussia." It concluded in the May following. The "club," as it is called, consisted of at least ten members, including Francis Turner of New College, afterwards Bishop of Ely, Benjamin Woodruff, who became Canon of Christ Church, and John Locke, "afterwards a noted writer." Peter Sthael was a Lutheran and "a great hater of women," which is one of Wood's favourite formulæ in describing a supposed Rosicrucian. He was brought to Oxford by Robert Boyle in 1659, where he erected a laboratory and took pupils. He went to London in 1664 "and became operator to the Royal Society." His death occurred about 1675 and he was buried in the church of St. Clement's Dane. Wood says that personally he gained some knowledge and experience, but his mind "still hung after antiquities."

Ashmolean Museum at Oxford, while his notable work on the ORDER OF THE GARTER is his chief title to consideration as an authority on British antiquities. It lies outside our subject, but he was also—as I have intimated—a collector of alchemical literature and an editor of priceless English texts. Furthermore, he was an amateur of the Art itself. He considered that its " Elected Sons " were " given to know the Mysteries of the Kingdom of God," as " our Saviour said to his disciples," thus suggesting that he concurred with FAMA FRATERNITATIS in maintaining that there is a higher side of Alchemy, comparable to a detection of all Nature.[1] As a fact, in distinguishing the four Stones of Philosophy, which are like corner-stones at the four angles of the House of Hermetic Wisdom, he

[1] THEATRUM CHEMICUM BRITANNICUM, *containing several Pieces of our famous English Philosophers, who have written the Hermetic Mysteries in their own Ancient Language. Faithfully collected into one volume, with annotations, by* ELIAS ASHMOLE, ESQ. *Qui est Mercurius Anglicus.* London: Printed by John Grismond for Nathaniel Brook, at the Angel in Cornhill. 1652. It is termed the First Part. Ashmole always intended to make a further ingarnering, presumably in several sections or volumes, and the Bodleian Library shews that he had ample materials. Six years later he published a single tract, explaining his hindrances and saying that it was designed " to be included in one of the later parts of THEATRUM CHEMICUM BRITANNICUM." See THE WAY TO BLISS. *In Three Books. Made public by* ELIAS ASHMOLE, ESQ. London, 1658. The editor is now described as *Mercuriophilus Anglicus*, the printer and publisher being as in the previous case. The motto on the title-page is: *Deus nobis hæc otia fecit.* The tract is of unknown authorship and is referred by Ashmole to the end of the fifteenth or beginning of the sixteenth century; but—as printed at least—the text bears few marks of such a considerable antiquity. It is not of our concern otherwise, except in the very subsidiary sense of the editor's prefatory remarks. In these he tells us (1) that " the author was without doubt an Englishman " ; (2) that the text is printed from a perfect copy ; (3) that he has included the annotations of Dr. Everard, translator of the DIVINE PYMANDER ; (4) that the copy is a transcript of an original, discovered by a " laborious searcher," who found also " three grains of the powder closed up between two leaves thereof, with which he made projection " ; (5) that a " pretended " text, imperfect and interpolated, had appeared previously in THE WISE MAN'S CROWN, under the editorship of Eugenius Theodidactus, about whom we shall hear at length in the present chapter.

quotes from the FAMA verbatim: "And certainly he to whom the whole course of Nature lies open rejoiceth not so much that he can make gold and silver or the devils be made subject to him as that he sees the heavens open, the angels of God ascending and descending, and that his own name is fairly written in the Book of Life." [1] This citation is made without reference to source in the prolegomena to THEATRUM CHEMICUM BRITANNICUM. The preface alludes also to Frater I∴O∴, "one of the first four Fellows of the *Fratres R∴C∴*, who cured the young Earl of Norfolk of the leprosy." Finally, it mentions Michael Maier and his translation of Thomas Norton's ORDINAL into Latin, from an independent codex.[2]

It follows that Ashmole had the mind of the Rosy Cross, and that he believed himself to have proceeded a certain distance on the path of attainment in the physics of the Hermetic subject emerges from certain autobiographical fragments which appeared many years after his death. Some one has remarked previously that the so-called LIFE, by way of Diary, is filled with his minor ailments, and this is true enough. It might be said also that it registers religiously his presence at the annual Astrologer's Feast,[3]

[1] It may be noted that there is an English version of the FAMA among the Ashmolean MSS., No. 1459, fols. 284–99. It is entitled FAMA FRATERNITATIS, *or a Discovery of the Fraternity of the Laudable Order of the Rose Crosse, from us the Brethren of the Fraternity R. C. to all that with a Christian-like censure shall reade this our fame, be our salutation, love and prayers.* It is followed by the CONFESSIO, which seems to end on p. 311. Mr. F. N. Pryce informs me that it proves on examination to be in the hand of Elias Ashmole. There is also Ashmole, 1478, fol. 125–30, containing both texts. It is not possible in either case to identify the translation with that edited by Vaughan.

[2] A collation of Ashmole's text with the Latin of Maier produces innumerable variations of a verbal kind but little essential difference. On the contrary both versions are the same substantially and reflect creditably upon the German alchemist's familiarity with the English language.

[3] He was chosen Steward on August 8th, 1650. There was also a Mathematical Feast, which he attended on at least one occasion.

his infrequent journeys in England, his occasional preferments, his differences with Lady Mainwaring, who became his second wife but applied for a separation and failed therein. It is poor and lean enough, the entries, as printed, being in the proportion of two or three in each month of the period covered; but it is quite certain that it was never intended for publication, and we must therefore be content with what we have, as it fills a gap which would otherwise have remained vacant.[1] Moreover, it specifies certain salient points or red-letter days of his relations with William Backhouse, the alchemist already referred to. For Ashmole, in view of his interests, they were no doubt the most important events of his intellectual life. Backhouse is mentioned first on April 3, 1651, and is described as of Swallowfield in Berkshire. It is said that on this date he caused his pupil to call him Father thenceforward. On June 10 of the same year it is noted that his teacher had communicated many secrets to him. The entry of October 10, 1651, states that "this morning my Father Backhouse opened himself very freely, touching the Great Secret." Again, on April 12, 1652: "This morning I received more satisfaction from my Father Backhouse, in answer to the questions I proposed." But finally and most important, there is the entry of May 13, 1653: "My Father Backhouse, lying sick in Fleet Street, over against St. Dunstan's Church, and not knowing whether he should live or die, about eleven of the clock, told me in syllables the True Matter of the Philosopher's Stone."[2] Among the age-long

[1] See MEMOIRS OF THE LIFE *of that Learned Antiquary*, ELIAS ASHMOLE, *drawn up by Himself, by way of Diary*. London, 1717. The text is said to be printed from a copy in the handwriting of Dr. Robert Plot.

[2] The Catalogue of Ashmolean MSS., No. 58, shews that William Backhouse was of Swallowfield in Berkshire, esquire—as stated in the text above. In 1644 he translated THE PLEASANT FOUNTAIN OF KNOWLEDGE, written in French by John de la Fountaine, *anno* 1413, and it appears in this MS. The translator's name is an addition by Ashmole. See also No. 1395, col. 1089,

memorials of alchemy on the historical side, this last record may be said to stand alone : I know of no other in which an adopted pupil and chosen Son of the Art confesses how and from whom he received the secret. Ashmole lived for forty years after this great event and pursued his researches as an antiquary. There is not the least reason to suppose that he proceeded to any practice ; presumably the secret was physical and a knowledge of the matter may have left him dependent on texts for the *modus operandi*. Whether Backhouse himself had succeeded is a problem which lies behind the darkness of our ignorance concerning him, while over and above this doubt there is the far more fatal question whether that which he passed on represented certitude based on experimental knowledge or on hypothesis only. On the other hand, supposing—perhaps against all likelihood—that Backhouse revealed the First Matter of the work in alchemy as a work on the soul, not on the body of things, it may be that the pursuit of such an experiment lay outside the calling of Ashmole and that the revelation was a dead secret. However this may be, the preface of THE WAY TO BLISS, published some years after the key had been put into his hands, is a poor and negligible performance in comparison with the *prolegomena* to THEATRUM CHEMICUM BRITANNICUM, which was prior to the great event. Thereafter he published no further Hermetic texts.

containing THE GOLDEN FLEECE, *or the Flower of Treasures*, described as translated out of French by William Backhouse, the original author calling himself Solomon Trismosin. The work is of considerable length and the translation is an extract only. It should be mentioned that Heydon ascribed to Backhouse his version of THE WAY TO BLISS and bibliographers unacquainted with Ashmole's text have been misled accordingly. So also was the Rev. A. F. R. Woodford in his ENCYCLOPÆDIA OF FREEMASONRY. Ashmole's account of the work has obviously mythical elements, but there is no reason to suppose that he would suppress wilfully the fact of its authorship had he been acquainted therewith. Backhouse provided the copy for printing. See Gould : HISTORY OF FREEMASONRY, II, 132. It may be added that Backhouse did not die till May 30, 1662.

This is the case as it stands for Elias Ashmole as a Brother of the Rosy Cross: he had been instructed in alchemy; on one occasion he borrowed without acknowledgment from one of the manifestoes; and he reproduces notions from a so-called BOOK OF ST. DUNSTAN, couching them in language which has a distinct flavour of the Rosicrucian manner of writing. I continue to think that if there were living members of the Order in England between the death of Fludd and the date of his own passing, it is probable that he was one of them; but it is all high speculation, and there is little ground for supposing that things may be discovered hereafter which will open a door to certitude hereupon. As we know that he was a theoretical alchemist, we know also that he was a Mason, that he was initiated in 1646 and long years after attended a Meeting of Lodge or Acception at Mason's Hall in London.[1] Out of his Hermetic interests has arisen his Rosicrucian legend and out of the fact that he who was a non-operative became—for reasons unknown but probably of an antiquarian kind—the member of a guild of craftsmen, there has arisen that other legend, according to which he was the father of Speculative Masonry. They are of the same value and essentially speaking this value is *nil*. I conclude that, Rosicrucian or not, there is no evidence for the awakening of the Rosy Cross in England under the auspices of Elias Ashmole.

I pass now to the case of his contemporary, Thomas Vaughan, and as I do not propose to retrace a ground which I have travelled previously through its whole length, I must either presuppose acquaintance with my study of the Vaughan question or refer thereto.[2] On this

[1] Sir Robert Moray, who was initiated in the North prior to Ashmole, and was first President of the Royal Society, is called by Wood "a great patron of the Rosicrucians."

[2] THE WORKS OF THOMAS VAUGHAN: Eugenius Philalethes. Edited, annotated and introduced by Arthur Edward Waite. Issued by the

understanding, let us make a beginning at the year 1650, when the twin-brother of Henry Vaughan, called the Silurist poet, issued two tracts in a minute volume, under the pseudonym of Eugenius Philalethes. It follows that he preceded Ashmole, and so far as I am directly aware he makes the first reference to the Rosy Cross in the English language in England.[1] It had been made previously in Scotland, so far back—speaking comparatively—as the year 1638.[2] In the case of Vaughan his reference takes the form of a dedication prefixed to his first tract, a " salutation from the Centre of Peace " to the " regenerated Brethren R∴C∴," who are described otherwise as " elders of election," upright, noble and " peaceable apostles of the Church," those, namely, " who behold in open day the threefold record of the Spirit, the Water and the Blood." This is the judgment concerning them, more than thirty years after they had ceased practically to testify on their own part; and the dedication itself is prefixed, as I have said, to a minute publication in England, far from the German centre of the Rosy Cross, as if Vaughan took it for granted that they could see with the eyes and hear with ears of the spirit all the wide world over. But it may

Theosophical Publishing House for the Library Committee of the Theosophical Society in the year 1919.

[1] There is, however, an ESSAY ON SPIRIT, referred to 1647 and described as a scarce black letter tract, dedicated to John Locke. It is said by King in THE GNOSTICS, second edition, p. 398, to contain a Rosicrucian Creed, of which he gives three clauses. They are identical with the first three Magical Aphorisms printed by Vaughan at the end of LUMEN DE LUMINE, 1651. I have failed to trace the ESSAY, but King derived from Edward Clarkson's ESSAY ON THE SYMBOLIC EVIDENCES OF THE TEMPLE CHURCH, prefixed to R. W. Billing's ARCHITECTURAL ILLUSTRATIONS AND ACCOUNT OF THE TEMPLE CHURCH, 1838. It is an open question whether Vaughan reproduced his Aphorisms from the black letter tract or both from a common source.

[2] See Henry Adamson's MUSE'S THRENODIA, in which are the well-known lines:

> For we are Brethren of the Rosie Cross.
> We have the Masons' word and second sight.

be suggested alternatively that there were members or emissaries in Britain and that he was acquainted with the fact. We have seen that there is nothing to support this view. In any case Thomas Vaughan lays the offering of his tract, concerned with the nature of man and the state after death, on the threshold of the House of the Holy Spirit, not indeed as that which he would bring but as all that he has. It is not to be regarded as a gift but as the homage of a suppliant. It follows from the last words that it was also a bid for initiation, and that there might be no needless hindrance, in view of German adeptship, the dedication is written in Latin.

So opened the life of Thomas Vaughan in the Hermetic paths of literature, and nothing followed thereon, as if a door swung back in hidden House or Temple to admit a candidate. The author of ANTHROPOSOPHIA THEOMAGICA and the little books that followed did not become a Brother of the Rosy Cross. In a later publication he tells us that he has " no acquaintance with this Fraternity as to their persons " and that no one should suppose in their distraction that he belongs to the Order. He does not much " desire their acquaintance " and owns " no relation to them," though he is not a stranger to their doctrine, on the basis of which he holds that they are " masters of great mysteries," while recognising the amplitude of Nature, in which respect they may receive as well as give, meaning that other schools and other personalities might offer instruction to them on lines distinct from theirs. " It will be expected perhaps that I should speak something as to their persons and habitations, but in this my cold acquaintance will excuse me." It is so cold, however, that for the fact of their existence, which he affirms, there is no better evidence offered than that they write and publish books. It is obvious therefore that Thomas Vaughan contributes nothing to the history of the Order, but he marks a date in the English concern therein. The denials and affirmations which I have quoted are drawn from the preface to the first and only published translation of the FAMA ET CONFESSIO FRATERNITATIS[1] in English, date 1652, or approaching forty years after their appearance in Germany. The version itself was not his own work but that of " an unknown hand," and " the copy was communicated to me by a gentleman more learned than myself."[2]

It must be said that the Preface of Vaughan is far enough from its presumed subject, but he institutes a parallel between the Rosicrucian House of the Holy Spirit and that clouded habitation on a hill where Apollonius of Tyana visited the Indian Brotherhood, and in this connection he offers the quotation already cited from Michael Maier, but without naming the source. "I beheld on a day the Olympian Towers shining by a certain stream and famous city, which we have hallowed by the name of the Holy Spirit. I speak of Helicon—or double-peaked Parnassus—wherein the steed Pegasus opened a fountain of perennial water, flowing unto this day. Therein Diana bathes; therewith are associated Venus as a waiting-maid and Saturn as a patient client. These are words which will say too much to those who understand, but to the unversed little or nothing." This, I suppose, is the first time that any words of the German Rosicrucian alchemist were put into an English vesture, for LUSUS SERIUS and THEMIS AUREA had not as yet been translated. As an illustration of doctrine, Vaughan

[1] THE FAME AND CONFESSION OF THE FRATERNITY OF R. C., *commonly, of the* ROSIE CROSS. *With a Preface annexed thereto and a Short Declaration of their Physical Work.* By EUGENIUS PHILALETHES. 1652. W. J. Hughan displays his knowledge of Rosicrucian literature by thinking that the FAME AND CONFESSION were " written by Thomas Vaughan."—THE ROSICRUCIAN, Vol. I, p. 9.

[2] It is a miracle that occultists of the pseudo-Rosicrucian type have not identified the unnamed "gentleman" with Elias Ashmole, whose THEATRUM CHEMICUM BRITANNICUM came out in the same year as THE FAME AND CONFESSION.

tells us that according to the Brotherhood, the Fire and Spirit of God worked upon earth and water at the beginning of things, extracting a pure and clear substance, on which that Holy Spirit expressed its own image, and so formed man. This "clarified extract" is the First Matter of Hermetic Philosophy, otherwise a liquid, transparent salt, which is the minera of all creatures; "and this Society doth acknowledge it to be their very basis and the first gate which leads to all their secrets." It is a living water, in which there is a Divine Fire, and that Fire is life. In the absence of all reference, I am unable to verify the source of this reverie, but it speaks the common language of Hermetic philosophy and is not typically Rosicrucian in character.[1]

In earlier texts of Thomas Vaughan there are certain direct quotations from Rosicrucian texts, and though again they cannot be identified, they are important on the spiritual side and both must be analysed at length. The author of the first is presented as "he to whom the Brothers of R∴C∴ gave the title of SAPIENS and from whose writings they borrowed most of their instructions to a certain German postulant." The extracts are in Latin and may be summarised in the following terms: (1) Truth is the highest excellence and an impregnable fortress, while it seems to be understood in the text, not as an intellectual acquirement but as a state of being, or in other words that the seeker becomes in its attainment at once the good and the true: it is the translation of truth into life. (2) In such fortress is contained that Stone which is the Treasure of Philosophers, and there should be no need to point out that here is a complete separation of the Great Work, in the light of the

[1] As stated already, I have not been able to trace a second issue of THE FAME AND CONFESSION, as edited by Vaughan, under the date of 1658, or alternatively 1659, but it is mentioned by more than one writer.

Rosy Cross, from any work in *Chemia.* (3) The matter of this Stone is found everywhere, yet is scarcely discovered by any ; it is precious to the wise and accounted vile by the crowd ; it overcomes all and is itself overcome by nothing ; it confronts us all, proclaiming with uplifted voice : "I am the Way of Truth." (4) It transmutes dead stones into Living Philosophical Stones, and is the true, rectifying Medicine. (5) It stands night and day, knocking at the door of conscience. (6) It is a fount of inexhaustible riches, without money and without price, to those who are athirst for truth and justice. (7) It is life and the light of men, shining in the darkness within us, and is planted within us by Him Who dwelleth in light inaccessible. (8) It follows that within us and not without is that which we seek in our folly without instead of within. (9) True knowledge begins when the soul elects to be united with the Higher Soul and the Eternal. (10) The body itself is brought into the harmony of union, and there is effected in this manner "the philosophical transmutation of body into spirit and of spirit into body," which is the valid process of the Mastery.[1] (11) Hereof is the gold of the Philosophers, "not that which is coined." (12) But it is also the Stone which is rejected. (13) The counsel of true schooling is to know Heaven by Heaven, not by earth, and earth itself by Heaven. (14) In Heaven, and so only, is found the Incorruptible Medicine which sets free the body from corruption and thus preserves it continually. (15) Thou wilt never make out of others that one thing which thou needest unless first there shall be made out of thyself that one thing of which thou hast heard. (16) So is the counsel brought to its last point and returns to its first imagery, the

[1] This is a remarkable passage and should be taken in connection with No. 14 in the present enumeration. They refer to the arch-natural body, otherwise the body of adeptship, on which see my introduction to the WORKS OF THOMAS VAUGHAN.

impregnable tower or fortress, where shines the Sun of Holiness and Justice, wherein is "Philosophical Love." (17) Beyond it there is such a place as is scarcely reached by mortals, "unless they are raised by the Divine Will to the state of immortality," above all fear of death. (18) Whosoever advances further than this state passes from the sight of men into a "realm of abiding happiness," filled with "perpetual joy."

On the faith of this testimony Thomas Vaughan terms the Rosy Cross "a most Christian and famous Society."[1] Let it be said on my own part that the voice of this witness is perhaps greater than the voice of Fludd, even in his most inspired moments. The extract contains, as one may say, in a nutshell the whole progress of the Christ-Life in man; and if I leave the speaking parable at this point it is because I must return thereto at the very end of our research. I have said that the source of this extract is withheld. There is, however, in the pseudonymous SUMMUM BONUM of Joachim Fritz that very curious letter described as addressed by the Order to a certain German candidate for reception and obtained by Fludd from a Polish friend at Dantzic. To this I have referred previously. Compared with the text which I have summarised, it is a poor and incoherent performance, and has been so characterised by Dr. Craven, but the notable point about it is that it reproduces almost verbally many passages of the alleged SAPIENS and is actually the document to which Vaughan refers when introducing his citations. It would serve no purpose to enumerate the identities and analogies—as for example, regarding the School of Philosophical Love and the conversion of dead into Living Stones. But over and above these there are a few points which may be drawn together, because if we are justified in regarding the document as an official communi-

[1] See ANIMA MAGICA ABSCONDITA, p. 107 of my WORKS OF THOMAS VAUGHAN, 1919.

cation of the Order it is an indication of its mind prior to 1629, the unknown SAPIENS himself of course anteceding any date that can be ascribed to the epistle, which offers on its own part no acknowledgments to place and time.

The EPISTOLA in SUMMUM BONUM[1] affirms (1) that the Fellowship of the Rosy Cross is with the Father and Jesus, but this has been quoted already; (2) that it walks in that Supreme Light which is God, according to St. John; (3) that Jesus dwells in the vile body of man; (4) that those who adhere to Him are with Him made one spirit; (5) that those who are alienated from God, are in opposition to the Order, and hence it comes about that "we give not answer to all"; (6) that its endeavour—this notwithstanding—is to lead back lost sheep to the true sheepfold; (7) that the only light in which the Order is manifested is the light of God and that "it is impossible for thee to see us—unless of our own will—in another"; (8) that the immovable palace of the Order is the centre of all things; (9) that Supreme Truth is a spark of fiery spirit, "dwelling in every created being," purging, sustaining, governing, an essential virtue; (10) that the work of the novice is to adorn and beautify himself with "sacramental graces," that the soul may enliven "the vile ashes and vulgar body," rendering it incorruptible and impassible by the resurrection of our Lord Jesus Christ; (11) that unity in spirit with Christ is possible here and now, and so also, even in this temporal state, "will appear the glory of the Lord and Jesus glorified"; (12) that this way is not

[1] Compare Reghellini, who speaks of an analogy and bond of union between the Rose-Croix of Germany and those of England and elsewhere. He is not easy to follow but seems to think that there were mystical Rosicrucians, during the Wars of Religion, who wrote for the illumination of humanity on pure Christian doctrine, as opposed to dogmatic intolerance. There were several systems differing among themselves but one as to their object and also as to the concealment of discoveries made in physical things, for which reason recourse must be had to emblems and allegories.

"walked in through dying," but is the way of conversion from dead to Philosophical Stones and the way of Christ, shewn to the favoured apostles on the Mount of Transfiguration.

On the faith of this document and the greater text from which it draws, we can see as through a glass and darkly how the Work of Spiritual Alchemy was understood in the Rosy Cross, as against that which passed at the period "under the name of *Chymia*," or "the ungodly and accursed gold-making," set forth by many "books and pictures" *in contumeliam gloriæ Dei*. That it attained any term in the mystery of the arch-natural body is another question and beyond the scope of our research at this point: it is sufficient to establish that it looked for the glory of adeptship, manifested to inward eyes, through whatever atmosphere of perfervid zealotry the vision was contemplated, as the exclamatory and disjointed language of the communication suggests too well. I should add that the German postulant, as Vaughan terms him, though addressed as "Worshipful and Honourable Sir" must have been at least on his probation, as the opening words speak of "the first year of his nativity" which can mean only his reception into some circle of the Order, some threshold or gate of initiation, however external. It is said to him also at the end that "these things the Lady Virtue hath commanded should be told to thee" and that he shall be "more largely taught" hereafter—according to his deserts.

The second citation made by Thomas Vaughan purports—like that of Fludd—to be another letter from the Brothers of the Rosy Cross addressed to one chosen out of thousands as worthy of some answer to his appeal for admission within their ranks.[1] His affirmed qualifications were diligence in the study of Holy Scripture and zeal in quest

[1] It is in reality drawn from GRUNDLICHER BERICHT *von dem Vorhaben Gelegenheit und Inhalt der Löblichen Bruderschaft, etc.*, 1617. This text has been the subject of previous reference.

after true knowledge of God. There is firstly a kind of preamble, containing a comment on the unworthy reception of FAMA FRATERNITATIS by those who looked for instruction on the art of making gold, so that they might "live pompously in the face of the world," and who "brand us with infinite calumnies" because nothing follows their demand. The truth is that no one looks for treasures in the place where God has stored them up. It is hidden from most of the world but not from those that are of God. The second part describes an Invisible Mountain of the Wise and the way to arrive thereat. (1) It is in the midst of the earth or centre, at once far off and near, containing most ample treasures, but such as the world does not value. (2) It is reached only by a man's toil and endeavour. (3) On a certain night, described as most long and dark—compare the "Dark Night of the Soul"—the seeker shall set out to find it, prayer being the preparation for his journey. (4) A Guide will offer his service and shall be followed, asking nothing of any man. (5) The Mountain shall be reached at midnight—meaning when the dark night is darkest. (6) On arrival thereat a great wind shall shake the mountain and shatter its rocks to pieces. (7) The adventurer will be attacked by "lions, dragons and other terrible beasts," but the Guide will suffer no evil to befall him. (8) The tempest will be followed by earthquake, and in the destruction thereafter of the terrene rubbish by fire the treasure will be discovered. (9) But it will not become manifest till the night and its darkness are over, or otherwise until the Day-star rises. (10) The treasure includes "a certain exalted Tincture, with which the world —if it served God and were worthy of such gifts—might be tinged and turned into most pure gold." [1]

[1] THE ROSICRUCIAN AND MASONIC RECORD for March 15, 1875, prints this Rosicrucian letter in full, without comment of any kind, and describes it as translated by Kenneth Mackenzie. It compares unfavourably with the antique and beautiful version of Thomas Vaughan.

It is obvious that this is alchemy of parable, the gold of Robert Fludd and the spiritual transmutation of the unknown SAPIENS. But the incoherent and confusing text proceeds to affirm that if used as directed by the Guide it will make the old young, and there shall be no disease of the body. Moreover, " by means of this Tincture you shall find pearls of that excellency which cannot be imagined." It is like the doctrine of the kingdom presented in the trade-terms of a cheap-jack ; but I conceive that so far as flesh is concerned, it is the Lord that raises up, while the pearls are not marketable in any house of exchange, though they are beyond price. In the view of Thomas Vaughan this Invisible Mountain of the Wise is the Mount of God and the mystical, philosophical Horeb ; but occultists would dwell upon the Rosicrucian use of the term " magical " in connection therewith and would regard the " wild beasts " as signifying that " Dweller on the Threshold " which is the enemy to overcome by those who would follow the path of occult practice. I know only that in far later and—as I am sure—more condign Mysteries of the Rosy Cross, the Secret Mountain, the Mountain situated at the centre—that is to say, in the midst of the earth—is clothed about with a greater grace of symbolism, whether or not it contains a higher meaning. In the seventeenth century German parable at its best had by no means emerged from the uncouth forms and manners of thought and language which were native to the Meistersingers. We know therefore better where we are when in the hands of the theosophist SAPIENS, who was not writing parable, than in those of presumed official letter-writers of the Rosy Cross, addressing their German or other postulants and neophytes.

In any case, Thomas Vaughan is the first English writer who made known the Order and its claims in vernacular language, apart from unprinted versions of FAMA and

Confessio. He represents therefore the awakening of the subject. The publication of Fama and Confessio under his auspices marked an epoch for those who came after him, like John Heydon, or those who were in evidence concurrently, like Elias Ashmole. I have shewn elsewhere that he appears to have been concerned largely on his own part with what I have called the body of adeptship, and he gives prominence, as we have seen, to citations from Rosicrucian writers who seem to deal in the same subject, in other words, the state of Enoch and Elias, "who were translated."

I suppose that the Rosicrucian history of Thomas Vaughan might be regarded as incomplete by a few persons who are acquainted with the by-ways of modern occult imposture if I did not refer briefly to the inventions of Leo Taxil when he produced his mock conspiracy against Freemasonry for the benefit of the Latin Church in France. It was he who created Diana Vaughan, a "Palladist" of perfect initiation, Grand Mistress of the Temple of Occult Freemasonry and Grand Inspectress of the New and Reformed Palladium, having its headquarters at Charleston, U.S.A., under the supreme pontificate of Albert Pike. It was devoted to the worship of Lucifer and the hierarchy of lost angels, with whom it was in uninterrupted communion by the aid of sorcery. Wealthy, beautiful and highly placed, the Palladian Diana was a lineal descendant of Thomas Vaughan, whose birth—for the purposes of the mendacious story—is placed in 1612, or ten years earlier than it occurred in fact. In 1636, at the age of twenty-four years, he came out of Wales to London and there entered into communication with Robert Fludd, by whom he was received into the first Grade of the Rosicrucian Brotherhood. He obtained also a letter of introduction to its Grand Master, Johann Valentin Andreæ, which he took over to Stuttgart and there presented it.

In 1637 he returned to London and was present at the death of Fludd, which occurred in that year. Being represented throughout as identical with the pseudonymous alchemist who is known as Eirenæus Philalethes,[1] and as using this pseudonym in succession to that of Eugenius, he is said to have undertaken a first voyage to America in 1638. At this period he is described as a Puritan impregnated with the secret doctrine of Robert Fludd. In 1640 he made further progress in the Order of the Rosy Cross, being advanced to the Grade of ADEPTUS MINOR by Amos Komensky. A year later he visited Italy and made acquaintance with a fellow-alchemist, the well-known Berigard de Pisa; but in reality the journey was undertaken as a pious pilgrimage which testified his devotion to Faustus Socinus, who was the actual founder of the Rosicrucian Order. A little later on he is said to have been tarrying in France, when he conceived the project of organising Freemasonry in the speculative form under which it flourishes at the present day. He returned to England, and with this object in view he joined the Accepted Masons, some of whom were Rosicrucians already, and among them he set to work. In the year 1644 he presided over a Rosicrucian assembly at which Elias Ashmole was present, he having entered the Order in 1640.

With the exception of Thomas Vaughan, it is to be

[1] This piece of confusion is not only recurrent among old writers but is characteristic also of several who in recent times lay claim on knowledge. It is found persistently in Westcott's tract on the SCIENCE OF ALCHEMY; Kieswetter's problematical collection of Order MSS. not only allows him to make it but is his authority for so doing; and Alexander Wilder, writing in THE THEOSOPHIST, refers to Vaughan the experience of Eirenæus Philalethes with a certain goldsmith to whom he had offered bars of precious metal produced by alchemy—a story recited in AN OPEN ENTRANCE TO THE CLOSED PALACE OF THE KING. Finally, Wilder and C. W. King, in THE GNOSTICS AND THEIR REMAINS, both appeal to an unnamed writer of the year 1749 in support of a story that Thomas Vaughan was then living at Nuremberg and was President of the Illuminated in Europe according to Wilder but throughout the world according to King.

understood that all the personalities mentioned so far in the narrative were addicted to the cultus of Lucifer as the true god, and in the year 1645 Vaughan himself made a blood-offering to Satan, who appeared in response to an evocation and with whom he concluded a compact, receiving the Philosopher's Stone and a guaranteed period of mundane existence extending to some twenty-two years from the alleged date. Thereafter he was to be transported without dying into the Kingdom of Lucifer, to live with a glorified body in the pure flames of the heaven of fire. It was subsequent to this undertaking that he wrote the OPEN ENTRANCE TO THE CLOSED PALACE OF THE KING. Moreover, he collaborated with Ashmole over the institution of Symbolical Masonry and the composition of the Craft Rituals. In the year 1646 he paid another visit to America, and there on a certain cloudless night of a New England summer he entered into a marriage-union with Venus Astarte, who came down on a crescent-moon to earth. The fruit of these nuptials was a daughter, who was consigned to the care of an Indian tribe, and from her in fine descended the Diana of the French memoirs. Astarte returned to the skies, while Thomas Vaughan placed the broad ocean between himself and the scene of his amours. In 1650 he began to issue the alchemical writings which pass under the name of Eugenius Philalethes, and four years later he succeeded Andreæ as Grand Master of the Rosicrucian Order. Between this date and the year 1667, which was that of his translation to the paradise of Lucifer, he issued his later Hermetic tracts under the pseudonym of Eirenæus Philalethes. He was succeeded by John Frederick Helvetius, whom he had introduced to the Rosy Cross. Such is the secret history and informal romance of Thomas Vaughan, as certified by his lineal descendant, Diana Vaughan of Louisville, on the faith of family papers. But Diana and all her *dossier* were invented by Leo Taxil, as in the last resource he admitted *coram publico*.

The last genuine Rosicrucian episode which connects with the name of Thomas Vaughan is unknown to all his biographers and arose out of his edition of the FAMA and CONFESSIO in English. It prompted two interesting aspirants towards the benefits and consolations of the Order to make a formal application for admission in a printed letter, after the manner of those who had preceded them earlier in the seventeenth century. Their identities were veiled under the sacramental names of Theodosius Verax and Theophilus Cælnatus,[1] and as their communication appeared apart from date or place, but presumably in England, I conceive that not even the Brotherhood of the Rosy Cross in the sanctuaries or crypts of their House of the Holy Spirit had taken better pains to place themselves out of reach. Such precautions may have commended them to the Order and yet the Invisibles *par excellence* may have failed to find them out, unless there was help from the ROTA. Perhaps in this case that " sacred voice " which assured and consoled the postulants was true as well as sacred and they found that which they desired, " by the grace of God." [2] The memorial contains nothing

[1] Compare the dedication of Maier's Preface to Themis Aurea, mentioned in my note on p. 329.

[2] The text of the communication is as follows: AN EPISTLE TO THE ROSICRUCIAN FRATERNITY. To the Most Perfectly United, Most Eminent, Most Wise and True Philosophers and Brothers R.·.C.·. Theodosius Verax and Theophilus Cælnatus wish Health and Peace.—We have no small comfort in beholding those things of which the possession itself would be unlawful. Ambition does oftentimes proceed by impulse where we on our own part should be afraid to go. We seek now to exalt ourselves, supported both by piety and your candour, as it were with wings, above sordid envy and ignorance. Whatsoever judgment ye may form concerning us must be to our profit. If favourable, we shall enjoy shortly an easy boon; but if harsh, the greater our necessities are the better will be the opportunity of benevolence. While we are considering seriously how philosophy has been corrupted by the schools and produces daily more dread monsters than Africa

of particular importance, but it is notable as (1) the only direct application for admission made by aspirants in England, though one of an implied or indirect kind will be found—as we have seen—in Thomas Vaughan's dedication of ANTHROPOSOPHIA THEOMAGICA in 1650, while there is also anything that can be inferred from Fludd's epistle to the Fraternity appended to his APOLOGIA COMPENDIARIA and TRACTATUS APOLOGETICUS ; (2) the very last that was made by any postulant in any country and language ; (3) an addition to our bibliographical knowledge concerning Thomas Vaughan, and everything that can be gleaned respecting him is of moment not only to the mystical and occult activities in England of the seventeenth century but to the history of English literature during the Protectorate.

Contemporary with Thomas Vaughan, but a little later

herself, we begin to feel terrified. Aristotle and others of his school have compelled our philosophy to become a mere servant of its own glory, recognising no truth but their proper inventions. We do not deplore the loss of so many secret writings which having perished in the fire did only at their destruction shew signs of brilliancy. Truth is naked ; it wears not any mask and, incapable of deceit itself, uncovers false persons. Those who pursue truth not only reach the goal but leave a track behind which may be followed by others. For our own part, unless we receive assistance, old age will overtake us and yet we shall be no further than the threshold. Nevertheless, we prefer to die seeking the goal rather than yield to shameful idleness. We will accordingly, O most prudent men, continue in earnest desire, looking towards you in whom our help lies. We are conscious sufficiently of our weakness and we seek therefore a remedy. The gentle ray of your humanity has animated our sterile hopes and encouraged the vintage-song. Where others finished have ye begun. Pardon us, most excellent men, if we speak of those things whereof we are still ignorant. Whatsoever is brought forth into the light under your auspices is deserving of praise. We believe that your book is so much what we need that it might have been written for us alone ; we recognise that no ordinary providence has taken us from cimmerian darkness and placed us in a twilight which will be flooded shortly by the rising day. We are not of those conceited Peripatetics who swear by Aristotle, while their books swarm with stupidities. Your philosophy, O most learned men, is not full of kindred absurdities. It displays the greatest secrets in light, and the darkness which blinds most men has sharpened your own eyesight. Furthermore, it is modest and truly learned, and—having

in respect of his published writings, there is John Heydon, who was a kinsman of Sir Christopher Heydon, well enough known, if not overmuch esteemed among English astrologers of the period. He was of the Lilly and Gadbury contingent and, I believe, of no vital consequence to the speculative science of the stars, though not without bibliographical importance among progenitors of ephemerides and horary handbooks. I suppose that John Heydon is the prototypical thief of English occult literature. It was a free world in those days in the matter of author's rights, for there was no protection of any kind and no way of redress. As if he carried some libertine's charter, Heydon stole from everyone, and perhaps from his contemporaries

fallen from heaven—derives its origin from the Holy Scriptures, wherein nothing is suspicious or erring. Whoever studies these writings will arrive at a knowledge of that Matter from which all that lives has been derived. Those who persistently deny that there are men whom God has elected to a knowledge of the intimate mysteries suspect the solicitude of the Creator, Who withholds nothing useful or necessary. He Who fabricated the whole machine of the universe for the human race willed—both for His own glory and our benefit—that His works should be understood. There is, however, no profit in mere study without light from God. Therefore, as God—thrice excellent and most great—created the light wherein all creatures flourish, so a light was kindled over the chaos of letters; a great cosmos has been produced; heaven has descended to earth; and—the superficies being removed—the centre itself comes into view; while, if we spoke of even greater things, there are some from whom the meaning would not be hidden. For we have good reason to believe that there is a true Society—your own—unto which God has revealed the oracles. It is much more probable that He would discover such mysteries to His Church than to the heathen, and those who possess Divine Truth are not likely to be ignorant of Nature's secrets. Ye also are few and wise, while the multitude is rude and hurtful; and wise Nature has hidden her treasures deeply, that they may not become common. In like manner, art hath also its penetralia: its gems are to be sought, its gold is to be dug up, and the divine operation is an assistant in the investigation of both. Your FAMA—translated into the English tongue—has come into our hands, being edited with a preface by the illustrious gentleman, E. P. Therein ye have invited worthy persons to join your Society—but hence, ye profane! Meanwhile a bitter strife has risen up amongst us, because we are well aware that we deserved not so great a blessing; and yet our weakness gave way before your favour, and we

especially, with unblushing assiduity. The victims included Thomas Vaughan himself, Sir Thomas Browne, Elias Ashmole and Bacon. There can be very little question that he helped himself in like manner from the stores of anterior Latin occult writers, but as in that direction he had an illimitable poacher's ground it would be difficult to follow in his tracks, as well as unproductive in consequence, for his proclivities in these matters are notorious and beyond dispute. His English piracies are complicated by the fact that he altered his authors to suit his purpose at the moment, which was usually one of mendacity and the kind of imposture which exposes itself on the open surface of the tale. For example, he took Bacon's ATLANTIS

rejoiced at being thus overcome. Another difficulty, notwithstanding, appeared presently, concerning where or to whom we shall apply, and we were plunged again into sadness. There was no comfort in the conviction of your wisdom and benevolence if we could not reach you. But in the silence which followed a sacred voice assured us that the Fraternity we desired so anxiously we should find at length by the grace of God. We have therefore cast away fear and again breathe hopefully. Mere gold-seekers have doubtless inquired after you, and so also have the votaries of pleasure, whose brains have turned into a belly, while they apply arts to their orgies. But we have followed on the path of Mercury. There are many also who are given over to much writing, who discourse of the Elixir and the Panacea in an enigmatic manner, purposing deception, while others coming after them have pretended to find therein what the writers themselves did not know. Let us not be considered thoughtless who have scorned the promises of psuedo-philosophers, that we might give ourselves to truth. Those versed in Nature's secrets are taciturn : they do not write much or attractively. Hence little can be gained from books, which are less means of instruction than of mental confusion. We ask you therefore to take pity on us ; we are still young men and novices, as our nervous epistle indicates ; but perhaps an elder mind has been infused into us. As regards religion, we believe in the Creator God and recognise Him in His works. We smile at all which you have said concerning the Pope : that religion—if so it can be called—will be involved in the same ruin as other sects and heresies. We trust that there are no other obstacles which separate us from your Society : we ask much, but it is within your power. Pardon us, most loving brethren, if with open arms we seem to force ourselves upon you ; and if our desire in itself be pleasing to you, may there be no difficulty from the length of this our epistle.

bodily but called it A VOYAGE TO THE LAND OF THE ROSICRUCIANS and varied the text throughout, as if he himself had visited the Order at its headquarters and was authorised to unveil its mysteries. These peccadilloes notwithstanding, it was the custom in Victorian days for occultists belonging to the MacGregor Mathers type to affirm that Heydon "knew something"—as for example, no doubt, in respect of geomancy or other purlieus on the threshold of irredeemable folly, some deeps of which they had sounded on their own part.

Subject to all his deviations, which in the impression they produce at this day are not without a touch of comedy, Heydon's contribution to the matter of the Rosy Cross in Commonwealth England and later may be brought within a small compass. It incorporates also a medley of stolen goods. (1) The father of Rosicrucians was Moses, though according to some opinions they belong to the Order of Elias or are followers of Ezekiel, while for Heydon himself they "have been since Christ." (2) They are seraphically illuminated, like Moses, and possess not only a great power in working miracles, but can be transported wherever they please, while they can assume any shape, like Proteus. (3) They stay the plague in cities, silence tempests, calm the rage of the sea, pass through the air, countercheck the powers of witchcraft and cure all diseases. (4) They are truly inspired and are comparable to Aholiab and Bezaleel, who were filled with the Spirit of God, as Moses testifies. (5) The sum and essence of their teaching is that the perfection of a virtuous soul resides in the accomplishment of her own nature in true wisdom and Divine Love. (6) Heydon himself, according to his plain statement, was neither a physician nor a member of the Rosicrucian Order, and he pillages Thomas Vaughan in his eagerness to deny the suggestion; yet he is in a position to discover their Temples, Holy

Houses, Castles and Invisible Mountains. (7) It comes about for this reason that the Governor of the House of Strangers in the NEW ATLANTIS is made to describe himself in Heydon's mendacious version as " a Christian priest of the Order of the Rosy Cross " and that the mysterious City of Damcar mentioned in FAMA FRATERNITATIS is said to be on the eastern side of Bacon's Island of Apanna. (8) Like some other literary impostors, Heydon had a short memory and, previous affirmations notwithstanding, represents that " Order or Society which we call the Temple of the Rosy Cross " as having been founded at Apanna some nineteen hundred years previously by a king who had reigned therein. (9) Its warders at the period of the story were possessors of the BOOK M∴, though according to the FAMA it was treasured in the German Fatherland. (10) So much for pretended headquarters, a place " in God's bosom, a land unknown "—as Bacon described his island. (11) But the Order was also in England—according to another account of Heydon—and abode in the West Country, where the Brethren had power to renew their youth. (12) I do not know what author has been taxed for the account of their Castle ; [1] but we hear of its rich halls, its chambers of white marble, its pillars of jasper, its pavements of fine amber and lintels of emeralds. (13) We hear also of rich hangings, benches of white ivory, beds garnished royally and presses containing gowns of cloth of gold and mantles furred with sable. (14) There was in fine a vault which was " bigger than that in Germany " and was lighted after the same miraculous manner, " as though the sun in the midst of the day had entered in at ten windows," and yet the building was " seven score steps underground." (15) But as regards the mysteries of the Castle we are told only of the banqueting hall,

[1] In some of the details it recalls the Rosicrucian Epistle issued by F. G. Menapius on July 15, 1617. See Chapter IX, p. 247.

which provided a feast like that of the Holy Graal on the earthly side of its ministry, for there was " all manner of meat in the world," as well as golden flagons, garnished with precious stones and filled to the brim with wine. (16) It is said that this castle was built of crystal, painted with gold and azure, while all things past, present and to come were inscribed on the walls, together with recipes for the diseased, characterised as golden medicines. (17) In fine the pavement was strewn with roses and sweet smelling herbs, " above all savours in the world." (18) Heydon concludes his story by another theft, this time from Michael Maier, perhaps through Vaughan: it gives expression to his desire for the place and to live therein.

These gleanings are chiefly from Heydon's version of the NEW ATLANTIS,[1] but his account of the Rosicrucians in England is in THE ROSIE CRUCIAN INFALLIBLE AXIOMATA (1660) which—howsoever compiled—is an exceedingly curious text and contains some further notable fictions belonging to our subject. I pass over a garbled version of the traditional history concerning Christian Rosy Cross, for which Heydon no doubt depended on the FAMA translation edited by Thomas Vaughan. (1) The Order is said to inhabit the suburbs of heaven, and its Brethren are " officers of the generalissimo of the world," even as " the eyes and ears of the great King, seeing and hearing all, things "—this being stolen from Henry More the Platonist, who is speaking of beneficent genii. (2) The happiness which they esteem above all is the gift of healing and of medicine. (3) But a long time, great labour and travail preceded the attainment of this their chief bliss. (4) They were at first poor gentlemen, the humble students of God and Nature. (5) Their infallible axioms purge the

[1] It is found in his preface to THE HOLY GUIDE, *leading the way to the Wonder of the World, etc.* 1662. The said preface includes also a theft from Sir Thomas Browne.

mind from errors and render it divine, teaching us so to labour in this life that the excellency of the mental part may be saved from all degeneration. (6) It is said that the Rosicrucians are acquainted with those angels and spirits which are empowered to rule over numbers. (7) They pay especial attention to the number four, as if it had been like a seal set upon them by God. (8) They deliver charms against devils and their bonds, against diseases and so forth. (9) A certain Theophilus Fullwood, either at that time or recently a resident in England, is described as a Brother of the Rosy Cross. (10) His familiarity with *Daimones Metallici* and Guardian Genii is affirmed by Heydon. (11) Among Rosicrucians of the past there was Pherecydes Syrus, who was acquainted with *Fauni* and *Sylvani*, being moreover the master of Pythagoras.

Much of the pretended information here summarised is reproduced in THE HOLY GUIDE. Heydon's next publication was a treatise on geomancy, disguised by a magnificent title.[1] It describes in its first chapter the manner of projecting a figure according to Rosicrucian rule, but about the Order itself there are no further statements. THEOMAGIA was followed by a treatise on the HARMONY OF THE WORLD [2] which claims to unfold the Art of preparing Rosicrucian Medicines, but otherwise there is no information, real or alleged.[3] It may be mentioned, however,

[1] THEOMAGIA, *or the Temple of Wisdom.* In Three Parts: Celestial, Spiritual and Elemental, 1662–4.

[2] THE HARMONY OF THE WORLD, *being a Discourse wherein the Phenomena of Nature are consonantly salved and adapted to Inferior Intellects.* By John Heydon, Gent. Φιλονομος, a Servant of God and Secretary of Nature. 1662.

[3] There was an earlier volume entitled A NEW METHOD OF ROSICRUCIAN PHYSIC, 1658. It speaks of Mr. Walfoord and T. Williams, who performed miracles in his presence and were Rosicrucians "by election"; of himself as not of the Order; of the "Rosicrucian physic" which he met with in Arabia; of the Brethren in England, who taught him "excellent predictions of astrology," were learned in the signatures of plants and the secret

that the preface admits his debt to other writers in a manner which condemns him further. "I have borrowed no man's authority," he assures his readers, "but such as is eminent and quotations I have left out purposely, because I am not controversial. . . . Besides I do not profess myself a scholar." His dedication to the Duke of Ormond is largely a theft from Vaughan and very curious as illustrating an anxiety to avoid controversy. So also the opening part of his preface and much else therein is pirated from LUMEN DE LUMINE. I pass over THE WISE MAN'S CROWN [1] because its Rosicrucian materials are reproduced from Heydon's previous works; while his next two publications [2] contain nothing to our purpose. But in 1665 he issued THE ROSICRUCIAN CROWN,[3] in the Epistle Dedicatory of which he describes the philosophy of the Order as (1) to know God Himself; (2) to pass into Him "by a whole image of likeness"; whereby (3) we may be transformed and made as God. It is probably stolen goods, but I have not identified the source. He says also, elsewhere in the book, (1) that the Rosicrucians exact an oath of silence, "with a certain terrible authority of religion"—as if there were a heavy penal clause; (2) that this precedes the initiation of Candidates into the "Arts of Astronomy, Geomancy and Telesmatical Images"; (3) that the dead are raised to life by means of these; (4) that the Brethren

mysteries hidden in their seeds; of baths of wine, which served vitalising in place of food; and of his kinsman Sir Christopher Heydon, who was "a seraphically illuminated Rosicrucian" as well as a learned astrologer.

[1] THE WISE MAN'S CROWN, *or the Glory of the Rosy Cross. . . . With the full Discovery of the True* CŒLUM TERRÆ *or First Matter of the Philosophers. . . . With the* REGIO LUCIS *and Holy Household of Rosicrucian Philosophers.* 1664.

[2] EL HAVAREUNA, *or the English Physician's Tutor in the Astrobolisms of Metals Rosicrucian*, 1665, and A QUINTUPLE ROSICRUCIAN SCOURGE, *for the due correction of . . . George Thomson.* 1665.

[3] HAMMEGULEH HAMPAANEAH, *or the Rosicrucian Crown, set with Seven Angels, Seven Genii, etc.* 1665.

of the Order change and amend bodies, prolong life, renew youth, make dwarfs grow into the stature of tall men, communicate wisdom and virtue to fools and madmen; (5) that they insure good fortune in play, lawsuits, love and warfare, as also in commerce and maritime expeditions; (6) that in fine they know all things and " resolve all manner of questions, present and to come." It is the Rosy Cross in the ashpits, proclaimed by an itinerant quack who is also something of a buffoon. And yet I suppose that there is nothing more curious in the annals of occult literature than the output of Eugenius Theodidactus, taken as a whole. He is remarkable for the great heaps of his rubbish, swept in from far and near, with a few stars glittering oddly in the dust-heaps. He is curious even in his thieveries and in the adaptation of his stolen goods.

It follows that John Heydon is in no sense a witness to the Rosy Cross in England, either as to the fact of its existence as one who presented its claims, at whatever value, or made commentary on its doctrine and theosophy, whether it were possible or not to accept or tolerate his views. Such as we may hold it to be, the evidence began and ended with Robert Fludd. After his mortal remains were carried, as we have seen, from Coleman Street to Bearsted, if there was anything at work in the hiddenness it did not emerge therefrom, not even as Speculative Freemasonry. I have made in this manner what may be termed a complete clearance, a considerable number of lying witnesses being driven out of court, carrying with them the baggage of their mischievous or idle fictions. Thomas Vaughan was not an Imperator of the Order; Elias Ashmole mentioned it on two occasions only and then in a manner which shewed no acquaintance with the subject; William Backhouse may or may not have discovered the First Matter of the physical universe or of the Philosopher's Stone, but he is no more likely, in view of the facts before us, to have been a brother of the Secret Order than any of the occult rag-fair who frequented the Astrologer's Feast. And the seventeenth century died in the arms of its successor, during the whole course of which no one remembered Fludd, while it is exceedingly difficult to find even a casual reference to the Rosy Cross in any branch whatsoever of English literature till the High Grades of Masonry began to drift over from France and to be worked in this country, unobtrusively for the most part and only here and there. The sole evidential English Rosicrucianism of the eighteenth century is the imported Grade of Rose-Croix, the place and import of which will be a subject of consideration later.

It remains to add that Heydon had autobiographical moods, of which the benefit remains with us in some of his writings. I conceive that they are largely mendacious and are certainly in a thief's setting, for in the course of his story he levies contributions as usual from there and here, like reflections to relieve the discourse. For want of other sources, the biographical dictionaries, late and early, have depended chiefly on himself, nor am I in a better position, and it would be of little consequence if research could carry the subject further. I summarise therefore from available sources briefly: (1) John Heydon belonged to the Devonshire branch of the Norfolk stock which bore this name and the fact establishes his kinship with the astrologer, Sir Christopher Heydon, already mentioned. (2) He was born at Green Arbour, London, in the house of his father, who was Francis Heydon of Sidmouth, the mother being Mary Chandler, described as of Worcestershire. (3) The date of his birth was September 10, 1629, according to his own statement. (4) The same authority tells us that he was educated somewhere in Worcestershire. (5) When the civil war broke out he claims to have joined the King's army and to have commanded a troop at Edgehill, being then about fifteen years of age, on the basis of his birth-story.

(6) He went abroad in 1651 but was in England in the following year and began to study for the law. (7) Even by his own account he could have obtained a mere smattering, but in 1655 he was practising at Clifford's Inn, combining professional business, if any, with the casting of nativities. (8) He is said to have been intimate with all astrologers of the Restoration, including Lilly and Gadbury, both of whom he vilified. (9) On August 4, 1656, it is on record that he married the widow of Nicholas Culpeper, the well-known herbalist. (10) About and after this date he seems to have been frequently in prison. (11) His books were burnt and he was committed to Lambeth House for two years, by order of the Lord Protector, Heydon's explanation being that he had foretold the date of Cromwell's death by hanging. The false prophet and his memorials on the art of divination naturally suffered together. (12) A rumour that he was putting treasonable matter into the hands of printers secured him a shorter term in 1663. (13) In the year following he suffered imprisonment for the common failing of debt. (14) In 1667 he was accused of being concerned in a conspiracy to seize the Tower of London, but he protested his innocence, affirming that he was the victim of false witnesses hired to inform against him. (15) This is the last record that I have met with concerning John Heydon, the date of whose death is unknown. His compilations are excessively rare and would form altogether a most curious miscellaneous collection, though dregs and lees enough for the better part, the penny-dreadfuls of occult literature. He is self-described on his title-pages as "a Servant of God and Secretary of Nature." So far as his books are concerned, the service might have been more honoured in suspension than observance, and I think that *Domina Natura* must have dismissed her scribe at an early stage of his proceedings.

It remains to mention the curious collection of Rudd

MSS. in the British Museum, Harleian, Nos. 6481-6. According to Kenneth Mackenzie, following the texts themselves, Rudd belonged to the West of England "and there is very little known concerning him," which notwithstanding Mackenzie affirms that he was a "mystic and quietist," denominations which his extant remains by no means justify. The bulk of the collection belongs to Peter Smart, Master of Arts, and was made up in the years 1712–14, but he describes nearly all the tracts as those of Dr. Rudd. In one place he mentions "an ancient manuscript" of this person, adding that it has been methodised by himself. In the absence of all knowledge otherwise there is only one fact which emerges clearly, namely, that the Rudd activities, in so far as he was not Smart's *alter ego*, are not earlier than the close of the seventeenth century, some of his materials coming from Vaughan and Heydon. What he left behind him was copies of printed books, and as the six volumes are not all in the same hand but in one also which seems to be older, it is possible that some sections are in his autograph. A summary analysis of their contents will exhibit the limits of their Rosicrucian character and claims, which have been exaggerated in certain quarters.

HARL. 6481. I. This is called Dr. Rudd's TREATISE OF THE MIRACULOUS DESCENSIONS AND ASCENSIONS OF SPIRITS, *verified by a practical examination of Principles in the Great World*. It opens with a so-called Vision of Dr. Rudd in an orchard at Sidmouth in Devonshire and is actually Vaughan's account of his experience with Beata at the beginning of LUMEN DE LUMINE. Whether mystic or quietist therefore, we see that Dr. Rudd belongs to the Heydon School of piracy, and indeed his garbled version reflects Heydon's "encounter" with the Spirit Euterpe rather than the original. The sections which follow are: (1) Of the Sympathetical Concord of the Macrocosm with the Microcosm, being a Discourse of Divine Names, Angels and Sephiroth, the whole, as it is said, Christianised. (2) Of the nature of God and spirits. (3) The Macrocosm and Microcosm. (4) Harmony of the Great World. (5) The Motion and Harmony of the Heavens and Planets as the Work of Angels. (6) The Harmony of Planetary Aspects. (7) Of Seminal Forms, the Souls of Brutes and the Soul of Man. (8) How Virtues are impressed by the Influence of Heaven, Stars and Planets, shewing Geomantic Figures and Seals of Spirits. (9) How Genii are united to their Vehicles. (10) The Harmony of the Microcosm. (11) The chief Seat of the Soul. II. The Harmony of the Microcosm, called otherwise the Second Part. (1) The nature and composition of Man. (2) Medicines to prolong life. (3) The separation of the Soul from the body. (4) Political Order and Laws of Air Demons. (5) The Bodies of the Dead. Here ends Harl. 6481, both divisions being dated 1714. I do not pretend to identify all their unacknowledged sources, but a great deal is derived through the Heydon channels from Cornelius Agrippa, from the forged Fourth Book of his PHILOSOPHIA OCCULTA, from Petrus de Abano and the early Grimoire-makers.

HARL. 6482. The general title is TABULA SANCTA CUM TABULIS ENOCHI and the several sections follow. (1) Characters of the Sixteen Figures of Geomancy, expressed in the Greater and Lesser Squares of *Tabula Sancta*: compare HARL. 6481, Pt. I, § 9. (2) The Seven Tables of Enoch, corresponding to the Planets. (3) The *Shemahamphoras*. (4) The Names of Good and Evil Spirits, according to the Seven Tables of Enoch. (5) Dr. Rudd's Nine Hierarchies of Angels, with their Invocations to Visible Appearance. (6) The Olympic Spirits. The first four sections are in another and older hand, their sources being referable to Casaubon's FAITHFUL RELATION, the other Dee MSS. not included therein, the so-called

LESSER KEY OF SOLOMON THE KING and Cornelius Agrippa: they include an account of Elementary Spirits. The prime source of the fifth section is, of course, the CELESTIAL HIERARCHY of Pseudo-Dionysius, but the Rudd codex derives from debased magical and especially Goëtic versions. After two "introductions" there follow certain Keys or "Provocations" and then "the Nine Great Celestial Keys," otherwise Angelic Invocations, including that of Metatron, the Kabalistic Angel of the Presence, illustrated by elaborate "Seals of the Angels." This section claims to be Smart's transcript and is dated July, 1712. The source of the sixth section is DE MAGIA VETERUM, under the name ARBATEL, first printed in 1575.

HARL. 6483. The general title is LIBER MALORUM SPIRITUUM, SEU GOËTIA, comprising the KEYS OF SOLOMON, the ALMADEL and ARS NOTORIA. The sources are therefore familiar, and I need add only that the sections are full of Seals and Diagrams, excellently drawn. HARL. 6484. THE TALISMANIC SCULPTURE OF THE PERSIANS. This depends from the English translation of Gaffarel's CURIOSTEZ INOUYES, first published in 1629. HARL. 6485 is a very curious volume, the general title of which is ROSICRUCIAN SECRETS: their Excellent Method of Making Medicines of Metals, also their Laws and Mysteries.[1] The date is March 12, 1713, presumably that of completion. The text is alchemical as far as folio 352 and draws much from Heydon. The VITULUS AUREUS of Helvetius follows as a letter to Dr. Dee and then an extract from the AMPHITHEATRUM of Heinrich Khunrath. On folio 370 there is a citation from Helmont. The next item is called CLAVIS CHYMICUS and purports to explain "hard words" in the writings of Dr. Dee: in reality it is a short alchemical lexicon. The last section is called the Laws and Mysteries

[1] In the corner of the title-page are these unaccountable words: "The first sheet Dr. Dee."

of the Rosicrucians, for which see the English translation of Maier's THEMIS AUREA.[1] HARL. 6486. The title is HERMETIS TRISMEGISTI : SPONSALIA CELEBERRIMA. *The Famous Nuptials of the Thrice-Great Hermes, allegorically describing the Mystical Union and Communion of Christ with every Regenerate Soul.* Composed by C∴R∴, a German of the Order of the Rosie Cross about 255 years past, and from the Latin MS. faithfully translated into English by Peter Smart, Master of Arts, 1714. Notwithstanding its title, there was never a Latin edition of NUPTIÆ CHYMICÆ and English is the sole language into which I can trace its translation from the original German. The inference is that Smart as a false witness is in the category of Heydon and Rudd. The version which he used is that of the English translation by E. Foxcroft, published in 1690. On the reverse of the title it is said that in the margin are brief notes by the late Dr. Rudd, explaining some hard words and sentences, but they are the marginalia of the English rendering and these derive in their turn from the German text. This additional and gratuitous mendacity suggests that Rudd is a figment of the brain of Smart. The cryptic figures of THE CHEMICAL NUPTIALS are reproduced and of course are not decoded. At the end there is a Table summarising the episodes of the romance, but nothing appears to justify the mystical meaning ascribed to it in the title. As a contribution to Rosicrucian literature, I conclude that the Rudd MSS. might be commended to the notice of the American Rosy Cross in some of its developments as an early example of its own dispositions in the art of occult fraud.

[1] As regards the third Law of the FAMA which—according to the Rudd transcript—" enjoins each Brother to appear on a particular day at a certain place every year, that they may meet all together and consult about their affairs," there is no mention of *Dies C* but it is suggested that the place of gathering is spiritual, and Maier's remarks follow concerning Olympic Houses, Helicon and Parnassus.

CHAPTER XIV

GERMAN ROSICRUCIANISM IN THE EIGHTEENTH CENTURY

WHEN John Heydon carried his weakling voice and his principles of petty piracy over the visible border, the Rosy Cross as presented to the mind of Fludd and reflected faintly—in almost casual references—scattered through the texts of Vaughan, appears, on the surface at least, to have fallen asleep once more in England, even as the Figurative Master of its Legend slept in the House of the Holy Spirit during that mystical period of one hundred and twenty years. What I have called the awakening in this country was perhaps rather a stirring in dream. So also in Germany, if there was activity in any of the Houses there was practically no echo in the world without. The occasional reproduction of an old text alone excepted, the written word, like the voice of rumour, was nowhere abroad in the land.[1]

[1] For the sake of an accuracy to which no consequence attaches it may be noted that a Salzbourg physician, named Adam Lebenswald published in 1680 ACHT TRACTATLEIN VON DES TEUFELS LIST UND BETRUG etc, and that the fourth of these eight treatises on the guile and imposture of the devil was concerned with the claims and traditional history of the Rosy Cross, regarded as fabricated doctrine and lying pretence. The Order is represented as divided into various groups or classes: Mathematicians, Magi, Kabalists, Physicians, Alchemists, Necromancers, and so forth. When men of learning enter the ranks it is affirmed that they are required to set aside their knowledge and become Paracelsists. Lebenswald believes that he was visited on one occasion by two who belonged to the " sect." Their discourse turned on the Philosophical Stone, the Universal Tincture, etc. Their expression was strange, their eyes gleamed, their manner was restless, they spoke hurriedly and seemed to read his thoughts. They impressed him as

The silence in the hidden heaven of German adeptship was prolonged for a period of at least seventy years, or till the year 1710, when Sigmund Richter emerged from the sacred precincts, bearing the Sacramental Name of SINCERUS RENATUS, as one who might testify from experience concerning the Second Birth and the mysteries of a new life. What he did, however, was to publish the Laws of the Brotherhood,[1] but not as they were formulated at first and not as we find them justified and expounded in the work of Michael Maier—the Book of a Golden Law, line upon line unfolded. We shall find that a notable change has come over the spirit and form of the Order and that it has passed under a methodised rule, suggesting something behind it which had been growing up in the silence, far from the common ken. An alternative view would be obviously that it was a new or recent creation developing from the old seed.[2] The salient points may be collected thus together: (1) The Brotherhood subsists under the government of an Imperator and *ex hypothesi* had been so doing

being possessed by some horrible kind of phantom in addition to the native soul of humanity. Lebenswald was a champion of Latin orthodoxy, and the views of the Rosicrucian CONFESSIO on the Pope and Antichrist were blasphemy in his eyes. He was incensed with Adam Haselmeyer for dreaming that the Brethren might be Jesuits and recalls that he was condemned to the galleys by the Archduke Maximilian—presumably not on account of his opinions in this matter.

[1] THE PERFECT AND TRUE PREPARATION OF THE PHILOSOPHER'S STONE *by the Brotherhood of the Golden and Rosy Cross, issued for the Profit of Sons of the Doctrine.* Breslau, 1710. A tract under the same assumed name appeared at the same place in 1711 and was entitled THEO-PHILOSOPHIA THEORETICA-PRACTICA.

[2] I must not omit to mention that Sincerus Renatus in the preface to his PERFECT AND TRUE PREPARATION furnishes the surprising information that the Masters of the Rosy Cross had taken their departure to India "some years ago" and that none remained in Europe—himself excepted presumably, as if one who was left to unveil the veridic method of preparing Stone and Tincture and of making known the Laws. I take it that this pretence was designed to baffle enquiry from unwelcome quarters. It was first put forward, nearly a century before, by Neuhusius in his PIA ET UTILIS ADMONITIO, as we have seen.

for possibly a considerable period, during which the custom was that he should be elected for ten years. This ordinance is now abolished, and he is elected for life. (2) The Society has been divided into two branches, called respectively the Rosy and the Golden Cross, the badge or jewel being a green cross in the first case and a red in the second. There is nothing to indicate the reason for constituting two branches, as it seems clear that they were under one rule and had the same object in view, being the physical work of alchemy. (3) The Brotherhood in both associations combined is restricted to sixty-three members, or presumably thirty-one in each branch and the Imperator at their head. (4) The anti-papal spirit of the FAMA and CONFESSIO has become a nightmare of the past, and it is laid down expressly (*a*) that the initiation of Roman Catholics shall be and is hereby allowed, while (*b*) no one is permitted to question another respecting his form of faith. This is part of a larger ordinance, which enjoined the Brethren to refrain from stirring up strife and discord—as " among men " generally, so obviously in their own Temples or Houses. (5) Members of religious, meaning monastic and kindred societies, shall not be accepted, however, under any pretence: it is noted that through past indiscretion in respect of such persons two Brethren were " lost " in the year 1641.[1]

[1] With these internal arrangements, which signify at most the genesis of a certain tolerant spirit, we may compare the affirmations of Findel on the position of the Rosicrucian Order in the early part of the eighteenth century. He says (1) that it differed essentially from the chief characteristics of the preceding period ; (2) that it was dedicated to the support and advancement of Roman Catholicism, citing Professor Woog : JOURNAL FÜR FREIMAURER, IIIrd year, 3rd quarter, p. 147, Vienna, 1786 ; (3) that when the Church endeavoured to repress liberty of thought and so forth, " the Rosicrucians enlarged their designs to check the progress of enlightenment," for which no evidence is offered and none exists ; (4) that the Laws of the Order published by Richter " bear unmistakable evidences of Jesuitical intervention," the answer to which may be found in the text above ; (5) that in particular the removal of " seven tufts of hair " from the heads of Candidates means that

The ordinances concerning the Imperator may be grouped as follows : (1) He shall change his name, patronymic and place of abode every ten years, or more often at his discretion, in case of need, secret information of the fact being conveyed to all members, especially by way of communication from one to another. (2) He shall keep the name and address of each individual Brother, so that they can help one another in case of necessity. There shall be a record, moreover, respecting places of birth. (3) It is laid down that " the eldest Brother shall always be Imperator," which seems to void the election implied and expressed in a previous clause.

It follows from the Laws *passim* that the Rosy and Golden Cross is an Order of Adepts in plenary possession of the Stone and the Great Elixir, not on the quest thereof. This fact is exhibited by several clauses. (1) Each Brother, after his acception, receives a sufficient portion of the Stone to insure his life for the space of sixty years : whether the period in question dates from his birth or initiation is an open question. (2) The Stone may be bestowed freely by one upon another, " lest it might be said that this so great gift of God could be bought with a price." (3) The Stone in the sixth projection shall be administered only to sick brethren and never to strangers. (4) Every member shall change his name and patronymic and shall alter his years with the Stone. (5) When the Brethren desire " to renew themselves," they must proceed in the first place to another country and must remain absent from their previous

they were tonsured like priests, but this is nonsense, for priestly tonsure has to be repeated continually by the process of shaving, while this was obviously an emblematic observance done once and for all. The only possible conclusion to be drawn from these views is that Findel was one of many people in the past and of a very few still remaining for whom the hand of the Jesuits can be traced everywhere : they are perfectly sincere and it is a matter of personal delusion which must be left to work itself out, if possible, as it is increased rather than reduced by debate thereon.

abode after the renovation has been accomplished. (6) No Brother on his travels shall carry the Treasure of Philosophy in " the form of oil " but only in that of " powder of the first projection, the same being contained in a metal box, having a metal stopper." (7) If invited to the table of a stranger, Brethren shall not eat " unless their host has first tasted the food," or if this be impracticable they shall take in the morning " one grain of our medicine of the sixth projection," fortified by which they can eat without fear. (8) The Stone shall not be administered to a woman in labour, for " she would be brought prematurely to bed." (9) He who has the Stone in his possession shall ask no favour of any one. (10) He shall not manufacture pearls or other precious gems " larger than the natural size "—meaning presumably not abnormally large, as it is obvious that gem differs from gem in magnitude. (11) It is forbidden under the penalties of the Order for any one to divulge " the sacred and secret matter, or any manipulation, coagulation or solution thereof." (12) Lastly, and of all things most fantastic, it is laid down that " the Stone shall not be used at the chase." I must confess that the meaning—if any—of this instruction escapes me utterly, though I know that Diana was a huntress and that according to Alexander Seton, he and some others, both of high and mean estate, had in his day of the seventeenth century beheld Diana unveiled. For the rest, it will be seen that these Laws concerning the Stone make mention nowhere of the transmutation of metals.

I will take in the next place—and almost as they come in the series—those regulations which concern the admission of new members. (1) When a Brother dies to preserve the secret, especially at the hands of a prince, it is laid down that a relative shall be received in his place—his vocation being presumed, I suppose, but the rule does not specify this or any other condition. (2) The warrant of the Imperator must antecede any election, which is void otherwise. (3) An earnest desire to attain the Art, a part taken in its practice and full experience of all its workings are essential qualifications before any one makes his profession to the Order. (4) No married man shall be eligible for initiation. (5) Each Brother is apparently permitted to choose and appoint an heir, the procedure being regulated by several clauses scattered promiscuously through the text. (6) A father is prohibited to elect his son or brother unless he shall have proved him well. (7) It is better to choose strangers, lest the Art should become hereditary. (8) The choice should fall on those who are " unencumbered by many friends." (9) Howsoever selected, the heir shall make his confession " in one of the Houses built at our expense " and shall serve as an apprentice for two years, actually or approximately. (10) During this period he shall be made known to the Congregation, the Imperator being informed of his name, origin, profession and country, so that two or three members can be despatched at the proper time—carrying the Seal of Office—to make the apprentice a Brother. (11) As it is permissible for Brethren to employ servants in their work when they are unable to operate with a Brother, so they may select those whom they have chosen for their heirs, provided that they are at least ten years old, the same to make profession as usual. (12) It is only by the warrant of the Imperator that any one can be constituted an heir. (13) The apprentice shall be obedient to his master, even unto death.

The following procedure is to be adopted at the initiation or making of members : (1) Reception into the Order can take place only " in one of the Houses built at our expense " and in the presence of six Brethren. (2) The postulant is instructed for three months previously and is provided with all things needful. (3) On the day and at the place appointed a vesture is placed upon him ; he is given the

Sign of Peace, together with a Branch of Palm ; he is kissed three times, and one of the companions says to him : " Beloved Brother, we enjoin silence upon you." Thereafter he kneels before the Imperator, having his own Master or Father and some second Brother on either side, and in this position he takes (4)

THE SOLEMN PLEDGE OF THE ORDER

I, FRATER NON NOBIS (*vel nomen aliud*), do swear by the Living and Eternal God that I will never reveal the Mystery which has been unto me communicated (*uplifting two fingers*) to any human being whomsoever ; but will preserve it in hiddenness, under the natural seal, all the days of my life. I will keep secret likewise all things belonging thereto, so far as they shall be made known to me. I will discover nothing concerning the position of our Order and the abode, name or surname of our Imperator, nor will I shew the Stone to anyone. All these things I promise to preserve eternally in holy silence, at the peril of my life, as God and His Word shall help me.

(5) The Master or Father then cuts seven locks of hair from the head of his pupil ; they are sealed up in separate papers, with the name and surname of the new brother written on each, and are placed in charge of the Imperator. This concludes the procedure and constitutes the first trace of Ritual in the observances of the Rosy Cross. (6) On the day following it is said that the Brethren—but those presumably who were present at his reception—visit the abode of the new Brother " and eat therein, but without saluting one another or speaking," until they prepare to depart, when one of them says : *Frater Aureæ* (*vel Roseæ*) *Crucis, Deus sit tecum, cum perpetuo silentio Deo promisso et nostræ sanctæ Congregationi.* (7) This sombre observance takes place three days in succession, after which gifts are distributed to the poor, according to the intention

and discretion of those concerned therein. (8) It is added that after a certain period of time, not otherwise distinguished, " the Brethren shall be on a more familiar footing with the novice and shall instruct him as much as possible." (9) After his acception every Brother shall set to work in—?one of—" our large houses " and shall recommend himself to God, undertaking not to use his Secret Art to offend the Divine Majesty, to corrupt or destroy the empire, or for tyrannical and ambitious ends. (10) It is further part of his pledge that he shall always seem to be ignorant, maintaining that the existence of such Secret Arts is affirmed only by impostors. So also each Brother who is at work with a servant or any stranger whomsoever, if questioned as to his status, shall plead that he is a novice and uninstructed.

The following rules are laid down as regards Brethren generally. I place them practically in the order of their appearance : (1) The Brethren shall not eat together, except on Sundays, unless they are working together, when they may live in common. (2) The rule of salutation on meeting is as follows : The first Brother shall say : *Ave, Frater*, to which the second shall respond : *Roseæ et Aureæ*, the first concluding with *Crucis*. Having thus exhibited their status, they shall exclaim one to another : *Benedictus Dominus Deus noster Qui dedit nobis signum* and suit the action to the word by uncovering their seals. (3) No secret writings can be printed and no extracts taken without the permit of the Congregation, nor can any document be signed with the name or Sacramental Name of any member. (4) Discussions on the Secret Art can take place only in rooms that are sealed against all intrusion. (5) No member of the Order shall kneel before any person, unless he be also a Brother. (6) It is said that Brethren shall not be given to much talking and that they shall not marry, but the regulation—which has been cited already—is stultified by adding that it shall be lawful to take a wife, should a Brother very much desire it, the conditions being these : (*a*) that he shall live with her according to a philosophical mind, the significance of which is doubtful, as it certainly does not connote the abomination of a so-called Hermetic Marriage ; (*b*) that he shall esteem the honour of his children even as his own ; (*c*) that his wife shall not practise overmuch with the young Brethren but rather with the old. It seems to follow that women might be novices at least of the Order and perhaps full members, being the earliest indication on the subject offered by the documents of the Rosy Cross. (7) It is laid down that no married man shall be eligible for initiation, which is not altogether an idle rule in view of the previous clauses, as *ex hypothesi* a Brother of the Order would choose his wife warily. (8) As it may befall that several Brethren are tarrying in the same town, it is recommended, yet not enjoined, that wheresoever a Brother is staying on Whitsunday he shall proceed to the eastern end of the town and there hang up a green Cross if he be integrated in that branch which is denominated the Rosy Cross, or alternatively a Red Cross if he be a Brother of the Golden Cross. Having so done, he shall remain in proximity till sunset, in case another should arrive and exhibit his own symbol, when they shall exchange salutations as usual, make or renew acquaintance and advise the Imperator in due course. Here it should be noted that green is the complementary of red, but no such relation exists between red and golden. The complementary of the latter is purple, so that the colour-symbolism of the Rosy Cross, which became important in later days, seems doubtful at this period. (9) In travelling from country to country a Brother shall change his name in each, " to avoid recognition, always giving notice of his destination to headquarters and of the designation that he has selected. (10) He shall not be absent for more than ten years from his own land. (11) He shall not begin to work in any town till he has been resident there for a year and has come to know the inhabitants, taking care to avoid all dealings with ignorant professors of *chemia*. (12) In his work he shall select persons of sober years, rather than the young. (13) He shall have no intercourse or conversation with women, but shall choose one or two friends, " generally not of the Order." (14) On deciding to leave a given place he shall not disclose his destination to outsiders, neither shall he sell anything which he cannot carry away, but shall direct his landlord to divide it among the poor, failing his return in six weeks. (15) When Brethren dine together their host shall endeavour to instruct his guests as much as possible. (16) They shall assemble as often as may prove practical in the great Houses of the Order, but shall not remain therein more than two months together. (17) During this time it shall not be incumbent on anyone to make more than three " projections," the reason being that certain operations belong to the Masters. (18) The Brethren shall be known among themselves by their Sacramental Titles, but among strangers by their ordinary names. (19) Finally, a new Brother shall receive the Sacramental Name of him who is last deceased, and all and several shall be bound by these Rules from the moment of their acception by the Order and on taking the Pledge of Fidelity *In Nomine Jesu Christi Domini Nostri*.

The method by which I have grouped these Laws together for the sake of perspicuity presents them in a more favourable aspect than they exhibit on their own part. In the original German text they are set down in no other order than that in which they occurred to the maker, and the result is complete chaos. My notes shew further that they are by no means in harmony with each other, while the fact of their publication makes it certain—at least to my own mind—that they belong to an Association which was not in a literal sense that which it claimed to be. About the last course that would be taken by a Congregation of *Adepti* in possession of the Philosophical Stone would be to publish their Rules of Membership, while there is nothing that lends colour to the hypothesis that Sigmund Richter had stolen the documents or betrayed his trust by printing them. If he belonged to such a Brotherhood, in possession of such a treasure, no purpose of his own could be served by a renegade course : he had everything to lose thereby and the gain was nothing. My conclusion is that he followed an agreed policy ; but this is of course tentative and must stand always as such, since we are never likely to know. Out of it arises the idea that the published claims of the Order call for drastic reduction. On the other hand, it does not connote untinctured and complete imposture. It is not unreasonable to suppose that secret chemistry at the beginning of the eighteenth century had tonic and recuperative medicines, the value of which was exaggerated, though in the case under notice we have seen that sickness and death were not overcome thereby. In like manner it is by no means improbable that there were means of producing colourable imitations of precious stones, which the ill-instructed minds of the makers may have thought of as corresponding in Art to the work of Nature and as genuine therefore in their way, even if the experienced jeweller could apply some fatal tests. In this connection we shall observe the prudence which forbade manufactured gems to exceed the average size. As regards the transmutation of metals, though there is one reference to projections and one injunction never to expose treasures of gold and silver to profane eyes, the Laws are otherwise silent on this subject, as we have seen, and the Stone appears in the main as a human medicine. In the first projection it was a safeguard of errant *adepti*, and was reserved in the sixth for the use of sick Brethren, or as a preservative against poison.

On the whole, I am inclined to think that the BOOK OF PREPARATION, according to the method of the Golden and Rosy Cross, was meant to indicate a certain stage of real or supposed progress in the occult arts concerned, and that it was put forward by Sigmund Richter and his associates from a genuine anxiety to incorporate other secret chemists, sons of the doctrine, philosophers by fire, and so forth, in the hope of securing its own position on the basis of extending knowledge. Having regard to the period, it is at least a hypothesis which seems entitled to toleration. The Laws may not only have been published with this object in view, but may have been framed or modified on account thereof. The PREPARATION is, of course, an impossible book to dream of presenting in English at this day. I could wish that it were otherwise, because it would exhibit it as a work of sincerity within its own lines, amidst all extravagance of process and the flush of its hectic claims. Those who see imposture or unrelieved delusion only and everywhere in such cases are no better than the occultist who descries great adepts and hidden Masters in all the highways and byways of the "secret sciences." Speaking generally, I believe that in those days there were numbers of ardent seekers after Mysteries of Nature and Science in the paths of *chemia*, and that they strove by every means in their power to reach an end therein. Secret association was obviously a not unlikely means, and it is possible that the Golden and Rosy Cross was brought over from the seventeenth into the eighteenth century;[1] that it may have taken some steps in chemistry; and that in its own opinion there was work in the world to do when its Laws were

[1] Kieswetter affirms that the work of Sigmund Richter was issued to commemorate "the centennial jubilee" of the Order and its work, from the time of the great impetus given thereto by the publication of FAMA FRATERNITATIS. But the PREPARATION appeared in 1710 and not, as Keiswetter states, in 1714, and it follows that the centennial was not due for another four years.

published at Breslau in 1710, under the ægis of Sigmund Richter. Such work was to extend the circle of initiation and at the same time that of the lore and practice, on the hypothesis that the great treasure—*Magnalia Dei et Naturæ*—would in this manner, and perhaps soon, be committed to their hands.

Such is the speculative but not exaggerated position at the date in question, and the other memorials are few. We hear of the great Houses, but the chances are that they were erected only in the hearts of those who made the Laws, though there must have been places of meeting. They are not otherwise in view, even in any scheme of texts. The Hague gave forth no sign; that city of great encounters and magnetic associations which is Nuremburg put up no banners of the Rosy Cross, and the echo of *adepti* was not heard through its streets and waterways. The period of general suspension is not of course without mythical rumours and more or less dubious records, among which a brief selection may be made. (1) It is said that Michael Sendivogius, pupil of Alexander Seton and reputed author of A NEW LIGHT OF ALCHEMY, spoke of Sincerus Renatus as one of the Brethren and also of an alleged admission by Philalethes that he had not received the secret of the Order. This is given on the authority of J. Michael Faustius, of Frankfurt-on-the-Main, in his preface to PHILALETHA ILLUSTRATA, 1706. But there is something seriously at fault with both sides of the statement, for Sendivogius died at Parma in 1646 and could have known nothing of Richter, who was probably unborn, and he could have known nothing of Philalethes, whose first printed testimony belongs to the year 1667. Moreover, the great pseudonymous alchemist never mentioned the Rosy Cross in any of his writings. The allusion applies probably to Thomas Vaughan, Eugenius Philalethes, who stated in 1659 that he knew nothing of the Rosicrucian Brethren " as to their persons ";

but Sendivogius at this date had been dead for thirteen years.[1] (2) We hear on the authority of M. Sédir[2] that there was renewed activity in Rosicrucian Lodges about 1730 and that the Ram appeared on the jewel, recalling the Golden Fleece of the CHEMICAL NUPTIALS; but no authority is given, and I have found no evidence on my own part. (3) The same French historian quotes Hermogenes: SPAGYRISCHER UND PHILOSOPHISCHER BRUNLEIN, 1741, and ARCA APERTA as reciting the history of a certain Adolphus Magnus, who was Emperor of the Rosy Cross in Cambodia and had attained the age of 967 years. As unfortunately neither text is available for reference, I need only add that M. Sédir recognises in both the intervention of a tale of faërie. (4) Duke Ernest Augustus of Saxe-Weimar brought out some THEOSOPHICAL DEVOTIONS in 1742,[3] in which work he is said to have affirmed that he had been received into the Order and refers to "the last great union of Brethren." We may be approaching here a question of historical fact, and I regret my inability to carry it any further, having failed to find such a statement anywhere in the work cited. (5) There is the evidence at its value of Nicolai that after the Society of Jesus was dissolved in 1744 by Pope Clement XIV it began to permeate the Rosicrucian Order, but opportunity is wanting to check this statement. (6) The *fabulator magnus* Kieswetter testifies that in 1762 his great-grandfather was admitted into the Order by one Tobias Schulze, who was Imperator at that date and was resident in Amsterdam; that in 1769 the ancestor in question himself became Imperator; that

[1] See my LIVES OF ALCHEMYSTICAL PHILOSOPHER, pp. 179, 180, for the fabulous account of a visit received by Sendivogius, in his castle of Groverna, on the part of a Rosicrucian deputation, bearing their warrants and proposing his reception into the Order.

[2] HISTOIRE DES ROSE-CROIX, p. 111.

[3] *Zu dem hoechsten alleinigen* JEHOVAH Gerichtete THEOSOPHISCHE HERZENS ANDACHTEN.

he—Kieswetter—possessed a seal belonging to his progenitor in the alleged official capacity, but that it was destroyed by fire in 1874, a characteristic fatality in stories of this kind; that the seal was of brass about the size of a mark, shewing a shield within a circle, a cross on the shield, a rose of five petals at the foot of the cross, while at the top, bottom and sides of the shield appeared the letter C, signifying: *Crux Christi Corona Christianorum.*

CHAPTER XV

THE RITUAL AND MASONIC PERIOD

THERE is nothing to shew that the Order of the Rosy Cross had entered into the Sacramental Kingdom of the Rites during its earlier epochs. We know by FAMA FRATERNITATIS that the master who chose a pupil sent him in one instance to the House of the Holy Spirit, where he took a " solemn oath of fidelity and secrecy " and thereafter served a novitiate, or—as it is said—" performed his school " ; but there is no account of ritual procedure in any real sense of the term. Now, in the year 1717 there was put up—a great omen and sign—the banner of Speculative Masonry among the tavern-haunts of London, and under circumstances with which we are all or may be well acquainted the taverns became Temples and London like a City of the Great King in symbolism. How it came about is a mystery in respect of nothing else but the unaccountable likelihood of things. Yet a greater wonder followed when the Masonic banner passed over the English Channel and began to be erected there and here in France, as elsewhere on the Continent, in the rapid succession of time. I have treated this subject at large in an immediately preceding work,[1] and it shall stand as my witness when I say here and now that the Craft of Masonry underwent a transmutation abroad which seems to me not less strange and unaccountable than anything that was hoped for by Benedictus Figulus when *Deo volante* he expected shortly to reach the desired goal

[1] A NEW ENCYCLOPÆDIA OF FREEMASONRY, Vol. I, pp. 290–9.

in Philosophy and Medicine, or Sigmund Richter propounding as *Sincerus Renatus*—him who is reborn—that perfect and true preparation of the Philosophical Stone which he looked to achieve in the hermitages and mystical retreats of the Golden and Rosy Cross. Assuredly Speculative Masonry—*Ars Latomorum*—was *Ars renata sincere*, in France and the Germanic kingdoms, under Écossais and Elect Rites, Rites of the Strict Observance, Councils of Emperors, Princes of the East and Grades of Perfect Masonry.

In the volumes to which I refer there is a critical survey of the various hypotheses by which it has been proposed to explain the origin of Emblematic or Speculative Freemasonry, since there began to be an approximate scholarship of the subject after several generations of romance and reverie. The conclusion which I have reached is that justifiable evidence for accepting any of them must be declared wanting, though a considerable inherent probability attaches to one at least. I believe that this conclusion, left to stand at its value, will take rank in respect of sincerity the more readily as I have had no personal axe to grind in the form of a counter-hypothesis put forward on my own part with any claim upon novelty. I have shewn that the practice of assuming the presence of a speculative element in Masonry prior to the year 1717 is not connoted by the fact, otherwise beyond question, that the doors of Operative Lodges had been opened to reputable persons of all kinds unconnected with the building trades. Long prior to the so-called Revival at the date just cited those Lodges had to all intents and purposes survived their *raison d'être*. They remained in considerable numbers, scattered there and here over the whole country, Scotland and parts of Ireland included; but they were mostly in a languishing state, and in the natural order of things there is sufficient reason to believe that they would have been numbered sooner or later among memorials of the past. That which came forward and saved them from such extinction was the pregnant event of 1717, when four London Lodges, neither more nor less obscure than the rest in South Britain, thought to improve their position by the unprecedented act of forming themselves into a Grand Lodge and proclaiming their intention to restore the quarterly communications. There had never been a Grand Lodge previously, and if there is very full evidence of an Annual Assembly as a rule in the Old Charges there is neither practice nor statute to quote as regards the more frequent meetings. The intention seems therefore to register that the four Lodges were accustomed respectively to meet at those periods but had fallen into such a state of inanition that the procedure was not maintained. This speculative explanation is rendered the more probable by the further fact that after Grand Lodge had been established its activities were so desultory, and the inanition so far from ended, that several years elapsed before the communications were actually restored and maintained in continuity thenceforward.

It was not, however, the fact of a Grand Lodge, and much less of its Meetings held according to law, that saved itself or Masonic Lodges at large from extinction. Nor is an explanation to be sought in the somewhat later fact that Freemasonry began to be a thing of public knowledge, coming into a certain repute and favour, when peers of the realm accepted the position of Grand Master, however indifferently or not they may have filled the office. The element of redemption, of awakening, of new life is to be sought in the Ritual element. So far as there is evidence before us—it has to be gathered from many quarters—ceremonial procedure prior to 1717 was a mere vestige; it corresponded no doubt to the trifling so-called "Mystery" enacted at the admission of Candidates—

then, since and still—in several of our City Companies. It is certain that six years after the foundation of Grand Lodge there was a great movement in Ritual, a very important development. I am not going to discuss this thorny question, which after the debate of years may be said practically to have been settled by common consent. Prior to 1717 there was whatever attached to the process of making Apprentice Masons—simple, primitive, short, so far as it is possible to tell. It is evident also that there were Fellows as well as Apprentices, but there is nothing to shew that there was any ceremony by which to mark their advancement. According to his Diary, Elias Ashmole was made a Mason at Warrington in 1646, and sixteen years later when he was called to a Lodge at Mason's Hall in London, he was in his own words "the oldest Fellow present," though there is nothing in his Diary or elsewhere to indicate that he had attended any Meeting during the intervening period. The Lodge in those days was governed usually or frequently by a Warden or Wardens, though we hear also of a Master, especially in Scotland. When such an Officer was installed there was no secret procedure of any kind: whatsoever took place was in the presence and with the assistance—supposing such to be required—of Apprentices and Fellows. There was above all no Master-Grade in the sense which we now attach to the Third Degree. The three great Masonic events in Ritual which constitute Craft Masonry—meaning Entered Apprentice, Fellow Craft and Master Mason—in the present elaborate form of the First and Second and of the Third as to root and development—must and can be only, in the present state of our knowledge, relegated to post 1717, and most probably are the work of the period between 1724 and 1726. I have shewn elsewhere, and it is also of common knowledge, that in the literary, conventional and moral sense they carry the ineradicable marks and tincture of that period.

So far on the historical and textual side; but that which remains over is the question whether outside Ritual there are traces of a speculative element in the body general of Operative Masonry, as shewn by any documents, wheresoever dispersed over the face of the United Kingdom, or the world at large. Was there any moralisation otherwise on building tools? Were lessons drawn from square and compass? Was there any allusion to a figurative meaning of stones? The answer is yes—in a casual, scattered, sporadic sense—if we appeal to the literature of the ages, far and wide. They were obvious subjects for lessons in allegory and ethics; I do not see how they could escape from the world-wide drag-net of the symbolists, and in any case escape they did not. But the answer is no, if we appeal to Operative documents—to the Old Charges and to the Constitutions, so termed. There are something approaching one hundred of these memorials now known to students and available to research almost without exception. They have been my subject of special study, in the hope that I should find some clear traces of an old system of morality, "veiled in allegory and illustrated by symbols." It would have served my general purpose far better to antedate the speculative element than observe it emerge at the dullest of all periods. To me and those for whom I speak this work of figuration must have appealed how far more strongly, had the great art and mystery of Gothic architecture been brought *sub specie æternitatis* in holy catholic times. So also here and now my hope for long was to find inexpugnable vestiges of the Rosy Cross long years before the protestant theologian Andreæ, before that zealot who was Studion. I could wish that one or other of the vain dreams was true which have been shattered in my early chapters. But in either case there is neither trace nor vestige: the Old Charges and Constitutions are not less silent over an art of building symbolised than is *Ars*

Lulliana over the union of Rose and Cross or the hidden city of Damcar.

It comes about therefore that we know certainly concerning a shadow of Ritual procedure in the Rosicrucian Laws of 1710, as published by Sigmund Richter, and that just as much and as little can be found in operative documents in respect of Masonic procedure. There was no reality in either case, and there was no borrowing one from another, since neither had aught to lend. There is yet a certain natural parallel, not alone in the fact that each institution administered a pledge to Candidates, but that both had something to impart which they would communicate only in secret to those who would keep it secretly. The Apprentice Mason learned the mystery of his trade, the things denied to a cowan, and the Novice of the Rosy Cross acquired Hermetic Secrets, to be hidden from the world at large, whatever their imputed or real value. The correspondence is slight enough and is common to all associations which work under a veil of secrecy. In any case this is how Masonry stood in relation to the Rosy Cross, until the former had earned its titles, had become a fashion and a certain power in the world—of that kind more especially which belongs to glamour and enchantment. The titles were earned by the high magic of Rites and there grew up an endless galaxy of these on the Continent of Europe—conceived, begotten and fostered there, but also destined to be carried over thence to the original home in England. There came a time when the Rosy Cross put up its own banner beside the manifold standards of Masonry; there came a time when in a certain sense, and for reasons proper to itself, it passed under the Masonic ægis; there came a time when it exacted the qualification of Master Mason from those who passed its threshold. The truth is, as we shall see in the next chapter, it had learned something from the great cohort of Orders which--secret, like itself—had developed suddenly about it. This lesson was the value of ceremonial procedure, the adornment and pomp of Rite.[1] After initiation of pupil by Master, after the simple bond sealed in the presence of an assembly or placed in the hands of a Hermetic Chief who ruled a particular House of the Holy Spirit, there came the day of Grades and of solemn reception and advancement, according to an established form. We shall find that the Rosy Cross, or at least one of its branches then most in evidence, underwent a great transformation in Ritual. There can be very little question that it was actuated by a spirit of imitation, that it followed the fashion of a time, but that which it did—as we shall see also—was done with a purpose in view.

The Rite of the Strict Observance—which originated in Germany—had practically overrun Europe and was out to capture all Masonry in the name of Unknown Superiors. There were also Ecossais and Elect Grades by the score and hundred, making great claims on precedence. But all these things and Speculative Masonry itself were but younger sisters at best of the Rosy Cross. It came about therefore that the House of the Holy Spirit, with a time-immemorial line of alchemists, magi, kabalists behind it, with Hermes—older than Solomon—and all Hermetic Egypt in the dusk of grey ages, began to reflect upon its warrants. It found quite naturally that behind the Templar claims, the chivalrous origins, the Holy House of Solomon, there loomed in the dawn of time, " before the Olympiads," the Temple of the Rosy Cross and its truly Unknown Masters. In all this panoply of tradition it

[1] It follows that if the Rosy Cross, under the ægis of Robert Fludd, gave anything to Freemasonry, the donor was recompensed and the advance refunded by gifts pressed down and flowing over in a great horn of plenty. The reason is that—as indicated in the text above—Freemasonry at a later period communicated to the Rosy Cross, out of its own dedications, a high passion for Ritual.

entered the lists to compete, according to the fashion of the moment, for a prize more or less open to all comers, that of being the nursing mother of Speculative Masonry. On very different considerations indeed this claim remains among us as one of the possibilities on a remote horizon of scholarship.[1] So far as the records go, we shall see that it was put forward *in Ordine Aureæ et Roseæ Crucis* with the uttermost detachment and the indifference of complete certitude, as one who might say in his heart : *De minimis nor curat lex magna et occulta.* Of such is the Rosicrucian Order in its relation to Masonry during the second half of the eighteenth century. They stood otherwise apart. Of whatever kind or degree, a Hermetic claim or a theosophy arising therefrom could appeal only to Hermetic students, and though there were many at the period, the active—or most active—Masonic centre was in France, wherein the Rosicrucian Rite—though some of it existed on paper—never seems to have penetrated in any living sense—that is to say, according to its German form. Out of this qualification there arises, however, the next point of my story.

When rumours concerning the Order first passed over to France the German denomination was translated as *Rose-Croix*, *L'Ordre des Rose-Croix* and so forth. We have met with these renderings already, when it was unnecessary to dwell thereon. I recur to them of set purpose and specify that they denote either the catholic symbol of the Order or are the technical title of persons enrolled therein. From the beginning of things they have never meant anything else in the French language. Now, it happens that

[1] Those who are concerned with the pursuit of this thorny question further may consult, among several aspects of the debate, (1) Ossian Lang : REPORT TO THE GRAND LODGE OF THE STATE OF NEW YORK, 1918, on the Rosicrucian origin of Freemasonry, and (2) TRANSACTIONS of the Manchester Association for Masonic Research, Vol. I, 1911, containing a paper on the Relations between Freemasonry and the Rosicrucians, by F. Brockbank.

in or about the year 1754 there arose in France a Masonic Grade entitled ROSE-CROIX—that is to say, a Rosicrucian Grade or Grade of the Rosy Cross. It is first heard of under the obedience of a Council of Emperors of the East and West, which either possessed from the beginning or acquired by invention or importation a sequence of twenty-five Grades, that of Rose-Croix being numbered eighteen in the series—Apprentice, Companion and Master, otherwise Craft Masonry included therein. It can be stated with absolute certainty that only the Eighteenth Degree or Grade had any Rosicrucian complexion,[1] and the question arises how did it originate or whence was it imported therein. I have explored in all directions and have found no answer, except by analysis of the Ritual in that form which I conceive to correspond most closely to an original that no one has seen. Before having recourse to this there is a preliminary consideration that should help to clear the issues. For at least one hundred years prior to 1754 there is no trace whatever of the Rosy Cross in France, nor can I remember even a sporadic allusion to the subject, outside encyclopædic dictionaries—like that, for example, of Bayle. I have no pre-judgment in the matter, no speculative cause at stake, when I say that antecedently the sudden appearance of a Rosicrucian Grade in France seems one of the most unlikely things that ever occurred in the course of Masonic history. Nothing led up thereto, and nothing followed therefrom, except variations of the Grade and developments, for it earned great repute.[2] It seems to me

[1] There are alchemical elements in old codices of the Twenty-third Degree, being that of KNIGHT OF THE SUN.

[2] The most important developments follow in the text above. See also Thory, ACTA LATOMORUM, I, pp. 335 *et seq.*, for a short tabulation, s.v. Rose-Croix, the heads of which are (1) Rose-Croix, being the fourth and final "Order" or High Grade of the French Rite. But at the present day—unless there have been recent changes—the French Rite comprises Seven Degrees, of which Rose-Croix is the last. (2) *Ibid.*, *i.e.*, Knight Sovereign

therefore that the best provisional answer to the question—however speculative and tentative—is that it came from a Rosicrucian source. As it stands at the present day, as I believe that it stood then, it is the Christian answer to Masonry, the Christian intent and meaning impressed upon the Craft Grades, their completion and their crown. When twenty-three years later we are in a position to speak with certainty as to the Grade content of an established Rosicrucian Rite in Germany, we shall find that like the French Rose-Croix, it was almost militantly Christian and accounted, though after another manner, for the matter in chief of the Craft. How it stood with the Rosy Cross as regards Ritual immediately prior to the year 1777 we do not know; but the nine Degrees of that date—which was one of reformation—were not the growth of a moment, as may be inferred from internal evidence. It is probable that they grew up gradually within the secret circles. On the other hand, it is not probable that the French Ritual ever belonged to any German branch of the Rosy Cross: it

Prince, being Seventh Grade in the old system of the Royal York Lodge at Berlin. (3) Knight Rose-Croix, being the Third—read Second—Degree in the Order of Heredom and Kilwinning, meaning the Royal Order of Scotland. (4) Brethren of the Golden Rose-Croix, an Alchemical Society of 1777 founded in Germany, for which see my next chapter: Thory's title is inexact. (5) Rose-Croix of the Grand Rosary, being a Grade of the Primitive Rite—presumably that of Narbonne—and classified a second time in error by Thory, s.v., No. 10, as Rose and Gold Grade. (6) Knight Rose-Croix of Heredom, being 46th Grade of the Rite of Mizraim. (7) Philosophical Rose-Croix, an alleged German Grade in the collection of Pyron and in the archives of the Scottish Philosophical Rite. (8) Brother of the Rose-Croix, otherwise Adept Grade, in the archives of the Mother Lodge of the Scottish Philosophical Rite. (9) Sovereign Prince Rose-Croix, Eighteenth Degree of the Ancient and Accepted Scottish Rite, also and previously of the Chapter of Emperors of the East and West. The variants outside Thory's list are very numerous, but their recitation would serve no purpose. In 1787 we hear of a Chapter of Rose-Croix, called Sovereign Chapter of Savoy, said to have been established by the Loge Parfait Union of Chamberg. I may add that the great Paris Lodge of Philalethes is said to have included four Rosicrucian Chapters in its system of Degrees.

seems to me rather a reflection from that source, after it had passed through the alembic of a Masonic mind turned to spiritual things.

The Rosicrucian symbol-in-chief, otherwise the Rosy Cross, is for the Eighteenth Degree of the old Rite of Perfection precisely that which it was for Robert Fludd,[1] namely, the Cross of Calvary steeped in the mediatorial blood of Christ, and connected also with red roses, as Fludd himself connected it.[2] On this evidence alone it is certain that the Rose-Croix is a Rosicrucian Grade, either by reflection and borrowing from the Germanic Order or because the Mason who composed it belonged to one of the branches, as there is no difficulty in supposing that he did at the period of its origin. On either assumption, we are entitled further to remember that the Grade is denominated Rose-Croix of Heredom at the present day and also in the year 1761—if not *ab origine symboli*—as there is indisputable evidence to prove. But this emblematical and altogether figurative Mountain of Rose-Cross Masonry, which never existed on earth, connotes the Rosicrucian Mountain of Initiation, about which we have heard otherwise and which is equally symbolic in character. There is no object in labouring the question of source, because nothing follows therefrom. My sole concern is to establish that the Rosicrucian Order, which undoubtedly owed to Masonry its development by imitation into a Ceremonial Rite, gave something in return, and that which it gave happens to be a contribution to Christian Masonry at its highest—for long and how often denominated *ne plus ultra*. I am personally convinced that the whole arrangement of the Rose-Croix

[1] The recurrence to Fludd's name in my text above enables me to repudiate again a statement, according to which it follows from the Kentish philosopher's CLAVIS PHILOSOPHIÆ, folio 50, that the members of the Rosicrucian Order passed into Freemasonry. I only wish that it did.

[2] The heraldic emblem of the pelican is placed beneath the Cross, but in symbolical significance as in place is subsidiary thereunto.

Grade, its clothing, its jewel, its entire *mise-en-scène*, the chambers in which it is worked are reminiscent of the older Order. The three Points are in crude correspondence with the Hermetic Work in Alchemy—blackness, death and finally resurrection into the red or perfect state, it being understood that in the Eighteenth Degree—as now known among us—the work is of course spiritualised, as all Higher Alchemy had done long before it.[1] I could carry these intimations much further and will do so elsewhere should a real need arise, exhibiting parallels drawn from Rosicrucian and Hermetic texts on the Cubic Stone, the seven mystical circles, the Rose of Sharon, the Lily of the Valley, the Eagle, and outside matters of symbolism, on Resurrection, Ascension and the Second Advent of Christ—all of which things belong, in one sense or another to Rose-Croix Masonry. It follows that the various Masonic writers who have denied any connection between the Eighteenth Degree and the Rosicrucian Order have either spoken with an extraordinary absence of even elementary

[1] The alchemical correspondences of Rose-Croix Masonry are developed especially in L'EMINENT ORDRE DES CHEVALIERS DE L'AIGLE NOIR, a Sovereign Chapter of which is claimed to have been established at the Orient of Marseilles in 1761. It was a Rite of two Degrees, the first of which offers a very curious blend of Kabalistic and Hermetic symbolism, while the second is a codex of the Eighteenth Degree, having marked developments to connect its emblematic period with the Death and Resurrection of Jesus Christ. In a Discourse attached to the First Degree, we hear of Raymund Lully, described as a great philosopher who accomplished the heavenly marriage of the Spouse with Six Virgins, from which union was begotten the Messias by him expected, a perfect gold of transmutation. He presented this treasure to the King of England, who made coins thereof, bearing a Cross on one side and on the other a Rose. It is an old story and historically the truth is not in it ; but it is useful for my purpose at the moment, which is to shew that when the Masonic Grade of Rose-Croix was explained in the past by Masons, they referred back, naturally and inevitably, to that for which the German Order stood in their own minds. In the case of the AIGLE NOIR it stood for the work of alchemy on its physical side. As regards the alleged treasure presented to an English king, see my RAYMUND LULLY, *Illuminated Doctor, Alchemist and Christian Mystic*, 1922.

knowledge or with considerable want of sincerity. The bond of kinship lies upon the surface of the subject, and those who have eyes can scarcely fail to see.

I do not propose to consider at particular length the story of the Eighteenth Degree in its developments *à rebours* and its decadence. There seems reason to believe that as originally formulated it stood at its own value, making no claims upon the past and presenting no traditional history. It has passed through successive phases of corruption, owing to the modifications which it has suffered at the hands of the makers of Rites. There and here it has reduced or expunged altogether the Christian elements which constituted its titles in chief. It carries no longer the Craft Degrees to their completion by the finding in Christ of that Lost Word which is sought in vain by all Master Masons. In some cases it has forgotten that there is a Word at all. The old language-symbols have become shibboleths in several hands or when emptied of their proper meaning have been filled with dead expatiation. The speaking pictorial signs have been furnished with new *signata* and with the testimony which they now carry they may be likened to bells which having rung out the true are now ringing in the false. It is practically only under English obediences in Great Britain and its Colonies that the validity of the Grade is maintained, unless there may be something in the hiddenness of Norway, Sweden and Denmark, about which little seems known at first hand.

There is no need to say that most vestiges, such as they were, of the original Rosy Cross have disappeared in the course of transformation under the ægis of false Masonries. Yet an isolated remnant is met with at times in strange places, at an unexpected moment. When the "Ancient French Rose-Croix" was set aside, *circa* 1850, in favour of a spurious Philosophical Grade, the mystic formula

I∴N∴R∴I∴ was rendered no longer *Jesus Nazaræus Rex Judæorum*,[1] and one of its familiar Hermetic alternatives was adopted, namely, *Igne Natura Renovatur Integra*=All Nature is renewed by fire. A gloss, however, was added and reads curiously enough: I=India, considered as a chief source of knowledge; N=Nature, the safeguard and guide of those on the quest of science; R=Regeneration, which comes to those who know, but it is not understood spiritually; I=Ignorance, being that which it is the business of seekers to combat and overcome. As regards the Lost Word, it is explained that the sun at autumn has lost its power and Nature is rendered mute, but the star of day at the springtide resumes its vital force, and this is the recovery of the Word, when Nature, with all her voices, speaks and sings, even as the Sons of God shouted for joy in the perfect morning of the cosmos. It is like the dead and forgotten Boulanger testifying from the tomb of his Deism. But after all the verbiage the Password of the Grade is formulated with the response thereto, and these are *Deus nobiscum*, *Pax profunda*. It is the old Rosicrucian salutation: "Peace profound, my Brethren: Immanuel, God is with us."

After such ways was the Eighteenth Degree rectified, and there seems no end to the story of its radical and casual variations. We have seen how France scouted and libelled the supposed Order prior to 1650, but it would seem that in the High Grade movement of the eighteenth century it could scarcely do enough to atone and reverse, as it were, the judgment. The Rite of Memphis was launched in the early part of the nineteenth century, and its ninety-four Degrees did not fail to include a *Maçonnerie des Chevaliers de Rose-Croix*, which produces a Rosicrucian

[1] Dr. Franz Hartmann suggested, now long ago, that the Rosicrucian reading was *In nobis regnat Iesus*, for which I should like to find the authority that he fails to give.—See MAGIC: WHITE AND BLACK, pp. 294–96.

history at large in the course of a Catechism.[1] The heads of it are worth noting on the score of fantastic invention.

(1) It distinguishes several Orders of the Rosy Cross, of which the first has been known in Europe onward from the twelfth century, being formed of Hermetic Philosophers who came from the East to propagate the occult sciences. (2) Three of them established a Philosophical Athenæum in Scotland, denominated Masons of the East. (3) Many members of the Academy which arose in this manner joined the Crusaders in the attempt to conquer Palestine and hence they obtained the designation of Knights. (4) In connection with this branch, it is added, however, that there were Rosicrucians prior to the twelfth century, that their origin is lost in the night of time and that they were devoted to natural philosophy. (5) There was also the German Order or Rite of Princes Rose-Croix founded by Christian Rosencreutz, whose traditional history is subjected to various modifications. (6) At Damascus he had conferences with Chaldæan sages; he mastered the occult sciences and perfected himself in the Lodges of Egypt and Lybia. (7) On his return he instituted the system of Princes of Rose-Croix, in three Degrees. (8) Their doctrine turned upon the attainment of human perfection and ascent to the Divine by virtue, the science of hidden things and mystical theology. (9) It is stated that this Rite had affinity with the Mysteries of Eleusis. (10) The decorations of the Rite were a golden compass suspended from a large white ribbon, and a silver ring engraven with the letters I∴A∴A∴T∴, signifying *Ignis*, *Aer*, *Aqua*, *Terra*. (11) The chief symbols were the Sun, Moon

[1] There is also the Antient and Primitive Rite of Mizraim, comprising ninety Degrees, the forty-sixth of which is called Sovereign Prince Rose-Croix of Heredom and Kilwinning. As on the one hand it has no likeness to the Eighteenth Degree of the Scottish Rite, so on the other, amidst many curious inventions, it reflects the Royal Order of Scotland.

and Double Triangle, emblazoned with a Rose. (12) It is said that this Rite claimed to be the depository and custodian of Masonic dogma. (13) There is further some account of an Alchemical Rite of Rose-Croix established at Padua at the end of the thirteenth century for the discovery of the Philosopher's Stone and the Elixir of Life ; but it was in search also of the Lost Word by means of oracles, meaning " magnetic science." From which of these branches the Memphis *Maçonnerie des Chevaliers de Rose-Croix* elects to descend does not appear in the reverie, which is a blend, in about equal proportions, of antecedent fables and inventions peculiar to the Rite.

It is necessary in the present connection to mention the Degree of Rosy Cross appended to that of Heredom of Kilwinning and constituting therewith the Royal Order of Scotland. It is, however, a mere shadow of procedure, reflecting nothing from the Eighteenth Degree in any of its codices and nothing from the non-Masonic Rosicrucian Rites. It is mentioned therefore to set aside. As much may be said of *Chevalier de La Rose Croissante* which still lingers, I believe, in the purlieus of French High Grade Masonry. It is a system of three Degrees.

Having mentioned on the authority of the Order of Memphis an Alchemical Rite of Rose-Croix which is purely mythical, it may be added that in the records of French Hermetic Masonry, there is a Degree denominated Sublime or Unknown Philosopher, otherwise Knight Rose-Croix. It was dignified by the title of Order and included three classes of members : (1) those who were dedicated to the work of healing ; (2) those who were students of the stars ; and (3) those who were said to contemplate the secrets of the Deity. It is certified, however, that all indifferently followed the quest of the Philosopher's Stone. It is obvious that by intention at least this alleged Order reflected the original Rosy Cross, and perhaps made claims thereon, rather than on the Eighteenth Degree, to which it bears no likeness, except in its alternative title, for according to this it is ranged among the putative Masonic chivalries. The procedure of the Grade is a mere nothing and the consequences are also *nil*: there are few things more negligible in all the cloud and mist of Masonic Ritual, but it is another illustration of my root fact, that the makers of Rose-Croix Grades never put them forward or thought of them as anything else than Grades of the Rosy Cross, in other words, that they were making a definite levy upon the one source which originated the symbolic denomination, and that the Eighteenth Degree is a palmary case in point, for we have seen that it draws from Robert Fludd and interprets its characteristic symbol in his very words.

There is no question that the Eighteenth Degree, in its valid and orthodox form as the Word discovered and communicated, carries on the Rosicrucian claim to possess the Key of Masonry, to be actually its *fons et origo* and to deliver its final message. It would be unreasonable to suppose that at the beginning it did not transmit consciously and with full intent. Its great success is to be accounted for (1) by the fact of this claim; (2) because that which it had to communicate was eloquent and convincing within its own measures; and (3) in view of the talismanic magic which has always and everywhere encompassed the title of Rosy Cross. It was not only annexed by the great majority of Rites which worked a sequence of Degrees but led to a multitude of developments, making great claims on exclusive truth and authenticity. It is this which lies behind the assertion of Barruel as to the number of Prussian Lodges which worked Rosicrucian Grades before the German *Illuminati* made a bid for recognition at their hands.[1] It is the vogue of Rose-Croix Masonry which must perhaps

[1] Abbé Barruel: MEMOIRS OF ANTI-JACOBINISM, English edition, II, 324.

be understood more especially when Von Andrée says that about five per cent of the entire German population belonged to the Freemasons, Rosicrucians and "other allied societies," among which must be included of course that Reformed Order which is the subject of my next chapter and the circle of adeptship which preceded it, a presumable continuation of the Sincerus Renatus establishment, or something derived therefrom.[1] The fashion of the time which made possible such claims as were advanced in and on behalf of Ritual led naturally and almost inevitably to many of a personal kind. An example sufficient for my purpose is that of the Austrian "Rosicrucian and Freemason," named Seefels or Sehfeld, represented or representing himself as one of "seven true adepts" who were to appear in Europe during the course of the eighteenth century.[2]

The Rosicrucian claim in respect of Masonic origins obtained an extraordinary currency, as if envoys of the Order were at work in Lodges,[3] Chapters and above all at Conventions. Moreover, after 1777, it passed into writing by means of a few works unfolding the Secret Tradition in Freemasonry from this point of view. Seeing also that the alternative fashion of hypothesis and invention put forward a Templar origin the Rosicrucian interest was strengthened by a fantastic marriage between the

[1] FREIMAUER, *Heft* I, p. 10, 1789.

[2] C. C. Schmieder: GESCHICHTE DER ALCHEMIE, 1832, pp. 527–42. Mackenzie mentions a Masonic impostor of about the same period whose pretensions connote false Rosicrucian claims. This was Magnus Paulus Schindler, son of a physician at Nurnberg, but he is said to have been born at Baireuth. He represented himself as belonging to the Directory of the Order at Cologne and posed as possessing the Philosophical Stone. He is reported as having been unmasked by Gerhard von Swieten and having died at Innspruck.—ROYAL MASONIC CYCLOPÆDIA, p. 652.

[3] The important French Loge des Amis Réunis is said to have had a strong element of true Rosicrucian tradition, owing to the presence of members belonging to both Orders.

Hermetic Order and the Christian Chivalry. As time went on the claim acquired a kind of traditional atmosphere and was tolerated or adopted early in the nineteenth century by serious writers. In addition to Bühle and Nicolai, Mr. Wigston mentions Meiners, Gatterer, Dornden and Semler as holding the Rosicrucian view respecting Masonic origins, as also Fustier, Peuvret and Pyron, but on I know not what ground as regards these industrious collectors of Grades.[1] Gould is most certainly correct on the point of fact when he speaks of the view being held widely that the mystical knowledge or symbolism of the Masonic Craft was "introduced into Lodges by the Hermetical Philosophers or Rosicrucian Adepts."[2] In more recent days it has afforded abundant material for the reveries of uncritical minds. Yarker regarded it as certain that prior to 1700 there were two Societies more or less related and eventually merged together[3]: (1) Accepted Masonry, which he believed even in those days to have had three Degrees, and (2) the Hermetic Order of the Rosy Cross, which was kept distinct from Freemasonry in the German Fatherland until a period vaguely denominated modern times.[4] In his opinion the FAMA legend has symbolical

[1] W. F. C. Wigston: THE COLUMBUS OF LITERATUR, p. 203E.

[2] C. F. Gould: CONCISE HISTORY OF FREEMASONRY, p. 62. Compare Clavel: HISTOIRE PITTORESQUE DE LA FRANC MAÇONNERIE, p. 181. He affirms that Rosicrucians introduced their "vain practices" into Freemasonry.

[3] See Yarker's organ of the Antient and Primitive Rite, entitled THE KNEPH, No. 45, February, 1886.

[4] We may compare the views of Reghellini, another and earlier fantasiast who had less opportunities for knowledge. (1) He accepts implicitly and affirms as matter of fact that the Rosicrucians first became known in the fifteenth century. (2) His evidence is apparently that *anno* 1459 is written at the head of the CHEMICAL NUPTIALS. (3) He is aware, however, that according to Nicolai, the romance was antedated and is the work of Andreæ early in the seventeenth century. (4) He says on his own part that it exhibits the manners of the earlier period, exposing the vices of theology (*sic*) and the abuse of the power of the popes, a statement which proves that he is confusing its contents with that of CONFESSIO FRATERNITATIS. (5) He

points of contact with the Degree of Master Mason and was indeed "an allegorical way of recording that the Brethren established the Masonic Rite," his reasons in either case not, however, emerging. The Rite in question was one of Seven Degrees, which of course is pure romance, but we are saved unprofitable speculation by the fact that they are not enumerated. As regards the Royal Arch it was a revision of some Rosicrucian Grade, while that late invention called Sovereign Prince Adept was extant unaccountably in the elusive period prior to 1700 and was Rosicrucian pure and simple. The Degree of Templar Priest is "an embodied expression of the Rosicrucian Robert Fludd." The Rosicrucian Order itself had apparently Seven Degrees, as from 1618 onward, the evidence being (1) the Heptagonal Vault of Christian Rosy Cross

sees traces also of doctrines ascribed to Crusaders, but does not specify on the subject. (6) In his view the fifteenth century saw the birth of several Rosicrucian Societies, under different denominations and distinguishable by the sciences which they cultivated. (7) There were Mystics or Theosophists, in opposition to "the dogmatic intolerance of the Roman clergy," and these based their doctrine on FAMA FRATERNITATIS, though it is legend pure and simple, not to speak of its historical position as a post-Reformation document. The branch in question had only three Grades originally, though these were subdivided at a later time. They were concerned with the study of Nature and her secret virtues, and with research into supernatural things. Their Mysteries are said to have been in striking analogy with those of Eleusis, but the exhibited symbols were identical with those of Rose-Croix Masonry, unfolding the universal harmony by which man is united to man, as man is united to the universe and the universe to God. They were called —in virtue of doctrine and science—the Brahmins of the North, though this happens to be a post-Baconian catchword expression. These Brahmins claimed to be the depositaries and preservers of Masonic dogma. (8) Philosophical Doctors, whose system came from Gnostics and Kabalists. The ethics of Jesus and Manes were side by side therein. They followed Paracelsus in medicine, though he does not happen to have been born. Their teaching was made public by Fludd, and indeed certain Germans are affirmed to have maintained that this Rite derived from England and went back to King Arthur. (9) Theosophical Alchemists, who were diffused widely under the name of Rosicrucians of the East, and these worked Nine Degrees, but they are a confused version of the Reformed Rite belonging to 1777, an account of which will appear in my next chapter.

and (2) an alleged intimation, not otherwise specified, in NUPTIÆ CHYMICÆ. The first four corresponded to the four elements and the fifth to the ether. They began with Theoricus [*sic*], proceeding thence to Junior, thus reversing the sequence which we shall meet with under date of 1777—not to speak of the logic of things. The three highest Degrees represented a triangle. The teaching is said to have been communicated under a triple veil of languages—operative, philosophical and religious. The Secret Mystery of the Order claimed transmission from the time of the Apostles. THE WISE MAN'S CROWN of John Heydon is quoted at second hand on the law of silence and so also is the Oath from the BREVIARY OF PHILOSOPHY in THEATRUM CHEMICUM BRITANNICUM, but the second is not Rosicrucian and the first is fraudulent. It may well appear incredible that speculations like these and many others which I have omitted are piled one upon another as matters of pure certitude when they are not only devoid of authority but are contradicted by all that is known. But Yarker was a man of muddled information, with a mass of confused inferences from reams of undigested materials, and I suppose that the things which he evolved from note-books and clouded memories passed in his mind for true.

I must omit his lucubrations on floor-cloths, tracing boards and banners in Rosicrucian Lodges, as also on the aprons worn by the Brethren. His decisions are recited in another place and may be summarised shortly thus: (1) The High Grades of Freemasonry derive from the Rosicrucians who claimed in turn to draw them from Thoth or Hermes Trismegistus, and more remotely from India.[1] (2) The word Heredom, as applied to the Rosy Cross, signifies inheritance. (3) Certain Hermetic Philosophers came from the East to propagate their secret doctrine under pledges. (4) There were originally three Degrees or Classes, advance-

[1] THE KNEPH, Vol. III, No. 10, October, 1883.

ment from one to another being a reward of merit. (5) The Candidate for the First Degree must have received preparatory instructions and must have rendered service to humanity. It inculcated an ardent desire for perfection and sought to shield the studies of enlightened men from the hostility of vulgar prejudice. (6) The qualifications for the Second Degree were sincere chivalry of heart and enthusiasm for true philosophy. (7) The Third Degree was bestowed on those who united wisdom of spirit with nobility of soul, constancy, morality and firmness.

After such manner was the Rosy Cross manufactured at Withington in the last quarter of the nineteenth century and issued with the *imprimatur* of the Antient and Primitive Rite of Freemasonry. I have only to add that—*ex hypothesi*—it flourished in the thirteenth century at Padua and is otherwise of the highest antiquity. On the whole I prefer M. Oswald Wirth, who affirms that the most striking analogies with Masonry are presented by Philosophical Alchemy, as this was conceived by the Rosicrucians of the seventeenth century.[1]

[1] See SYMBOLISME HERMÉTIQUE, p. 86.

CHAPTER XVI

THE ROSY AND GOLDEN CROSS

We have seen that according to the evidence of Sigmund Richter there existed in Germany prior to the year 1710—as doubtless then and thereafter—a dual Rosicrucian Order, denominated respectively the Brotherhood of the Rosy and Brotherhood of the Golden Cross, that they flourished under one headship, whether or not they worked for one end. It is to be wished that it were possible to suggest on the basis of this division that there was a dual understanding and pursuit of the Magnum Opus, respectively on the spiritual and physical side ; but in the absence of all evidence such a hypothesis is likely to prove intolerable. In the simple nature of things it is more colourable to suppose that the dedications of one branch were represented by Elixir Vitæ, the Medicine of Men, and of the other by the Medicine of Metals ; but the Laws published by Richter offer no warrant for inference in this or any other direction. We have seen also that according to the same Laws there was a certain manner of acception—presumably into the joint Order—and it was so simple in character that it can be scarcely called ceremonial. It was comparable—as I have said—to the method of conferring the Liveries still prevalent in certain City Companies of London ; it was probably not unlike the mode of making an Entered Apprentice and communicating the Mason's Word in Scotland ; finally—*cœteris paribus*—it recalls exactly the procedure indicated by some of the Old Charges of

English origin. But Sigmund Richter wrote and his Rosicrucian Orders worked prior to the foundation of the first Grand Lodge of Freemasons in 1717, and it was subsequent to this date that the Speculative Art or Science developed in the mode of Ritual and raised up that great beacon of the Craft Degrees which has since filled the world with its speaking light of ceremonial.

After what manner it was propagated and to what additional Rites it gave rise I have shewn elsewhere and recently. The continent of Europe, but above all France and Germany, was like a garden planted everywhere with exotic flowers of Ritual. Between 1737 and 1777 the growth of Masonic Rites and Grades, and of Grades and Rites which passed under the name of Masonry, however little they belonged thereto in the facts of their purport and symbolism, is a thing without precedent in history. The Ancient Mysteries were numerous and widely spread, but in comparison herewith they were few and far between. During the sixty years which elapsed between Sigmund Richter's publication of the Laws of the Brotherhood in 1710 and the next epoch in the German Rosy Cross, which belongs to 1777, there is no evidence before us as to the nature of the secret workings in the Holy Houses,[1] but as regards that year there is the fullest material in print and rare manuscript to shew that the Rosicrucian Brotherhood had developed ceremonial forms and had

[1] Particulars of any nature are few and far between. According to the German SPECTATOR, Vol. VI, No. 17, p. 198, the Society of True and Ancient Rosicrucians became extinct in the Fatherland after the death of a leader named Abraham von Bruna or Brun in 1748. It is not to be supposed, however, that the Order was represented by a single group; the existence of several independent bodies is antecedently probable and there may be said to be vague traces. For example, the record which I have just quoted refers—at least on the surface—to another foundation than that of Sigmund Richter, while the Reformation of 1777, with which I am about to deal, represents by its hypothesis a change in an organisation then in being, as it might be, that of Richter, the denomination of which was preserved.

passed, moreover, under the Masonic ægis. I shall give in the first place an account of the palmary Rite and its content, proceeding thence to a brief consideration of its historical aspects, so far as materials are available.

The Association still flourished as the Brotherhood of the Rosy and Golden Cross, but the denomination was generic and there is no evidence of division into two branches. It is termed otherwise the Most Laudable Order and the Sublime, Most Ancient, Genuine and Honourable Society of the Golden Rosy Cross, abiding in the Providence of God. In the documents on which I depend there is a traditional history, otherwise a Legend of Foundation, presented in various forms to authenticate the Rite, and it may be summarised thus: (1) That Adam received immediately from his Creator the Gift of Wisdom, in virtue of which he understood universal Nature. (2) That this is intimated by Genesis when it is said that he gave names to all creatures. (3) That such knowledge was transmitted by him to his children. (4) That it has descended through all generations to the Brotherhood of the Golden and Rosy Cross and will remain in their custody, seeing that they are the chosen Sons of Wisdom. (5) That many are called but few elected, for few only are inspired by a valid fear of God and enlightened by the science of Nature. (6) That the succession of Wise Masters included Noah, Isaac, Moses, Aaron, Joshua, David, Solomon, as well as Hiram Abiff and Hermes Trismegistus. (7) That the Keepers of the Secret Tradition separated themselves from the profane multitude and that a law of deepest silence was established in Egypt and Arabia in the days of Moses. (8) That the secret association flourished in those of Solomon and Hermes. (9) That it continued to exist in Syria during the Babylonian captivity. (10) That in course of time the hidden science which it connoted was spread over the whole globe. (11) That this diffusion led, however, to its deterioration through the wickedness of mankind. (12) That on such account it was reformed in the sixth century, A.D., by Seven Wise Masters and was brought in fine to its present position and development. (13) That the better to conceal their real purpose the Superiors of the Order established those lower Degrees which pass under the name of Freemasonry. (14) That they served, moreover, as a seminary or preparation for the higher curriculum of the Rosicrucian Order and as a kind of symbolical prolegomenon. (15) That at the same time Masonry has deteriorated on its own part and has passed almost beyond recognition, being profaned and adulterated by so many idle and useless *additamenta.* (16) That all this notwithstanding it remains the preparatory school of the Rosy Cross and from this source only can the Order itself be recruited.[1]

[1] See ARCHIVES MYTHOHERMÉTIQUES. It will be observed that the twelfth clause of this traditional history passes over twelve hundred years in a sentence. It happens, however, that the work entitled DER ROSENKREUTZER IN SEINER BLÖSSE, under the name of Magister Pianco, fills part of this great gap with supplementary legend which belongs to the same source, and these are the heads of its instruction: (1) That a time came when the Confederacy of Initiates—being those otherwise described in the text above—began to feel the need of a general unification, in which Christian teaching should be joined to the old wisdom of the Magi; (2) that a new alliance arose in this manner and framed its laws in accordance with the doctrine of Christ; (3) that under this form it suffered many changes and adopted many names; (4) that in 1115 it was known as the Magical Alliance of Magical Brothers and Associates; (5) that this was the period of the Crusades and that the Knights Templar were formed with the help of the Alliance; (6) that the Templars were associated with the Magical Brothers and shared their secrets; (7) that they stood, however, in the same rank as the last and youngest Grade of the Secret Knowledge, under the rule of the Alliance; (8) that when the Templars were practically exterminated in 1311 these Apprentices or Neophytes were "overlooked in the cruelties of the time" and escaped the evil days; (9) that they incorporated subsequently with the remnant of surviving Templars and founded a permanent Brotherhood, with definite rules for its maintenance; (10) that like the Magical Alliance at large—which recedes into the background and is said to have suffered a decline—this institution assumed different names at different epochs; (11) that it was called the Order of the Cross, the Brothers of the Cross,

Those who are acquainted with the broad elements of the Secret Tradition in Israel and what may be called its charter of transmission will see that this Legend of Foundation is varied but slightly therefrom, the Brotherhood of the Rosy Cross being substituted for other equally mythical keepers, such as the Sons of Doctrine in the ZOHAR. The Legend is notable otherwise as formulating for the first time, and on the authority of the Order itself, what may be called the once familiar and even popular thesis which represented Speculative Masonry as emerging from a Rosicrucian centre. Assuredly those writers of the early nineteenth century, such as Bühle and Nicolai, who put forward this view were unacquainted with these unprinted sources from which my account is drawn, and it is interesting that they were forestalled by the Brotherhood some twenty-five years at least. It should be added that the

Noachites, and finally Freemasons; (12) that under the Masonic guise the headquarters were situated at Berlin; (13) that in the capacity of a Head Lodge it promulgated the true and fundamental system of Masonry, but the statement is worded so vaguely that the significance of the affirmation escapes; (14) that in addition to the three Craft Grades which were of universal recognition there were also High Grades subsisting from time immemorial and involving apparently many local differences of practice, claim and privilege; (15) that the High Grade Masons included many earnest students of the Secret Knowledge, who knew that Freemasonry was rooted in the Ancient Mysteries; (16) that an incorporation was formed by these for the extension and application of knowledge derived from those sources and from the Magical Alliance of antiquity; (17) that it was known as the Alliance of the Wise and then as the Golden Alliance, in succession to the Templars and the fallen Magical Brotherhood; (18) that it received only the highest class of Master Masons or Masters of the Appearance of Light; (19) that the foundation of this Alliance belongs to the twelfth century; (20) that by reflection on the Jewish and Christian Scriptures in conjunction with 72 MSS. and other writings of the Magi transmitted from the past of ancient wisdom, they produced a new book, "adorned with the halo of religion"; (21) that they assumed another title thereupon, to mark, as it were, a new epoch or dispensation, and became in this manner Brothers of the Golden and Rosy Cross, otherwise true Freemasons; (22) and that they have been known under this denomination since 1510. It must not be thought that this involved fable is the invention—so to speak—of a moment or of a single person: it grew up out of several reveries, and, so far as

qualification required for JUNIORES of the Rosy Cross was that of Master Masons, who were termed Masters of the Appearance of Light, otherwise Masters of the Dawn of Light and of the Lost Word. At the beginning of his experience as a Novice the Candidate received a summary explanation of the Craft Grades in the light of Hermetic science. The Pillars J∴ and B∴ are significant of far more than simple Beauty and Strength: they connote eternity and time, the male and female principles, the two everlasting seeds, the active and passive which rule in all created Nature. The Sun, Moon and Stars represent the Three Philosophical Principles, being Salt, Sulphur and Mercury. These are clear issues at their value, but it is said also—and in a more strained, artificial manner—that the seven steps set forth the wisdom of Solomon in his recognition of the Trinity and the four active qualities. They are typical also of the seven planets and seven metals. As regards Masonic tools—the gavel, compasses, trowel, square and so forth—they do not refer to the building of any earthly temple but to the work of erecting furnaces and the making of vessels which are necessary to the science of physics. In the Third Degree the dead body of Hiram alludes to philosophical putrefaction; the three lights

Rosicrucianism is concerned, the roots of it go back to Michael Maier and his SYMBOLA AUREÆ MENSÆ. The work from which I have quoted appeared at Amsterdam in 1781, just prior to which Count Hans Heinrich Ecker und Eckhoffen is said to have been expelled from the Rosicrucian Order, but under circumstances which do not seem to affect his honour in any real sense. We shall see that in the same year he founded a new association called the Asiatic Brethren—as it is affirmed, by way of reprisals. He is credited also with the authorship of THE ROSICRUCIAN UNVEILED, as part of his alleged policy of revenge, because it is a revelatory work. It is a difficult and very dubious question on several accounts and among them because he has been regarded alternatively as having written a reply to Magister Pianco. I suppose—in the absence of direct knowledge concerning it, as there is no copy available—that this is the work which appeared at Leipsic in 1782 under the title of A ROSICRUCIAN SHINING IN THE LIGHT OF TRUTH, and I am in the same position regarding DAS GANZE ALLER GEHEIMEN ORDENSVER-

mean God, Christ and Man, the beginning, middle and end of all things, and finally soul, spirit and body. As regards the Substituted Word in the Third Degree, the Novice is taught thereby that the inferior Brethren—who walk in parabolic darkness—have lost the Word, which is the Name applied to the true matter of the Stone, connoting also the valid understanding thereof and how it is to be sought and found, namely, through God and His wisdom, according to the blessing of Jacob[1]—that is, in the dew of heaven and the fat of the earth. The philosophical matter is said further to bear record of those who are three and one, yet not God, but the principle of the world and the end of all things. I conceive that this is an allusion to the three alchemical principles already mentioned, embroidered on Rosicrucian vestments.

The validity of these interpretations is not a question at issue, but the fact that they were communicated to neophytes as of faith in the Order, combined with the Masonic qualification and the claim that Speculative Masonry originated within the secret circle, are obvious warrants for affirming that whatever Grades were administered by the Golden and Rosy Cross can be regarded only as superposed on the Craft Degrees.[2] It was therefore

BINDUNGEN, Leipzig, 1805—otherwise a FULL ACCOUNT OF ALL SECRET ORDERS, which is said to contain particulars of Magister Pianco. It is alleged also alternatively that THE ROSICRUCIAN UNVEILED—or literally, "in all his nakedness"—was the work of Friedrich Gottlieb Ephraim Weisse. According to Findel, this is on the authority of Hans Heinrich, who also wrote a pamphlet denying his own connection with the work. By whomsoever written it is notable as a record of revelation, and I have drawn from it there and here. Among the qualifications of a Candidate for the Rosy and Golden Cross it is said that he must be a man of honour, of true spiritual power and considerable knowledge, because so only could he be of service to the Sacred Alliance—a clear indication, as it seems to me, that the Order was hoping to attain its objects by the help of its members. By the hypothesis it was the donor, but actually it hoped to receive.

[1] See GENESIS XXVII, 28.

[2] At the Masonic Convention of Paris, held in 1785, Baron de Gleichen

within its own measures and subject to its distinctive characters a High Grade movement, comparable as such to the Rite of Perfection, the Scottish Philosophical Rite and others by scores. Like genuine Rose-Croix Masonry, it was also Christian and maintained the doctrine of the Blessed Trinity, as we have indeed seen otherwise. The Grades were nine in number, being (1) *Fratres Zelatores vel Juniores*, (2) *Fratres Theoretici*, (3) *Fratres Practici*, (4) *Fratres Philosophici*, (5) *Adepti Minores*, (6) *Adepti Majores*, (7) *Adepti Exempti*, (8) *Magistri*, (9) *Magi*. The authority for this sequence rests in part on the documents, to some of which I have alluded, and in part on that work under the name of Magister Pianco, entitled THE ROSICRUCIAN UNVEILED, published at Hamburg in 1782, the content of which has been discussed in my previous note.

The Masonic qualification was not in itself a sole and sufficient warrant for reception into the Rosy and Golden Cross. The petitioner having made his formal application for admission, and this having been entertained by the Directorate of the Order, he was supplied with a list of questions designed to test his fitness, and put by some texts in the following terms: (1) What in your opinion are the ends of this Sacred Order and in virtue of what motives do you seek admission? (2) Are you acquainted with the aims and dedications of our laudable Brotherhood and

affirmed (1) that the Rosicrucians claim to be the Superiors and Founders of Freemasonry; (2) that they explain all its emblems Hermetically; (3) that it was brought in their hypothesis to England during the reign of King Arthur; (4) that Raymund Lully initiated Henry IV, King of England; (5) that the Grand Masters of the Order—then as now—were designated by the titles of John I, II, III and so onward; (6) that the jewel was a golden compass suspended on a white ribbon, as a symbol of purity and wisdom; (7) that the emblems of the "floor-cloth," or Tracing Board in modern parlance, included Sun, Moon and Double Triangle, with an *Aleph* placed in the centre; (8) that the Grades at this period were three in number; and (9) that the Master-Grade, as practised now among us, is the shadow of something which was then of great significance.

what are those qualities by which, in your own expectation, you hope to be found worthy to share therein? (3) Have you diligently examined your own capacity? (4) Are you conscious of such courage and firmness as will enable you to withstand those trials by which the Superiors of the Order may search your heart and prove your strength of mind? (5) Do you commit yourself with confidence to the Venerable Superiors of the Order, putting trust in their wisdom and love, notwithstanding that they have the power of life and death over those who are under their obedience? (6) Do you confess that the Holy and Worshipful Order is endowed with knowledge and wisdom, that it possesses the highest secrets of Nature, including true cognition of the image of our Principle, and that it can communicate them to zealous disciples, according to their abilities and desert? (7) Do you believe that the elevation of base metals into gold and silver can be performed by the processes of the Order? (8) Have you made any study of the works which treat of true physics, the high science of chemistry founded thereupon, and Natural and Divine Magic? What books do you know—meaning obviously on Hermetic subjects—and what are your views concerning them? (9) Have you made any practical experiments in chemistry, in which case what was the object in view and what was the result attained? (10) Do you enjoy any secret knowledge whatever, and if so in what does it consist? (11) Are you ready and willing to attain the truth and to learn the refinement of metals by operative practice? (12) Are you pure in your intentions? Are you solely in search of wisdom, knowledge and virtue, according to the good pleasure of God and for the service of your neighbour? (13) Have you, in fine, resolved, of your own free will and apart from all compulsion, to petition for admission to the Genuine, Most Ancient and Laudable Order of the Rosy and Golden Cross, submitting to its Laws and Bye-Laws, pledging yourself to inviolable secrecy and unconditional obedience, that you may become a true Son of Wisdom?

As regards the Form of Application which preceded the communication of these test questions, it appears to have been brief and informal, the postulant being left to express it in his own terms. A typical example is as follows: "I, N∴N∴, being a Master of the Shadow of Light and of the Lost Word, do petition hereby and herein, and by the Holy Number of the Order, to be received into the most Ancient and Genuine Order of True Rosicrucians, according to the old System." In respect of the questions themselves, supposing that the particular Order of the Rosy Cross, whether of the old or another system, were veridic *Adepti*, familiar with the secrets of transmutation, it is—as we have seen in the case of the Sigmund Richter foundation—an incredible hypothesis that they should have been anxious to receive members and should have devised an elaborate system for the initiation and advancement of Candidates. They had nothing to gain thereby and they ran a considerable risk in respect of the Great Secret, which all alchemists were supposed to guard so jealously, while it was obviously possible that their science could be transmitted in a simpler and safer manner, according to the old traditional method of communication from master to pupil, and could in this way be kept alive equally in the world. I am led therefore to conclude that as this particular branch of the Rosy Cross was at least concerned mainly with the physical work on metals, it was an association on the quest and not at the term of attainment. Its position, in other words, was similar to that of Sigmund Richter, whether or not it had made a certain progress during the intervening sixty years.[1]

[1] Compare Thory's ACTA LATOMORUM, which affirms that the Brotherhood of 1777 promised the Secret of the Great Work and the Universal Medicine. It would be the current report of the period.

I pass now to the Rituals of the several Grades, of which there are five codices within my own knowledge, premising that they present the earlier stages at full length, while they disclose nothing whatever as regards the status of *Magistri* and *Magi* or the method of induction into these exalted positions. Concerning postulants for the Novitiate, otherwise the Grade of Zelator, it is laid down (1) that the special qualifications are intelligence, sincerity, a disposition towards peace, desire of knowledge and the virtue of willing obedience ; (2) that each applicant must be warned against fostering false and illusory notions ; (3) that there must be no thought of riches or greatness ; (4) that the heart must be set on the path of quickening virtue, realising (5) that it is the duty of one and all to carry the doctrines of the Order by their own diligence into practical experience. On the day for reception, the Candidate was provided with Bread and Wine in a vestibule and was required to wash his hands. There also he was asked whether it was his sincere wish to become a humble Apprentice of the True Wisdom and a zealous Brother of the Rosy Cross. Having satisfied his conductor, he was led into a second room and was called upon to affirm (1) that he had no vain or evil purpose in view ; (2) that he was not covetous of material wealth ; (3) that he thirsted after wisdom, virtue and the secret art for the better fulfilment of Christian duty. He was then bound with cords about the hands and neck, a white veil being also placed over his head. In this condition he was led to the third and innermost apartment, where he was presented as one whose spiritual being was imprisoned by an earthly body, which however could be rendered perfect and thus justified by the spirit. He was subjected to further questioning and placed within a fourfold circle to take the pledge of the Grade. The circles were respectively coloured black, white, yellow and red, by allusion to the successive states and stages which appear in the Philosophical

Work, being (1) Putrefaction ; (2) Albation ; (3) Gradation ; (4) Rubification, or the achievement of the Highest Arcanum of Nature. But the fourfold circle as a whole is said also to be a symbol of eternity—compare the Masonic Grade of Rose Croix—and of the everlasting covenant into which the Candidate enters with God and the Brethren.

The Pledge was taken on the New Testament and—according to one of the codices—was couched in the following terms : "I, Brother X, Y, Z, in the Name of the Triune God, Omnipotent and Omnipresent, in the presence of this Illustrious Order, and before its Worshipful Masters, do hereby and hereon vow, promise and swear : (1) That I will work steadfastly in the fear of God and to His honour ; (2) That I will never cause distress to my neighbour of my own will and intent ; (3) That I will maintain inviolable secrecy in all that concerns the Brotherhood ; (4) That I will always pay due obedience to my Superiors ; (5) That I will act with perfect faith in respect of the Order ; (6) That I will reserve no secret from the Honourable Fraternity which belongs to the business thereof ; (7) And finally, that I will live for the Creator, His Divine Wisdom and for the Order. So help me God Almighty and His Holy Word."[1]

[1] One alternative version was as follows and was taken on the Gospel according to St. John : I, N. N., of my own free will and accord, after due and mature consideration, do vow hereby and hereon to worship the Eternal Jehovah from this day forward, even to my life's end, in spirit and in truth ; so far as in me lies, to seek out the Wisdom of God Almighty in Nature ; to forego the vanities of this world ; to strive for the welfare of my Brethren ; to love them ; to aid them in their necessity with my counsel and consolation ; and finally, to maintain inviolable secrecy. As God is everlasting. See H. G. Albrecht : Secret History of the Rosicrucians, 1792, p. 103. We may compare also a Pledge which seems to have been written and signed by the Novice with his own hand after Reception : "I, A. B., of my own free will and accord, in sincerity and truth of heart, do obligate and dedicate myself, soul and body, to God and to the Most Ancient and Venerable Fraternity of the Golden and Rosy Cross, dwelling under Divine Protection. I acknowledge my integration therein by virtue

It is obvious that this undertaking lies within the general measures of simple piety and good faith, there being nothing—on the surface—of an occult and much less of a Hermetic character, except in so far as the latter is connoted by the reference to " business " of the Order. In respect of Ritual procedure the Golden and Rosy Cross has not made any signal advance upon the Laws published in 1710, for the matter of its First Grade is practically before the reader. That which remains is concerned with the communication of Official Secrets, the Symbolic Name, the Arms bestowed on the Novice, and the payment of fees.

Reception to the Grade of Theoreticus is even more like a shadow of procedure. The Candidate is led into the place of convocation, where he undertakes to maintain the Pledge of the Order and submit to all its Laws, after which he receives the Word and Token, together with a special Cipher, the necessity or reason of which does not appear in the text. The Grade of Practicus was important, at least, by its name ; therein it was the duty of a Superior to instruct the lower Brethren and to prove all their mental powers, because the praxis of true philosophy must rest on a sound theory. On the day and in the place of his

of reception into the First Degree of *Juniores* and that the same has been ratified in the Supreme Degrees by the Secret Name and Coat of Arms conferred upon me. I submit myself cheerfully and with my whole heart to the ordinances and commands of my Superiors. I undertake to maintain the Seven Points of Obligation, as imposed already upon me, to the best of my ability ; and to act as a true Son of Wisdom, deferring to my Director with all patience and obedience. I will keep inviolable the Laws and Regulations of the High Illustrious Brotherhood. I will love and be true thereto. I will preserve everything concerning it in profound and eternal secrecy, in accordance with the third sworn Point of Obligation. So help me God and His Holy Word.—See OSTERR. FREIMAURER ZEITUNG. It is probable that this post-initiation Pledge was dictated to the Novice, thus accounting for its correspondences and variations in several cases. It is on record that one new member was required to keep silence about certain aberrations and differences, referring presumably to those events which I have cited already as having caused a revolution in the Order *circa* 1777.

reception the Candidate certifies (1) that in his experience of the Order he has found nothing in opposition to the commands of God, the love of others or the welfare of the State ; (2) that he will abide by the customs of the Fellowship ; (3) that he desires to be numbered among the Practici ; (4) that this is of his own free will and (5) that he covenants once more to maintain inviolably the Seven Points Major of his original Pledge. These undertakings are sealed by the threefold Grip of the Grade and the corresponding Secret Words. When the Grade of Philosophus is worked in ample form there is an elaborate arrangement of apartments and furniture therein, but the essential procedure in most versions lies within a moderate compass. The Candidate is caused to partake of Bread and Wine, and is reminded that the medial or vegetable kingdom of Nature produces nothing more exalted than are these gifts of Heaven, by which also God made and confirmed an Eternal Covenant with the race of man. He is then directed to wash in pure water and to remember in so doing that the Portals leading to the Higher Wisdom are closed to the impure and open only to virtuous and spiritual men. He is asked in formal terms whether he will become a Philosophus, is instructed in that case to pay the fee of the Grade and is welcomed by the Philosophical Brethren, who pray that wisdom, peace and joy in God may be with him. He testifies that he has looked for promotion, as on the previous occasions, that he may attain Wisdom, Art and Virtue, for the service of God and his neighbour. He repeats the Pledge of the Grade, which is one of obedience to the particular Laws thereof, and is anointed with oil in confirmation of his covenant, made with God and with the Order. It is prayed that the Spirit of Wisdom may strengthen his senses, enlighten his mind and rule in all his heart. He is given a new Word and another manner of token, after which he offers incense to the glory of God and

His wisdom and for the welfare of all the Brethren. In fine he is declared a Philosophical Brother in the name of the whole Order and is embraced by all present.

The Candidate for Rosicrucian advancement passes from the Grade of Philosophus to that of Adeptus Minor. It is the taking of an important step and preparations in all cases are made with solemn care. The President or Superior of his district makes known to him the fact of his election, or a messenger, who is himself an Adept, may be sent to him from the general centre. On the eve of the day of advancement he devotes himself to pious meditations on the Divine Goodness, on the immortality of the soul and its royal race. When the day itself arrives he repairs to the place of assembly in his richest vestures. The Ceremony in most codices, but not throughout the series, recalls that of the Eighteenth Degree in the Scottish Rite, otherwise Rose-Croix of Heredom, and in the summary account which follows I shall omit all descriptions of interiors by reason of this resemblance. In the part which belongs to the Portal: (1) The Candidate certifies in the presence of chosen *Philosophi* that he has been called to the rank of *Adeptus*; (2) The Brethren give him God speed and bid him remember them, even in the Higher Wisdom. (3) The Spokesman of *Adepti* enters in full regalia and with his face veiled. (4) He wishes all present the blessed fruits alike of eternity and time. (5) He informs the Philosophi that they have been cited as witnesses of a great and holy event, being the transit of one of their number from the fourth to the fifth Grade. (6) He invites them to testify concerning him. (7) They give expression to their approval and bear good witness. (8) The Spokesman of Adepti places a gold circlet on the table, puts his right finger therein and directs them to do likewise. (9) They swear to keep secret all that has been performed so far and all that remains to be done. (10) He bids them close the Hall of Assembly in the Philosophical Grade. (11) Thereafter he says that they are about to be deprived of a beloved Brother, but he leaves them in the certain hope that each of them shall be called to advancement in his due turn. (12) The *Philosophi* are dismissed, and here ends the First Point. In the Second Point the Spokesman of *Adepti* is alone with the Candidate and what takes place is discourse between them. (1) The Spokesman dwells upon the symbolical contrasts of Darkness and Light, Death and Life, Corruption and Resurrection or Rebirth, Time and Eternity. (2) He speaks of the righteous man and of the state in which all creation becomes an open book, revealing past, present and future. (3) He affirms that the Grade of Adeptus Minor gives increased knowledge of Nature. (4) There is also philosophical and theosophical contemplation, leading to the attainment of the Blessed Stone. (5) The Stone is triune. (6) It proves the existence of God and the Divine Transmutation of Souls in Christ by the regenerating illumination of the Holy Spirit. (7) The Candidate is asked whether he has sinned against the Order, its Holy Covenant and the Seven Points of Obligation. (8) In the event of him making acknowledgment, the free confession is taken as a sign of goodwill and he is asked whether he repents. (9) Supposing that he has nothing to confess he is invited to be sorry in respect of all human errors. (10) The required acknowledgment being made in either case, the Spokesman of the *Adepti* pronounces absolution in the name of the Order and seals the Candidate in a particular manner on forehead, mouth and breast, after which he is declared made pure and entitled to the Fifth Degree. Here ends the Second Point. The Third takes place in the presence of all the *Adepti*, amidst incense, lights and the offering of praises to the Glory of God in the Highest, all present being veiled, the Candidate only excepted. (1) The Spokesman of *Adepti* testifies concerning his charge. (2) The Master of the Temple welcomes him as one who has been created, called and chosen for the work of their Holy Assembly. (3) He is exhorted to manifest the Christian man within him and to unite with them in the praise of the Most High. (4) A curtain is drawn aside from a Representation of the Most Holy Trinity, before which they kneel and worship. (5) The Candidate is pledged in respect of the Fifth, Sixth and Seventh Degrees, which would seem to be like a trinity in unity of Ritual. (6) He promises to esteem Divine Wisdom above all earthly treasures, applying the riches of this world to the Glory of God and the salvation of his soul. (7) All present unveil and the Candidate is clothed in the vestments of an Adept, which include an apron, after the Masonic manner, to which a special explanation attaches. (8) He receives the Official Jewels. (9) He is told that during the present Decennium the High Superiors have suspended the Astral Works because of their great difficulty and that they abide in the Mineral Realm. (10) So far as the wording of this observation goes, it appears to apply only to the Grades of Adeptship. (11) Above these there is the eighth, which we know—on other authority than the MSS. from which I derive—to be that of *Magistri*. (12) It is said concerning this that the Eighth Degree can never be changed, for therein is the great and unique work which is called Treasure of Treasures, otherwise *Lapis Philosophorum*. (13) It is the magnalian Jewel of Nature, and as such it can be understood why the High Superiors have placed this *Mysterium Magnum* at the summit of so many steps—a reference to the staircase of Degrees. (14) The last words addressed to the Candidate, now an Adept of the Golden Rosy Cross, pray that he may be blessed, directed, ruled and crowned with the fear of God, love of humanity, long life, health and wisdom, to the Glory of the Eternal Name, for the salvation of his own soul and to the honour of the Order, through Christ his Lord and Saviour.

An Adeptus Minor had a right to petition for advancement to the Sixth Degree, in which there is no Ritual procedure that can be said to deserve the name. It is wanting in some codices. As a fact, he is pledged simply, receives the Grip or Token and hears the Secret Word. There is a Cipher attached to the Grade of *Adeptus Major* and another to that of *Adeptus Exemptus*. So far as records are concerned this and a New Word are the sole communications received on attaining these exalted positions. The mode of Opening and Closing the House or Hall of Assembly is identical in the Three Grades of Adeptship.[1] *Ex hypothesi* at least, the Eighth Degree is a Grade of the Mastery, and there is no other reference thereto than that which I have cited, either in manuscript or printed sources. The Ninth is the Grade of Magus, which by a colourable supposition may represent solely the status of the Headship and is therefore a Degree in numeration, but without procedure. It would be comparable in this case to the last and highest Grade of the Swedish Masonic Rite, being that of *Vicarius Salomonis*, held by one person only, who is the King of Sweden. It

[1] According to Clavel, the Reformation of 1777 was comprised in three Grades, the inexactitude of which statement is now evident and is characteristic of the Histoire Pittoresque in all its sections. Probably the author had heard a report concerning the Grades of Adeptship. He makes four statements otherwise, which must be left to stand at their value : (1) that the Golden and Rosy Cross spread into Sweden ; (2) that it claimed to be under the direction of Unknown Superiors, thus recalling the Rite of the Strict Observance ; (3) that these Superiors were said to be located at Cyprus, Naples, Florence and Russia ; and (4) that in 1784 one of the known chiefs was at Ratisbon and was in fact that Baron de Westerode of whom we have heard otherwise. He acted certainly as if in the capacity of an Envoy at the Convention of Wilhelmsbad. As regards the alleged abodes of Superiors they may be compared with those published by Magister Pianco in The Rosicrucian Unveiled and reproduced in a folding plate facing p. 218, Vol. II, of my Secret Tradition in Freemasonry. It should be added that according to Pianco the Brethren of the Ninth Degree—i.e., Magi or Wise Masters—gave instruction in Divine Things.

would appear, however, that there were several Superiors ruling the Rosicrucian Order in that particular branch or obedience with which I am at present dealing. It will be remembered that we hear of an Imperator as sole and supreme head in another and earlier school.

Were any reader at this point to intervene and advance that the "Sublime, Most Ancient, Genuine and Honourable Society of the Golden and Rosy Cross," as it is called in the extracts cited by the FREIMAURER ZEITUNG, was alchemical on the evidence of its Rituals but that its alchemy was of a spiritual and moral kind, it must be admitted that so far as my analysis has proceeded the presumption may seem in this direction, notwithstanding some physical allusions, nor is it reduced by the reference to *Lapis Philosophorum* as the *Summum Bonum* reserved to the Eighth Degree, for we may compare at need all that has been cited on this subject from the testimony of Robert Fludd. But as it is important above all to reach a clear issue hereon the analysis has been arranged with this purpose in view, and we must now proceed further. The Ritual content of the Order is before us, with its references—few and far between—to the Three Alchemical Principles, the matter of the Stone and the stages through which it passes in the process of the Great Work. There are, however, certain documents connected with the earlier Grades, and there are certain things which were communicated to *Adepti* outside Rituals: the intimations concerning these and their analysis may perhaps afford us light. (1) The *Zelatores* received an instruction concerning the four elements and the familiar symbols by which they are represented in old physics. The origin of these characters is referred traditionally to Solomon in the lectures attached to the First Degree. According to that wise king and the Kabalists, the primal manifestation of God originated in a first movement of the Eternal Being. This movement is represented by \, and the Divine Name belonging thereto is ADONAI, held to signify Creator and Omnipotent. The next event was the fall of the rebellious angels, represented by >. The Divine Name ELOHIM is connected therewith, and is said to mean Judge and Just. The third epoch was the creation of Adam and the promise of a Deliverer to come, represented by △. Hereunto is referred the Divine Name JEHOVAH. The Triangle signifies also Beginning, Middle and End. It was adopted afterwards as the *Signum Magnum* of creation and was taken by ethnic philosophy to denote celestial and earthly fire. The discourse goes on to affirm that fire produces smoke, steam and air; that air 🜁, if caught up, changes to water ▽; and that water separates itself in earth 🜃. Air and fire lie occult in water and earth. If this is Rosicrucian physics in the year 1777, it must be characterised as raving mania. The reverie is developed on the cosmic side by affirming that the Lord God kindled a mighty fire, that a dreadful steam went forth therefrom, and the same was changed into water. These opposing elements—meaning fire and water—were united by Omnipotence in a chaos ✡, from which air and earth were separated. As regards the Hermetic side of the thesis, it is said that he who understands the four elements, who can bring forth therefrom Salt, Sulphur and Mercury, who can also recombine the three, he it is who stands on the seventh step—a reference to the Grade of Exempt Adept—but it is to be known that the Mastery is reserved to a higher Degree. (2) In a General Regulation which is attached to the First Degree, it is affirmed that the fundamental law of the Order is to seek the Kingdom of God and not Mammon, to strive after wisdom and virtue rather than to abide as mere Midas Brethren. This is to be impressed upon every Candidate, who shall be promised no more at reception than he may attain (*a*) by the mercy of God, (*b*) by the instruction of his

Superiors, and (*c*) by his own industry. He shall above all and for ever be refused the sight of any other transmutation than that which is prepared by himself. (3) It is laid down otherwise that the cost of experiments undertaken in any House of Initiation shall be on a restricted and economical scale so that the material resources of members may not be imperilled, above all by extravagance on the part of individuals, working with others in the circle. The infringement of this rule is to be visited by heavy penalties, including suspension and expulsion.

So far in respect of *Zelatores.* The *Fratres Theoretici*, as the title of their Grade implies, were concerned with instruction, that they might formulate a theory of the work, but they were entrusted with no apparatus. Basil Valentine and his TRIUMPHAL CHARIOT, the ROSARIUM MAGNUM and other notable texts of Arnold de Villanova, the AUREA CATENA HOMERI, and the works of the great master Raymund Lully were commended to their studious care. The convocation of assemblies apart from advancements took place in this Grade, when such authors as these were read and discussed, or there were conversations on the physical sciences, all being intended as preparations for the work awaiting members when they attained the status of *Practici.* The sole point of theosophical doctrine which emerges in connection with the *Ars Theorica* is that the fire of Divine Love prepared the Heavenly Quintessence and Eternal Tincture of Souls from the cosmic cross of the four elements, and that by this *Medicina Catholica* the whole human race is liberated from the yoke of hell, delivered from death and transmuted by spiritual regeneration, so that the soul is clothed with the splendour of everlasting being. It will be seen that this is the doctrine of the radiant or resurrection body of adeptship, about which we have heard briefly in connection with Thomas Vaughan, but it is expressed here in language which is curiously reminiscent of Jacob Böhme in those moments when he reflects from Hermetic writers.

A Rosicrucian instruction concerning the seven planets and metals corresponding thereto in old physics is more particularly developed. (1) Quicksilver is in familiar analogy with the planet Mercury, but as it is not to be identified with the star shining in heaven, so it is to be distinguished most carefully from Philosophical Mercury, the true *Mercurius vivus*. Common quicksilver is called the Flying Slave, and this *ignis fatuus* has led sophists and unlettered amateurs into every kind of marsh and pitfall. Its true nature is well indicated by the character which represents it in chemical formulæ.

☿

The crescent denotes its lunar part, which is feminine and volatile in nature: this is the *Spiritus Mercurii*. The medial circle has no point in the centre, signifying the immature state of mercurial *Sulphur Solis*: this is the *Anima Mundi* of quicksilver. The cross at the base represents the volatile body of this metallic substance. It is the Water of Quicksilver, otherwise *Aqua Permanens*; it is also the *Sal Centrale* and *Menstruum Naturale*.[1] In a word, quicksilver is an immature metal, an extremely volatile *ens*, separated from a fixed state as pole from pole. As regards *Mercurius Philosophicus*, it is not described in the text, but the fact emerging from a cloud of Hermetic verbiage is that the so-called work of the wise is really a work in quicksilver, which must be separated from its *Humidum Superfluum* and must be animated by its *Homogenium*. It is said further that whosoever can prepare its medium, so that it becomes *Mercurius Duplicatus* and *Mercurius Animatus* shall be able to combine therewith that which is *Res Perfectissima* and will so produce *Lapis Mineralis*, the end of all research,

[1] Compare Dee's MONAS HIEROGLYPHICA *passim*.

otherwise *Aurum plusquam perfectum.* The chemical sign of *Mercurius Currens* stands also for *Mercurius Astralis*, meaning on the surface the planet Mercury, but there is an intimation behind this, the key to which must be sought in the astral workings followed by the Brothers of the Golden and Rosy Cross in the *decennium* or period which preceded 1777. Finally, there are *Mercurius Animalis* and *Mercurius Vegetabilis*, because there is its own Mercury in every *genus* and *species.* There is, moreover, an attainable adeptship in the three Kingdoms of Nature, and those who wear its triple crown can produce in all *Mercurius Duplicatus*, *Mercurius Triplicatus* and *Mercurius Philosophicus.* This is physical alchemy *in excelsis*, and it must be acknowledged that the *Fratres Theoretici* received a rare instruction, whether or not they proved able, at a later stage, to proceed thereby to the practice. It is missing in several versions.

(2) Mars is in correspondence with iron and the chemical sign of this metal shewing an arrow emerging sideways

♂

from a circle, signifies that the *Sal Martis* is celestial rather than terrestrial, while its cross—or sign of corrosion—has been broken up into an open angle, and this is a symbol of fire. On such basis it is affirmed that the inward nature of iron is fiery, active and magnetically attractive, all which appears to indicate that Hermetic operations can be performed thereon with at least comparative facility. Now, in the work of wisdom the task before the Adept is to purify the externally adherent Celestial Salt from the Terrestrial Sulphur and locate it within the circle. There will appear a great star which is said in the confused imagery to devour all its brethren, transforming their shapes into its own, then raising them—as it were—from death and crowning them with highest honour. For the Mars of the philosophers has earned such rank on its own part by the spiritual power resident in its sword of fire. This process is like a *chaos magnum informatum*, but an undertaking is given that it will be demonstrated *manipulando modo* in the Grade of *Practicus*.

(3) The character of Venus, to which copper corresponds, is explained in *la grande manière* and is shewn to exhibit the supreme operation which must be performed thereon in alchemy. The sign indicates that copper is an imperfect metal, for the point of perfection within the circle from which gold cannot err has been removed from the circle of Venus and has changed into the cross which appears in the lower part of the symbol. This cross signifies the

♀

corrosive salts which render copper of a perishable nature. Whosoever can purify these salts will reduce the cross to a point and if he can place that point again within the circle, he will see the sun at its meridian, instead of the Morning Star, and possess a treasure of gold instead of Venusian copper. One text speaks of Divine attainments.

(4) The chemical sign of Jupiter bears witness to the great immaturity of the metal tin, which is in correspondence with this planet. The crescent or half circle indicates

♃

that it is essentially of lunar nature, while the cross attached thereto, which is the invariable sign of the *sal centrale et fundamentum subjecti*, points out that the earth of this metal is mercurial and lunar, the salt arsenical and the sulphur volatile. It follows that the *corpus totum* can be brought with considerable facility to a state of liquefaction.

(5) Lead is in correspondence with the planet Saturn and is described in the text as an odd and morose fellow, whose disposition is exhibited by his symbol. We learn in this manner that the salt of lead is mercurial and lunar,

♄

as also pure and celestial, while the sulphur is terrestrial and solar. It is said further (*a*) that the *pars salis* liquifies all bodies, but can neither fix nor render them volatile; (*b*) that the *pars sulphuris* devours all metals—gold and silver excepted—penetrating them by the help of Vulcan-like lightning, purifying and imparting the highest splendour, but again leaving them; (*c*) that Mercury is coagulated by the *fumus Saturni*, while *vitrum Saturni* renders it fixed and fire-proof. The *corpus Saturni* is actually a conglomerated and exsiccated Mercury and can be easily changed back thereto. The Hermetic Secret of Saturn is formulated in the following terms: (*a*) Salt, Sulphur and Mercury; (*b*) Separate these Three Principles in *Subjectum Saturni*; (*c*) Make out of the Salt a menstruum; (*d*) Dissolve the Mercury therein; (*e*) Fix it by the *principium* of Sulphur. Whosoever can perform this operation conjoins the two crescents or half-circles in the character of Saturn, inserts the cross therein, concentrates the cross into a point within the circle and transmutes ♄ into ☉—i.e., lead into gold.

(6) The point within a circle denotes the state of perfection. In the character of the Moon and silver the circle is broken, and as the text says confusedly the missing half is put inward but the point is still in the vicinity. The

·☽

explanation is that silver is like unto gold, as woman is like unto man; but gold as the male part is hot and dry, while silver, the female part, is moist and cold. The imperfection of silver is indicated by the ease with which it blackens, but gold is free from this failing. It is, moreover, the Child of the Sun, while silver is the Daughter of the Moon, the light of which is borrowed from the solar orb. The Hermetic Arcanum is this: Communicate the male *Sperma Solis* to the female matrix of the Moon, or in other words turn the light inward and draw out the inward half-circle. The artist who so does kindles an independent fire or light and transmutes ☽ into ☉—i.e., silver into gold. The true meaning of this emerges in one case.

(7) Gold is *Principium Solis* and the end of all metals is gold, the great intent of Nature in the work of mines.

☉

The character of the Sun and gold is also that of eternity. As the visible Sun in the heavens is the most splendid of all the luminaries, so is gold—otherwise the terrestrial sun—most noble among all metals. The point within the circle of eternity denotes Divinity; but when this circle is used to signify the precious metal the connotation is imperishable and pure being. The Son of the Sun is the product also of profoundly concentrated fire.

The Rosicrucians were neither the first nor last among philosophers by fire to dismember the planetary signs or analyse them as they stand and discover mysteries of alchemy therein, but the work has never been performed so well and attractively as in this text. After such manner the *Fratres Theoretici* were prepared for the Grade of Practicus, but they were expected moreover to be well acquainted with the three kingdoms of Nature and the harmony which subsists between them. This is a clear issue, but when it is added that they must also have knowledge of manipulations, stones, vessels and so forth, we are reminded of the fact that, as recorded already, they were entrusted with no apparatus. Presumably they fared as they could, and when they became *Fratres Practici* they had the use of a *Laboratorium* in the particular House of the Order to which they were attached, making up a common purse for the costs of experiments, under the guidance of their Superior. They were instructed also in the following official processes: (1) Preparation of the Mineral Radical Menstruum; (2) Preparation of the Vegetable Radical Menstruum; (3) Preparation of the Animal Radical Menstruum; and (4) The preparation of an Universal Menstruum. By the hypothesis, each of these Menstrua contains its three principles, from which the Stone could be prepared, according to the nature of the kingdom. It was *Lapis Mineralis*, *Lapis Vegetabilis*, or *Lapis Animalis*, as the case might be. There was in fine *Lapis Universalis ;* but as to their properties, uses and effects there is no indication whatever, except in respect of the first, which belongs to the transmutation of metals.

There were general and special instructions on the Hermetic Operations which took place in the Grade of Practicus, but I have met with mere vestiges, whether in printed or private sources. In the Fifth Degree, which is that of Adeptus Minor, the Candidate, at the end of his reception, is handed a process drawn up by the Most Worshipful Superiors at the last reformation of the Order. It is certified as true and concordant according to the agreed scheme of procedure adopted at that time. It enables those who possess it to discriminate respecting previous operations and to prepare under favourable circumstances for those which are designed to follow. There is no indication whatever concerning its character. In the Grade of Adeptus Major there is another process presented, and it is affirmed concerning it (1) that it is a secret which has never been obtained and much less examined or worked, except by a few exalted Brethren of the Order ; (2) that it is an approved masterpiece discovered to *Adepti Majores* on account of utility and exactitude. It must be applied and dedicated to the glory of God, for the welfare of others and one's own benefit. It does not appear that *Adepti Exempti* received anything but the peculiar cipher attached to that Grade, and the general instructions on procedure in the alchemical experiments pursued therein. It may be presumed that from the lowest to the highest stage of his advancement a Rosicrucian Brother was taught throughout in symbols and that it depended on his own perseverance, skill and ability whether he decoded the formulæ. If he did a title was earned to the Eighth Grade, or that of Mastery: alternatively he remained where he was.[1]

When the message of these instructions is compared with that of the Rituals it emerges with considerable clearness that the concern of the Golden and Rosy Cross in the year 1777, notwithstanding the spiritual and religious atmosphere by which it was encompassed, had no other purpose than the physical medicine of men and metals. The archives of the Order fall after this manner into their proper place as a part integral of alchemical literature. To the alchemist in his laboratory, among alembics and Mary Baths, the work of chemistry was in consanguinity with the work of prayer. *Laborare est orare.* The quest was a divine quest; it called for a pure heart and a devout mind; success therein was peculiarly a gift of God, and good intention on the part of the operator was the first and an essential qualification. When therefore the Superior in the Grade

[1] The question of good faith is assumed in this statement, and it is of course the point at issue. I am not affirming it, having no evidence before me on either side. The case is supposed for a moment. In the contrary event it is obvious that there would be no advancements. Hostile criticism is likely to suggest that the whole Ritual scheme was astutely arranged to lead its dupes onward, always left to their own devices, always failing of the desired term, and permanently ignorant that the ruling headship occupied no better position. I have indicated already my own view that it may have been a headship of ardent alchemists with generations of processes behind them, on the threshold—in their own opinion—of the great, unrealised secret and hoping that the activities in the lower Grades might bring the quest to its issue in the accident or providence of things. There is no need to add that I hold this view fluidically and that it is speculative, like its alternatives. But I am very certain that among the errors and enthusiasms of criticism there must be included that disposition which sees knavery or advanced mental delusion only in the highways and byways of all occult history. We have found that the early memorials of the Rosy Cross offer eloquent and valuable testimony to the frauds of alchemical literature, but their authors knew that there was another side of the subject, and I have certified to its existence on my own part there and here in these pages.

of Adeptus Minor informed the Candidate that the astral workings of the preceding *decennium* had been suspended in favour of operations in the mineral realm for the advancement of metallurgical knowledge, it follows that this statement is to be taken in its literal construction, whatever we may elect to understand by astral processes, and however we may interpret that "highest secret of Nature," in virtue of which it is affirmed that the Master Grade can suffer no change. It was always alchemical and (or) always divine. In later days it became wholly spiritual.

This is probably my last word on the purely alchemical subject in the course of the present volume, and as it belongs hereto only in an incidental sense, it must be left unavoidably at a loose end. It may be possible barely at some later date and in yet another work that I can throw some light on the comparative problems of spiritual and physical alchemy, albeit in the natural order it might be said that the day is far spent for the planning of great undertakings. But He Who overwatches undertakings and is the Warden of those which are conceived and done in His service is the Judge in this respect and *in spiritu humilitatis* I commend it therefore to Him. There is but a word to add here. To the fact that there are two alchemies in Hermetic literature I have borne witness in many writings; but although they are sufficiently distinct from one another, alike as to path and term, their use of the same symbolism, in a varied sense, of necessity creates a difficulty in respect of their memorials. It is possible to discriminate broadly and to reach a grade of certitude about the comparative position and intent of certain texts, but the difficulty in other cases is either insuperable or I have failed in my own endeavours, at least for the time being, to take it out of the way. Those who are entitled to speak on these branches of Hermetic literature know that the Latin Geber belongs to physical alchemy and that the AMPHITHEATRUM of Heinrich Khunrath is concerned with the spiritual side; but at this present time I am acquainted with no canon of criticism which will enable us to speak with certainty as to Zosimus the Panopolite and the inward sense of his prolific contributions to the texts of Byzantine alchemy. So also in the Rituals of the Golden and Rosy Cross I confess to a sense of dissatisfaction over one point, and it remains in my mind as if the quest were yet unfinished. It abides in that solitary reference to the Eighth Degree which I have cited twice already and now recur thereto. From *decennium* to *decennium* the lower Grades might suffer a variation of concern, and there is nothing to assure us that the measure of change lay only between things astral and things metallurgical. But the Mastery of the Eighth Degree was without change or shadow of vicissitude, and the decades had no power thereon. To what did it belong therefore and in what medium did it work? Was it possible that the inferior ranks might be busy over that or this, and that they were like a series of sifting nets which brought a few only, chosen out of many, over a certain bridge built beyond the Grade of Adeptus Exemptus? Was it possible that this bridge gave upon the threshold of a Sanctuary where transmutation was wrought in souls, no longer *in re metallica*, where *res tingens* was Art of the Spirit of God and the Medicine administered was drawn from no other Pierian Spring than that of Eternal Life? There is nothing before us, not even a forlorn hope of light from the sifting of a false witness, and we may be never likely to know. Could it be said that there were chances they would be all against the view, so I leave this part of the debate concerning the Golden and Rosy Cross in that winter of discontent which comes from something remaining over and that something unknown.

The Grade of Adeptus Minor, according to the German Order of the Golden and Rosy Cross may be compared with an almost unknown French Ritual under the title of Brothers of the Rose-Cross, otherwise the Adepts. It is evidently part of a series, representing the same procession of Degrees, and is in fact termed the fifth. It is possible that it reflects the Rite prior to its reformation in 1777, or alternatively it may be a later variant. The following points are from sources outside the Ritual but attached thereto by way of annotation, and it will be seen that they are of considerable importance. (1) It is said that the renowned Order of *Princes Chevaliers de Rose-Croix* is classified in two distinct categories, corresponding to the two classes of Rosicrucian Science itself. (2) The Great Mystery is one, being the Stone of the Wise, which notwithstanding it is of two kinds, or Theological and Philosophical. (3) Theology—which calls to be understood here in the sense of *Theosophia*—has in view the transmutation of man from the state of sin and its corruption, according to the Law of Nature, into the state of perfect sanctity which qualifies for Eternal Life, according to the Law of Grace. (4) The Stone of the Philosophers gives health to diseased bodies—human, animal, vegetable and even mineral, thus procuring temporal felicity of being. (5) But the Stone of the Theosophists communicates eternal beatitude, to be preferred before all things else. (6) The Elementary Stone unfolds the greatest Mysteries of Nature. (7) The Theological or Theosophical Stone leads into the Most Sublime Mystery of Incarnate Divinity. (8) The majority of *Frères Chevaliers de Rose-Croix* are said to hold the temporal aspect of the work in disdain, while admitting its necessity, for which reason they belonged to both branches of the Order. It is said finally (9) that the ancient salutation was *Ave, Frater*, the answer to which was *Roseæ Crucis*, on the part of those who were Rose-Croix Brethren only, but subjoining *Aureæ Crucis* in the case of those belonging to both classes. It will be seen that from this unexpected source we derive an intelligible explanation of the separation into two classes for which we looked in vain either in the account of Sigmund Richter or the Reformed Rite of 1777. My inference is that we might add substantially to our knowledge were the whole French series available.

It cannot be said that the Ritual procedure corresponds in any wise to the German Grade of Adeptship. The Candidate is counselled to lay aside all preconceived opinions, so that he may be free to receive the truth. Having been veiled and hoodwinked, he is placed between two Pillars on the threshold of the Sanctuary and is admitted after a battery of five knocks. The Temple is in charge of a Grand Master, to whom he is brought in ceremonial form and by whom he is asked (1) whether he is resolved to sacrifice life itself rather than reveal the least of those Mysteries, whatsoever they may be, which are now about to be communicated; (2) whether he will renounce cheerfully all his worldly possessions; or alternatively (3) whether he will accept with gratitude that which the Lord of Lords may permit him to retain thereof. Having assented, he is called upon to pray (1) for liberation from all sophistry; (2) for the kindling fire of Divine Love; (3) for the Gift of the Holy Spirit; (4) for knowledge of the true Mercury of Philosophers; (5) for separation from all aims except the glory of God, desire of the soul's salvation, the splendour of holy religion and the relief of the poor.

The Obligation is taken in the Name of the Holy Trinity and includes the following clauses: (1) To preserve inviolate whatever may be made known in this Sublime Degree; (2) To keep faith with the Sovereign and observe the laws of the realm; (3) To love all Brethren; And (4) to let them "share in the Great Work if God permits me to accomplish it." It follows that the adeptship of the Fifth Degree was nominal or symbolical in character and that its members were on the Great Quest but not in the Great Attainment. The Pledge is followed by that curious observance which has been met with in the Laws of the Golden and Rosy Cross, according to Sincerus Renatus. One of the officers cuts off seven locks from the hair of the Candidate, places them in separate sealed packets and the whole in a single packet, which is also sealed and handed to the Grand Master, the officer affirming that they are "seven branches from the head of that Tree which God planted in the Earthly Paradise." The Grand Master answers in taking them: "Every tree which bringeth not forth good fruit shall be cut down and cast into the fire."

It is now only that the hoodwink is removed, after which the Candidate is clothed with a linen ephod and girdle and is told that "these are symbols of that purity which gives entrance into the Sanctuary of God, for we are not only the elect but also priests of the Most High, even the priestly kingdom of Levi, into which we were adopted from the tribe of Judah." [1] It should be explained here that the Grand Master is himself clothed somewhat after the manner of a priest of the Old Law,[2] his Assistants representing Abiathar, son of Abimelech, "for the things which are of God," and Joab for those of the King.[3] The salutation offered to the new Adept Brother is: "God be with thee, on the faith of perpetual silence, according to the promise of God, in the bonds of our Holy Society." A discourse on the nature of man follows and insists on the necessity of his transformation into a New Adam, the old body being destroyed.[4] So only,

[1] As if from the Kingdom of those who are chosen in this world to the spiritual Kingdom of an everlasting priesthood.

[2] That is to say, with an ephod of white linen, but the Grand Master wore also an imperial crown, as one who is king and priest.

[3] See, however, I KINGS ii, 26, 28.

[4] It is difficult to see why the WISDOM OF SOLOMON is quoted in this connection as follows: *Occultum faceat manifestum, et manifestum occultum.*

it is said cryptically, shall God give him the power to contain all things. The text presents what is done in a shortened form, and it is difficult to codify the next event of the Ritual, being a solemn Prayer on the part of the Grand Master. The heads of its thesis are seemingly (1) that Man is the Temple of God;[1] (2) that three worlds are within him, as they are also in God;[2] (3) that man moreover contains the true Matter from which the Stone is formed. It will be observed that this is important for the spiritual side of the Great Work. There is a final exhortation to the Brethren on the duties attached to the Grade, being the tenderness and charity of the Pelican towards all men but especially those who are within the sacred circle, and the uttermost secrecy not only in respect of the "profane" but also towards Masons who are not of Rosicrucian Grades. It is affirmed specifically that "we look upon Master Masons of the first three Degrees as but little above the profane." If they are "found worthy to search for the Truth at its source, which is God Himself," they are to be led into the light, but this failing the very name of Adepts must be concealed, the reason being that otherwise "we should be in danger of our lives." As regards the furniture of the Temple, I need say only that the Tracing-Board—as we should call it in Craft Masonry—represents the Sanctuary and Sanctum Sanctorum of the first Temple, with the things contained therein.

The Ritual concludes with a Catechism, according to the prevailing custom of Masonic and Super-Masonic Grades in France. Like the Lectures attached to the Craft Degrees, most of them covered the Ritual procedure for a second time, with occasional explanatory developments. In the case of the *Frères Chevaliers* there is another manner of instruction which is not only exceedingly

[1] Citing the testimony of St. Paul.

[2] Presumably an allusion to the Holy Trinity.

curious, but so unlike anything amidst all the cloud of Rituals that I propose to append it in full.

(1) Are you of the number of the Reformed?[1]—That is my belief, because I know the Truth. (2) What is Truth?—It is the Great Architect of the Universe. (3) What has declared it unto you?—His works, and the work of my hands. (4) How in His works?—All His creatures testify concerning Him. (5) How by the work of your hands?—Because I have seen the likeness of His creation.[2] (6) Who taught you this work?—Our Excellent Master. (7) What did he teach you?—That in Salt and Sol we have all things. (8) What is this Sun?—It is the Work of the Philosophers. (9) How many Principles do you recognise?—Three, that is to say, Salt, Sulphur and Mercury. (10) In what are they contained?—In one only thing. (11) What is this one thing?—It is that Matter out of which all things, Man included, are formed. (12) What is its name?—APHAR-MIN ADAMA.[3] (13) How can this be the First Matter?—If it be not, it at least contains it. (14) It is not then the First Matter?—It is the Second, which contains it. (15) How do you describe it?—As a Circle encompassed by a Square.[4] (16) What does the Circle symbolise?—Unity, from which the Quaternary Number results. (17) What does this enigma signify?—That from One there were made Four. (18) What are these Four?—They are the Four Elements. (19) What do these become?—A Triangle, and this must be enclosed in a Circle. (20) What does this become in

[1] This appears to connote the Reformation of *circa* 1777, but there is no certitude on the subject. There may have been an earlier development of Ritual under Masonic influence, and it would have constituted an earlier reform.

[2] The progress of the Great Work in the crucible was often likened to the work of creation, and the generation of the spiritual man is in analogy with that of the natural man.

[3] A parenthesis explains that this signifies Adamic Powder.

[4] This part of the Questioning should be followed in comparison with some important symbolism of the Holy Royal Arch.

its turn?—It suffers no further change, for this is all. (21) Have you any other Mystic Figures?—We have the Blazing Star and the Interlaced Equilateral Triangles. (22) What is symbolised by the Blazing Star?—That subtle Quintessence which penetrates all things in a moment by its moist and temperate fire, and so communicates its virtues. (23) What is signified by the Interlaced Triangles?—Our ALKAHEST. (24) What is your ALKAHEST?—It is our Fire. (25) And what is this Fire?—It is our Water and very powerful Dissolvent. (26) What is this Water?—It is our Salt. (27) What is this Salt?—It is our Sulphur. (28) What is this Sulphur?—It is our Mercury. (29) You are speaking to me of incredible things.—I could tell you more if you were older. (30) What is your age?—It is like that of Methuselah. (31) Yet you appear to be very young.—It is the effect of the King crowned with glory, even of Him Who died and rose again perfect. (32) Do you know the Root?—I know its Bath, being that of its Spouse, and I have seen him naked therein, bathing with his Wife. (33) Why do you speak so obscurely?—So that only the Sons of God may understand me. (34) Who are these?—They are those who do His will. (35) How long have you been born?—From the moment that I died. (36) What is the hour?—It is a great day which knows no darkness. (37) Why do you answer my question indirectly?—How can I determine the hour of a perpetual day? (38) Where did you find the Light?—In Darkness. (39) When do you work?—When I take my rest. (40) What is your Wage?—The perfection of my work. (41) What ambition do you cherish in view of all this wealth?—The joy of supplying the needs of men of good report. (42) Have you no further wishes?—Only to be ignored by the world, only to live for God, Who is the sole aim of our true Brethren.

It will be seen that this Catechism combines the symbolical language of Alchemy with the geometrical emblems of Craft and Arch Masonry, but that it abandons both in the end and passes to the terms which veil a purely mystical research, pursued in the experience of mystical death and the illumination which follows thereon. The work that is performed in rest is an intimation of the activity at the centre, and it is known that the realisation therein is the plenary reward thereof.

It remains only to say that whether the Grade of *Frères Chevaliers* derived approximately or remotely from Rosicrucian sources prior to 1777 or whether it represented a variant in Ritual from that epoch of reform, it was subsequent to the Rite of Perfection and to that Eighteenth Degree which developed out of Rosicrucian elements a Grade of princely knighthood.

In the year 1785 there began to appear at Altona a work of extraordinary interest under the title of SECRET SYMBOLS OF THE ROSICRUCIANS OF THE SIXTEENTH AND SEVENTEENTH CENTURIES.[1] The text included AUREUM SECULUM REDIVIVUM—otherwise THE GOLDEN AGE RESTORED of Henricus Madathanus—and the TRACTATUS AUREUS of an anonymous German Adept. Both had been translated into Latin and published previously in MUSEUM HERMETICUM REFORMATUM ET AMPLIFICATUM at Frankfurt so far back as 1678, and prior to this in the original edition of the same work, which belongs to 1625, and contains nine tracts against twenty-two of the enlarged collection. Both also had appeared originally in German. They were reissued under the Rosicrucian auspices as if made public for the first time, but adding a reference to the Brethren of the Golden Cross in the sub-title of *The Golden Treatise* and describing Mada-

[1] The fore-title of Part I reads GEHEIME FIGUREN DER ROSENKREUZER AUS DEM 16TEN UND 17TEN JAHRHUNDERT. The title itself is as follows: DIE LEHREN DE ROSENKREUZER AUS DEM 16TEN UND 17TEN JAHRHUNDERT, *Oder Einfaltig A B C Buchlein* für Junge Schülerso sich taglich fleissig üben in der Schule des H. Geistes, etc. Part II, which was not issued till 1788, has no fore-title and appears in the full title as GEHEIME FIGUREN, etc.

thanus as *Theosophus, Medicus et tandem Dei Gratia Aureæ Crucis Frater.* Whereas also he subscribed his preface " to the worthy and Christian reader " as " written at Taunenberg, March 23, 1622, it is represented in the *Secret Symbols* as *datum in Monte Abiegno, die* 25 *Martii, anno* 1621, as if put forward by authority from the Holy House of the Brotherhood. The original text of Madathanus had certain Order references,[1] and it is the subject of allusion in the preface of the anonymous German. It points out rather cryptically that he " could more easily have composed this treatise " and made himself " known to the Brethren of the Golden Cross," if he had not verified his references for the convenience of his readers. His address concludes with an appeal to " the Beloved Brethren of the Golden Cross, who are about to learn how to enjoy and use this most precious gift of God in secret "—presumably owing to his instruction. The appeal is : " Do not remain unknown to me," adding : " If ye know me not, be sure that the faithful will be approved and their faith become known through the Cross, while security and pleasure overshadow it." These allusions are valuable as a further testimony to the fact that Rosicrucians had begun so early to be known no longer under their original title but under that of the Golden Cross. I need add only that THE GOLDEN TREATISE is an interesting collated catena of alchemical authorities, with a parable placed at the end, while THE GOLDEN AGE is an allegorical story to which is attached an Epilogue, wherein Madathanus beseeches " the Creator of this Art " that he may not " speak of this Mystery or make it known to the wicked " lest he be found " unmindful " of his vow, " a breaker of the Heavenly Seal, a perjured Brother of the Golden Cross, and guilty of the sin against the Holy Ghost.

It follows that this tract is important to our purpose

[1] It described the author, moreover, as *Aureæ Crucis Frater.*

from the standpoint of its own hypothesis, as speaking from the seat of authority on the subject of Hermetic Doctrine and Practice.[1] It is unfortunately by the hypothesis only, for THE GOLDEN AGE RESTORED is the story of a dream and a waking in which the matter of dream continues. It tells of a virgin in the court and harem of Solomon who is described in the terms of the SONG OR CANTICLE OF CANTICLES and is therefore all beautiful; but her garments—which lie at her feet—are "rancid, ill-savoured and full of venom." The virgin is "Nature bared and the most secret of all secrets that is found beneath the sky and earth." The duty imposed on the dreamer was to cleanse the garments with a certain lye, the recompense of which would be the hand of the virgin, together with "a flowing salt, an incombustible oil and an inestimable treasure." At this point the dreamer awakes and finds the foul garments in his chamber. As he does not know how to proceed he changes his room and leaves them untouched for five years, when he is on the point of burning them but is hindered by another dream, in which he is reproached bitterly as having caused the virgin's death. Having protested his innocence, he is told of a box beneath the garments and of great treasures therein. He discovers it in the waking state and after further failure as the fruit of ignorance he is able to open the casket and gaze upon "brilliant lunar diamonds and solar rubies." Thereafter the dawn breaks, which is that of the restored Golden Age; all who see it rejoice in the Lord, while the dreamer kneels down and glorifies His Holy Name.

An Epilogue explains that this is the Great Mystery of the Sages, "the power and glory thereof and the Revelation of the Spirit." It is otherwise an exposition of "the Most Precious Philosophical Stone and the Arcanum of the Sages."

[1] According to Sédir, Madathanus gives accounts of Rosicrucian statutes and jewels, but he has been misled by materials which he did not collect himself.

On the surface at least it is concerned with the work on metals, and the Preface derides those who seek the Blessed Matter among animal or vegetable substances and anywhere indeed apparently except in the House of the Seven Metals. But it is difficult to say, for all the processes and apparatus of Alchemy are condemned as plausible impostures—the purgations, sublimations, putrefactions, solutions, coagulations and so also the athanors, alembics and retorts. Nature, it is affirmed, " delights in her own proper substance " and " knows nothing of these futilities." The work is not therefore performed by processes comparable to those of chemistry and would not seem to be a material work. Yet an Epigram at the end of the Preface affirms as follows: " I have sought; I have found; I have purified often . . . I have matured it. Then has followed that Golden Tincture which is called the Centre of Nature. . . . It is the Remedy . . . for all metals and for all sick persons." On this understanding it can be only a physical Elixir, and Madathanus testifies: that he has " seen with these eyes and handled with these hands." We are therefore in the usual medley of words and symbols which are all at issue with each other. I note only as regards " the Centre of Nature " that it was shewn to the dreamer " in the Triangle of the Centre " by Solomon, when accompanied by all his queens, concubines and virgins, while in the course of a later episode " his whole harem was stripped naked," expecting that in this manner some light on the Great Mystery would come to the dreamer. If therefore AUREUM SECULUM was issued as pretended from a House of the Rosy Cross, it would look as if that House were at work on a mystery of sex and that owing to its nature Madathanus may have been justified in saying that " the laws which obtain in the Republic of the Chemists forbade me to write more openly or plainly," the reason being that " many evils would arise from a profanation of the Arcanum " and that it " would be manifestly contrary to God's will." He intimates further that in the enjoyment of such " hidden fruits of philosophy " the " Brethren of the True Golden Cross and the elect Members of the Philosophical Communion are and remain joined together in a great Confederation."

So far as regards the main texts of THE SECRET SYMBOLS, but the work opens with an untitled section concerning the Magistery of the Philosophical Stone, the Universal Tincture of all metals, the cryptic language and parables of the Art, the First Matter, the Three Principles, the putative Elements and the several processes which succeed one another in the course of the Great Work. Stress is laid upon the innate Sulphur of Mercury, by which the latter is stilled and fixed. It is said to be a secret and hidden fire which—according to Crebrerus—digests the cold and moisture of Mercury in the long procession of time. This preface, if it may be so called, is followed by eleven elaborate plates in colour, the majority of which are closely set about with German text. The next item is an octosyllabic poem on the Emerald Table of Hermes, after which comes THE GOLDEN AGE RESTORED, succeeded by thirteen further plates, coloured in like manner and also inscribed heavily within and without. They complete the first part, published at Altona in 1785. The second part followed at the same place in 1788 and it opens with THE GOLDEN TREATISE, to which are appended twelve final plates. The entire work is said to have been found and translated by J. D. A. Eckhardt, about whom I can report nothing.

As regards the scheme of colour there are certain broad lines less or more followed, but in several cases it is difficult to see that there is any real order at all or that the arrangement—if any—is not a matter of fantasy. The four elements, Fire, Air, Water and Earth are respectively red, yellow, green and blue, which obtains generally, but not without exceptions, for on one occasion Water is represented white. The Holy Trinity in Its relation to temporal things is referred to elemental colourings, the Father to the Red of Fire, the Son to terrestial blue, the Holy Spirit to yellow and Air, while the circle which represents Jesus Christ as God and Man, Alpha and Omega, is coloured green and is thus attributed to Water. The allocations in respect of the Son and the Son of Man are explicable only on very fantastic lines. Among other attributions there are some which are not explicable at all, as for example the Cross in one of its representations to a drab cinnamon-brown, minerals to blue and the Light of Nature to blue also. In fine there are some and many which call for no interpretation, being plain upon the face of their symbolism because it draws from the nature of things. All things which connect with the Sun and with gold, its metallic correspondence, are coloured golden yellow: so also are the Sun of Righteousness and other types of Christ. Salt, Sulphur and Mercury, the three Philosophical Principles, are Blue, Reddish and pale Yellow. So also there are traditional grounds for connecting Saturn with Indigo, Jupiter with Blue, Mars with Red, the Sun with Orange, Venus with Green, Mercury with Brown and the Moon with White. The subject and its variants could be pursued further but it would serve no purpose here. I am acquainted with other Rosicrucian schemes of colour which have been developed in a logical order, and there is one of them which I regard as important because of certain analogies with the modes and gifts of grace; but they are not those of the *Secret Symbols*. However they are allocated and whether reflecting tradition or not, it must be said that they are all arbitrary in the last resource, and their eloquence—such as it is—is that of agreed signs.

I have dwelt at some length on the subject of THE SECRET SYMBOLS, because of that which is intimated by their letterpress, apart from the text of the work. Whether it was issued by the same House or Temple which adopted the Reformation of 1777, it is impossible to say, but it may be observed that there is no trace of Emblematic Freemasonry. We are in the presence of a school or system which drew in part from Paracelsus, in part from Jacob Böhme, which did not despise the secret of *Tinctura Philosophica*, but regarded this evidently as the least of its accredited treasures. It may or may not have been acquainted with the eloquent memorials of Robert Fludd, but it was carrying on the tradition established or adopted by him. It has the aspect of a text produced by an occult and theosophical Church in Christendom, and it reflects so closely the mystical House of Election pictured by Eckhartshausen a few years later on that when we remember his dedications in Alchemy, the higher Magia and the mystery of numbers it seems by no means impossible either that he was the concealed author or alternatively that it emanated from a foundation to which he belonged and about which he wrote otherwise subsequently. However possible, it must be understood at the same time that there is nothing overt in his acknowledged writings to connect him with the Rosy Cross.[1]

It remains to be said that in 1888 and at Boston, U.S.A., Dr. Franz Hartmann produced an English edition of THE SECRET SYMBOLS, stating that it was "copied and translated from an old German MS." Dr. Hartmann added material of his own, outside the original text, which represents the views and speculations of modern Theo-

[1] In THE THEOSOPHIST, Vols. 8 and 9, there appeared long ago certain ROSICRUCIAN LETTERS, signed F.H. and H. in the case of the last. It is affirmed that No. 6 was addressed to Eckartshausen. They have been republished since in an American periodical, the initials suppressed and the whole series described as written to Eckartshausen between 1792 and 1801. It is claimed that they are translated from the Spanish. The initials suggest obviously the hand of Dr. Franz Hartmann.

sophical schools, and which can hardly be held to accord with the Rosicrucianism of the eighteenth century. It is just, however, to add that the colour-printing is much better than was the case in the original work. About a third of the plates are omitted, and part of the German text is wanting in the translation.

CHAPTER XVII

SAINT-GERMAIN AND CAGLIOSTRO

THE romance of the Rosy Cross has formed for generations which have almost passed into centuries a prolific fund of suggestion in the fact that its early history obtained for the Brethren a title as mysterious as that which they had assumed on their own part. They were called—as we all know—the Invisibles. It mattered little to romance that the denomination was applied originally by way of derision, for those who manufactured and those who marketed in that creative world carried a hallowing wand. All the problematical personalities who emerged for periods or moments from the background of history, carrying a knapsack or wallet of strange pretensions, were sealed by imagination with the symbol of the Rosy Cross. The apparitions and occultations of the Comte de Saint-Germain would have earned him the title had he made only a small percentage of his imputed claims. It is interesting to note how the myth has grown concerning him, till at this day he has received his crown and nimbus in the form of a cultus. We shall see that there is no cultus which is so utterly its own and no other as that of Saint-Germain. For the purpose, however, of this sketch, the most notable reports concerning him can be reduced within a small compass. It is by reason only of his growing importance from the cultus point of view that it is desirable to notice him at all.

I will make a beginning with unquestioned matters of fact, contained in certain diplomatic correspondence preserved in the British Museum under the title of MITCHELL PAPERS. (1) On March 14, 1760, Major-General Joseph Yorke, English Envoy at the Hague, wrote to the Earl of Holdernesse, reminding him that he was acquainted with the history of an extraordinary man, known as the Comte de Saint-Germain, who had resided some time in England, where, however, he had done nothing. Since that period, and during a space of two or three years, he had been living in France, on the most familiar footing with the French King, Mme. de Pompadour, M. de Belleisle and others. He had been granted an apartment in the Castle of Chambord and had made a certain figure in the country. More recently he had been at Amsterdam, "where he was much caressed and talked of," and on the marriage of Princess Caroline he had arrived at the Hague, where he called on General Yorke, who returned his visit. Subsequently he desired to speak with the English Envoy, and the appointment was kept on the date of Yorke's letter. Saint-Germain produced two communications from Marshal Belleisle, by way of credentials, and proceeded to explain that the French King, the Dauphin, Mme. de Pompadour and practically all the Court, except the Duc de Choiseul, desired peace with England. They wished to know the real feeling of England and to adjust matters with some honour. Madame de Pompadour and Marshal Belleisle had sent this "political adventurer" with the King's knowledge. The conversation with Yorke lasted for three hours, but we are concerned neither with the generalities of the English Envoy nor with the needs of France.

(2) On March 21 the Earl of Holdernesse informed General Yorke that George II entirely approved the manner in which he had conducted the conversation with Comte de Saint-Germain. The King did not regard it as improbable that the latter was authorised to talk as he had

done by persons of weight in the Councils of France, and even possibly with the King's knowledge. Yorke was directed, however, to inform Saint-Germain that he could not discuss further such " interesting subjects " unless Saint-Germain produced some authentic proof that he was " being really employed with the knowledge and consent of His Most Christian Majesty." On that understanding only King George II would be ready to " open himself " as to the conditions of peace.

(3) On April 4 General Yorke reported that Saint-Germain was still at the Hague but that the Duc de Choiseul had instructed the French Ambassador to forbid his interference with anything relating to the political affairs of France and to threaten him with the consequences if he did.

(4) On May 6 the Earl of Holdernesse wrote to Mr. Andrew Mitchell, the English Envoy in Prussia, referring to all that had passed between General Yorke and Comte Saint-Germain at the Hague; to the formal disavowal of Saint-Germain by the Duc de Choiseul; and to Saint-Germain's decision that he would pass over to England " in order to avoid the further resentment of the French minister." The Earl mentioned also the fact of his arrival; his immediate apprehension on the ground that he was not authorised, " even by that part of the French Ministry in whose name he pretended to talk "; his examination, which produced little, his conduct and language being " artful "; and the decision that he should not be allowed to remain in England, in accordance with which he had apparently been released and had set out " with an intention to take shelter in some part of his Prussian Majesty's Dominions," which intention Mr. Andrew Mitchell was desired, on the King of England's part, to communicate to the King of Prussia.

The Mitchell papers by no means stand alone. There is also extant in the French Record Office of Foreign Affairs certain correspondence on the same subject at the same period between the Duc de Choiseul and Comte d'Affry, who will be distinguished in the following summary by the letters A and B. (1) The Hague: February 22nd, 1760. From B to A. Saint-Germain is reported at Amsterdam, claiming to be entrusted with an important mission on the financial position of France. He is said to have spent a long time formerly in England and to affect many peculiarities. (2) March 7th. From B to A. It is said that Saint-Germain "continues to make the most extraordinary assertions in Amsterdam." (3) March 10th. From B to A, stating that Saint-Germain had visited him at the Hague, using much the same language as he was said to have used at Amsterdam on the state of French finances and his intention to save the kingdom, in part by securing for France the credit of the principal bankers of Holland. (4) March 14th. From B to A, stating that he had seen the scheme of Saint-Germain and intends to tell him that affairs of the kind have nothing to do with the Ministry with which he—A—is honoured. (5) Versailles: March 19th. From A to B, enclosing a letter from Saint-Germain to the Marquise de Pompadour, which is described as sufficiently exposing "the absurdity of the personage." He is an adventurer of the first order and seems also to be exceedingly foolish. B is to warn Saint-Germain that if he chooses to meddle in politics "he shall be placed for the rest of his days in an underground dungeon." He is to be forbidden B's house, and all the foreign ministers as well as the Amsterdam bankers are to be informed. (6) April 3rd. From B to A, reporting that M. de Bentinck, "no longer seeing M. de Saint-Germain coming to my house, and knowing that I have openly discredited him, is ready to disavow him." (7) April 5th. From B to A. Reports a visit from Saint-Germain, to whom B communicated the instructions which he had received from A. Saint-Germain is said to have been overwhelmed, and the two parted, meeting only on one occasion further by the request of B. (8) April 8th. From B to A. Saint-Germain is reported as continuing to see Bentinck and as claiming to have a place in his French Majesty's councils. Saint-Germain is said otherwise to be absolutely discredited. (9) Versailles: April 11th. From A to B. The latter is required by the King to discredit the so-called Comte de Saint-Germain in the most humiliating and emphatic manner; and to arrange for his arrest "through the friendliness of the States General," so that he may be transported to France and "punished in accordance with the heinousness of his offence." (10) April 17th. From B to A. Reports the flight of Saint-Germain by the help of M. de Bentinck, and expresses a belief that he is sorely pressed for money, having borrowed two thousand florins from a Jew on the security of three opals. (11) April 25th. From B to A. Expresses a belief that Saint-Germain has gone to England and reflects upon the conduct of Bentinck. (12) May 1st. From A to B. The writer doubts that the Comte de Saint-Germain has gone to England, where he is already too well known. (13) May 12th. From B to A. It transpires that Saint-Germain did reach England but was met by a State messenger who forbade him to proceed further and caused him to re-embark on the first vessel outward bound, it being the English minister's opinion notwithstanding that the displeasure of French diplomatists against Saint-Germain was simulated and that he was in reality sent to assist the cause of France in London. (14) May 14th. From B to A. Contradicts the report specified in the previous letter. Saint-Germain was not stopped at Harwich but was arrested in London under an order from Pitt; but having been examined by one of this minister's chief clerks, the latter regarded him as a kind of lunatic who had no evil intention. Saint-Germain was therefore taken back to Harwich and warned to quit the English shores. He was now thought to be on his way to Berlin. (15) From B to A. March 23rd, 1762. Recalls the Comte de Saint-Germain, says that he is again in Holland under assumed names, that he has purchased an estate in Guelders and suggests that he is making dupes of people, with chemical secrets, in order to earn a living.

It will be seen that the papers in the French Record Office of Foreign Affairs give the inner significance of facts and proceedings to which the Mitchell papers bear witness. It remains to say concerning the French documents that my knowledge is derived from Appendix II of a work entitled THE COMTE DE SAINT-GERMAIN published at Milan in 1912 by Mrs. Cooper-Oakley. It contains also some very full abstracts from the Mitchell papers, but these have been examined on my own part at the British Museum, as well as other important documents cited by her at various points of her monograph. It is obvious that their subject-matter lies far away from the concern of the present work; but in view of modern theosophical claims concerning Saint-Germain and his alleged place in the history of the Rosy Cross it is desirable to shew under what circumstances and in what environment we begin to meet with authentic particulars concerning him.

There is full documentary evidence for the fact that Louis XV assigned him the Castle of Chambord in 1758 as a place of abode and that he was actually installed thereat in the month of May. There is also extant a letter from Saint-Germain to the Marquise de Pompadour, dated March 11, 1760, which most certainly exhibits his relations with the Court of Versailles in no uncertain manner and justifies what is said upon this subject in the Mitchell correspondence. Furthermore, it presents the writer as anxious to act in the cause of peace apart from personal interest. It does not shew, however, that he was accredited by Versailles after any manner, however informal. This notwithstanding, at the value of such a tentative view, it seems to me quite possible that he had a private verbal commission to see if he could arrange anything in the matter of peace with England behind the back of the Duc de Choiseul, and that when his attempted intervention became known to that minister he was thrown over by the French King, after the best manner of Louis XV. Whether Saint-Germain shewed any considerable ability and tact on his own part is another question. Experience in these later days tells us that the rôle of the professional occultist is seldom set aside by those who have once adopted it, and it would appear that he had failed signally at an interview with Pitt's clerk. However this may be, Saint-Germain comes before us as an unsuccessful political emissary who was used at best as a cat's-paw, and it must be added that when he addressed the King's mistress it was not *ut adeptis appareat me illis parem et fratrem*, or

> Lofty and passionless as date-palm's bride,
> Set on the topmost summit of his soul.

He tells her that he has spoken to Bentinck of " the charming Marquise de Pompadour " from " the fullness of a heart " whose sentiments have been long known to herself, reminds her of the " loyalty " that he has sworn to her and alludes to Louis XV as " the best and worthiest of kings." It is not at such cost that adeptship repays the favour even of a palace at Chambord. Let us now glance briefly at some other records.

(1) December 9, 1745. Horace Walpole writes to Sir Horace Mann, stating that " the other day they seized an odd man who goes by the name of Count St.-Germain." He is said to have been in England for two years and had confessed that he was not passing under his real name, while refusing all information as to his origin and identity.

Walpole acknowledged his great musical abilities but testifies otherwise that he was mad.[1] We hear from a later source that he was arrested because some one who was "jealous of him with a lady slipt a letter in his pocket as from the Young Pretender . . . and immediately had him taken up." It is said that his innocence was proved and that he was discharged. See Read's WEEKLY JOURNAL OR BRITISH GAZETTEER, May 17, 1760, the reminiscence of 1745 arising out of Saint-Germain's second visit to England. (2) He is heard of next at Vienna, "from 1745 to 1746," with Prince Ferdinand von Lobkowitz, "first minister of the Emperor," as his intimate friend. He became acquainted with the Maréchal de Belle-Isle, who "persuaded him to accompany him on a visit to Paris." The authority is J. van Sypesteyn: HISTORISCHE ERINNERUNGEN, 1869. (3) On his own testimony at its value he was in India for a second time in 1755. (4) It would appear that he revisited Paris about 1757 and according to Madame de Genlis her father was a great admirer of his skill in chemistry.[2] (5) April 15, 1758. Writing to Frederick the Great, Voltaire mentions Saint-Germain, "who will probably have the honour of seeing Your Majesty in the course of fifty years. He is a man who never dies and who knows everything."[3] (6) Notwithstanding the events of 1760, Saint-Germain is said to have been in Paris in 1761, and when the Marquise d'Urfé mentioned the fact to the Duc de Choiseul the latter answered: *il a passé la nuit dans mon cabinet.*[4] (7) Saint-Germain is

[1] LETTERS OF HORACE WALPOLE, EARL OF ORFORD, TO SIR HORACE MANN, 1833, Vol. II, pp. 108, 109.

[2] Comtesse de Genlis: MÉMOIRES INÉDITS POUR SERVIR À L'HISTOIRE DES XVIIIe ET XIXe SIÈCLES, 1825, p. 88.

[3] See Beuchot's edition of Voltaire: ŒUVRES, Vol. LVIII, p. 360. The letter is numbered cxviii.

[4] F. W. Barthold: DIE GESCHICHTLICHEN PERSÖNLICHKEITEN IN JACOB CASANOVA'S MEMOIREN, 1846, Vol. II, p. 94. The Marquise d'Urfé's story seems evidently mythical.

reported at St. Petersburg, presumably *circa* 1761–2, and according to the Graf Gregor Orloff he "played a great part" in the Russian Revolution.[1] (8) In 1763 he was at Brussels, as appears in a letter of Graf Karl Coblenz, who regarded him as the most singular man whom he had ever seen, affirms that he witnessed his transmutation of iron "into a metal as beautiful as gold," his preparation and dyeing of skins, silk, wool, etc., all carried to an extraordinary degree of perfection, as also his composition of colours for painting.[2] There is no need to particularise further: considerable evidence exists for the fact that Saint-Germain had signal skill in chemistry. (9) If we can trust the MEMOIRS of Casanova, and research has placed them in a better position than criticism had assigned formerly, Saint-Germain was at Tournay at some later time in the same year and permitted the famous adventurer to visit him, when Casanova found him wearing a long beard and an Armenian dress. (10) Between 1763 and 1769 we have the authority of Dieudonné Thiébault for the fact that Saint-Germain spent a year in Berlin, where he became acquainted with Abbé Pernety, who was a considerable figure in Hermeticism and High Grade Masonry at that period and later.[3] (11) The Graf Max von Lamberg met him in Venice under an assumed name, engaged in experiments on flax, and in July, 1770, they were staying together at Tunis.[4] (12) He is said also to have been at Leghorn in the same year during a visit of the Russian fleet, when he wore a Russian uniform "and was called Graf Saltikoff by the Graf Alexis Orloff." I have not met

[1] C. A. Vulpius: CURIOSITÄTEN DER LITERARISCH HISTORISCHEN VOR UND MITWELT, 1818, pp. 285, 286.

[2] A. Ritter von Arneth: GRAF PHILIPP COBLENZ UND SEINE MEMOIREN, 1889. See annotation to p. 9.

[3] See Thiébault's SOUVENIRS DE VINGT ANS DE SÉJOUR À BERLIN, 1813.

[4] See von Lamberg's MÉMORIAL D'UN MONDAIN, 1775.

with confirmation of this story.[1] (13) According to Von Sypesteyn, 1770 is another year in which the Count revisited Paris, being after the fall of the Duc de Choiseul.[2] (14) The same writer states that Saint-Germain was again at the Hague in 1774, after the death of Louis XV, and proceeded thence to Schwalbach, where he carried on alchemical experiments with the Markgraf, but their nature and results do not appear. (15) In 1776 it is certain that he was at Leipzig and at Dresden in the following year, when Graf Marcolini offered him an important post in that city, which, however, Saint-Germain refused. According to a letter of Baron von Wurmb, written on May 19, 1777, the Count was at that date between sixty and seventy years old. There is also extant a communication in his own hand which shews that he was acquainted with Baron de Bischoffswerder,[3] whom we shall meet with again as an active member of the Rosicrucian Order at the Court of Frederick William II of Prussia. (16) In or about 1777 Saint-Germain was at Hamburg and afterwards on a visit to Prince Karl of Hesse, with whom he engaged in experiments, presumably on various herbs, but the particulars are vague. (17) The last authentic record is that of the Church Register of Eckrenförde, which has this entry : " Deceased on February 27th, buried on March 2nd, 1784, the so-called Comte de St. Germain and Weldon —further information not known—privately deposited in this Church." On April 3rd the Mayor and Council of the town certified that " his effects have been legally sealed," that nothing had been ascertained as to the exist-

[1] There is no authority in this case beyond that of Mrs. Cooper-Oakley *op. cit.*, p. 60. It is one of the few instances in which she fails to provide a reference.

[2] Cornelius Ascanius von Sypesteyn : VOLTAIRE, SAINT-GERMAIN, etc., 1869.

[3] Karl von Weber : AUS VIER JAHRHUNDERTEN, 1857, pp. 317 *et seq.*

ence of a will, and that his creditors were called upon to come forward, "with their claims," on October 14th. The result of this notice is unknown.[1]

There are foolish persons who challenge the truth of these later records, because, according to the protestant Anti-Mason Eckert, Saint-Germain was invited to attend the Masonic Congress at Paris in 1785 and that of Wilhelmsbad in February of the same year, according to another account. It has not occurred to them that such invitations could be issued without knowledge that a mysterious and unaccountable individual, ever travelling under assumed names, and ever vanishing out of view with great suddenness, had at last departed this life in a private manner.[2] There are other uncritical persons, and Mrs. Cooper-Oakley is among them, who take the Comtesse d'Adhémar's SOUVENIRS SUR MARIE-ANTOINETTE[3] seriously, instead of as an exaggerated and largely fictitious narrative, no important statement in which can be accepted, unless it has been checked independently. They certify among other marvels innumerable to the appearance of Saint-Germain and to the fact that she saw him with her own eyes (1) at the execution of Marie Antoinette; (2) "at the coming of the 18th Brumaire"; (3) on the day after the death of the Duc d'Enghien; (4) in the month of January, 1813; and (5)

[1] Louis Bobé: JOHAN CASPAR LAVATER'S REISE TIL DANMARK I SOMMEREN, 1793, published at Copenhagen in 1898, Vol. III, p. 156, cited by Mrs. Cooper-Oakley, who refers also to BERLINISCHE MONATSCHRIFT for June, 1785. It may be added that no less a friend than Prince Karl of Hesse is said to have been not only acquainted with the fact of Saint-Germain's death at Eckrenförde but that his illness began while pursuing experiments in colours, his own apothecary preparing innumerable medicaments for his cure in vain.—See THE THEOSOPHIST, May, 1881, reproducing an article from ALL THE YEAR ROUND.

[2] It may be mentioned that Louis Claude de Saint-Martin was certainly invited to these Conventions and as certainly did not attend, though many unequipped writers have said that he did.

[3] Published in 1836.

"on the eve of the murder of the Duc de Berri," in 1820. According to his alleged promise, she was to see him yet once more and was not to wish for the meeting, meaning evidently on the eve of her own death. In any case, on the basis of these statements Saint-Germain survived his recorded burial in Germany by at least thirty-six years, and by as many more as we may choose to imagine after 1820. He may have even attended his own funeral in 1784. It is also on Madame d'Adhémar's unsupported authority that we hear of Saint-Germain being present at the Court of Versailles long before herself—that is to say, in 1743. Notwithstanding her absence she is able to give an almost microscopical account of his appearance and especially of his apparel.

We may compare the CHRONIQUES DE L'ŒIL DE BŒUF,[1] which is equally explicit on appearances and not less mendacious after its own manner.

We hear of a Countess von Gergy, who met him at Venice in 1710, looking about forty-five years, and fifty years later she talked to him at the Court of Louis XV, no older to outward seeming by a single day. When she said that he must be a devil he was "seized with a cramp-like trembling in every limb, and left the room immediately."[2] The Baron de Gleichen bears witness also to the Count's presence in Venice at the date in question but makes it clear in his sincerity that he has derived it at second hand.[3]

There are other fables besides those which have been

[1] Published in 1845 under the name of G. Touchard-Lafosse.

[2] *Loc. cit.* RÈGNE DE LOUIS XV, *chap.* XXII, *tome* III, pp. 407 *et seq.* Much as the supposed authoress of these memoirs, La Comtesse Douairière de B . . . ., is acquainted with the Court of Louis XV, she has heard nothing of Saint-Germain's residence at Chambord or of his political mission. In her story of the *Règne de Louis XVI*, cap. 4, pp. 450, 451, there is an account of his death, with fabulous details, especially regarding the terrors of his last moments.

[3] MÉMOIRES, published at Paris in 1868.

quoted, and when all have been set aside as accretions which accumulate invariably about occult and mysterious personalities, the facts which remain are (1) that Saint-Germain was a wanderer for a considerable period over the face of Europe; (2) that he had the entrée to most courts in the countries which he visited, and this could not have been the case apart from personal and other high credentials; (3) that although there are no occult sciences there are secret arts, and there is very full evidence that he was versed in these; (4) that for twenty-six years he was an occasional figure on the stage of public affairs and that this period was closed by his death. Here is the plain story, which invention has coloured to its liking. The inventions are much more interesting than the plain facts, and I should be very glad if there were evidence of their truth. There is none, however, and their rejection is inevitable on this ground, quite apart from *a priori* considerations of the possible and probable, in which I have no concern when I write as an historian.

I am of opinion otherwise that Saint-Germain was not an adventurer in the ordinary sense of the term, that he was not living by his wits, that during the whole period of his known activities there is no evidence of dishonourable conduct and that he was a gentleman of his time who acted throughout as such. Those who represent him as making preposterous claims on his own behalf are those precisely whose accounts in particular and in general cannot be accepted on their own warrants and no others are forthcoming. At the same time it is well within possibility that he may have claimed considerable occult powers and may perhaps have possessed some, seeing that such powers exist. Voltaire's scoffing allusion indicates the kind of rumours that were abroad, and whatever they owed to invention their opportunity could have been provided only by Saint-Germain himself. His chemical and herbal knowledge is vouched for fairly well, but does not enter into the consideration. On the other hand, there is also no evidence that he was a man of spiritual experience and much less a mystic in the sense, let us say, of Saint-Martin. He was an occult personality of his period, and whatever his faculties of this kind—if indeed he had such faculties—they could count for nothing on the mystic path of adeptship. For these reasons and on these grounds I do not accept the judgment of his personal friend, the Landgrave Charles, Prince of Hesse, when he affirms that Saint-Germain "was perhaps one of the greatest philosophers who ever lived":[1] it is open to question whether the deponent had any valid canon of distinction on such a subject. But as nothing can be found to the contrary in authentic records of the past, and as it postulates nothing that is in the least unlikely or the least uncommon, I accept and welcome the judgment when the Prince of Hesse affirms otherwise (1) that Saint-Germain was "the friend of humanity," desiring money only that he might give to the poor; (2) that he was a friend to animals; and (3) that "his heart was concerned only with the happiness of others." For the rest, it seems to me that his own account of himself, which is not wholly unsupported and has reasonable inferences in its favour, may be accepted provisionally, and according to this he was a son of Prince Rákóczy of Transylvania. It seems fairly certain also that in his earlier life he was under the powerful protection of the Duc de Medici. He adopted innumerable aliases during his life-long travels, and some of them may have been dictated by prudence, but others are more readily explicable by the love of mystery for its own sake. It is inalienable from the professional occultist, especially of that period, and if its connotation is a passion for pose, it must be said that Saint-Germain had dispositions of this kind. They are significant of

[1] Mémoires de mon Temps, 1861.

folly, but I have followed the tracks of occult adeptship through all the Christian centuries and I have not found wisdom.

Saint-Germain was a man of his period and a figure in the great world. As such in the eighteenth century he was of course a Freemason. I have quoted elsewhere Casanova's shrewd advice to those who in his time—being that time—had an ambition to make their way: if they were not Masons already, they must become such; it was a condition of future prosperity. Saint-Germain had obviously no way to make, but he had a position to maintain, being that of a great occult virtuoso and master of his period, and all sorts and conditions of occultism were gathered in that day under one or other of the Masonic banners. He is described as an "eager" Freemason by the Landgraf von Hessen-Phillips-Barchfeld, but I find no record of activities, except in suspicious sources. There is nothing to shew that Cadet de Gassicourt was speaking from first-hand knowledge when he describes Saint-Germain as travelling for the Knights Templar, to establish communication between their various Chapters or Preceptories——a reference either to the Rite of Perfection or the Strict Observance. On the other hand, the great vogue of the Strict Observance makes it not antecedently improbable that he belonged to it as part of his concern, though I cannot regard as genuine a letter which he is supposed to have written to Count Görtz and in which there is reference to this Rite. If, however, Saint-Germain was drawn into Masonry as part of his business, it must be confessed that he would be attracted still more strongly by the Rosicrucian Order, and there is evidence that on one occasion he appeals to Bischoffswerder, a militant member of the Fraternity, as one who knew and would speak for him. There is nothing to be inferred from this except a precarious possibility, and otherwise there is a complete blank in all the records, which never mention the Rosy Cross, in connection with Saint-Germain or otherwise.

The lacuna thus created has been filled, however, to the brim by occult speculation, expressed as usual in terms of more or less complete certitude. We know too well already that whensoever it has proved convenient every one who practised alchemy was *ipso facto* a Rosicrucian, every one who wrote about elementary spirits or was supposed to have commerce with these belonged to the Order. The flagitious rule obtained naturally enough in the case of Saint-Germain, but the myth of his membership has been the subject of special effort in the forcing-house of modern theosophy. Out of a casual and unsupported affirmation of Madame Blavatsky, who says that Saint-Germain was in possession of a Rosicrucian cipher-manuscript, Mrs. Cooper-Oakley leaps to the conclusion that he occupied a high position in the Brotherhood and talks vaguely of his connection with alleged branches of the Order or developments therefrom in Bohemia, Austria and Hungary. She maintains that these things are proven, but how or by whom does not appear in the statement. It is presumably the kind of proof which she met with in a German occult periodical, according to which Vienna at that period was swarming with Rosicrucians, Illuminati, Alchemists and Templars, whence it follows that during his visits to that city he could not fail to come in touch with many "mystagogues," especially in a certain Rosicrucian laboratory, where he is said to have instructed his Brethren "in the science of Solomon." She may have remembered also that LE LOTUS BLEU (1895), a French Theosophical Review, described the Rosicrucians as "perhaps the most mysterious Fraternity ever established on western soil," and obviously therefore a fitting asylum for a professional man of mystery.

It would serve little purpose to quote the fantastic memorials at large, but they have grown from more to more with the effluxion of time, and so it comes about that in the foolish account of the Order published as No. 2 of the Golden Rule Manuals[1] we hear of the hand of Saint-Germain being traceable in the formation or guidance not only of Mystic and Masonic, but of many Rosicrucian bodies, as it would seem, anywhere and everywhere at the end of the eighteenth century. The source of these inventions is not in the records of the past which are known to history but rather in those Akasic Records to which I have referred in my first chapter. They must be left or taken as such, remembering the kind of deponent who skries in that psychic sea. If the Graf Rákóczy is known to certain theosophists at this day in a physical body; if he testifies that he is the Comte de Saint-Germain; if Saint-Germain was Francis, Lord Verulam; and if Verulam was Christian Rosy Cross; it is obvious that the French occult personality of the eighteenth century knew better and more about the mysterious Order than any one else in the world and must have come into his own in every Lodge and House of Initiation that he happened to visit. But outside the Akasic Records there are those of German Rosicrucianism at the close of the eighteenth century, and they have not one word to tell us on the presence or activities of the Comte de Saint-Germain. In this dilemma I am content to leave the issue.

I have now to consider for a moment the case of Count Cagliostro. Whether he is to be identified with Joseph Balsamo—that cheerful Sicilian rogue—as affirmed by the Holy Inquisition, or whether he appeared suddenly in France and London in the rôle of an occult personality, his antecedents and identity unknown, as Mr. Trowbridge has tried earnestly to prove,[2] are not alternatives which call

[1] THE ROSICRUCIANS, already cited on several occasions.

[2] This apologist for Cagliostro weaves a thin romance of his own about the Rosicrucians and has scarcely a vestige of evidence for anything that he

for discussion in this place. The question is whether he also, like Saint-Germain, came out of the hiddenness as a Master of the Rosy Cross, for this is the story concerning him, and though it has been in no wise invented by modern occultists it is cherished near to their hearts. The original of the mythos is to be found in a sensational romance, published anonymously but attributed to the Marquis de Luchet.[1] It belongs to the year 1785, and the scene of the episode is Holstein, where Cagliostro and Lorenza, his wife, are represented as visiting Saint-Germain and being received by him into the " sect " of the Rosy Cross. That which they learned, however, was (1) that the Great Art is the government of men ; (2) that its secret is never to tell them the truth ; (3) that they must get wealth but dupes above all. In a word the account is a comedy, but it set in motion a belief that Cagliostro claimed connection with the Order. There is no particle of evidence that he did. On the contrary the Rosy Cross would have dissolved for him in the higher and more ancient light of Egyptian Mysteries, and what he actually pretended was that he had been initiated at the foot of the Pyramids into the secret wisdom of Osiris, Isis and Anubis. His Rite of Masonry drew, by its hypothesis, from these sources and owes nothing to the later institution. When a catechism attached to its Second Degree describes the Sacred Rose as a symbol of the First Matter of Alchemy we are far removed from the field of Rosicrucian symbolism.

Having disposed in this manner of the chief occult personalities who figured in France during the second half of the eighteenth century there remains only Martines de

says, as, e.g., concerning their far-reaching influence. He explains that " contentment " was the Philosophical Stone of the Order, which is taking Addison's rather dubious story literally.

[1] Mémoires Authentiques pour servir à l'Histoire du Comte Cagliostro.

Pasqually, whose Rite of the Elected Priesthood had at least one Rosicrucian Grade high up in its Ritual sequence. We know practically nothing concerning it, though John Yarker in one of his most confused moments seems to suggest that he has seen it.[1] In such case, the procedure included a baptism and apparently a rank in chivalry, for the candidate became in his reception a Knight Rose-Croix, as in the Eighteenth Degree. There was also an Historical Discourse in which it was affirmed (1) that natural philosophy was the object of research in the Order; (2) that its origin was lost in remote time; (3) that the Rose and other symbols, displayed in the Lodge or Temple, represented the vivifying light which renews itself incessantly, but also the everlasting benevolence of the Divine Source; (4) that the Rose in union with the Cross signified the mixed joys and pains of life, "indicating that our pleasures, to be lasting, should have delicacy, and that they are of short duration when delivered over to excess." I think better of Pasqually than to believe that these puerilities entered into the highest Grade of his Rite. They have the flavour of Memphis or Mizraim in the annals of Masonic folly. I should add that Pasqually claimed to derive from Unknown Superiors and at the beginning of his Masonic career he carried a hieroglyphical charter. It may be mere speculation to suggest that it had a Rosicrucian source, but it does not offend probability, and at need I should take this view rather than conclude that a man of his blameless life sought to make capital out of a forged document. Otherwise he drew from elsewhere, and in such case his Rose-Croix Grade may have been one more item added to the long list of developments from the Eighteenth Degree. It would doubtless owe much also to

[1] This at least is the inference to be drawn from an account of the Rite which appeared in THE KNEPH, No. 45.

himself, a suggestion which obtains in respect of his Rite at large.

It follows from my whole consideration that France on the eve of Revolution knew little of the Rosy Cross except by filtration through Masonic channels.

CHAPTER XVIII

FRATRES LUCIS

I HAVE met with no first-hand memorials of the Golden and Rosy Cross in the second half of the eighteenth century, excepting the Rituals which arose out of the Reformation of or about 1777.[1] We do not know certainly whether that reform came about in the course of a natural development, as for example in exchanging the astral workings for those of alchemical experiment, or whether it was the result of disruption. It was a stormy period, and the history of Secret Societies—Masonic or otherwise—indicates that titles of adeptship may have had many claims on the good pleasure of Divine favour and recognition but they had few upon the peace of God. I conclude that the Golden and Rosy Cross underwent a revolution which it characterised by a different name. There is another point of uncertainty. We have no means of determining whether the circle about which we have

[1] My reference is to official documents, actual or assumed. An important memorial belonging to the period itself, although at the last end, is H. C. Albrecht's GEHEIME GESCHICHTE EINES ROSENKREUZERS, from their own documents, published at Hamburg in 1792. It is concerned entirely with the *post* 1777 period and in particular with (1) the revelations of a certain Cedrinus; (2) the history of Freemasonry; (3) the Order of the Temple; (4) the Convention of Wilhelmsbad; (5) a Rosicrucian romance called DON SYLVIO; (6) an ADDRESS to the Rosicrucians of the Old System, belonging to the year 1781 and connected with an attempt by Fraxinus to establish or revive the Rosy Cross in Vienna, the nature of which experiment was exposed by Cedrinus; (7) the activities of Theoretical Brethren; and (8) the PHYSICA MYSTICA and PHYSICA SACRA SANCTISSIMA of Johann Gottfried Jugel.

learned so much owing to the survival of its Rituals was the only one of its kind in Germany and otherwhere on the Continent of that period. There may have been several branches admitting no allegiance to one another, but following their own path. In any case the Order survived, and there came a time when two of its important members—who were not, however, Supreme Superiors within the initiated circle—were the chief advisers of Frederick William II, with their hands on the helm of the Prussian ship of state. I refer to Johann Rudolf Bischoffswerder and Johann Christoph Wöllner.[1] The King himself had been received within the ranks, and for a period of eleven years there was the strange spectacle of a Rosicrucian triad ruling over the destinies of an European kingdom. But this period began in 1786 and the initiation of Bischoffswerder must have taken place—under whatever Obedience of the Order—prior to 1773; that of Wöllner is altogether uncertain; it may have been subsequent to the King's reception, which is referable to *circa* 1780. I do not propose to pursue this subject because it offers nothing to my purpose and information concerning it is available in many quarters.[2] We are told that the King was a tool

[1] Bischoffswerder was a native of Saxony, and was born on Nov. 13, 1741. He had been in the service of the Duke of Courland prior to that of the King, and before he became a Rosicrucian he belonged to the Strict Observance and many of the Secret Rites. He died in 1803. Wöllner was born at Dobritz in 1732 and belonged to the Lutheran ministry. He entered the service of the Prussian King in 1786 as Privy Councillor of Finance. He died on September 11, 1800.

[2] Mr. Gilbert Stanhope's MYSTIC ON THE PRUSSIAN THRONE, 1912, gives an excellent general account, with a long list of authorities; but it should be understood that the writer neither has nor claims acquaintance with Rosicrucian history, outside the place and period with which he is concerned. As regards these the following summary particulars will clear up the chief issues, and those who are concerned further may be referred to Mr. Stanhope's work. (1) Bischoffswerder had served during the Seven Years' War and again in the Bavarian campaign, at the end of which he was attached to the suite of Frederick William, then Prince of Prussia. (2) He had attained already a high position in the Rosicrucian Fraternity and was

in the hands of his brother-adepts and that Wöllner in particular must be called his evil genius. In both cases, however, they were working for their own ends and not for those of the Order. This point seems perfectly clear from all that we know of their history. I set aside, of course, the bare possibility that the King's treasury might at need have furnished money to the heads of the Rosy Cross through the influence of his two advisors, but no suggestion of the

a firm believer in the healing power of an elixir known to the Order. (3) It was used in an illness which befell the Prince, and his recovery was attributed to its virtues. (4) Bischoffswerder thereupon induced him to join the Order, concerning which it is said that the real leaders worked in secrecy, exacting implicit obedience : in a word, they were Unknown Superiors. (5) Delighted as they were—this is of course speculation—at the advent of a royal recruit, they imposed on him a year's probation—as it is said, "to impress him more deeply with the sanctity and seriousness of their authority." (6) On their own part, as stated at an Order-Convocation and mentioned in the text above, they looked upon his advent from the standpoint of its possible spiritual profit, in view of his exalted position. (7) Bischoffswerder is regarded as sincere, at least at that time ; but Wöllner, the son of a pastor, had belonged to the rationalistic party which flourished under Frederick the Great, and is thought to have entered the Order for the furtherance of his own schemes. (8) When Frederick William ascended the throne in 1786 he desired a return to the "orthodox religion," and Wöllner cooperated. (9) The number of Rosicrucians and mystics multiplied about the new King, and their influence was resented by many of the German princes, including Duke Frederick of Brunswick and Prince Eugène of Würtemberg. (10) Such was the *entourage* of Frederick William II, so far as occult circles were concerned ; but if the Rosy Cross in Prussia does not shine in any favourable light, there is nothing to shew that its representatives at the German Court were doing anything but play for their own hands. Mr. Stanhope says that the reactionary tendency of Austria made it sympathetic to Bischoffswerder, who regarded it as "a bulwark of monarchical and ecclesiastical authority against the approaching tide of liberalism in religion and politics." But this at least exhibits a Rosicrucian on the less intolerable of two sides when neither made for goodness. Moreover, the case against Wöllner may call for amendment. It is possible for a rationalist to be sincere when he turns to things represented by the religious side of the Rosy Cross. When he said in a Circle of the Order : "O my Brethren, the time is not far off when we may hope that the long-expected Wise Ones will teach us and bring us into communion with High and Invisible Beings"—it is scarcely fair to suggest that this was a mere pose. In any case the statement is valuable for my own purpose, as it shews that he was addressing a Lodge of Expectation, a Lodge of Quest, not one of attainment.

kind has been made from any direction. On the contrary, it would seem that the advantage of a royal patron and member was regarded in another light, for—at the value of such records—it is in evidence that the Master of a House or Temple at Hamburg, speaking in the name of the Highest Superiors, welcomed *in absentia* a Brother, then newly joined, under the name of Ormesus Magnus, as one who might be able to advance the Kingdom of Christ and the spread of the Order—presumably as a herald of His reign to come. Now Ormesus Magnus was the mystic name of Frederick William II as a Brother of the Rosy Cross.[1]

Meanwhile the Reformation of 1777 had by no means eliminated undesirables or malcontents.[2] The impostor

[1] That of Bischoffswerder was Farferus Phocus Vibron de Hudlohn, while Wöllner was known as Chrysophiron in outer circles and Helioconus at the ruling centre. The King's sacramental title, having regard to its claim on fabulous inventions of the past was most certainly provided or conferred and not chosen by himself. It indicates the hope of the Order in his respect.

[2] Though Findel knew little of the Rosicrucian subject, and in view of his Masonic hypotheses found little reason for knowing, he has drawn facts belonging to the period under review from various quarters and aids in the extension of our knowledge. (1) We hear of Dr. Schluss of Löwenfeld, Sulzbach, Bavaria, called Phocon in the Order, and Dr. Doppelmayer of Hof as "stars of the first magnitude" in what is denominated "the new Order"—otherwise in "the latter half of the eighteenth century." (2) As regards Schrepfer, who was a native of Nürnberg, it is said that he was the first who became a public apostle of the "Golden Rosicrucian Order," but this was before the Reformation—an event with which Findel seems unacquainted—and before it is possible to speak, even incorrectly, of a new Order. (3) Schrepfer shot himself on October 8, 1774, at the age of thirty-five. (4) He is said to have confessed previously that he was an emissary of the Jesuits, Findel having a mania in this direction, and almost anything served as evidence. (5) There is a story of Schröder—but I know not which is intended of the two Masonic celebrities who bore the name—and according to this he became acquainted with the Rosicrucians and "their first three Degrees" through an unknown alchemist. (6) He is said to have propagated the Order zealously till he lost the address of the person with whom he was directed to communicate. (7) This is on the authority of Lenning, and if the story is not a myth, the Schröder in question can hardly be he whom we shall meet with in the next chapter. (8) The activities of the

Schrepfer is an example of the first class; his pretended evocations made him the comet of a season and there must be some ground on which he called himself a Rosicrucian, for he seems to have been acknowledged by Bischoffswerder, who ought to have known a fellow-initiate. The malcontents also were in evidence, and this fact led to the establishment of other Rites and Orders by what may be called a process of segregation. They were made in the likeness of their original and advanced corresponding claims, e.g., to hold the key of Masonic Symbolism, possessing therefore all its secrets, or to represent the true and original Order of the Rosy Cross. We have seen that there were similar pretensions in France, but they owed nothing to each other and in all probability knew nothing of each other's existence. Three years after the Reformation, or

Brotherhood caused the Order to take root in Lower Germany—especially Hamburg; it appeared in Silesia *circa* 1773, at Berlin in 1777, and soon after at Potsdam, which became its headquarters. (9) The members claimed direct derivation from the old establishment, and the inheritance of all its secrets, including the only solution of Masonic symbols. (10) About 1782 it is stated that Wöllner placed himself at the head of the "new Order," using three different names in the three different Degrees: this is exceedingly doubtful and Findel has admitted previously that the Degrees were nine. (11) According to certain MSS. in the possession of a Dr. Puhlmann, Wöllner corresponded with members at a distance and promoted greatly the extension of the Order. (12) But the BERLINER MONATSCHRIFT exposed the propaganda and declared the whole thing an invention of the Jesuits. (13) In addition to attacks like this, the Order is affirmed to have carried within it the seeds of its own destruction—of what kind does not appear. (14) But when it became evident that the subjection of German Masonic Lodges to its yoke was beyond all expectation, a command went forth in 1787 from Southern Germany, enjoining the suspension of activities. (15) The event coincided with the time when "the credulous were anticipating the last and most important disclosures of that new and general plan which had been promised them." (16) In the North the Rosicrucians survived till the Prussian crown "changed hands," dying out in 1797–98. (17) I can see no reason for reliance upon these statements, which indicate a Rosicrucian headship in the South apart from that of the North, after placing Wöllner in charge of the whole Order. (18) As a fact, there seems no evidence for regarding Potsdam as the Rosicrucian headquarters or Wöllner as more than the chief of a single province.

circa 1780, Clavel says that a last schism in the Order produced the Initiated Brothers of Asia in Austria and Italy, but coincidently therewith or proceeding immediately therefrom was an association of *Fratres Lucis*, otherwise Knights of Light, and this shall be the subject of investigation in the first place as considerable consequence has been attached to it in some modern occult circles. It has been named by a few continental historians of Freemasonry and has figured in a few lists, like those of Ragon, but there was no knowledge concerning it till the late Mrs. Isabel Cooper-Oakley took up the subject with that earnestness which always characterised her excursions in research. She had unfortunately no critical faculty and her sense of evidential values made her judgments worthless, but she was to be trusted implicitly about facts within her first-hand knowledge, and if she said that a document was in her hands, it was most certainly there. The point is of vital importance in the present connection.

Her study of the *Fratres Lucis* was based by Mrs. Oakley on one of many rare MSS. which were once in the library of the late Count Wilkoroki of Warsaw. In connection with the Rosy Cross in Russia, we shall see that this library was looted by Catherine II, but Mrs. Oakley found access to the collection, which is or was in the Imperial Library at Petrograd. It would seem also that she was permitted or found it possible to make extracts or a transcript in full, for she states that the documents belonging to the *Fratres Lucis* passed—apparently from herself—into the charge of a member of the Theosophical Society, "having been committed to his care for possible future use." Many years have elapsed, however, and it does not appear that any result has followed. The original MS. claimed to comprise or embody the system of the Wise, Mighty and Reverend Order of the Knights or Brothers of Light, working five Degrees, the titles and content of which will appear immediately.[1] It was either divided formally or falls naturally for purposes of consideration into two main sections—otherwise the Laws of the Order and the Rituals worked thereby.

The second division of the manuscript contains the Ceremonies of the Order in what is presumably a rough outline or at least summary form. Preliminary to the whole appear the general conditions on which reception is possible and may become actual. They may be enumerated in the following order: (1) As in the Brotherhood of the Golden and Rosy Cross, Candidates must be Master Masons, raised in a regular Lodge; (2) they must be free from physical defects, thus recalling the whole manhood required by the Craft itself, but the stipulation in the present case connotes something more than perfect limbs, this being insured already by the first condition: it is possible that there is a sex-implicit; (3) they must not be initiates of any other Secret Order: alternatively they must resign therefrom, but it is unlikely that this undertaking was fulfilled by the Heads of the *Fratres Lucis*; (4) they must be at least twenty-seven years of age or otherwise Master Masons of seven years' standing, thus intimating that minors were eligible for Masonic initiations at the place and time; (5) they must not be oppressors of the poor; (6) they must not be disputatious and quarrelsome, or must have repented sincerely, as the banal clause adds; (7) they must submit to a probation of seven months, five of which would be

[1] Each Degree was called a Chapter and membership was graded on reducing multiples of the number 27. That of the First Degree was $27 \times 5 = 135$; of the Second $27 \times 4 = 108$; of the Third $27 \times 3 = 81$; of the Fourth $27 \times 2 = 54$; of the Fifth $27 \times 1 = 27$. It will be seen that according to so-called theosophical addition the number 9 ruled throughout, e.g., $27 = 2 + 7 = 9$, and so forward. According to Éliphas Lévi, the number 9 is that of initiation, while in Martinism it is of evil import; but there is neither harmony nor analogy between the numerous competitive systems of occult numerology, except in the sense that they appear to be at once arbitrary and worthless.

occupied by the Superiors of the Order with inquiries into their Masonic conduct and reputation. The significance of these rules is to be sought in all that is omitted rather than anything that is expressed: it will be seen that they turn upon questions of moral fitness, Craft status and tolerably good citizenship. There is no word as to spiritual qualifications, religious aims or attainments, although—by the hypothesis of its Grades—the Rite was one of priesthood. Supposing that the Intelligence Department reported favourably the seven-months' child of its concern might then be born into the Order.

On the day fixed for his reception the Candidate was placed in a vestibule, where he was proved in the Three Craft Degrees, after which he was passed to the Chamber of Reception, otherwise the Chapter House, and there signed the following preliminary Pledge: "I, N. N., Master Mason, do promise in the Name of the one God, and by the duty of an honest man, that I will respect all the Mysteries and will observe all the Statutes which shall be imposed upon me by the Reverend, Wise and Worthy Chapter of Knights and Brothers of Light, Novices of the third year, and will hold them as a revelation of the ultimate forces of Nature, even if they seem difficult to follow and dealing with unheard of things." The execution of this undertaking entitled the Candidate to be acquainted with the Laws under which he must abide as a Novice. These may be summarised as follows: (1) He was required to abstain from any action which might militate against the Order itself, its Chapters or its Grades; (2) to exhibit dutiful submission—as pledged—in respect of all its Laws; (3) to prosecute its Mysteries throughout the days of his life, because they emanate from the True Light; (4) to ask nothing respecting their source or those by whom they have been delivered; (5) to maintain, so far as may be possible, the Three Degrees of Freemasonry, seeing that they are the Elementary School of the Sublime Order; (6) to guard and shield the Reverend, Mighty and Wise Order itself.

Having signified his adhesion to these undertakings in writing, the Novice was then escorted into the Chapter itself, where he was questioned as to when and by whom he had been made a Mason, and as to his age in the Master Grade. The Headship being familiar already with these points of his career, the testimony was exacted presumably for the information of those who were auditors. Having been given and approved, an Officer denominated the Corrector of Novices called the Chapter to prayer by sounding a bell. The Invocation which follows has, however, been mangled in translation or is represented badly by the original.[1] "Thy Name, O God our Creator, is known throughout the earth,[2] and we give Thee thanks in Heaven. Out of the mouth of babes Thou hast established Thy strength against Thine enemies, that Thou mightest put to silence the accuser and the avenger.[3] I behold the heavens, the work of Thine hands, the moon and the stars which Thou hast made.[4] They that have ears let them hear what the Spirit saith unto the Churches: To him that overcometh I will give to eat of the Tree of Life which is in the Paradise of God.[5] And to the Angel of the Church of Smyrna write, saying: This is the first and the last, He that was dead and shall live again.[6] They

[1] I speak under certain reserves: there it no end to the follies and confusions of minor Masonic Rituals, as there is no end to the commonplaces and ineptitudes of those which rank as major. The Invocation above is, in any case, a mere chaos of Scripture-quotations.

[2] Cf. Ps. viii, 1: "How excellent is Thy Name in all the earth."

[3] *Ibid.*, 2: "Out of the mouths of babes and sucklings hast Thou ordained strength because of Thine enemies, that Thou mightest still the enemy and the avenger."

[4] Cf. *ibid.*, 3.

[5] Apocalypse i, 7.

[6] *Ibid.*, 8, but read: "which was dead and is alive."

that have ears, etc. (*repeated*). To him that overcometh I will give of the hidden manna, and I will give him a good testimony written in his name (*sic*), but none shall know it save he that owneth it.[1] For all this hath the Lord spoken, and the word of the Lord is pure, even as pure silver, purged seven times."[2]

The Corrector of Novices then exhorted the Candidate, bidding him pray to "the good elements of all creatures that the One and the Three and the Five and* * * * * * * may be with us and that they may direct thee on the path which thou hast entered." Robing and unrobing followed, with the recitation of a Psalm, which is not otherwise specified. The Candidate was then warned that he had been brought within the secret circle in order that he might study the Laws of Divine Wisdom, Justice, Mercy and Power. He was called upon to abide among his Brethren in sincerity of heart, with the spirit of goodwill and submission, with love and devotion to the true ends of the Order. In the fulfilment of these conditions it was said that he would be taught "our Mysteries" fully and would be directed to that point when he himself should enter the light. On the faith of this prospect he ratified another Pledge as follows: "I, N. N., do swear by the one law of the True and Unknown Being that I will continue through all my life in fidelity to the duties of Knights and Brothers of Light. If I violate even one of them, may my Superiors, by the miraculous power of Magic, render me the most pitiable of all creatures. May the powers of evil rise up against me for ever, the cruel spirits which hide themselves from the light. May the powerful Princes of Darkness assemble about me all terrors of darkness, to encompass me as with a cloud. May they expel all light from my spirit, my

[1] APOCALYPSE, 17, but read: "will give him a white stone, and in the stone a new name written, which no man knoweth saving he that receiveth it."

[2] Cf. Ps. xvii, 6.

soul and my body, and may the Source of Good, which is One and Three, shut me out for ever from its mercy."[1]

The Signs and Passwords are communicated in the next place, after which another Master of Novices delivers the Historical Discourse. It affirms the existence of various occult Societies from past times immemorial and under various names. In all cases their knowledge and objects were concealed in hieroglyphics, and thus reserved to the elect. The centre was always in Asia, and there on a day it came about that certain Knights were admitted who took part in the war against Saracens under the Banner of the Cross. They learned after this manner many mysteries in Asia, but the time came when part of them perished under a thousand tortures. The reference is of course to the suppression of the Knights Templar, whose story is told in brief. It is added that out of this ruin there arose what is called the *Radiz*, otherwise Knights of St John, as also " the German Order "—presumably Teutonic Knights—and the Golden Fleece.[2] The wreckage of the Templar Mysteries was inherited by these Associations. Apparently, however, they were not the only heirs, for it is said that the Order of Freemasons, more ancient than any of the above, is that which has best preserved the hieroglyphics of Templar Knights. The Temple of Solomon was their most catholic symbol of all, yet it was used by the Chivalry itself, the Sanctuary of Israel being divided apparently into symbolic portions corresponding to the Grades of the Knighthood.

[1] In the imposition of such a Pledge the Order of *Fratres Lucis* is condemned out of its own mouth, for it is certain that nothing true and of good report would require a Candidate to invoke an eternal judgment on himself. The Masonic Rites and Degrees are content with penal clauses which threaten the destruction or maiming of the body.

[2] We have seen that the Order of the Golden Fleece originated in 1429 in connection with an event belonging to that date and to nothing else ; the Knights of St. John were founded in 1124 ; and the Teutonic Knights in 1191. It follows that none of these institutions " arose " out of the suppression of the Templars in 1307.

The discourse is confused at this point and it is scarcely possible to understand what is intended. We hear of moral interpretations applied by Templars to sacraments and picture-symbols. It recurs then to Masonry and affirms without further preface that its real objects have been invariably those of Alchemy, Theosophy and Magia, but they have not been pursued owing to the ignorance of Brethren. The *Fratres Lucis* were, however, in a position to intervene and atone for this deficiency, by means of clear instructions, which would be given to deserving Novices.

In this manner the claim of the Order itself begins to emerge distinctly for the first time, and thereafter the Discourse proceeds to explain the Entered Apprentice Degree of Craft Masonry. The dark room used prior to reception signifies that the First Matter of the Great Work is found in a black earth. It is an earth which contains no metals, and these are removed from the Candidate prior to his reception for this reason. When he is divested of various garments the reason is that " Our Matter is stripped of the veil that Nature has given it." It is said also that it can be " drawn as from the breast of a mother." When the shoe also is removed the reference is to a certain mystical severance and is " one of the most ancient hieroglyphics known to the Israelites," being connected with the refusal to take the wife of a deceased brother, the renunciation of an inheritance, and so forth. The battery which is made upon the floor as a token of affirmation or consent to the reception of Candidates " signifies that we procure our Matter from its habitation in a volcano and that the Order has for its chief objects the physical mysteries wrought by fire." The hoodwink indicates that although the First Matter is luminous, shining and clear in itself, yet it can be found only in a most darksome abode—meaning the black earth already mentioned. The three circumambulations which are made in the course of reception are called "laborious journeys" and with their connected discourses and procedure are not interpreted alchemically: they signify[1] the obedience, fidelity and silence which must be shewn towards Chiefs, as well as "the toils, reflections, upright heart and open soul," by which only the Novice can hope to rise towards them. But it is obvious that this is a blundering digression which has forgotten that its business of interpretation is at work on a Craft Grade. The confusion persists throughout the following clauses. The point of the sword making contact with the breast is a reminder that "no two-edged weapon must ever be used to slay our Hiram and obtain his precious blood, which is shewn afterwards by a 'weak' Brother and his blood-stained handkerchief." It is affirmed that this unintelligible reference—which has no Masonic application in our own day—is explained to the Knight-Novice of the seventh year. The silence preserved in the Lodge intimates that "our Matter," after its due preparation, operates the dissolution of all metals in stillness. The compasses brought forward on a plate of blood and afterwards applied to the Candidate, with the subsequent elevation of the plate, intimate that "we have another poniard," being that which "we thrust into the bosom of our matter" and cause it to pour forth blood." Whatsoever is repeated thrice indicates that the Matter is animal, vegetable and mineral. Finally, the name of Thooelkam (*sic*), conferred on the Candidate in virtue of his admission, is another reference to the fact that "our Matter lies where the volcano has its fire and its dwelling."

The Tracing-Board offers an opportunity for further confusion between Masonic symbolism and that of the

[1] It is said alternatively that the path, according to its affirmed significance, can be found only in secrecy, after great trials, and by firm and fearless constancy.

Fratres Lucis. The four cardinal points or quarters intimate that God has endowed the Chiefs of the Order with such wisdom that they are raised above all mortality, and that to them nothing is unknown. The four principal winds, considered as symbols, offer the same lesson. When the Smaragdine Tablet testifies that " the wind bears it in its belly," the meaning is : " I carry the Matter, for it is the source and end of all things." The border and the pointing finger are said to denote " our unchangeableness," but this seems pure nonsense. The Masonic flooring reveals the well-known magic squares.

The Sign of the Hexagram appeared on the Tracing-Board and is connected with the words *Aesh Mazor*, whence it is said to signify the watery-flame or flaming water which belongs to the Hermetic work. The Sun and Moon typify the male and female elements, active and passive, corresponding to Jakin and Boaz. But it is affirmed that these have also their meaning in the operations of Divine Magic, to which statement is appended an unintelligible sentence, referring presumably to the Pillars of the Sephirotic Tree, the Mystery of MERCABA, being the Symbolic Chariot of Kabalism. The last episode of the Grade was a further historical recitation, dealing more especially with the Order of *Fratres Lucis* and including a sketch of the *Theosophia*, *Magia* and *Chemia* belonging to the First Degree.

It seems that according to the ridiculous nomenclature of the Rite the Mason admitted to the First Degree became a Knight-Novice of the Third Year and that having been proved as such for a period of three years he was entitled to the Second Degree, which is Knight-Novice of the Fifth Year. It is difficult to believe that such a contradictory symbolical scheme of times could have obtained in any sane Ritual, and my inference is that Mrs. Cooper-Oakley, who was always a confused writer, has mismanaged her material. The ceremonial of the Second Degree is said to be substantially the same as the first, and it comes about for this reason that she presents some selections only from certain addresses delivered in the Chapter. They would appear to be explanations of Fellow-Craft Symbolism, though this is little better than speculation in the state of the summaries given. We hear of the "entrance"—whether of the Chapter or the Candidate it is impossible to say—and that it signifies an approaching union of those principles that are separate in themselves. The letter F, placed in the centre of a Blazing Star, signifies the active principle of the Creative Elohim. There is also an allusion to "the Seven Degrees," which are not specified by name and it is impossible therefore to identify the Masonic Rite: they correspond, however, to the seven metals which have to be perfected in the Hermetic Work and to the least number of "the true Jewish name of our Matter." The following cryptic sentence is appended to this statement: "Thus Zechariah saw one stone with seven eyes and finally seven wheels, which are our last workmen, by means of whom we raise ourselves to perfection."[1] The Degrees, moreover, signify seven stars, "the power of which is explained in our Kabalistic science, for Natural Magic is very useful and indeed necessary to our Chiefs in their work."

The time of probation for the Third Degree is not specified, but its title is Knight-Novice of the Seventh Year, and it is either in analogy with the Craft Master Grade or the latter is expounded as to its inner meaning therein. (1) The Temple of Solomon is declared to be the general synthesis of the Hermetic Art. (2) It is affirmed to be clear from Ezekiel that Hiram has an universal

[1] For the stone with seven eyes see ZECHARIAH iii, 9, but the prophecy has no reference to wheels. In the Vision of Ezekiel the wheels are four in number.

meaning—namely, NEPHESH, URIM, THUMMIM—and also that he was slain.[1] (3) He signifies "our Matter, killed by three workmen in order that they may obtain the Word," which Word is Jehovah, otherwise the Central Fire.[2] (4) He was buried and the murderers secured his *caput mortuum*: it is said to appear "as if the spirit were excited by rage" and that the Acacia is an illustration of the fact. (5) As to the nature of the Matter, this is shewn in the Master Grade: it comprises three kingdoms, and these are symbolised in that Grade by (a) the touchstone,[3] corresponding to the mineral kingdom; (b) the "dead-head," corresponding to the animal; and (c) by the Acacia, which represents the vegetable kingdom. (6) The Name or Symbol of Jehovah, which appears in the centre of a triangle, denotes the fulfilment of the Work, and this itself is called the Central Fire, otherwise "the greatest light." After these explanations, however they may happen to have been communicated in the course of addresses, the Candidate is told as follows: "This Matter, Reverend Brother, is our book, which is here exhibited before thee, and after close study thou shalt find that it is adorned with all these qualities." Mrs. Cooper-Oakley makes tiresome omissions and at points which seem to be vital, but I conceive it possible that some of them were actuated by a desire to reserve what she might regard as Masonic

[1] There is no reference to Hiram in Ezekiel, whether the king or the builder and artificer. It is impossible therefore to speculate on the meaning of this statement. Hiram the worker in brass is mentioned only in I KINGS, vii, and 2 CHRONICLES iv.

[2] I conclude that this is an attempt to allegorise in a Hermetic sense for the purpose of saving the Masonic situation when it communicates familiar Divine Names and other formulæ as great secrets protected by solemn pledges and Words or Names of power.

[3] I conclude from this interpretation that German Craft Masonry must have incorporated stone-symbolism into the Third Degree; but it may be mentioned for the benefit of non-Masons that it is not to be found in any English working, wheresoever practised.

Secrets. If the Philosophical Matter of the *Fratres Lucis* was literally a book, it is obvious that the work was not physical—in the sense of metallic transmutation—and if the qualities which it is said to contain are a reference to the three kingdoms specified above, then the latter must be understood in an allegorical or mystical sense. One is inclined to speculate whether the Knight-Novice of the Seventh Year had the Bible held up before him and was told that this was the touchstone—otherwise a key to all things—a " dead-head " or *caput mortuum* in respect of the cortex or external meaning, and the Acacia or sign of life and resurrection, a gage of immortality in respect of its inner meaning. As regards the Third Degree of the Order, I may add that there is one reference to Hiram, King of Tyre, of whom it is said that according to the Chaldæan book JALKOT he gained inexhaustible riches by his wisdom and was eight hundred years old. But a time came when he thought himself equal with God, and this led to his destruction. He fashioned two " beams " by his art and raised seven heavens upon them, in which he caused an altar to be erected, after the fashion of the Altar of God. The purpose of this adventure in emblematic building does not transpire, nor why it was counted against him as an evil work ; but the story says that God sent Ezekiel to pronounce judgment upon him, that he fell from the height which he had raised and was slain subsequently by men.

In the Fourth Degree the Candidate passes from Grades of supposed Knighthood into offices of priesthood, but as no one can see why his previous experiences should connect with the idea of chivalry, so now there is no reason on the surface, or perhaps beneath it, to account for him becoming a Levite. There may be, however, an explanation in the procedure which does not appear in the extracts. A Catechism contains the following unconnected and mostly inexplicable points. (1) Perfection is 1, 2, 3 and 4, but the sum of these numbers is 10, and the meaning may be that perfection is in the keeping of the whole Law: alternatively the allusion may be to the denary scale of the *Sephiroth* and the emblematic mystery of their ascent. (2) The Perfect Flame is that which illuminates, blazes and destroys not. (3) The word *Majim* must not be pronounced while proving pure stones of marble. (4) Elohim is *Eli* and *Ki*, the light without will and the light with will, otherwise colourless and coloured, will being the source of colour. (5) The serpent which flies through the air and burns is represented by the ant found within its scale—referring, I think, to some rabbinical myth. (6) Moses was forty days with *Schamajim* and brought back the natural laws, inscribed on a stone. Mrs. Oakley says that there are many more questions and answers, after which the officiating Brother offers the following Prayer: "I beseech Thee, O Lord, to grant me two graces, and may they abide with me through all my life. Take away my idolatry and falsehood; give me neither poverty nor riches, but only my daily bread. Vouchsafe unto me reason and wisdom, that I may learn both good and evil." It may be added that the whole Ceremony is much shorter than those of the previous Degrees. Considerable stress is laid upon the ethical side of the Candidate's life.

In the Fifth Degree and last the Levite becomes a Priest and is told that he has reached the end of the Secret Mysteries of a Royal and Sacerdotal Order. It is said also that he is approaching a barrier, through which he may pass, if God wills, being "enlightened by the light." He is caused to perform certain ceremonial acts before a Sacred Fire which has been kindled with religious observances. Thereafter the Closing is taken. After making every allowance for a piecemeal translation which may be also indifferently done, it will be seen that on the surface at least the Candidate has learned little enough throughout and that there is practically nothing in the Degrees to deserve calling Ritual. In view of the references to light Mrs. Oakley cherished an opinion that the teaching of the *Fratres Lucis* was designed to lead members from the darkness of sense-life into that illumination of spiritual being which is our heritage. Her opinion on any subject having debatable elements cannot be said to count, and there is nothing apparently in her original to support the view. The barrier referred to in the Ritual most probably means the guarded threshold of the Fifth Degree, or alternatively the threshold of that secret knowledge which would have been held to lie behind the whole Rite. The intimations concerning it point to a medley of doctrine in combination with a medley of occult practices. As such the Order of *Fratres Lucis* does not stand alone: there are other Rites in its likeness, though there is nothing to indicate that they have drawn therefrom. The characteristic, I am afraid, of all is that they lead nowhere. The highest Orders and Degrees of Masonry are shadows of things which have never passed into plenary expression, but they can open great vistas of symbolism beyond their own measures: this is the distinction between them and a thousand others which were dead before they were born, which contain nothing and impart nothing in themselves, and have no windows from which we can look beyond.

Having exhibited the general Ritual-horizon of the *Fratres Lucis*, I will complete the available information concerning them by reference to the same source. The Order was divided into Provinces, particulars of which are wanting. If the scheme, as it may have been, was laid out on an elaborate scale, it will be understood that most of them were in a state of potential subsistence only, awaiting a day to come when *Fratres Lucis* would have acquired the Masonic world. Actually or hypothetically, each Province was governed by a Head elected by the Brethren over whom he was subsequently to rule. The Chapter on such occasion was in the hands of a Provincial Administrator, who sounded a bell seven times. The process of election began, the votes were taken, the result was announced in due course and the Head-Elect was installed immediately after. Psalm ii: "Why do the heathen rage?" was recited, after which the Chancellor-Assessor and Sword-Bearer uncovered the breast and head of the elected Knight. The questions of the time were then put, namely, (1) Whether he promised to have faith in the Good Author of all creatures to the end of his life; (2) whether he would observe the Statutes of the Order and maintain the same inviolate; (3) whether he would love the Brethren more than he loved himself. When the Assembly had been satisfied on these points, the Chancellor took a golden cup containing oil and anointed the head of the Knight-Elect crosswise on the crown, saying: "God chooses thee as the Chief of His Elect." Afterwards the left hand and breast were anointed, with the words: "David said unto the Philistines,[1] etc. He was also and finally anointed on the right hand, but seemingly with no verbal formula. He was invested thereafter with the robes of his Office and with the Cap, the Chancellor saying: "He who is the Chief Priest among his Brethren, on whose head has been poured the holy chrism and whose hands have been anointed, shall be clothed with this sacerdotal garment, and let him not uncover his head or rend his robe." There were other exhortations, ending with this Prayer: "They who have ears to hear let them hear: he that overcometh shall have the first Tree of Life [*sic*]

[1] The use of the plural notwithstanding it is not unlikely that reference is intended to I SAMUEL, xviii, 45–47: "Then said David to the Philistine," i.e. to Goliath. Compare *ibid.*, xxix, 8: "and David said unto Achish," i.e. the King of Gath, who was a Philistine; but this is without application.

in the Paradise of God. And to the Angel of the Church [*sic*, meaning the Church in Smyrna] he shall write: This is the First and the Last, Who shall die and live again [*sic*]. To him that overcometh I will give of the Hidden Manna, and I will give him a good certificate[1] [*sic*], and this certificate he alone that hath shall know it [*sic*]. The lightning shall arise from the Altar, and also the Thunder and the Voice. And seven lighted candlesticks shall be before the Altar which represent the Seven Spirits of God. May God bless thee and keep thee: may God teach thee and be gracious unto thee: may God turn His countenance and give unto thee peace therefrom."[2]

As regards the Laws of the Order they may be extracted thus: (1) The Grades comprised by the Rite, as already given; (2) Regulations concerning voting, election and so forth; (3) The decorations of the Temple, in the centre of which there was to be a seven-branched candlestick of gold; (4) Offences against the Order and complaints; (5) Rules for the preservation of right and order; (6) The vestments used in the Rite, but they are omitted by the translator; (7) Concerning alms; (8) Dues payable in the Order; (9) The Chronology of the Order, and this is given as follows: The Chronology begins with the year of the reform which was inaugurated by John the Evangelist, Founder and Head of the Seven Unknown Churches of Asia, seven years after the death of Christ. By subtracting from A.D. 1781, the year in which the Order was founded, the 33 years of Christ's life on earth and the seven which elapsed before St. John began his work, making 40 years, we arrive at the symbolical or rather mythical year which was arrogated to itself by the Order, namely, 1741. Were it revived at this day on the same basis it

[1] Cf. the "testimony" of the previous prayer.
[2] Cf. Ps. iv, 6: "Lift up the light of Thy countenance upon us."

would assume the age of 1883 years. The subsequent Laws are devoted to questions of correspondence and business details.

It remains to be said that the manuscript on which Mrs. Cooper-Oakley depended was addressed to the Seven Wise Fathers, Heads of the Seven Churches of Asia, wishing "peace in the Holy Number"—presumably the number seven. The Order comes therefore before us as that of a Hidden Church or Holy Assembly, *ex hypothesi* like that of Eckartshausen, but passing into substituted manifestation by virtue of its ceremonial workings. The analogy ends at this point; but the reference to the Seven Churches opens a further question. We are taken back to the Asiatic Brethren or Initiated Brothers of Asia, otherwise the Knights and Brethren of St. John the Evangelist for Asia in Europe, which claimed to possess and to propagate the only true Freemasonry. According to Findel, the system consisted of two probationary Degrees of seeking and suffering,[1] which were followed by (1) Consecrated Knight and Brother, (2) Wise Master, (3) Royal Priest or Perfect Rosicrucian, called otherwise the Degree of Melchisedek. It should be understood as regards the last that it was neither the Eighteenth Degree of the Rite of Perfection nor any variant thereof but that it drew from the Golden and Rosy Cross of *circa* 1777 and from Rosicrucian things antecedent thereto in Ritual, so far as served its purpose.[2] The proof is that the Initiated Brothers of Asia

[1] There were three, according to Mrs. Cooper-Oakley, namely, (1) Seekers, (2) Endurers, (3) Probationers, all classed under the general denomination of Sufferers. She does not cite her authority. See THEOSOPHICAL REVIEW, Vol. XXIV, 1899.

[2] A Grade of Melchisedek connotes Eucharistic procedure and symbolism, but, according to Findel, Hans Heinrich established a Melchisedek Lodge at Hamburg into which non-Christians were admitted, as they were also in Berlin. He promised to unfold the meaning of all Masonic "hieroglyphics."

were almost beyond question a foundation of the Brothers Ecker und Eckhoffen prior to the Knights of Light. Findel seems to be the only writer who has thrown any doubt upon the point, but he has created uncertainty solely by contradicting himself. He says in one place that Baron Hans Heinrich was propagator rather than founder and that he was helped by an Israelite named Hirschmann in recasting the Rituals; but in another place we are told that because he had failed in "obedience, trust and peaceful behaviour" he had been expelled from the Rosy Cross and that in revenge he founded the Asiatic Order. It is possible that this is a correct version of the matter and it seems certain also that the only Rituals to remodel were those of the Rosy Cross.

There is no trace of the Initiated Brothers prior to 1780,[1] and by Findel's own shewing the expulsion of Hans Heinrich could not have taken place till very late in the previous year, for in 1779 he is said to have been editing for the Rosicrucians a "collection of Masonic [*sic*] speeches," delivered in the "ancient system," that is, prior to the Reformation of 1777. But the *Fratres Lucis* based their symbolic chronology, as we have seen, on 1781. It is clear therefore that they arose concurrently with the Initiated Brothers, or alternatively that they were different branches or names of one thing. In support of the latter possibility we find that the heads of the Initiated Brothers claimed to have been Directors of the Seven Invisible Churches of Asia, or in other words that they are the very persons to whom the Wilkoroki manuscript was addressed. Moreover, the chief stipulation with Candidates was the same in both cases, or "not to inquire by whom the secrets were communicated, whence they came now or might emanate in the future." Finally, the Initiated Brothers dated by

[1] This is the date of organisation given by Mackey, an American historian of Masonry. He terms the Asiatic Brothers a Rosicrucian schism.

their hypothesis from the year A.D. 40, when the *Fratres Lucis* originated under the auspices of St. John the Evangelist. There could be no two emblematical peas more like unto each other in one pod of the Mysteries. It ought not to need adding that nothing attaches to the identity or distinction between the two groups. In modern occult circles of the theosophical type a considerable rumour of importance has grown up about the *Fratres Lucis*, but—against all intention on her part—it has been dispersed by the publication of Mrs. Cooper-Oakley's analysis of the Warsaw document. The two Orders concern us only as derivatives of the Rosy Cross in the eighteenth century under the Masonic ægis. They are serviceable as illustrating the circumstances under which new branches of the Order or things made in its likeness came suddenly into being, making great claims on present possession of knowledge and on an immemorial past, but with very little behind them and, as it happened in both these cases, with no horizon in front. According to Clavel, the Initiated Brothers were in trouble with the police in 1785—where, however, being omitted—and in 1787 a writer named Rollig put an end to them by revealing their secrets. My experience of Secret Orders, Masonic and otherwise, shews that they do not suffer death in this manner: more often they undergo change.

It is reported also that the *Fratres Lucis* were broken up in 1795, but the fact is exceedingly doubtful on other considerations than are adduced by Mrs. Cooper-Oakley. She refers to a publication entitled DER SIGNATSTERN, and terms it an official organ of the Order. It began to appear in small volumes about 1804 and continued for several years, but was not a periodical publication in numbers or in any way corresponding to Transactions. It is in reality a collection of archives, and according to these and the general title of the work there were Seven Grades of

Mystical Freemasonry, otherwise of the Order of Knights of Light. I can speak with certainty only of the ninth part or division, comprised in a duodecimo volume of three hundred pages and containing (1) a long disquisition on the Mysteries of Egypt and their alleged analogies with those of Freemasonry; (2) the Constitution and Laws or Statutes of the St. John's Lodge Ferdinand zum Felsen at the Orient of Hamburg, dated in 1790 and signed by Hans Karl Freyherr von Ecker und Eckhoffen; (3) a sheaf of orations emanating from the Grand Lodge Royal York of Friendship. If the archives as a whole are to be judged by these examples, they offer no evidence on the perpetuation of the *Fratres Lucis*. I have no doubt that the Asiatic Brethren survived the revelations of Rollig, and I should regard it as exceedingly doubtful that the concordant or identical association was actually broken up in 1795. It is probable that both lapsed gradually and that the second had passed out of sight at the beginning of the nineteenth century.

As regards the fraudulent antiquity claimed by both Orders, it is alleged concerning the Asiatic Brethren (1) that it underwent some kind of reform in 1541; (2) that it was working at Prague in 1608; (3) that it was closely connected with the Rosicrucians and had been helped by Christian Rosencreutz from time to time—a reference to its supposed activities, in the early fifteenth century; (4) that according to one of its traditions it was to continue till the Head should return—presumably C∴R∴C∴. The Jew Hirschmann is said to have supplied Kabalistic and Talmudic elements, including instructions on the four worlds of *Atziluth*, *Briah*, *Yetzirah* and *Assiah*. According to Mrs. Oakley the *Fratres Lucis* were incorporated originally at Berlin, but were first made public as an Order at Vienna in 1780, or immediately after the death of the Empress Maria Theresa. The evidence does not appear, and we have seen that their own chronology points to the year 1781. It appears from the Warsaw manuscript that few Rosicrucians were admitted, it being alleged that they had fallen away from their original ideal, were tainted with the thirst for gold and the search after power.

It remains to say that Hans Heinrich von Ecker und Eckhoffen—who seems to have worked always in conjunction with Karl his brother—was a gentleman of the bedchamber and counsellor of the Duke of Coburg-Saalfeld. According to his own statements, he became a Freemason in his sixteenth year and a Rosicrucian at no long date after. We have seen that he was expelled from the latter Order, or such is the recurring allegation, whatever its value.

CHAPTER XIX

THE ROSY CROSS IN RUSSIA

ACCORDING to one of the legends which have grown up around the name of Louis Claude de Saint-Martin, that illustrious French mystic is supposed to have visited Russia at some uncertain period between the publication of his work on the correspondence between God, Man and the Universe[1] in 1782 and his journey to England in 1787. It would follow in such case that a Brother of the Rosy Cross, under the obedience of Martines de Pasqually and his Rite of Elect Priesthood, had tarried in the Muscovite Empire. While there is no truth in the story it is certain that then and subsequently he was abiding there in the spirit, for at Petrograd and Moscow, if not otherwhere in Russia, Martinism was the fashion of a period, a philosophical and mystical influence. It was reflected, moreover, from the illuminations of DES ERREURS ET DE LA VÉRITÉ, Saint-Martin's first work and not from the occult Rite of his teacher Martines de Pasqually. I am about to give account briefly of the Rosy Cross in Russia, and not unfortunately on warrants depending from independent research of my own.[2] We shall see that it entered Russia under the auspices of German *adepti* who were also Masons, responsible to a German obedience, and that it worked hand in hand with the Emblematic Society, more expecially

[1] TABLEAU NATUREL DES RAPPORTS *qui existent entre Dieu, l'Homme et l'Univers.* Lyon, 1782.

[2] I depend on four articles "by a Russian" published in THE THEOSOPHICAL REVIEW, Vols. 38, 39.

in its *Écossais* developments.[1] We shall see also that Masonry and the Rosy Cross were known in common parlance and were identified, politically speaking, under the generic name of Martinism. It is a testimony to the extent of the fashion which I have just mentioned[2] and which was illustrated further by a Court farce produced to ridicule the subject and most probably played under the eyes of Catherine II.[3] We shall see firstly that it was the Golden and Rosy Cross of the post-reformation variety which made its bid for conquest. The emissaries and chartered Brethren were all indifferently members of the STRICT OBSERVANCE, but holding from Germany, not from Russia, where the great Rite of Baron von Hund had effected an entrance so far back as 1765, but had found no soil in which to take permanent root. The fact of this membership must not be understood as connoting a second effort to find a place for the OBSERVANCE, which indeed may have been lingering still within the walls of a few unrecorded Lodges or Chapters.[4]

The account of the anonymous Russian, mentioned in my note, derives in part from Russian MSS. which are described as " inaccessible for verification by ordinary readers " and for the rest on Russian printed books which have not been translated and are therefore equally

[1] The history of Freemasonry in Russia begins *circa* 1731 and is in the usual cloud of uncertainty. It has no part in my subject, but it may clear the issues to say that fifty years later there were several Rites or combinations of Rites at work.

[2] It seems to have permeated all Masonic systems in Russia, as it did in a number of French Rites and in the German Strict Observance, when the latter came over to France.

[3] It may have been written by the Empress or under her supervision, as a *ieu d'esprit* with a motive. On the farce itself and on Martinism in Russia see the MÉMOIRES of Baronne Henriette Louise d'Oberkirch, first published at Paris *circa* 1850 and translated into English in 1852.

[4] It should be understood that the Strict Observance influenced the Swedish Rite and the Rite of Zinnendorf, both of which played their parts for a period in Russia.

sealed—except to a very few—in England. It is characterised as an attempt to study "the almost unknown occult group which worked behind Masonry and in its midst under the sign and the name of the Rosy Cross" —meaning in Russia itself and to some extent in Germany. There is no doubt in my own mind as to its utter sincerity,[1] under circumstances, moreover, when there could be no ulterior purpose to serve, and as it throws light not only on its own immediate subject—or on the Rosy Cross in Russia—but also on the Order in Germany about the period of the Reformation and thence onward, it is of high and unquestionable importance. I must therefore take the only course which is open and rest satisfied with an analysis of the several papers into which the account is divided, adding only such occasional notes as arise out of the text. Their publication many years ago in a class periodical, which has been numbered long since with the dead, means that they have passed out of sight, and I hope that their presentation here in a readily available form may induce some competent person to undertake a further investigation and make the results public.

The central personality of the papers is N. Novikoff,[2] of whom it is said that his life-story is that of Freemasonry and still more of the Rosy Cross in Russia. In the epoch-making year 1777 we are told that he met Prince Peter Repinno and was told something of the Order—of the fact, let us say, of its existence; but the Prince died before Novikoff could pursue his inquiries. This notwithstanding he contrived to proceed further, and we hear of Elaguin, a Russian noble of French education, who became his director or chief, but whether in things Masonic or otherwise is left uncertain.[3] Elaguin had met with an English-

[1] I have been at the pains of ascertaining the name and character of the writer, but have no authority to make them public.

[2] Otherwise, Novikov.

[3] Elaguin or Yelaguin according to the FREEMASONS' CALENDAR, 1777,

man travelling in Russia and had been assured by him that "real Masonry was a mysterious science seldom communicated to any one"; that it was passed orally from one to another in his own country; that the home of the secret was a very ancient London Lodge, the existence of which was known to but few Brethren; and that it was difficult to gain admission therein. It must be said that this looks like mendacity, but the story goes on to affirm that the unnamed and perhaps anonymous Englishman gave Elaguin five years in which to make acquaintance with wisdom and that the Russian became a student, the lines followed in his adventure not being otherwise specified, till the time came when he received as his teacher and friend, a certain Dr. Stanislas Ely, author of a work entitled BROTHERLY ADVICE and said to have been well known at the period. He is affirmed further to have been a Kabalist, and under his auspices Elaguin began the study of Robert Fludd—among other writers. Whether he continued and how he fared the deposition does not tell us, for Ely passes out of sight as well as the other mysterious Englishman, and when we next encounter the pupil he is in the position of master and leader. We hear of a "vast library" belonging to Lodges under his system and of MSS. in his own collection. The latter included an alleged translation from Eugenius Philalethes under the title of A WORD ON BEING, which seems to have contained a Diagram of the Tree of Life in Kabalism, shewing the allocation of planets to *Sephiroth*, "worked out in a most interesting way."[1]

was appointed Provincial Grand Master of Russia by the Grand Lodge of England in 1772. He was a Court official and a favourite of the Empress.

[1] Though he speaks in one place of Ten Secret Principles, which suggest the *Ten Sephiroth*, it must be said that there is no reference to the Tree of Life in Kabalism anywhere in the writings of Eugenius Philalethes, and much less a Diagram of the Tree. As it would be intolerable to suppose that a Russian student had access to an unprinted and utterly unknown text, I conclude that there is some mistake in the attribution.

There were notes also written by Elaguin himself, in which he quoted from the MYSTERIES OF CHRISTIANITY, also translated from the English and said to have been printed at London in 1775.

As regards the "vast library," two of its items—presumably both in MS.—were a THEOSOPHICAL-MAGICAL-KABALISTIC EXPLANATION, by Wöllner, the so-called evil genius of Frederick William II, and the anonymous DIARY of a German Mason. It emerges from the latter document (1) that the author had visited Russia to help the Masonic Brethren in that country; (2) that he returned to Berlin; (3) that in Berlin he assisted at studies of the Rosy Cross Degree [*sic*]; (4) that at one of the Rosicrucian conventions a member named Simson reported having heard that true Masonry was to come once more from the Kingdom of Tibet; but (5) that another named Ritch had been told of its expected advent from Eastern Russia. The date of this second MS. was 1784.

It does not transpire after what manner Elaguin promoted the aspirations of Novikoff, who came next under the influence of John George Schwarz, described as born on Slav soil in Transylvania. Being one of two Russian deputies at the Masonic Convention of Wilhelmsbad in 1782, it is said that at those epoch-making deliberations, when the Rite of the Strict Observance was weighed in the balance, he met with persons who "hid from the other Masons."[1] They were in fact Rosicrucians but distinguished apparently by a different policy than was followed by Baron Ecker und Eckhoffen at the same time in the same

[1] The German Rosicrucians at Wilhelmsbad do not figure as such in the history of the Masonic Congress, and it is more likely that they were absent than moving mysteriously about as people hiding from observation. They were Masons as well as Rosicrucians and could mix with other Masons as such. It is on record that Baron Hans Heinrich von Ecker und Eckhoffen was engaged actively in the precincts of the Congress conferring his Grade called True Rosicrucian, being part of the system known as Asiatic Brethren.

place. However this may be, they found no difficulty in advising Professor Schwarz that "the hour to bless Russia had arrived" or to entrust him with papers for the organisation of the Rosy Cross therein, namely, the First or Theoretical Degree of Solomon's Science.[1] Their facility is explained by the fact that Schwarz had been received previously into the Order at Berlin, by no less an adept than Wöllner. He was now constituted Chief of the Theoretical Degree for Russia, and as far as it is possible to reach an intelligible mean amidst the confusion of the various statements, it is clear that a warrant was conveyed also to Novikoff, who by this time was already a member of the Masonic Strict Observance. Rules of Procedure were established in writing to the following effect: (1) That the qualification of Rosicrucian Candidates should be the rank of Ancient Scottish Master[2]; (2) That no copies were to be taken of any documents; (3) That the teachings peculiar to the Degree should be communicated once in every nine Meetings—meaning, I presume, that the rest were to be concerned with ceremonial; (4) That Schwarz was to explain and interpret on his own authority in the best manner that he could; (5) That there was to be absolute secrecy, with prudent choice of members; (6) That Novikoff was to be admitted, having bound himself in the presence of at least three Theoretical Brethren to recognise Schwarz as his head; (7) That he was not to receive anyone without the permission of Schwarz; (8) That other Russian Wardens were to obey Novikoff. The document

[1] There is certainly a confusion here, presumably on the part of the anonymous Russian. We have seen that *Zelator* was the first Grade of the Golden and Rosy Cross.

[2] On the multitude of Écossais Grades see my New Encyclopædia of Freemasonry, I, 208–13. The particular variety which we know to have existed in Russia at the Novikoff period was called Scottish Master. There is no need to say that all Écossais Grades, like all Masonic Rites everywhere, were ancient by their hypothesis or that this hypothesis is false.

which embodied these undertakings is described as "given" in the Palace of the Theoretical Degree at Berlin on October 1st, 1781, and was executed by Johann Christian, *Eques a Tarda*, and Franciscus Wilhelmus, *Eques a Castra.* It is to be observed that these titles of symbolical chivalry shewed that the signatories belonged to the Strict Observance. Their use in place of Sacramental Names signifying Rosicrucian initiation serves to indicate that the two Orders were working at that time under some kind of concordat. It corresponded probably to a later arrangement, in virtue of which my own Warrant as a member of the great spiritual chivalry is countersigned by the Supreme Council of the Thirty-third Degree in the particular jurisdiction concerned.

It is said that in virtue of his appointment Schwarz returned to Russia, bearing a new and unheard of teaching —so far as that country was concerned. The objects were (1) to seek the Great Mystery of Perfection; (2) to attain therein all heights accessible to man; (3) to found a new Church which should unify all nations and make peace between all governments.[1] It is affirmed by the anonymous writer that spiritual life in Russia "rose to unknown heights" when Moscow took its place as the heart of the "new teaching." Having discounted this extravagance of language as that of an enthusiasm which betrays its own folly, we shall find some food for reflection in the political aspects of the third clause, and may feel disposed to recognise that the German Rosy Cross had profited by intention at least from the astuteness of Wöllner; that it had a programme to develop in Russia; and that when Catherine of Russia intervened, as she did presently, it

[1] The point is notable, when we remember FAMA FRATERNITATIS and its profession of the faith maintained at that time in Germany and other reformed countries. But we shall see that out of the Rosy Cross in Russia there was produced the idea of an Interior Church as conceived by the mystic Lopukhin.

may be that her action was not apart from knowledge. On the other hand, if we can forget Wöllner, it might seem possible that within the measures of the three clauses there lay expressed rather than concealed a "glorious great intent" belonging to a policy of God, in which case Catherine might have known something, but it was enough to miss the meaning. It would seem meanwhile that Professor Schwarz and his coadjutor went to work in real earnest, for we hear of Rosicrucian Lodges or Temples established at Moscow, Petrograd, Orel, Simbirsk, Mohileff, Vologda and in the ancient city of Yaroslav.

As regards the teaching of the Order, its elementary part, or that of the Lower Degrees, recalls the little that we know of things communicated within the circle of the Golden and Rosy Cross, *post* 1777. There was instruction on the elements in general, or Fire, Air, Water and Earth; on things of the body and on spirits; on Sulphur, Mercury and Salt; on the sperm of all things; on Birth, Death and Resurrection; on the action of Superior Stars; on the generation of metals, on metals and precious stones; on plants and the animal kingdom; on maladies of the human body, mental maladies and those of the soul; and on the perfect state of all things. But there were instructions also on God and Nature, on chaos, on the duties of those admitted to the Inner Temple of the Sciences of Solomon, with extracts from Böhme and other "God-taught" men. We are told also of a printing-press attached to the Degree and of works issued therefrom, such as the RING OF PLATO and SIMPLE INSTRUCTIONS ON PRAYER. The latter spoke of preparing the heart by inner meditation to realise that Christ, like the old Adam, is within us and not without. The Theoretical Degree was called a Rosicrucian School of Nature's Mysteries, for the education of members in love of God and their

Brethren and for the encouragement of the work of charity.

The Kabalah, Magic and practical Alchemy were studied in the Higher Degrees, the Russian writer speculating whether the last was to be understood spiritually. The same question might be raised about all three branches, when we learn that the mystic Lopukhin belonged to the Order, and it is on record that according to him its true mark or seal was that love in which the inner body grows up. His work on the INTERIOR CHURCH[1] appeared at Petrograd in 1798, issuing—as I have suggested in a recent note—from within the secret circle. The speculation sheds strange light on the possible purpose of the Rosy Cross in Russia. According to its own claims, it taught Divine Wisdom, Chemistry as known to science, but also a Divine Chemistry, said to be "unrivalled in its discoveries." That, I take it, was a chemistry of the soul, the transmutation of soul by the Divine Spirit, or there may be a key in the observation of Lopukhin, just quoted, on the growth of the inner body. The reference is to the radiant body of adeptship, about which we have seen that there are intimations in the writings of Thomas Vaughan.[2]

There are vestiges, however, of more direct mystical instruction, as for example in certain intimations concerning

[1] See SOME CHARACTERISTICS OF THE INTERIOR CHURCH, by I. V.; Lopukhin, translated by D. H. S. Nicholson and introduced by myself. 1912. Mr. Nicholson was unacquainted with the fact that the reference to "Novikoff's Society" in his preface was a reference to the Rosy Cross, as he had not met with the Russian's contributions to THE THEOSOPHICAL REVIEW. It may be added that at the time of my collaboration I was in the same position.

[2] See my Introduction to THE WORKS OF THOMAS VAUGHAN, pp. xxxi–xxxv. There are allusions also in SOME CHARACTERISTICS. Lopukhin speaks of love as "the true sign of regeneration in Jesus Christ," adding that it is the soul of the regenerated interior body and that "this soul is manifested in proportion as the body grows."—Chapter IV. Elsewhere he says that it is the body of Jesus Christ which must be "reborn in us."—Chapter V.

a "supernatural state," so-called. The affirmation is that those who attain it are recipients of great mercies and exceptional gifts from God. "It is not possible to express the outpouring of love and beatitude which flows down upon them. . . . They become sensible of Christ and find union with Him and with the Holy Spirit. . . . They receive God and His peace." It is said also that in their liberation from the animal creature they forget—as it were—their embodiment and the sense of self is not with them. "They are transfigured into Christ; they are as one spirit with Him, annihilated in God, even in the depth of His being. . . . Henceforth their life on earth is a progress towards Heaven only."[1] There is some advice as to the means of reaching this state. Supposing that the record is one of aspiration towards attainment rather than a memorial thereof, it remains of great importance as to object and intention. It is expressed, however, in the terms of experience and may be compared with the substance of another memorial, which affirms that Christ, operating through faith, brings us to birth as Sons of Light. "In such light we communicate with Father and with Son, as well as with each other."[2] The Son manifested within us by the Father is described as "the source of water flowing into the eternal womb." There is also the following invocation. "Brethren, we call you into the holy union, into the communion with Holy Ones who are in the true light . . ., the Fire-Ring of Loving Intelligence." The hearers of this address were reminded that the life

[1] A more direct teaching of the purely mystical kind than is met with in—I think—any other published memorial of the Rosy Cross.

[2] There are similar intimations in Lopukhin's SOME CHARACTERISTICS. Compare also the hints scattered here and there through the strange account of a Hidden Temple in the PHILADELPHIAN TRANSACTIONS. I should add that the MS. quoted in my text is or was preserved in the Petrograd Imperial Library, MSS. Section, O, III, 63. It is described as Masonic, but belongs obviously to the archives of the Rosy Cross.

of sense is temporal and comparable as such to the strings of a lute, "which vibrate only so long as the hand strikes." It would seem therefore that the *adepti* if not the initiators of the Rosy Cross in Russia were " mystic citizens of the eternal kingdom," whether or not their charter was signed by the crafty and time-serving Wöllner.

I proceed now to the Rite itself in its working, so far as the information in the memorial can be harmonised and drawn together. The headquarters—otherwise the Directory of the Order—were located at Moscow, presumably in a Lodge called *Eparchy*, which represented an union of all circles of the Rosy Cross in Russia. The question of headship is not a little complicated according to the piecemeal accounts. It appears that Schwarz died in 1784 at the age of thirty-three years.[1] The leadership of the Theoretical Degree was then assumed by a Directory, which was responsible to Wöllner and another German Rosicrucian, named Theden, who is not more particularly described. I learn from independent sources that he was a surgeon at Berlin, of whom it is said that he " tried to catch falling stars, believing that from their substance might be distilled the *prima materia*, a tincture for universal use."[2] In any case he was one of the secret heads who had charge of the Russian branch represented by Schwarz, when alive, at Moscow and at Berlin by Wöllner. The Directory was apparently constituted on April 30, 1784, " by order of the High

[1] He is said to have been buried in a church in Otchakov, close to the altar. He affirmed on his death-bed that he had been judged and found without guilt, wherefore he asked those about him to take part in his gladness. Only a very high state of attainment could warrant such a conviction ! It is said that in 1820 a meeting was held at Moscow to commemorate his services. The expressed sentiment was that the teacher was still present in the grace of his influence.

[2] See Gilbert Stanhope : A Mystic on the Prussian Throne, 1912, p. 128.

Teachers." The three chosen leaders gave each other their hands and swore loyalty to the Order, "having prayed on their knees to the Triune God." Their names in full, with their chivalrous denominations in the Strict Observance were: (1) Nicolaï Novikoff, *Eques ab Ancora*; (2) Prince Nicolaï Troubetzkoï, *Eques ab Aquila Boreali*; (3) Pierre Taticheff, *Eques a Signo Triumphante*. The secret name of Novikoff in the Rosicrucian Order was *Colomir*. It would seem that when the Charter was issued he was admitted at once into the highest Degrees. It is impossible to adjust dates, and they are few and far between in the narrative, but there was a time subsequently when the famous Baron Schröder[1] was Wöllner's delegate for Moscow, and he would seem to have acquired a position at the head of the whole movement. The fact is challenged, however, by the Russian writer on considerations which are open to criticism, if anything attached to the question.

As regards the Laws or Statutes by which the Directory governed its members, they emerge only here and there, and may be grouped in the following order: (1) Unques-

[1] The reference is to Baron F. J. W. Schröder, 1733–92, whom Masonic writers connect with a Rectified Rose-Croix, possibly an occult version of the Eighteenth Degree, possibly another attempted reformation of the German Rosy Cross. He was concerned with Alchemy and Magic. But in all probability it is a confused reference to his connection with the Order of 1777. Baron F. L. Schröder, his brother, was Provincial Grand Master of the Provincial Grand Lodge of Lower Saxony at Hamburg. See my NEW ENCYCLOPÆDIA OF FREEMASONRY, II, 28. As regards the delegate of Wöllner, the anonymous Russian tells us (1) that a time came when he fell deeply; (2) that he was led astray by many temptations; (3) that Novikoff thwarted his financial schemes; (4) that Schröder seems to have attempted reprisals; (5) that Koutouzoff, a high Mason and pupil of Wöllner at Berlin, warned the Russian Rosicrucians to suspend relations with the former delegate, who ultimately left Russia; (6) that Catherine received news of his death in 1792, when Novikoff was in prison; and (7) that he admitted in his will having deceived the Rosicrucians of Moscow, but in what manner or to what extent does not appear in the story.

tioning obedience was due to the Head of the Order, apart from knowledge concerning him and without asking who he was.[1] (2) Candidates must be approved by the Directory prior to their reception, even the Warden-in-Chief of Petrograd submitting names to Moscow. (3) The existence of the Directory was kept secret from members of lower Grades. (4) The Masonic qualification of Candidates obtained throughout.[2] There were also rules which governed the Theoretical Degree, and these are given *seriatim.* (1) Receptions were in the hands of the Warden, from which it would seem to follow that there was no Master of the Lodge.[3] (2) Before going on leave it was his duty to provide a substitute, pledged to return all papers on demand and to copy none. (3) He was required further to make provisions for the records in case of death. (4) Instructions in the Theoretical Degree were to be read and explained according to the best lights of the Warden. (5) A record was to be kept by the Secretary of everything said and done. (6) At Meetings apart from receptions the Brethren were to take their seats at a table for study, same being covered with a black cloth and having a seven-branched candlestick in the centre. (7) Meetings were to be held monthly. (8) It was laid down that every "pupil"—meaning Candidate—must belong to some branch of the Christian Religion, discharging his duties as such with zeal and earnestness, but shewing tolerance towards all forms of sincere belief.

[1] It will be remembered that a similar stipulation was made by the Asiatic Brethren and may have arisen from the bitter lesson taught by the experience of the Strict Observance, which foundered on the rock of its claim concerning Unknown Superiors.

[2] It follows that there were no Women of the Rosy Cross in Russia. Compare the Rituals of 1777 as regards the Masonic qualification.

[3] The distinction is idle, for the information available does not acquaint us with the Russian term which is rendered as Warden.

The Degrees incorporated by the Rite are set out in a schedule as follows:

THE ROSY CROSS

Degrees	Magical Progression	Titles	Number of Members
1	9	Magi	7
2	8	Masters	77
3	7	Adepts (Probationers)	777
4	6	Majores	788
5	5	Minores	779
6	4	Philosophi	822
7	3	Practici	833
8	2	Theoretici	844
9	1	Juniores	929
			5856

This is the Ritual succession as established by Magister Pianco in THE ROSICRUCIAN UNVEILED and as verified by the various Rituals of the reformation epoch, but it is muddled in respect of the Adept Grades. It will be seen that the Grade number added to its corresponding magical progression always produces the denary, which is therefore the suggested number of the system, but the Grades are nine. There is another Rosicrucian Grade-succession which always suggests eleven but the attained number is ten. As regards the number of members, it seems to me that some items have miscarried in transcription: they differ in any case from those of the German Rosy Cross. By the hypothesis of the symbolism the grace and power of the Order proceeded downward from unity, whereas the Candidate proceeded from unity upward. The Theoretical Degree, of which we hear so much in the memorials, was therefore second in the scheme, and we only learn vaguely of any other being worked in Russia. The first, or that of Juniores, is never mentioned. It is said that in the Fifth

Degree the Candidate partook of Wine and Bread, as in the Holy Eucharist ; that he was anointed and clothed in a kind of priestly garb ; and that he received a name and crest. Of those in the Sixth Degree we are told that they were on the level of angels and that thence upward the whole life was consecrated, as in official religion, meaning life under conventual rule and observing a rule of silence—at least as far as possible. If this is to be understood literally and as obtaining throughout the Order, it is certain that Bischoffswerder and Wöllner carried great dispensations.[1] It seems clear otherwise that there were advancements up to a certain point, for we hear that the conditions were humility, modesty and love of Brethren. Moreover, each member of the " Assembly " was required to be loyal towards the Government, obedient to Superiors, peace-loving as a citizen and an apostle of peace in strife. The reference is to the Theoretical Degree, which appears from the beginning of the account as of great importance in the system : we are told of " that splendid group of high minds, of high souls who bore the humble title."

A writer named Parowky is reported as stating that a terrible pledge was given by every Rosicrucian—namely, to die rather than reveal the Rosy Cross, even under torture. That of the Theoretical Degree was, however, short and simple : " I, N∴N∴, testifying in complete freedom and after due deliberation, do promise hereby (1) to worship the Eternal, Omnipotent Jehovah through all my days ; (2) so far as in me lies, to become acquainted with His wisdom and omnipotence by the study of Nature ; (3) to renounce the vanities of this world ; (4) to promote

[1] We have seen that above the Grade of Adeptus Minor there are practically no particulars of procedure in the Golden and Rosy Cross. We can make no inference therefore as to what was required of Members or what was implied by the Mastery of the Eighth Grade. Novikoff is supposed to have enjoyed the freedom of the whole Rite, but so far from leading a conventual life, he was a husband and father.

whatsoever is profitable for my Brethren, to love them in word and deed and serve them in all their needs; (5) to observe unbroken silence, as God is true and eternal." There are no particulars of the Ceremony, but it required three apartments and a vestibule or place of preparation. The inscription over the first door was KNOW THYSELF, over the second FLY EVIL and over the third SEEK GOOD.[1] There was work about an Altar.

The following additional points may be drawn thus together: (1) The Order was affirmed to come from the East—meaning Palestine—and to have been brought into Scotland by ten Brothers, who are said also to have restored it. It should be observed that this is a variant of the Strict Observance legend, according to which the Knights Templar were preserved and perpetuated by Aumont, the Prior of Auvergne. (2) The connection between the Rosy Cross and Masonry was very close at the time in Russia; the Masonic membership was no doubt comparatively small and the government in a few hands; the important personalities probably belonged to both. (3) The Directory at Moscow seems to have exercised jurisdiction over the Johannite or Craft Degrees and Écossais Masonry. (4) The name of Martinism covered both activities in the profane or popular world—as we have seen. (5) According to M. V. Longuinoff, one of the biographers of Novikoff, the Chief of the Ninth or Highest Rosicrucian Degree was one of the Seven Magi, or Magus Major, but we know that Magus was the title of every member in this exalted position. It is said of one of them that he was born in Venice and lived in Egypt; but this

[1] It is conceivable that counsels like these which to us are commonplaces of spiritual life may have signified differently and even perhaps deeply when they were set up in Russia accompanied by great claims. There seems no question that Martinism, Masonry and the Rosy Cross came with glad tidings to Petrograd and Moscow, like a spirit of life breathing on bones of formalism, speaking of liberation and light dawning in the heart.

is doubtless to be understood symbolically, there being various emblematical or mythical locations for the different Degrees. The name ascribed to the personality in question is Lucianus Rinaldus de Perfectis, but this is a mystical title belonging to the Ninth Degree. The nine Chiefs are represented as living in Cyprus, Palestine, Mexico, Italy, Persia, Germany, India and England, but according to Magister Pianco they were to be found in Egypt, Persia, Venice, Madrid, London, Amsterdam and Cologne. None of the ascriptions can be taken literally. THE ROSICRUCIAN UNVEILED tells us that it is explained orally why they are scattered through the world.[1] Other allocations, which are many, stand at the same value and are explicable in the same manner.

Such is the story of the Rosy Cross in Russia, the only country in which it was enabled to illustrate the thesis that it was *fons et origo* of ancient Freemasonry by having Masonry under its wing.[2] There was, however, a Nemesis on the threshold. On April 21, 1792, the Empress Catherine II issued an ukase for the arrest of Novikoff. We are told that Lopukhin and Tourgureff burned their papers at night, as also Prince Troubetzkoï—the latter at his country seat. There is no need to say that the central book-collection was also seized. The accused himself is described as almost in a dying state when the blow fell, but his young nephews are supposed to have carried off the " dangerous " secret documents, and very few things were found. It could not have been an unexpected blow, for Novikoff had been examined previously—though only as to the Christian

[1] Magister Pianco's entire scheme of Rosicrucian Grades, their titles, symbols, sacramental names and places of distribution will be found in my SECRET TRADITION IN FREEMASONRY. See the folding diagram facing p. 218 of the second volume, to which I have referred on p. 456.

[2] The reference is perhaps more especially to Johannite and Écossais Grades, but it would include the Strict Observance, supposing that this was at work.

Creed and his position respecting it—by the Metropolitan Archbishop Platon, who told Catherine in writing that " he wished there might be, all the world over, such Christians as Novikoff." The process began and was directed nominally against the Martinists, but we are told that it was not formal and that no judgment was passed. Certain people were banished to their country estates after written examinations and were threatened in the event of their leaving them or inducing others to join " the evil sect." The German Lodges are said to have continued undisturbed: in a word, according to the anonymous Russian, everything proves that the Empress feared Novikoff alone. We learn also the reason. It is said that " Catherine sought to discover the measure of her heir's engagements to Masonry, and the test question to Novikoff was therefore : " What were your relations with a certain person of high rank ? " That person was the Grand Duke Paul, afterwards Paul I. The desired information was not obtained, and on May 17 or 18 Novikoff was taken secretly to " the living tomb " of the Schlüsselburg Fortress, being condemned to fifteen years' imprisonment, though the sentence was not signed by the Empress till August 8. His fate was shared voluntarily by his doctor—Michail Bagriansky—and by his valet. Those who are concerned must be referred to my original for the story of this imprisonment, and of things connected therewith and arising therefrom. It ended on November 6, 1796, with the death of Catherine and the succession of Paul I, who threw open the doors of the prison. That the new Emperor was indeed a Mason, if not also a member of the Rosy Cross, there is perhaps no need to say. His roposition was therefore one of full liberty for the Masonic Lodges and their work. It is suggested that he might even have taken the Office of Grand Master, but there were other interests at work. He became instead Grand Master of the Order of Malta, and to Masonry he was lost.

The story of the Rosy Cross in Russia ends at this point, so far as my records are concerned, but the life of Novikoff continued till July 31, 1818, when "he passed away peacefully" in his seventy-fourth year. He had seen an interdict laid on all Masonry in 1797 by his Imperial Liberator. He had seen the ban removed in part and in brief—or so the story goes—by the Czar Alexander. We know that suppressions of this kind do not kill institutions which have anything vital in them: they disappear from public gaze and find a place in catacombs or in the very crypts of palaces. After the greater light on the further side of mortality had dawned upon the soul of Novikoff, or in 1822, there followed a more rigid and much more prolonged interdict on all the Secret Rites; but there can be no one so unwary as to say that from the year mentioned and onward to 1916 there was no Masonry at work in Russia. And in whatsoever places of hiddenness there was also and remained the Russian Rosy Cross. I have had reports concerning it by word of mouth, testifying to a time when it reposed in the bosom, so to speak, of certain families, as if it were a family tradition, a skeleton in the cupboard of certain noble houses, a secret abiding under their armorial bearings. I have had reports of it later still, also by word of mouth, and according to these some branch or phase or remnant was subsisting under a rose of many petals in Petrograd, prior to the War. In both cases, so far as I am justified in surmising, it had degenerated once again into the occult activities of old, presumably the so-called astral workings. It is highly probable that it had outlived all interest and all consequence, but in some sense or other it remained and may rise again out of its ashes when the present reign of terror is over.[1]

[1] There are said to be Rosicrucian documents in the Petrograd Library and in the Roumianzeff Museum at Moscow, which contains also various letters of Novikoff.

CHAPTER XX

ENGLISH ROSICRUCIANISM OF THE NINETEENTH CENTURY

So far as this work has proceeded the Woman of the Rosy Cross has scarcely been met with therein. The possibilities of her membership, her qualifications, if any, have not emerged for consideration. It would appear as if they had not so much as occurred to the mind of the original Brotherhood, though the Lady Lucifera and her trains of radiant virgins were *personæ* of manifold importance in the dramatic pageant of the CHEMICAL NUPTIALS, and though it follows from the Laws of 1710 that a Brother in wedlock could work on alchemy with his wife. When the Golden and Rosy Cross laid out a private plan to take all Masonry for its province, providing Unknown Superiors as inscrutable as those of the Strict Observance, its rule of Masonic qualification would have put up a barrier to the initiation of both sexes, supposing that such a question arose, but there is not the least evidence or indeed likelihood that it did. On antecedent and *a priori* considerations there was something to be said against the exclusion of women from the peculiar mysteries of the Order, for in the traditional history of alchemy—not to speak of the fraudulent ascriptions of certain texts—there was Miriam the sister of Moses and there was Mary the Egyptian, both of whom had attained the Grade of Adeptship. We are now brought into touch with another method of procedure, appealing also to tradition, and with presumably another branch of the Rosicrucian Mystery, emerging not unfitly from a past which gives up no clue as to its genesis, connections or history. On September 12 in the year 1794 a certain Comte de Chazal, then resident or sojourning in the district of Pampelavuso, Isle of Mauritius, received Dr. Sigismund Bacstrom, who is known otherwise to Hermetic students, into a *Societas Roseæ Crucis*, personally and on the spot, by what is known as the mode of communication. The record of this admission remains in the form of an undertaking or certificate, signed by the neophyte and countersigned by his initiator over the seal of the Society. It is a remarkable document from several points of view, and I proceed to summarise its contents with reasonable fullness, under the following heads.

On the historical side of the subject, it affirms (1) that the Society is most ancient, most learned and comprises investigators of Divine, Spiritual and Natural Truth; (2) that in the year 1490 it separated from the Freemasons; (3) that it reunited subsequently and formed one spirit with the Masonic Brotherhood; (4) that at this time the Society assumed the denomination of *Fratres Roseæ Crucis*. These statements are substantially identical with those of Magister Pianco, in THE ROSICRUCIAN UNVEILED, concerning the Magical Brethren. At the end of the eighteenth century they seem to have obtained a kind of traditional value by repetition from mouth to mouth. The fact that they were countenanced and advanced by and under the authority of some given branch of the Rosicrucian Order offers no evidence that they were in vogue prior to the first printed work in which they were presented, nor does it signify that the branch in question was producing an intentionally fraudulent history. It was an utterly uncritical period, so far as occultism and its personalities were concerned, and it seems possible that people, otherwise of sincere minds, invented traditional histories because certain things seemed explicable along such lines, especially in regard to supposed

Secret Tradition and the mode of its transmission through centuries. They expressed them in terms of certitude, because they came to believe in them on their own part, amidst all their contradictions and notwithstanding all unlikelihood.

It follows otherwise from the document (1) that the Society was concerned solely and only with the work of physical alchemy; (2) that it pretended to the possession of secret knowledge on this subject; (3) that it pledged its members not only to keep its secrets sacred but any discoveries of their own connected therewith; (4) that those who entered the Order undertook to make a beginning in the Great Work as soon after as circumstances, health, opportunity and time permitted; (5) that this beginning was to be made with their own hands and was not therefore to be deputed; (6) that every individual discovery relating to the Great Work must be communicated to that Brother who was nearest at hand; (7) that if it should please God to permit of the Great Work being accomplished by a member with his own hands, the same should give thanks to God, should do and promote all possible good to others and be dedicated himself to the pursuit of true and useful knowledge; (8) that it was most especially forbidden to administer *Aurum Potabile* to any person infected with venereal disease; and (9) that every member was pledged on his admission never to give the Fermented Metallic Medicine for transmutation—not even a single grain—to any person unless that person was an initiated and received Brother of the Rosy Cross.

It will be seen that this branch of the Order, like the Golden and Rosy Cross of 1777, gave certain instructions to its members, who were left to work them out; if they came to any good by so doing, the Society was to share in the result; if they failed, on the other hand, there was no undertaking on the part of the Society to instruct them further or to extricate them from any difficulties consequent on the cost of experiment. In this case, as in two others that have preceded, my conclusion is that the Society existed to exploit the wits and industry of the rank and file of Brethren, hoping that in this manner the Great Work might be in fine accomplished within the secret circle and redound to its everlasting credit.[1] The occult fool is still extant, however, and I may as well register briefly his inevitable counterview. He will believe that all these branches of the Rosy Cross had true Masters ruling in the inmost circle ; that they were in possession of the Metallic Medicine and the Elixir Vitæ ; but at the same time and rightly they promised nothing to their neophytes but that which might result from their own industry, guided, however, from above. This reservation notwithstanding, in the case of a properly prepared and truly deserving novice, discovered to be such by the unerring illumination of the Masters, these latter in their perfect compassion did so guide their elect children, so lead them from point to point of instruction, that at a right and proper time the mastery was in fine attained by them. My answer is : *Quod erat demonstrandum demonstratum non est.* In other words, the evidence for this view is in the folly of the belief which prompts it, for other witness there is none. I might as reasonably advance on my own part that the Golden and Rosy Cross, and the particular *Societas* now under consideration were secret political centres—working, e.g. for universal revolution—and that they derived their revenues from the subscriptions of Hermetic enthusiasts, whom they led to expect great things without actually promising them. There is again no evidence and antecedently in both

[1] It is obvious that the personal claims of Comte de Chazal are opposed to this view, but there is no evidence that, however genuinely held, they represented truth in fact. The best comment upon them is that the Count received his income from Bordeaux, as we shall see.

cases there is no likelihood. My own hypothesis of quest is in harmony with the facts on record, as also with the probability of things, while it saves the several associations from that charge of flagrant imposture which would be the resource of extreme criticism. An intimate study of the documents leads me to conclude that there is something which calls to be saved from aspersions of this kind, for however unconvincing they are in various and several respects, it is impossible not to recognise a heart of sincerity at their root. This is eminently the case with the Rituals of 1777, but it is the case also with the Bacstrom Certificate, countersigned by de Chazal.

The position of the association in respect of official religion and political matters is indicated by the following undertakings on the part of Novices : (1) That they would not build churches, chapels or hospitals ; (2) That they would not establish public charities, there being already a sufficient number of such institutions, if only they were regulated efficiently; (3) That they would provide no salary for a priest or churchman as such, thereby tending to make him yet more proud and insolent; (4) That if they relieved any worthy clergyman in distress they were to regard him in the light of a private person only;[1] (5) That they would not assist or support with gold or silver any king, potentate or government whatsoever, save only by payment of taxes ; (6) That they would not help any popular movement or private cabal in revolt against any government; (7) That they would leave public affairs in the hands of God, Who will bring to pass the events foretold in the Apocalypse of *St. John*, which events are even now in the course of rapid fulfilment. It will be seen that the old Second Advent thesis recurs herein.

[1] The Order in that branch with which de Chazal was connected seems to have been militantly anti-clerical : it would be difficult to think that its certificates in Russia embodied such requirements.

There are three further points which call for particular notice. (1) The Bacstrom Certificate defines the Brethren of the Rosy Cross as a Company of those who believe in the great atonement made by Jesus Christ on the Rosy Cross, described as "stained and marked with His blood," for the redemption of spiritual natures. This determines the judgment of a branch of the Order on the significance of its own symbol as formulated in the last years of the eighteenth century. It does not explain, however, in virtue of what necessity an association of physical alchemists should be incorporated under the bond of Christian faith. Supposing that metals can be transmuted by a chemical process it is difficult to credit that a Jew, as Jew, is incapable of performing the experiment with success. It seems to follow either that the Brethren of the Rosy Cross arrogated to themselves a special and divine election to the *ars magna* of secret chemistry by reason of their Christian faith or that behind and beyond the physical work there was one of a spiritual nature which could only be performed in Christ.

(2) It is especially laid down that the Order does not exclude a worthy woman from initiation and on the contrary will not hesitate to receive her as an Apprentice, or even as a practical member and master, if she possesses the work practically and has herself accomplished it. The reasons given are: that there is no distinction of sexes in the spiritual world, whether among blessed angels or rational spirits of the human race; that redemption was manifested to mankind by means of the Blessed Virgin; that salvation—"which is of more value infinitely than our whole Art"—is granted to the female sex as well as to the male; that Semiramis Queen of Egypt, Miriam the prophetess and Peronella the wife of Nicolas Flamel are believed to have been all possessors of the Great Work; and lastly that Leona Constantia, Abbess of Clermont, was

actually received into the Order as a practical member and "master" in the year 1736. If we take the last statement for a moment at its face value and the date as it stands, the year 1736 would mark a period prior to any probable connection between Freemasonry and the Rosy Cross, all later claims notwithstanding. No Masonic qualification was therefore required, and—as shewn already—there was no reason why women should be excluded. Whether or not the story of Leona Constantia is a mere legend or pious fiction, there came a time when the only known Rosicrucian Order of 1736 passed under the Masonic ægis and *ipso facto* would have ceased to receive women. But in 1794 it was just emerging from the alembics of the French Revolution, and notwithstanding its claim on Masonic connection *ab origine*, it may have dropped the Masonic qualification. It seems a tolerable hypothesis therefore that the *Societas Roseæ Crucis*, as represented by one of its "worthy members" then located at Mauritius, was another development of the Golden and Rosy Cross. We shall see, however, that if in such case it had abandoned Masonic qualifications it had also abandoned Ritual, and this strains the hypothesis.

(3) There was a promise on the part of every member that—for the benefit, as it is observed, of worthy men—each of them before he departed this life would instruct one or at the most two persons in the secret knowledge, he or they being worthy, upright, well-meaning and desirous of secret science; that he would also initiate and receive him or them into the Society as members or apprentices, after the same manner that he had been received himself. It is obvious that this undertaking connotes a pre-Ritual period of the Order, such as may have corresponded to the procedure of 1710, or even earlier. There are traces also in general alchemical history of the Secret Art being perpetuated in this manner from Master to chosen pupil.

The *Societas Roseæ Crucis* was obviously securing its transmission from age to age. It may be noted in this connection that Sigismund Bacstrom promised in the tenth clause of his undertaking ever to remember with gratitude that worthy friend and Brother by whom he had been initiated and received, to respect and " oblige " him so far as lay in his power, after the same manner as, on his own part, he who had admitted him was pledged to some earlier Brother who had received himself. My conclusion is that the Comte de Chazal belonged to a branch of the Order which is not to be identified with the Golden and Rosy Cross, as the latter existed in 1777 ; its root may perhaps be referable to the system of which Sigmund Richter became the spokesman in his work on the Philosophical Stone, or to some still earlier development.

There is one word more on the document and it arises out of the manner laid down for the examination of persons who called themselves Brothers of the Rosy Cross. It does not appear that vouchers of initiation were carried in the form of a particular jewel or cross, or that certain formulæ were interchanged as a test of status. The claimant was called upon to shew (1) a precise explanation of the Universal Fire of Nature ; (2) of the Rosicrucian magnet for attracting and magnifying this fire under the form of a salt ; (3) adequate acquaintance with the work of the Order ; and (4) knowledge of the universal dissolvent, including the use thereof. The inference is that at least some further acquaintance with these secret things was communicated to the neophyte, or he was put in the way of attaining them at an early period of his novitiate. Were it a tolerable hypothesis—which I do not indeed think—to advance that such arcana call to be understood allegorically, then the meaning concealed behind them would be that which he was taught or was at least led to discover, and thereon in his turn he would test the claimants whom he met. Till the eve and night before the French Revolution gave place to its tempestuous dawn, the eighteenth century had been an age of errant adepts, of professional masters and claimants to the Rosy Cross in many a land and city. The cataclysm swallowed up the last generation, and the memorial dated from Mauritius is like a solitary survival.

As to the whereabouts, if still extant, of the original Bacstrom Certificate I have no knowledge. I am acquainted with two copies, in manuscript, one belonging to the year 1842 and in my possession, while the other has passed through my hands. Included with the first in the same volume there is a separate manuscript, entitled ANECDOTES OF LE COMTE DE CHAZAL, F∴R∴C∴ and containing what I presume to be the only available particulars concerning him. It should be explained that the title is a device of the scribe who made the copy and that the document comprises a single letter of considerable length, addressed by Dr. Sigismund Bacstrom to a correspondent, named Alexander Tilloch, who had asked for particulars concerning the late Louis de Chazal. I propose to summarise in full that which was furnished, premising that the content of the letter forms a consecutive narrative.

(1) The acquaintance with de Chazal began in Mauritius. (2) He is described as the most learned as well as the most opulent man in the island, his landed estate and other property being worth three million Spanish piastres, though he followed no profession or business. (3) He is said to have educated a hundred orphan girls and to have provided them with marriage dowries totalling another million piastres. (4) His more private charities were also very numerous. (5) As to the source of his revenues, he received annually considerable sums from Bordeaux. (6) Dr. Bacstrom affirms that he had inspected a manuscript in the Count's autograph, containing an account of his experiments and cures by means of animal magnetism,

electricity and galvanism. (7) Though resident at the time in Mauritius he was cognisant of all that took place in Paris during the horrors of the French Revolution, including the execution of the French King and Queen, while all communication was suspended between France, Mauritius and the adjacent island of Bourbon. (8) He kept a journal of that which he saw or learned, and its accuracy was verified twelve months after when news from Europe was brought by an American ship. (9) Bacstrom was introduced to de Chazal by Dr. Petit Radel, a learned Parisian physician who escaped the guillotine by flight, leaving all that he possessed behind him, so that he was now secretly supported by the Count. (10) Bacstrom paid three visits to de Chazal, the last of which extended over eight days. (11) He became an intimate friend, inspected his rich collection of gold medals, precious stones, philosophical, astronomical and mathematical instruments, his library and laboratory. (12) De Chazal informed him that he possessed the *Lapis Philosophorum* and also the Animal Stone. (13) The text at this point is doubtful, but I understand it to mean that he owed to the one all the wealth at his command and to the other his robust health at the age of ninety-seven. (14) The Count kept the best table in the island, and one day after dinner he took Bacstrom into his laboratory and caused him to perform in his presence an alchemical experiment, under his supervision and direction, as a result of which there was produced (*a*) gold of thirty carats, but exceedingly brittle; (*b*) most glorious, soft and ductile gold of twenty-four carats; (*c*) a gold of yet more glorious colour, somewhat heavier than the former. (15) The memorial relates further that Comte de Chazal found by frequent conversations that Bacstrom was acquainted with the theory of the *Lapis Philosophorum* and with the classic writers on alchemy. (16) He therefore initiated him and then communicated his practical labours. (17) Bacstrom "wrote down from his mouth" the whole procedure of the *Lapis Animalis*, there being five or six different methods, all leading to the same end. (18) The Count affirmed that *Lapis Animalis* was the easiest of all works; that it was best elaborated by Nature alone, apart from artificial heat, because the subject was so extremely tender; that he had succeeded in his first attempt during the second year after his arrival at Port Louis; and that in proceeding he had followed the instructions which he had received in Paris, *anno* 1740. (19) Finally, the Count offered Bacstrom 30,000 Spanish dollars if he would prolong his stay for a year, "in order to work the process once more from the beginning." (20) Whether or not Bacstrom was a ship's doctor does not explicitly appear, but it is said that he dared not comply, having orders from the President of the Colonial Assembly to go on board the *Harriet* (Captain Daddy), bound for New York. (21) At this news, it is added that the worthy old man wept like a child and lamented that he had not been introduced to him three months sooner. (22) Subsequently he mustered up all the money there was in the house, amounting to about three hundred dollars, and begged Bacstrom to accept it as a small token of his sincere friendship. (23) It remains only to add that the Comte de Chazal was married and that Madame la Comtesse is mentioned once during the course of the narrative.

The letter of Sigismund Bacstrom is dated March 16, 1804, and concludes by assuring his correspondent that it contains practically all that he can remember of his different conversations with him who was his father in alchemy. The next question before us is to ascertain what is possible concerning the pupil who became under such exceptional circumstances a neophyte of the Rosy Cross. It happens that he wrote much upon alchemy, and I have met with amateurs of the art who prized his texts, but the devotion paid to them was entirely of a private kind, among a few who had secured copies, for so far as I am able to trace not a line of them has entered into print. The Rev. W. Alexander Ayton, the student part of whose life was spent among the rarities of all occult literature, but perhaps especially of alchemy, had not only an intimate acquaintance with the Bacstrom manuscripts but had attempted to follow some of their practical processes—without success, however, as there should be no need to say. His transcripts passed into hands where it has proved impossible to follow them ; but there are others, I believe, if not the original autographs, which are somewhere in theosophical keeping and are said to be jealously guarded. One does not get further commonly in this kind of quest, but the fact may be registered with detachment, as any possible importance would be only of the textual kind, and we have texts enough and to spare against any future experiment in decoding the symbolism or separating the wheat from the chaff in the *chaos magnum* of the literature.

It is doubtless unnecessary to add that biographical dictionaries do not concern themselves with Sigismund Bacstrom and that I have found no allusion to him in the ordinary or extraordinary sources of reference in occult literature, with the sole exception of THE ROSICRUCIAN AND MASONIC RECORD, but that is by derivation from the Certificate countersigned by de Chazal, which I printed *in extenso* over thirty years ago. It is barely possible that a DIARY OF A ROSICRUCIAN PHILOSOPHER, which I once transcribed from a copy in the autograph of Frederick Hockley may have been drawn from the Bacstrom manuscripts. It belongs to the year 1797 and contains very curious notes on diurnal proceedings in a laboratory undertaken for the purposes of the Great Work. The text is accompanied by crude diagrams of an explanatory kind, but it breaks off abruptly, leaving the experiments unfinished. I suppose that believers—if any at this day—in the occult arts and especially of those branches represented by the Hockley collections would aver that the adept was brought to a pause of necessity by the fact that subsequent to his last entry he accomplished the *Magnum Opus*, and could therefore put nothing in writing. The evidence for this is like the evidence for the assertion in the title—that the Diary was actually that of a Rosicrucian Philosopher. It may be added that there was a William Bacstrom, who also appears to have been concerned in occult activities, but whether he was related to Sigismund there is no means of knowing.

It is to be presumed that the communication which has been summarised here at length was written in England to a correspondent who was also in England, and as I have no doubt whatever that the Bacstrom Certificate is a genuine document of its period, it follows that a Brother of the Rosy Cross was resident in these islands at the beginning of the nineteenth century. Moreover, as an earnest alchemist, student and operator of the art he would have fulfilled the simple conditions imposed upon him at his reception into the particular branch of the Order: in other words, he would have appointed his successor. A transmission could have been established in this manner, but there is of course no evidence that it was.

To the period of Bacstrom there belongs the Baal Shem of London, Dr. Samuel Jacob Falk, a Kabalist who claimed to possess thaumaturgic powers, and is rumoured to have been connected with some association or brotherhood, the name and nature of which do not emerge. On such authority as this the makers of myth have integrated him in the Rosicrucian Order.[1] He appears to have died in 1782.[2]

[1] See a most explicit statement to this effect in Westcott's HISTORY OF THE SOC. ROS., p. 5.

[2] See Abbé Fournier, p. 84, for an account of Dr. Falc (or Falk) in England. He states that some people regarded him as Chief of all the Jews and his ministry as purely political.

He is a subject of reference in the important Rainsford Papers, to which I shall advert immediately; but General Rainsford—whose record they are—remained in doubt whether he was a knave or not, though his banker's son at the Hague testified that he was not only a profound Kabalist but a very holy man.[1] There was also—according to Kenneth Mackenzie—a certain Cain Schenul Falk, otherwise Dr. Falcon,[2] who is represented as possibly or probably distinct from the former and as living in London *circa* 1788. Either he or his son Johann Friedrich Falk is affirmed to have been the head of a Kabalistic College and to have died about 1824.[3] He is included by Kenneth Mackenzie among known members of the Rosy Cross, the warrants being wanting as usual. Occultists and Masonic speculators in the past and now have failed to realise that the Rosy Cross was a Christian Order always and only; the Jew, therefore, had no place in its ranks, whatever his qualifications as a Kabalist and whatever his thaumaturgic powers. It remained for spurious High Grade Masonry, drawing unawares from Rosicrucian sources in the Eighteenth Degree, to cast out the essential Christian elements from the Rose-Croix of Heredom for the admission of Jews and Deists.

The Rosicrucian allusions in the Rainsford Papers[4] are comparatively few, but they serve to establish the following points: (1) That General Rainsford was on the quest of the Rosy Cross, understood presumably as an occult and magical Order; (2) That he was evidently received into a Society of this kind, the particulars of place and time being alike wanting; (3) That there is some ground for inferring that his admission took place in London; (4) That in 1785

[1] See Chevalier de Rampson: MÉMOIRES, for a Falk reference and some curious details.

[2] The Baal Shem of London was known under this name.

[3] The JEWISH ENCYCLOPÆDIA knows nothing of this alleged personality.

[4] See British Museum, Additional MSS, 23644–680.

he was apparently attached to something of the same kind then working in Paris and made use of its cipher on one occasion; (5) That the English society is referred to under the denomination R∴Cru∴✡; (6) That in this case it was probably working the scheme of Degrees adopted at the German reformation of 1777; (7) That some German Notes on Alchemy, entitled *Instructio et Manipulatio ex Ordinatione et Concordia Fratrum*, were signed by Rainsford with the Mystic Name *Spheræ fondus in Salis*, which is not translatable but belongs to a high Grade of the Rite in question; (8) That in a letter written at Harwich in October, 1782, he mentions having met with certain Hebrew MSS. at Algiers, and that they related to the Society of Rosicrucians, "which exists at present under another name with the same forms"; (9) That he refers on another occasion to a *respectable, honorable et très vénérable Fraternité*. This is the sum of the allusions, and they leave no doubt in my mind that the writer was received into some branch of the Golden and Rosy Cross. We know by the evidence of one of its Adept Rituals that a variation of the German Rite was extant in France prior to the Revolution, and it is possible that there was an English branch, but our sole source of information on the subject is the single Rainsford reference, unfortunately of the vaguest kind. It is impossible to base even the most tentative hypothesis on such an allusion.

We do not meet with any further reference to the Order in England till the year 1836, when Godfrey Higgins published ANACALYPSIS, in the course of which he remarks that he had not sought admission among Rosicrucians or Templars, because it would involve pledges which might be detrimental to his work of research. It has been concluded by unwise speculation that a branch of the old Order was at that time established in England, but there is no evidence for the view. The Templars cited in the passage were the Masonic Order of that denomination, and the legitimate inference is that the Rosicrucians were the Knights Rose-Croix, whom we know to have been at work at the period both within and without the jurisdiction of a Supreme Council, otherwise of the Scottish Rite. Alternatively, Higgins may have referred to the Rosy Cross connected with the Royal Order of Scotland. He was a Craft Mason, acquainted with Masonic activities, and there is the fullest evidence in his writings that he had no canon of distinction between things which differed from one another, though they passed under the same name. A typical case in point is the Masonic Knights Templar, whose descent from the old chivalry was accepted implicitly by Higgins. It remains to say that those who have put forward the counter-view, talking glibly of a Rosicrucian College ruled by a Magus and conferring Degrees during the first half of the nineteenth century, on the authority of Godfrey Higgins, are persons whose opinion on any question of scholarship or ordinary research can be set aside at once and utterly.

Before proceeding to the final concern of the present chapter it is interesting and curious to note that about 1860, and in Manchester above all places, there flourished a Rosicrucian Brotherhood for a considerable number of years. The particulars verifiable concerning it are, however, (1) that it was an Antiquarian Society, without pretensions of any kind; (2) that the only mystery concerning it is its choice of the particular name; (3) that it met at the houses of members; (4) that its convocations were called chapters; (5) that reports of its activities appeared occasionally in THE MANCHESTER GUARDIAN, one explanation being (6) that the editor of this newspaper, John Harland, belonged to the Brotherhood; (7) that it was concerned with topographical, historical, architectural questions and so forth; (8) that it knew and cared nothing for so-called occult sciences and had no views on the legend of Christian Rosy Cross ; (9) that on one occasion at least there was a volume of antiquarian interest published under its auspices ; (10) that its occasional meetings continued till the end of 1869, if not later.

The next event in this country was the foundation of the Masonic Rosicrucian Society, otherwise *Societas Rosicruciana in Anglia*, usually abbreviated by familiars, who speak of it as the *Soc. Ros.* It has been taken over by unfriendly critics and applied in a derisive sense. The chronological story of this institution, with many of its Minutes in abstract, will be found in occasional TRANSACTIONS—S.V. London—at the British Museum. But as regards the circumstances of its origin recourse must be had to two publications issued by the present " Supreme Magus," Dr. W. Wynn Westcott, the first being HISTORY OF THE SOCIETAS ROSICRUCIANA IN ANGLIA, 1900 and the second DATA OF THE HISTORY OF THE ROSICRUCIANS, 1916. It appears from these pamphlets that the *Soc. Ros.* was projected in 1865 and started in 1866 by Robert Wentworth Little, described as originally a clerk at Freemasons' Hall and subsequently Secretary of the Royal Institution for Girls.

The allegations are (1) that Little found and borrowed or abstracted certain papers, containing " Ritual information," preserved in the Grand Lodge Library ; (2) that they had been discovered before him by William Henry White, who was Grand Secretary till 1857 ; (3) that White himself was among " the last survivors " of an English Rosicrucian Society, holding from a Venetian Ambassador to England in the eighteenth century who had " conferred Rosicrucian Grades " on students in England, and the said students had handed " on the rule and tradition to others " ; (4) that according to Dr. Westcott, White " made no use " of the Grand Lodge MSS., but according to another deponent, who will be cited presently, White admitted Little, not apparently by the powers committed to him as an initiate and from "Ritual information" in his own possession but from the papers in Grand Lodge; (5) that this notwithstanding these papers were "imperfect for ceremonial open use"; (6) that on finding them after White's "retirement from office"—as stated by the other deponent—Little called to his assistance Kenneth R. H. Mackenzie, who claimed that when in Germany he had been admitted by some "German Adepts" into certain Grades of a Rosicrucian system and had been licensed to form a group of Masonic students in England, "under the Rosicrucian name."

The critical position of these statements may be summarised thus: (1) There is some slender ground for believing that papers were abstracted from Grand Lodge, because in the month of September, 1871, Matthew Cooke "raised a complaint in Grand Lodge against Masonic officials for discovering, using and removing old MSS. from the Record Rooms of Freemasons' Hall." This is on the authority of Dr. Westcott, who adds that the missing documents were applied to a reconstruction of the Red Cross of Rome and Constantine as well as the foundation of the *Soc. Ros.* It will be observed, however, that Cooke's complaint was about the removal of old MSS., not otherwise specified. If reference to Rosicrucian documents was intended, there is negative evidence that they were not returned to Grand Lodge as they are not to be found therein. They have also disappeared otherwise, as Dr. Westcott tells us that they did not come into the possession of either Supreme Magus in succession to Little, who assumed or received that title in 1866. I should add that the only evidence for Little personally discovering or removing MSS. rests on the second deponent. (2) Dr. Westcott cites a letter from the Rev. T. F. Ravenshaw, once a Grand

Chaplain of England, no information emerging concerning the person to whom it was addressed. It is the authority for the story concerning a nameless Venetian Ambassador, for White as a last survivor of some English Society, for Little's admission by him, and for the alleged papers coming into the possession of Little after White's retirement. But without prejudice to the *bona fides* of Ravenshaw the depositions in this letter admittedly represent explanations made to the writer by Little himself. It follows that the whole story depends on the latter's good faith, and this is the question at issue.[1] (3) As regards Kenneth Mackenzie, his share in the foundation or reconstruction is not mentioned apparently in the record of Ravenshaw. Dr. Westcott tells us that it depends on letters from Mackenzie to himself and Dr. Woodman, the second Supreme Magus. We are again in the same position, reposing on a question of good faith, and in the present case it is precisely and very much at issue. On Rosicrucian subjects at least the record of Kenneth Mackenzie is one of recurring mendacity, a typical instance of which is the Table of Rosicrucian Degrees published in his ROYAL MASONIC CYCLOPÆDIA, for the first time as he states, but it appeared at the close of the eighteenth century in THE ROSICRUCIAN UNVEILED of Magister Pianco, and I have referred to it on previous occasions. It follows therefore—and this is the historical state of the case concerning the *Soc. Ros.* (1) That any representations on Rosicrucian matters made verbally or in writing to any one by Mackenzie must be set aside decisively in the absence of collateral evidence.

[1] Dr. Westcott confuses his own case, either by citing a letter distinct from that of Ravenshaw as "literary extant evidence . . . in possession of the Society," without explaining its source and tenour, or by quoting the Ravenshaw Script at two points of his story, once in the absence of details and once with content summarised. See *loc. cit.*, pp. 6, 7. My inference is that he is alluding to one document, which—as I have shewn above—is not evidential by itself.

But in the case there is none forthcoming. (2) That Little's credentials, if any, reside in the fact that he removed papers from Freemasons' Hall and that there is no evidence of their return. A certain probability attaches to the point of fact, owing to the vague accusation of Matthew Cooke, but there is nothing evidential. (3) That Little's story to Ravenshaw is without probability in itself, is contradicted by Dr. Westcott, and it does not appear that Ravenshaw had opportunity or sought to check the statements. (4) That in 1866 Mackenzie was a Mason only under some foreign and apparently unacknowledged Obedience, and, because of the Masonic qualification enacted from Candidates and Members he could not belong to the Society which according to his unsupported story, he had helped to found. He was made a regular Mason in 1870 and joined the *Soc. Ros.* towards the close of 1872. According to the Minutes, he was proposed on April 11th and "initiated" on October 17th. I gather that Dr. Westcott did not become a member till some time after the death of Little in 1878, and I suggest that Mackenzie's communications to him and Wood. man were subsequent to that date.

Such is the clouded story of the *Soc. Ros.* in respect of its origin. Its history is in the trivial TRANSACTIONS, about which and on the scholarship of early members I gave adequate views in 1888, and there is no need to repeat. The Metropolitan and other Colleges work the scheme of Grades which we know by the Rituals of the Order Reformation in 1777. But they are not those Rituals, nor are they the work of one who has seen them. They are mere vestiges of procedure, a frivolous and childish pretence. Let those who belong to the Society compare their Grades of Philosophus and Adeptus Minor with my summaries of the corresponding German and other Rituals in the present volume.

CHAPTER XXI

A MODERN ROSICRUCIAN ORDER

For a period of about twenty-five years, dating approximately from 1860, the existence of amateur manufactories of Rites in England is made evident by the facts of their output, otherwise by certain successive products, for which all antecedent history is wanting, except in the pseudo-traditional sense, which is that of occult invention. My statement does not signify that in the various coinages produced by the mints in question there was no attempt to collect materials from the past, so that they might make some colourable claim thereon. There were begotten under these circumstances at the beginning of the period in question the Red Cross of Constantine and its appurtenances, laying claim upon archives in the possession of Waller Rodwell Wright—not to speak of the alleged document abstracted from Grand Lodge, as already noted. It does not belong to our subject and is passed over for this reason. Much about the same time there emerged also that Societas Rosicruciana in Anglia with which I have dealt adequately in the previous chapter. The manufactory, mint or studio of Degrees—if I may venture so far to mix and confuse images—was not precisely the same in both cases, but some artificer or alchemist of the one was not absent from the other. Kenneth Mackenzie might be one of the connecting links, and there are other names which it would be possible to quote at need, giving reasons in each case, but again their activities are outside the present issues. I am concerned now with another centre, actuated by very different motives. It was situated in the West of England and connects with the interesting name of Major F. G. Irwin, who in 1863 was Eminent Commander of the William Stuart Encampment and Grand Standard Bearer of the Grand Conclave of Knights Templar. So far as my present purpose is concerned, the record begins in 1874 and there is some evidence that the activity of the people in question went on to the year 1887 at least. Major Irwin began life as a private soldier, but his abilities were such and their recognition also was such that he received a commission in the regiment to which he belonged, an exceedingly rare honour in those days. His name became known to me when I discovered that he was third—so to speak—in a race of collectors concerned with occult manuscripts. The first was Frederick Hockley, who was devoted more especially to magical and alchemical texts, and whose transcripts of less or more documents in a good scribe's hands were illustrated for the most part with seals, sigils, signatures and symbolical drawings, sometimes of a very elaborate kind. The collection thus made by his own skill and industry has become almost historical, but it was unfortunately dispersed at his death in 1887. Most of it was purchased by Walter Moseley, who was thus second in succession and was like his predecessor what is called a practical student; but whereas Hockley appears to have been content with employing clairvoyant subjects, skryers in crystals and persons who could be passed into the magnetic trance, Moseley is said to have tried more dangerous paths. The particulars are vague and as the authority is second-hand, I give it under all reserves, but I have been told that his health was injured seriously by the use of drugs for occult purposes, under the guidance of Paschal B. Randolph, about whom we shall hear in the next chapter but one. It is of course wholly possible that the story is an idle fabrication. As intimated, the third in succession was F. G. Irwin, to whom many Hockley manuscripts passed over by purchase on the death of Moseley. He was a believer in occult arts within the measure of a thinking and reading person of his particular mental class, but for the rest was satisfied apparently with the pursuits of spiritualism, to the truth of which his circle bears witness in unpublished writings. For the rest, it is obvious from all I have ascertained concerning him that he was a zealous and amiable Mason, with a passion for Rites and an ambition to add to their number. He seems to have worked with others of some ability and of some inventive power in these paths, but through lack of education they were uncertain in the use of English and in their ill-starred fascination for Latin formulæ were always at sea.

In the year 1874 it seems to have dawned upon them that the time was at hand to launch upon an unenlightened world the revelations of a new Order of the Rosy Cross, and they saw to it that there should be not only a claim made upon the known past of the subject but upon many centuries behind it. The manuscript which embodies the first experimental draft extends to 383 quarto pages and was begun on December 7 of the year in question. It was called THE STAR RISING IN THE EAST, *or a brilliant Light Revealed unto all men* by S. N. These letters can be construed as one likes into suggestive Latin mottoes, but they happen to be the terminals of an illustrious occult name, that of Thomas Vaughan and even used by him in 1651 on the title-page of AULA LUCIS. Passing onward, the introduction to the manuscript is signed Thomas Vaughan, and his name or initials can be found throughout the text. The intention was therefore to present it as his actual work. In virtue of what ignorance and illiteracy any person could have supposed that this pretence would impose on anyone is beyond apprehension, at least on my part. There is no attempt—colourable or otherwise—to reproduce the manner of seventeenth century writing, for it would have exceeded the capacity of the circle. The bulk of the document consists of feeble disquisition of a sentimental religious kind, teeming with grammatical blunders and orthographic curiosities, interwoven with which are (1) occult theses which betray no grasp of their subject; (2) the long story of an Italian monk who became a Rosicrucian but fell into the hands of the Inquisition and escaped the extreme penalty only by the intervention of the Brotherhood: it is the poorest quality of invention, apart from all verisimilitude; (3) notions on Rosicrucian doctrine, mostly reflections and ridiculous when they are not; (4) a traditional history of the Rosy Cross; and (5) sketches of secret receptions into the Order, including fragments of Ritual, with very indifferent prayers and invocations. The work is accompanied by diagrams and variations of familiar occult symbols. It might seem desirable to dismiss it at this point, but it happens that I have an ulterior purpose in view, apart from which the autograph volume would call for no further reference than a brief bibliographical note. Because of this purpose I proceed to a summary account of the central idea concerning the Rosy Cross and what it is shewn to have been doing in 1874.

It is a most reverend, ancient and sacred Society which has existed for a great space of time in silence and hidden light but it is at last emerging from darkness because of false pretenders. The name of Rosy Cross refers to the sacrifice of Jesus Christ upon the Tree and to the pouring forth of His blood thereon. This sacrifice was typified in all the Ancient Mysteries, and as those who belong to the Order look upon Jesus as the long-expected Messiah—though not apparently as God manifested in flesh—He may be called their Founder, and He it is Who is the Master of the Rosy Cross. He was an Angel of the Third Hierarchy before coming into this world. The origin of the Order is to be sought in Egypt and India, among a body of priest-philosophers who were called Searchers of Light and who pursued the study of theosophy and mystic chemistry under strict pledges of silence, some 1700 years B.C. Candidates for admission into their sanctuaries passed through seven years of preparation. Those who attained the higher Grades were entrusted with all the secret knowledge and were bound to select some worthy person to succeed them in the event of their death. About 800 B.C. this association was established in Greece and later on among the Jews, where the name of Essenes was assumed. When Jesus of Nazareth attained the due age he was received in one of their convents. Some time after the destruction of Jerusalem members were transferred into another Order in Europe, being that of the Rosy Cross, and as time went on men of knowledge and influence entered the ranks. Rumours went abroad concerning them during the course of the fifteenth century, and ultimately their claims were set forth in certain official proclamations. Their object was to unite the Rose and the Cross, to seek the Mountain of Light and to erect a Spiritual Temple thereupon. They were workers also in metals, for the elevation of those which are base into the state of pure gold by means of fire. The process of such transmutation is typical of the search after God and His light, and it is presumably in this sense that the procedure is said to be both physical and spiritual, the alchemy of metals and that of the soul or spirit.

After this manner does the traditional history of the Order—which is apart from all novelty—merge into the quests pursued therein. It is said further that in the fourteenth century it was divided into two sodalities, being (1) Seekers of Theosophical or Divine Knowledge and (2) Seekers of Gold. In the seventeenth century these Brethren assumed the titles respectively of Fratres Aureæ Crucis and Fratres Roseæ Crucis. In the eighteenth century they were unified once more and so remain as the true Order of the Rosy Cross, entirely unconnected with political and other bodies in Germany which have assumed this name and have brought dishonour thereon. There arose also a *Societas Rubeæ Crucis*—otherwise *Rouge Croix*—which adopted the symbolic jewel of the Order in its higher Grades—namely, a pelican in its piety, typical of the Great Mysteries. This was incorporated later on with the Society of Speculative Masons ; but the true Brotherhood of the Rosy Cross has never been merged in any other Society, and by the grace of God will ever maintain its individuality and its secret existence.

Upon what may be called the doctrinal instructions of this mythical Order there is little reason to dwell. There are disquisitions on the Godhead prior to creation, the Trinity in unity, the idea of creation and the development of cosmic order out of the first chaos. There are theses on the soul and immortality, on the experience of death and preparation for life to come. There was also a species of Magia practised by the Brotherhood, concerning which it is said that those who would commune face to face with the denizens of the inner world must prepare themselves according to true rules. The allusion is to those creatures of the elements which are a subject of vague allusion in FAMA FRATERNITATIS, but are treated at large in the tale of the COMTE DE GABALIS. It is on this comic romance rather than on anterior tracts of Paracelsus that the text appears to depend, for the very simple reason that—for the most part—the latter had not been translated in 1874. On this basis, as if on a rock of truth, we are told that the spirits of the elements are kind, beneficent and willing to aid man in his search for knowledge. This is especially the case with those of fire, who are apparently like the letter H in the rhymed apologue: they assist "at his birth and attend him in death"—fire being the hope of the alchemist and a great aid of the magus. For this reason the Order appears to have practised cremation. It is said that at the burial of a Frater R∴C∴ he was received into the communion of fire, his disused garment being laid to rest therein, while "prayers of more than mortal sweetness" were recited over it. Finally, there is much alchemical speculation, but it is the record of persons who are astray in the Hermetic labyrinth and do not know what they say. I pass therefore to the hypothetical scheme of initiation and things leading up thereto.

There are seven cardinal precepts of the Rosy Cross which appertain as much to the preparation of a postulant as to self conduct within the secret circles. They are these, expressed briefly: (1) To be ductile and pure as a child, giving prompt obedience to all lawful commands of Superiors. (2) To eschew unprofitable speculations, especially those of the mystics, or so-called "Watchers for God," and to weigh all things carefully for the attainment of that truth which is the sole object of research. (3) To adore the Great Sun, remembering that a Brother of the Rosy Cross can worship in all Temples, so only that there is no sacrifice of living creatures performed therein. (4) To treat all men in a spirit of gentleness and love, whatever their form of faith. (5) To follow earnestly the quest of light and knowledge, alike in spiritual and material things. (6) To seek the Good and the True in all things and to proclaim it everywhere. (7) When the end of quest has come; when that powder has been found which is priceless above all powders, the elixir which is more than all known medicines—transmuting the base into the pure and evil into good; when the seeker stands at the Gate of Life, let him remember that beyond the darkness of the threshold and the dweller thereby, the glorious light is shining on the Angel of light and glory and the company of the elect. They are the elect of the Rosy Cross; and at their hands shall the seeker receive his guerdon, or otherwise the Grade of Master for him who by his own efforts and their instruction has attained the threshold thereof.

Now, it is said that the New Jerusalem, of the Crown and Fountain of Light, may be compared to a Temple, and it is this Temple which all true Brethren of the Rosy Cross desire to erect on earth, in the grace of the Rose of Sharon. It is represented by the Holy Sanctuary of the Order, wherein the Conventions are held. Wheresoever the Brethren meet for the ceremonial purposes of the Rite is said to be in the City of Jerusalem, under the shadow of the Mount of Olives. It is otherwise an oblong room and comparable therefore to the authorised configuration of a Masonic Lodge. As regards the content of the Rite there are said to be three primary and six secondary Grades, and though only two of them are named—being those of *Magi* and *Magistri*—it is obvious that they are the sequence of the Golden and Rosy Cross as established at the Reformation of 1777, though I should infer that the circle derived them from the shadowy reflection of the SOCIETAS ROSICRUCIANA IN ANGLIA, of which they were aware. It is said also that "the number of the Brethren who meet under the shadow of the Mount of Olives is limited to the progressions of the number three," as e.g. 27, 36, 72, 81, 144, or—as it is added by way of precaution—"a lesser number." The general jewel of the Order is described as an emblem of the Heavenly City; but whereas this is represented descending four-square out of heaven, that is said to have sixteen sides or faces, bearing many characters and emblems which the authors did not "dare" to put on record at the time of writing. Had the scheme gone further they would probably have thought them out. We hear also of a room in reservation for the meetings of Superiors and representing "the Sepulchre of Jesus," where "secret instructions were obtained from the Governing Spirits." It was a place of prayer and meditation, fixed upon the glory of the Eastern Star and on the significance of those mystic letters which are "emblematic of the Divinity of Jesus Christ."

There is neither diagram nor description to indicate the arrangement of the ordinary place of reception, except that it contains an altar, whereon is a White Stone, representing (1) the Spirit of Life, (2) that great Temple which is erected in the Land of Souls, (3) "our Beloved Brother, Master and Saviour Jesus Christ." Like Him, it is "perfect in all its parts" and in correspondence therefore with that state to which every Brother of the Rosy Cross should aspire. There are several sections which claim to be extracted from the Ceremonial of Secret Reception, but their complete chaos represents stages in the manufacture of a Grade, devised by those who were uncertain where to begin or what they might wish to do. To bring something of order out of confusion grounded in incapacity is doing too much honour; but—as I have said—there is a purpose in view, and by a process of sorting and piecing a tentative conspectus of intended procedure may be evolved and left to stand at its value, which is little enough in any ceremonial sense. It is understood that there were certain qualifications required on the part of the Candidate, as for instance, that he should shew himself ready to receive the light.

In this connection we hear of a probationary period, the length of which might be varied according to circumstances. The object was (1) that the current of his life might be made known to the Superior; (2) that his mind and soul should be fitted to receive the teachings; (3) that he might be uplifted by the higher branches of science.

It was essential that he should be free from prejudice and bigotry: otherwise the "terrible negations" of the first instructions might undo him. It is said that the first ceremonial utterances heard by the Candidate are (1) *Deus non est*; (2) *Pax non est*; (3) *Vita non est*; (4) *Omnia vanitas est* (*sic*); (5) *Quod superius est sicut quod inferius*—the last not apparently in the sense of Hermetic correspondence but the identity of good and bad, right and might, vice and virtue, matter and spirit. It may be added, however, that the said negations are an afterthought in the process, reflected from Éliphas Lévi, and that elsewhere there is no trace of them in the initial procedure. One is left unconcerned therefore by the suggestion that they are developed subsequently into higher and nobler teachings, by which the Candidate is led to see "the littleness of his knowledge and of himself." Either the compilers forebore wisely from delineating the kind of instruction because they would have produced a puerility or refrained of necessity because they could produce nothing.

On the day of reception I presume that in the mind of the writers there would be the opening of the Temple according to some ceremonial form, but it does not seem to have been excogitated. We hear of the Candidate when he is already in the presence of the assembled Brotherhood, and he responds *Et cum spiritu tuo* to the *Lux vobiscum* of the Master, pronounced by way of benediction. There is then recited Ps. cxlv; and when it is finished the Master places on the Candidate's head a chaplet of red and white roses, on his shoulders the white robe of the Order, the "mystic cross" upon his breast and in his hand a wand, specified as having peculiar virtue but not otherwise described. The Recipient being clothed in this manner, the Master places his own hand in the middle of the Seal of Solomon—presumably on a pedestal before him—and offers up two prayers in succession, referring to the Sacrifice on Calvary as that essential condition by virtue of which the Rose might be seen of all, for the illumination and refreshment of all, and imploring help to follow in the path of the Master, but most especially in the contest with "priestly bigotry and tyranny." It happens unfortunately that in the zeal "to overturn that power which bars our progress," the fact of a Candidate who, by the hypothesis is also deserving light and liberation, passes altogether out of view and nothing is besought of the Almighty in his respect. The omission is atoned for, however, at a later stage of the proceedings in the course of a further prayer, but it offers otherwise nothing that demands remark. As much or as little can be said for several further orisons which intervene amidst a variety of rambling and unconnected discourse.

There is a point at which questions and warnings are addressed to the Candidate. What does he hope to attain in the mystic Temple? Is it wealth, honour and power? If so, let him desist from the attempt. Does he come as a child, humbly, seeking light in the Eternal East? Is his heart turned to the Father of all, desiring wisdom from above? Is he filled with the love of God and of that Blessed One Who was crucified? Then shall he be blessed and received among them, in the Name of Him Who suffered little children to approach Him. But let every Aspirant realise that those who enter the Assembly must renounce all worldly affections, for the world will be ever at war with them. After these and other lucubrations the uppermost point of a Pentagram was pressed against his breast; he was told to trust in Adonai and to be centred in the thought of God; to take heed lest he prove a traitor, whether to God and His light or the Brethren, for the two avenging points of the Pentagram would then be turned against him and the powers of the evil ones let loose. Thereafter he is again questioned. Will he listen to the voices of the Cherubim when they come forth from the Eternal Presence? Does he long to penetrate into the Sanctuary of angelic Governors of space? Has he been in warfare with himself and overcome all his passions? Has he fitted himself spiritually, as those must do who would converse with even the lowest among angels, and much more therefore with the glorious spirits of fire? Above all, is he willing to take upon himself the burden of the Master Jesus, bringing offerings of gold, frankincense and myrrh —that is to say of the true light which he hopes to obtain, of universal love, and of tears shed in the bitter valley of darkness and of doubt? If so, let him raise up the Holy Cross and pledge himself solemnly to follow the quest of God, of the Most Holy Son and of that Divine Light Which is the Holy Spirit. This is the undertaking of the Grade and this its sacred obligation.

It is perhaps at this stage that a crown is offered to him, which he is expected or caused to reject. It is balanced on the point of a sword, which signifies that those who aspire to earthly power must be prepared to reckon with its dangers. The renunciation, on the other hand, indicates that those who join the Brotherhood must resign all earthly ambitions, as they must renounce also whatsoever would reduce them to the common level. The only aristocracy recognised in the Order is that of knowledge, and the only wealth is intellect. For the rest, he who is now a Novice of the Order is admonished to remember the penalty which he has invoked upon himself, should he wilfully prove a traitor in word or deed to the Brotherhood and its doctrine. With the point of the magical sword let him repel all powers of evil, tempting him to forsake the path chosen and dishonour the light therein. It were better to have shunned the light than to embrace and then abandon it.

At the end of this and some other orations, the new

Brother of the Order is hailed as a true priest, to whom the key of knowledge is extended with complete trust concerning it. He is blessed in the Name of the Eternal Father; the Powers of the Spirit are implored to descend upon him, that he may be filled with its glorious knowledge. In the Name of JEHOVAH, of ON, of ADONAI the Almighty, he is admitted as a secret member of the Sacred Temple and Order. This is obviously the term attained of the Ceremony, but there follows a final discourse of the Master, in which the Novice is told that after the trials of his initiation there are the ordeals belonging to the fulfilment of those vows which he has taken upon himself. He cannot truly belong to the Brotherhood of Light and still be counted among those Children of Earth who strive for material gain. The science of the Rosy Cross is a jealous science, admitting of no rivals and no compromise. Progression therein connotes the toil and application of intense perseverance, qualifications indispensable to success in sublunary things, but how much more to advancement in Universal Life.

Such are the West of England Mysteries of the Rosy Cross, produced in the name of Thomas Vaughan by the West of England centre and introducing in its theses such anachronisms as Modern Spiritualism. I have mentioned that it is a large MS., extending, as I found, to nearly four hundred quarto pages, when submitted to my examination. It must be said that the one Grade which is delineated piecemeal in the course of errant disquisitions compares favourably with that of Zelator under the obedience of the *Soc. Ros.* But, as there should be no need to specify, it reflects practically nothing from the past of Rosicrucian history, while—as it happens—there is nothing also in the likeness of the Little foundation. THE STAR IN THE EAST was by no means the sole excursion in the manufacture of Rites and Grades. There is another less elaborate and less curious invention, claiming to be translated from the French but unquestionably of like production. It is concerned with Judges in Israel and extends to Seven Degrees, but it is no part of our concern. In view of yet other MSS., it seems possible, however, that from this centre came also the Warrants of another Secret Order or Association of Occult Students to which there are occasional allusions in the TRANSACTIONS of the *Soc. Ros.* and which acquired at a later period much undesirable notoriety in the public press, owing to successive misfortunes. According to the terminology of the period in circles dedicated to the subjects, it was supposed to be "very occult" and all allusion to membership, or even the fact of its existence, was expressly prohibited. This notwithstanding, the official organ in question is the first source of information concerning it, as shewn by the summary references which now follow.

(1) It appears by the TRANSACTIONS that a copy of the German SECRET SYMBOLS was exhibited at a Meeting of the *Soc. Ros.* on October 11, 1888, as once in the possession of the Rev. A. F. A. Woodford, described as "a very learned Hermetist and member of a very ancient universal Rosicrucian Society, composed of students of both sexes, whose—*sic*, meaning the Society's—English name even is unknown, except to Members." The account proceeds to specify that the "Hebrew title" was CHaBRaT LeReCH AUR BOQR and that the sodality was known otherwise as Hermetic Students of the G. D. It was explained further that his association with this body accounted for Woodford ignoring repeated requests to join the *Soc. Ros.*, "which he deemed a mere exoteric institution." (2) In the course of a lecture delivered on July 5, 1894, it was stated that Éliphas Lévi's supposed "Kabalistic Exhortation of Solomon to his Son Rehoboam" was the key to "a vast mass of information still studied

by large Colleges of Rosicrucians, both on the Continent and in England." The Colleges in question were those of the G. D., but they do not happen to have been known under the scholastic title. (3) So far the TRANSACTIONS, but I do not claim to have exhausted all the references. (4) The next point of information occurs in the HISTORY OF THE SOCIETAS ROSICRUCIANA, 1900, which I have had occasion to cite at length. It is stated that S. Liddell MacGregor Mathers, "in association with Dr. Wynn Westcott and Dr. Woodman," "founded the Isis-Urania Temple of the Hermetic Students of the G. D." (5) The date of this event is not given in the HISTORY, but it appears in Dr. Westcott's DATA of 1916, by which we learn (*a*) that "a Continental adept," identified as S. D. A., authorised the formation of the Isis-Urania Temple in 1887; (*b*) that the object was instruction in mediæval occult sciences; (*c*) that the Chiefs were Fratres M. E. V., then Supreme Magus of the *Soc. Ros.*, S. A. and S. R. M. D.; (*d*) that the third of this triad "wrote the Rituals in modern English," deriving from old R∴C∴ MSS. There is further information of consequence on cognate matters and it can be materially extended at need, but for the moment it lies outside the field of inquiry. The last points are (*a*) that S. A. "resigned from this Association in 1897," and (*b*) that "the English Temples soon after fell into abeyance," which, however, was not the case.

It is a matter of common knowledge at this day that the "Association" thus referred to is the Hermetic Order of the Golden Dawn, which in addition to a Neophyte Grade conferred the following sequence, common to the *Soc. Ros.* and the German Rite of 1777; (1) Zelator, (2) Theoricus, (3) Practicus, (4) Philosophus, and—beyond these—a certain sub-Grade, leading in Ritual directions beyond the Golden Dawn.

It appears therefore on the surface that the "very

ancient universal Rosicrucian Society" started in 1887. As regards its "vast mass of information," the bulk of this—and everything counted as of consequence—was produced by the person whose identity is no longer veiled by the letters S. R. M. D. Finally, the lecturer who spoke so mysteriously on October 11, 1888, was not only a member of the Order but one of its Chiefs. There remains, however, the reference to old Rosicrucian MSS., as the basis of Rituals written "in modern English." They are so-called ciphers, or Ritual Summaries in a certain Magical Alphabet, existing in several codices, the paper of some bearing the water-mark of 1809, but so far from belonging to that period—which, by the way, is one of reasonably modern date—they refer to the Egyptian RITUAL OF THE DEAD, then unknown by name and undeciphered, much as the Thomas Vaughan of another MS. referred to Modern Spiritualism. Moreover, with one variation about which the Ciphers are wrong, they contain an attribution of Tarot Trumps Major to letters of the Hebrew Alphabet, which they owe to Éliphas Lévi, subject, however, to the fact that his attribution is also wrong.

There are several stories about these Ciphers when they were—so to speak—on their travels—that they were picked up on a book-barrow, and so forth. It is agreed generally that they came into the possession of Woodford and that they were decoded easily by the help of a book in the British Museum. The last statement at least is true. A photographic reproduction of one page of the Ciphers, made from a codex in possession of one of the earliest members, faces this account, and I have selected that which includes the reference to the Egyptian Funerary Ritual. It calls to be added that the MS. contains words which had not been incorporated into English dictionaries till after 1879. The first example of use in one case seems to be Madame Blavatsky's ISIS UNVEILED. My conclusion is that the Ciphers are *post* 1880, notwithstanding the faded ink of certain originals. My information concerning one codex referred it to the West of England, on which account I have dwelt at considerable length upon the Rosicrucian activities of that district. Moreover, THE STAR RISING IN THE EAST teems with allusions which recall the Rituals of the G.D., and its reference to the sepulchre of Jesus is especially significant in this connection. But if these things signify only a long sequence of curious coincidences, and if G.D. ciphers did not originate somewhere at this centre, then, alternatively, one of the codices may have been found among the papers of Kenneth Mackenzie, who died in 1886. They are replete with Tarot symbolism of the inferior, magical kind, and we have Dr. Westcott's authority that Mackenzie claimed "special knowledge" on this subject.

CHAPTER XXII

A KABALISTIC ORDER OF THE ROSE-CROIX

NOT only are great subjects encircled, for the most part by an external penumbra which, in comparison with themselves, is a region of trifles, but the subjects themselves, when approached, not so much in an unserious spirit as in the mood of the light mind, seem, under such auspices, to abdicate their proper office and to manifest on their fantastic side. They enter to this extent the region of comedy, and as he must be a cross-grained poet who cannot be diverted by the skilful parody of his own work, so it is in no sense outside the law that the true mystic—who is saved by many things, including a sense of humour—should be the first perhaps to appreciate the motley appearance of his own interests, when seen under the reflections of travesty. From the days of Eugène Sue and his epical romances, and thenceforward to Zola, a long line of poets, prophets, and makers of revelations have formulated and expounded to us the greater mysteries of Paris, all of which have gone as far as might be possible to shew that it is the one city now situated in Europe wherein a man of parts may take up his abode with every consideration for his dignity. Of the lesser mysteries, some, at least, may be supposed to reflect the same sentiment, or to intimate, if you prefer it, the same polite lesson. Their name, however, is legion, and it is in their midst only that it is possible for the man of parts to forget occasionally, and for a period, that he is almost of necessity a Frenchman.

When he has forgotten this, it is open for him to become many things, but always to the exaltation of his honour, and it will be a matter of astonishment with many persons not actually its residents, who believe that they know their Paris, including the Quartier Latin, to learn shortly what ambitions and what aspirations have been cherished in the hearts of certain Parisians, for something like forty years past, and are still recapitulated silently when, catching his reflection in the looking-glass, each of them says devoutly, though not always audibly, *adveniat regnum tuum* !

We may take among the legion of these lesser mysteries a single broad group, being modern developments of things that belong to our subject. It has at least the advantage of being curious and would deserve to rank as important if its varied claims might be assumed to admit of verification. The records of these mysteries exist in a literature which, beyond its particular field, is even now little known in Paris, and scarcely at all outside it, with the possible exception of things which the Sar Péladan once dared to certify as possible to French genius when offering to the women of Paris his instructions on the art of becoming a fairy—*comment on devient fée*—and to the men of that gay capital his grave, if unserious, treatise on the best means of becoming a magician—*comment on devient mage*. It follows that the lesser mysteries of which I am speaking here are otherwise occult mysteries, and here it is necessary to distinguish. That there is occultism in Paris, as in London or New York, is known of course to the world ; but as in London it signifies in the eyes of the vain multitude an interest in psychical research, a desire to investigate the *poltergeist* and to believe in spiritism ; as in New York it connotes a regard for trance oratory and a tendency to accept mediumship for materialisations and the direct voice ; so in Paris it means probably, for this same multitude, if it means anything definitely, the investigations of Richet and Gely on the subject of ectoplasm ; a certain disposition towards the doctrines of Allan Kardec, including reincarnation as established by messages from the " hither hereafter," a certain leaning towards theosophical notions modified by pantheism, not inelegantly expressed in modern French and led in the direction of demonstration by the less obtrusive phenomena of the " circle." As to all of these, they are lesser mysteries of Paris, of London, or of New York, but specifically they are not those to which reference is intended here. The latter are not, perhaps, fundamentally, more curious, and they are not, perhaps, less insincere, within the horizon of the vain multitude ; but they are less obvious among the many things which rank as mysteries, and they are less conspicuously diluted, though they are not without those aids to reflection which are furnished by the *conversazione*, the *soirée*, the *séance tenue* and the *compte rendu*. For the man of parts is deliberate after his own fashion, even when he has exchanged the Frenchman of his period for the mystic citizen of an eternal kingdom, and has so, without exactly designing it, ceased from being republican and materialist.

It appears, from an analysis of the documents, that there has been a choice of courses open to him and that among these is the pursuit of alchemy, which has been long flourishing in Paris, is not unknown at Lyons, and has been reported at Bordeaux. The interest in this pursuit has been focussed possibly by a handbook prepared for its disciples, containing full instructions for becoming an alchemist—*Comment on devient Alchimiste*. Mons. F. Jolivet Castelot is the writer of this manual, and his predecessor in the same mystery appears to have been Albert Poisson, who is termed the Restorer of Alchemy. The work descends even to minute particulars concerning the daily life of an alchemist, as this may be lived in Paris and the environs, even in the matter of ablutions, so it may be thought tolerably complete ; yet the further direction of students in the same subject has been secured by founding an Alchemical Society of France, being a section of the Faculty of Hermetic Sciences, a body which once dispensed degrees, titles and the certificates that are evidences of each—*magnifiques diplômes*—and certain initiated authors prior to the Great War were not afraid to add the words *Docteur en Alchimie* after their name on a title-page. It is reported that the Alchemical Society has a regular course of study and a decisive laboratory practice. As regards the term of its labours it would seem that " gold has been furnished, but only in small quantities, differing in this respect from that which is produced by the Philosophical Stone," because mere science can deal only with those *minima* of which *non curat lex magna* of the old adepts. In other words, Paracelsus and Raymund Lully are masters still, while the man of parts, although he is a Frenchman and has contrived to become an alchemist, can reproduce their traditional achievements *en petite quantité seulement*. But, as Mons. Jolivet Castelot explains, he is for all that on the right road, on the road which leads to ecstasy, " that privilege of the adept." And for his further guidance there has existed, these many years past, a monthly review under various titles, which may not contain the proof positive of metallic transmutation as now performed in France but is undeniable evidence of the extent to which these lesser mysteries must be prosecuted in secret by persons well acquainted with the terms, experiments and development of modern chemistry, for it calls very often to be classed as a highly technical periodical. Its latest denomination is La Rose-Croix, and though in all its chameleon changes it has been silent, I believe, on the spiritual aspects of alchemy, there is no question that its *direction* and its earnest subscribers generally would regard it as dedicated to the time-immemorial object of all Rosicrucian research. Outside these centralised and perhaps vested interests of modern French alchemy, there are traces also of isolated and more mysterious researches which can be scarcely named here, but are at work in the same direction, and it is not so long since an American visitor to Paris was shewn the "menstrual water of alchemy," the dissolvent of all metals, in the form of a limpid fluid having a slightly acid flavour. In such ways does one section of *la France spirituelle* qualify, beyond the doctorates of its Hermetic Faculties, for the mystic citizenship of the eternal kingdom already mentioned, and I may add that, in the mind of Mons. Jolivet Castelot, it seems impossible for a right-thinking alchemist to be other than monarchical in politics, while it is, further, a canon of perfection that he should adhere to the dynasty of Orléans.

Here therefore is one aspect of the substituted Rosy Cross, as it is understood and followed in France. It knows little enough of the Brotherhood from which its name derives, unless it be through Sédir and his rather slight monograph; but it is following a practical, experimental research and is not concerned with history.

Now, the occult sciences are, in the minds of their disciples, all inter-connected; it is impossible to pursue one without becoming tinctured by another; and thus he who is, before all things, an alchemist, will, at least after a secondary manner, be familiar with the heads of that particular mystical tradition which, under the name of the Kabalah, has been cherished both in East and West for something like ten centuries upon the most moderate computation, and from time immemorial according to the opinion of its adepts. I have had little occasion—except in connection with the Rose—to speak of it in this volume, except by way of allusion, but I have established in other books that on the Godward side it is a great theosophical medley and in its degeneration a magical art. It originated among the Jews at some undetermined period of the Christian dispensation, and it has a very large literature in Jewry. When it first attracted attention among Christian scholars in Europe, so many points of comparison seemed possible between its philosophical portion and the chief doctrines of Christianity, that it was regarded as an eirenicon between the two religions, and it was held that Christianity Kabalistically interpreted would ensure the conversion of all Israel. Though we still—or some of us—have our missions to the Jews, it would seem incredible at this day with what fever of enthusiasm this false light was followed by many learned and sincere persons who had no interests *per se* in any transcendental philosophy and still less in any occult or magical art. I must not say that no conversions took place as the consequence of all this zeal misplaced, but the value of the instrument was assuredly out of all proportion to the machinery which was required for its manufacture, and it fell into disuse accordingly. It was then that the Kabalah passed over among the Christian scholars of Europe to that use for which only a single phase of it was originally designed; it became part of the intellectual baggage of the occultist, to whom its externals belong properly, and outside this interest it ceased to concern any one. It entered into connection with alchemy, probably in the seventeenth century, and with other secret systems, including some of the Masonic Rites, during the course of the eighteenth century; it fell asleep at the Napoleonic period, like all the connected interests, and, so far as France was concerned, it awoke in 1850, for the purely academical work of Adolphe Franck, published a few years previously, scarcely calls for consideration from this point of view. About 1885 it became one of the leading interests of those lesser mysteries of Paris with which we are here concerned, and is regarded as one of the important depositaries of hidden truths which have come down to us from antiquity, though its highest claims are missed rather than realised. Gérard Encausse, otherwise Dr. Papus, who was a great light of these byways prior to the War, has done what he could to simplify its "occult" and magical side, and it was not at all necessary for the man of parts in Paris who was disposed towards such studies to embarrass himself by the study of Aramaic, in which dialect the chief books of the Kabalah were originally written, or even of Hebrew, for sufficient of their substance was rendered into French, usually out of anterior Latin versions, and it is never essential for this kind of scholarship to go actually to the root of the matter.

When a day came for the vast *midrash* of the ZOHAR to be put at full length into French outside occult circles, and when they learned for the first time the import of true Kabalism, a silence fell upon the circles, for their great oracle was voided. It was not for consultations like theirs, and I believe that to this day the translation is never mentioned.

It must be confessed that the French occult Kabalist is, for the most part, a dull person of preternatural gravity, and the authors who once catered for him did not know their subject. The alchemist of Paris was and is much to be preferred before him, even though he can make gold *en petite quantité seulement*, if actually at all; but his existence made it possible to establish—as we are about to see—a Kabalistic Order of the Rose-Cross, admission into which being obtained with considerable difficulty was much prized in consequence. And this Order did something to redeem the dullness, for it elaborated—as one of its activities—a system of occult man-hunting, and was very busy behind its guarded vestibules in tracing to their doom the Black Magicians of Paris, whose evil practices were counteracted by the higher arts of the Kabalistic Order. Here then is a second and perhaps unexpected aspect of the Rosy Cross in France, and its consideration brings us to the last class of those lesser mysteries with which I am concerned here.

Though the alchemist in Paris may desire to make gold possessing a commercial value, he is, ostensibly at least, actuated by grander aims. He is in search of that mastery of Nature which gives gold to the Alchemist, a familiar spirit to the magicians, and the wisdom of the stellar influences to the searcher of the starry heavens. The pursuits of the occult Kabalist are of a still more lofty order, for he is learned in the emanations of Deity and in the virtues of those mysterious letters and numbers by which he believes that all things were made originally, whether in heaven or on earth. Or if he does not believe precisely, he is convinced at least that his old masters in Kabalah were veiling great mysteries in this strange symbolism. There might seem some ground also for supposing that he is concerned after his own manner in the conversion of that Israel which the exponents of other mysteries, also located in Paris, would extirpate if possible, even by fire and by sword. The ground is that old books of the Latin-writing scholars who tormented themselves with this subject, have been put into French. But after reading a version of ADUMBRATIO KABBALÆ CHRISTIANÆ, first published in the seventeenth century, wherein a Kabalist and a Christian philosopher compare their respective tenets, one can imagine a man of parts and a Frenchman excusing his indifference as an evangelist only by a reasonable uncertainty whether it would not serve as well if personally he became a Jew, Christianity, in this curious tract, having converted itself already into Kabalism, so that the Kabalist might turn Christian.

But the lesser mysteries which produced all these high, if occasionally stultifying ambitions, produced also the revival of Black Magic, in which flippant Paris, so far as it concerns itself with any, found much more for its entertainment than in the Alchemical Society of France, though it was patronised by Mons. Berthelot, or in the Kabalistic Order of the Rose Cross, though it has been tolerated, in the person of one of its chief spokesmen, by Mons. Adolphe Franck.

The Black Magician does evil for the sake of evil, according to the hypothesis which explains him, and in this he is unlike the Jesuit, by the terms of another hypothesis. The peculiar nature of his pursuits lead him to be more occult and mysterious than either Kabalist or Alchemist, though these also believe that there is wisdom in mystery. The latter, however, pursue it largely for its own sake—mystery for the sake of mystery—but the former of necessity. That which he dares to attempt must, for his own safety, remain hidden and obscure, since it is nothing less than a league with the powers of evil. The reports concerning such practices have passed into literature and even into history, and though originally their actual basis in fact may have been so thin as to be more than elusive, they did not fail to act in a country like France much as suggestion acts on a subject in the hypnotic state : in other words, they created their object. As we heard of them in the last decades of the nineteenth century, they offered elements which are not to be found in old legends of the Black Sabbath and in old records of sorcery. These were a coarse and crass phantasmagoria produced upon a scale which befitted the nature of the participants. Their horrors were chiefly ridiculous—the peasant's dream exteriorised. But in later days the grace of literary skill exercised itself upon the subject ; the romantic writer adorned it, as a Parisian who is a man of parts, for the Parisians who were his brethren and were fitted to appreciate exotics. In this way, a *cultus diabolicus*, a religion of the evil principle, was invented, firstly on paper, and was put subsequently into practice in those secret places where lesser mysteries of this kind can be celebrated. Into the motives which prompted the frenzy on either side it is unnecessary here to enter, but the worship of Lucifer was based broadly on the presumption that in place of the Satan of Milton, he is a tolerant combination of the Satyr and Silenus, under whose rule the Decalogue is abolished. It is perhaps manifestly unfair towards the occult circles of Paris to include this kind of aberration among the number of their pursuits, as if it were recognised and professed, but it is in evidence after its own manner, it comes out of the occult past, and the pathological consequences which are supposed to result therefrom are of the kind which were said to follow the Black Magic of the past ; what has been done is to civilise the process. Moreover, evocations, divinations, and all the hundred and one rites of White Magic have abounded in the same city ; secret and other societies existed and exist to practise them ; they had and they have still their weekly journals as well as their monthly reviews. To any one unconversant with such matters, they must sound incredible enough, and yet they are a very small parcel only of the whole truth. Materialism, the anti-clerical movement and liberty as it is interpreted by the Republic, have produced more wonders than all phenomena of faith ; and the expatriated Religious Orders might smile at that which has come into possession after them.

Now, this is a third aspect of things which encompass the idea of the Rosy Cross in Paris, but the Cross has been defiled and the Rose is black. It is not only "the flesh in rebellion against the spirit," but in revolt against Nature itself. I do not propose to specify its records in books, but the books exist, though now withdrawn from circulation. Whether the circles and their orgies are still maintained I do not know : many things died in the War, and these—it is to be hoped—among them.

Of such are the lesser mysteries of Paris. They do not

appear on the surface, at least officiously, though they ware not unknown in *salons*, and occasionally some episode of the moment gives them a moment's vogue. It remains to say that, with their connections and derivations innumerable, they all issued from or were revived by that one epoch-making apostle of the "occult" sciences who began writing about the year 1850, using truly a pen of magic, under the name, already mentioned, of Éliphas Lévi. In spite of his pseudonym and of the fact that he was a Kabalist among other things, he was not a Jew, but actually a brilliant and unfortunate Abbé, who lost his clerical position and turned to the secret sciences, possibly in search of consolation, possibly as a part of his doom, or, in the opinion of the censorious, for more material reasons. The explanation matters nothing; *vous savez qu'il faut vivre*, and the important fact is that this personage, equally in England —where he is now well known—and in France, has created what is termed generally the occult movement. Without him, it would be impossible to write on these lesser mysteries, for to speak in the language of the occultist, they would only have existed negatively. Assuredly there are more things in Paris than are dreamed of in the philosophy of its normal visitors, whether from England or America, or further across the seas.

The purpose so far in this chapter has been to indicate what has passed as belonging to the Rosicrucian subject in the mind of modern France; but I have yet to deal with the attempt, so far barely signalised, to establish a working Order of the Rosy Cross. We shall find that it owed nothing to the past, even by claim, and the explanation is that Parisian occultism cares little for the past in history. We have seen that there are bibliographical legends of the FAMA FRATERNITATIS and CHEMICAL NUPTIALS being translated into French at a very early period and in the case of the latter—according to one report—about or before the time that it appears to have been written. So far as evidence goes there is no truth in any of these legends. For some unaccountable reason the claims and traditional history of the Rosy Cross did not appeal to French occult imagination, and there is no trace of any House of the Holy Spirit having been built in France, not even in the heart, though the Eighteenth Degree had its Sovereign Chapters and conferred its rank of chivalry. From 1860 and onwards—as we have just seen—Éliphas Lévi, in several brilliant writings, clothed his imagined "occult sciences" in a new vesture and gave them a new philosophical setting; but even in his HISTOIRE DE LA MAGIE it is curious to note how few and far between are his references to the German Order and how utterly wanting he is in all knowledge of the subject. Neither before nor after his period has any manifesto of the Rosy Cross ever been published in French, though one would have thought that a decorative romance like the CHEMICAL NUPTIALS could have hardly escaped this honour. The great revival of 1885, at the head of which was Dr. Papus, brought with it a certain sentimental feeling of concern in the subject, but it was little more than instinctive. I remember Papus in a mood of prophecy affirming that the whole secret mystery of the Rosy Cross would be unfolded within a given number of years—how many I forget—but their limit has been passed long since in the flight of historical time, and the Elias of this revelation is still to come.

Some years prior to this suggestive advertisement and actually in or before 1889 an ORDRE KABBALISTIQUE DE LA ROSE-CROIX was founded at Paris by the Marquis Stanislas de Guaita, whose literary life began with exotic verse—FLEURS DU MAL—and who ultimately closed his career at comparatively an early age, fortified by the last Rites of the Holy Roman Church. Between these events he became famous in France by the issue of monumental works on occult subjects and especially on Magic. La Clef de la Magie Noire is an important case in point, but there were several other volumes, all speaking with authority and accepted in France at the face value of their personal claim, yet a little pretentious in manner, as the claim exhibits, and not a little inaccurate on points of fact, as is common, if not inevitable, with French occultists. De Guaita was President *ad vitam* of that which he had established until his death on December 19, 1897, when he was succeeded by F. C. Barlet, who apparently resigned and his place was taken by Dr. Gérard Encausse, otherwise Papus. The President was assisted by a Council of Twelve—six, as we are told, known and six unknown, *Philosophes Inconnus*, I presume, in memory of Saint-Martin and perhaps of that mysterious association the Laws of which were published by Baron Tschoudy. Papus was a member *ab origine* and so also was the fantastic celebrity Sar Péladan. He was in fact one of the Council till the early part of 1890, when he severed connection, finding it intolerable, I believe, to be second, or in any minor part whatsoever, even in an occult Rome. He did more, however, than this, for he created a newer Ordre de la Rose-Croix, which was also an Order of the Temple and of the Holy Graal. It was characterised otherwise and especially as a Catholic Rose-Croix, for I believe that Sar Péladan—like the fairies of Bishop Corbet—amidst all his vagaries, was and remained of "the old religion." It is said that in 1899 there was a proposal to amalgamate the two bodies, but it came to nothing, as might be expected. Whether the junior creation deserved to be called a body in any organised sense remains doubtful, but whether it was Rosicrucian at all in the sense which attaches to the term is, past all question, to be decided in the negative. I remember that its originator once issued a book under the title of Quête du Saint Graal; it contained nothing about the Sacred Vessel or anything related thereto, but—as the author confessed naïvely—it secured the title to himself, forgetting perchance or ignoring the Chronicle of Galahad. The Quest, in a word, was Péladan. So also, I conceive, when he founded his new Order, Sar Péladan was the Rose-Croix. It was his portrait in any position, his views on occult subjects, his last book or any other. It was COMMENT ON DEVIENT FÉE and perhaps above all it was COMMENT ON DEVIENT MAGE, but it was he, his and of all else nothing. When, therefore, L'ORDRE KABBALISTIQUE proposed to amalgamate with his Rose-Croix it proposed to amalgamate with Sar Péladan or—in other words—invite him back to the fold. And the scheme fell through.

Two things remain to be said on the external side: (1) That in 1910, according to Sédir, the Kabalistic Order had deviated from its original character, but we know and have seen that there were precedents for this in the past; (2) That when the institution lost its third Grand Master towards the close of the War it seems to have dissolved entirely. Other occult societies of the immediate preceding past have been restored in whole or in part, but this is heard of no longer. As regards the characteristics from which it fell away, I have no means of knowing; but in L'INITIATION for 1907—being the President or Grand Master's monthly magazine—there appeared a statement on Rosicrucian Hopes by Dr. Fulgence Bruni, who, I conceive, knew something at first hand concerning L'ORDRE KABBALISTIQUE. The heads of his discourse follow. (1) The ignorant fanatic, who believes and does not know, is vanquished by the Kabalah, grafting itself on each branch of philosophical evolution. (2) After the great Fall there remained in the human breast a feeble spark of uncreated fire, like a vague remembrance of celestial spheres, and in hours of repose and liberation it makes war upon our lower instincts. (3) The Great Work is the redemption of man, bent under the yoke of evil and superstition. (4) The truly initiated priesthood cannot be separated from the work of artists, art being the cultus of beauty. (5) Love is the eldest Son of the Absolute. (6) The three degrees of initiation are Purification, Illumination, Union. (7) The luminous resurrection of the Rose ✠ Croix is mentioned at the end and is understood as "a most exalted Order of veritable western initiates," depositaries of Kabalistic tradition. The proof is that the mere name of its Chief offers a complete guarantee, "the superiority of Papus" being known throughout the world. The final peroration affirms as follows: "Sons of light and love, the Rose ✠ Croix destroy everywhere the efforts of obscurantists and the wicked. They are at once iconoclasts and architects. Silent and unknown . . . they seek no other recompense than the "lawful satisfaction of accomplished duty." Rough designations are not as a rule politic, but the proper definition of diatribe like this is rant. If it stood for a predominant sentiment within the confraternity, we can understand the finding of Sédir, who was probably himself a member.

As regards interior constitution, we learn on more sober authority, which shall stand, however, at its value, owing to the first clauses: (1) That between 1880 and 1887 the "initiates" had cause to bestir themselves because foreign societies were seeking to strip France and transfer the direction of European occultism to London.[1] (2) That they may have designed even to annihilate the work of true masters in the West. (3) That a reforming movement began in France and was carried to a good term by Stanislas de Guaita. (4) That L'Ordre Kabbalistique de la Rose-Croix "emerged from the darkness." (5) That it comprised three Grades, or baccalaureate, licentiate and doctorate in

[1] The reference is probably to the Theosophical Society, established at this period in London. It is to be noted that Papus joined the Paris branch early in his career, but came into opposition thereto and left it with embittered feelings.

Kabalah—attainable by examination. (6) That de Guaita was Grand Master and administered the Order, aided by a Council consisting of three Chambers. (7) That he proposed a threefold task, being study of the classics of the occult, effort to establish spiritual communion with Divine Unity, and propaganda.[1] These being the original "characteristics," it is to be noted on our own part: (1) That the foundations made no appeal to the past and no claim thereon in respect of descent. (2) That the adopted designation was purely fantastic or conventional in respect of the words Rose-Croix. (3) That it did not work in Ritual after the manner pursued by the Reformation of 1777, or after any manner. (4) That by intention it was primarily and above all a learned Faculty, which applied tests of knowledge and granted diplomas. (5) That it planned the formation of what may be called an Inner Circle for certain experiments or practices which on the surface seem mystical, but in view of the Grand Master's pursuits it is impossible to specify what he understood by "spiritual communion with Divine Unity." The followers of so-called theurgic paths used language of this kind from time to time.

[1] Maurice Barrès: UN RENOVATEUR DE L'OCCULTISME: Stanislas de Guaita (1861–98). Paris, 1898.

CHAPTER XXIII

THE AMERICAN ROSY CROSS

THE story of this chapter begins in Germany, and it may be mentioned in the first place that there is a considerable literature of the subject, though to all intents and purposes it is unknown among us. As a part of American history it has grown up there and thereunto belongs. The early memorials are concerned, among many personalities, with Johannes Kelpius, who was born in the vicinity of Denndorf, probably at Halwegen, *anno* 1673, and was son of a pastor named George Kelp. After the death of his father in 1685 Johannes was sent to Altdorf, near Nüremberg in Bavaria, to continue and complete his education at the University of that town. In 1689, or at the age of sixteen, he became a Doctor of Philosophy and the Liberal Arts, the thesis which earned this title being on Natural Theology.[1] In the course of his scholastic career he made acquaintance with Baron Knorr von Rosenroth, the author of KABBALA DEUNDATA and a famous theosophist of his period. It is a matter of speculation only, but the reasonable inference is that Kelpius owed to Rosenroth the beginning of those dedications which characterised his subsequent life.

Kelpius became also a friend of his tutor, D. Johannes Fabricius of Altdorf and Helmstadt, and seems to have been in bonds of intimacy with Johann Jacob Zimmerman,

[1] The authority is Sievert's NACHRICHTEN, VON SIEBENBÜRGISCHEN GELEHRTEN UND IHREN SCHRIFTEN, 1785, but I know it only through J. F. Sachse: THE GERMAN PIETISTS OF PROVINCIAL PENNSYLVANIA, 1895, who is also my chief source of reference in respect of Kelpius.

a mathematician and astronomer of European distinction, who in one notable respect became the guiding star of his destiny. Zimmerman is said also to have been skilled in astrology and geomancy, not to speak of theological knowledge presupposed in the pastor of a Lutheran Church in Würtemberg. In 1684 he lost his ecclesiastical position owing to his expressed views on a coming millennium and subsequently the chair of mathematics at Heidelberg on account of other " mystical speculations " described as deeper. He has been characterised by Brecklingius as a magician, Kabalist and partisan of Jacob Böhme.[1] It follows that when Kelpius made his acquaintance in the vicinity of Nüremberg, Zimmerman was under a cloud in the worldly sense, and at one period acted as proof-corrector to a Hamburg publisher of " mystical and theosophical works," in which manner he became familiar with persons whose enthusiasms were similar to his own. They seem to be enumerated indifferently as Pietists, Mystics, Chiliasts,[2] Rosicrucians and Illuminati. It was the day of *Collegia Pietatis*, reminiscent remotely of Tauler and his Friends of God, of Chapters of Perfection, the keynote of which was a deeper sense of personal religion, but they were in bonds of union with many kinds of extravagance, from the pursuit of physical alchemy to Second Advent zealotry. Except for its anti-papal spirit, of which there is no vestige in the memorials before me, the chief text-book of all might well have been Studion's NAOMETRIA.[3]

[1] One of his published works demonstrated the truth of the Copernican system from Holy Scripture.

[2] It is curious that this fantastic designation should have been perpetuated from the days of Andreæ—see MEMORIALIA, 1619—apparently to those of Kelpius.

[3] As Studion predicted the crucifixion of the Sovereign Pontiff on an all too definite date, so Zimmerman foretold " the exact time " of a coming millennium by the help of " astronomical observations." This fatal facility in computation seems to have been more obnoxious to Church and State than his divergences on doctrinal subjects.

The mental and spiritual environment which encompassed Kelpius in Bavaria was analogous in all respects to that of Würtemberg at the close of the sixteenth century and throughout the first epoch of the Rosy Cross. The Lutheran Church and its recognised competitors in the common mesh of particular vested interests, having manufactured their respective titles of working orthodoxy, followed the gentle art of persecution and hounding: if torture and burning had passed out of fashion as the Holy Roman Rite fell into comparative desuetude, there was hardness enough in yokes that were still imposed, and heavy enough were the burdens on those who dared to differ. It was far indeed to the day of liberation in Germany and far to the reign of tolerance. Zimmerman "denounced the Established Church as a Babel" and cast doubts on the Augsbourg Confession.[1] He proceeded to Erfurth and there established—*circa* 1690—a Chapter of Perfection, presumably within the bosom of a *Collegium Pietatis* antecedently existing at that active centre. Its personalities included Daniel Falkner, an university licentiate; A. H. Francke, a Deacon; and Anna Maria Schuckart, an ecstatic, who was called the Erfurth Prophetess. This *Collegium* was suppressed and the Chapter decided on departing from the German "Babylon" and seeking the "American Plantations"—so called in a contemporary account[2]—under the guidance of the Divine Spirit.

There is ground for inferring that the Chapter was founded with this interest at heart and Zimmerman stood at its head, the controlling and inspiring spirit, the *Magister* of the work in hand, Kelpius being second in command or influence. There was also Heinrich Bernard Köster,

[1] See Zimmerman's Mundus Copernizans, 1684.

[2] I refer to a State pamphlet of this period, issued in 1708 under the title of Carolus Wirtembergische, *Unschuld Act*, and quoted at length by J. F. Sachse.

described as throughout a champion of "the orthodox Lutheran faith" but imbued with "mystical doctrines and Rosicrucian speculations," which led him to join another *Collegium Pietatis* when at Berlin and afterwards to promote the emigration scheme of the Erfurt Chapter. The companions of that which for them and in their day was a great and perilous venture were some forty-seven in all, according to the DIARY of Kelpius, and from two rallying points—being Magdeburg and Halberstadt, they made a beginning of their pilgrimage, joining forces at Rotterdam. This was in 1693, and there—on the eve of embarkation for England—Zimmerman died. We know little of the delays which followed, but the party were in London[1] on February 7th, 1694, when Magister Kelpius, now in supreme command, chartered the "Sarah Maria," under Captain John Tanner, and the voyage down Thames began on February 14th. The events and perils which followed are pictured at full length in the Kelpius DIARY,[2] but they do not concern us here. It shall be sufficient for my purpose to say that the "Sarah Maria"—of good hope, as Kelpius called her—was "made fast to the public wharf of Philadelphia" on June 23rd, 1694.

Before speaking briefly of that life which awaited the pilgrims in their new land and home, the question arises as to how and why they and their leader or master have come to concern us at all in connection with the Rosy Cross. We have seen that they have been labelled Rosicrucians, as alternative to Illuminati and Chiliasts, but the term seems used in that old fluidic, inexact or arbitrary

[1] It is said that while in London the leaders of the expedition made acquaintance with the Philadelphian Society, under Dr. Pordage and Jane Lead. There was even a surface disposition on the part of the English pietists to join forces with the Chapter of Perfection, but it came to nothing.

[2] See THE DIARIUM OF MAGISTER JOHANNES KELPIUS, with Annotations by Julius Friedrich Sachse. Published by the Pennsylvania-German Society, Lancaster, Pa., 1917.

sense which we have met with on many occasions. Were they or any of them actually initiated Brethren of an Order which in the year 1694 seems to have been otherwise asleep, like Christian Rosy Cross in his vaulted sepulchre? Mr. J. F. Sachse, who was an heir by birth of the pilgrims, had many treasures as such in the muniment room of his family and acquired many more by research in the four quarters, affirms that in a certain retired valley at Ephrata in Pennsylvania, on the banks of the flowing brook, "the Secret Rites and Mysteries of the true Rosicrucian Philosophy flourished unmolested for years." He says also of those who practised them that they were a true theosophical or Rosicrucian community, "whose tenets were founded upon the dogmas of the Kabalah and esoteric philosophy." But all this, on the surface at least, looks like poetic imagery, and is used, moreover, by one who neither knows nor professes knowledge concerning the Order, except in a very casual sense. Because certain people of the early seventeenth century who might have been called Pietists—had such a denomination existed—were among witnesses to an incorporated Order of the Rosy Cross, it seems counted tolerable to call the historical Pietists of 1694 the Rosicrucians of their own day. Now, if this is how the case stands, Magister Kelpius and his fellow-pilgrims have no place in the present volume.

It happens, however, that there is another side of the question and that although the designation is a loose and inaccurate label of the Chapter of Perfection at large—like that of Illuminati, which was not current at the period—and although there is no real evidence that its members practised any Rites or Mysteries which can be called Rosicrucian in complexion, it seems colourable that a few among them, or—let us say—Kelpius at least, were after some manner integrated in the Order and may have communicated that which was theirs to all or many of the pilgrims. The reason is that they are said to have carried with them, and to have followed, the rule of a priceless Rosicrucian MS. In the account of Sachse and in the illustrations which accompany it there may be nothing to show that this document answers conclusively to its technical description: it might be mainly theosophical or pietistic in character. As a fact, however, it represents an early stage of the SECRET SYMBOLS, published at Altona in 1785–8, analysed in my sixteenth chapter and utilised for many illustrations of the present work.[1] Historically and bibliographically it is therefore of the first importance, as apparently a real Rosicrucian text and seeming to indicate (1) that the German Rosy Cross in the hiddenness of the late seventeenth century was that Christian Theosophical Order which Fludd represented it to be in his earlier day, indeed *ab origine symboli*, and (2) that the Altona circle did not produce an invention on their own part nearly one hundred years later but had developed and extended only.

There is one possible consideration which militates against this view and must be left to stand at its value (1) because of the inadequate account which J. F. Sachse has bequeathed of his literary treasure, outside the photographic reproduction of four leaves; (2) because he is no longer with us in earthly life; and (3) because it is understood that his heirs decline to produce it for inspection. The consideration is that if the thirty pages or leaves of the Kelpius MS. are as suggested in my note pages containing symbols, then the illustrations of GEHEIME FIGUREN may be almost reduced to this number by subtracting peculiarly Rosicrucian

[1] Mr. Sachse describes the "ancient manuscript" as an heirloom in his family, the only "perfect copy" extant, so far as is known, a folio measuring 12 x 18 inches, consisting of "thirty pages exquisitely written and embellished with illuminated symbols." As an inference from a photographic reproduction facing his p. 10, it might be suggested that the ancient manuscript has no letterpress except that which is grouped about the designs; that GEHEIME FIGUREN is approximately of the same size; and that it is extended to 57 pp. by the help of AUREUM SECULUM REDIVIVUM, AUREUS TRACTATUS, a purely alchemical preface, a fore-title and a few extra designs.

designs and designs accompanying the alchemical texts reprinted in the work. I submit that this is arbitrary on the surface, though it is not inconceivable that the bulk of the plates in the Altona publication could have been taken over from an antecedent work which was not Rosicrucian at all. There is, however, one piece of direct evidence. The Golden and Rosy Cross which appears on the title-page of GEHEIME FIGUREN is wanting in that of the Kelpius MS.,[1] and so also are Rosicrucian references throughout its letterpress.

Moreover, although Sachse almost invariably refers to his manuscript as Rosicrucian only,[2] and in so doing one would think that he might, or must have, been guided by something evidential therein, we must remember that in 1888, or seven years prior to THE GERMAN PIETISTS OF PENNSYLVANIA, Dr. Franz Hartmann had published at Boston his dismembered edition of THE SECRET SYMBOLS; that it is quoted on one occasion by Sachse;[3] and that as he was

[1] It reads as follows: PHISICA, METAPHISICA ET HYPERPHISICA. D.O.M.A. *Deo Omnipotenti sit Laus, Honos et Gloria in Seculorum Secula, Amen. Einfaltig A.B.C. Büchel, für junge Schuler, so sich fleissig üben im der Schule des Heiligen Geistes, ganz einfaltig Bildnissweise für Augen gemählet, zum Neuen Jahres Exercitio in dem Naturlichen und Theologischen Lichte.* Compare the crowded sub-title of GEHEIME FIGUREN, describing it as also an ABC Booklet for young pupils in the same School, much as we have seen that cryptic texts of alchemy are termed *Ludus Puerorum* or *Opus Mulierum*.

[2] On two occasions he calls it a Theosophical MS., and one of his photographic reproductions is termed "a page of Rosicrucian Theosophy." The Theosophy was Rosicrucian in his view, and the Rosy Cross was for him a THEOSOPHIA at large.

[3] See annotation on p. 37 of THE GERMAN PIETISTS, giving an extract from Hartmann's publication, which is described under the name of COSMOLOGY and nothing more. Hartmann altered the title of the Altona work, calling it COSMOLOGY; OR, UNIVERSAL SCIENCE . . . , *containing the Mysteries of the Universe . . . , explained according to the Religion of Christ, by means of the Secret Symbols of the Rosicrucians of the Sixteenth and Seventeenth Centuries.* Sachse has described his MS. as the only perfect one known, which statement seems obviously untrue in the light of the Altona folio. About this publication Sachse did not know, and in what must be called a disingenuous manner he gives no account of Hartmann's, its illustrations or

not a very critical person his use of the term Rosicrucian may be a mere reflection from that work. All this is likely enough, but after full reflection on the confused issues I question whether we can hold a decided view. I cannot make up a full thirty designs in THE SECRET SYMBOLS without including some that are partly Rosicrucian, and with scarcely a single exception—pietistic, theosophic or cosmological—they are all alchemical. But that which weighs with me most is the fact that if Kelpius carried a text of the Rosy Cross and belonged to that Order I can understand tolerably what is otherwise past comprehension in a Lutheran community, namely, that the Philadelphian pilgrims—as Sachse and his sources shew—were pledged to celibacy, like the early traditional Brethren, of whom it is said that they were " all bachelors and of vowed virginity."

I cannot help thinking that this is an important point, and here I must leave the debate. Unless and until my tentative disposition calls to be revised by a fuller acquaintance with the Sachse MS., it is at least possible that there are grounds therein for the use of that descriptive term which he applies so often.

I pass on to sketch briefly that which befell the pilgrims in the Quaker Province of Philadelphia. They reached the German settlement now called Germantown and there established themselves on the banks of the Wissahickon, Magister Kelpius taking up his abode in a cave among the rocks of the hillside. The object of all was " to live apart from the vices and temptations of the world " and thus be

real purport. But he could not fail to see that his precious heirloom was less or more facing him in public print. It may be added that the order of the plates differs in the Altona work and the Sachse MS. That which is numbered 3 in PHISICA, METAPHISICA ET HYPERPHISICA occupies leaf 35 of GEHEIME FIGUREN, No. 7 answers to 26, and 24 to 32. Moreover, those words which constitute the title in chief of the Kelpius document are omitted in the other case, but are found later on in leaf 35, while they are absent from the corresponding plate, No. 3 of the earlier text.

prepared for expected revelations " in the silence and solitude of the wilderness." The isolation was not complete, for they had also a mission in teaching and religious services were held. Kelpius on his own part strove to unite the German sects of Pennsylvania in one Christian Church, and there was zeal also for the conversion of Indian tribes. According to Sachse, the pilgrims lived in their virgin forest of the New World " for a period of at least ten years, a strictly Theosophical Fraternity, whose tenets were founded upon the dogmas of the Kabalah and esoteric philosophy." In the outer world they were called " The Woman in the Wilderness." It was not, however, a period of unbroken harmony, for the presence of a strict Lutheran element did not work in that direction and the pledge of celibacy led to several separations. When Kelpius himself died of consumption in 1708 at the early age of thirty-five it is said that " such of the brethren as were left of the original community performed the last rites according to the impressive ritual of the Mystic Fraternity." It follows that the Master saw the decline of his Company; the communal life came gradually to an end; the solitude was colonised by settlers; and the remnant " followed each other to the shades of death."

I have searched in vain for traces of the alleged Kabalism in the tenets of the so-called Chapter and for any characteristic Rosicrucian vestiges in the letters of Kelpius. The emigration to the New World was in search of a place of peace and contemplation in view of the coming Millennium, " which, according to Zimmerman's astronomical calculations, was to take place in the fall of the year of grace, 1694." The pilgrims find therefore their natural place in the succession of German Second Adventists whose forecasts were as false as Studion's. Kelpius and the more advanced members are affirmed to have studied Hermetic Arts, not, however, in search of metallic transmutation but rather the Elixir of Life, " to provide remedies and preparations for the alleviation of human suffering." They cast horoscopes also, used the Divining Rod, and prepared astrological amulets or talismans—to be worn upon the person. It is said further that they " scouted the idea of physical death," and Kelpius above all believed almost to the end that he would be transfigured like Elijah and " translated bodily into the spiritual world." We can see now where we stand, that is to say, in the presence of a group of religious and occult enthusiasts who may have carried a Rosicrucian MS. and some of whom may have belonged to the Order in one of its circles, but their real location is in MILITIA CRUCIFERA EVANGELICA and not in the *Collegium Mysticum* of him who, according to Vaughan, was called SAPIENS by earlier Brothers of the Rosy Cross.

On the faith of available testimonies I have now dealt with what may have been the advent of a German Rosicrucian Chapter into the United States. The evidence is faulty enough, but if such it was we must recognise that it stands alone, and we have now to glance briefly at things which have paraded in the name but have in all cases assumed it without a warrant and have sometimes supported their pretence by imposture and mendacity. The credulity of the American mind on this subject is comparable to that of England over other occult claims.

As I have not taken all imposture for my province, I am not in a position to affirm that Paschal Beverley Randolph produced the first putative Order of the Rosy Cross in America, but I have failed to trace anything anterior to his date, and he will answer as the first witness in a line of occult adventurers who are typically characteristic of their place and circumstances. It should be understood that in the account which follows I have set aside entirely all references to Rose-Croix Masonry as exceeding my present province. There is a Southern Jurisdiction of the Scottish

Rite, having its headquarters at Charleston, and there is also a Northern Jurisdiction seated at Chicago, both of them working Thirty-three Degrees which are identical in name and purport. The Eighteenth in each case is that of Rose-Croix, as it was in the old days of that French Rite of Perfection which has been mentioned at some length in my fifteenth chapter. To make use of Masonic terminology, I believe that both have been philosophised: this at least is the case assuredly respecting the Ritual of the Southern Jurisdiction, once ruled by the famous Albert Pike. The designation signifies that the original Christian elements have been removed—wholly or in part—and it follows that from my point of view the validity of the Grade has been destroyed. It offers no longer the Lost Word of the Craft Degrees restored in the light of Christ, but such a substitution as is represented by the Hermetic formula—IGNE NATURA RENOVATUR INTEGRA—in place of JESUS NAZARAZÆUS REX JUDÆORUM. However this may be, the two Grand Obediences constitute together the authentic Scottish Rite in the American Republic, and this not only by the hypothesis of their claim, but in virtue of general recognition and the success of an accomplished fact. It is desirable to mention this because it happens that there are other claimants, who also work and administer the Grade of Rose-Croix, under I know not what warrants and apparently in various forms. There seems in any case no evidence to indicate that they or any of them represent the Rite of Perfection or preserve the Christian elements. Like the orthodox Scottish Jurisdictions, they do not enter therefore into an historical consideration of the Rosy Cross in America.

I have spoken of putative Orders and false witnesses, with Randolph and his fantastic association standing at the head of both as equally "false in sentiment and fictitious in story." My readers shall judge, however, on their own part, for the case is characterised by several conflicting elements, and the Randolph dossier is not entirely that of a vagrant travelling in occult arts. In respect of deception there is no question that he was his own and his first victim if he thought that his views and lucubrations might stand for authentic Rosicrucian teachings. But in a judgment which makes for justice it must be added that he revoked his own claim on a vast antiquity. He was also a man of enthusiasm and of great personal zeal. It is said finally that he was a seer from childhood, like his mother before him, and that he had passed through the horrors of mediumship, as he describes them, adding that he turned with loathing from the bare recollection of conditions implied thereby. He was further what is called in America a "half-breed" and he entered this life in consequence with something approaching a stigma in America at that time. The fact was likely to react on a highly psychic nature, and there is evidence that it did. The dual disability may help to account for the peculiar cast of his dedications in the life that he led, the books that he produced, perhaps even for his ultimate end.

It does not appear that in the matter of the Rosy Cross he did more than give a fresh circulation to some of the old reveries, to the extent that he was acquainted with these by common report and otherwise. It appears to have been presented mainly as of Essenian origin, though it must be acknowledged that there were other fantasies. In other and more hectic stories he paraded flaming accounts of the Brotherhood, its immemorial antiquity, its diffusion throughout the world, with suggestions that its ramifications extended to unseen spheres. In perhaps the worst of these performances—a thing called RAVALETTE—he affirmed the existence of American Lodges, working under a Grand Charter granted by a Third Temple of the Order which dated from Atlantis; but the particulars are banal, and

I suppose that in such productions he was directing attention sensationally to the fact that he had brought something into existence under an historical label, had placed himself at its head, and that it charged substantial fees. I have worked through such of his volumes as are available here in England, from so-called Rosicrucian dream-books to declamatory sex-reveries, and have concluded that, mountebank as he was, he believed in all his rant and was not lying consciously when this stuff of sorry dreams was put forward unfailingly as the wisdom of the Rosy Cross. This is how it loomed in his mind and this is what it was in dream, for it was a thing of his own making. On this subject he is his own irrefutable witness, affirming that " very nearly all which I have given as Rosicrucian originated in my own soul."[1] When he talks of initiations, " officiating girls " and " strange oaths," we may infer that he held meetings of some kind, but I have failed to obtain particulars.[2] It is, I think, sufficient for our purpose to recall that he signed as " Supreme Grand Master of Eulis, Pythianæ and Rosicrucia, Hierarch of the Triple Order."

One of his admirers and fellow-workers was F. B. Dowd, subsidiary no doubt to himself, yet claiming the titular position of " Grand Master Imperial Order of Rosicrucia." In 1882 he issued a small volume entitled THE TEMPLE OF THE ROSY CROSS,[3] otherwise concerning " the soul, its powers, migrations and transmigrations." The references to the Order are few and far between, and there is nothing on the historical side, but there is one excursion in prophecy

[1] See EULIS, ed. of 1874, p. 47. In Randolph's opinion, expressed in this volume, Hargrave Jennings was " the chief Rosicrucian of all England," and he quotes in this connection from CURIOUS THINGS OF THE OUTSIDE WORLD.

[2] According to Sédir, the Randolph incorporation was a *société d'éditions*, which may be substantially true, but on the understanding that the " editions " meant works by the author of EULIS.

[3] Its substance seems to have been reproduced by Dowd in THE GNOSTIC, edited by George Chainey and W. J. Colville, eleven issues of which appeared at Oakland and San Francisco, between 1885 and 1888.

concerning a day to come when a great, peace-bringing power shall be poured from the Temples of the Rosy Cross and no one thereafter will be disposed towards evil. On the point of fact, while abiding with things as they are, the Rosy Cross is described as a Fraternity rather than an Order, though attempts have been made to establish it on the latter lines, and some of these have succeeded. The intimation is useful as a probable side-light on the inchoate state of the Randolph institute. And so is that which follows: "I meet many Rosicrucians, and although total strangers, we know each other at sight." The so-called membership was therefore a matter of disposition, not of integration in a given mystic circle, under which circumstances we can understand easily that the Brethren are said to be numerous, indeed "of all nationalities and all climes," but also scattered, as they would obviously be. It is added that they meet occasionally, but are not summoned, being drawn together by the spirit, "as of one accord." Reflecting from Randolph, the author affirms that prior to the times of Christian Rosencreutz, they were called Essenes, Illuminati and so forth, apparently by any title which has ever been held to distinguish "intensely and transcendentally spiritual" men. For the rest, Dowd affirms (1) that there is a virtue in the human soul which is capable of eternally renewing "youth and beauty": otherwise there is an Elixir of Life; (2) that the transmutation of metals is possible but is no longer of any service to the true Rosicrucian. This approximately is the sum of the allusions, and the rest of the volume is filled with moony vapourings on the principles of Nature, on body and spirit, mind, faith and knowledge, the soul and its transmigrations, will and spiritual gifts. They are a little after the manner of Andrew Jackson Davis. Dowd has been mentioned only because of his relations with Randolph, whose occult activities began about 1859, and after his unfortunate suicide—with the date of which I am unacquainted—his wife published new editions of his works till near the end of the nineteenth century.

Meanwhile the *Societas Rosicruciana in Scotia*, holding from that *in Anglia*, chartered a Philadelphia College for Pennsylvania in 1879 and a New York College in 1880 " for New York State." My authority[1] proceeds to record that in April of the latter year these two bodies established a High Council for the whole of America, and that it chartered Colleges in Boston for Massachusetts, 1880; in Baltimore for Maryland, 1880; and Burlington for Vermont at a date not given. The New York, Baltimore and Boston branches became dormant, the last in August, 1896. One of its members was Sylvester C. Gould, editor of an American NOTES AND QUERIES and of a quarterly periodical called THE ROSICRUCIAN BROTHERHOOD, 1907–9.[2] It is affirmed that " from the moment " that the Boston College suspended " his chief ambition was to hold the work fast," looking " beyond the ideas which dominated the fraters (*sic*) of his day." He did nothing, however, till November, 1908, when he laid plans in conjunction with a few *Soc. Ros.* members, apparently of New York, for the formation of a body on broad principles " and opening its doors to all true seekers." A *Societas Rosicruciana in America* is described as having begun in this manner, its " rituals, traditions, landmarks, customs and practices " having been " carefully gathered " by Gould, who died, however, in July, 1909, so that the work and its developments passed into other hands. It has abandoned the Masonic qualification, originally and elsewhere required for membership, and

[1] MERCURY, the " Official Messenger of Metropolitan College, S∴ R∴ I∴ A∴," Vol. ii, No. 5.

[2] I have inspected a complete file, which contains practically no original matter, while its reprints are drawn from readily available sources. Mr. Gould had evidently sincere interest in his subject, but he seems to have known nothing about it.

it initiates both sexes. So far as I am acquainted with its activities, the work undertaken is done in an earnest spirit ; it has gradually rectified its Latin—at least to a certain point—and is an exponent of esoteric Christianity, as this is understood by its leading spirit. But it has obviously no tradition, no claim on the past and no knowledge thereof. The Transactions—now apparently available to any subscribers—are amazing reading from the standpoint of things put forward under the denomination of the Rosy Cross. Of recent times it seems to have borrowed Grade and Order titles from connections of the Hermetic Order of the G∴D∴. The headquarters are at New York, and there are branches in various places.

It would serve no useful purpose to enlarge upon later foundations, like that of Dr. R. Swinburne Clymer, who seems to have assumed the mantle laid down by Randolph, or Max Heindel's Rosicrucian Fellowship of California. They represent individual enterprises which have no roots in the past.

CHAPTER XXIV

LAST DEVELOPMENTS OF THE MYSTERY

We have seen that from an early period in the disjointed pageant of Rosicrucian history there are traces of a spiritual intent. Though he carries a heavy yoke of physical alchemy, there are a few saving intimations in the long literary record of Michael Maier that he knew of other gold than that which is found in earthly mines and of other transmutations than those that are wrought in crucibles. He had heard at least of a Medicine which is not administered to men through lips of sense. Robert Fludd is like a prophet of the Rosy Cross on an uplifted platform of lucid Christian Theosophy. We remember also some pearls of a certain price among too few citations in the little books of Thomas Vaughan. The eighteenth century offers some curious lights, too few also and very far between. It would seem that there were several schools within the general circle of the Order and so far as the available records are concerned, they offer but little to our purpose in the connection which is here in view. They were (1) those of the astral workings, activities and fruits of the magical paths in their distinction from the Higher Magia: the Order of the Golden Dawn offers a late witness or example concerning them; (2) those which confessed only to dedications in physical alchemy, like the Reformation of 1777; and (3) those for which the Kentish philosopher Fludd stood up a most valiant champion more than one hundred years before: they diffused a welcome light, but in the period which followed it shewed only occasional gleams.

About the Rosy Cross in Russia, it is difficult to speak, except on the external side. It appears to connote a purely spiritual movement, but it must be confessed that the life behind that movement escapes in the analysis of its overt and documentary side. The Rosy Cross in Germany during the reign of Frederick William II leaves us also with an uncomfortable feeling of having missed something, though it can scarcely lie in the direction of Wöllner and his immediate associates, who seem to have been grinding no other axes than those of their personal advancement and who inspire a profound distrust. Thereafter it is a complete blank, so far as memorials are concerned, till Rudolf Steiner began, some twenty years since, to use the name and symbols of the Rosy Cross in his reproductions of a qualified modern theosophy. I have reflected on his claims and have left them, because the path of occult science is not the path of God and because any putative marriage between things occult and mystic is more like a marriage of heaven and hell than anything met with otherwise in the world of disordered experiment. For the rest, it is not to be supposed that Dr. Steiner, though it has been reported that he derives from some German Order of the Rosy Cross, could produce any definite historical connection with the past, supposing that he wished to do so, which it seems fairly certain that he does not—being his own authority, at its value.[1]

It seems undeniable therefore that the links are broken everywhere. The various associations and sodalities which have claimed the generic title exhibited in the early seventeenth century, rose up in their day, advancing their particular claims, and they died also in their day—again so far at least as any records are concerned. It is above all

[1] At the root it is a modern occult adventure in akasic records, and we have the means of presuming its value by the light of other adventures in the same field.

things probable that their connection one with another was in the bond of union furnished by an identical name and a certain consanguinity of intention, whatever the intention was. As it seems entirely certain that the physical alchemists who, in one and another generation, worked under the style and title of the Golden and Rosy Cross, did not attain their physical end in the Medicine of men or metals, and that those—if any—who followed the dubious paths of Ceremonial Magic made no advance therein, so it is of little consequence if the links between them are of name and purpose only. Having regard to the voided term, it would be of no real moment were the chain of succession complete, however considerable the interest which might reside in the established point of fact.

I have dealt as an historian throughout this work and so far as little else, developing the records of the Rosicrucian *mysterium magnum* to the best of my ability and knowledge from the standpoint of simple scholarship and critically as to all mendacious claims or romantic reveries, including the theses of writers who—in one or another interest—have had their particular axes to grind. It may be thought that the Order itself has evaporated under such a process. That which remains, however, is the Rosy Cross, a body of Christian symbolism, variously interwoven and clothed in various forms. As to the fact of its existence there is a broken but recurring witness. To each epoch its own particular manifestation and its special concern of the moment, but in the background of all there looms vaguely, or is bodied forth in distinguishable if unaccountable shapes, the orm of a Godward side. After the pure Christian Theosophy of Robert Fludd, to which I have just adverted, a luminous body of doctrine suggesting a certain basis in mystical experience, there is the clouded sanctuary of the Sigmund Richter school, dealing in nothing but physics, yet holding that these are a work on the Divine side and demand a Divine motive in the art thereof. I must set aside the Magia belonging to astral workings because there are no particulars: it connotes the activities of seers who had never passed through the Mystic Cloud of Unknowing; but we have heard of a Higher Magia, and though it happens seldom enough that God is in the visions or auditions, the tactions or psychic messages, it may follow on not less rare occasions that those who are sanctified before they travel in the spirit vision will find a door open and a path of issue towards the world of another order. So here also there is a kind of background, though for us it can offer only a field of tentative speculation. Again alchemy prevailed and again it was in the physical realm, but with certain oracular voices sounding from a void behind in the Ritual vestiges of 1777. The SECRET SYMBOLS may be telling another story amidst the Hermetic motley of their vestures.[1] Within a Masonic

[1] As I have been told that in Russia, prior to the recent revolution and indeed before the War there was still a Rosy Cross which was a kind of family inheritance, concerned solely with Magic and have set it aside for want of evidence, though the communication was made in good faith, so I have heard and left over some vague rumours that the chief secret of the Order was a sex-mystery. It does not happen to come from those who, groping in the dark over cryptic texts, have suggested to themselves and others that the Key to alchemical literature should be sought in this direction. There is a broad sense in which many and most of our problems have sex at their root, but the historical problem of the Rosy Cross has no traces of this kind and its literature above all has none. There is of course a sex-side in the psychic which belongs to the hallucinations of Black Magic and has an echo in LE COMTE DE GABALIS. This very curious document has been represented as a betrayal of Rosicrucian secrets, which is not the case, and there is an old story that its author, the Abbé de Villars, was assassinated by the Invisibles on account of it, but his death was the result of a vendetta which avenged a similar crime on his own part, as his latest biographer tells. The sex-side of Black Magic is like the rest of it, abomination and infamy. I have heard of modern practices in the guise of experiences on the astral plane. That evil side of German Rosicrucianism at which a German witness hinted, some few years since, to myself, may have to do with these sense-welterings, and the circles concerned would bear the same relation to the true Rosy Cross as the *petit résurrection des Templiers* in Paris bore to the Masonic Grade of *Kadosh* or to the Military and Religious Order of the Temple.

circle in the meantime there had arisen the Grade of Rose-Croix, which—in another form of language—might have come out of a quiet study in a beloved manor at Bearsted. Hereof is the succession before us and so far as evidence is concerned it is suggestive of new things grafted on the original root of the early seventeenth century, or—as I have intimated—that there were many Orders of the Rosy Cross rather than one obedience continually varied and transformed. Now, in the sense of such grafting I testify that the Rosy Cross is in activity at this memorable day and new epoch of the world under greater warrants than the past held up in its beacons to any of the old *Adepti*, and clothed also in other and more radiant vestures. I have taken all Ritual as my province and the Great Rites and Hierarchic Orders have written their messages in my heart. I have loved the beauty of their Temples and the hallowed walls whereon their symbols shine. I know their secret language and the still deep wells of life which lie concealed within them. But there is nothing in the world of Ritual to compare with the high pageant of the Rosy Cross, transformed by the Light of the Spirit into a Hidden House of God. It is a place of valid sacraments, abiding within the measures of sacrament, and the grace of their meaning shines through the outward veils. There is nothing in the catholic world of instituted symbolism to compare with the gospel thus conveyed, gospel of quest, gospel of path and term, of the soul in separation and in union, and of That Which is All in All—the Life Which is hidden with Christ in God.

The question being how such a transformation has come about, let it be recalled in the first place that I have, in Masonic parlance, most especially excepted all question of continuity because there is no vestige of evidence to support it in the long story of succession.[1] In the second

[1] It should be added that, alike within and without the Circle here

place, and as something of living importance to the subject at large, I appeal to that which lies behind—as it lies also within—Rosicrucian history—I mean, the Secret Tradition in Christian Times, to the various departments of which I have devoted so many volumes during the years of my literary life. One and all are witnesses to a process of development or transformation which took place within them. I do not speak here and now of that which historically and theosophically is at the root of all, the renewal which was suffered by the world-Mysteries of old under the light of the Christian ægis. The great religion which began its career of conquest in A.D. I adopted, adapted and gave a new birth in time to whatsoever of Greece or Rome could be bent and shaped to its purpose and to whatsoever from eastern sanctuaries of old found meeting-points at Alexandria and Byzantium. I am very sure that the great antique tradition of Egypt was, as to living essentials, absorbed in Christ. I am not less certain that through all those years when the schools of neo-Platonism made their stand against Christianity they were doing unawares the work of Christian formation, that when dying Plotinus bore the Divine within him to the Divine in the universe, the theosophy which he left on earth, in respect of all its vitality and all its Godward side, was carried into the Christian Sanctuaries, to dissolve and be reborn therein. The world of thought and the world of action were then alike in the crucible, and that crucible was Christ. They came out therefrom in the soul and body of a new order, having also a new spirit within them. They were no longer of Egypt and the East, of Rome or the Greece behind it : all these had suffered transformation.

Let us look at some other and—within their own measures

referred to, the claim of antiquity could not only offer no test of value, as it does not justify itself, but the affirmation, wheresoever it is made, conveys unawares a strong counsel of caution.

—very typical conversions. There is that of chivalry by the spirit of romance, converting crude and predatory feudal knighthoods into a great ideal, mystical and holy order, as much and as little on outward land and sea as are the light of "consecration and the poet's dream." It produced a great tradition of impossible books, a world, moreover, of quests and attainments, and high dwellers therein: Arthur and his companies of kings; the Round Table and its "flower of all the world"; Charlemagne, Roland and Oliver, shining among the peers of France; above all Lancelot; and in fine Perceval, and Galahad as more than he. This golden tradition gave us Christian womanhood, the type above all womanhood. Now the point is that it took over the rough knighthood and transformed it in its own alembic.

But the makers of chivalrous romance did much more than this and earned yet a higher title to immortal fame. There had come to them strange tidings as from some mystical Carmel or holy Horeb, like unto that Mountain of Initiation and Hill of Wisdom, about which we have heard otherwise in Thomas Vaughan's strange fragment from a rescript of the Rosy Cross. They were tidings of a great mystery behind the Sacred Eucharist and Mass-Words not found in liturgies, whether of Rome or Sarum. This is on the one side and the other is Celtic lore, telling of the Cauldron of Ceridwen, Cauldron of the Dagda, Broth and Wine of Wisdom, myths of quest and venture, wild enchanting tales of exile and return. They drew these medleys of early folk-tale together and raised them into the light of the Holy One by interweaving the Eucharistic Mystery, legends of Passion-relics and legends of conversion. Out of such marriages there issued the romance-literature of the Holy Graal, the later quests of Perceval and the sacro-saintly quest of Galahad, the high prince. Again the point is that folk-lore was taken over, saturated with pre-Christian elements, and was transformed by another tincture, in another alembic, presenting a new and gloriously emblazoned aspect, for those who can see and hear, of legend and tradition in Christian times.

There was also, coming down from comparatively early Christian centuries, the Secret Tradition in Israel, of the SEPHER HA ZOHAR and other memorials of Kabalism. Before it was formalised by Rabbinical doctors of the sixteenth and seventeenth centuries it constituted within its own measures a luminous, if inchoate, theosophy. I know of few literatures which radiate such startling lights of speculation. They are reflected there and here into the doctrine of the Rosy Cross. Now there came a time in the fourteenth century and from this date onward when Zoharic literature fell into the hands of Christian scholars. I have cited them so often that it shall be held needless here even to repeat their names. I have shewn also how it appealed to them and how it was used by them, as an independent and unexpected demonstration of Christian root-doctrine grown up in Jewry itself during the exile of those terrible centuries when persecution followed persecution, after the fall of Jerusalem. It came about in this manner that the Kabalah was Christianised. Once more the point is that a traditional teaching was taken over, was informed with another meaning, adapted to another purpose and in this sense transmuted.

The position of alchemy has been made plain already in these pages, but its mystical body of symbolism was not so much taken over as used concurrently by two schools. In fine there was old Operative Freemasonry, its art and craft, its body of moral duty, and the sweet savour and incense of its religious atmosphere. That which befell it was long posterior to the genesis of the Rosy Cross, but there is nothing more signal in the secret traditional records than the transformation of Operative into Speculative Masonry, while there is no more marvellous and golden chronicle than the true and literal history of the growth of Rite and Grade which developed from that root through all the spacious epoch of the eighteenth century. After two volumes devoted recently to this subject my only point here is—yet once more and now last of all—the fact of transformation.

Hereof in brief outline is the career of the Secret Tradition in Christian Times, over against which is the devolution of Catholic doctrinal tradition under the ægis of the protestant reformation. It is none of our concern here. The transformation of the Rosy Cross came about, I conceive, in the same manner and for the same reasons that ruled in the other conversions. In each case there was a material tolerant to the change involved and, so to speak, there was a predisposition also in the direction of the kind of change. Under the providence of Latin Christianity that which is understood among us as the Mystic Quest came forth bearing the signs and sigils of a valid sacrament, and the transformation of chivalry by romance was like an epoch in its natural evolution. The matter of folk-lore for the creation of Graal literature was already in the world of symbol. Zoharic Kabalism was theosophy *ab origine symboli* and the outward body of theosophy is plastic and transforms easily. So also the many veils of the Great Mystery in physical alchemy, peculiar and unique as they were, constituted a broidery of images derived from Art and Nature, the elements of which had been in use from time immemorial in *Magna Mysteria Dei*. Witness the Stone and the Medicine. It was the same in respect of images belonging to the art and craft of building, including the art itself.

And so also with the matter of the Rosy Cross. The elements comprised therein were already in the course of transformation, *Magia* into Higher *Magia*, the metamorphosis of alchemy into the conversion of souls. It seems to have stood for these new births more or less from the beginning. Kabalism was incorporated therein, but long after Mirandula and Reuchlin had begun their work upon it. Moreover, the great central sign and symbol of the Rose placed upon a Cross could never, as we have seen, have signified anything but a spiritual and as such a Christian Mystery. The Cross was typically that of Calvary, from the days of Robert Fludd, and the Rose was the Rose of Sharon. My position is therefore that though many associations sprang up successively and concurrently under the implied and expressed claims connoted by the same recurring denomination, though their history is chequered enough, though that which was called originally the House of the Holy Spirit may have been occasionally a den of thieves, the sacramentalism of the sign remained, and—again in the natural evolution of things—it was antecedently and above all things probable that there would come about (1) a reversion to the one only and valid message of the sign; (2) a desire on the part of some who knew and were of the elect that the Rosicrucian House of the Holy Spirit should become or again be consecrated to the Holy Spirit of God.

It is this transformation which has come to pass in fact. The old Rosicrucian Tree of Life in Kabalism has become the Tree of Life in mystical experience on the ascent of the soul to God. The light of the Rosy Cross under such new birth in time is the light of the world in Christ. The path of progress through mystical Grades and Worlds is the path of the soul's return to that centre from which it came forth, or even to God Who is its end. After this manner is adeptship transformed by sanctity, the key and secret of all being the translation of Ritual into life. The term and crown of all is a great mystery of attainment, and he who is called Sapiens in the records of the seventeenth century is one witness concerning it. The new spirit has changed not the old name, which is of catholic and perfect meaning in the world of types, but it has changed the body of the thing and has given it a robe of glory.[1]

There is a sense also, but as if unawares, in which the whole Secret Tradition of Christian Times has passed through its alembic. It is not officially or conventionally an Order of Chivalry; there are no accolades or titles of knighthood; yet is it a Spiritual Chivalry, a Chivalry of the City of God and a *Militia Templi*. It is not in competition with external Christian Churches, and yet it is a Church of the Elect, a Hidden and Holy Assembly. It is not a College of dogmatic Theology, but it is a House of Christ Mystical.

[1] It may help to avoid misconceptions, though they are avoided seldom enough in subjects of this kind, if I state categorically that in the text above there is no reference whatever to that "exalted Rosicrucian centre" mentioned by Sédir—HISTOIRE DES ROSE-CROIX, pp. 128, 129—and referred by him to the year 1898. Its location and mode of recruiting are said never to have transpired, which notwithstanding the deponent seems qualified to affirm that "the initiation is very pure and essentially Christian." At p. 139 of L'INITIATION for 1912, Papus speaks of a mysterious association of "developed men under the title of Rosicrucians," used as an exoteric name which conceals another in the hiddenness. He says also that there are only ten true Rosicrucians—presumably of this association—and that he is acquainted with them, though he does not belong to the number. We may compare Édouard Schuré: L'ÉVOLUTION DIVINE DU SPHINX AU CHRIST, Paris, 1912, p. 350. As a point of Rosicrucian tradition he affirms that "the Spirit who spoke to the world under the name of Christ and by the mouth of the Master Jesus is spiritually joined to the King-Star of our system"—*i.e.*, the Sun. But this is the Rosicrucianism of Dr. Steiner, who is reported in THE VAHAN as once lecturing at a German Theosophical Congress on "The Initiation of the Rosicrucians." It appears to have been presented as a "sevenfold scheme," and this scheme was said to be expressed symbolically in the Gospel of St. John. There is no such Grade-progression known or heard of in the Order prior to Dr. Steiner; I conclude therefore that he alludes to a system of his own, and I have long understood that he works something of the kind in secret. To make an end of these miscellaneous garnerings, the Theosophical Society of England and Wales started a Temple of the Rosy Cross in London, from which were developed branches in Manchester, Edinburgh, the Hague, Krotona and Adyar. It appears to have been moribund in 1918. It was looking for a new Teacher, and claimed, I believe, no connection with the past. Among those who belonged to it I know one at least who found no light therein.

There is a form of government, but the Head of all is Christ, the Hidden Master of the Rosy Cross. It has no claim on Apostolical Succession, looking rather to that superordination which is conferred otherwise than by imposition of hands. And yet it is a House of the Holy Graal in the sanctity of a High Symbolism, where the sacred intent of the Order is sealed upon Bread and Wine. The reason is that they are primary among signs efficacious of things signified in the consecrations of the natural order, for the realisation of the inward truth that Divine Substance may be communicated to the soul through outward channels of grace. But beyond this normal mode there is recognised also another and more direct communion, between the Divine in the universe and the Divine in man, *videlicet*, God and the soul, by the way of channels that are within. So is the Graal manifested, and so also is withdrawn.

Moreover, the theosophy of the Rosy Cross is not a rabbinical theosophy in what may be called the rabbinical sense, as any doctor in Jewry and any scholar on MIDRASHIM would be quick to recognise, and yet the purest of those Zoharic lights to which I have referred are woven into its veil of symbolism, because they happen to serve its purpose and help to perform its work. For the Order is a path of symbolism, as it was indeed from the beginning,[1] and it remembers how long ago the Golden and Rosy Cross made appeal in its Ritual procedure to the Sephirotic scheme of Kabalism. There is also an alchemy of the spirit, as Robert Fludd understood it within the measures of his particular illumination; but it has passed beyond SUMMUM BONUM and PHILOSOPHIA FLUDDANA, to find a higher light of transmutation and a yet more catholic Medicine. It calls

[1] It is a path of symbolism at its highest and has cut itself adrift as such from all occult adventures, the mendacious inventions and fradulent connotations of the past. It should be understood therefore that it does not belong to history.

to be added that this also is a sacro-saintly veil of something behind or within which is not indeed more holy but is a yet brighter sign-post set up over the rock of ages.

To make an end in fine of these spiritual consanguinities, the Rosy Cross is not a Rite in Masonry and does not demand now, as it did once, a Masonic qualification of members, yet the key of Masonry is there, for it is a mystery of new life, of figurative or mystical death, and after these experiences there is a Great Mystery of Raising. But it is all in the light of the Sun of Christ, shining at the zenith-altitude in a heaven of soul, no longer in the substituted and penumbral rays of the Craft Mason, which have been called darkness visible. So also there is a Quest of the Word, pursued from Grade to Grade; but the instructed Brother of the Rosy Cross knows that albeit the journey is taken from East to West, those quarters of heaven are *termini* of another cosmos. If he reaches the Grade of Master, he finds the Word, but it is not uttered with lips of the body of this world or heard with the ears thereof.

I may seem to have cited as one speaking unawares that pregnant formula concerning the Quest of the Word, but it leads to my last point, which is another story of transformation, and this in a dual sense. There are few things older in myth and symbolism than the Great Word, the Word of power, which appears sometimes as the secret of the gods, or of some one or other among them. There are many variations of its story and it is met with in many environments, perhaps the most unlikely of which might seem to be Operative Masonry. It is there, however, or at least in the Scottish Craft, emerging as a Masons' Word, the earliest reference to which connects it with Jakin and Boaz. It was, of course, a secret, and the Entered Apprentice seems to have been taught concerning it. The palmary fact about it is that of its possession. From the standpoint of the old Mystery of the Word, it is the last transformation or reduction into the lowest possible term: in place of a secret of the gods, it has become the palladium of a common craftsman and a right earned by his reception into a worker's guild. The communication to this extent may even be called automatic. When, however, Emblematic Freemasonry came upon the scene in London there took place also—but post 1717—a remarkable transformation in respect of the Word. The palmary fact concerning it was no longer that of its possession but of its loss rather and the communication in its place of more or less idle substitutes. We may speculate as we like upon the grounds and reasons of this change, and I have shewn elsewhere that it connotes an acquaintance—somewhat through a glass and darkly—with the Secret Tradition in Israel. There must have been other sources, however, or other influences at work, for out of the specific loss there arose also a quest which has been called—rightly or otherwise—the Mystical Quest in Freemasonry.

"From small beginnings unto greater ends" is an old, it may be, an honoured adage. Hereof is the Mystery of the Rosy Cross in origin, history and development. At the last close of all, there is something that remains to be intimated, and it is of two kinds: (1) There is that which is left over for want of available materials, and here it is an open question whether there is any way in which our knowledge is likely to be extended, unless it be in respect of accidents and *minima*, in days to come; (2) There is something which belongs to the Holy Assembly, is reserved thereto and can be found only by those who are without when he who is now a Stranger at the Gate receives that call which takes him across the threshold. But this is of the spirit, is indeed the inward life, and not matter of history. *Benedictus Dominus Deus noster qui dedit nobis signum.* For those who know or can discover the authorised battery of the Rite, it may happen that the door will open and that he—*Ostiarius Magnus*—by whom they are admitted will be Christian Rosy

Cross, who after witnessing the Hermetic Marriage left the Palace of the King, expecting that next day he should be Door Keeper. *Introitus Apertus est ad Occlusum Regis Palatium.* The ways indeed are many, but the Gate is one. *Valete, Fratres.*

APPENDIX

ADDITIONAL EXPOSITORY NOTES

I. ASTRAL WORKINGS, p. 3. The first distinct allusions are *circa* 1777, and it is indicated—p. 620—that their nature does not emerge. Among early records, there is something behind the FAMA reference to Elementary Spirits, and its nature is indicated by the kind of activities which came out from the PHILOSOPHIA SAGAX of Paracelsus: it might be called EXPERIENTIA SAGAX. But in the last quarter of the eighteenth century Pasqually was already in the world, and his Rite of Election is a strange finger-post pointing towards such paths. There are, moreover, certain things in the hiddenness, of which I do not speak here because of their dangers, and because their claim upon a Rosicrucian source cannot be established, though the roots may be older than appears likely on the surface.

II. PHILOSOPHER'S STONE, p. 3. In the course of our research we have seen and heard continually of *Lapis Mineralis* in its contrast with the Spiritual Stone. The Rosy Cross is like alchemical literature, in the sense that the one is not without the other all through its chequered history. Nothing better or clearer will be found upon this subject than is the discourse appertaining to the Order of *Princes Chevaliers de Rose-Croix*, pp. 469, 470.

III. ROSICRUCIAN OF ROMANCE, p. 4. On the one hand, Robert Fludd and the unknown SAPIENS are not in the likeness of Mejnour because the Occult Adept is not a Spiritual Master: on the other, the long procession of late and early mountebanks cannot be compared with Zanoni because they do not recall Saint-Germain, or even Cagliostro.

IV. SCOTTISH PHILOSOPHICAL RITE, p. 7. On this subject see my NEW ENCYCLOPÆDIA OF FREEMASONRY, II, 411. The Catalogue is important and I append particulars, hoping that a copy may be found. Title: CATALOGUE DE LA BIBLIOTHÈQUE DES ARCHIVES G . . . DU RIT ÉCOSSAIS PHILOSOPHIQUE. *Orné d'une planche.* Annotation: *Catalogue d'une précieuse collection des livres anciens, manuscrits et imprimés, de documents originaux, etc. Vente de* 23 *février,* 1860, *et jours suivants.* Paris. Tross, 1860, in 8 de 111 pages.

V. NAOMETRIA, p. 38. The Librarian of the Landesbibliothek, Professor Leuze, has been good enough to look at one of the Studion MSS. and has derived an impression that the account of it in the REPERTORIUM seems substantially correct, but the unconditional identification of its reveries with so-called "Rosicrucian wisdom" seems exaggerated in his view. He claims, however, no special knowledge of the subject, and has not been able to do more than glance at the text. He has found many references to the Cross and *Cruce signati*, but the index gives two only regarding the Rose. It is obvious, however, that these may stand for many pages of disquisition in the work itself. I am justified therefore in saying that the results are negative, and it is obvious for the rest that a considerable acquaintance with early Rosicrucian dreams and speculations is necessary to determine their analogies—if any—in a still earlier text. Professor Leuze has recognised this and has conveyed his impression tentatively and under all reserves. As regards Studion's methods of calculation for prophetic and other purposes, he proceeds from the beginning of the Christian era, from the foundation of the City of Rome, or from the Creation of the World, as one or the other happens to suit his purpose, and he connects historical events which in reality are widely separated by the help of these chronologies, though they do not belong to one another. It seems probable that a thorough examination of NAOMETRIA would exonerate the witnesses concerning it in a general sense, being that with which I am concerned, yet not in every particular.

VI. MILITIA CRUCIFERA EVANGELICA, p. 41. Bühle, on the other hand, takes an opposite view and considers that the sect can have been neither very large nor important. He suggests also that he had found no account of Rosicrucian meetings in NAOMETRIA; but (1) so far as I am aware, no one has said that they were there, and (2) no first-hand acquaintance worth naming with the text of that vast MS. is shewn anywhere in the Bühle monograph. I hope that on my part I have done nothing to put it forward as other than a Rosicrucian precursor, characterised by similar concerns, the same spirit and analogous forms of symbolism. The MILITIA was no more than a field in which the Order may have sprung up.

VII. FAMA TRADITIONAL HISTORY, p. 47. The transformation of the Rosy Cross is delineated in my last chapter, dealing with things as they are, though there is that also which is to come. The traditional history develops in this process and emerges as a real legend of initiation. It could not be otherwise when the whole symbolism is embraced by the work of conversion. According to John Yarker, the Jerusalem Encampment—presumably of Knights Templar—working at Manchester about 1827, practised not only their own Order or Degree but a version of the Rose-Croix, in which the FAMA legend was recited and at a certain point of the narration the Most Wise President touched a concealed spring, upon which the representation of "Sir Knight Rosenkreutz" is said to have "started from the tomb in symbolic resurrection." See S. C. Gould's Quarterly, THE ROSICRUCIAN BROTHERHOOD, Vol. I, p. 115. I quote this as one who puts up a casual sign of direction.

VIII. PIANCO MS., p. 55. I have promised a further reference to this subject, but it can be only to note that in his chronological account of the Order and its history the concealed author does not cite his supposed source of information referred to 1374. That date, in view of his hypothesis, signified nothing of itself, and the fact that it antecedes the mythical birth-period of Christian Rosycross according to the CONFESSIO would also signify nothing, for Magister Pianco had obviously set aside the FAMA legend.

IX. ROSE OF LIGHT, p. 67. As regards the Christ-figure suspended in the sun with extended arms, my annotation says that there is no distinction between the Cross in this form—*i.e.*, the cruciform human figure—and the Rose in the state of attainment. The explanation is that a Calvary Cross is a symbol of human nature in the manifested state, and in that which is called attainment humanity becomes the Rose, that is to say, the Christhood. *Rosa Christus est.* Herein also is the Incarnation understood mystically.

X. THESAURUS THESAURORUM, p. 70. I am glad to add that the Supreme Council MS. under this title has proved to be only misplaced, that it is now restored to the proper shelf, and that I have had an opportunity for its examination by the courtesy of the Secretary-General. The body of the work is entirely alchemical, the processes described therein being identified throughout as those of the Rosy Cross. It recalls in this manner and otherwise the PERFECT AND TRUE PREPARATION of Sigmund Richter. There is a preface concerned with traditional history and the descent of Hermetic Alchemical Mysteries from the days of Abraham, Isaac and Jacob to those of Moses and Aaron, thence to Joshua, David, Solomon and so forward into Christian Times. The preface is followed by certain Rules of the Brotherhood, to the number of 35, after which there is the JURAMENTUM FRATERNITATIS. These Laws also recall, though they are not identical with those published by Richter: it must be said that they are substantially the same; so are the modes of salutation; and we hear also of an Imperator ruling the Order. As regards A.D. 1580, being the date which appears on the title-page, that inference which my note draws, a little in the dark, from the denomination of Rosy and Golden Cross is justified, not alone generally by my examination of the MS. but specifically by the fact that it quotes Sendivogius, who was not born till 1566, while the NOVUM LUMEN CHYMICUM, which passes under his name, was first printed at Prague—but said to signify Frankfurt—in 1604.

XI. ROSE-SYMBOL, p. 95. The Beatific Rose of Dante, in which those who behold the Vision are represented as if rising and sinking, appearing and passing out of sight, is said in my text to have another meaning, belonging also to another category than that of early Rosicrucian symbolism. This highest mode is adumbrated only in the most exalted Grades, when the spirit of man at the end of all the sacraments quivers on the threshold of absorption, dissolves, as it were, therein, but returns inevitably therefrom. In the sensuous imagery of the ZOHAR it seems intimated by the sex changes of the Great Angel Metatron, trembling before the last Veil of the Presence and vibrating with the ineffable ecstasy. Nature was not ashamed of her emblems for the doctors of the Higher Kabalism, but in such types the essence of the subject escapes: the sense-images have passed before that threshold is reached, even in thought.

XII. SIMON STUDION. p. 182. Professor Leŭze tells me that I do not stand alone in regarding this name as assumed. There seems no question on the subject in the minds of Ferdinand Haug and Gustav Sisel, who state that "his real German name is unknown," and suggest that it was perhaps Eifest. See THE ROMAN INSCRIPTIONS AND SCULPTURES AT WÜRTTEMBERG. 2nd ed., Stuttgart, 1914, p. 2. In the opinion of Professor Leŭze, "it must have been the son, the student scholar, who latinised the name, and not the father." But he cites a notable passage on p. 1170 of NAOMETRIA, in which Studion speaks of his descent, mentions that he had been assistant in the school at Stuttgart, and was transferred to Marpach as Preceptor. In Marpach his father, Jacob Studion, had a house built by himself, and he had become *Coquus Aulicus*—*i.e.*, Court Cook—there being a ducal castle in that town. The father was born in 1517 in the village of Flechdorf, in the county of Waldeck.

XIII. DECLARATIO BREVIS, p. 281 *et seq.* The existence of this MS. and the nature of its content were made known for the first time in 1895, when I contributed an article on the subject to THE UNKNOWN WORLD, a magazine under my editorship. See Vol. I, pp. 134, 135.

XIV. VAUGHAN'S FAME AND CONFESSION, p. 376. With reference to my annotation on this page, the date 1658 (alternatively 1659 in some records), which has given rise to the idea of a second edition, is evidently a scribe's blunder or a misprint. See Gould's ROSICRUCIAN BROTHERHOOD Quarterly, Vol. I, p. 71, where the full title is given. It is described as printed by J. M. for Giles Calvert, at the Black Spread Eagle, at the West end of St. Paul's, 1659. But—date excepted—these are the very words of the 1652 and doubtless sole issue. Gould's title does not specify that it is a second or new edition.

XV. LAWS OF THE FAMA, p. 401, note. The six rules observed by the early Brethren should have been given in my descriptive account of the FAMA, but they are matters of common knowledge and may be now summarised thus: (1) The Brethren should profess only to cure the sick, "and that gratis"; (2) They should wear no distinctive habit; (3) They should meet annually at the House of the Holy Spirit on *Dies C.˙.*, "or write the cause of absence"; (4) Each of them should endeavour to find a worthy successor; (5) The letters C.˙.R.˙. should constitute their seal or mark; (6) The Fraternity should remain secret for 120 years.

XVI. THE SILENCE OF THE ROSY CROSS, p. 402. Of the activities, such as they were, and the records—if indeed any—it is impossible to give account, apart from the resources of continental libraries. There may be something in DISPUTATIO HISTORICA DE ROSÆ-CRUCIANIS, of C. S. Kazauer, published in 1715, and there are several other tracts which it is not worth while to enumerate, as none of them seem available in England. Towards the end of the eighteenth century there were attempts to reconstruct the past, but one is in the same position concerning them in most cases. A few others—which are available—offer mere vestiges, apart from all evidences.

XVII. THE ROSY AND GOLDEN CROSS, pp. 441 *et seq.* The sources of this monograph are a collection of many years, and I am hoping still to extend them, in case an opportunity should enable me to go further than is possible in this volume. I am looking also for other Rituals, and especially for additional German versions of *circa* 1850 and later. It must be understood that the archives otherwise are extensive, as they now exist. It should be possible also to go further into the Rosicrucian claims on Masonry from 1780 to the period of the French Revolution. I infer from Gould's larger history—section on the Golden Rosicrucians, in his third volume—that he had met with rumours of other sources. There are casual references in many places. In respect of the Secret Tradition which I have summarised, pp. 441, 442, my most important materials are in Codex No. 3 of a Grade of First or Lesser Adept: it differs substantially from Nos. 1 and 2, these varying only verbally from one another. All of them demand comparison with secret developments of the Strict Observance, *circa* 1780, included in my collection. As regards Egypt, there are strange intimations in two secret Degrees entitled respectively S.'.O.'.S.'. and G.'.O.'.T.'.S.'., the real names of which are believed never to have transpired. The variants of *Adeptus Minor* are very striking, both as to procedure and the additional instructions which have grown up round them. This applies also to *Adeptus Major*, which, in one version, being that of Senior Adept, is concerned with the black state of the Spiritual Stone and the passing from that state. There is also Supreme Adept, corresponding in other codices to *Adeptus Exemptus*, and therein the Candidate receives in his hands, actually and not symbolically, the prepared Matter of the Work. It happens sometimes that what is put literally in one sequence may be found expressed by emblems in another. The instruction on planets and metals, as adapted in my text, is fantastic apart from the light furnished by an alternative codex. The ASTRONOMIA INFERIOR of M. Fried, 1674, claims to be the work of a Rosicrucian, as well as an astrologer, chemist and amateur of Natural Magic. The seven metals are symbolised as seven earthly planets, corresponding to those in the heavens. It is difficult to accept the claim made on the Order or to take the writer seriously in other respects; but the speculative lore is curious and it may have reflected something from the alleged source. From this point of view, Fried is useful for purposes of comparison with Rosicrucian formulæ of the Reformation and later periods, scattered through various texts. It remains to say that THE ROSICRUCIAN UNVEILED of Magister Pianco gives account of the Zelator or *Juniores* Grade, while DIE THEORITISCHEN BRÜDER, of 1785, attributed to Graf von Lohrbach, has a mass of reliable information on the second Grade of the series, though it claims to be published by a "profane." There is an Appendix also on the third and fifth Grades. A third printed work, fullest and most important of all, is the STARKE ERWEISE, etc., of J. J. Ch. Bode, published in 1788 and containing the "genuine Rituals" of the Order of the Golden Rose Cross, "amended according to the last supreme and Reformatory Convention for the use of all worthy Brothers, as well as other Masters of the Appearance of Light and the Lost Word." The Reformation out of which they arose, and with which I have dealt so fully, is described here as authorised by the Superiors of the Order in 1777, *cum cordantia Fratrum* at Leipzig, Vienna, Regensburg and Berlin. Bode claims that they have been brought forth at the close of the first subsequent Decennium " by a genuine lover of the True Light." As regards the STARKE ERWEISE, or Strong Proofs of his title, they are to the effect that " the authentic writings of the Most Holy Order " exhibit its destinies as of " eternal efficacy and activity," seeing that they are centred in God. So far as printed documents are concerned, my appeal is to these three sources for the authenticity of my account of the Golden and Rosy Cross in and after 1777, though it draws from wider archives.

XVIII. FRATRES LUCIS, pp. 508 *et seq.* I have omitted to mention that Mrs. Cooper-Oakley's account of this Brotherhood appeared in THE THEOSOPHICAL REVIEW, Vol. 41.

XIX. THE RUSSIAN ROSY CROSS, p. 547. It is to be hoped that some qualified person will take up the work which calls to be done on the Rosy Cross in Russia. There is a vast mass of material available, at Petrograd and Moscow, if ever the star of peace should dawn on that tortured country. The connection of the mystic Lopukhin with its brief season of activity is significant from my own standpoint ; and outside his CHARACTERISTICS OF THE INTERIOR CHURCH, which I have helped to make known in England, there is not only his Masonic CATECHISM, but above all his Ritual of THE SPIRITUAL KNIGHT, to a modern reprint of which in the British Museum my attention was drawn some years since by a reference in a theosophical magazine. It seems probable that both may offer some light—direct or reflected—on the subject of this chapter. The Candidate for Spiritual Knighthood is described as a " searcher after supreme wisdom," and he is pledged to the maintenance of seven rules, concerned with Fidelity to God and to the Order. The maxims are : " Know thyself " and " Happiness is within." As regards ceremonial, this seems to have been exceedingly simple, but at the end there was an Eucharistic observance, in which salt signified wisdom, while Bread and Wine were emblematic of the Secret Work. The jewel was a gold heart, inscribed with a Cross. A white mantle was worn, embroidered with golden roses.

XX. ROSICRUCIAN BROTHERHOOD OF MANCHESTER, pp. 563, 564. The volume of " antiquarian interest " mentioned in my text is THE TREE OF COMMONWEALTH, by Edmunde Dudley, described as written in 1509–10, and " now first printed for the Brotherhood of the Rosy Cross." It appeared in 1859. At the time of composition the author was a prisoner in the Tower, having been sentenced to death for treason.

XXI. Additamentum Magnum. As the final and most important of these Expository Notes, I am now able to add that the providence which overwatches undertakings of this kind has, at the last moment, fulfilled itself and that the Landesbibliothek of Stuttgart has sent for my inspection the original quarto copy of Simon Studion's Naometria, in two volumes, so that I can make at first hand an examination of its content and check the reports concerning it of the late eighteenth and early nineteenth centuries. The collation is as follows: (1) General title, for which see p. 48 of my text, but after *anno* 1604 appears the word *Consistorium*, as if the debate between Nathanael and Cleophas belonged to official proceedings. (2) Dedication to Frederic Duke of Wirtemberg, pp. 1–177. (3) *Vatidicæ et antiquæ imagines tres, quibus totius hujus Naometrici voluminis prognosticum comprehenditur et confirmatur*, pp. 178–189. (4) *Corollarium Naometricum de Friderico Secundo Romanorum Imperatore*, pp. 190–205. (5) Second Title: *Naometriæ Novæ et Prognostici Pars Prior*, unpaged. (6) The Dialogue which comprises the work begins on new p. 1, after which the names disappear, but it follows from the questions embodied in sub-headings that Nathanael continues to ask and that Cleophas answers. *Pars Prior* ends on p. 877, and so also does Vol. I. (7) Third Title, unpaged: *Naometriæ Novæ et Prognostici Pars Posterior: In Cruciferæ Militiæ Evangelicæ gratiam, Authore Simone Studione, inter Scorpiones, Anno* 1604. *Consistorium.* (8) After Title the pagination of Part I continues from p. 879 onward, ending on p. 1790. (9) 16 pp. blank. (10) *Hieroglyphicus Simonis Studionis*, entitled *Versus de instantis temporis fato imminente*, being six lines unpaged. (11) The same, set to music, unpaged. (12) Full Index, also unpaged.

I proceed now to check the representations cited in my second chapter from Repertorium Literarium and the later witnesses with the results of my own examination. (1) As regards the Militia there is no evidence that Studion attended the Meeting at Lüneburg and much less that he convened it. (2) When the Repertorium states that it was a branch of the Rosicrucians, " as is well known," it calls to be said that the evidence is not in Naometria. (3) When it affirms that the Militia became " a strong sect," the evidence must be sought elsewhere. (4) On the other hand, the Meeting itself was of some note and moment, as Studion tells us—MS. pp. 149, 150—that it was attended by German Princes and by legates of the King of Navarre, Queen of England and King of Denmark. (5) It took place on July 27, 1586, and is termed in the marginal reference CRUCE SIGNATORUM CONVENTUS. (6) The business in hand was help and defence in common, in case of hostility on the part of the Holy League—presumably the Catholic League of 1576–93, founded at Peronne to prevent the accession of Henry of Navarre to the Throne of France. It came to an end when this Prince was reconciled to the Latin Church. There was an earlier Holy League, 1511–13. (7) It follows that the Convention was political and summoned as such in the interests of Protestant Powers, though religious convictions are implied. (8) Studion calls it *Fundamentum Confederationis Evangelicorum* and *Initium Fœderis Evangelicorum Principum Protestantium*, terms which appear to imply only a Political Alliance. (9) But the allusions in his titles to MILITIA CRUCIFERA EVANGELICA might connote a military and religious foundation in the likeness of the Teutonic Order and the Christian Chivalries of crusading times, to both of which he refers elsewhere in his text. (10) I leave it an open question whether the REPERTORIUM, von Murr and Bühle are right in calling it a sect: it is quite possible that a perfervid dreamer like Studion saw a great army of God arising out of such an understanding as is said to have been reached at Lüneburg.

(11) However this may be, the remaining affirmations concerning the views of the MILITIA must be taken for references to NAOMETRIA, as our only source of information concerning it. (12) It offers no trace whatever of Paracelsian influence; it never mentions chemistry; its only astronomy is that of signs in the heavens, applied to prophetic purposes with the help of numbers. (13) It is an apocalyptic work, based mainly on the BOOK OF REVELATION, but at need taking all Scripture for its province. (14) It is not an occult work in the sense of being magical, alchemical, Hermetic and so forth: there is no vestige of these things in all its pages. (15) On the other hand, the REPERTORIUM and its successors bear true witness when they say that Studion and those for whom he stood were looking for a renovation of the earth, for a general reform to come; that they regarded Scripture as "written within and without"; that they were ultra-Protestant, "heated by apocalyptic dreams," and regarded the Pope as Antichrist.

When the occult element is thus removed from NAOMETRIA we seem to be taken a great distance from the FAMA and CONFESSIO: let us test therefore the reports of the witnesses concerning Rose and Cross. It is true, as the REPERTORIUM says, that Studion derives long predictions from Rose Symbolism, though his references to the Rose are two. The basis of all is the numerical value of the Hebrew letters comprised in the word חבצלת, which he translates Rose. The value in question is 530, and he connects it with that of שושנה =661, translated as Lily. The sum of these numbers is 1191, and this he regards as a date, being approximately that on which the Teutonic Order was founded, which Order is a type of his MILITIA EVANGELICA, dwelling *sub Rosa et Lilio* (p. 1673). So also Godfrey de Bouillon, who took Jerusalem, *cum principibus cruce signatis*, is a type of " our new King," namely, Him who is to come (p. 1689). As regards Cross Symbolism, the text is full of its mysteries : there are pen drawings of the Rose, but the Tau Sign, the Sign of the Cross is everywhere. It is the Sign of the Living God (p. 565) ; the *Crux Salvatoris* is the name of a star in heaven (p. 955) ; we hear also of the Exaltation of the Cross (p. 292), of the Feast under that name, and the finding of " the Cross of the Lord " after it had been taken into Persia. Of the Cross in Studion's numerology and the predictions drawn therefrom I forbear to speak. And now as to the test question, whether there is a marriage of the Rose and Cross in symbolism, the answer—to my surprise—is affirmative. It is found in a diagram on p. 271, the description of which is : *Hierichuntis Rosa ex quatuor ejus portis*. The Cross is in the centre, encompassed by a crude whorl of five petals and this by another whorl of eight petals. Four of these correspond to the Four Living Creatures and the four gates of the Mystic City, which city " lieth four-square," as we know, and there is a square about the whole diagram. It follows that I have searched vainly everywhere in my fourth chapter for an example of the Rosy Cross prior to the publication of the FAMA—Luther and his seal excepted—and that I have found it at last in NAOMETRIA. I care nothing how Studion interprets his symbol, or that it is covered with groups of figures, that these figures are dates and belong to the prophetic business of the work. He calls the symbol *Rosa* and he places a Cross in its centre : the analogies are in THE SECRET SYMBOLS.

I have reached a main point of this study, and there is little space to go further. The new stars of the CONFESSIO are like the Cross, all over the text, and they are that which the CONFESSIO says, signs of great council, for those of 1572 and 1602 have reference to the year 1620, " which is fatal to the Man of Sin," otherwise the Sovereign Pontiff (p. 146). It is true that in another prophecy he is to be crucified in 1612 (p. 417) and that 1620 is the coming of the Kingdom (p. 85), an event, I suppose, by which his spirit is overthrown for ever. There is scarcely an end also to prophetic tales concerning the Morning Star, the Star Lucifer and Vesper, and the mysteries of the planet Venus. The CONFESSIO is like a short excerpt from the greater text. The renovation to come is a renovation of kingdoms and churches (p. 491): it connotes the New Jerusalem, the renewal of the whole world, the *Regnum Dei et Christi* (p. 1615). And *Regnum mundi dabitur Evangelicis*. My conclusion is that REPERTORIUM never spoke more truly than when NAOMETRIA is said to breathe the Rosicrucian spirit—apart as it is from that of Paracelsus, dwellers in the elements, ever-burning lamps and "rogues and runagates" of alchemy.

It should be added that the *Cruce Signati*, who also recur everywhere, are scarcely an incorporated Fraternity: they are Lutherans and Zwinglians (p. 386); they are the saints and martyrs of APOC. VII, 14, and those who bore the sign upon their foreheads (p. 379): their type is the patriarch Joseph (p. 975). Not only the concealed author of CONFESSIO but those who wrote several later official documents would agree with the REPERTORIUM that all this "embodies real Rosicrucian doctrine." And I think also that I am justified in stating, on p. 50 of this work, that the R∴C∴ was in embryo *circa* 1604, as also that NAOMETRIA is its first memorial, in the sense of a precursor. The bibliolatry and sectarian zeal, the fever of false prophecy and the war of separation in Christendom were things in which it began and Studion is the protagonist of these; out of these it had to come and it emerged slowly enough, as the CONFESSIO shews. It assumed occult dedications and married them to current theosophy, which was raised in the person of Fludd and a few less known witnesses beyond all normal modes. That in all the Hidden Houses it had not emerged entirely even at the end of the seventeenth century is suggested by the case of Kelpius: that it was occult rather than mystical throughout the eighteenth century is clear from its general history, though another and sacred leaven was at work in Russia. And so the tale goes on, to the threshold of the last developments.

I have sketched once more the career of the Rosy Cross, and as one who has followed it through long years in all its paths I bear my faithful witness that it is impossible in the light of my knowledge to read the work of Studion without seeing that its beginnings are there. And the Anabaptist charge which was raised so early against the Rosy Cross was raised also against him by Melchior Fischlin. It follows that REPERTORIUM and the other witnesses are, as I expected, justified in a general sense, though I shall never understand how the philosophy of Paracelsus could be traced in NAOMETRIA. It follows also that its reflections in the FAMA are not drawn therefrom, as I have suggested at p. 211 on the basis of the German Repository. There is, however, little else to correct, save an error in my third note on p. 41. The Rosicrucian thesis in REPERTORIUM is pseudonymous, not anonymous, appearing under the assumed name of Wilhelmus ab Indagine. It must be added that in the quarto recension NAOMETRIA is impertect wanting pp. 1407–1454, inclusive ; but I have checked their content with the aid of the plenary index and find that there seems to be nothing which belongs to the subject of this notice. I give thanks in conclusion to the Würt-Landesbibliothek for the generous help which has been extended to me of its own free will.

INDEX

Index

Index

Index

Index

Index